I0761888

# Sam Spallucci Omnibus: Volume One

A.S.Chambers

This edition published in 2022.


ISBN: 978-1-8384573-9-6

# Dedication

For all those who have supported me over the past ten years.
I owe you an eternal debt of gratitude.

## Also by A.S.Chambers

Sam Spallucci Series.
The Casebook of Sam Spallucci - 2012
Sam Spallucci: Ghosts From The Past - 2014
Sam Spallucci: Shadows of Lancaster – 2016
Sam Spallucci: The Case of The Belligerent Bard - 2016
Sam Spallucci: Dark Justice – 2018
Sam Spallucci: Troubled Souls - 2020
Sam Spallucci: Bloodline - Prologues & Epilogue – 2021
Sam Spallucci: Bloodline – 2021
Sam Spallucci: Fury of the Fallen - Due 2022
Sam Spallucci : Lux Æterna - Due 2023

Short Story Anthologies.
Oh Taste And See – 2014
All Things Dark And Dangerous – 2015
Let All Mortal Flesh – 2016
Mourning Has Broken – 2018
Hide Not Thou Thy Face – 2020
If Ye Loathe Me - 2022
Out of the Depths - Due 2023

Ebook short stories.
High Moon - 2013
Girls Just Wanna Have Fun – 2013
Needs Must - 2019

Novellas.
Songbird – 2019
Bobby Normal and The Eternal Talisman - 2021
Bobby Normal and the Virtuous Man - 2021
Bobby Normal and the Children of Cain - 2022
Bobby Normal and the Fallen - Due 2023

Omnibuses.
Children of Cain - 2019
Macabre Collection: Volume One - 2022
Macabre Collection: Volume Two - Due 2022

## Acknowledgements

A very special thanks to the Seraph tier members of my Book Club for their continued and valued support:
Paul Lewis
Gemma Innes.

For more details about my Book Club and how you can receive signed copies of my books when they are published, please visit my website:
www.aschambers.co.uk.

# Contents

# Foreword

Greetings one and all and welcome to this, my collection of the first three Sam Spallucci books.

When I first conceived the idea of a whiskey-drinking, chain-smoking, fedora and mac-wearing paranormal investigator all those years ago whilst sitting in the back of a long, tedious chemistry lesson, I don't think I imagined what a well-loved character I would create or just how large the universe would end up that surrounded him. At the time of writing this foreword, I currently have eighteen books in print and, in two hours' time, I will be launching the Kickstarter campaign for my nineteenth (*Bobby Normal and the Children of Cain*).

I think it is fair to say that the last ten years have been a good old-fashioned clichéd rollercoaster of a ride. My original idea was to get a few books under my belt, make a name for myself then start looking for a mainstream publisher. It soon became apparent, after meeting many stressed authors with contracts, that I did not want that career. I needed my writing to be something that was true to what I wanted to create, to tell the story that I wanted to tell and not be dictated to either by a publisher looking to fill a certain hole in a market, or a generic editor stating that my style had to be non-threatening and not at all challenging in order to sell my books.

As a result, it has not been an easy process. The first five years were exceptionally hard as I attended event after event to *get my book out there* to Joe and Josephine Public. I found it gruelling and exhausting. It eventually took a toll on my health and I had to step back from appearing at so many nationwide outings. However, by this point, I had developed a dedicated and amazing following of readers and fans of my work. People were engaging with me over social media. They were asking questions about plotlines and characters, enquiring as to when the next book in the series would be out. This, to me, was the panacea that I needed. It reinvigorated me and drove me onward. Sam's Spallucciverse expanded outward in ways that I had never previously imagined. Characters took on lives of their own as they developed on the page. Ideas for new stories set in the far future miraculously appeared out of the ether along with novels and novellas concerning side characters. And, in the wings of the dark, brooding stage, the hooded menace of Kanor sits and rubs his hands awaiting his big reveal in the very last book, *Divergent Lands: Dragon* (currently slotted for publication about 2030).

Anyway, I don't want to ramble on too much here. You've got enough of my words to plough through as it is. You don't need to sit there skim-reading my self-indulgent witterings. All I want to say, before you dive into the world of Lancaster's sort-of-finest, is a big thank you to you for buying this book and to all those who have supported me over the years. Strap yourself in and keep your hands clear of the sides because this rollercoaster is nowhere near finished with its exciting spin around the tracks just yet.

ASC 2022.

# The Casebook of Sam Spallucci

# Introduction

My name is Samuel C. Spallucci. I am an investigator of the paranormal. As I sit here typing at my laptop, the moon hangs full and white in the night sky that envelops Dalton Square, Lancaster sometime after two in the morning.

In the last week, I have witnessed visions of what seem to be the past and the future, seen three dead bodies, been abducted twice, knocked unconscious (also twice), conversed with supposedly mythological creatures and had at least seven people eagerly expect my death.

Oh, and I think I may have also gunned someone down in cold blood.

So would you like to know some more about my first few days on the job?

You would?

Okay. Walk this way…

# The Case of the Satanic Suburban Sitcom

So, may I ask you what is the weirdest question you've ever been asked? You know the sort of thing. You're normally sat in a quiet corner of your favourite bar or pub (the Borough, in my case, as it's just over the road from my office) supping away at your favourite brew, enjoying the peace and solitude of your own inner ramblings when you notice that someone is stood next to you.

Even before you look up from your alcoholic musings, you just know that it's going to be trouble. There's that air of "Oh, dear God," hanging in the air, but you do the polite thing and look up at the person looming into your personal space whilst smiling expectantly.

Now, if it was a normal person stood there, perhaps wanting to share a table due to the lack of space or wanting to ask you what the time might be as their watch had stopped, then they would smile back and make polite conversation.

No, the sort of person stood there now does not smile, they gawp. They have that faraway look in their eye that tasted far too many magic mushrooms in their youth or tells of a childhood climbing electric pylons on long, hot summer days. Also, they tend to dribble somewhat, don't they? Not much. Just a drip from the corner of their slack-jawed mouth.

Then they pop the question.

There's no reason or rationale to their request. It's just totally random. It might be something like, "I hit badgers with teaspoons. Wanna join in?" or "You wanna see my collection of belly button fluff? The yellow ones are really interesting."

Yeah. Weird. Really weird.

Well the other week I got asked a question that topped all of those: "Will you investigate the cast of a high-profile sitcom? I think they're all Satanists."

I suppose it began as an ordinary day. It was a mundane Monday morning in October and I was in the process of readying myself for opening up to the public at large. I had finally gotten around to assembling my desk. Well, when I say "assembling" what I really mean is swearing loudly and throwing pieces of chipboard around my office in Dalton Square. I guess the internet is a wonderful thing, but when you use it to buy flat-pack furniture, you really ought to check that the instructions come in your native language or at least with a phrase book for Mandarin or Cantonese. Also, why is it that those long black screws they supply always seem to have the knack of lurching to the side just as you try to screw them in so that you gash your hand with a Phillips screwdriver? Until I saw *Revenge of the Sith* I was convinced that Anakin Skywalker would end up as the suited Darth Vader after a near-fatal wrestling match with a self-assembly hi-fi unit from the star system of Ikea.

So it was that my screwdriver was making a satisfying clattering noise as it smashed against the far wall when my office door opened and a diminutive, grey-suited man shuffled in. He stood in silence, peering through his large, dark-rimmed glasses as he tried to decide whether it was worth his life to enter what was quite obviously an unofficial war zone. After a brief pause he ventured, "Mr Spallucci?"

I looked up from my DIY carnage and smiled. "That's me." I stood, enthusiastically brushed my clothes down and stepped over the wreckage of the victorious desk before sticking out my hand. "Samuel C Spallucci, investigator of the paranormal." At last, some semblance of relief from the frustration of fascist furnishings. A little bit of normality, I thought.

Then he asked his question.

Well I have to admit that it threw me somewhat. I mean, it's not the sort of question that one might expect from a chap who looks like Moleman out of *The Simpsons*. Now, "Can you help me find my biro?" or "Is this the public lavatory?" Those I would have expected, but "Will you investigate the cast of a high-profile sitcom? I think they're all Satanists." Well that is just what Grace, the young bar-maid at the Borough, would call somewhat "random."

I was rapidly becoming aware of an ever-increasingly embarrassing silence permeating the room, so I shoved some evil pieces of Chinese wood out of the way with my shoe and motioned for the man to come in.

"Thank you," he mumbled. "Mr Spallucci, my name is Roger Philips. I'm the producer of the television series *More Tea Vicar*. Perhaps you've heard of it?"

I nodded. Of course I'd heard of it! Everyone's heard of that little gem. It has single-handedly revived the fortunes of Wednesday nights on prime time commercial television. What was once the domain of dull, mundane repetitive soaps or banal, obtrusive docu-dramas has now been transformed into a comedic jewel in the schedules. "Please. Please come in," I gestured once more, sweeping some deadly, black screws off the comfy sofa. It would not do to impale a potential client.

Philips shambled into my office. He was quite obviously a man on the edge of a nervous breakdown. He constantly fiddled with the frayed cuffs of his cheap, grey polyester suit and his eyes fidgeted around the room taking in my "obsession".

"You seem to have a lot of clocks," he commented, gazing up at the old railway station time-piece that hangs on my wall opposite the main door.

"I like to know what the time is," I shrugged noncommittally, patting my trousers for a packet of cigarettes.

Philips' mouth hung open as his eyes passed from the station clock to the long-case clock, the brass carriage clock, the library clock and the napoleon hat – to name but a few. "But so many? How many are there?"

I extricated a pack of Luckies and tapped one out. "Dunno. I lost count years ago." That was somewhat of a lie. In the office there are, in fact, twelve. Upstairs, in the flat, another ten. I think.

"He stood agape for a minute watching the slow swing of the pendulum in the long-case before saying what everyone else has always said when confronted with my collection. "But doesn't the ticking drive you mad? All that noise?"

I flipped the Lucky into my mouth and lit it with my Zippo. "Trust me," I said, "There are far worse noises you can listen to all day. Now," I gestured to the comfy sofa, "why don't you tell me exactly what it is that I can do for you?"

Philips shambled over to the brand new, soft-fabric sofa and studied it as if it would sprout some sort of demonic mouth and devour him. His sad eyes looked at me as if seeking reassurance.

"It's okay," I volunteered. "It's not an Auton."

He smiled slightly and perched himself on the edge of the comfy chair, smoothed out his trousers, coughed and began to explain his situation. "Mr Spallucci, like I said, I am the producer of *More Tea Vicar*. It is a somewhat successful situation comedy that has turned my company, John O'Gaunt Media, into a rather profitable venture."

"I'm familiar with the story," I nodded, seating myself across from him in my swivel chair. "You singlehandedly badgered the executives at ITV to take on an idea that they described as 'insanely outdated' by offering them the show gratis for three months. It subsequently torched all the soap-opera and reality shows in its back-draft as it rocketed up the ratings. They are now saying that you have single-handedly altered the way that the public view mid-week television. Quite an achievement for someone who started out with not much more than a simple idea and a hand-held video camera. You're based over on White Cross aren't you?"

He nodded. "For now, yes. We hope to move to larger premises soon, what with all the promised redevelopment down on the quay."

"You said 'we'?"

He gave an embarrassed smile. "Yes. Contrary to public belief, John O'Gaunt Media is not just one man in a suit. We are actually more of a partnership of five: myself, Malcolm Haversham, Howard Baines, Maggie Sothwell and Melanie Brande."

"The main cast of Vicar?" I raised an eyebrow. "I wasn't aware of this?"

"Not many people are. We keep our business dealings very close to our chest."

I tapped the nails of my fingers against my teeth. "And you think that your partners are Satanists? I can see how that would be awkward at a church tea party, but in the echelons of high business..? Not really an economical sin, just a cardinal one."

Philips shook his head, frantically. "I know what you mean, Mr Spallucci, and normally I would say live and let live, it's just that it appears Haversham has been abducted," he rummaged inside his jacket and produced a long envelope, "and this was left in his dressing room."

I took the manila envelope and studied the front. It was embellished with a five-pointed star drawn in black ink. I looked back up at Philips. "If this is evidence, why don't the police have it?"

He scratched his ear and stared at the floor.

"Shit," I groaned. "They don't know, do they?" I waved the letter at him furiously. "This is a criminal matter. If someone has been kidnapped, then the police need to know. You can't just come running in here and expect me to bypass the due process of law!" I stood up sharply and thrust the letter towards him. "I think you'd better take this back."

Philips raised his head and his rheumy eyes behind those large glasses looked absolutely pitiful. "Please, Mr Spallucci, read the letter. I know I should have gone to the police, but the things they say in there..." He shook his head and buried it in his hands. "It's awful. Absolutely awful. I can't go to the police. They say they will sacrifice him tonight!"

I looked back at the five-pointed star. It looked so neat, so stark – one point facing up, two on either side. It didn't look like it had been penned by a lunatic that wanted to sacrifice a TV vicar, but then apparently Jack the Ripper's handiwork had also been very neat.

"Why do you think the rest of the cast are involved?" I asked.

"Recently there has been unrest, dissent between the partners," he explained. "I don't know the ins or outs of it but yesterday Haversham telephoned me to say that he had worrying news about the others and that I should meet him in his dressing room this morning. When I got there..."

"You found this instead?"

He nodded.

"I still don't see why you haven't gone to the police."

"I told you, they say that they will sacrifice him!" he wailed. "They also said that they have eyes everywhere and would know if I went to the authorities. I used to know the old Detective Chief Inspector quite well, but the new chap who's filled his shoes is somewhat of an unknown quantity." Philips paused. "Besides, he's a, you know?"

My mouth fell open. I couldn't believe what I was hearing. The new Detective Chief Inspector, Jitendra Patel had taken up his position just two weeks ago and the local rags had already fanned the flames of latent racism that burnt in the uneducated masses, but to hear it from an allegedly intelligent man such as Philips made me see red. I didn't say a word. I couldn't say a word. I just dragged him up by his lapels, manhandled him across my office and jettisoned him down a flight of stairs before slamming the door behind him.

I lashed out at the partly-assembled desk, swore as I barked my shin and slumped into my swivel chair before catching sight of the thin, white rectangle that lay discarded on the floor. It was Philips' envelope. I picked it up and stared at the five-pointed star, licking my lips as my mouth felt dry. I needed a drink. I picked up the phone and started to dial.

I think the thing I like most about my office (and also my flat, which is situated just upstairs) is the handy location. 15a Dalton Square is close to just about everything that I really need. It's a three storey building with my flat on the top floor (although there is an attic space which I might find a use for at some point), my office on the middle floor and the Paradise Dragon Chinese restaurant on the ground floor, opening out onto Dalton Square. The Dragon is owned and run by one Mr Harry Kim. Now any *Star Trek* nuts out there will be jumping up and down at the coincidence of my landlord having the same name as the chief of engineering from *Voyager*. Trust me, even though he talks incessantly about his folks back home, I have never seen him fall disastrously in love with either a hologram or a shape-shifting alien. Harry is just Harry – a damn decent bloke. I mean, who else would let me take up so much room rent free? Okay, I did rid his kitchens of a poltergeist a couple of months ago for which he was, and still is, eternally grateful, but that gratitude goes both ways as a lack of monthly rent certainly helps my finances stretch that bit further.

If you come out of the stairs leading down from my office to the side of the Dragon, then turn either left or right, you can follow the road round into the centre of town. Lancaster is not the biggest of cities and is easily navigable by foot, which suits me down to the ground as my 1983 VW Polo Classic is somewhat temperamental. I sometimes wonder if it is possessed, but then I shrug and think, "Nah. Stephen King's already done that one."

If you cross over the one-way road in front of the Dragon, then you are in Dalton Square proper. This was the direction I had taken after making one quick phone call and stuffing the dratted envelope in my mac pocket. Now most people would normally cross over the road using one of the two sets of pedestrian crossings at either end of the square, but I prefer the more direct route. Why not live life to the max, I say. The cars that screeched to a halt and blasted their horns did not seem to agree. I just thrust my hands in my mac, kept my eyes straight ahead and hopped onto the opposite path. I was now on the island that makes up the centre of Dalton Square. It is, as it were, a small park decked out with four large flower beds, recently renovated benches and a large copper statue of Queen Victoria which faces the Town Hall. I carried on walking past the late queen and hurried in the direction away from the local politicians towards my ultimate destination: the Borough.

The Borough lounges on the corner of Dalton Square and Sulyard Street. Look for it on Google Maps. You'll see it immediately. It's one of the few pubs that are actually marked on there. Quite right too as it's my little haven of calm and worthy of such recognition. I bounced up the front steps, pushed the doors open, breathed in the warm, welcoming atmosphere and smiled.

I was home.

I slipped off my mac and lay it on the back of my chair near the window then popped my fedora hat on top before wandering up to the bar. It was about mid-day so it wasn't too busy. I smiled at the barmaid. "Hi, Grace."

Grace beamed her infectious, little smile straight back at me. She's a nice kid, a post-grad at Luneside University down on the Quay. Like most students, she is normally broke and hence supplements her funding with a few hours here and there working behind the bar.

"Hello, trouble," she grinned from under her woolly brown hat that never seems to be parted from her curly red hair. "You on your own today?" She reached under the bar and pulled out a bottle of Jack Daniel's and one crystal tumbler.

I shook my head. "Nah. He'll be here in just a bit. You know Spliff. He'll be late for his own funeral, that one."

Grace chuckled and reached under the bar again. This time she produced a bottle of Gordon's as well as another tumbler. "That chilled?" I asked as I poured myself a whiskey.

"It bloody well better had be!" boomed a clipped baritone voice from behind my shoulder as I heard the doors swing open and shut, "but then that gorgeous little pre-Raphaelite picture knows just how I like my gin..."

"Chilled and straight, just like your men?" Grace grinned, pouring a measure of alcohol.

"Exactly!" beamed Spliff as he downed the drink in one. "Much more of a challenge. Now Samuel, dear. What seems to be the problem on this fine autumnal day?"

I smiled, raised my eyebrows at Grace and took my drink over to our table in the bay window where the portly frame of Reverend James Francis MacIntyre (or "Spliff" to his friends) joined me. He slumped down into his chair opposite and slipped his dog collar from out of the slit in the neck of his clericals and flipped it onto the small table between us. "Off duty," he smiled and raised his glass to me. "Your good health, Sam. Now, what's got your g-string all knotted up around your testicles?"

I reached into my jacket pocket, pulled out the envelope and slid it across the table. Spliff's grey eyes twinkled as he picked the item up and turned it over in his hands.

"A valentine's card? It's not even Hallowe'en yet, let alone Christmas. Mind you, I always knew you'd come round to my way of thinking."

"Behave," I sighed. "What do you make of that? I got given it this morning?"

Spliff held the envelope between his thumbs and index fingers and smiled. "Was the deliverer of this a good, god-fearing Christian?"

"I didn't get the chance to find out. I threw the bigoted little racist out of my office." I sipped at my whiskey. "He said he was sent it by Satanists."

Spliff harrumphed.

"What? What's the matter?" I asked.

He turned the envelope around, making sure that it was facing the right way up. "Samuel, what do you see here?"

"A pentagram," I shrugged.

"Indeed. Now tell me which way it is facing. Where is it pointing?"

"Upwards. The point goes up."

"Exactly." He tossed the envelope onto the table and downed his gin before waving the empty glass in Grace's direction. "That's no devil symbol there, Sam. It's the five wounds of Christ, a Christian symbol. They drew it the wrong way up, the imbeciles!"

Grace approached the table with our bottles of drink. I flipped the envelope face down. She's a sweet kid. I didn't want to freak her. "You do know it's only you two who get waitress service in here, don't you?" she smiled.

"Ah, and what lovely service it is, my dear," Spliff beamed.

Grace giggled. "Stop it, you old queen. Now what else can I get you?"

"DRPs?"

"No probs. Coming right up."

She trotted off to the bar and returned shortly with a bowl of peanuts. After she had returned to work, Spliff palmed a few nuts into his mouth and asked, whilst chewing, "So what does it say?"

"Hmmm?"

"The letter? What does it say? Really Sam, I do sometimes wonder how you managed a first back at uni."

"Oh. I don't know. Like I said, it was given to me this... Hey! Spliff!"

He yanked the envelope out of my reach as I lunged forward to stop him opening it. He whipped the enclosed letter out, slipped on his spectacles and peered gleefully at its contents. "My, my," he murmured. "Ooo, nasty. Urgh. Wouldn't have done that in front of my mother, that's for sure. Is that physically possible?" When he had finished, he waved the letter under my nose and said, "Well they may not have much knowledge of arcane imagery, but they certainly have a graphic imagination. James Herbert would be proud of them. Want to see?"

I snatched the letter from his hand and glowered at him before having a read for myself. As there might be children reading this, I won't go into too much detail, but let's just say that the writers of the letter seemed quite determined to ensure that the next time Haversham ate a three-course meal he would be able to watch it travelling all the way down his oesophagus, into his stomach and then onto his bowels. Nice. "Sick bastards," I grumbled. "You think they mean it?"

Spliff had been steadily munching his way through the bowl of nuts and was now tipping the dusty remains into his hand. "Who knows?" he shrugged. "But can you take the risk that they don't? If I had a student come to me in floods of tears saying that their teddy bear had been stolen and had found this in its place then I would tell them to stop whinging and get a new teddy bear," (I always admired Spliff's loving touch and pastoral care for his charges as a university chaplain), "but this is a real-life person, albeit a hack, has-been actor who had to marry into money to save his dying, lack-lustre career."

"Tell me again, why they appointed you? Was it your ability to empathise with those in need or just your, kind, caring manner?"

He leant forward and grinned, "Sam, you know it was because the bursar couldn't take his eyes off my finely-toned arse. Now, what are you going to do about that poor hack, Haversham?"

I sighed and pulled out my mobile. I had another phone call to make and a good dose of humble pie to eat.

One hour later I was munching on a falafel panini I had grabbed in Market Square and I was making my way up Penny Street towards the White Cross industrial estate where John O'Gaunt Media had its offices and studios. I was feeling somewhat perplexed. When I had rung Philips I had been expecting the cold shoulder treatment. I had thrown him unceremoniously out of my office, after all. Instead he was very warm and welcoming. He understood my anger at his silly off-hand comment. He had come from an old working class background, he explained, and deep prejudices were hard to be relieved of even in this cosmopolitan age. So he had arranged for me to visit the studios and meet with the three other members of the production team: Baines, Sothwell and Brande.

I wrapped my humble pie in cling wrap and stashed it in the freezer for a later date. My stomach, however, had been rumbling at the lack of more tangible fodder following my mid-day drink, so I had opted for the panini and quite delicious it was too. I was just finishing it when I crossed over the lights from Penny Street to South Road with the imposing stone built edifice that is White Cross Industrial Estate looming in front of me. Like many of the older buildings in Lancaster, it has a link to the Victorian mills. I think this one used to be a linen mill, but I might be mistaken. I'm not from round these parts originally and my local history is somewhat patchy. It was revamped in the eighties and split up into numerous offices and warehouses. John O'Gaunt occupy the main building on the front which overlooks the main road that crosses the canal bound for Preston and Glasson Dock.

It was quite a blustery day and I pulled my coat up tight to keep out the chill. The number two bus was just dropping gaggles of students off on the opposite side of the road outside the infirmary. Looking at the young, fresh-faced learners made me think of my desk in pieces back at the office. What was I going to do about those infernal instructions? Could I get an English set off the internet?

I froze. A chill ran down my back that wasn't being directed by the wind. I glanced over my shoulder and saw a youth stood a few metres behind me. He looked like he had come up the canal tow-path and was leaning casually against its stone entrance by the rambling ivy. I was sure I hadn't seen him as I'd passed it, but then my thoughts had been somewhat elsewhere. I stopped in my tracks and let my eyes study him. He was of average height and seemed slim of build, clothed in shabby jeans and a grey hoodie. What really grabbed my attention were his pale, grey-blue eyes that just stared at me from under his mop of dark, brown hair. I'm sure he didn't blink once.

I started to take a step towards him when I heard someone calling my name. I spun round towards the source of the voice and saw Philips hurrying towards me from White Cross. I flicked my eyes back round to the canal tow path and, surprise surprise, the boy was gone. I swore under my breath. I don't like mysteries and I don't like being spied on, but there was nothing that I could do about it right now, so I fixed my professional smile on my face and walked over towards my host.

I have to say that the John O'Gaunt studios were not at all how I expected them to be. I guess it was Philips' slightly careworn appearance that had somewhat coloured my expectations, but the insides were rather quite swanky. The producer showed me in through the main entrance where I was smiled at and greeted by a pretty young receptionist who handed me a visitor's badge. Various bodies were milling around, traversing from one important location or office to another. I had to dodge quite a few people in my journey across the foyer. Philips led me down a bright, white corridor past a number of purple doors. "What's behind these?" I asked.

"Oh, these are our sets." He explained. "We have a limited amount of space here, obviously, so we only use five rooms and rotate the sets in them. The rest of the time the sets are stored away in the props department. They're sort of flat-pack, I guess."

I cringed at the use of the term "flat-pack", thinking once more about my desk-shaped nemesis, but he didn't seem to notice. I pointed to the nearest door. "So what's set up in here at the moment?"

"That would be 52, Acacia Drive – Mrs Haddock's house."

I looked blank.

"Mrs Haddock is played by Maggie."

"Ah," I said, and opened the door. Philips bustled behind me explaining that we really ought to go straight to his office as the actors were very busy and were waiting for us, but I just ignored him. I'd never been on a film set before so I wanted to have a look. It was a rather weird experience. When I walked through I was directly behind the cameras (there were two of them). Beyond that was a room that looked for all intents and purposes like my mother's living room: photos of relatives on the wall and toby jugs in a small corner cabinet.

"Mr Spallucci, time really is of the essence. We should be..."

Philips continued to blabber on as I entered the living room. I smiled.

Yes, it really was like my mum's house. There was the gas fire and the hearth rug. There was the faded three-piece suite facing the telly. The curtains were drawn back and held in place with little ties.

I sat down on the sofa and stroked my chin. Well this certainly didn't feel satanic at all did it? I was suddenly aware that Philips had stopped yammering on. He was just stood staring at me. "Is there a problem? I asked.

"Mr Spallucci, I know that you are not accustomed to this environment, but please, please don't touch anything. Every item here will have been set out at the end of the last take and will be prepared for the next shooting."

I raised my arms, slightly worried that I may have inadvertently ruined the artistic forming of the sofa. "How come it's not being filmed on today?"

"Because its occupant is currently waiting outside my office," he sighed. "Now if you would kindly follow me?"

I stood up, making sure not to do anything as clumsy as kick the hearth rug and made to follow Philips. Just as I was passing the fire-place I stopped and glanced at a small ornament on the mantel. Now, on my *mum's* mantel, you will find a profusion of Leonardo figurines or china dogs. I was sure that she had never owned anything quite like this. It was a silver piece about ten centimetres tall. It seemed to be a lion with a long, serpentine tail and an extra head in the shape of a goat. Instinctively, I reached out and picked up the little figurine.

"Mr Spallucci!" Philips stomped over, grabbed the ornament and very carefully set it back in its exact position. "I told you not to touch anything. Now please, can we go?"

I gave the statuette a hard stare then nodded and walked out of the set.

Philips' office was not too far away – just through a couple of double doors and down a bending corridor. My sense of direction is not very good at the best of times and, away from natural light, I was completely lost. However, I knew that we had arrived before he could say anything, just by the sight that met my aching eyes. At first I thought I was imagining things. There in front of his office door, bickering maniacally was a woman who had been cloned and then subsequently been both aged and rejuvenated so that there were two versions of her – one in its late sixties and one in its early twenties. Not only that, but every seemingly decent cell had been sucked from her body and replaced by ones which screamed "Strumpet!" Such were the phenomena of Melanie Brande and Maggie Sothwell.

"Philips!" screeched the younger actress, Brande. "Where the hell have you been? I've been waiting ages. I haven't got all day, you know? I have a function to attend in two hours and I have to get myself ready." She shot me a filthy look. "Who's this perv? He looks like a dirty mac man."

"This is Mr Samuel Spallucci. The investigator I told you about, Mel," Philips explained in a placatory manner. "He's here to talk to the thr-" He stopped short and frowned. "Where's Howard?"

"He's gone home, dear," said Sothwell. "Said he had important business to attend to. You know how impatient he can be." Her eyes fell on me and I saw an unmistakable twinkle in their pupils that made my libido want to run screaming for the middle of the Antarctic. "Well, hello, Mr Spallucci," she purred, offering her bejewelled hand. "Wonderful to meet you."

I politely shook her hand whilst my libido continued to hurriedly pack its belongings into a large suitcase. "Pleased to meet you too, Mrs Sothwell."

"Oh, please, young man. Call me Maggie," she giggled in a coquettish manner.

I smiled the smile a terrified rabbit gives the headlights of a large, oncoming truck and looked hopefully at Philips.

He coughed. "Perhaps, you would like to start by asking Melanie a few questions in my office? I will try to track down Howard whilst you do so."

I nodded quickly, gave Sothwell another quick smile of fear and rushed into Philips' office, followed by the sulky Miss Brande.

"You got a cigarette?"

"Pardon?" The question caught me off-guard. I was still trying to accustom myself to my latest set of surroundings. The office was small but impeccably neat. There were photographs of Philips posing with various actors plastered across one wall and awards displayed on another. The third wall was home to his desk and a number of filing cabinets. There were two chairs: Philips' desk chair and a red, leather sofa. Brande had folded herself onto the sofa and crossed her legs provocatively. I could not help but notice the top of a stocking peeking out from under her incredibly short skirt.

"I said, 'You got a cigarette?' You a retard as well as a perv?" She crossed her legs again.

I blushed and fished into my mac, drawing out a pack of Lucky Strikes. I flipped the lid and offered her one. She took it without so much as a thank-you. My guess was that Miss Brande was not very forthcoming in gratitude.

She popped the cigarette in her mouth and lifted an eyebrow expectantly? "What?" I asked.

She sighed and removed the cigarette. "A light?"

I reached into another pocket and retrieved my Zippo. I tossed it over to the brunette and sat on the desk chair. "Knock yourself out. Please," I grumbled.

She lit the Lucky then studied the lighter. "Fancy. Quite esoteric," she commented. "I've always liked pyramids. So... potent." She threw the Zippo back. I had better explain that it has a design of a pyramid with an eye emblazoned across the front wall. I've had it since it caught my eye as a student. It was a gift from... well let's just say "a friend" for now, shall we?

I pocketed the Zippo. "Well, here we are," I said.

"Indeed we are," Brande blew a smoke ring. "One young starlet and one ageing dirty mac man. Do you get over to Rylands park much?"

I ignored the quip and pressed on. "What can you tell me about Haversham?"

"Apart from the fact that he was a dirty old man?"

I groaned. "Do you think all men are perverts then?"

She shrugged and the shoulders of her red dress rose and fell causing her necklace to glint in the light of the office. "Only those over twenty-five. Those under are normally quite buff."

Buff? Did people still use that as a description? I shook my head and continued. "So? Tell me about Haversham." She opened her mouth to speak and I held up my hand with the smoking Lucky between my fingers. "Without any comments about his perviness."

Brande grimaced, inhaled heavily on her cigarette and pouted. "Not much to tell really. He was quiet, boring. Kept himself to himself really."

"What about his interests?"

"Dunno. Like I said. He kept himself to himself."

I was getting nowhere fast. "When was the last time you saw him?" I asked.

"On set two days ago. He seemed somewhat anxious." Brande fiddled with the hem of her red dress.

"What do you mean by anxious?"

"He was fidgety, jumpy. He kept snapping at us."

"Us?"

"Me, Maggie and Baines."

"What about the rest of the cast? What about the crew?"

She shook her head. "Nope. He was okay with them. Perhaps he was just having a luvvie fit?" She looked at her watch and stubbed the cigarette out on Philips' desk. "Can I go now? This is boring."

I had to admit that I was hardly enthralled myself. I nodded and stood up. As the actress made to stand, she leant forward and her pendant glinted in the light once more. I frowned and reached out, grasping it in my hand.

"Hey!" she shouted. "Get your filthy hands off of me!"

I twisted the pendant around and dangled it in front of her green eyes. "Do you know what this is?" I demanded, my face in front of hers.

"A necklace," she sneered and tried to wriggle free.

I pulled tighter. Brande gasped as the chain cinched around her neck. "Don't get smart with me. A man is missing and I have to find him." I pointed to the two-headed creature made from silver. "This is a chimera and I've seen another one of these quite recently."

There was a sharp slapping sound as Brande's palm connected with my cheek and I staggered backwards, dropping the pendant. She spat at me, turned and stormed out of the room. As I wiped her spit from my face I decided that perhaps the interview could have gone somewhat better.

I collapsed onto Philips' desk chair and groaned inwardly. This was sheer lunacy! What was I doing here? Earning a living, that's what, I told myself. It couldn't get any worse, I told myself. It couldn't.

There was a gentle knock at the door.

"Come on in!" I called.

The door swung open and the ageing figure of Maggie Sothwell swept in, a radiant, beaming smile filling her heavily made-up face. “Mr Spallucci, darling,” she flounced, “I have been dying to meet you.”

*I bet you have*, I thought.

“Roger has told me all about you.”

“Roger?”

“Roger, darling. Roger Philips.”

“Ah,” I nodded. My *chat* with the fiery Brande had obviously disturbed my memory. “Please, Mrs Sothwell, take a seat.” I waved towards the sofa.

Sothwell luxuriated herself down onto the forgiving upholstery. “Please, darling, like I said before, call me Maggie. Oh, this is so exciting. A real-life detective, here at our little studio. Have you solved many crimes, Mr Spallucci?”

I coughed and mumbled something placatory. I hardly had the heart to tell her that this was my first professional case since setting up in Dalton Square. “Well, Maggie, as you know, I'm investigating the disappearance of Malcolm Haversham. What can you tell me about him?”

“Oh, Malcolm was a delightful man. So attentive,” her eyes glimmered.

I shuddered at just how attentive Sothwell liked her men to be. “You said ‘was’. Do you think he's dead?”

“Who's to know, darling?” she shrugged making her voluminous bosom ripple under her tight–fitting dress. “I would imagine that things don't look very good for him though?”

“Why would that be?”

She leant forward conspiratorially, “Because of a phone call I overheard the other day, that's why?”

I nodded for her to continue.

“Well, darling, it was before we were about to go on set and Malcolm was missing, so I volunteered to go and find him. I was just about to knock on his dressing room door when I heard raised voices. I stood and listened, trying to make out the words, but it was no good. My other faculties may still all be there, but my hearing's not what it used to be. Then I heard him stomping up to the dressing room door so I hid round the corner. He came out in quite the fury, darling. He was shouting obscenities into the mobile and just before he hung up he said something like, ‘You don't scare me. You're all mad, I say. Mad!’ Then he pocketed the phone and marched off to the set. Most peculiar, don't you think?”

I tapped my teeth with my nails. Peculiar? I wasn't so sure. Convenient seemed more likely. I could smell a proverbial rat. Something here was about as phoney as a sun-tan in Lytham-St-Annes.

I asked Sothwell a few more questions and dodged a few of her more personal inquiries then graciously allowed her to get on with her life. I picked my hat up from Philips' desk and twisted it round and round between my hands. My investigation was moving in a similar direction to my fedora: in circles. Two interviews and all I had achieved was an overwhelming feeling that the two female leads of *More Tea Vicar* were more concerned with their sex lives than the disappearance of Haversham.

I stood up and kicked the sofa. I was frustrated. Totally frustrated. There was nothing, just spurious hints and futile dead ends.

Except...

As I made my way to the office door I turned over in my mind the image of the two-headed chimera. Brande had the necklace and there was the statue in Sothwell's fictional home. Was there a connection?

I didn't know, but if Baines appeared to possess such a symbol then perhaps... just perhaps. I walked out of the office and went to hunt down Philips. I needed Baines' address.

Sociologists may argue against me, but I believe that Lancaster can be divided into four really distinct social groups. At the bottom and, as in most cities, most prolific are the working class. This is itself split into two groups. There are those who are either looking for or have jobs (such as in the high street shops or on the numerous industrial estates), then there are those who don't want a job and will never look for one until the day that the council throws them into a pauper's grave. The workers/work-seekers in this group are the salt of the earth. They may not be the most academically intelligent but they are grafters and make sure that their families are well-fed and cared for. The work-shy ones, well, how can I put it politely? Hmmm. I can't. They're losers. They will harass you for a quid with some sob story about needing to save up for a train ticket or a meal and then go and piss it up a wall or shoot it up their arm. Both of these sub-groups tend to live in areas dominated by small terraces or semis that used be council housing but have been gradually sold off to make quick capital for the permanently broke local authorities. The former group hate the latter and the latter just don't give a shit.

The second class of Lancastrians tend to be the imports. They are, on the whole, the liberal middle-class. Normally, they are university graduates who liked the area so much that they decided that it would be a wonderful place to settle down, co-habit and raise three bratty children called Louis, Penny and Lyle. In the early eighties they were solid Labour. Now they are true Green and would happily have solar panels on every inch of the roof of their converted Victorian terrace house if it wasn't going to look just so very unsightly. I don't have much time for this class, the pompous, sanctimonious floating voters. In fact, I probably have to say I prefer the jobless winos to these folk-singing, arran clad, body-shopping hypocrites.

Anyway, onto the third class. These are the ones whose families have been here the longest. These are the old money in Lancaster. They vote Tory but I just can't hold it against them as they quietly get on with their lives. They will normally have a rambling pile out in Scotforth somewhere or a family farm on the edge of the city. I will never be able to agree with their political views but I respect them for holding true to what they actually believe rather than following the latest fad or trying to stab someone in the back to climb up the social ladder. Which brings me onto the fourth class.

These are what would have been called the bourgeoisie many years ago. Marx would have hated them. These would originally have been in the working class or the middle class. However, somewhere along the line, the greed for money and power has infected them. They have turned their backs on those who supported them when times were hard. They have scurried off to a private estate somewhere and surrounded themselves in their own personal red brick fortress complete with a trampoline for the snobby offspring. These they ship out to Cumbria for schooling rather than pollute them with anti-social ideas from local children. They shop in Preston or Manchester and the husband works even further afield whilst the wife stays at home to cook, clean and drink gin.

Needless to say, when I drew up outside Baines' spacious mock Tudor house, my view of him was already somewhat coloured. As I crunched my way up his winding gravel path, I glanced over my shoulder at my 1983 Polo and sighed. Perhaps my animosity to this sort of set up was jealousy. Perhaps it was a feeling of injustice. Whatever it was, I knew that I would end up giving the guy a hard time and thoroughly enjoy it. I rapped the ornate door-knocker and waited a few moments until the door opened. A tall, grey man with a slight stoop peered down at me with a condescending glare. No, honest! He was! I'm not letting my prejudices colour your first encounter of him. He had the look of someone who feels that everyone else is totally beneath him. "Philips said you were coming," he sneered. "I suppose you'd better come in."

So I did.

I have to be truthful here, the inside of the house was rather nice. I had expected fake wooden panelling and a roaring fire, but it was quite minimalist with a distinct lack of clutter accentuated by crisp, sharp edges. Nice and tidy, just how I like my living spaces myself. "You were late at the studio so I had to leave," Baines explained as he walked ahead of me, giving me plenty of opportunity to study the back of his stooped, black-clad figure. He really was quite tall, a good head height above me. It was no wonder that he stooped. "Damned inconsiderate keeping us all hanging about like that. I really don't see what all the fuss is." He opened a stark, white door and gestured for me to enter.

"I would have thought that you would be concerned for Haversham," I commented as I entered the room which was a mixture of office-cum-study. There was a large grey desk positioned slap bang in the middle of the floor with one wall full to the brim of books opposing a wall that was complete glass, overlooking an expansive garden.

What really caught my eye, though, was a sketched drawing mounted in a large frame on the wall behind the desk. I crossed the room, all thoughts of Haversham momentarily swept from my mind, my eyes fixed to the picture.

"You like that?" Baines asked, a touch of warmth in his voice. "Curious piece, isn't it? It was a gift. Apparently it's from Greek mythology. It's a..."

"Chimera," I finished as I let my eyes skip from the goat's to the lion's head and down the serpentine tail. It was truly a fine piece of work. I could make out every muscle, every sinew down the twisting spine of the creature as it rose up on its hind legs to attack me. "Who was it a gift from?" I asked.

"No one that you would know," Baines answered dreamily as he drew level and gazed lovingly at the piece of artwork. "I'm not normally one for receiving gifts as, all too often, they come with a price – but I just couldn't say, 'No,' to this. The picture was calling out to me. Does that make sense?"

I nodded, unable to speak as I continued to be drawn into every last detail of the artist's vivid imagination.

"It's not the first time I've seen this chap today." I whispered, "Melanie Brande wears one round her neck and there is a statue of one on the set of *More Tea Vicar*."

Baines turned to face me. "Really?" I tore my eyes away from the creature and studied his response. He seemed genuinely surprised. "That's funny. I've not noticed." He moved away and sat behind his desk, his hands clasped together. I gave the picture one last glance and walked back around in front of him.

"So why is it you're not concerned for Haversham?" I asked once more.

Baines gave a non-committal shrug of his rounded shoulders. "The man's an oaf, a drama queen. He will have suffered some sort of hissy fit and flounced off somewhere for a week or two before gliding back in all sweetness and light, saying how he has missed us all, his dear friends, so terribly, terribly much."

Baines' voice dripped acid and contempt.

"Are you saying this has happened before?"

"God yes!" Baines harrumphed. "A number of times. "The man is completely unreliable. Something normally sets him off and he goes walkabout."

I tapped my teeth and considered Sothwell's description of Haversham's phone conversation. It did seem to fit with what Baines was saying. I reached into my inside pocket and pulled out the envelope containing the letter. "What do you make of this?" I asked as I passed it over.

Baines peered down at the pentagram then slowly opened the envelope and withdrew the letter. He gave it a quick glance and snorted his contempt. "Did Philips give you this?"

I nodded.

He slowly shook his head. "That man is a complete cretin." He waved the letter in the air and said, "I'd recognise this handwriting anywhere. It's Haversham's!"

By the time I slumped down into my armchair in my flat above my Dalton Square office, my head hurt. I grabbed the stereo remote and flicked it on. The calming sounds of Mike Oldfield wafted around my living room and I closed my eyes. I was stressed. I could tell this because the sound of multi-instrumental genius was not the only accompaniment playing in my ears.

The infernal sound of the tiniest bells ever cast were jangling furiously in my head. I suffer from tinnitus. I've had it since I was a kid and it's more or less constant, but it's normally a background noise, a whisper that I hardly ever register. However, when things start to stress me out, it's all that I can hear, all that I really notice. Everything else gets swept aside in the rushing waves of tintinnabulation and my head screams for quiet. So as I sat there, my eyes clenched tight, I did what I normally do in this situation: I turned the music up loud and grabbed the bottle of Jack Daniel's from its space on the floor next to my chair. I poured a large measure and downed it in one then lit myself a Lucky Strike. The smoke sank deep into my lungs and I coughed, but it was a good cough, a satisfying cough. A deep harsh sound that could punch through those wretched bells!

I poured another glass of whiskey and sat deep in thought. Something smelt as fishy as the docks at Glasson. I pulled the now well-read letter out of my pocket and scanned its scrawling script once more. Baines claimed that this was Haversham's hand-writing. This meant one of two things: either Haversham had faked his own abduction or Baines was lying. As I sipped at the bourbon I considered both of these points. Brande hated Haversham, but then she seemed to hate most people of the opposite sex from a certain age upwards. Sothwell claimed that Haversham had been arguing on the phone the day before he disappeared. Was that connected? Was it fabricated? Philips claimed that Brande, Haversham and Sothwell were all Satanists. Was this true or just speculation?

The truth of the matter was that I had no hard and fast facts to base anything on. There was just a possibly fabricated letter and a bunch of hearsay. Marvellous! I drained the whiskey glass and looked outside the window across the square. It was getting dark, twilight. A good time to go snooping around when no one would spot you. If you try and snoop during the night, then you might as well wear a black and white striped sweater and carry a bag marked "swag". Someone will instantly spot you in the empty street and either call the police or confront you. If you venture out when day is just ending and night is falling, then there are enough people around for background cover. You can blend into the last stragglers as they wend their tired way home from a long hard day's work. You are just another faceless, nameless body swept along in the daily grind.

It was time for a good snoop around the John O'Gaunt studios. This was the only place I had which was tangible, which linked the players in my little drama together. I got up and made my way to the door when my mobile started to vibrate in my pocket. I fished it out and flicked it on. "Hello?" I asked.

"Mr Spallucci?" It was Philips. I raised an eyebrow. Don't you just love synchronicity?

"Speaking. What can I do for you Mr Philips?"

"I... I'm at the studio," he whispered. "There's something going on. There's something you ought to see. Please come quickly. Please... Oh no!" The phone clicked dead.

I stood staring into my mobile as if it could explain to me what had just happened. "The plot thickens," I muttered to myself and walked out of my flat.

I was back at John O'Gaunt studios in approximately ten minutes. The sky was turning a deep indigo shade of purple and Venus was hovering over the stone crenellations of White Cross Industrial Estate. Quite apt, I thought to myself, that the Daystar known in antiquity as Lucifer should be watching over a supposed satanic cult.

I cut away from the meandering traffic of late commuters and wandering students and made down the approach towards the entrance to the studios outside the main gate of the estate. I made sure that I did not look suspicious and refrained from checking over my shoulder before trying the front door – I was just another employee entering the studio on mundane business.

The door swung inwards and I was left peering into a dark corridor. "No lights on, but there must be somebody home," I muttered to myself and quickly stepped inside. I closed the door behind me and drew a small penlight out from my mac. The small beam flicked across the plush, carpeted floor of the main corridor and exposed no stumbling blocks or protrusions so I carefully ventured along the gloomy passage. The corridor was, dare I say, deathly quiet. The sound of my footfalls were cushioned by the pile of the well-trodden but immaculately clean carpet. All I was aware of was the sound of my breath and the tinny ringing in my ears. I'm not one for dark spaces. I used to wake screaming as a child, crying for my poor parents to turn all the lights on before I would even try to return to some semblance of infant slumbering. As I cautiously edged my way through the premises towards Philips' office, my mind kept telling me that creatures of unimaginable grotesqueness would leap out from around a blind corner and proceed to rip my head off then devour my innards. I could feel tension starting to increase in my body. My shoulders were starting to ache and I was aware of my heart pounding. This was not good; higher blood pressure affects tinnitus. I stopped for a moment as I drew near to Philips' office and leant against a wall. Sure enough, the ringing in my ears was gradually crescendoing. I concentrated and tried to slow my heart rate by breathing slowly, but it was no use, the old ticker was beating faster than ever.

Damn it! I swung the pen light around the corner and, after seeing nothing, decided I just had to press on regardless of the irritation in my ears. I leant up against the office door and pressed my already overloaded ear up against the purple painted wood. I could hear nothing apart from those noises that existed purely in my head. I swore and slowly edged the door open. It silently swung half way then came to an abrupt stop. I pushed a bit harder but it did not budge an iota. My hand was shaking as I swept the light around behind the door. First, it found a pair of black, highly polished shoes, then the legs of a grey suit lying limp on the floor. I rushed in and bent to grab Philips by the shoulders. I gripped the penlight in my mouth as I used both hands to turn his body over. It almost dropped from the grip of my teeth when he opened his eyes and smiled at me.

The next thing I knew was a heavy blow to the back of my neck, then there was just darkness.

When I came to, I realised that I was in a most unfortunate predicament. Aside from the fact that the back of my neck was throbbing, I was also somehow bound hand and foot to the floor. As I wrestled with my bonds I dared to move my head in order to survey my situation.

It was dire.

I was tied down in the centre of a pentagram.

The day just seemed to be getting worse.

As I tugged hopelessly I heard the steady, confident footsteps that I knew would be Baines. Even the sound of his shoes sounded as smooth as his crooning baritone. “Ah, Mr Spallucci. I see you are awake. Very good. We would not want you to miss the fun now, would we?”

“You call this fun?” I asked. “This is about as much fun as a Saturday night in Skerton. Ow!”

My left side erupted in pain as the sharp toe-end of a patent high heel shoe jabbed into me. “I grew up in Skerton, you old git!” The delightful Miss Brande.

“Well that explains a lot,” I shot back. I received another sharp kick, but it was worth it to see her riled. I really hated that little bitch. Like Baines, she was adorned in a long, flowing scarlet red robe, although hers was cut short enough to show off a decent amount of leg. Didn’t people only wear that sort of thing on dodgy websites? You know the sort – www.saucy-wiccans.com.

I could hear hushed voices from my right and turned my head to see the source. There was the miraculously not-dead Philips and the blue-rinsed Sothwell conversing with an elderly man adorned in a shock of white hair. “Ah, the eponymous Malcolm Haversham, I presume?” I called out cheerfully.

The white-haired man turned round and his blue eyes twinkled as they fixed on me. “The hardly-renowned Mr Samuel C Spallucci, I presume?” he returned as he bowed his head slightly.

I shrugged as best as I could with my arms at obtuse angles from my body, “It’s been a short career so far.”

“And it will remain so,” Haversham commented as he held out his right hand, palm up. Baines shuffled up beside him and placed a cruel looking dagger in his grasp. “You see, Mr Spallucci, we really cannot allow a gentleman of your profession to wander aimlessly around our little city whilst we practice our dark, nefarious deeds, can we, hmmm? You might inadvertently cause us some sort of bother. So we decided that we ought to lure you here somehow to despatch you quickly and quietly. At first we thought that my abduction would suffice but, alas, our acting could not have been of great merit as you did not readily devour the bait. So we had to resort to another staged abduction over the telephone, and quite a performance it was too," he said towards Philips, who stood and beamed as the others actually began to clap him.

"No, please. You're too kind," Philips protested. "It was nothing, really."

I shook my head in despair. Apparently I was about to be sacrificed by a cult of self-congratulating luvvies. "But you had me here this afternoon. Why didn't you just kill me then?"

Haversham looked genuinely horrified at the suggestion. "What? In just the second act? Where would be the build-up? Where would be the suspense? No, Mr Spallucci, you had to leave us and go away to brood over the matter for a while whilst the viewer tried to piece the mystery together with you." He smiled the sort of smile an old uncle gives a young lad who is trying to ride his wobbly little bike down the street for the first time.

"The viewer?"

"Yes, the viewer, Mr Spallucci. It is always about engaging the viewer in the story. Anyway, you are now at the end of the show and about to be removed from the picture, as it were. No hard feelings."

My blood ran cold. "None taken," I croaked and began yanking hard at the fastenings around my wrists.

Haversham casually polished the wicked edge of the curved blade with a golden-coloured cloth. "I really wouldn't exert yourself, Mr Spallucci. Those fastenings are quite secure. You would only hurt yourself, and we wouldn't want that would we, hmmm?"

I stared at him incredulously. Wouldn't want me to hurt myself? What the hell did he think the knife would do? Give me a soothing back massage? The guy was a complete fruit cake! They all were. How had I managed to let myself be snared in by bunch of five imbeciles.

Five.

Imbeciles.

Those words rang a bell. Why? Why did they sound so vitally important? As the five Satanists rounded on me and Haversham started to chant in a low, menacing voice, I desperately tried to wrack my fear-stricken memory for a glimmer of hope. However, my memory was currently curled up in a dark corner gibbering into its jumper which was pulled up over its head. As Haversham raised the knife I imagined myself bending down to coax my poor little memory out of its paralysis with a small packet of peanuts.

Peanuts.

Dry roasted peanuts.

Spliff!

The Satanists were now stood at the five points of the pentagram. I double-checked the lines on the floor. My head was in one of the points and Haversham was behind me which meant the symbol was facing upwards, not down.

The knife started to arc down through the air of the film set.

"YOUR PENTAGRAM IS THE WRONG WAY UP!!!" I shrieked and

closed my eyes.

There was silence and no searing pain in my chest - which I took to be a good thing. Tentatively I squeezed an eyelid open and peered through. Haversham's outstretched arms were being held in place by the strong grip of Howard Baines. It appeared that I had been granted a reprieve, if only momentarily. I would have to think fast.

"What do you mean that it's the wrong way up?" growled the deep baritone of Baines.

"I would have thought you would have done your research," I said, my mind racing ten to the dozen.

Haversham had now lowered the knife and was peering at me from a rather surreal upside down angle. "In what way, hmmm? It is the Sigil of Baphomet, a most dark image indeed."

I shook my head. "Sorry to disappoint you, but not the way you're using it. With my head here, it's the five wounds of Christ. You have me tied down the wrong way."

Brande swore such words that were most unbecoming of a young lady and spat, "He's lying! The old git's lying to save his worthless neck."

Sothwell waved a pacifying hand at her to calm the firebrand down. "But what if he isn't dear? What if we make a pointless sacrifice? Surely that would displease the dark lord?"

Baines towered above me. "How are we supposed to believe you, Spallucci? Melanie has a very valid point. You could just be trying to trick us."

I smiled. "Surely one of you has a phone on you? Go online and check Wikipedia. I bet it's on there. There you go. Wikipedia, the fount of all knowledge, scientific and arcane."

"There's no need."

I turned my head and frowned. It was Philips that had spoken, but there was something about his voice. It seemed distant, far away.

"He speaks the truth. He is positioned wrong. We must move him," and in one graceful move he had knelt down and unhitched from the floor the clasp that held my left wrist. This would be my only chance. I gripped the fabric and whipped the heavy clasp around behind my head. It lashed around Haversham's ankles and I pulled hard. Normally, I don't think it would have worked, but he must have been caught off guard and he toppled over to his left into Baines who was too busy shouting at Philips to see the white-haired actor collapse on top of him.

I yanked my left hand free, lashing and all, and scrabbled to free my right hand. Just as my fingers had prised the clasp open I felt a weight pounce on me and a sharp set of nails dug into my neck. I rolled back and slammed Brande heavily onto the floor. She shrieked and fell limp, winded.

I pulled myself to my feet and quickly assessed the situation. Brande was winded. Haversham seemed to have struck his head and was out cold. Sothwell was staggering over to try and help Baines to his feet. Philips... Philips was just stood staring into thin air.

I shrugged. I had no time to wonder what was going on there. I caught sight of the knife and flew at it. Just as I grasped its cold hilt, a black polished shoe crunched down on my wrist. I yelped in agony then cried out as another shoe kicked me in the face. I fell back down on the floor and felt blood welling up in my left nostril as a fully recovered Baines reached down and prised the knife from my weakened grip. "Mr Spallucci," he menaced, "you appear to be far more resourceful than we had imagined. Sacrifice be damned! I'm finishing you now!" His face glowered as he fished a small revolver out of his robes and levelled it at my face. Then something rather peculiar happened. His aim faltered and he blinked as he dropped the gun with a loud clatter and backed off quickly. "No. No. No!" he shouted, waving his hands in front of him. "It can't be. You can't be that! It's not real. I only did it for the kudos. I never really believed in you." He was staring right at me and tears were streaming down his face as terror held him fast. He sank to his knees and buried his head in his hands and wept loudly. Puzzled, I drew myself up off the floor and instinctively slipped the revolver into my coat pocket before taking in my surroundings. Sothwell was the only other person not incapacitated or a gibbering wreck. She shot a worried frown at the gun-shaped bulge in my pocket before deciding that enough was enough and darted for the set's exit. She didn't get very far as the door was flung open and a group of uniformed policemen barged through, sending her flying. They raced into the room, batons raised and an authoritative voice boomed from behind them, "Nobody move! Police!" A tall, dark-skinned plain-clothes officer strode commandingly between the bobbies as they took up position around the varying members of the cast. "What the hell have we got here?" he demanded.

"DCI Patel?" I asked as I wobbled to my feet and stretched my hand out. "Sam Spallucci. Pleased to meet you."

Jitendra Patel grabbed my hand and helped me up. His dark eyes scanned the five actors then fixed themselves on me. "You have the office in Dalton Square, yes?"

I nodded.

"Would you care to enlighten me as to why we received a 999 call saying that you were about to be murdered here?"

I frowned and watched in a state of bewilderment as the policemen started to cuff my captors and read them their rights. Haversham took quite a bit of rousing and Philips seemed as if someone had laced his tea with Diazepam, but the most disturbing sight was that of Baines. As he was bundled past me he screamed in absolute terror. "Get me away from him! He will kill us all! He will kill us all!"

My spine felt icicles slide down its vertebrae. I looked back at DCI Patel. "I have no idea who rang you. I didn't tell anyone I was coming."

"It would seem that you have a guardian angel, then, Mr Spallucci," he smiled.

I smiled back and grimaced. My face hurt. "Please, call me Sam." I stuck out my right hand, this time in friendship, rather than a call for assistance.

The detective took it and shook it firmly. "Jitendra. Pleased to make your acquaintance. Listen, you look pretty beat up and we have a few questions to ask, obviously. Would you mind if one of my men dropped you off at your place to clean up then bring you back to the station?"

I ran my hand through my hair. "Sure," I agreed. "Get it out of me while it's still fresh."

"That's the idea. We'll go over this place with a fine tooth-comb." He strode over to Brande and hoisted her to her feet. "Come on you. Time for another show, and no play-acting." Brande said nothing. She just scowled as Jitendra and another officer led her away. As they walked past I saw something glint and tinkle as it hit the wooden floor. I bent down and scooped it up. It was Brande's silver pendant of the chimera. I looked at the mythological creature and ran a fingernail over my teeth. This little fellow seemed to have been everywhere, but it seemed to bear no significance to the Satanists at all. No one was watching me so I slipped it into my mac pocket next to the purloined revolver and headed towards the door of the studio where a policeman stood talking on his radio.

Thirty minutes later I was walking stiffly up the stairs to my flat whilst a bobby was parked up outside the Paradise Dragon. I felt as if had spent twenty-four hours in a gigantic tumble-dryer. I was hot and sweaty and my muscles screamed at every movement. I fished my keys out of my pocket and made to insert them into my lock.

I paused.

There was an envelope tacked to my door. It was addressed, "Sam."

I groaned inwardly. I had endured my fill of mysterious envelopes for the day, but I pulled it down and thumbed it open. When I realised what it contained, I could not help but smile. Whether the smile was one of joy or worry I was not totally sure, but I was certainly glad of the item that I now held in my hand. It was the assembly instructions for my office desk, in English. Scrawled across the bottom was a short message. "Sam. If you are reading this then the police arrived in the nick of time." I groaned at the awful pun. "I hope this will be of use to you as you seemed very troubled on the matter of your desk earlier. We shall meet soon. Alec."

Alec?

Who the hell was Alec?

Then it struck me, the boy standing outside White Cross when I was on my way to meet Philips. I had been thinking about the desk when he had been watching me. But how had he known my thoughts?

I shuddered. It was creepy. Very creepy. Nonetheless, I apparently owed the young man my life and more importantly, I decided as I looked at the plans for the desk, my sanity. Yes, young Alec, I thought to myself, I look forward to meeting you soon. I opened my flat door and stepped inside. There was a policeman waiting for me downstairs and I still needed to finish building my desk.

# The Case of the Vexed Vampire

Needless to say, after my little escapade with the five bungling Satanists, I decided that I needed to relax, to chill out, to curl up in a ball and cry "Mummy!" So, after tightening up the final screw of my chipboard nemesis, I did what I normally do when I'm stressed, I slipped downstairs to the Paradise Dragon to eat until I felt fit to burst.

"Sam!" cried Harry Kim, the restaurant's owner, as I walked through the glass doors that were adorned with red and black dragons, "Good to see you, old man. How are you?" He frowned then said, "No, don't tell me. You look like shit!"

I chuckled and removed my hat and mac which the restaurateur went and hung up by the kitchens. "Observant as ever, Harry," I called as I wandered over to my usual corner just behind the reception area, giving me a clear view of Dalton Square.

A bottle of sake in a warming jug was placed on the table next to me along with a small china cup as Harry came and sat down opposite. "You been working too hard, my friend?" he asked, his face obviously worried. "Too many..." he wiggled his fingers in front of me like epileptic worms, "ghosties and goblins?"

I poured a cup of sake and downed it in one. "I wish," I grumbled. "Too many bloody actors."

"Actors? Actors?" Harry gave a feigned look of amazement. "Already you going into movies, my friend? You should write a book."

I laughed. Good old Harry. He always cheers me up.

"So what will it be then, Harrison Ford?" he winked. "Spicy bean curd and boiled rice, am I right?"

"As ever Harry." I downed two more cups of sake and waved the half-empty bottle, "Another one of these beauties too, eh?"

"Of course, my friend. I'm sure you've earned it." Harry bustled off shouting in Cantonese at waiters and kitchen staff alike, sending them into a frenzy of chopstick polishing and napkin arranging. I reached into my jacket pocket and pulled out a thin wallet that I had brought downstairs with me and pulled out my own personal chopsticks. Whereas most chopsticks are either a light type of wood or plastic, these are made from ebony. Their blunt ends are capped in sterling silver and their business ends are sharpened to a fine point, enabling even the clumsiest of diners to skewer the most difficult to grab piece of bean curd. I slowly polished them on my napkin before laying them down on the table next to my right hand. They were a present from my parents when I graduated. Neither of them had ever tasted Chinese food in their lives and had no idea as to why I loved the stuff, but they just accepted that it was my thing and they bought me the best present that they could afford. I clicked my teeth together and ran a finger along the sleek, dark wood. I thought about my mobile sat in my pocket next to my hip. I could get it out and speed dial number 2. I could talk to Mum and see how she was. I could ask about the neighbours and what the weather was like down there.

But I wouldn't.

She would want to talk about Dad. She always wanted to talk about Dad. It had been almost twenty years and still the conversation came back to him. So my phone stayed in my pocket and words were left unsaid.

Instead I finished off the first bottle of sake.

Half an hour later and I was feeling warm and content. I had a belly full of bean curd and a liver full of sake. I sank back in my chair and stretched my arms out above me. My Tissot watch slipped down my wrist into my shirt sleeve. I slipped it back out and glanced at the time. Eight thirty. The night was still young. It was only Monday but town would still be relatively busy in an hour or so. I peered through the entrance of the shop out towards Dalton Square. The sky was dark and the street lights were bright. A large pair of googly eyes was bouncing up and down the windows of the office block opposite. God, I hated them. When they built that monstrosity about four years ago, some idiot had the great idea to install programmable light bulbs on the windows. Not only is it a complete waste of electricity, but some of the designs they come up with are totally pathetic. Rain in April, snow in December, fireworks in November. Then for the rest of the year great big googly eyes wandering from left to right, staring inanely at passers-by. It's like big brother stoned out on the biggest ever joint of marijuana.

I had to get away from their lunatic scrutiny. There was only one obvious place to go. I slipped a tenner onto the table, grabbed my hat and coat, waved goodbye to Harry, lit myself a Lucky Strike and headed off towards the Borough.

Only a couple of cars had to brake and honk their horns at me tonight. Much fewer than normal. I waved cheerily at the angered drivers. It was the least that I could do. I finished the cigarette as I reached the Borough and stubbed it out on the bin outside the pub then entered inside. It was already quite busy. People were milling around and ordering drinks. I looked over to the window and my heart sank. There was someone sat in my chair. Now, normally when this happens I pull the old, "There's a phone call for you at the bar," routine. Tonight, however, the couple sat in the window seats did not look like they would fall for such an old line. They were a man and a woman. He looked like he was in his forties or fifties, immaculately dressed and a fine claret-coloured cravat adorned his neck. She seemed quite a bit younger with short, dark hair, pale skin and a youthful complexion. They were sat silently, watching the world outside, quite oblivious to the humdrum of the pub. They were firmly rooted. I was sure they would not move.

So I dragged myself disconsolately to the bar. This was even worse. It was absolutely heaving. There must have been a function going on upstairs as loads of suited and booted types were jostling for drinks whilst painted ladies preened themselves and gossiped over fancy handbags. I sighed and was about to give up hope when I felt a finger tap on my shoulder.

"Hey you!"

I turned and saw Grace's little face beaming up at me from under her woolly hat. "Hi," I said. I noticed that she was in her civvies. "You not working tonight?"

"Just knocked off," she said. Her eyes wandered over to the window. "Oh no! You, like, lost your seat. Bummer!"

"I know. Quite the odd couple, aren't they?"

Grace nodded, little bangs of ginger curls bobbing up and down from under her hat. "You can say that again. They came in about fifteen minutes ago, ordered their drinks and have just sat there not saying a word. Creepazoids, if you ask me."

I smiled, then looked back at the bar. It was still solid. I sighed.

"You could always come clubbing with me," Grace volunteered. "I'm off to the Sugar House in about an hour or so. I could come and call for you... if you wanted that is?" Her young, innocent face smiled up expectantly.

The Sugar House is the local student-run night club. It is full of loud, ramshackle music, sweaty bodies and herbal-smelling toilets. "Thanks for the offer, but it's not really my thing."

"Oh." Grace looked somewhat disappointed, then her eyes twinkled and she motioned to the crowd at the bar. "It's a rugby do. I've heard they're planning, you know, karaoke later."

I looked down at the grinning little face and laughed. "Why on earth would you want to drag an old fogey like me to one of your hip and trendy night-clubs? Won't I ruin your street cred?"

She shrugged. "Doesn't bother me. Besides, you'll be miserable if you stay here tonight and you know it."

I looked at the bar then at the two creepazoids and nodded. She was right. It felt like my sanctuary had been violated. "What time did you say?"

"Call for you about ten?"

I looked at my watch. It was just coming up to nine. "Okay," I relented, "but the first drink's on you."

The happy student grinned and flicked me a little salute. "No problemo!" she chirped. "I'll see ya laters!"

I smiled as she bounced out of the Borough. She really is a nice kid. I gave the busy pub one more miserable sweep with my eyes and walked out into the night air.

Half an hour later I had showered, smoked about four Luckies, downed a couple of glasses of Jack and sat on the edge of my bed looking at various arrangements of clothes. I'm not a big fashionista and I tend to keep it simple: suit, mac and fedora. That's all I've ever needed. They keep me warm and dry and to me that is the main function of clothing, but tonight I was apparently going clubbing and I felt that I needed to change my attire somewhat. I held up a pair of plain, black trousers. They seemed okay to me, but would they be somewhat formal? I held up a pair of jeans next to them. Am I too old to wear denim these days? I am almost forty after all. I clicked my teeth together as I mulled the quandary over, then thought, "Sod it!" and pulled the jeans on. I hadn't worn them for a while and was worried that they might suffer from middle-aged snugness, but the zip pulled up fine and showed no signs of going south on its own.

Okay, so that was the leg department. What should I wear on top? I was just evaluating the merits of a plain, green tee over a lightweight shirt with buttons when I heard a pounding from downstairs. I paused with the shirts in my hands and listened. There it was again. Someone was hammering on my office door. I dragged the t-shirt over my head and ventured to the door of my flat.

Now there was a raised voice accompanying the knocking. A male voice was calling out my name. Slowly, I opened the flat door and peered over the banister. The voice and the knocking continued, but I could not see far enough to make out who was the source of the racket so I had to venture down to the half-landing between my flat and the office level. The sight that met my eyes was not really what I had been expecting.

There, hammering on my office door was a tall man in his late twenties/early thirties wearing a basin cut dark-haired wig (at least I hoped it was a wig – would anyone have their hair cut like that?) a tattered tight blue top, black trousers that stopped above his ankles and (this is the best bit) plastic pointy ears.

I coughed loudly and the stranger turned to face me. His features were neat and angular and his shirt really was quite messed up. He fixed his eyes on me and stared up the staircase. Silence hung between us waiting for one of us to speak. He looked kind of nervous and worry creased his basin-topped forehead, so I decided to break the ice. I lifted up my right hand, spread my ring and little fingers to the right and said, "Live long and prosper?"

For a moment the stranger stood looking up at my hand then he just slumped to the floor and started banging his head against my door before burying it into his hands and sobbing loudly. Not the effect that I had hoped for, I had to admit.

Cautiously I descended the stairs and approached the crying man. I crouched down and reached a hand onto his juddering shoulder. "Hey, calm down. I'm sure it's not that bad," I reassured him.

He kept his face buried in his hands and wailed, "Live long and prosper! Live long and prosper! What a joke! What an absolute joke!"

"Sorry, mate. I didn't mean to upset you."

"It's not you. It's me."

"Why's that then?"

"I'm going to live long, that's for sure, but I don't think I'll prosper."

I was now feeling as confused as a dairy farmer at a Vegan Society convention. "Why do you say that?"

You know how they say that the cheetah is the fastest land animal on the planet? Well that night I think I broke the big cat's record when I shot back up the stairs into my flat after the crying man turned his face towards me, bared a very sharp pair of fangs and said, "Because I'm a vampire, that's why."

Okay, so I've read *Dracula* and I've seen *Buffy the Vampire Slayer*. Vampires can't enter your house without an invitation. I was just hoping that applied to rented properties too. I mean, it had to, surely? My name was on the lease, wasn't it? I had signed a lease. I was sure I'd signed a lease. I scanned my living room for something I could use to defend myself with. Holy water was out, as was garlic. A cross? As the sound of footsteps trudged wearily up the wooden staircase I darted across the room and took a wooden crucifix down from the wall. Not very big, but then size wasn't important was it? I certainly hoped not and if it was I would go and haunt the descendants of Sigmund Freud.

I turned and saw him stood in the doorway. He was shaking his head. "I was kind of hoping that you would respond a bit different to that," he sulked. "I thought you were a specialist in this field?"

"What? In bloodsuckers?" I asked, and held the crucifix in front of me.

The vampire looked at the cross then back at me and shook his head. He ran his long fingers through his black wig and groaned, "Oh, this is all going so wrong. I'm not here to suck your blood. I'm here for your help."

I slightly lowered the crucifix and said, "My help?"

He nodded and I could see small red rivulets forming in the corner of his eyes. "I had nowhere to go, no one to turn to. You seemed like my best bet. I got one of your fliers in my shop."

Now I was really confused. "Your shop? Vampires are in the retail business?"

The vampire sighed. "I've only just been made a vampire. I own the sci-fi book shop down on North Road. Last night I was hit by a car. The last thing I remember was an awful lot of pain and this woman bending down over me. Then tonight I woke up like this."

"She dressed you up as Zachary Quinto?"

He placed his hands on his hips and glowered at me. "No! I was on my way back from a sci-fi convention when the car hit me. I woke up as a vampire." He paused. "Anyway, for your information I am dressed as Leonard Nimoy, the original and true Spock, not some psychotic brain stealer from *Heroes*."

"Sorry," I apologised. Jeez, the guy had issues. "So what am I supposed to do for you then?"

He shrugged. "Help me find out what I'm supposed to do now. It's not as if she left me a manual or anything. I guess there must be certain rules and procedures."

My fingers drummed my teeth as I looked at the door-frame between us. "Yeah... rules and procedures." I looked at the crucifix in my hand. I looked back at the vampire. He didn't seem like a crazed blood-sucker and the ripped top certainly seemed to weigh out his story about the car accident. "Okay, I'll help."

He smiled slightly. "Thank you. Now hadn't you better invite me in?"

"Oh, because of the door thing?"

"No! Because it's very rude keeping me stood out here in the cold."

I hesitated as I processed this little snippet of information and he sighed, "Never mind," and just walked straight across the threshold. "You might as well put that away too," he commented, taking the crucifix out of my hand. "Apparently, apart from the sunlight thing, a lot of the myths about vampires are just that: myths."

I suddenly felt like a rabbit having invited a fox to afternoon tea in its burrow. For Christ's sake I had a bona fide blood-feasting monster in my flat! What the hell was I thinking? Would he turn on me and have himself a little night-time snack? Was I a walking pantry, full of delectable midnight feasts? I sincerely hoped not. I watched him intently as he paced around the living room, his eyes scanning his surroundings. "You have a lot of clocks," he commented. "Doesn't the ticking drive you mad?"

"There are worse things to hear," I shrugged.

He raised his Vulcan eyebrows in agreement and placed his hands behind his back before rising up and down on the balls of his feet. "Well?" he asked.

"Well what?"

"What are you going to do?"

What was I going to do? Good question. I needed to think fast. "Well... First things first. What's your name?"

"Dave. Dave Nichols."

"Dave?" I creased my forehead in obvious disbelief. "Shouldn't it be something more like Vlad or Lestat?"

Dave placed his hands on his hips and gave a deep sigh. "Do I look Transylvanian or French? You really shouldn't believe all you read in books you know."

"And this coming from someone dressed as the science officer of the USS Enterprise?" I shot back. Dave was about to say something else when I heard the worst possible sound I could and my blood turned to ice as a thousand geese were strolled across my granny's grave.

It was a knock at the door.

My eyes locked onto the carriage clock on the windowsill. Five to ten.

Grace.

Shit!

"Oh, this is not good," I wailed. I looked at the door then I looked at the vampire. I grimaced. What was worse. That I had a vampire in my flat or a sodding Vulcan? "Bugger, bugger, bugger..."

"What's the matter?" Dave asked, "Aren't you going to answer the door?"

I gave him my best withering stare but it just slipped off his fixed Vulcan exterior. Either he actually had no social skills whatsoever or he really went for the method acting approach to role-play. My money was on the former. "It's a friend of mine. She's come to take me to a night club."

"You're going out on a date?"

"No I'm bloody not!" I snapped, temper suddenly flushing my cheeks, "I'm old enough to be her father. I think." I tried a quick mental calculation, but all the numbers were running around in the vacuous space between my ears waving their arms in the air and screaming, "Run away! Run away!"

The door knocked again. "Sam!" a female voice called. "It's me. You in there?"

I stared at the vampire and levelled a finger at him. "You owe me big time, mister," I said and opened the door.

"I thought you were never going to answer." Grace was adorned with her normal cheery smile and her woolly hat. She was also wearing a small denim dress over a pair of those thick black tights that seem fashionable today. "Were you on the loo?"

In spite of the insanity of my predicament I couldn't help but smile. She's somewhat infectious. "No," I explained. "I was just with a client."

Being somewhat shorter than me, Grace stood on tip toe and peered over my shoulder. Now whereas most people, if they saw a battered-looking Vulcan or indeed any other species from a 1960s sci-fi series, would probably take a double-take and make some sort of disparaging comment, Grace just waved cheerily and said, "Hi! I'm Grace!"

Dave gave a perplexed little wave back and introduced himself. "I'm Dave."

"Pleased to meet'cha," the perky little student beamed. "So, Sam. You gonna, like, invite me in?" For a moment I had one of those curious feelings of déjà-vu then I recovered and let Grace inside.

Her eyes scanned my obsession and she opened her mouth to speak. I held up a finger. "With *Doctor Who* it's 'Oh, it's so large.' With me it's 'What's with the clocks?' Why can't anyone ever say 'It's so large,' to me?" I stopped and realised what I had just said. Grace was snickering into her hand and Dave was looking at me somewhat perplexed. Apparently Vulcans (or is it vampires) don't get accidental innuendo.

When she had controlled herself, Grace just about managed, "Actually, I was going to ask you if you were nearly ready. We get into the Sugar House free before ten thirty."

I felt my ire deflate and started to smile, but then I caught sight of Dave and my amusement faltered somewhat.

Grace seemed to pick up on my thoughts. "Bring him too, if you like. He looks like he could use a good night out." I was about to say that was a really bad idea, but she had swept past me and grabbed Dave's hand, pulling him off in the direction of my bedroom. "Have to get you changed first. It's not a character night. You been to like a fancy dress thing already?"

Dave gave me a bewildered look that was an obvious plea for help and I just shrugged. One cannot stop a whirlwind that's in motion.

"You don't mind him borrowing these clothes, do you Sam?" Grace called out as she closed my bedroom door. I puffed out a long breath of air. It was going to be a long night. I needed a drink.

A little while later we were headed through town, swimming through the streams of clubbers as they made their way to the various late night hostelries. I kept casting a bewildered eye over my recently acquired client. It was weird enough seeing someone dressed in my clothes, let alone knowing that they did not possess a pulse. The idea of taking him out into the darkened streets was somewhat disconcerting. It wasn't as if I knew him. I didn't even know if I could trust him. Part of me kept expecting him to go all William the Bloody on me and start chasing blonde teenage girls.

He seemed totally in awe of his surroundings. His eyes did not stay fixed on one point for more than a couple of seconds. First he would watch a party-goer, then a lamp-post, then a shop sign. He seemed to be like a child taking his first steps out into the big, wide world. It was quite obvious that the change in him had heightened his senses and they were taking some getting used to.

Grace, on the other hand, was totally oblivious to my worries and Dave's voyage of discovery, bless her little cotton socks. She was whiffling on about her day at work and an essay that she was writing. I vaguely heard her say that she was really pleased that I had agreed to come out with her and that, perhaps, if I enjoyed the evening, we ought to do it again sometime.

I stopped and watched Dave as he came to a halt and his eyes stayed fixed on one particular shop front on North Road. I followed his gaze and realisation dawned. "Grace?" I asked.

"What?" she replied her eyes tracking back and forth from me to Dave. "Something up?"

"No. It just looks like there's a queue forming up there. You sure we're going to get in?"

The Sugar House was just up North Road from where we were standing and a line of people were already forming outside it back onto the main road. "It'll be fine," she beamed. "I'll just go and check, though. Okay?"

I nodded and she wandered off.

"That part of your life's gone now," I whispered to Dave. "You've got to let it go."

His hand touched the glass window of the sci-fi shop. "I can't," he said. "I just can't. It's all I have. You know? Like the Galacticans as they travel through space, all they really have is the Battlestar, all alone in the dark."

"Are we talking about the old *Battlestar Galactica* or the new one?" I asked.

"Oh, definitely the new one. It's far superior."

"I only watched a few. Found it a bit too post 9-11 for my taste. You know, reds under the bed and all that. I find the idea of people looking like us but actually being sleeper monsters quite disturbing. People you think you know suddenly turning then being complete killers."

"They would have to be rooted out and destroyed before they were activated."

I took a step back. "That's a bit harsh, don't you think?" Well this was a sudden and unexpected not-so-welcome turn to the conversation. His voice was at once firm and hard, most unlike he had been earlier.

Dave faced me and the streetlights shone yellow in his dark eyes. "They are everywhere. They have been sent to cause chaos and destruction. They appear harmless and look just like everybody else, but when the time comes their masks shall fall and death will come by their hands. They must be eradicated." He paused, breathing heavily for a second, then all tension seemed to leave his body as his features became softer, less cruel. His voice lost its edge as he smiled and said, "But you've got to admit Number Six is reason alone for watching the series though, haven't you?" His smile faltered. "Sam? You okay there? You look a bit pale."

"I'm fine, Dave," I reassured him, pulling myself back together. He hadn't even noticed. He had slipped into this other persona without so much as a skip of a heartbeat (or whatever it is that vampires used to measure small amounts of time), then once again it was gone and here was the mild-mannered sci-fi shop owner. What was going on inside his head? What seed had been planted in him to germinate and grow? "Look," I motioned over his shoulder, "here comes Grace."

Grace bounced back along North Road from the corner of Sugar House Alley. She was grinning and waving maniacally. "Come on, slow coaches!" she shouted.

I turned to Dave and shrugged. "I think she means us."

"I guess she does," he agreed.

We strolled leisurely up to the little red-head. "I guess you've got us all in then?"

Her grin was even wider than normal. "Oh yes! The Gracester strikes lucky. It was Barry on the door and he's a pushover. Just fluttered my little green eyes at him and, you know, putty in my hands." She giggled. "Now come on, before he so changes his mind."

Dave and I followed her around the corner and down the alley towards the entrance. We could see Barry standing cross-armed on the door with a group of annoyed looking punters lined up against a graffitied wall. Dave paused. "Curious," he commented.

"What?"

"You don't normally see such grammatically correct graffiti."

The words were impressively large, covering most of the sizeable, grey wall. "Spud was here." it read. "I see what you mean," I agreed, watching Grace chatting to Barry out of the corner of my eye. If he had been any more closely related to a gorilla, he would have been sticking bananas up his nose and thumping his chest. "*Was* has been spelt correctly and they've even used punctuation," I noted, indicating the full stop.

"Are you two going in or what?" It was a crass-sounding voice and it emanated from an even crasser-looking female. She was stood with her mates in the queue who were all seemingly desperate to catch hyperthermia due to the lack of clothing. Her hair was dyed dark violet and her midriff seemed to ooze over the top of her impossibly small skirt. "Bit old for her, ain't you? Bloody paedo, I bet."

I was good. Very good. Normally, I'd shout something back. I'm very bad at controlling my temper like that, but Grace was there and I didn't want to show her up after she had gotten us into the nightclub. My mouth worked silently, trying to find something civil to say. I had to say something. Something. My eyes fixed on her voluminous belly and I frowned at the sight of the expansive, smooth skin. "Where's your belly button?"

"What?" the harpy shrieked. "Damn perv!" (What was it with women calling me a perv today?) "Get your filthy eyes off a me!" She tried to hitch her skirt up but failed miserably due to the fact that there was no way she could bend the laws of physical matter. I shook my head and set off towards Grace.

I realised that I was walking on my own. "Dave?" I called. "Coming?"

The vampire snapped out of some sort of reverie. He had been staring intently at the fat woman as she had started to talk to her friends again. I walked over and touched him on the elbow. "Dave? You okay?" I asked.

"Yeah. Sure," he whispered, his throat cracking. "Just... Nothing. Let's go."

I gently led him down the alley away from the queue of irate punters and precisely grammatised graffiti.

As I'm sure you have probably realised by now, nightclubs are not really my idea of fun. My idea of fun is more a quiet night in with a glass of bourbon, a take-away and something daft on the TV. Clubbing it, for me, is right up there with such things as letting rats eat your toes and shoving cocktail sticks coated in tabasco sauce up your nose. Why I had agreed to let Grace drag me along to this was quite beyond me, let alone why I had decided to bring a worrisome vampire with issues regarding his identity.

I knew from the start that it was not going to go well. I decided to just make sure my seat belt was secure, brace myself and await the oncoming crash.

Now, I have nothing against clubs, per se. If people want to spend a night bashing their heads away to incredibly loud music and getting hammered on drinks or high on other such stuff, then that's up to them. It just doesn't work for me. I guess it's probably the ear thing. I have enough going on behind my ear drums to assail the poor overworked timpani. They don't need anything else to barrage them. So it was that, after checking my hat and coat in at the cloakroom, I entered the main room of the club and the aching sensation started to niggle away at the front of my head.

Grace turned and grinned at me. She looked so happy she could explode with glee. She was obviously excited at the prospect of boogieing the night away so I returned the smile and forced myself to ignore the encroaching agony that I knew would undoubtedly follow.

"I'm gonna grab a drink," she hollered across the pounding beat of rhythmic music that was stamping on the egg shell of my ear-drums with a pair of size twelve Doc Marten boots. "You want one?"

I nodded and tapped Dave on the shoulder then mimed a drinking motion. He nodded then let his eyes wander across the busy room. I signalled to Grace that we needed two and, as she bounced off to the bar like a young lamb across a fragrant meadow, I turned my attention to the vampire. Ice seeped slowly down my spine. Watching him was like watching a wolf sat silently calculating how many sheep it could carry away from an unguarded pasture. He was stood rigid, his eyes wandering slowly from left to right across the mass of gyrating dancers. Not once did he blink. Not once did he flicker. He was silent, steady and cocked like the firing mechanism of a loaded gun.

What had I done?

"Dave?" I asked tentatively, waving my hand in front of those piercing eyes, "Talk to me. You in there, mate?"

He let out such a sigh that I had not heard for some time. It was the sound of longing, neediness and desire. I had sighed like that so many times when Caroline had walked out of my life. "It's just so...beautiful," he finally managed, his voice barely audible. "All this life. It's enthralling, intoxicating, Sam. I wish you could see it like I do."

"You're not going to go all fangy on me, are you?"

He turned to me, his face looked horrified. "God, no! That would be like going to the Dark Side and you saw how that turned out for Anakin, didn't you?" He shuddered. "No molten lava of Mustafar for me, Sam. These creatures are here to be protected. They have no idea what is coming, what awaits them."

"What's that then?"

He shook his head. "I have absolutely no idea, my friend. None whatsoever. Here come our drinks."

Grace joined us holding three drinks and managing to not spill a drop as she weaved through the crowd. Ever the professional, I thought. "I got you a beer, Sam. Sorry, no hard stuff here," she winked. "Got you one too, Dave. That okay?"

"Fine by me," he said and took a sip from the bottle. "Wow!" he cried as he pulled the glass container away from his mouth and stared at it in complete amazement. He then drained the rest in one fell swoop. "That was good! I need another," and he waded off towards the bar.

Grace sipped at her orange-coloured drink and gave a small grin. "He's a bit weird but rather sweet, isn't he? Where did you meet him?"

"He turned up at my place this evening," I told her, carefully watching Dave as he bought not one, but five bottles of beer.

"What's his, like, story, if you don't mind me asking?"

"It's complicated," I said, "and I think we'd better just leave it at that for now, okay?"

She nodded her little nod, her woolly hat bouncing up and down. "No probs."

I peered at the drink. "What's that? Vodka and orange or some strange sort of fruity cocktail that's lost its umbrella?"

"No, silly," Grace giggled demurely, "just orange. I don't drink."

"Oh." It was all I could say. The possibility that the young girl never touched alcohol had never crossed my mind. I suppose what with her working at a pub and being a student, I had just taken it for granted that she would party like there was no tomorrow, just like the majority of her peer group did.

"Here he comes."

I looked up and saw that indeed Dave was on his way back. He had already drained one of the bottles and was onto his third of the evening.

"I'm gonna dance," Grace said, backing up to the dance-floor. "You wanna, you know, join me?" Her head was cocked inquisitively to one side and her mouth radiated a pretty smile in the gloom of the club.

I laughed. "No. Go on, dance yourself silly. I have two left feet, you know. Besides, I think I'll be needed here." I motioned with an incline of my head towards Dave.

"Okay," she called out as she entered the heaving throng, "but I expect more later, Mr Spallucci."

Sweet kid, I thought to myself and smiled quietly.

"Christ, she fancies the pants off of you!" The rather squiffy vampire thrust another bottle of beer into my spare hand. I drank heavily from my original one then faced him. "Yep, she really thinks you're the bee's knees, that one. It's kind of like when Deanna Troi wanted to get back with Riker but she was all shy about it. She had to wait until Worf was off on DS9 and settled in with Dax before she could make a move. At least you don't have a beard to shave off."

I emptied my first bottle and sat it on a nearby table. "First," I counted on my now free hand, "you are way off the mark there. Grace is a sweet kid. There's no way she would fancy an old fart like me." I ignored the rude snorting noise that the vampire's rasping lips produced and continued, "Second, you are so, so pissed. Third, what is it with you and sci-fi?"

He shrugged, almost dropping two of his bottles of beer. "It's a life," he stated matter-of-factly.

"But it's all fiction."

"I didn't say it was my life, did I?"

I let him have that one.

"And she so does fancy you," he smirked, emptying another bottle. "I can smell it. Heightened vampire senses, you know." He tapped the side of his nose with a beer bottle and almost jabbed his eye out. "Improved taste too," he grinned and started on the next bottle.

"So I noticed," I frowned. "So what does your bloodhound nose tell you right now? That I haven't used the correct deodorant? That the group of students over there are smoking some very unusual mixture of tobacco?"

Dave harrumphed and drew his head back then inhaled with great aplomb. Then his head snapped forwards and his eyes targeted on someone out of my line of sight across the dance floor. He was suddenly very still, completely focussed and quite eerie. For an instant, all traces of alcohol seemed to have left him, then there was a crash of glass as the beer bottles smashed to the floor and he was no longer stood by my side.

"Shit!" I cursed and started to scan the room. I had been a complete muppet and I'd let my guard drop. I just hoped that someone would not pay the price for my carelessness.

People. Lots of people. Most of them young, lots of them dancing. All of them unaware that an inebriated, undead killer was lurking in their midst.

As the pounding beat of music shook the room, hands waved gleefully in the air swaying to its deafening pulse and rhythm. My eyes squinted through the melee and my ears screamed in protest at the torture that was being inflicted upon them. The bells were ringing. Louder and louder they grew, making me feel like a modern-day Quasimodo. So high, so sonorous, so beguiling, dragging me away from the here and now, pulling me away from my purpose. I slapped myself around the face. "Get a grip! Get a grip!" I told myself. I had to find him. I had to concentrate.

Grace!

Where was Grace? She was in there! Somewhere in that throng of revellers, she was enjoying herself, oblivious to the danger that she was in. I had let her bring him. I had led him here like a friend, damn it! If he had harmed her...

I saw a flash of red under a green woolly hat and pushed my way towards it. There she was, side on, grinning away like a loon with a couple of other girls dancing and whooping like there was no tomorrow. Her friends saw me and shouted something to her which I couldn't hear under the din. She turned and smiled at me with her little radiant smile, then beckoned for me to join her. I shook my head and ploughed further into the crowd. I tore my eyes away from the look of disappointment that settled on her young face.

I had to focus.

I had to find the vampire.

I spun round and round frantically trying to spy him, but it was no good, there were just too many people in the way, spinning past my vision. I drew in a deep breath and braced myself. I was going to have to try and listen. I was going to inflict excruciating pain on my senses and open up my ears to the noise around me. I stood still and prepared myself, then above the pounding and the drumming of the relentless music I heard it.

A scream.

I bolted towards its source.

The crazy thing was, most people in the room seemed completely oblivious to the shriek. They continued to dance to the thumping and banging din that they called music. Most seemed wrapped up in their own little piece of heaven, grins on their faces and hands in the air. They didn't even protest when I barged past or elbowed them out of the way. They just continued to sway in time to the rhythm – totally blissed out.

One person who wasn't blissed out was the source of the scream, only now the scream seemed to have changed into a tirade of verbal abuse, all of it aimed at Dave. "You disgusting pervert! What d'you think you're bloody doing? Get your filthy hands offa me!" and so it went on and on. I won't burn your ears with the rest of the vitriolic outpouring.

I recognised the voice instantly. It was the badly dressed woman from the queue outside the nightclub. She was bouncing around inside her clothes that were at least two sizes too small and was jabbing a furious finger at the vampire who was stood to one side looking decidedly perplexed. With her other hand she had a tissue clasped to her neck. Even in the dim light of the nightclub I could make out a dark flower blossoming on the white paper.

"What's going on?" I asked as I made my way over towards Dave.

"Oh, I might've guessed *Paedo Boy* would be in on this!" she spat at me, her eyes rolling upwards.

I ignored the insult. Now was not the time for a slanging match. "In on what?"

"Here I was, dancing with me mates," she waved her free hand to her gaggle of cronies who were stood around with their arms folded and looks of disgust painted on their heavily made-up faces, "when I feel someone sidle up behind me. Well, naturally I think that me luck's in, what with being the stunner that I am." I refrained from laughing. "Then all of a sudden your pervy mate bloody well bites me neck." She turned back to Dave and lunged forward. "I'll have you for that! It's... it's..." I could practically hear the rusted cogs turning in her head as she tried to find the right word. "Bullying!" she shrieked. "Bullying! That's what it is."

I caught eyelock with Dave and raised an eyebrow. His shoulders shrugged and his face said, "Help."

"Well, what you gonna do then? Ay? Ay?" she shouted at me. "Look at my neck. I bet it's gonna scar. I'll lose all my good looks, I will. I want compensation!" she bellowed.

I had had enough. I walked over to Dave then turned to face the overweight harridan. I took a deep breath, leant forward into her face and said, "Look. I'll tell you what you can do right now."

"What?" she asked, curious.

"Just piss off."

I turned on my heel, grabbed Dave and headed for the toilets. For the first time in a little while I actually felt like smiling.

"What the hell happened there?" My smugness at flipping off the overweight tart had subsided as I was now stood in the gents with a door wedged shut behind me and a shamefaced vampire in front. Could the night get any worse?

"I... I don't know," Dave stammered. He looked even paler than he had done earlier although there was a slight blush to his cheeks and his lips had a definite scarlet tinge to them. "I just knew that I had to attack her. I couldn't stop myself."

I leant against a sink and frowned. "What do you mean you had to attack her? You only had an inclination to take a chunk out of her neck and no one else's?"

"I swear to God, Sam. No one else. It was just her. I felt her from across the dance floor and I couldn't stop myself." Dave looked wretched. A slick sheen of perspiration had formed on his forehead. He wiped it away with the back of his hand then stared in horror at the result. His hand was smeared red. He was sweating blood. He fell very silent and looked like he was swaying slightly.

I recognised that look. "Dave? You okay?"

"I think... I think I'm gonna be..." He turned and bolted for a cubicle. Whilst he was getting acquainted with Hughie on the big white telephone I fished out a Lucky and lit it. This was insane. I had a newly-created vampire who seemed to attack people at random them threw up at the sight of blood. Bloody marvellous!

I finished the fag in four long puffs and stubbed it out on the floor before marching over to the stricken vamp. "You alright?"

The retching stopped and he managed to raise a feeble thumbs up. I shoved my hands under his arm pits and hefted him up. The pan was full of blood. "Don't look, just don't look," I urged him as I flushed the toilet and grabbed a handful of loo roll to wipe his face down. When I'd finished his ablutions, I flushed that away too and clapped him on the shoulder. "There we go, mate. Looking good, feeling great!"

Dave smiled weakly and there was a banging at the door to the gents followed by some cursing and swearing. "We need to get out of here," I stated, "and fast, I think."

Dave nodded.

I looked around. There was a fire exit at the far end of the cubicles. Perfect. "Come on. Let's get you some fresh air."

I half pushed, half carried the swaying vampire towards the fire door, then lifted a foot and booted the escape bar. The door swung open and an alarm started to shriek. The hammering on the other door stopped suddenly and I could hear screams of panic. Ah well, I thought, at least it created a diversion, and I heaved Dave out into the night air. We had barely gone three steps when we almost stumbled over something lying in our way.

"Shit!" I shouted as I toppled forwards and fought to regain my balance. Dave grunted as he landed in a heap on the obstruction.

I straightened myself up and heard my back creak. Oh, what a night, I thought, then I realised that Dave hadn't moved.

"You okay?"

Slowly, the vampire lifted himself off the obstacle before turning and running for a corner in which to be sick once more. I just stood and stared at the dead body of the overweight girl from the nightclub. There, on her neck next to where Dave had bitten her, was a deeper and much nastier, fatal wound. The night had just gotten even more worse.

"Sam! Sam! Is that you?"

My heart sank at the sound of the female voice. Grace! Bloody hell. I had completely forgotten about Grace! I glanced down at the body then at Dave vomiting violently before walking quickly round the corner to greet her. She bustled up to me brandishing our coats and my hat. "I thought it was you. I, like, heard your voice. Is your friend with you?"

Even now, although I had abandoned her in the Sugar House, she was still smiling out from under that woolly hat. She made to walk past me. I grabbed her by the arm and pulled her back. "I wouldn't go round there, if I was you," I cautioned the little student. "It's not that pretty."

"Why? What's up?"

I paused. What could I tell her? That there was a body round there that had been killed by a vampire and another creature of the night was busy throwing up blood in the corner of a yard? No. So I bent the truth a bit. "It's Dave. Those beers have sort of caught up with him, you know?"

Grace grimaced. "Oh," she said quietly, "Yuk. Listen, do you need any, you know, help?"

I could tell from her voice that the offer was the obligatory type from one friend to another which hoped it wouldn't be called upon. I smiled inwardly and shook my head. "No, I'll be alright. I'll get him back to his place and clean him up." I popped my hat back on my head and slipped into my coat. "Thanks for these, though." Then something dreadful crossed my mind. There was a killer vampire out there. "What are you going to do now?"

"Oh, I've met a couple of guys, you know. So we'll find somewhere to party." She rocked back and forth on her heels. "You could text me when you've sorted him out, you know? Come and join us?"

I smiled and shook my head. "No thanks. I think I'm partied out for the night, so I'll get Dave home then head back to my place. Just make sure you stay with the others, okay? Don't wander off on your own. What?"

Grace was giggling behind her hand. "It's okay, Sam. You sound just like my dad. That's a bit weird."

I turned to go back to the car crash hidden round the corner. "Look, I've got to sort this mess out okay? You just be careful, you hear. I know what you students are like. I was one myself once, you know?"

She flipped me a little salute, then ran off towards her mates who were gathered down the road. They giggled to each other and pointed at me as Grace joined them before they all wandered off together in the opposite direction. I chewed my bottom lip and went to find Dave. He had stopped throwing up and was sat in a heap on the floor by the body of the dead woman. "It wasn't me!" he moaned. "I didn't do it."

"I know, Dave. I know. You were with me remember?" His brown eyes looked up at me and red streaks were drying on his cheeks. I remembered that he cried blood as well as sweated it and puked it. "Right," I said, pulling him to his feet. "We need to get to the bottom of this. We need to find out just what's going on with you. I find it far too much of a coincidence that you are vamped then a dead body turns up the next night which is someone who you yourself had attacked a few minutes earlier. There has to be a connection."

He peered glumly at the pale corpse. "What are we gonna do with her?"

"She's beyond our help. Someone else can deal with the aftermath. You're my client, not her. I know somewhere safe I can take you. I have a friend who can help us."

Dave nodded like an infant does when they have been told that everything will be alright and someone would make it all better again. After wiping his face down with a handkerchief, I led him away from the scene of the murder and off towards Saint George's Quay – to Luneside University.

First, I rang Spliff's doorbell. The dulcet tones of *Ode to Joy* rang from within his apartment. Dave looked at me and raised his eyebrows. "Don't," I warned him. "If you were still wearing that wig you would look so completely Vulcan."

He shrugged and considered the various blue and white flags of Saint Andrew that hung on the stairwell. "Are these the property of your friend?"

"Uh-huh," I rolled up my sleeve and swore. "Shit, it's past midnight."

"Is that a problem?"

"Spliff values his beauty sleep. He'll be cranky if we've woken him."

"Oh."

I jigged up and down then tried the bell again and hammered on the glass door for good measure. There was still no reply. "Come on, you old sod. Where are you?" I fumbled into my pocket and pulled out my phone, unlocked it and hit speed dial. I heard the receiving phone ring in stereo; in my ear and in the apartment. It rang about seven times then an educated Scottish voice spoke into my ear, "You have reached the phone-line of Father James MacIntyre. This is not a recording. It is the middle of the night. I am very busy. It had better be good."

I grimaced and mouthed "cranky" to Dave then said into my phone, "Spliff, it's Sam. I'm outside your flat. I'm in a pickle. Please let me in. I need help."

"You need your bloody head read," he sighed down the phone. "It's past bloody midnight and I'm busy." There was a short silence which I didn't dare fill, then he continued, "Is it a matter of life and death?"

"Yes."

"Does it require the services of a middle-aged but still nonetheless rakishly attractive priest?"

I smiled. "Yes."

"Does it require doing unspeakable things with half a cucumber and a tub of Chivers marmalade?"

"Sorry, Spliff. Not tonight."

Dave's face was a picture of bewilderment. I guess that was down to the vampiric power of a heightened sense of hearing. I winked at him. He shook his head a little and looked somewhat worried.

"Ah well, I suppose I really ought to help," Spliff relented. "The key's under the dead begonia, as usual. Let yourself in."

"Thanks Spliff." I reached under the blue pot that sat adjacent to the door and contained the withered stem of a once beautiful plant. A brass Yale key jangled on its small fob as I bounced it in my palm. Spliff has always had one stashed there ever since he went sleepwalking once in the altogether. It is also why he has the large Scottish flags. They just about cover the essentials if he's forgotten to replace the key and has to go and get help from the university porter's lodge. That reminded me; "Oh, by the way. I've got company, so you'd better be decent."

"I always am, dear boy," he replied. "I always am." Then he hung up.

I unlocked the door and let myself and Dave in.

So how can I describe Spliff's chaplain's flat atop Grizedale Block at Luneside University? One word will probably suffice: decadent. Most vicarages or rectories have that slight musty smell of old books and deadly committee meetings. There will be pretty little arrangements of roses and lavender or other English garden flowers decoratively vased around the rooms in an attempt by an ageing housekeeper to lighten the mood of the rambling house.

Spliff's flat has a decidedly different ambience.

"Oh, my!" Dave exclaimed when he came face to face with a life-size gold-painted statue of Michelangelo's *David* in the foyer. It had a long black coat draped over its shoulders and Spliff's Panama hat placed at a jaunty angle on its head. It had a couple of sagging helium balloons tied to its arm and was adorned with a leopard skin thong. "I take it your friend is hardly conventional?" Dave enquired, his eyes unable to part company with the underwear.

I chuckled. "That would be somewhat of an understatement. They tried him in a normal parish for a while but when you start to forget to turn up for services," I shrugged as I removed my hat and coat, before precariously balancing them with Spliff's on *David*, "people tend to be rather unforgiving. Oh, and there was an incident with the Rural Dean, a Chihuahua puppy and a stick of salami."

Dave paused, where he stood and turned to consider the front door. "If I leave now will he forget I ever came?"

I moved him back round and led him towards Spliff's living room. "Oh, you ain't seen nothing yet, my Vulcan friend," I grinned. Then the vampire's face fell as he passed through the vestibule and watched Spliff saunter through his living room. I wasn't sure what was causing the vampire more consternation: Spliff in his black silk kimono, emblazoned with a bright red dragon entwined around a naked geisha girl, or the general decor of the room.

First, there's the books, journals and newspapers. They are absolutely everywhere: on bookshelves, tables, chairs and scattered liberally across the floor. There is always a pile of discarded reading material in an unceremonious heap by the kitchen door. These are the ones that have offended Spliff and his own individualistic sense of morals. They have caused him to shout "Bollocks!" exceptionally loudly before tossing them across the room onto his "burn at midnight" pile.

Next there is the artwork. Spliff likes his artwork. It ranges from reproductions and photographs of the works of artists such as the aforementioned Michelangelo through to common little bits of tat that you can buy along the Prom in Morecambe at the height of summer. They all have one thing in common, though: nudity. There are more tits, willies and bums than you can shake a stick at in Spliff's living room, and if you did try to shake your stick at them all you would probably end up very sore and extremely blind.

Then finally there is the general mess. Apparently Spliff's last cleaner resigned when her doctor informed her that the marks around her ankles were not, in fact, a bad case of eczema but were in fact flea bites. That was about twelve months ago. The university has since given up. Apparently they arranged to have his carpets taken out and burnt whilst his room was fumigated, but mud sticks and no other campus cleaner has been brave enough to climb that flight of stairs since. I won't go into too much detail but needless to say that Spliff likes his cigarettes, his coffee and his fine alcoholic beverages but I don't think I've ever seen him use a sink let alone washing up liquid. There is a dishwasher in the kitchen, but it was never the same again after Dante urinated in there.

That thought brought me up short. I had brought a stranger into the flat. My eyes scanned the room quickly, but not fast enough. Dave screamed and started to hop wildly on one leg, whilst a black fury that was all teeth and claws started to shred my borrowed trousers. "Get it off!" he clamoured. "Get it off!"

Spliff bustled over and scooped the cat up in one easy gesture. It immediately turned into a black ball of soppiness, purring and pummelling at his neatly-trimmed beard. "Oh, my poor little fluffy-wuffy-puff-ball, did the nasty man fwighten you?" He glowered at Dave as he continued to tickle the black spawn of Satan's belly. "I mean what does he expect coming up here and disturbing us at this hour?"

"That thing's vicious!" Dave shouted. "It's got longer claws than Wolverine!"

Spliff was about to proffer a retort when a muffled cough came from his bedroom. "I'll... just settle Dante down in the spare room," he tried as a diversion, heading over the other side of the flat towards the vestibule.

I eyed my old friend up and down. "You said you were busy."

His eyes darted nervously to his bedroom as he shooed Dante out of the living room and shut the door. I groaned and marched off in the direction of his boudoir. "Sam!" he called out. "Don't!" but it was too late. I had already flung the bedroom door open and had marched in. A pretty young male was curled up under Spliff's red, satin bed sheets. "You made them leave, lover?" he murmured without even opening his eyes.

"Nope," I said, gathering up what I hoped were his clothes, "but you are." I dragged the sheets back and forcibly removed the butt-naked youth from the bed.

"Hey!" he screamed, "Who the hell are you?"

"Someone who knows jail bait when he sees it," I shot back as I frog-marched him through the lounge and towards the open front door.

"Get your greasy hands off me!" he swore as I propelled him out of the flat.

"Glad to," I spat and threw his crumpled threads at him. "Now piss off back to nursery-school and don't come back you little arse-wipe!" I yelled and I slammed the door.

"Well that was uncalled for," Spliff commented sulkily as he meandered over to his drinks cabinet, "and after I agreed to see you at such an inconvenient hour. I need a brandy. Don't think that I'll be offering *you* one, though."

"Bloody hell, James!" I exploded. "How many times do I have to tell you? The young ones are trouble! Not to mention illegal."

Spliff half-filled a large brandy glass and swirled the alcohol round to warm it up. "For your information, he *was* legal. He's a first year."

"And that makes it okay does it?"

Spliff shrugged and proceeded to light a cigarette in a "Who gives a damn?" sort of attitude.

"You know what they say, you muppet." I stalked over to him and snatched the fag out of his hand and proceeded to punctuate each word with a jab of the small, white tube: "Don't stick your pen in the company ink!"

"Hah!" he flounced. "You're a fine one to talk!"

"And what's that supposed to mean?"

"They also say, 'Don't sleep with the daughter of the priest whose parish you're on placement with!' I know it's not as catchy, but it rings true doesn't it?"

I seethed with rage as I crumpled the cigarette up in my hand. "Bastard," was all I could manage.

"Git!" he retorted, then, "Damn, you've made me hungry now." He pushed past me and headed off into the kitchen.

"Erm, I thought he was supposed to be helping us?" Dave tried, tentatively. He made to follow Spliff but stopped in his tracks as the priest flipped a one finger salute over his shoulder. "Sam?"

This was not going to plan, but then things rarely did with Spliff. I manoeuvred the vampire into a precariously small amount of space between some coffee cups and some old books on one of Spliff's gaudy red leather sofas. "Sit there and don't touch anything. You might catch something," I warned him. "I'll go and reason with the old queen."

Spliff was banging about in his tiny kitchen as he slammed a sliced bloomer onto the cluttered counter before kneeling down to rummage around in the overfull fridge. "Mayo, mayo, mayo... Where's the bloody mayo?" he chuntered to himself.

"In the bedroom?" I volunteered sarcastically.

The silk-robed clergyman stood up, pondered this and replied, "No. Today it was Philadelphia. I distinctly remember putting the mayo away last night. Damn senior moment! See what you've done to me, Sam?" He knelt down again and moved a jar of expensive-looking mustard. "Aha! Doctor Hellman's I presume!" he exclaimed and came out brandishing a white jar which he then proceeded to open and lather onto a thick slice of bread before stuffing it in his face.

I winced. "That is totally gross, you know? Most people put something else on the bread first."

"You're a fine one to talk, dear," he sniffed. "You don't even eat eggs." He masticated for a few seconds then nodded past my shoulder. "So what's with him, then? A waif and stray you found down by the docks?"

I shook my head. "I'd ask you to sit down, but as there's not even any room to swing a cat in here... Not that I'd want to swing Dante, mind. He'd have my eyes out on the first pass." As you have seen, Dante is an exceptionally vicious tom cat. Vicious to everyone that is except for Spliff who coos over the furry razor blade and calls him his little "fluffy-wuffy-puff-ball." This little "fluffy-wuffy-puff-ball" is in the habit of sitting on the window ledge of Spliff's apartment and catching sparrows as they fly by. It is a fiend and a menace and I very rarely make it out of the flat without getting at least my ankles pounced on and punctured. Dave got off somewhat lightly considering its neurotic hatred and suspicion of strangers.

"Fluffy-wuff was just upset because you came and disturbed his sleep." Spliff finished his mayo sandwich and ceremoniously licked his fingers. "I know how he feels. Now, dish the dirt on Mister Dull and Uninteresting out there."

"Mister Dull and Uninteresting is actually called Dave, and Dave is a vampire."

"A vampire?"

I nodded.

"Called Dave?"

I nodded again.

Spliff peered over my shoulder at Dave who was still sat on the sofa.

The priest smiled and wiggled his fingers at his nocturnal houseguest who gave a rather bemused wave back. "Crap name for a ruddy vampire," Spliff hissed through a forced smile whilst absentmindedly wiping mayonnaise from his beard with the back of his hand.

"I dunno," I turned and motioned for Spliff to follow me back into the living room, "there are vamps in *True Blood* called Bill and Eric. I mean, Eric the vampire? You've got to admit that's worse than Dave."

Spliff shrugged in a non-committal form of agreement and proceeded to re-enter the living room. He had finally calmed down and his curiosity had obviously been piqued. "So, Dave," he began as he sat himself down atop the pile of books on the sofa next to the vampire and started to inspect him quite closely, "Sam, here, tells me that you are, in fact, a vampire."

Dave nodded, hesitantly. "I am."

"Hmmm..." Spliff tapped an index finger against his lips. "Tell me Dave, can you prove this claim?" As I stood to one side I saw Spliff's hand slip down the side of the sofa and latch onto something. I made to speak, but he shot me a sharp glare with his grey eyes.

"Well," Dave started, "I have a pair of fangs." He opened his mouth wide and the sharp teeth slid out ominously.

"Impressive," Spliff pondered, "but my cat has fangs and he only drinks the blood of birds, small rodents and those who piss him off in the middle of the night." I made a snorting noise and those steel-grey eyes shot me another glare. "I think we need a bit more proof than that."

"Such as?" Dave asked."

"This," and in a swish of black silk, Spliff had pulled out a pair of dress-making scissors and had driven them into the back of Dave's hand.

"Ow! Jesus! You lunatic!" Dave shouted as he jumped up and began to hop around the flat for the second time that night - this time waving his hand maniacally in the air. "That bloody hurt. That's gonna scar. It'll... It'll..." He stopped and stared at the back of his hand. So did Spliff and I. "Bugger me," the vampire whispered as the wound slid shut and the blood absorbed back into his skin.

"Not tonight, dear," Spliff purred. "Not tonight."

So I brought Spliff up to date with the events of that night: Dave turning up at my office with his story of the female vampire at the car accident, biting the girl at the Sugar House and finding the same girl dead from a vampire attack shortly afterwards. "Obviously, I don't believe that Dave killed her," I said, "as he was with me at the time of death."

Spliff lounged back in his armchair and ponderously stroked his small, dark goatee beard. "So it would seem. So it would seem," he mused. Then he leant forward and addressed Dave, "So you know nothing about the vampire who," he formed quotation marks with his fingers, "created you? You'd never seen her before or had any previous contact?"

Wearily, Dave shook his head. "I just run a small sci-fi bookshop. I may read fantasy, but I'd never dreamed of actually becoming part of that world. Hell, I never even thought it existed."

"Oh, it exists alright, Dave." Spliff looked over at me. "You'd be surprised what we've seen before now, old boy."

I quietly nodded my head. I remembered the first time we encountered the paranormal back at university. It had been a hell of a shock and was still an unresolved matter in my book, at least.

"Can you help me?" Dave pleaded. His hands were clasped tight together and his skin was as pale as the moon and as taut as his nerves. "Please. You've got to help me."

I walked over and sat on the edge of the armchair. "It strikes me that we could do with knowing more about the vampire that created you. Like I said earlier, it seems quite a coincidence that there should be a vampire attack the night after you were made. Perhaps she was involved. If we knew her identity, then perhaps we could track her down."

"But I don't know her name."

Spliff spoke in a soft, soothing manner. "You may think you don't, Dave, but you were at the centre of a traumatic experience and very near to death. Your mind had other things to deal with at the time. However, your brain may have picked up on something and it may be buried in your subconscious. We could try to extricate it."

Dave's eyes narrowed as he thought this over. "You want to hypnotise me?"

Spliff nodded.

"It didn't work when Doctor McCoy used it on Kirk in *The Prometheus Design*," Dave protested.

Spliff sighed. I groaned. "Look, I don't care what you've been reading or watching in your little Trekkie world," Spliff snapped. "That's fiction. This is reality. Hypnosis will help you relax and help you open your mind to me, allowing me to share your thoughts."

Dave suddenly perked up. "You mean like a mind meld?"

Spliff's mouth dropped open and was about to let loose a vile expletive so I pre-empted him to diffuse the situation, "Yes Dave. A mind meld. Spliff will perform a Vulcan mind meld on you just like Sarek performed on Jean-Luc Picard in *Star Trek: The Next Generation*."

There was silence again as the vampire thought this over then he grinned. "Cool!"

Spliff's eyes narrowed and he sidled up to me. "Never took you for a Trekkie," he observed.

"Insomnia and re-runs on late night TV," I whispered.

"Ah!" He turned towards Dave and attired himself in his most serious looking face. "Now, then, I'm going to need you to lie back on this couch and relax."

The sandy-haired vampire did as was requested once Spliff had made some space by pushing the various bits of detritus onto the floor. He slipped a pink furry cushion under Dave's neck as the patient lay out on the red leather sofa. "Be careful with that," Spliff warned, gesturing to the cushion,

"It's Dante's girlfriend."

Dave looked somewhat horrified at the idea that a cat's love-toy had been placed under his neck and I glowered at Spliff. The portly priest ignored me and carried on: "Now, Dave, I want you to focus on this." He slipped a ten pence piece from a nearby coffee table and held it in front of the vampire's face. "It is really, really important that your eyes do not leave this coin. Do you understand me?"

Dave nodded, silently.

"Good boy," Spliff patronised. "Sam, could you be a dear and dim the lights please?" I wandered over to the light switch and did as I was asked. The room was suddenly lit in the sort of manner that Spliff reserved for entertaining young, male students with an essay crisis. "Look at the coin, Dave." Spliff continued in a low, soothing baritone voice. "See how the light glints off its finely polished surface. See how it dances over my knuckles." He started to flick the coin over the back of his hand. First to the left, then back to the right. Over and over it went. Back and forth across his knuckles. I sat down on the edge of the coffee table and watched the coin bob up and down. I had seen Spliff perform this neat little trick a number of times, and it always fascinated me. "See the coin walking up and down, Dave. See it walking over my fingers, just like it walks from person to person in its little, impersonal life. From one wallet to another. From one cash register to another. See it bobbing up and down, faster and faster. Then slower and slower." Dave's eyes were fixed on the coin. I could see in the glint of the dim lights that his pupils were tracking its path. They were glued to the shiny, silver metal disc.

"Imagine this coin is your life, Dave. Lots of little steps making one big journey. Lots of little steps bringing you right here now to this room, to this sofa."

"Lots of little steps." Dave's voice was not much more than a murmur.

"That's right, my dear. Little steps. Your mind is my mind."

"My mind is your mind," Dave whispered.

"Spliff!" I hissed. "Behave."

"What?" he protested. "I'm tapping into his subconscious. Jungian archetypes and all that."

"You're dicking about, more like."

He shrugged. "Same difference. Anyhoo, he's deeply under now. Where do you want to begin?"

"At the beginning I guess. When he was knocked down."

Spliff nodded. "Dave?"

"Uh-huh?" His eyes were completely glazed over and seemed to burn a deep red in the dim light.

"I want you to tell me about your accident the other day. When the car hit you, what were you doing?"

"I was walking down Caton Road."

"Why were you there?"

"There was a convention at the Holiday Inn. I was on my way home after handing out some fliers for the business."

Spliff looked at me for confirmation. "Sounds about right," I concurred. "What with the book shop and all."

Spliff continued the interrogation. "Where did the car hit you, Dave?"

"Outside the Holiday Inn. It jumped the lights. Didn't even see it until it was under me."

Spliff and I both grimaced. "Ouch!" Spliff whispered, then asked, "What happened next?"

"I was lying on the pavement. I could feel a lot of pain in my chest and I think I was bleeding from somewhere. Then I knew I wasn't alone. Someone was with me. I could hear voices."

Spliff gave me a warning look. I inhaled and let my breath out slowly. This made something quite clear. There must have been more than one vampire.

"Tell me about the voices," Spliff asked, his Scottish baritone soft and coaxing.

"There were two. One a deep-sounding male. Very refined. The other a female. Sounded quite young. They were arguing."

"What about?"

"Me." Dave frowned. "The man said they had to go, but the woman said that they couldn't just leave me there. The woman came over to me and placed her fingers on my neck. She said that my pulse was weak."

"Dave, did you see the woman?"

"Yes. She was very pretty."

Spliff raised his eyebrows. "Aren't they always? What did she look like?"

A soppy smile filled the vampire's dreamy face. "T'pol."

Spliff paused and looked at me with a contorted look of confusion on his face. "What?" he mouthed to me.

"The science officer on the Enterprise," I whispered.

"I thought that was Spock?" Spliff whispered back. "Does he cross-dress these days?"

I smiled. "It's from another series," I informed him.

"You really need to get out more, Sam," Spliff muttered as he turned back to Dave. "What does this T'pol look like? Apart from the pointy ears."

"Petite, slim, nice... you know..." I gesticulated appropriately with my hands, "and short, dark hair."

"Sounds adorable," Spliff huffed.

"Ideal insomnia fodder," I smiled back at him.

"Quite. Now, Dave. What happened next?"

"The man said they had to go. He said others would be there soon. She said that I was near death and she had to save me. He wasn't happy about that. She said, 'Stop being so stuck-up and keep watch.' Then she bent over me and sank her teeth into me. I felt really light headed. I thought I was going to pass out but she placed her wrist over my mouth and I felt her blood seeping into my mouth. It tasted sweet, like honey."

"Lovely," Spliff grimaced. "What happened next?"

"There was the sound of a car and the man shouted, 'Nightingale! We have to go, now!' She pulled her wrist away and looked worried. 'He's not finished,' she said, but the man was insistent. She gave in but bent over and whispered instructions into my ear."

"What were they, Dave?" Spliff asked, then out of the side of his mouth, "Live long and prosper? Make it so? Ow!" He rubbed his leg where I'd kicked him. "Uncalled for, Samuel."

"She said, 'Find the Eternals. Protect the Twins. Await the Divergence.'"

Spliff gave me a puzzled look. I shrugged. It meant nothing to me, either. "Ask about the male vampire," I whispered.

Spliff nodded. "Dave, did you see the other vampire? The one with Nightingale."

Dave nodded wearily. "Yes. Just after she had whispered in my ear he came over and grabbed her by the arm to pull her away."

"What did he look like? Captain Kirk?"

I slapped my hand to my head and groaned.

"No." Dave's voice was still far away, oblivious to sarcasm. "He was taller. Grey hair and well dressed. I remember he had a red cravat."

I recalled the man and the woman sat in my window seats. "Damn!" I cursed. "I saw them earlier today in the Borough."

"Seriously? What were they drinking?" Spliff asked.

"Well it wasn't blood, that's for sure. I need a fag." I patted my pockets. "Bloody hell, where are they? You got any?"

"Silk Cut."

"You pissing about? You know I hate those."

He shrugged.

"I'll pass. I think you'd better wake him up."

Spliff grinned wickedly. "Dave I'm going to count backwards from five and when I reach zero you will..." he shot me a quick grin, "be a Klingon warrior with a hunger for *gagh*."

"Spliff!"

"Okay, okay. Dave, time to wake up baby," he cooed, "Up we get. Time for school."

The vampire yawned and rubbed his eyes. "Hey guys. We learn anything?"

I got up and stretched my arms. I was suddenly rather tired. "Yep. We sure did. It would appear that you were taken out of the oven before you were fully baked."

Five minutes later we were all sat in silence, each holding a very large brandy. Dante, retrieved from the spare room, was curled up asleep on Spliff's knee and Dave was staring out into space. "Well I guess that's just bloody typical," he eventually sighed as he upended his wide-bowled glass. "Not only do I get hit by a car, but a vampire does a Friday night special on me." He gave an involuntary shudder as the expensive cognac slid down.

"Bugger!"

Spliff and I exchanged glances. The sandy-haired vampire seemed exceptionally down and there didn't seem to be anything that we could really do about it. We could neither finish the job nor reverse it. We had reached a somewhat unexpected impasse. Spliff scratched his black cat thoughtfully behind its ear as it purred loudly. "My concern," he mused, peering through his little, round glasses at Dave, "is that these vampires are still out there. Think about that dead girl at the Sugar House, hmmm? Goblins and fairies didn't do for her, did they? No, I think your saviours are still out there."

I nodded. "I agree. Don't forget, I saw them in the Borough. For all we know, they could have been watching my place, waiting for you. They might have second guessed that you would look for help."

"What do you think they would want with me?" Dave asked.

"My guess," said Spliff, "is one of two things. They would either want to finish the job, or..." he paused a bit too dramatically.

"What?"

"How might one put it?" Spliff stroked his beard and grinned wickedly from ear to ear. "Correct their mistake?"

Dave's face fell. "You think they might want to kill me?" he wailed. "Why on earth would they do that?"

"Loose ends? Cheap kicks?" Spliff shrugged and stood up, causing an annoyed cat to tumble to the floor. Dante shot his owner a dark scowl then began to vigorously wash his privates in annoyance. "How should I know? I'm not a vampire."

"I think Spliff has a point," I interjected. "We don't know how they think, do we? Also, we have to presume that my place is off limits for you. So I have a suggestion. We hole up here for the night and keep watch over you, then tomorrow, when it's light, Spliff and I can safely do a bit more digging. I can find out if there have been any more deaths recently and he can, I don't know, look into other stuff." I yawned and looked at my watch. It was past one in the morning. I was starting to feel dead on my feet.

"You don't look fit to keep watch over anyone, Samuel, old bean," Spliff observed, pouring himself another brandy. "Look, why don't we take it in turns? You get some kip for a couple of hours and I'll wake you up at, say, three a.m.? Then I'll take a turn at shut eye. That way we'll both be fresh in the morning for our little field trip."

I yawned again and nodded. "Sounds like a plan. You okay with that?" I asked Dave.

My client's thoughts seemed momentarily elsewhere, but he snapped back to us. "Yeah. Sure," he said. "It sounds fine, I guess."

"Okay," I said, settling down into my armchair, "wake me at three." I was asleep as soon as I shut my eyes.

I felt an insidious chill bite into me. I shivered, drew my trench coat tighter and hung onto my fedora as the wind tried to tease it away. An old, stained newspaper skipped along the pavement: "Spud was here and chased by Cylons!" the headline read.

I realised it was a dream. I decided to go with the flow.

I was walking down Cheapside. I passed Burger Bob and his grill whilst wondering what he was doing selling burgers in the middle of the night. I waved cheerily at him. He screamed and ran off down Lower Church Street. Curious, I thought.

The wind was screaming up Damside Street as I walked past the Wetherspoons pub. Lots of people were sat stock still at the tables. They all held empty glasses. There were no cars around so I walked over North Road and looked into the window of Dave's shop. It was dark inside and I could see next to nothing. There just seemed to be piles and piles of books. They all had the same title: "It's Coming." There were big books, small books, pamphlets, comics. There were even games still wrapped in their cling-filmed boxes. They all bore the same title: "It's Coming."

What was coming?

"Wouldn't you like to know?"

My heart jumped into my throat and I jerked out into the road. It was a good job that there were no cars there. I would have been hit and, dream or no dream, I'm sure it would have hurt.

"Yes, I would like to know," I said to the dead woman. The bite mark on her neck looked deep and ragged, but no blood seeped from it. Curious.

She laughed. Her laughter was joined by that of a milkman who was getting out of his float and a postman delivering letters to the shops along the street. All around me, normal looking people started to point at me then laugh. I turned to run. I wanted to get away, to leave this dream behind, but I knew I couldn't escape.

"It's coming!" they all shouted as I tried to drag my way away from them in the wet clay into which North Road had transmuted.

"It's coming!" they screamed at me as the viscous material dragged my legs down into the ground.

"It's coming!" they proclaimed as a loud roar snapped me from my sleep.

"Jesus!" I swore as I rolled out of the armchair and tumbled onto the floor. The floor, a nice solid, carpeted floor. No clay, just a fibrous pile of nylon with the occasional crumb of bread or pretzel. Praise the Lord of synthetic materials and midnight snack detritus.

I heard the roar again and flipped myself onto my back in panic, then smiled as I recognised its source.

Spliff was splayed out in his armchair, his head lolled back and his mouth open. That guy can snore for Hibernia.

My mouth straightened. Where was Dave? The sofa was empty apart from Spliff's usual junk. There was no other sound in the flat apart from Spliff's reverberating palate. I ran into the bedroom: empty. The kitchen: various bacterial life forms, but otherwise empty. The hallway: empty and the door open.

I stormed back into the living room and hefted a firm kick into Spliff's thigh.

He yelled and woke with a start. "What? What? Wasn't me? Who? Where? Sam?" He looked at the empty sofa. "Oh. Sorry. Shall I make some coffee?"

I raised a finger and started to shout.

Fifteen minutes later I was sipping the most lovingly made cup of coffee that I had ever tasted. I was sure that every drop was filled with the essence of absolute contrition and apology. There was also a decent slug of brandy in there for good measure.

"Sun's coming up," Spliff observed.

I said nothing and just stared out the window at the long shadows creeping their way out westwards.

"Is your coffee nice, Sam?"

Again I said nothing.

Spliff sat quietly, his fingers silently drumming on his leg, then he tried, "Perhaps he just popped out for a breath of fresh air? What do you think?"

I glowered at him from across the top of the coffee mug. "And perhaps he'll top up his tan whilst he's at it, do you think?" I snapped. "Jesus Christ, Spliff! All you had to do was stay awake! It's like Uni all over again. 'You grab five winks, Sam. I'll watch over the ghost, Sam.' Bloody hell, what was I thinking? You lost us that one and now you've lost us a neurotic, new-born bloodsucker. If he attacks anyone, God help me..." My words faltered at the sight of my best friend looking totally crest-fallen.

"Do you really think he could attack someone?" Spliff asked. His words were faint and weak. He looked pale and sick behind his goatee.

I sighed. There were white hairs in his beard. I hadn't noticed them before. A subtle sign of age creeping up on my best friend just as it was stalking me, too. A reminder that we were both, after all, only human.

"I don't know," I admitted and finished off the coffee. "I don't think he'd want to, but last night, he just homed in on that woman. There's stuff going on that we know nothing about, Spliff."

"Where do you think he's gone?"

I tapped my fingernail against my teeth and thought about this long and hard then words from the previous night came to me: "It's all I have." I placed the empty mug on the floor and stood to leave. "I think he's gone back to his mother ship," I said. "I'll see if I can find him. He can't go out in the daylight."

"You want me to come with you?" Spliff asked?

I looked at the sad, middle-aged cleric in the silk night-robe and the greying beard and shook my head. "No. It's okay, buddy. You get some proper sleep, okay?"

"Okay."

I turned and left the flat.

Lancaster is quite a calming place first thing in the morning. As I traipsed back along the river Lune and into the city centre, I watched the varying people going about their first-light business. Small trucks darted along the one-way system hurrying to deliver produce to local shops. Street cleaners whupper-whupped the gutters, hoovering up the detritus from the previous night's revellers - some of whom were shambling along the half-deserted streets back to their homes, back to where they belonged.

I was heading to where Dave thought he belonged. His life. His business. His obsession. I turned down Cable Street and walked past Sainsbury's as an articulated lorry pulled in to drop off its delivery. Opposite, I could see Sugar House Alley. I shuddered at the thought of the grim discovery Dave and I had made last night, then I frowned. Something was wrong. Where were the police? Where were the bands of blue and white tape? Where were the circling lights and the probing, inquiring reporters?

My feet picked up speed and I jogged down to the imposing, stone Gillow building that stood majestic in front of the Sugar House before venturing around to the rear car park. Surely someone must have stumbled across the body by now? But even before I reached the back yard, I already knew the truth. The body was gone. The yard was stark and bare, the white-washed walls clean and scrubbed. There was not a drop of blood, no sign of the murder that had occurred just a few hours before.

Someone had been here.

Someone had tidied up. Meticulously.

I heard a rustling noise behind me and I spun around a hundred and eighty degrees. A familiar pair of eyes met me from under a mop of dark hair.

"You!" I shouted, "Come here!" and I ran for my teenage stalker only to stop short after just a few paces, my heart in my mouth.

He had vanished.

Right in front of my eyes.

"What the...?" I removed my hat and ran my hand through my hair in confusion. He had been there. He had been there, the boy from in front of the White Cross.

Alec.

I reached into my trench coat and fished out a Lucky. I flicked my Zippo and inhaled deeply. Things were getting creepier and creepier and I needed to get out of the yard. I walked over to where he had been stood just a second ago and looked at the ground. There was nothing, not a trace. It was as if he hadn't even been there. Had I imagined it? Was I creeping myself out?

I closed my eyes and listened. At first there was just the light jingling of my own internal church tower with the background thrum of early morning traffic on North Road, but then, as I concentrated, I started to hear something else, something faint.

Breathing.

I opened my eyes and scowled. "I know you're there, Alec, but I don't have time for these games right now." I finished my cigarette and tossed the dog-end at where he had been standing then I walked out onto North Road and headed for Dave's shop.

Okay. So here goes, I suppose this is the appropriate time to confess something that you may have already guessed. I, Samuel C. Spallucci, am into sci-fi. Now, when I say *into*, I don't mean the sort of *into* that involves stalking cast members of *Star Trek* or dressing up as Spock (unlike a certain missing vampire). No, my sort of into stems from the memory of being a seven-year-old sat in a flea pit cinema with my dad watching a huge grey triangular star destroyer zoom into view from over my impressionable little head and blast the living daylights out of the Tantive IV before Darth Vader swaggered his black-suited arse into a clinically white corridor and captured the sexily demure Princess Leia.

I remember sitting in awe and wonder at the flashing laser bolts and thrumming lightsabres.

I remember grinning up at my Dad as he affectionately tousled my hair.

It was the last time we ever did anything together that was really fun. The last time that we did anything together before he got ill.

So yes, I'm into sci-fi, but not in the obsessive Trekkie kind of way, but in the way that a seven-year-old sees the world before it all goes horribly pear-shaped and gets turned completely on its head. As you get older you can hide yourself in your bedroom and watch Blake and his freedom fighters outrun Servalan whilst you ignore the shouting downstairs. You can watch Q running rings around Jean-Luc Picard on a flickering screen whilst the smell of disinfectant seeps into your nose in a hospital ward's day room.

You watch all of this knowing that there are other lives out there. Other lives that are not yours and you so want to be a part of them.

Anyway, time marches on and so do television schedules. Special effects improve and CGI rules as the great god of fantasy. One of the first sci-fi programs that embraced this new technology was *Babylon 5*. I won't bore you with the details, but needless to say it was a drama about life on a space station and one of the central characters was Commander Susan Ivanova played wonderfully by Claudia Christian. As I stood outside Dave's shop in the early light of the morning I pondered over the possibility that the newbie vampire might have a *thing* for the former commander of the *Babylon 5* space station. Sure there were pictures of other characters adorning his frontage, Kirk, a couple of Skywalkers, Rog Blake and the eponymous Number 6, but over and over my eyes were drawn to the blue-suited, brunette-haired figure of Commander Ivanova. There were at least ten posters of her not to mention a handful of framed and signed photographs and collectible cards.

As I knocked on the door I couldn't help but smile.

At first there was no answer, but then, as I lifted my hand to knock again, a voice called out from within, "It's open, Sam. Come on in."

I twisted the handle and the door swung in easily. It was dim inside.

There was no illumination and the posters and paraphernalia in the window were blocking out most of the encroaching daylight. "Shouldn't you be asleep?" I asked as I carefully closed the door behind me.

Dave was hunched up in the far corner of the shop as far away as possible from any stray sunbeams. "Apparently not," he noted. "Would you mind?" he motioned with his head towards a set of blinds on the front window. I nodded and rolled them down. The vampire noticeably relaxed somewhat.

"So how goes the very long night of Dave the vampire?" I asked.

A smile touched his pale lips. "Oh, very good. I thought you were just an insomniac." He stood up and brushed his clothes, sorry, *my* clothes, down. "Not many people know that episode was originally penned for Ivanova."

"You must have been gutted when she left before the fifth season."

He sighed. "Things change, I guess. It's just so hard to let go."

I scanned the shop. It wasn't very big, about the size of a suburban living-room, but every available space was crammed with books, games, memorabilia and much, much more. The stock must have been worth a considerable amount. "I guess you've put a lot of work into this place," I volunteered. "I can see why you wouldn't want to leave."

Dave picked up a plastic model of Boba Fett and absent-mindedly flicked a speck of dust from the bounty hunter's Mandalorian helmet. "It's not just that," he sighed. "It's the unknown. How am I supposed to find my way when I have so many questions left unanswered?"

I was about to say something when some primeval early warning system prodded my subconscious and my head turned to the back of the shop, allowing me to see a petite, dark-haired female lower a voluminous hood down from a black cloak that covered her from head to toe.

"Well," she smiled, "it's a good job that we're here to answer them then."

On registering the word "we" I made to move but felt two vice-like hands gripping my arms immobile from behind as a refined baritone voice purred, "I really wouldn't try anything stupid Mr Spallucci. It would be your last act, I promise you."

I was fluidly deposited in a nearby plastic-backed chair and the hands remained on my shoulders, keeping me safely prisoner. I sat motionless knowing that trying to escape would quickly cost me my life. I hadn't even heard these creatures enter the shop. Dressed in their long, light-shading, cloaks they had slipped silently onto the premises without so much as a whisper. I did all that I could for the moment and that was look at the female vampire in front of me as she smoothed the creases out of her cloak. She was fairly dainty - about five foot two, I would have estimated. She had short, brunette hair and looked in her early twenties, but then looks, I guessed, could be deceptive. "I would have said Dax, myself," I said to Dave who was stood motionless across the room, his mouth agape.

His head turned to me and he frowned, momentarily confused as to my meaning.

"Nightingale," I nodded towards the female vampire. "I'd say she looks more like Ezri Dax from *DS9* rather than T'Pol. She's cuter," I grinned disarmingly.

"I think I'll take that as a compliment, Sam," Nightingale smiled as she walked over towards Dave. "I wasn't born in the last few decades, so I don't find the term *cute* offensive. Although," she tapped a slender finger against her slim lips, "there are colleagues of mine who would have ripped your throat out for less." She placed a hand softly around the back of Dave's neck and peered up into his eyes. "How are you, my child?" she asked, her voice brimming with concern. "I have been so worried."

"I... I'm okay, I think," the infant vampire managed. He pointed in my direction. "Sam has been good to me. He has looked after me well. Please, please don't hurt him." He turned to me. "You won't do anything," a quick glance to my captor, "stupid, will you Sam?"

I gave as much of a shrug as the hands of steel would let me. "No more than normal," I volunteered.

Nightingale gave a wry little smile and nodded to her counterpart. "Marcus, if you wouldn't mind?"

I felt the weight leave my shoulders and I was able to stand up, stretching my arms. "Well," I began, "now we all know each other's names, perhaps someone could enlighten me as to what exactly is going on and just why a dead woman has vanished without a trace this morning?"

"Don't push it, Mr Spallucci," rumbled the deep voice of Marcus. "You are in no position to be flippant."

I carefully edged away from the tall vampire and let my eyes wander over him. Under the cloak, he was once more immaculately dressed, a tweed suit, highly polished brogue shoes and a silk cravat. Quite the English gentleman. All he needed were a couple of hounds and he could have been off to shoot a few defenceless birds, although I guess the prey he hunted were normally quite a bit bigger than a partridge and ran on two legs. "For your information, Marcus, old bean, I'm not being flippant in the slightest. Last night I found the body of a woman who had quite obviously been killed by a vampire. This morning, said body was gone. Poof," I flicked my fingers in front of me, "as if by magic, not a scrap of blood was left behind. Needless to say I find this quite disturbing."

"Looks can be deceptive, Sam," Nightingale said from behind me.

"Don't give me that crap, I know what I saw. Dave saw the body too, didn't you?"

He nodded slowly.

"I don't doubt you saw a body, Sam," Nightingale continued, "but just because it looked like one of your kind doesn't mean that's what it was."

"You're saying it was another vamp?" I frowned.

She shook her head. "No. Far from it, and right now it doesn't concern you. All I can say is that no innocent creature was killed last night. That is not what we do. That is not why we were created."

My mind ran back to Dave under hypnosis; "Find the Eternals. Protect the Twins. Await the Divergence," I repeated verbatim, then gasped as my feet left the floor and air struggled to reach my lungs.

"Where did you hear that?" Marcus stormed as I grappled with his hand clenched suffocatingly around my throat. Black dots formed in front of my eyes and everything started to turn grey.

"Marcus!" yelled a female voice from far, far away. Suddenly, air rushed into my burning lungs and my backside rushed into contact with the unforgiving floor. "That will achieve nothing."

"He is a threat, I tell you," the grey-haired vampire scowled, "I don't trust him."

Nightingale was next to my side, her cold hand calming my hot cheek. I hadn't even seen her leave Dave's side. "My apologies, Sam, but please tell us where you heard that. It's very important, as you might have surmised."

"Dave was talking in his sleep last night," I lied, not wanting to drag Spliff into this. "He mentioned you finding him dying and those were the words that you spoke to him before you left."

I could tell from the look on Nightingale's face that she knew I was hiding something, but after a short pause she stood up and helped me to my feet. "Then you probably already know that my child, here, is not fully born."

I nodded. "You were disturbed. A car drove past?"

"That is correct, so we have to finish the matter." The female undid the cuff of her jacket and rolled the sleeve up before biting down hard on her skin. Blood oozed through the puncture wounds and she offered the bleeding arm to Dave. "Here you are, my child. All you need to do is drink of this and you will become one of us. You will join our consciousness and all your questions will be answered. All your doubts will be banished away for good. If you do not drink then you will stay as you are, a bastardised halfling with one foot in the mortal world and one foot in the world of the Children of Cain. You will wander forever not knowing peace of mind. It will drive you mad."

"Hardly a choice," Dave murmured and he took Nightingale's wrist up to his mouth. He wrapped his hands tight around her arm and drank greedily, like a baby at its mother's breast. Marcus looked on with reserved concern whilst the female vampire slowly stroked at the new-born's sandy-brown hair. "There, there," she cooed. "Drink up. It'll be alright." Then slowly, Dave's slurping slowed down and his eyelids slid closed. He sank down onto the floor and started to breathe heavily.

"Is he asleep?" I asked.

Nightingale held up a finger for me to be quiet. I could see the puncture wounds in her wrist healing shut before my very eyes. "Just a minute, Sam. Marcus?"

The tall male approached the slumbering infant and placed a hand on his forehead. "Still cold," he commented

"That's good," Nightingale nodded.

Then Dave's eyes shot back and I swore. Loudly. His sockets were pools of blood. A bright scarlet film covered his eyeballs. "They're everywhere!" he wailed. "Everywhere. There's too many of them!" His head twisted from side to side under Marcus' restraining hand as if he were looking in fear at invisible people or creatures all around him.

"Who's there, Dave?" Nightingale asked calmly. "Tell us who's there?"

"Monsters. Faceless creatures. They've risen up out of the ground and they've taken us prisoner." He writhed under Marcus' grip, desperate to flee.

Nightingale gave her partner a look that held recognition then held Dave's wrists and spoke to him again, "Who's with you? Dave. Who is with you?"

"The boy," he whimpered.

"What's his name?"

Dave seemed to ignore the question and carried on with his hallucination. "They've taken us to *him*!" he spat the word out with such venom.

"Not another one," Marcus muttered. I felt like I had walked into a play somewhere in the middle and had missed the bulk of the plot so I just sat and watched enrapt.

"He's so dark," Dave hissed. "A soulless man with the heart of a black dragon. NO!" he shrieked, his entire body bucking against the restraint of the other vampires, "NO! Not him! God! Not him! It can't be him!" Tears of blood were now trickling down his cheeks. I'm not sure I'd ever seem someone in so much distress before.

Nightingale looked up inquiringly to Marcus. Marcus nodded for her to go on. "Dave. Who is he? Tell us who he is."

Dave's head shook violently from side to side. He was breathing heavily and erratically now. The words came with great effort. "His... name... is... Kanor!"

Then hell broke loose. Dave screamed so loudly that I had to cover my ears and things around the room actually shook. His legs started to slam up and down as red foam oozed from the side of his mouth. "He's burning up!" Marcus shouted as blood started to pour out of Dave's nostrils and his ears. "Night, we're losing him."

"What's happening?" I asked across the din.

"His body's rejecting the vampire blood," Nightingale explained as she hung desperately onto her child. "We left him too long. We need to stabilise him."

"How do you do that?"

Her face fell dark. "You won't like it," she growled and the next thing I knew, she had snatched my wrist and ripped it open with her sharp teeth before pushing it into Dave's open mouth.

Having the liquid that provided my brain with oxygen drained out of my body was a most surreal experience. As Dave sucked hard at my punctured wrist, my brain was screaming for me to pull away and get the hell out of there. My body, on the other hand, was remarking that this was a wonderfully blissful experience and why hadn't I ever tried it before?

As bright lights started to flicker in front of my eyes I felt my legs begin to buckle and I fell limply into Marcus' arms. Dave must have finished drinking because I was being curled up quite carefully on the plastic chair. I closed my eyes. I needed to sleep.

With the sleep came dreams, patchy, incoherent ones. I saw rank upon rank of faceless creatures made from clay marching across a barren land to fight with angels clad in brilliant white. At the head of the angels was a man clothed from head to toe in obsidian black. His face was covered by an eyeless hood. I marvelled at how he could see. Then I was stood in an old church. It was a ruin and stank of death. I was aware of a faint susurration coming from behind as a man stood in front of me and my companion. His shoulders were bent over in anger. Rage seemed to emanate from his very soul. There was something familiar about him. I knew this man. If only I could catch a glimpse of his face I would undoubtedly recognise him. Slowly, he turned round towards me, his face creeping out from under the shadows...

A rough shaking roused me from my fitful slumber. "Sam? Sam? Are you in there?" It was Nightingale. "Can you hear me?"

I slowly allowed my eyes to ease open and looked up into her small, pretty face framed by her short, brown hair. She smiled. "Hello sleepy-head."

"Screw you, bitch." I winked then motioned over to the newly-born vampire. "How's the patient?"

"All the better, thanks to you," she smiled, relief pouring off her. "Sorry about that. His body was dying. It was rejecting the vampire blood and needed an infusion of human blood to stabilise it. Normally the infant dies because there's not a willing donor."

I shifted myself up into a sitting position and looked at my wrist. Not a mark. "Nice trick," I grunted. "They could use you on the NHS, but I suggest you tell patients that you're going to operate first before you go in with the knife."

Nightingale took my wrist in her cold hands and examined her handiwork. "Our saliva contains a clotting agent, amongst other things. Think of us as glamorous, bipedal fleas."

I couldn't help but chuckle. A small snore from nearby made me ask, "So what happened before the rejection? What was he seeing?"

Nightingale's face frowned as she ran a finger lovingly over the back of Dave's hand. "The stories you read portray us as heartless creatures. Brash and foolhardy, afraid of no one." She sighed deeply. "That couldn't be further from the truth. When we are born to this life we suffer a vivid dream that we will not remember once we wake up. It is the moment that we stop being vampires. The moment that we die. You see, Sam, unlike a human child who comes into the world full of glee and mirth, unaware of their own mortality, we are born screaming in terror having seen the thing that will kill us." She wiped a red tear away from her porcelain cheek. "Oh, Dave. What have I burdened you with?"

"You knew what it was that he was seeing." I said. "What was it?"

There was a polite cough and Marcus said, "Many have seen the creatures of clay, and we know that they are deadly, brutal vermin, constructed to destroy us."

Nightingale glared at him and Marcus grimaced. He had obviously said something that was not for my ears. "I saw them," I said. "While I was sleeping just now."

The vampires looked at each other in stunned disbelief. "You saw them? Just now?" Marcus' voice was trembling. "What else did you see?"

I tapped my fingernail against my teeth as I tried to remember then continued, "I saw a man stood in a church. He felt totally evil."

"Sam," Nightingale was knelt in front of me, her blue eyes focussed intently on my face. "This is very, very important. What did he look like? Could you describe him to us?"

I shook my head. "Sorry, but you woke me before I could see his face."

Her head hung and her shoulders sagged in disappointment. "At least we know his name now," Marcus volunteered. "Kanor."

Nightingale nodded and stood up. "The thing is Sam, many of us have seen the image of the black dragon in our dreams, but none of us have actually met him. We feel he is important and extremely dangerous. We need as much information as is possible."

"I'm sorry I can't be of much help," I apologised. "All I can remember is that I was stood in an old, ruined church." I paused a moment. "Do you think they were actually my dreams?"

Nightingale shook her head. "No. They were undoubtedly Dave's. They must have passed through to you when he drank your blood." She stood and eyed the sleeping vampire with pure curiosity. "I wish he could tell us more, but when he wakes he will remember nothing. All he will have is what we can tell him."

I chewed at my lip and plucked up the courage to ask the obvious question. "What were you two told that you had seen, when you were born as vampires?"

A little smile touched Nightingale's slim lips. "Curious one for me. Apparently I saw a man dressed in black in an old barn with a pistol."

"Oh," was all I could manage at first. Then after a bit of thought, "But I thought bullets couldn't harm you."

"They can't. Sunlight, fire and extreme trauma to the heart or decapitation; that's all. We are impervious to everything else."

"Crosses? Garlic? Holy water?"

The female vampire shook her head. "Nada. Not a sausage."

"What about silver? The internet's full of silver hurting vamps."

"That's a very recent idea. I think it's down to *True Blood*," Marcus said in an informative manner. "Now if you were a werewolf..."

"Whoa! Werewolf?" I jolted upright so hard that I almost fell off my chair. "You say there are werewolves out there? Howl at the full moon and rip people to shreds lycanthropes?"

"I'm afraid the Bloodline of Abel is very much a reality, Sam," Marcus explained, his voice laced with informative concern, "and you should be on your guard now."

"Why?" I did not like where this was going at all. "What have I done?"

"You have helped one of the Children of Cain," Nightingale explained. "The Bloodline have eyes everywhere. They will know and they will come after you. Soon."

"By soon you mean, next full moon?"

"Sorry."

"Well you guys will be here to help me won't you?" I pleaded already fearing the answer.

"Sorry Sam. Our responsibility is to look after Dave, here," Nightingale placed a hand on my shoulder. "I truly am sorry, but we have to protect the infant, especially with what his dream showed."

I wrenched my packet of Luckies out of a pocket and lit one. "Talking of dreams... You didn't say what yours was, Marcus. Care to enlighten me?"

The tall vampire's normally serene visage took on a look of beatific adoration. "I saw the light of day," he whispered.

"Okay," I puffed on a Lucky, "but surely that's, you know, a bad thing?"

"Oh no, Sam!" His eyes twinkled in the light of the room and his whole body seemed animated. "Before I stepped out into the light I had met the most incredible person, a blonde girl filled with such presence. I knew that it was coming and that I was to be its harbinger."

I gesticulated with the cigarette, "What? What was coming?"

"The Divergence."

"Marcus! Watch your tongue. That's twice now," admonished the petite female.

"Ah!" I smiled. "Await the Divergence. What were the other two instructions again? Protect the Twins and find the Eternals?"

Nightingale glared at me.

I felt exceptionally smug and blew a smoke ring as the strong tobacco cleared my mind. "So, would I be right in guessing that Marcus' little blondie is, in fact, one of the aforementioned twins?"

"You know too much already," Nightingale grumbled. "To tell you any more would have consequences far more wide-reaching than you could ever imagine." She wrapped herself in her cloak before stomping over to Dave and swaddling him up in a blanket and lifting his sleeping form clean over her shoulder. "It's getting busy out there. We must be gone. Take care of yourself, Sam. Watch for the moon." She made for the back door then paused and called over her shoulder, "One more thing. Cut down on the drink. Your blood tastes like a distillery." Then, in the blink of an eye, the three of them were gone.

Half an hour later I had made my way back to Dalton Square. It was rush hour and the traffic was busy, snarled all the way down Great John Street. I was glad to be on foot. I had taken a rather circuitous route, wandering up Cheapside and along Penny Street. I wanted to be among living, breathing people rather than alone in a sea of lifeless, mechanised cars.

Right now, people felt good. Living, breathing, heart-beating humans. Creatures of the day rather than children of the night.

When I stepped out of Gage Street onto Dalton Square I glanced up at the clock tower on the town hall. It was just coming up to eight-thirty. I needed a drink and there was nowhere open at this time in the morning. I would just have to use my filing cabinet reserves.

I trudged up the flight of stairs to my office and let myself in before throwing my hat down onto the sofa. Wearily I meandered over to the filing cabinet and slid the top drawer open. I reached inside to grab the bottle of Jack Daniel's that resided therein and paused as my fingers alighted on something long and padded. My brow creased as I pulled the envelope out. In old, flowing and unmistakably feminine handwriting, my name was penned on its front. I slid the packet open and whistled as a large number of twenty pound notes fell out onto the floor along with a letter.

I squatted down on the sofa next to my hat and fished up the note. It read, "Sam, if you are reading this then you have just been very sensible and not angered Marcus too much. I apologise for his short temper but we have all been under a lot of strain recently. I just wanted to thank you for looking after my child. It is strange to think that I do not even know his mortal name yet, but that is of little consequence as he will have to choose a new name shortly. Anyway, as a token of my future appreciation, I have enclosed five thousand pounds in cash for your time and trouble. I trust that is a sufficient amount. I also enclose a warning in case I forgot or did not have chance to tell you of it: watch for the moon. Vampires are not the only supernatural creatures out there and others have much less of a conscience than we do. We, the Children of Cain, are in a continual struggle with the Bloodline of Abel. They have eyes everywhere and they will know that we have been in contact with you. They will seek you out and most probably try to hunt you down. For this I apologise, but it is a matter out of my hands. For now, I must tend to my new-born child. Take care and, once more, my eternal gratitude. We shall contact you again when it is possible. Regards, Nightingale."

I got up and grabbed the bottle of whiskey from the filing cabinet then downed five long slugs of its reassuringly harsh liquid. So, apparently, I had made enemies of some sort of supernatural crazy-gang. Brilliant. My eyes fell on the sea of money that lay at my feet. At least I had enough money to treat myself to a slap-up meal and a new bottle of whiskey, so the day wasn't going to be that bad after all.

# The Case of the Fastidious Phantom

I'm guessing that, by now, you're wondering how I got into all this sort of stuff? Was I traumatised as a child? Well, duh, yes, but aren't we all? Did I witness supernatural phenomena as an impressionable teen? Well, I saw Margaret Thatcher get re-elected time and time again when we all knew she was going to be really bad for the country, but I don't think that really counts.

No, I was not subjected to anything paranormal until my last term at Luneside University. I had lived your normal average life, with the normal average ups and downs that accompanied your normal average family. I was the only child from good, solid working-class stock and I worked as hard as I needed to in order to get the university place that I wanted. Then, for three years I worked as hard as I needed to in order to get my degree which would let me go off and start training for what I believed I was called to do.

I was going to be a priest. Does that surprise you? It tends to have a bit of a mixed reaction. Some folk go, "Oh yes. Of course. I see it now." Whereas others just say, "You pulling my leg or what?"

I'd felt the calling for some time and had regularly attended the Anglican parish church in my home town at least once a week. I had been involved with the youth fellowship and loved all the high church trappings. I was truly at home when the building was immersed in incense smoke and bells were ringing out (not the ones in my head, I might add). So I studied hard and got myself to university in order to obtain the degree that I needed before I could start the selection process for theological college.

Anyway, the first two and two thirds of my academic years were totally uneventful. Well, paranormally uneventful. I won't go into any detail here, but you've all heard as to what students get up to. Late nights, binge-drinking, friends duct-taped to statues and traffic cones deposited in the most unusual of places. That sort of stuff was commonplace and I participated in my fair share of it along with the thumping headaches of regret in the morning. But of ghosts, ghoulies and goblins I saw nothing.

That was, until I met Gerald.

Like I said before, I was in my last term. It was summertime, the skirt lengths were high and the work to attention ratio was low. We were down to our last few lectures and exams were imminent. We could taste the end of university approaching on the smorgasbord of life and it was skipping across the palate rather nicely. I was living in halls for my final year and there were ten of us sharing the corridor with a communal kitchenette area at one end. I had actually vowed never to live on campus again after my hell of a first year, when an American student named Kyle decided that it would be absolutely hilarious to get totally bladdered every Saturday and ram a loo roll down the toilets before flushing them. I spent the last few weeks of that year kipping on a mate's floor in town rather than shoulder the depression that such childishness caused. However, my second year proved to be even more of an absolute pain, as living in town meant trekking backwards and forwards to campus with bag loads of heavy books which damn near put my back out a number of times.

So, come the final year, I asked the campus residence officer if there was anywhere on campus where I could live without the threat of blocked toilets and loud flat-mates. So it was that I ended up in Borrowdale Hall.

There were ten of us in total. I won't drag on with the details, but we were all finalists studying a mixture of subjects. There were three physicists, one English major, a mathematician, one chemist, one performing arts and three theologians. The theologians consisted of me, Spliff and a guy by the name of Malcolm Wallace. I'd known Spliff since fresher's week in year one and we had sort of become acquainted with Malcolm over the next couple of years. I would like to have said that we "befriended" him, but that would be somewhat of an exaggeration as he didn't seem to make friends very easily. He kept himself to himself, studied hard and, unlike the rest of us, didn't spend the evenings in the bar. He had spent his second year living in rented rooms with an elderly spinster. This had seemed to suit him fine, so I was amazed when he approached Spliff and me towards the end of the year saying that he had heard we were coming back onto campus and asked if he could tag along. The others on the corridor paid him no attention whatsoever. I sometimes wondered if they even knew he existed. I have to say that I had never made it past the plain, brown wooden door into his room.

When I wasn't studying or letting off steam in the evening, I'd normally spend time in Spliff's room when he wasn't earning himself a bit of cash in the manner that gained him his nickname. Needless to say, he was never out of pocket and was always flush for the weekend. His room wasn't as untidy as his lodgings would be in later life, but looking back on it, this was probably just because he had not accumulated as much stuff yet or become a master in the art of acquired detritus.

His room, like mine which was next door, had a great view over the green quad area between Borrowdale and Windermere halls. I was always amazed when I looked out over this that the whole area had once been a hub of Victorian industry – it was built on the site of the old Williamson linoleum works down between the Marsh and Saint George's Quay. A lot of the campus consisted of recycled mill buildings such as warehouses or factories and it was dominated by the huge lecture block that stood near the old chimney house. Both were splendid examples of Victorian industrial architecture at its best: functional, but strangely worthy of awe and adoration.

It was on a day in late May, when I was sat on Spliff's bed watching clouds drift by the top of the chimney-stack behind Windermere, that the first of two things that would occur over the next couple of days and would change my life came about. I had just grabbed our mail from Stewart, the elderly porter at reception, and Spliff had filed his in the usual manner (dumped it with the accumulated heap on the edge of his desk over the top of the bin – the unimportant ones dropped to their doom and he eventually got around to doing something about the surviving remnant). I was opening the one letter that I had received that morning. It was in a heavy-weight manila envelope, so I had guessed it was important before I had looked inside.

"Now if it was me who had received an envelope like that," Spliff observed as he sipped on a strong cup of Earl Grey, "it would undoubtedly be a bill or some kind salesman inviting me to part with cash in a bloody timeshare apartment in Southern Spain. Whereas you, Samuel," he took another sip and grinned, "are the son of a gambler who has passed his luck on through your genes."

I smiled. "If I didn't know just how much my parents like you, I'd knock your Scottish block right off your... oh crap!" I sank down onto his bed and showed him the letter.

Spliff put his tea down, read the missive in silence and repeated what I had just said, "Oh crap indeed, Sam. What are you going to do?"

It had been a letter from the DDO: the Diocesan Director of Ordinands – the guy who oversaw those who wanted to wear their collars back to front and enter the clergy. He had written to tell me that my parochial placement had fallen through. I was supposed to be spending the three weeks after my exams trailing a local priest about his parish, but it seemed that said vicar had been caught in bed with the church-warden's wife and all hell had broken loose in the parish. Consequently, it would not be a suitable place for a raw recruit. Now, in most dioceses, the DDO is a kind, caring sort who holds the ordinands' hands and gets them ready for selection conference and the big wide world of the parish. Ours, however, was a self-righteous, self-serving git. None of the potential ordinands liked him. We all saw him for what he was - a promotion priest. He was young and wore his hair in the fashionable style of the day whilst rising quickly from curate to parish priest to rural dean. Now he was a canon at Blackburn Cathedral. Everyone was tipping him for a pointy hat in a few years' time and pity those who stood in his way.

"He says that you'll have to find another placement on your own," Spliff read out from the letter. "What a sod! He knows you haven't got time to do that right now, what with finals."

I shook my head. "He's never liked me. He's a pompous arse." I let myself fall back onto Spliff's bed, clutching my head in my hands. "What the hell am I going to do?"

My friend seemed to ponder this for a moment then said, "Call out for a she-male hooker? That would take your mind off it?"

I laughed. "Not tonight, buddy. I think I'll settle for a few beers around campus. You gonna come help me drown my sorrows?"

Spliff shook his head. "Unfortunately, my only idea of joy tonight will be the companionship of Messrs. Marx, Engels and Lenin." He waved his hand at a pile of text books that lay strewn around a sheet of empty A4 paper.

I winced. "You still not finished the Marxism paper?"

He shook his head.

"But it's due in tomorrow."

He nodded. "And hence the lack of coming out with you to ritually burn an effigy of our beloved DDO. I'm afraid this wee Scotsman will have to hitch up his kilt and write like fury all night."

I hopped off the bed and made to his door. "Okies. I'll have one for you, then. I'll just go and see if any of the others are up for a drink."

A few hours later I was climbing back up the stairwell of Borrowdale Hall. I had succeeded (without much effort, might I add) to persuade four of the others from my corridor to go out for a beer that evening then I had headed off to a terminally boring ethics lecture (to this day I do not know for the life of me why I actually took that course) before spending a couple of productive hours engrossed in the library. Apart from the letter, the day was following the course that most of my university life took. I worked hard and I played harder. By day I would be secreted away in some secluded corner of the library, multi-tasking amongst piles of dusty old books and the shiny, sparkly highways of the new-born love child of the *Encyclopaedia Britannica* and Alexander Graham Bell - that wonder known in hushed tones of awe as "The Internet". I had an obsession to unpick all the words from every text that I studied. I wanted to understand how the author had arrived at his or her particular conclusions, then I proceeded to challenge them and ultimately try to overturn them with the latest ideas that were bouncing around the end of the Twentieth Century. Later, as the afternoon would wear on, and my eyes began to scream, "No more! We can take no more!" I would shut down my terminal, tidy up my books, stuff my scrappy notes into my back pocket and saunter back to my room then get ready to frequent one of the uni bars, where I would chug my beers down with great gusto until I was the last man standing.

A typical day.

I guess I don't need a dramatic pause here, do I? If this day had been a typical day then it would be rather tedious watching some shmo going about the same old, same old before yawning loudly, scratching his backside and slouching off to bed.

No. Not a typical day.

As I rounded the corner of the stairwell onto our corridor, my stomach rumbled. I glanced at my watch. Six thirty. Christ, I had completely lost track of time. I needed to eat before heading out.

I diverted into the kitchen area and wandered over to the cupboards. When I was a first year, it had been terribly unadvisable to store one's food in the kitchen. If you did that, then it would be gone by the morning. All that would be left would be a few pitiful cornflake crumbs and some mouldering pieces of fruit. This year, though, was quite different. We all had our own shelves in the cupboards and no food ever got swiped in the middle of the night when someone had an attack of the munchies from some of Spliff's products. Also, amazingly, the kitchen was always spotless. Now, normally, when you group a bunch of late teens-early twenties males together, you are wading through crud, pants and unspeakable crunchy stuff that adheres itself to your feet. Our kitchen was always spick and span – never a dirty pot, never a tea towel out of place.

This meant that I was able to quickly find a sparklingly clean spoon for my pot noodle as the kettle boiled me some water. I poured the water on and let the snack stand before lifting the lid and deciding that I had in fact made it a bit thick, so a fork would be better for eating the snack. I grabbed a fork and turned to leave the kitchen when I realised that I had left the spoon on the side. Deciding that I had best keep the kitchen in the manner to which we were all accustomed, I turned and made to put the spoon away.

The work surface was empty. There was just the kettle. I frowned. I was sure I had put the spoon down there. I had a quick scout around and saw no obvious pieces of cutlery. I shrugged to myself, deciding that I had obviously put the spoon back in the drawer when I had taken the fork.

Munching on my pot noodle I meandered back to my room planning in my head what beer I was going to drink and where later on that evening.

The next morning my head hurt like hell. I banged and clattered my way along the corridor and stumbled into the gleaming, bright kitchen. Instinctively I shaded my eyes from the debilitating sunlight that bounced inconsiderately off the pristine surfaces. I reminded myself to knock back some paracetamol when I got back to my room.

"Morning sleepy-head," chirped a bright, Scottish accent from around a mouthful of muesli. "Good night last night?"

"I think so," I managed as I shambled across to the fridge. "I don't really remember much about it." As I crouched down to look for my milk, the room swayed. "Whoa! Who moved the planet?"

There was the gentle sound of chuckling from behind me.

"Knock it off, Spliff," I moaned as I stood up with my carton and started to hunt for some cereal. “Damn it! It’s too bright in here for me to think straight.”

“Hmmm,” my friend mused. “It is rather perky isn’t it? What time did you and the others pile in last night?”

I managed to tip most of my cereal into a nearby bowl. Some of the cornflakes waterfalled onto the counter. I made a mental note to clean them up later, when it wouldn’t feel like I was trying to scrub out the guts of a hippo. “Dunno. About four? Five?”

Spliff finished his breakfast and thoughtfully placed the spoon in the bowl. “And it is now about...” he glanced at the kitchen clock, “nine thirty.”

“Don’t remind me,” I grumbled around my cornflakes. “I’ve got a ten o’clock.”

“I guess you grabbed a bite to eat before you came back?”

“Yeah. Chinese I think. Might have been Indian, though.” I squinted through my heavy eyelids. “Look, what’s up? Why the questions?”

Spliff leant forwards across the dining table. “I take it you left your discarded packaging and other such things here to tidy up in the morning?”

I nodded. I winced. It hurt to move my head so much. “What of it?”

“Where are they now?” His eyes scanned the pristine room. Mine tried to follow, but gave up half way.

“The cleaners must have come in.”

“As you know, I had an appointment last night with the leaders of the revolution. Aided by sheer stubbornness, self-control and a steaming hot pot of tea – oh, and some rather delicious hob-nobs – I managed to rattle out three thousand words before midnight. After this I slept like a baby only to stir vaguely when a bunch of drunken hoo-hars bumbled along the corridor in the wee hours.”

“Sorry,” I mumbled.

He waved his hand dismissively. “Even with this nocturnal noise I was able to wake bright and early feeling refreshed and rejuvenated.” He looked me up and down. “Unlike someone else I might care to mention.”

“Looking good, feeling great.” I vaguely lifted my thumb up to illustrate the point but let it drop back down again with a crash after the exertion of too much effort.

“Indeed,” Spliff continued. “Anyway, I have been sat here since seven a.m. enjoying the beautiful rays of our god-given light and the pleasure of my own company. Not a discarded scrap of your refuse was here when I arrived and I have seen neither hide nor hair of a cleaner. In fact, I have been the only living soul in the room.” He paused. “Make that the corridor.”

My head was starting to pound and I was losing the will to live, let alone the appetite for my cereal. I staggered to my feet and walked over to the bin where I deposited the remains of my breakfast. “Look, Spliff, I really don’t get what you’re driving at. I’ve gotta go and get ready for my lecture.”

“Okay,” he smiled, “but hadn’t you better clean up those cornflakes you spilt, first?”

I grunted and turned to the worktop, grabbing a damp dishcloth on the way.

I stopped.

I stared.

I looked at Spliff, still sat at the dining table sipping his tea and smiling in a fashion that appeared both benevolent and smug.

I looked back at the spotless work-surface. There wasn't a crumb in sight.

"How?" I croaked.

"Tell me Sam," Spliff grinned, "do you believe in ghosts?"

"Do they have good painkillers?" I asked.

Spliff sighed and slipped a packet of paracetamol onto the kitchen table. "I thought you would need some of these."

"Thank you." I downed two and swallowed them with a swig of water.

"Now leave the glass on the side, sit down and watch," my friend instructed.

I did as I was told. I placed the half-full tumbler on the work surface, sat down at the table and watched in amazement as it simply vanished before my eyes.

"Jesus!" I shouted, leaping to my less-than-steady feet, then regretting the outburst as my synapses wept in agony.

"Serves you right for such blasphemy." Spliff placed his empty cup on the table.

I stuck two fingers up at him as the cup also disappeared.

This was far too much for my alcohol-abused grey matter. I was having difficulty focussing on the here and now let alone any apparent ghostly goings-on. "Where've they gone?" I finally managed when the pounding in my head had started to subside. Thank you, you great god Paracetamol!

Spliff rose to his feet and walked over to the crockery cupboard. "Allow me. I don't think you could tolerate any more sudden surprises this morning." He opened the melamine-coated door and there, washed and dried were my glass and his china cup, neatly positioned with all the rest. "Have you not wondered why this room is so clean and tidy, Sam? Look at it. It gleams brighter than Tom Cruise's teeth when he prattles on about Scientology!"

"I just thought that everyone tidied up after themselves," I shrugged pitifully.

Spliff shook his head in despair. "So bright, yet so naive. Honestly, Sam, one of these days someone will see you coming and squeeze you like a toddler squeezes a tube of toothpaste until there's nothing left inside. Have you ever put anything away in here?"

I thought about it then shook my head.

"Have you ever washed up?"

Again I shook my head.

"So why on earth would you presume that anyone else must have done so, either? You really do need to develop a more cynical side to your nature, young man."

The paracetamol was really starting to kick in now as I could open my eyes properly and was starting to be more capable of a logical thought process. "So have you seen this happen before?"

"Nope." He reached into the fridge and grabbed a square of white sliced bread which he proceeded to munch on. "I've always thought it a bit peculiar, but it wasn't until I came in this morning and saw the place spotless that I decided to investigate. I must have still been in the inquisitive zone from essay writing last night. I made myself a pot of tea and left the teaspoon on the side. I sat down and, when I looked up, the spoon was back in the drawer, clean and polished. Naturally my curiosity was piqued so I tried a few more things. Mugs: back in the cupboard. Cheese: stored in the fridge. Spilt food: in the bin. Everything neat and tidy, all where it should be."

"And you think it's a ghost?"

"You got any better ideas?"

The painkiller allowed me partial access to the depths of my consciousness. The rational side of me wanted to explain it away. It wanted to find something substantial to wave in the air and shout out "Poppycock!" as loudly as possible, but there was nothing. There was nothing that I could counter Spliff with whatsoever.

In the end I slowly shook my head. "But why?"

"I think, Samuel that is for you and your little bouncy brain cells to find out. Why don't you start by asking the one person we all know who's been here the longest?"

The porter's lodge was just inside the main foyer of Borrowdale Hall. It was a cramped little afterthought of a room that had been split into two. The front contained a small desk and the external mail pigeon holes. The back was crammed full with piles of sacks and an assortment of tool chests that seemed to envelop a small, overstuffed armchair. This was where I found Stewart, his head in a trashy crime novel.

"Sam!" the old boy crowed when I walked in. "Good to see you. Saw you wandering over to the bar last night. Had a good one?" He winked conspiratorially.

I chuckled. Stewart didn't miss a thing. He was the hub of the residence. Anything that happened always fell within his radar: the drunkenness, the partying, the celebrations, the commiserations. He was privy to everything and divulged nothing. There may have been a counselling service set up by the powers that be, but anyone with a real problem went and talked to Stewart. It was like having a friendly uncle on demand. The sort you went to unburden yourself to when your parents were at each other's throats again and home was unbearable. The sort who would sit and listen attentively whilst you just rambled on and on about how life was awful and pointless and how you had just about had it up to here with everything. The sort who, after they had sat listening to you for half an hour without saying so much as a word, just gave you the feeling that everything would turn out alright in the end.

"Well, I don't remember much..."

He spread his arms wide. "Says it all then. You not come down for your post?" His eyes twinkled knowingly.

"Actually, I was kind of after some information."

The old man rubbed his bristly chin. "Now you know I'm not one for gossip, Sam," he said, his brown eyes dancing like a ballerina fifty years his younger. "What gets told in this room, stays in this room."

I held up a pacifying hand. "No, no. I understand. It's not about anyone in this residence." I paused. "Well no one living that is."

Stewart seemed to ponder these words, half closing one eye as he absentmindedly patted his jacket pockets. "You know, Sam, I think it's time I went and got some fresh air." He fished out a battered packet of Golden Virginia and some Rizlas. "Perhaps you'd like to join me?"

I nodded.

He accompanied me out of the lodge, locked the door behind him and stuck up a sign saying, "Back in ten minutes."

"Eee it's warm today." Stewart pronounced "warm" as "wahrm" as most long-lived Lancastrians do.

"I think it's set in for summer now," I observed after taking a pull on one of the roll-ups the porter had made for me. I made sure I didn't cough my guts up. There was more tar in there than on the surface of the M6.

"Nah, lad. Storms are coming, I reckon." He tapped his tobacco packet against his left knee. "This 'ere tells me so." He drew heavily on his roll-up, causing it to burn brightly, then he blew a long smoke ring before saying, "Anyways, you didn't come to seek me advice on the weather, did you Sam?"

"How long have you been here, Stewart?" I asked.

He let out a long breath and scratched at his beard. "Well now, let's see. It was a few years after the place opened. I was just out of the army. Bert was retiring... Must be getting on forty years, I reckon. Why's that?"

"You seen anything odd?"

The old man let out a deep chuckle. "You mean apart from young lads walking home with their pants on their head or girls trying to climb stairs on their hands?"

I grinned. "Non-drink related events then."

He peered at me again through his half-closed eye. "I might have, Sam. It depends on what you mean."

"What about on our corridor? In the kitchen?"

A warm smile formed under Stewart's beard. "I think I know what you'd be getting at, Sam. You're referring to a kitchen that, no matter how untidy you leave it, always appears to be clean and spotless a short while later? Am I right?"

I nodded.

"Nothing to worry about there, young'un," he explained. "It's just old Gerald."

I waited for the porter to continue as he finished his cigarette and proceeded to roll up a new one.

"Yep." He tapped some tobacco into the paper. "Gerald's been dead some twenty-odd years now." He gently prodded the brown flakes down and moistened the gummed edge. "He was the best cleaner we ever had in the halls. You could see your face in any surface that he polished." His small, disposable lighter ignited the end of the cigarette and he took a long drag. "So clean. So proper, he was. Always on time. Never dawdled. Yep. The best cleaner I ever knew." He blew out some smoke and stared off into space.

"What happened?" I asked, when it became apparent that his thoughts were off hiking up a distant mountain. "How did he die?"

"His heart gave out, apparently," Stewart finally said, tapping ash off the small roll-up. "Nothing suspicious. Nothing unnatural. He just died." He turned and looked me in the eye. "In your kitchen, no less."

The look on my face must have been a picture as he chuckled quietly to himself before letting his thoughts ramble off again.

"Why's he still here?"

Stewart shrugged, finished his cigarette and made to stand up. "Not got a clue, Sam. Why don't you ask him yourself?"

The rest of the day just dragged. We were nearing the end of our university education and exams were looming. Rather than letting up on us, our lecturers were determined to cram in as many revision seminars as possible. I had five that day alone; each of them in a small, stuffy lecture theatre surrounded with other students all who kept giving wistful glances out of the window to the grounds of the converted linoleum factory.

It never ceases to amaze me just what the planners of the university managed to do with the old derelict grounds of the Williamson works. Many conversions of Victorian and Edwardian architecture tend to end up looking like the love child of two completely incompatible parents. Stone brick is encompassed in gaudy steel and neon giving you a migraine as you try to work out just where the main entrance to a building is or whether said building is an office block, an art museum or a public urinal. Luneside University, however, kept the heart of the old complex and sort of went with the flow. Those buildings that could be restored were perfectly renovated and those that were beyond repair were levelled in favour of tasteful lecture halls and grassy lawns. It's not a very large campus, but it does seem to have the TARDIS effect. You are constantly amazed at just how much stuff fits within its walls and how much space was created in its conception.

It is a great place to stretch out and relax on a warm summer's day. The sort of day when you just do not want to be stuck in a seminar going over and over the same material that you read up on only a few months ago. I knew that I would be better off curling up under a tree with a few books and a cold can of something fizzy and alcoholic rather than listening to the incessant drone of some old fart who loathed students and thought that undergrads were just an inconvenience that stopped him from his own research.

There was one student, I noticed, who was still lapping up these little hours of hell and that was Malcolm Wallace. Whereas the rest of us were adopting the fashionable stance of the apathetic slouch, he was upright, pen in hand and eyes transfixed on the latest lecturer. As I watched him, I noticed that not once did his pen touch paper, but his eyes never left the speaker. He was enrapt and enthralled. I cast my eyes over to the front of the lecture hall to see what had got him so unusually keyed up.

The lecturer was babbling on about the concepts of free will and predestination. The names of various philosophers and theologians were scribbled unintelligibly on the white board and he was pointing from one to the other with a big stick.

I raised my eyebrows. This was old hat. We had gone over this last year. Why was Malcolm so on tenterhooks about it? I shrugged and went back to inward speculation on the two subjects that were currently bugging me: the ghost of dearest Gerald and my lack of parish placement. I guessed that something would crop up for a placement. I could do the ring round or have a chat with the campus chaplain. I was sure that they had protocols for such things. Now, the ghost was a completely different matter. What was I going to do about that?

Should I do anything about it? I mean, it wasn't as if he was malevolent or evil, was it? In fact, he seemed quite the opposite; fastidious in his nature, constantly tidying up after us. That was no mean feat in a student halls of residence. I chuckled slightly as I imagined Casper the friendly ghost wandering around wearing a frilly pinny and a pair of Marigold rubber gloves. I was suddenly aware that the room was silent. I looked up and saw the lecturer scowling at me. I shrank further down into my seat. He coughed and carried on.

I decided that it would be best to save my ponderings on Gerald until later. I didn't realise just how fast things were going to move after the lecture. I really should have paid more attention to the concept of predestination and destiny.

The sun continued to beam down as I wandered back from the lecture rooms towards the halls of residence. Wallace had joined me and was in quite a chatty mood for someone who was normally so withdrawn that he usually made a wallflower look like John Barrowman's hyperactive twin brother. "That was fascinating, don't you think?" he beamed, the sun reflecting off the white streaks in his hair. "The notion that we are not really in control of our own actions, but at the beck and call of higher powers?"

I shrugged somewhat noncommittally, "It's old news, surely? I mean, right back to the Greeks and even before that, we were supposedly at the beck and call of the gods."

Wallace shook his head, "Yes, but what about today? What about the good old, post-modern here and now?" His eyes, with their curious hue of orangey-brown, were practically on fire with enthusiasm. The lecture had well and truly got him stirred up. "You ask a priest if they really believe that their god controls their life and they will cite 'free will' right back at you. They would say that we have the power to decide our own destiny and that nothing or no one can make you do otherwise."

"So?" I couldn't really see where this was going.

"Well I think it's baloney!" he exploded. A group of girls who were walking past us turned and giggled into their folders. Wallace was unperturbed. "Of course we can be controlled. All something needs is the power and the focus to achieve it."

I smiled and shook my head. "I think I'll leave that to the almighty. Perhaps he can steer me into the path of a parish placement?"

Wallace calmed down and looked at me seriously. "I thought you had one?"

"I did," I explained as we approached the glass doors to the foyer of our halls, "but it fell through. Besides, in hindsight they were probably a little bit too *evo* for my tastes."

"Ah, the 'God is a squirrel' brigade."

I paused with my hand on the door. "Pardon?"

He grinned. "You know the sort. When they talk to God, they do it with the wistful look in their eyes whilst they peer up into the trees or up at the rooftops, as if God was a squirrel nibbling on his nuts."

I chuckled. "Nice one."

"Thank you. Listen, if you're stuck, I'll have a word with the priest at my placement. With a bit of luck, I might be able to persuade him to take pity on you."

"Really?" A cool air-conditioned breeze wafted over us as we entered the stone building. "What's the church like?"

"High as a kite and barrels full of smoke," Wallace smiled. "You'd be right at home, Sam."

"Sounds perfect."

Wallace looked over his shoulder towards the porter's lodge. "I'm just going to check my mail. I'm waiting for something."

"Okay. See you upstairs later?"

He nodded agreement. "I'll take you to the parish tomorrow if you like? Oh, just one thing."

"What?" I asked, my voice suddenly wary.

"Watch out for his teenage daughter," he winked before he headed off to the porter's lodge. "Apparently she's a bit of a man-eater."

Looking back on that moment I wonder perhaps if I should have refused his offer, but I didn't and, anyway, Caroline is a story for another time and another book.

Isn't it great when things just seem to fit together. You feel like there's a purpose to life. All is hunky-dory and there's not a grey cloud on the horizon. The birds twitter in the treetops, no one shot Bambi's mother and Buffy settled down to a happy ever after with Spike. Okay, perhaps I should have stopped at the Bambi reference, but you know what I mean. You get that warm feeling deep down inside of you that doesn't feel like indigestion and you can't help but smile.

I think I even whistled as I made my way upstairs. That's how good a mood I was in. I don't do not being in control. I like all the pieces of my life to fit snugly and neatly together. When they don't, well things just fall apart. So, hearing that Malcolm could sort me out with a placement was a big deal to me. Things were back on track and everything was how it should be.

It's funny how life comes and punches you in the gut so quickly.

I dumped my stuff in my room and sauntered down the corridor to Spliff's door. I knocked three raps and let myself in, grinning.

Spliff was sat on his bed.

His glasses were held loosely in his hand and his eyes were red-rimmed.

The twittering birds fell quiet as the gunshot rang through Disney Forest.

"Oh Sam..." he started, his voice cracking as he held back more tears.

"What?"

"Sam... It's your dad... I'm so sorry."

I was sat on something. I didn't know what. It was hard and my knees were bent so it was probably a chair. It could have been a large rock for all I knew right then. There was a mug in my hand. It was exceptionally hot. It must have contained tea or something. I neither knew nor cared. The heat was burning my hands, scolding them.

I let it.

It felt real.

Disturbingly comforting.

The painful sensation on my hands.

It felt real.

Nothing else was real. It couldn't be.

It couldn't be.

Arthritis doesn't kill people. It just doesn't.

Does it?

I looked down into the brown liquid. Yes, it was tea. I could smell it. Strong, brown tea, piping hot in a white mug that was burning my hands.

That was real. That was real.

Arthritis doesn't kill people. It makes them sore and cranky. They have operations and take medication. They don't die.

"Tell me again what she said."

Spliff sighed as he steeled himself again for the umpteenth time. "Sam, perhaps you need to rest for a bit."

"Tell me!" I snapped, my eyes staring down into the brown liquid. "Just... tell me."

"Your mum said that the doc came round this morning. He told her there was nothing they could do. There's a build-up of crud on your dad's lungs caused by him being immobile. It's called pulmonary fibrosis..."

"Are you saying it's my dad's fault he's dying?" Venom. Pure, spiteful venom.

A pause. A breath. "No, Sam. It's just a complication. A bloody awful, dreadful complication. They tried him with oxygen, but that's only making him more comfortable."

I wanted to smash the mug of tea. I wanted to press my hands so hard that it would shatter, spilling hot liquid onto the carpeted floor and driving shards of ceramic into my hands. I wanted it to hurt. I wanted it to make me bleed. I wanted it to shock me.

I wanted to enjoy the pain.

My dad had been in pain so long. So long.

That was going to end soon.

Pause. Breath. I put the mug down on the floor away from my feet. "How long?"

"Not long. Probably a few weeks at the most. He's quite advanced."

"Is he toilet trained? Does he know his alphabet? Can he count backwards from a hundred? That's advanced, Spliff. Dad's not advanced, he's dying!"

"I know he is. I'm sorry, Sam. I truly am."

I opened my mouth to let something awful loose into the face of my friend, saw his wet, grey eyes and pressed my lips together.

Pause. Breathe. "I know you are. I know you are. I'm just..." I waved my hands around hopelessly then slapped them down on my knees.

"I know what you mean, Sam. There's nothing we can do."

Something prickled where my head met my neck. A thought clambered its way up into my brain. "Yes there is. We can talk to someone who's already been through it."

"You mean our friendly neighbourhood..." Spliff wiggled his fingers in the air.

In spite of how I felt right then, I laughed. The old bugger's the best friend a guy could ever have. He's always there for me when I'm down as well as always being keen to knock me back before I make a tit of myself. I don't know what I'd ever do without him.

"Our OCD ghostie? Yeah. I mean him." So I filled Spliff in on what Stewart had told me while he made a fresh pot of tea.

"I don't know, Sam," he said as we sat drinking more Earl Grey. "It all sounds a bit dark arts to me, you know?"

"It's not like we'd be raising a corpse or anything," I countered, "and he hardly seems malevolent does he?"

Spliff sipped his tea and nodded his head from side to side. "Okay, point taken, but how do you plan to go about communicating with the deceased? Hmmm? You ever spoken to the dead before? And stoned philosophy students don't count. Technically they still have a semblance of brain activity deep in their cerebral cortex."

"Well I guess we hold a séance, don't we?" I looked at him for approval as I brushed my fingernails over my teeth.

He looked back at me, his face a portrait of incredulity. "A séance?

The two of us? Now I'm no expert, but we do seem to be a bit thin on the numbers, don't you agree? And would you know where to begin?"

"I'm sure you could think of something appropriate to say."

He nearly choked on his tea. "Me? Why me?"

I shrugged. "You're better with words."

Spliff half shut his eyes and glared at me. "I could take that as your way of saying I talk too much. Okay. I guess I could think of something, as it's you, but I still think two is a lame number."

I nodded then thought back to a conversation on predestination and destiny. "I think I might know someone else who would be willing to join in."

I knocked rather tentatively on the door to Malcolm's room. At first there was no reply and I made to leave, but then I heard the sound of approaching feet and it opened just a crack. The quiet student's face appeared and, as the doorway framed his face, I noticed just how much white was starting to appear in his dark hair that framed those light-coloured eyes.

"Hello Sam," he said. "Can I help you?"

I ran my fingers through my hair. "Yeah, Malcolm. It's just, it's a bit..." I looked up and down the corridor. There was no one else around at the moment, but I didn't want to risk anyone stumbling onto our conversation. "Delicate," I finished. "Would you mind if I came in?"

The recluse hesitated as he mulled over the possibility of letting a stranger into his inner sanctum. Just when I thought he would refuse, he silently nodded and opened the door enough to let me in. I quickly stepped across the threshold before he changed his mind. The room was almost exactly how I imagined it to be; absolutely neat and pristine with classical music playing quietly from a small CD player. For a moment I actually wondered if Malcolm had his own little supernatural cleaner, but then I told myself off for jumping at ideas – he was obviously just a very tidy individual.

He was also quite the reader.

"Wow!" I gasped as I surveyed the numerous bookcases filled with hundreds of books of all sizes and appearance. "I thought Spliff was bad for books, but this..." I waved my hand towards the impressive library as my words trailed off, unable to complete the sentence with anything able to describe what was going through my head.

"I like to read," Malcolm shrugged. "You would be amazed at what one can uncover."

My head nodded slowly as I continued to let my eyes wander over the collection. I noted some large, leather-bound tomes on the bottom shelves. "Some of these look pretty old, and are those scrolls?" There was an expensive looking glass box with what looked like rolls of parchment sealed inside it. I turned my face round to Malcolm who was grinning with obvious joy.

"They're exceptionally old." He reached up and brought the box down with due reverence. Carefully he placed it on his over-sized desk and unsnapped the catches. The unmistakable smell of centuries wafted up to greet us. He slid a pair of protective gloves onto his hands and pulled out a couple of the ancient documents. As he rolled the first one out, I saw the unmistakable stylised pictograms of Egyptian hieroglyphs.

"This is genuine?"

He nodded. "It dates from the time of Rameses the Great. See, there's his cartouche." He pointed to a series of small symbols enclosed in a flat-sided oval.

I could make out a disc, a man sat on a throne and a wiggly line. The rest was all, well... not exactly Greek to me, but you get my drift? "I'll take your word for it. What's on the other?"

"Oh this," he was whispering now like someone venerating at a holy of holies. I felt like we should be burning incense and lighting candles whilst we perused the scrolls. "This is my pride and joy." He unfurled the small document across the table. I think I may have involuntarily given a little gasp. It was obviously very, very old, but it was immaculate. There were no tears, no missing edges. It was covered in a script that I had never seen before in my life.

"Where's this one from?"

"Canaan," Malcolm beamed. "It's one of the earliest examples of Proto-Canaanite script."

"But that must be..."

"Priceless," he finished.

For a while we just stood and stared at the most valuable item I had ever laid eyes on and then I asked the obvious question, "How did you end up with it? A rich uncle?"

A look of beatific joy spread across his face as he rolled the scrolls back up and sealed them once more in the case. "My benefactor."

"You have a benefactor?"

He nodded.

"How come you never told anyone?"

Malcolm shrugged. "You never asked."

"Fair enough." My eyes started to take in the rest of the small room and they found a small table which was located discretely in the corner. It was dressed in a white cloth upon which stood five votive candles around a small upright pole that was entwined in two strips of ribbon; one red, one black. I walked over to the table.

"You haven't said what you wanted," Malcolm said, a touch of apprehension sounding in his voice.

"Oh, sorry. Spliff and I are going to do something tonight and we wondered if you might be interested. What's this?" I made to pick up the decorated pole.

Malcolm's hand was suddenly like a vice around my wrist. "Something that's not to be touched." His voice was firm and his orange eyes were like deadly daggers.

I drew back, quickly. "Sorry," I apologised.

Slowly, he released my arm and recomposed himself. "What is it that you have in mind?"

I faced him and decided that, probably, the direct approach was for the best. "We believe that the kitchen is haunted."

"You mean Gerald?"

I was gobsmacked. "You already know?"

"You never asked."

I winced. "Okay, I see a pattern here. Anyway, we intend to communicate with him tonight. I have some questions."

"I doubt he'll help you. He's not the chatty type, apart from the weather. He's always interested in the weather."

I made to say that he had never told us he had actually spoken to the ghost before, but the look in Malcolm's eyes told me the answer that I would get, so instead I asked, "How did you communicate with him?"

"Oh, that was easy. First I used an invocation ritual then I used the old tried and tested method." He pulled a wooden box out from under his bed and took something out which he offered to me. "You can borrow it if you want to."

It was the essential ingredient to every teen horror flick - a Ouija board. I took it from him. "Thanks." I turned the board over in my hands and peered at it from varying angles. It was light and thin with the alphabet inscribed upon it along with numbers zero to nine and the words "yes" and "no". I couldn't help but feel somewhat apprehensive. "Is this thing safe?"

"Sam, it's a piece of wood, not a gun. You can't load it with bullets and shoot your foot off by accident."

"You know that's not what I meant."

Malcolm shrugged nonchalantly. "I'm still here, aren't I? Still got one head, two nostrils and no green goblin hanging onto my shoulders."

"Fair enough." I frowned as I pondered what I was holding in my hand. "I imagine the DDO doesn't know about all of this." I gesticulated with the board. "I imagine he would freak out somewhat."

Malcolm nodded slowly. "I guess he would. What he doesn't know doesn't hurt him. I see it all as... research."

There was a slight awkward silence until I said, "So as you're lending us this little baby, I'm guessing you won't be joining us tonight?"

He shook his head. "I'd love to but I'm meeting up with my benefactor. She's staying at a hotel in town so we'll go out for a meal and I'll be spending the night with her."

It actually took a little while for the inference to sink in.

Eventually, my brain prompted my mouth to say, "You're sleeping with your benefactor?"

Malcolm gave a little shrug. "It's complicated, but we both get what we want."

"Bloody hell," I swore, tucking the board under my arm. "It's always the quiet ones. Here we all are spending time in bars wondering whether some hot piece of skirt on the next table thinks we look cute and you've bagged yourself a rich, older woman."

"Older." Malcolm chuckled at the word. "Sam, you have no idea."

"Okay, so now you're creeping me out somewhat. I'm guessing that we're not talking late twenties, early thirties here?"

He burst into a fit of near uncontrollable laughter and had to sit down on his bed to bring himself to order. "No Sam, far from it."

Images of lustful nights spent in a quaint sitting room doused in the pervading aroma of lavender filled my head and I shuddered. "I'll take your word for it. Let's just leave it there, shall we?"

Malcolm spread his hands in a "as you wish" manner and changed the subject by asking, "So why do you want to talk to Gerald? Need a washer changing?"

"I wish."

Malcolm frowned. "What's wrong?"

"It's my dad. He's dying. I just found out. I just want to..." I wanted to what? I wasn't sure. It just seemed that I needed to do something, but I wasn't sure what. I felt impotent, and not in the Doctor Freud kind of way.

"You want to make sure that he'll still be around when he dies."

There it was. Plain. Matter of fact. I was terrified that, when Dad died, he would be gone for good, a piece of dust on the jacket of eternity ready to be scraped off with the Sellotape of time.

I needed to know that he hadn't been a waste.

I needed to know that he would go on forever. I needed to know that he would be there.

My mouth said nothing but my eyes must have spoken volumes.

"I know how you feel, Sam. I lost my parents when I was young. I was still at school. It was awful - a car crash. Some idiot rammed their car into a tree. They were burned alive. Burned alive, can you believe it? I went completely off the rails. I skipped school, spent my time in dive bars and got into all sorts of stuff that would make your toes curl.

"Then *she* found me.

"I was slumped on a park bench with a bottle of scotch in my hand and dubious stains down my shirt when she just sat down next to me and started to hum this tune. I can't for the life of me remember it now, but it sounded so good. It lifted all my cares away and I knew right there and then that she would save me. She stood up, took my hand and I followed her. She's been guiding me ever since."

"But you still don't know if your parents are, you know, in Heaven or whatever?"

He shrugged. "I don't need to. She's shown me that I don't need to worry about them anymore. I just need to live my life and follow my destiny."

I raised an eyebrow. "Your destiny? What might that be then?"

"Time will tell, Sam. Time will tell." He stood and pulled another box out from under his bed. It was full of tubs of herbs and various occult bric-a-brac. Definitely the sort of things that would make the DDO's coiffured hair stand on end. "For now, though, we need to solve your little problem, don't we?" He passed me a small plastic bag containing some brown powder. "This should help."

"It looks like something Spliff would sell," I said dubiously.

"It's althaea root. It attracts benevolent spirits. Burn it over a candle and say this enchantment," he handed me a piece of paper with writing on, "and Gerald will be bound. He won't be able to escape. That way you can ask him anything you want."

"This will definitely work?"

"Like a gem, Sam," Malcolm grinned. "Like a gem."

So the scene was set. The kitchen, as usual, was spotless. A white sheet had been spread over the dining table. The Ouija board was set central between myself and Spliff with a third, empty chair at the head of the table. (We weren't sure why we had set one for the ghost - it had just seemed like the right thing to do.) A large candle burned nearby and fragrant incense wafted around the room from some joss sticks that I had acquired from the Student Union shop a few weeks previous.

"You're sure we're not going to be disturbed?" Spliff was polishing the board's glass pointer with the back of his t-shirt. "That would be a bad mistake."

"It's cool," I reassured him as I smoothed a small crease out from the white linen. "Greg and the guys are off at an all-nighter at the Sugar House. They've been banging on about it for weeks."

My friend nodded and placed the pointer on the wooden board. "Shame Malcolm didn't come. What did you say he was doing?"

I chuckled to myself. "He told me he has a date, so he's somewhat unavailable."

Spliff's eyes twinkled in the flickering light of the candle. "Malcolm Wallace?" he grinned. "A date? Well, bugger me sideways with a ten-foot barge pole! The sly old dog. What's she like?"

I shrugged. "He wasn't for giving. Apparently she's older."

"A lecturer?"

"I don't think so. He wouldn't tell me, exactly. Apparently it's been going on for some time now. He says she's fascinating."

A low whistle left Spliff's lips. "I bet she is. You'll have to grill him tomorrow when he takes you to that parish." He stroked his downy chin. "Which one was it?"

"Dunno. He didn't say and I sort of forgot to ask."

"Bloody hell, Sam." Spliff shook his head in despair. "Sometimes you can be so crap at squeezing info out of people." He placed a finger on the glass pointer and tested that it slid smoothly. "When we contact this guy, just let me ask the questions, okay?"

I smiled and nodded then placed my finger next to Spliff's. The glass felt unnaturally cold to the touch. I took a deep breath and looked up at my friend. He looked back and raised his eyebrows. I nodded. It was time to start.

Spliff cleared his throat, laid his spare hand next to the Ouija board and lightly closed his eyes. "We beseech the invisible powers that walk amongst us to make themselves known this day."

I stifled a laugh. It burst into a short snort.

Spliff's eyes snapped open. "What is it?"

I smiled. "Beseech?" I asked. "Come on Spliff. The guy we want to talk to only died about twenty years ago. I think he understands modern English."

"You were the one who said I was good at the talky stuff. Besides, there is such a thing as protocol, Samuel." Spliff sounded rather sniffy. "One has to follow the rules as they are lain down. We are dealing with the supernatural here, not the bra strap of some first year sports science student."

"Hey!" I protested. "Those things are dangerous. Get it wrong and they could have your eyes out!"

"Quite. Get this wrong and you could lose your soul." He closed his eyes again. Matter over. "Shall we continue?"

"Sure." I made sure that my finger was in place on the pointer and my chuckle reflex was locked up tightly in a box.

"We have come here this night to communicate with a restless spirit that walks these halls. We wish to commune with this lonesome soul and ask if there is anything that we can do to assist its passing over." He paused. "Is there anybody there?" His right eye opened just a crack and lanced me with accusation.

I was very good. I looked down at the pointer and was about to hit my chuckle reflex over the head with a cricket bat when I felt movement under my finger and the glass pointer slid across the board to YES.

My head snapped up - my mouth open, about to tell Spliff to stop dicking about - when I saw the look of shock on his face. He has never been a good liar and I could tell right then that he had not moved the pointer. "Spliff?" I managed. "What's happening?"

He ignored the stupid question and carried on. "Thank you for making yourself known to us, restless one. Please tell us what your name is."

The pointer moved again G...E...R...A...L...D. I let out a low breath and started to feel sweaty under my shirt. This was really happening. We had contacted the dead cleaner. My spare hand slipped into my trouser pocket. It brushed against the piece of paper and packet of althea root. For some reason that I was unsure of, I had failed to inform Spliff about them. Something was bothering me. Something was niggling at me. I wasn't sure what, I just felt like I needed it as a backup plan. Obviously I had presented him with the Ouija board, which he had taken great delight in, mincing around like a camp Dennis Wheatley, but the spell and powder... I had memorised the incantation, two words in Latin, and decided to bide my time.

My attention jerked back to the here and now. "We welcome you Gerald," Spliff was saying. "Please stay with us a while. We would like to ask you some questions."

The glass pointer did not move. My hand twitched on the packet of root as I remembered Malcolm saying that the spook was not one for small-talk.

Spliff's brow creased. "Gerald, are you still there?"

"Do you think it's cold for this time of year?" I asked.

Spliff was about to admonish me when the slider slid over to YES, then rapidly:

"N...O...T...L...I...K...E...W...H...E...N...I...W...A...S...Y...O...U...N...G."

I smiled. *Thank you, Malcolm*, I thought.

"You must have seen a lot of changes."

"YES."

"Good ones?"

"S...O...M...E."

"Are the students much different?" I asked.

"No. S...T...I...L...L...U...N...T...I...D...Y."

I chuckled. "Well, thank you for keeping the place clean. It's appreciated."

"This is all very well and good, Sam, but what about your question?"

I frowned. Spliff was right. I knew he was. We had Gerald here for a more theological reason rather than to chew the fat over how things were better in the good old days.

"Gerald," I began. "I have a question to ask." The pointer stayed still. "I need to ask what it's like when you die."

The pointer hammered across to "NO."

"Please, it's important."

Again, "NO."

"Gerald, my father is dying. I need your help."

Spliff and I both swore in unison as the glass pointer suddenly superheated. We snatched our fingers away as it spun maniacally before hurtling across the room and smashing against the wall.

Now was the time for the backup plan. I stood, grabbed the althaea root, sprinkled it over the burning candle and shouted, "*Spiritus manere!*"

There was a blinding flash and a force shoved me so hard that I toppled over onto the floor. Slowly, I picked myself up and looked over at Spliff as he did the same. We then both turned and looked at the other chair, which was now occupied, and I groaned.

I can't exactly remember what was going through my mind at that moment, but I know I was not exactly in a happy place. Our "visitor" for want of a better word was just sat there at the head of the table, his head slouched forwards onto his chest. He was dressed in a grey boiler suit which was immaculately clean. There were even sharp creases in the legs. His hair was dark but starting to thin and he sported a carefully combed moustache.

I kept expecting his head to snap up and for him to lurch towards us groaning, "Brains! Brains!" à la George Romero.

But he just sat there, motionless.

I looked over at Spliff.

Spliff looked at me.

"This is all your fault," I said.

He opened his mouth in shock. "My fault?" The Scottish accent lay heavy on the second word. "And how might that be, Samuel?"

"It was all your idea."

"My idea? In which alternate reality have you been living? Who was the one who suggested a séance? Who went and got this blasted Ouija board? The finger of fate points at you Mr Spallucci." He got up and walked over to the caretaker.

"What are you doing?" I hissed.

He poked a finger onto a grey shoulder of the boiler suit. The digit didn't pass through.

"Spliff!"

He ignored me and carried on with his examination. "Fascinating." He crouched down and cast his twinkling eyes over the visitor. "He seems totally corporeal if somewhat dated."

"Have some respect."

"Well, would you wear a 'tash like that unless you were a backing singer for the Village People?"

I ran my hand through my hair. This was not good. What had happened? "It wasn't supposed to be like this. I was supposed to get answers. Malcolm said..."

"What exactly?" Spliff's eyes were focussed entirely on me now. They were distinctly lacking in his usual carefree joviality. "What did the marvellous Mr Wallace tell you when you kindly leant him your ear?"

I squirmed. "He said that he could get answers for me. He said that the incantation would ensure that Gerald was bound here."

Spliff's eyes softened. "Oh, Samuel. So bright yet oh, so dim. What exactly did you think he meant by Gerald being 'bound'?"

I felt the blood drain from my face as realisation dawned from on high. Malcolm hadn't meant bound as in kept captive. He had meant bound to the physical realm. "What was I thinking?" I ran my hand through my hair again then tapped my teeth with my fingers. "I need a fag." I grabbed my pack of cigarettes and struck one up.

There was a polite cough. "Excuse me, sonny, but smoking's not permitted in the kitchen."

I dropped the match as it burnt down to my fingers.

Gerald's head was now up and his eyes sparkled under the fluorescent lights of the kitchen. "If you don't put that thing out, I shall have to inform the Dean."

I didn't say a word. I stubbed the cigarette out on a saucer.

"That's better," said the caretaker. His moustache wobbled from side to side as he seemed to be thinking. Eventually he asked, "Now will one of you two lads please tell me what's going on?"

I have to say that he took it rather well. Personally, I would have gone a bit mental, what with all the being dead and altered state stuff.

"So you two young lads contacted my dead spirit to ask for advice about Sam's dying father, and somehow I ended up all physical again." He ran his finger and thumb thoughtfully along one of his perfect creases.

"That's the gist of it," Spliff said as he placed a mug of tea on the table in front of Gerald. "Sorry for disturbing you. Sugar?"

"No thanks." He peered at the mug. "You don't think it will go straight through me, do you?"

"The bathroom's next along the corridor," I volunteered. "Oh," I said when I realised what he had actually meant. "No. You should be okay. You appear physical."

Gerald picked up the drink. He placed it under his moustache, inhaled and grinned. "Now that's a smell I've missed." He drank the brew slowly and lovingly. I noticed Spliff leaning back in his chair and peering underneath where the caretaker sat. There were no puddles. Thank heaven for small mercies.

"What was it like," I asked when he had finished the drink and wiped his moustache dry with a neat, folded hankie from his pocket, "being dead?"

His facial hair performed the little bobbing motion again as he mulled it over. "Busy," he finally said. "There was always something that needed tidying or fixing. Mind you, at least I didn't need to sleep. I could crack on at all hours."

"Thank you for that."

"S'okay," he shrugged. "It's all part of the job."

"But it's not as if the university are paying you anymore, though," Spliff pointed out.

"Not as if I have anything to spend money on either."

"Good point."

"Besides, it was always more than the money. Someone had to do the job. Someone had to clean out the blocked loos. Someone had to wipe down the pizza-strewn surfaces. Someone had to stop that annoying little drip which would bug you for days on end as it plinked into the wash basin." He shrugged again. "That someone was me. Always was. Always will be." He drained the cup, set it down neatly on the table and asked, "So what did you young chaps want then?"

"My father's dying," I blurted out. "I don't know what to do."

The caretaker's brown eyes held mine and I could see a sorrowful compassion deep inside them. "You poor lad, you must be devastated. How old is he?"

"Sixty-three."

"What's wrong with him, so to speak?"

"To cut a story short, his brain's being starved of oxygen. He only has a couple of weeks." I looked down at my hands. My knuckles were clenched and white. "I... I... just need to know..." I felt heat in my throat and warmth behind my eyes. My vision was blurring. "I just need to know that he will be..." My voice cracked and dwindled out. "...okay."

Gerald's hand came into my blurred vision as it slipped around mine and squeezed softly. I looked up and saw him smiling gently. "Surely I'm proof of that for you now, Sam? Surely I prove that he'll still be around once he's passed over?"

"But why are you here? Where do all the others go?" Tears were now running down my cheeks.

"Don't know why I'm here, lad. Guess I still have work to do, but let me tell you this, when people die, they do normally pass over. I've seen it."

"When?" Spliff asked. He had been so quiet; I had almost forgotten he was there.

Gerald got up and walked to the windows. He looked out over the rooftops to the top of the boiler chimney poking up at the centre of campus. "Last summer, one poor soul decided that he'd had enough. Don't know why. Don't want to know why - none of my business. He took himself up to the top of that chimney - God knows how he managed it - and the poor bugger jumped. No one can survive a fall like that. After he hit the ground there was this almighty flash of light and I saw him glowing bright then fade away. There was this wonderful sense of peace when his spirit left his broken body. It was his time, so off he went. I'm guessing that only certain folk - by that, I mean dead ones - can see that sort of thing. If everyone could, then the papers would be full of it, wouldn't they?" He gave a little chuckle. "I imagine there would be a whole TV channel devoted to it too. Anyways, Sam, don't you fret about your old man. When his time comes he will pass over..." He paused. "Unless of course, he has a job to do here, like me, and if that's the case, don't you worry none 'cos I'm sure he'll be fine."

The kitchen was quiet for a short while. There it was, the finality of it all. There actually *was* life after death. We had proof sat in front of us.

Why would we need to worry anymore?

Why should we fear the unknown?

Why did I feel so cold inside?

Gerald coughed. "Well, if that's all you chaps needed to know, then I guess you'll be sending me on my way and all that."

The maudlin quiet turned to an awkward one.

"Ah," said Spliff.

"Ah," I echoed.

"Is there a problem?" Gerald asked.

"You mean I'm bloody well stuck here?"

This bit of news he did not take as well as the first. Gerald was storming around the kitchen like a pissed off tornado. He was waving his hands in the air, huffing, puffing and shooting us disbelieving glances.

"You stupid pair of numpties! Don't you know not to meddle in things you don't understand?"

"Things didn't exactly go as we'd planned," I tried.

"We?" Spliff spluttered. "Whoa there, cowboy! Don't drag me into this. You were the one who cocked up the spell."

"I did not cock it up. I read it exactly as it was written. We did everything to the letter."

"Making Super Mario here corporeal was not part of the deal. We were just supposed to bind him so that you could ask him questions. Why on Earth did you decide to do that? Tell me?"

"I didn't know that's what it would do!"

"You didn't know?" Gerald was totally stunned. "What sort of boy are you that uses magic spells that he doesn't know what they do? You could have turned me into a pig!"

"Malcolm said that the spell would tie you to this plane so that I could... just... ask..." I stuttered to a full stop as I saw Gerald's moustache twitch in his thinking manner.

"Malcolm?" Gerald asked. "Quiet lad. Dark hair going white? Funny looking eyes?"

We nodded.

Gerald twitched his moustache once more. "I think you've been had, sonny. He's been to see me a few times and each time it's with the 'What's it like on the other side?' or 'Do you feel you're not in control of your destiny?' Personally he gives me the creeps."

Two minutes later we were stood outside Malcolm's door whilst Spliff and I tried to work out our next course of action.

"We could knock."

Spliff shook his head. "One: he's out with the lady in lavender, remember? Two: as it was he who gave you this magical dumb-bell, do you really think he's going to be kind enough to bear the load? The smug little shit's probably sipping chamomile tea and eating bourbons with his..." he spun his hand maniacally trying to think of a suitably derogatory term, "his... sugar mummy whilst regaling her with a quaint little tale of how he duped a pair of ignorant Philistines."

I tapped a nail against my teeth. "Point taken. So how do we get in?"

"You could always break the door down," Spliff smiled viciously.

"Me? Why me?"

"Oh, I just thought all the lead that you keep in your brain case instead of grey matter might be heavy enough to smash through plywood."

"That's uncalled for." I wagged my finger at my spiteful friend. "He took advantage of me. I was in a state."

"Why don't I let us in?" Gerald suggested. "I could open the door."

Spliff squinted at him. "What? You think you could go all Casper the Friendly Cat-burglar, float through the wall and unlock the door from the inside? But you're corporeal! Solid!"

"Yes I am, which means I can use these." He fished around in his overall pocket and jangled a set of keys in front of Spliff's face. He turned to the door, selected a Yale key and inserted it into the lock. "Needs a touch of oil this. I'll have to sort it later." There was a click and the door swung inwards. "There we go. Let's have a look shall we?"

I followed him in and looked around. The room was more or less how it had been that afternoon: neat, precise, full of books and an aromatic pall of incense hanging in the air. Spliff was straight over to the bookcase. "Wallace, you old bugger, what have you got here?" He started to pull books off the shelves at random, flicking through them.

"Spliff!" I hissed. "Focus! We need to find what we came for. Stop messing his room up."

He ignored me and continued to paw over Malcolm's things. "Oh, hello."

I recognised that little croon. He had found something interesting - something that one would not expect to have found in a certain situation. You know, like a condom in the Pope's wallet - that sort of thing. "What is it?" I walked over to the desk and looked at what he was holding in his hand. It was the small stick of wood that had been decorated with coloured ribbons. "I saw that earlier. He was very protective of it."

"I'm not surprised. It's not really the sort of thing someone considering the clergy as an occupation should really have. It's an asherah."

"And that is?"

Spliff shook his head in despair. "Samuel, Samuel, when will you learn that religions are founded on their histories and not on what we pontificate about in the modern day. You've read the Old Testament?"

"Some of it."

It was my turn to receive a Paddington Bear stare. "You know the Canaanites? They inhabited the Holy Land before Moses and his bunch kicked them out."

I nodded. I wasn't completely illiterate. "Malcolm showed me an ancient scroll written by them."

"Humph. Nice bit of bed-time reading I'm sure. Well they had this rather fun practice of *erecting*," he savoured that word a bit too much, "big wooden poles then decorating them and dancing round them butt naked in the moonlight."

"You sure that's not your perverted imagination there?"

"Okay, okay, let's just go for scantily clad. But the Hebrews hated this so either made them convert or wiped them out. The whole thing was a fertility ritual. Freud must have loved it - big sticks and all that."

"Rather like a maypole," Gerald suggested.

Spliff nodded. "Exactly. It's all giving back to Mother Nature and that sort of crap. Anyway, the pole was called an asherah and, incidentally, so was their goddess."

I took the stick and frowned. "So what the hell is Malcolm doing with an ancient fertility symbol?"

Spliff shrugged. "God knows, but my guess is that it has something far more to do with his lady-friend than the Church of England."

I grimaced and placed the asherah back down where it had been lying on top of a large tome that was open on Malcolm's desk. I frowned. The book was open at "P" and there was a pencil mark in the margin next to an entry. I read it over and suddenly felt rather sick. "You'd better see this."

Gerald and Spliff peered over my shoulders and read the passage for themselves.

"Oh," said Gerald.

"Bugger," said Spliff.

The passage in question, to paraphrase, was regarding psychopomps. Psychopomps, explained the author of the encyclopaedia, were things that were used to guide the souls of those who have not fully passed over to "their final resting place on the other side". So all we needed was a psychopomp and that would be that - Gerald could wend his merry way on into the afterlife and we could get our lives back to normal.

There was, however, just one teensy-weensy, little problem.

A psychopomp was, itself, the soul of someone or something that had also died. Not really something that we had on our person - excluding Gerald of course.

There was only one thing that I could think to say at that moment: "I need a drink."

Apparently ghosts did have a problem with drinking after all. Gerald could touch things and manipulate things here on the material plane, but liquids did appear to pass straight through him. Not literally straight through him - puddle on the floor style - but it would seem that a ghostly bladder had no memory of what it was supposed to do. So, as soon as he had downed the first can, his distraught phantom insides caused him to run quickly to the toilet.

"Guess we'd better have his." I took a fresh can and passed it over to Spliff who ripped it open, necked it and held his hand out for another. I obliged. This time he drank more slowly.

"What about a pigeon?" he mused between sips.

I lowered my can. "Why? Are you hungry? Won't a frozen pizza suffice?"

"No, you dingbat! Not to eat. As a psychopomp."

"Can't say I've got any to hand."

"Campus is full of 'em." He nodded towards the kitchen window. "What say we nip out and, you know..." He waved his can in front of his neck.

"What? Offer it a beer?"

Spliff groaned theatrically and sank back into the kitchen chair. "For God's sake, Sam. I mean go and neck one. Use it as a psychopomp."

"Oh. I see." I finished my can as I mulled this over. "Not sure that would work. One: how do you propose we catch said pigeon. Two: if we did, would you have the balls to wring its feathery little neck whilst it sat there cooing cutely up at you. Three: if we did slay the little sky-rat, who's to say it would actually do what we wanted in its afterlife. If I was a dead pigeon, I would be more likely to want to go and evacuate ghost droppings in the eyes of my killers."

"Good point, Watson." Spliff waved a finger in the air. Then reached for another can. "Hadn't thought about that."

"Hadn't thought about what?" asked Gerald as he re-entered the room.

"The downside to using a murdered pigeon as a possible psychopomp," I explained, finishing off my own can. "Far too risky."

Gerald nodded slowly and sat down in a spare chair. "True. Dirty little blighters. Always making such a mess. Perhaps I could just spend the rest of eternity stalking the campus and exterminating the vile little fiends with their beady eyes and pointy beaks..."

I held my hand up. "Okay, okay. We get it. You don't like pigeons."

"You could be the Death of Pigeons," Spliff volunteered. "Make yourself a long, black cloak and go around throwing about bits of bread soaked in cola."

I looked at my rather drunk friend. "I beg your pardon? What the hell has that got to do with anything?"

He chuckled to himself. "You must have heard of what happens to pigeons when you feed them cola, Sam? Surely?"

I shook my head.

He whooshed his hands apart making an exploding noise and spraying beer liberally about his person.

"I'll take your word for it," I said, then yawned loudly.

"You tired, Sam?" Spliff asked, sipping more beer as I nodded. "Why don't you get forty winks? Gerald and I are still good to go. Perhaps we can figure something out?"

Okay, so you sort of know what happens here, but I was really, really tired. My shoulders were aching and my eyelids were drooping. I needed no encouragement to rest my head down on the kitchen table for five minutes.

Besides, Spliff was there to make sure nothing happened, wasn't he?

Yeah, right.

As I dozed, I was aware of everything spinning. I knew that the earth spun on its axis as it spun around the Sun that spun around the centre of the galaxy that most likely spun around a primal hub of the universe; but was I supposed to be so aware of it?

I tried to open my eyes.

I gave up.

I just lay there with my head on the nice, cool dining table whilst everything around me spun in a perpetual drift of the universe.

I swallowed and the contents of a dozen cat litter trays burnt their way down my oesophagus. I groaned. No more. I would imbibe no more lager. Why had it betrayed me? It had tasted so good when I had been drinking it just a while back. Now it was like the sandpaper-encrusted toilet paper of Satan's bottom. I'd have to change my drink of choice. No more artificial fizz for me. I'd take it neat and straight. Yes, whiskey in future. Nice, mellow, pure whiskey like my dad used to drink.

Dad.

I kept my eyes closed. Not even the welling tears could force me to open them as the weight of despair sank down into my alcohol-sodden stomach. How was I going to cope? He had always been there. Now he was going to be taken away from me. And what about Mum? He had done everything for her: brought in the money, paid the bills, decorated the house, burned the

Sunday lunch. I managed a little smile at the reminiscence of my dad grinning proudly as he carved into the remains of a charred cow, whilst my mum looked on in dread.

This little piece of positive thinking gave my eyelids the smallest amount of strength they needed to jack themselves apart from one another. It was as I pried them open and the smallest of tears trickled down my face that I heard the most abysmal noise.

It was a deep, threatening roar. At first, I thought a lion had stalked into Borrowdale Hall, but I soon chided myself for such a stupid idea. Only an idiot with the hangover from hell could possibly think that. Then, through a misty blear, I saw Spliff sprawled on his chair, his head slung back, his jaw slack and the mating call of a hippopotamus resonating from his mouth.

At first I smiled, amused at the sight, then I felt a wave of panic waft over me as I remembered Gerald. I spun my head round one hundred and eighty degrees without it losing contact to the table, felt my stomach lurch and closed my eyes once more to try and still the motion of all creation.

When I opened them again, I was aware that we were not alone. There was a fourth person, a man, stood in the kitchen. He was talking quietly to Gerald who was listening intently to what the newcomer had to say. My brain was having trouble catching up with what my eyes were telling it, so it adamantly refused to help out. All I could do was watch as a yellow glow enveloped the dead caretaker. Then, before my bleary eyes, he dissipated and became one with the mist which drifted up into the air and faded away.

I must have grunted or made some sort of noise because the stranger turned and looked straight at me. I tried without much success to focus my eyes, but the muscles around the sockets were playing havoc with my vision. I was sure that I could see straight through him and he seemed somewhat blurred. I could not make out his clothes or fully define the features of his face. I tried to speak, but he shook his head as if telling me not to exert myself, then the fog around his face cleared and I recognised his features.

They were the same ones that I saw every time I looked into a mirror.

My brain decided that it was now completely overloaded and gave up the ghost. I passed out.

I was to stir, albeit rather briefly, one more time - can't a guy sleep off a drunken stupor in peace? I heard the slow, precise clicking of heels on tiles. They were the sort of heels which said, “Hello boys,” and were worn by the sort of woman who would devour a man either as an object of desire, a morsel of nutrition or perhaps both.

They were what I refer to as “praying mantis heels”. They are normally glossy black or tart red and they are confident in their approach. There's not the slightest hint of wobble, no uncertainty. They are heels with a purpose, heels with a mission.

And they clicked to a stop right next to me.

By now, my brain had packed its bags and left for Acapulco. I didn't even try to move or open my eyes when I felt long, manicured fingers run up my neck and into my hair. "This one's rather cute," murmured their owner who owned the sort of voice that matched her dress sense: deep, slightly cruel and ever so sexy.

I was aware of someone else walking into the room and mutter something just out of earshot. Then the woman stroking my hair started to hum under her breath and lights suddenly exploded in my head. It was wonderful! I was in heaven! Paradise was my giving in to her every whim. All I had to do was follow her, obey her...

"Stop that!" hissed her companion, who sounded male and rather annoyed. "We don't have time."

The humming stopped and suddenly I was feeling like crap - empty and drunk on a hard kitchen table. There was a rustling of paper and something was thrust into my hand. I heard the man walk off, anger and jealousy resonating in his hard footfalls.

My head was stroked one more time and there was the scent of the most amazing perfume - fresh and warm at the same time, a blue ocean washing over a sun-baked sand dune - as the woman's mouth bent down to my ear and her lips whispered just one word. "Later."

Then she was gone, her killer heels carrying her out into the corridor.

When I awoke, the sun was streaming in through the large kitchen windows and my senses were being soothed by someone cooking eggs and bacon. I winced as the dining table clung desperately to my face and my back cracked harshly when I sat up. Spliff was no longer slouched, snoring in his chair. He was now over by the hob, industriously pouring love and contrition into my breakfast. He turned as he heard me stirring and said nothing. He dished up the aforementioned duo of food along with fried bread, grilled tomatoes and even some lovingly reheated baked beans. Quietly, he slipped the act of penance onto the table and laid out a knife and a fork. As I tucked into the food (I didn't turn vegan until a few months later), the kettle boiled and he poured us both a cup of coffee. I noticed that he shovelled six sugars into his. Boy, he really was full of self-loathing this morning.

He placed my mug next to me and I took a small sip then continued to fill my stomach up with something other than alcohol. Spliff sat down in his chair and waited.

I continued to eat.

I'm not a spiteful person by nature but that morning I wanted him to stew longer than my mum's extra-strong red label tea.

When I had finished the breakfast and was sat sipping my coffee, I let my eyes fall on him. My friend shifted uncomfortably in his seat and his eyes cast down to watch his hands clasped around his own mug.

"I fell asleep," he finally managed, his voice not much more than a whisper.

"I know," I said.

He hesitated, unsure how to proceed. His eyes glanced over to the empty chair and his face reddened with embarrassment.

"Gerald's gone." His eyes finally looked up at mine and the fear in them was pitiful.

"I know."

Spliff looked somewhat perplexed. "You don't sound too unhappy about it," he said.

I shrugged and winced as I un-kinked my neck a bit before sipping some more coffee. "There's not a lot we can do about it is there? And we were trying to help him on his way, weren't we?"

"But what if something happened to him? Something bad?"

"I don't think that's the case." I went on to explain what I had seen during the night during Spliff's little nap. "I think he's at peace now, so to speak."

"You really think that was you?"

I nodded. "I could hardly be mistaken about my own face, could I?"

Spliff stroked his cheek, his brain cells ticking over. "How old?"

"Sorry?"

"How old did you look?"

"Dunno. I'm crap with ages," I said. Then I frowned and looked down at my hand. "There was something else. Did you see a piece of paper lying around?"

"No. What was it?"

I started to look around the table. "There were other people here later. One male and one definitely female. They put something in my hand." I looked under the table. "Ah, there we are. It must have fallen out." I bent down, picked it up and opened it out. It was a note written in neat, cursive handwriting. Malcolm's handwriting.

"Samuel," I read aloud for Spliff's benefit, "if you are reading this then you have successfully sent your ghostly visitor on his way and I have left your life for the time being. I hope you got some answers to your questions, I truly do. I know I have. I have been asking questions for a long time now and, at last, someone will show me what I am yearning to know and understand - things that academia and the church could never satisfy my curiosity for. Talking of the church, I am sure that my placement will gratefully take you on now as I have no need for it. It's Saint Cuthbert's out in Caton. I hope it works out for you. Give them a ring but, like I said earlier, watch out for the vicar's daughter. She's rather feisty.

"Until we meet again, Malcolm."

"Well," said Spliff.

"Well," I agreed. "The old bugger. Didn't see that coming.

Spliff drained his coffee. "You think the woman with him was his benefactor."

"I guess so. She sounded rather hot."

"Well."

"Well."

So we sat there for a while finishing our coffees before sorting ourselves out for the morning. At nine, I gave Saint Cuthbert's a ring and arranged to visit them that afternoon.

That afternoon was probably even more momentous than the previous night.

That afternoon I met Caroline.

But that's another story.

# The Case of the Paranoid Poltergeist

The next day I had the hangover from hell. Now, I know what you're thinking, "Sure, Sam. We've all been there. A bit too much hard stuff and you have a dry mouth and a bit of a throbbing head." Well, let me tell you this, when it gets to about nine in the morning and the sunlight streaming through the open window is burning into your retinas when your eyelids are shut and the noise of passing traffic sounds like the four horsemen are partying on your eardrums, then you have a true hangover, my friend.

The worst of it was, the phone was ringing.

I was aware that there was this very loud, insistent din screaming at me and making my world shimmy and shake worse than a belly dancer atop of the Leaning Tower of Pisa, the trouble was that I could do nothing about it. I tried to move my hand but there were no muscles there, just jelly - fat wobbly jelly clinging to my heavy, heavy bones. Without opening my eyes, I put all my effort into my shoulders and tried to heave myself over.

I succeeded.

I fell off my office sofa and crashed downwards, smashing my nose on the floor.

I staggered to my feet and realised that there was blood dribbling from my left nostril. I weakly raised a finger towards it in a vain attempt to staunch the flow, whilst I reached for the phone with my free hand.

Where was the phone?

It had been on the desk yesterday. I was sure of it. I half staggered, half crawled across the room in search of the screeching little harpy, then tripped over one of three empty whiskey bottles. I crashed in a heap and nearly shoved my finger right up my nostril when I saw the dratted device lying on the floor at the foot of the sofa next to an empty Chinese take-away box.

As I fought back a rising tide of sweet and sour bean curd I grabbed the handset to my ear. "Sam Spallucci," I croaked down the line. The blood was now flowing quite freely out of my nose and I was trying to stop it from splattering onto the mouth piece with my handkerchief.

"Hello?" came a faint voice from a very long way away. "Is there anybody there?"

"Hello!" I shouted back, "I'm here."

"Hello? You're very faint," the other voice said.

I scowled, swayed, then noticed that I was talking into the ear-piece. I fumbled the phone around and asked, "Is this better?"

"Ah, yes. Much better."

"Sorry about that. You know what modern technology's like." I patted my pockets and found a crumpled packet of Luckies. The person on the other end said something as I fished one out and tried to light it. "Sorry?" I apologised. "Could you repeat that, please. I missed it."

"I said, 'Do you investigate matters of a paranormal nature?'"

"D'uh, I'm an Investigator of the Paranormal, read the sign" said my head. "I do. What seems to be the problem?" said my mouth.

"It's difficult to explain over the phone. I'm ringing from Edmund Campion School on Ashton Road. Would you be able to come and speak to me in person?"

I was having no luck at all lighting the damn cigarette and my nose was still streaming blood so I shoved the filter up my nostril to try and make a practical use of it. "Ashton Road? That's down by the RLI isn't it?"

"Yes it is."

I nodded. "Okay I should be there in an hour or so, I guess." On the way to the school I would pop into A&E and have someone look at my nose – kill two birds with one stone. Success!

Three hours later I was standing in the foyer of Edmund Campion High School with the receptionist eyeing me as if I was an unsuccessful stunt double for John Merrick. I have to admit she had every reason to view me with suspicion, the Accident and Emergency guys had done a real number on my nose. By the time I had staggered into the RLI my face had been covered in blood and my handkerchief had been sopping red (I had given the cigarette up as a bad idea when I sneezed crossing over South Road). They had taken one sniff of me and mockingly said that if they were to try and cauterise the inside of my nostril then my face might go up in flames from the alcohol vapours. Ha ha, medical humour is so droll.

So instead of nipping the problem in the bud, so to speak, they shoved wadding the size of an elephant's suppository up my nostril and taped it in place with plasters of some sort. They hadn't been very gentle with the process and, as a result, finger-spaced bruising was starting to bloom on my cheek bones and forehead.

Oh yes, I looked quite the picture, and here I was asking to be let within striking distance of teenage youths. I'm thankful the receptionist didn't ring the police there and then. Instead she asked, "Who is it you have an appointment with?"

I grimaced. "I don't know their name. They rang me this morning, about nineish."

"They didn't give you a name?"

"I didn't ask." I nervously rubbed the side of my inflamed nostril. It hurt and I winced.

The receptionist tapped a biro against her teeth. "Just let me ring someone, okay?"

I nodded as she picked up the phone and began to speak in hushed whispers. I scanned the area looking for the quickest way out if I was to be pursued by a bunch of prefects, security guards or whatever they used in schools these days. From what I'd seen in the press it would most probably be riot police with cattle prods – wasn't that what they used in the classrooms now? The tabloids were always banging on about the hallowed halls of education being out of control and run by undisciplined, knife-wielding hoodies.

As it was, I was confronted by none of these, but something far more potent. For a split second I was transported back thirty years. I was an eight-year-old boy stood outside the headmistress' office waiting to be scolded for dipping Lizzy Powell's blonde pig-tails in red paint and proceeding to use them to create a sunburst picture on her desk. Mrs Enfield, all green-suited five foot five of her was peering over her half-moon spectacles at me and saying "Samuel, I am so disappointed with you."

"Sorry, Miss," I mumbled.

"Pardon, Mr Spallucci?"

I snapped back to the here and now and gawped at the simulacrum of my childhood nightmare then stuttered, "I... I said... 'Sorry, I missed that.'" I smiled. At least I tried to. It hurt rather, so I guessed I must have looked like I was leering somewhat.

The head teacher gave me a curious look and repeated her original statement, "I'm Lindsay Wetherington. I'm glad you could make it," she glanced first at her watch, then my nose, "at last. Please, come into my office."

I tried to smile again and followed her whilst mentally telling myself over and over again, "I am not in trouble. I am not in trouble."

Her office was quite opulent. The walls were lined with a mixture of book-laden shelves, certificates and pictures of smiling pupils following their glorious sporting triumphs. Large ferns stood to the rear of the room, framing a panoramic picture window with a commanding view of the rugby field. The main attraction, however, was the desk. A grandiose mahogany affair topped with green leather and numerous filing trays. Next to a name plate sat a wood block carved with the old Trumanism "The Buck Stops Here." I had a feeling that Mrs (I had noticed a plain wedding band) Wetherington was somewhat of a pro-active head rather than the pen-pusher types that seem to be quite prevalent these days. She was the sort who, when faced with a problem, would grab it by the ears and bellow loudly at it until it cowered into submission. Now, as she seated herself in her high-backed leather office chair, she was faced with me – a somewhat scruffy-looking chap who pervaded an aroma of whiskey mixed with mints and sported an assortment of unfashionable facial bruises complemented by a rather extravagant nose-bandage.

"I must say, Mr Spallucci," she commented over the tips of her fingers that were steepled in front of her face, "that you are not quite what I had imagined. Did you fall out of bed the wrong side this morning, perchance?"

I grimaced and shrugged. "An industrial accident," I volunteered.

There was a short painful silence whilst her eyes bored into me. "Quite," she remarked. Short, to the point and extremely withering. I think that summed up both her use of words and her character in general. "Well, as it happens, come what may, I am in need of your services. Tell me, what do you know about poltergeists?"

I exhaled sharply and said, "Well, for starters, I'm sure that they're not covered by the National Curriculum."

There was a frosty silence.

The clock ticked.

Wetherington glared at me.

Oops.

I tried a more formal approach. "The term 'poltergeist' comes from the German for 'rumble ghost' referring to the noises often made by an invisible being knocking things about or moving them. In documented cases it has often been mentioned that the manifestation is centred around an individual, usually a teenager or adolescent." I paused. "I'm guessing that you have a lot of those here?"

"One thousand two-hundred and eighty-nine in years seven to eleven and two-hundred and eighty-seven in the sixth form, Mr Spallucci," she rolled off without a pause. "They are all in my care whilst they are in these four walls and I will not let anyone or anything bring them to harm. You understand me?"

I nodded sage-like. Then, when no more information was forthcoming, I asked, "And you think that one of them is at the centre of paranormal activity?"

"About two weeks ago," Wetherington began, "members of my staff noticed little peculiarities. Things would go missing. They would put something down on the desk and a moment later it would have been moved away by a few centimetres or so."

I shrugged. "Not necessarily a poltergeist. It could be absent-mindedness or, at worst, latent telekinesis. It could even be a childhood prank. We used to do that sort of thing all the time when I was a kid."

"My students do not play pranks, Mr Spallucci," Wetherington simmered. "They know how to behave themselves. Besides, the matter did not stop there. Things rapidly progressed. There were knocking noises, chairs falling over, doors inexplicably slamming. Then yesterday, this happened." She slid a digital photo across her desk to me. I let out a low whistle. It was a picture of a large ornate window with every single piece of glass smashed out.

"That looks expensive," I said, "and dangerous. Was anyone hurt?"

The teacher shook her head. "Fortunately not, but you can see my predicament here. I have to make sure that this does not happen again."

I nodded in agreement. If that glass had hit someone, it could have been very, very messy. Then something struck me as rather odd and I enquired, "Why have I not seen anything about this in the local press? The rags love a good, messy story about schools and safety to pupils? They must be lapping this up."

Wetherington paused and, for the first time since I entered the room, I sensed a certain amount of hesitation shroud her. She placed her hands flat on the desk and stated, "There will be no comments on this matter in the press. Of that I can assure you, Mr Spallucci."

There was a light knock at the door. "Ah." She rose from her seat, smoothing down her immaculate green suit. "That will be your escort. Enter!"

A teenage boy walked into the room. He was about average height and bore a mop of wavy, blonde hair that sat comfortably above his steel-rimmed spectacles. His uniform was moderately neat: a slight crook to the tie, a trace of shirt peering out from under his blazer and small scuffs to his shoes. The normal attire for a teenage school boy. He glanced quickly at me then focussed on his head-teacher. "You wanted me, Miss?" he asked, fear of retribution apparent in his voice.

"John," Mrs Wetherington began to explain, "Mr Spallucci here will be staying with us today to investigate certain matters. I need you to guide him around. Take him to your lessons and assist him, so to speak."

At the realisation that he wasn't in trouble, the boy visibly brightened. "Oh. Okay." He smiled at me. "Pleased to meet you, Mr Spallucci."

"Call me Sam," I insisted.

"He will call you Mr Spallucci," Wetherington interjected. "You are an adult. He is a child. Each must know their place."

I shrugged and slipped a covert wink to John. "Okay, Mr Spallucci it is then. Shall we be going, John?"

I immediately took to my young guide. John was the bouncy sort of lad who always seems to sport a lop-sided grin that can tease a smile out of the most mendacious grouch. As he led me along the stone corridors to his next lesson (Information Technology) he chattered on about school life and other such things. From the random little anecdotes that he leapt between like a frog on bouncy lily pads, I got the overall impression that Edmund Campion was a nice place to study. Sure, Mrs Wetherington was strict and bollocked anyone who vaguely stepped out of line, but, as a result, no one normally *did* step out of line so everyone bimbled along in their own sweet way going to lessons, enjoying the companionship of their peers.

"I'm in a band, you know," he said as we turned down what seemed to be the forty-second corridor – I was completely lost – "My mum taught me to play the piano when I was little and a few of us got together and started jamming at the weekends. It's well cool."

"Cool?"

"Yeah, you know. Cool." He frowned at me. "You do know what that means, don't you?"

I grinned. "I'm not that old, you know. I just thought kids wouldn't still be using the same words as I did when I was your age."

He quickly glanced over his shoulder as if checking the coast was clear then leant up towards me in a conspiratorial manner. "Are you here because of... you know?"

I raised an eyebrow then winced. It hurt my nose. "Because of... I know what?"

"The stuff that's been going on," he whispered. "Things going bump and that window breaking yesterday."

I stood still and carefully eyed the youth up and down. "You mean that window that was broken by a cricket ball?" I fished just to see what exactly he knew.

John snorted. "Cricket ball, my arse. That's not possible."

"Why?"

He counted on his fingers: "One, we don't play cricket in the autumn. Two, I was there when it happened." He crossed his arms and grinned. "So what do you think's going on?"

"Whoa, whoa cowboy," I shot my own furtive glance around the corridor. We were alone, for now. "Let's just rewind a bit here. You were there? When the window broke?"

"Uh huh."

"What happened exactly?"

"Well it was lunch time and a group of us were just hanging around, you know. Not doing anything. We weren't where we shouldn't have been. Anyways we were chatting and it just sort of broke. You know? Smash! Made a great noise."

I sighed. Oh brother! "And none of you threw anything at the window at all?" I asked.

"No!" He shook his head violently. "We'd be in trouble if we did that. But we ran away anyway 'cos we didn't want to get the blame." His eyes shot over my shoulder and he was suddenly silent as a pair of girls walked around the corner. "Come on," he said. "My lesson's just down here." He led me down the corridor to a blue-doored room.

The computer room was unlike anything I had ever known at school back in the eighties. As John led me in, I marvelled at the sheer spaciousness of the suite. Tall windows let sunlight weave its way through roman blinds catching the white surface of the huge interactive whiteboard at the front of the classroom. There were four rows of terminals: one down each side of the room and two back to back down the middle. Most of the monitors were slideshowing bright, colourful photographs of school life: smiling teachers, thoughtful pupils, that sort of stuff. Some terminals were already occupied by members of the class who had logged on and were industriously working away at spreadsheets and Word documents.

I frowned.

"What is it?" John enquired as he started to log onto a nearby machine.

"Nothing really," I replied, undoing my overcoat and removing my hat. "It's just that this is a far flung thing from the computing of my day. We were all networking and programming in dark, dingy rooms which stank of teenage body odour. This," I waved my hand around at the room in general, "seems more like an office than a schoolroom." I shook my head and tapped my fingernail against my front teeth in thought.

John shrugged. "I guess things move on." He removed his blazer and adjusted his sleeves before he began to type. I noticed a lilac coloured band on his wrist which bore the legend, "Anything is possible..."

"What's that?" I asked, curious.

He paused his typing. "The wristband?"

I nodded.

"It's a society I belong to. Surely you've seen the posters around town?"

I shook my head. I didn't tell him that satanic actors and new-born vampires had made me slightly distracted from the day-to-day recently. "I've been busy," I said instead.

"Wow." The boy's face was a picture of incredulity. "I can't believe you've missed this. It's really big. A lot of us are members." At this comment, a number of arms were raised and flashes of lilac wobbled down teenage wrists. "Here," he rummaged through his bag and dragged out a three-fold A4 leaflet, "take this. It's got all about the society. It'll change your life."

I smiled politely. I had heard all this before, many, many times. It was the big build up before either a financial sting or a catastrophic failing of faith. I glanced at the cover of the leaflet. It bore a lilac coloured emblem on it that seemed to resemble an upper-case letter "T" which was wrapped around by two spiralling lines. "I'll read it later," I smiled, carefully filing it in my inside jacket pocket. "I'm a bit busy at the moment."

John nodded and returned his attention to his screen.

I took a seat in the corner of the room just as a shrew-like little man with a sparsely haired head stalked in and slammed his things on the teacher's desk. He glared at me suspiciously and marched over. "You must be the investigator, I presume?" he snarled, eyeing me up and down the way an exterminator does an unfortunate rat that he has happened across in a dodgy restaurant.

"Sam Spallucci." I stuck out my hand. He gave it a withering glance then fixed his eyes on mine.

"You don't look like an Eyetie," he surmised, his fierce pupils darting over my face.

I groaned internally. "I'm not," I explained. "It's a long story, but my Dad..."

"Can it!" the teacher snapped, obviously not interested. "I don't give a flying fig for your life story. I'm Mr Crash and this is my lesson. Don't you dare get in the way. If you so much as step out of line, I'll throw you out the goddamn window. Is that understood?"

Part of me wanted to jump to attention and snap off a salute whilst shouting, "Yessir! Nossir!" but the sane side of me reeled it in and I just nodded my head. This seemed to appease Crash who turned his back on me and began the lesson. Well, I call it a lesson, it was more like a military drill. The teacher would bark out orders and the pupils would follow the instructions meticulously to the letter. Any who didn't keep up or dared to ask for an explanation were publicly humiliated in front of their peers. Needless to say there was no chatter, just the diligent click-clack-click of keyboard typing punctuated by the guttural bark of Mr Crash.

As Crash ranted on about files, folders and syntax I let my mind contemplate more ethereal matters, such as what was causing the disturbances here. So far I had seen nothing untoward whatsoever. The pupils hardly stepped out of line let alone allow their subconscious manifest itself as some sort of malevolent force and as for the window, well John himself had said that a group of lads had been there *doing nothing* when it had shattered. I was just starting to consider the possibility that all this was some sort of teenage prank which the school management in its blind disciplinarian style was unable to accept as reality when I felt a buzzing in my trouser pocket. This was followed by the raucous voice of Tom Waits singing about *swordfishtrombones*. I fished for my phone, saw the caller as "Unknown" and bounced it to voicemail.

When I looked up, the room was silent and most eyes were on me, especially those of Crash. "Sorry," I said out loud. "Bugger," I thought inwardly.

I had the image of a minotaur readying itself to charge and blowing sulphurous steam through its flared nostrils as Crash regarded me with complete and utter contempt. He lifted his finger and was about to shout at me when a dark-haired boy nervously raised his hand. "What is it Swarbrick?" snapped the teacher, flashing his wrathful energy between me and the unfortunate boy.

The boy muttered something that I couldn't make out, but Crash obviously heard quite clearly. "Well you've obviously opened the wrong file," he spat with complete lack of sympathy as he threw me a parting glance that was packed to the brim with hatred and warning before descending on the unfortunate boy.

I pulled my phone out and quickly turned it off. I valued my life too much to let anyone else disturb Crash's lesson.

I closed my eyes and rested my head against the wall as my nose throbbed in a way that told me it was going to be a long, long day.

I have to admit that I wasn't the most industrious of pupils during my time at school, and, as the lesson dragged on, I could feel the soporific effects of the warm room and the droning baritone of Mr Crash taking their toll on me. I was suddenly transported in time to the back row of a computing lesson where the monitors were small and green and where no light could penetrate the smog of underarms and fetid kit bags. I was supposed to be concentrating on setting up a simple subroutine, but the numbers and letters just kept darting around the dim screen refusing to stay still. My tired eyes began to drag and my lids started to droop.

I woke to the sound of tentative giggling and was aware of a voluminous shadow blocking out the calming light.

"Snoring tends to distract the pupils," rumbled the shadow.

I snapped up straight. "Wasn't snoring!" I managed as my dry lips prised apart and my parched throat gasped for air. There was a solid thud as the back of my head connected with a notice-board behind me, sending leaflets about cyber-bullying cascading down onto the floor. I muttered an apology and started to gather up the glossy pieces of paper.

"Typical!" Crash snorted. "Just what I thought. A loser. A waste of space. Look at you man. You're a wreck. A mess. You shouldn't be here disturbing my lesson."

He went on and on, piling heap upon heap of insult on my reddening cheeks. I could feel the eyes of all the students fixed on me and I wanted the ground to swallow me whole. It was so embarrassing.

But then, as the laughing paused whilst Crash stopped to draw a single breath, I heard a small voice say from somewhere in the room, "It wasn't his fault."

That was when all hell broke loose.

First, I felt a breeze rubbing against my cheeks, calming the flaming embarrassment, then I saw posters and carefully crafted work pulled free from the walls and start to spin around the air in the classroom. Next, the mouse on Crash's PC detached itself and flew at high speed before thumping him on the back of his head. He turned to see who had thrown it, only to be bombarded with every other mouse in the room as they levitated off the desks and rocketed towards him. He barely had enough time to cover his face from the barrage of plastic and cable. I grabbed the bulky man by the square shoulders and tried to drag him down, out of the way, but he shrugged me off and screamed, "Stop this, I say! Stop it at once!" He raised a finger to say something else, but a flying keyboard caught him on the temple and knocked him out cold. He fell like a stone that had been dropped from a great height and, quite appropriately, considering his name, crashed to the floor.

The uproar ceased and calm settled once more as pieces of students' work drifted down to the carpet. I glanced up at the bare walls.

Well, I say bare. *Almost* bare would be a better description. Here and there the occasional piece of work was still firmly attached and neatly presented for all to see. *Curious*: I thought, before venturing over to the sleeping teacher. I smiled to myself as I observed that it was now his turn to snore.

After the IT lesson, came lunch. John told me that he had a packed lunch so we went out of the school building onto the yard area where he rummaged around in vain. "It's in here somewhere," he said, his head immersed in the gaping mouth of the over-stuffed bag. "I was sure I packed it last night." I peered over his shoulder and saw a multitude of pen lids, worn books, an odd sock and an mp3 player but no lunch box. He zipped the bag shut. "Crap!" he moaned. "I must have left it on the kitchen side. Mum'll kill me."

"Always used to be my dad that bawled me out," I said. "Mum was the soft touch."

John shook his head. "It's just me and Mum. She works hard and I have to remember so much stuff. It keeps floating away." He mimed little clouds drifting out of his ears then slung the offending bag back onto his shoulder.

I looked over at the queue of students lining up by the canteen. "What's the food like here?" I asked.

"It's okay."

"Better than nothing?"

"Definitely better than nothing!"

I began to walk over to the queue. "Come on then, slowcoach. Guess I'd better feed you. Don't want you getting into trouble."

John gave his lop-sided grin and bounced along after me.

"So you think it's really a poltergeist?" John was talking around a large slice of pizza whilst wiggling a half-full tumbler of orange juice. "I mean what else could it have been this morning?"

I finished off a small jacket potato with beans and scanned the canteen. It was a hive of activity and not just in the physical sense. Various smells and aromas were jostling for attention in the distant memory synapses of my brain. There was the processed cheese, the over-boiled cabbage, the leathery beef and how could one forget that strange pink dessert. There they were, banging around in an old tin can and being poured over my face like a historical baptism.

Schools change. Pupils change. The food we feed them doesn't. It has to be quick, vaguely palatable and, most importantly of all, very, very cheap. People have tried to reform school dinners over the years but, at the end of the day, governments don't really give a toss. The kids don't vote yet and they will ultimately do what they are told. Sit down, shut up and eat or you go hungry - and there was a lot of eating going on here.

"Don't the teachers eat here?" I asked noting a distinct lack of adult presence. There were the odd one or two teachers prowling around, obviously on crowd control, but none were dining.

"They eat in the staff room, I guess," John finished the pizza and glugged the juice down. "But come on, is it a poltergeist?"

I didn't really want to go there. It was too early to say conclusively. "Things can sometimes be not what they seem, John," I explained. I took his unused napkin and held it out in front of him. "Look at this." I opened the napkin out and held it ready to drop down onto the table. John stared at it attentively, his brown eyes peering through his spectacles. I dropped the napkin and blew at it. The paper cloth wafted into his face. "Tell me, who moved that napkin?"

He picked it up, looked at the paper towel then at me, slightly bemused. "You did, of course. You blew on it."

I nodded. "Correct. Now watch again." I let it drop and this time I took my hat off and slammed it down on the canteen table. A number of heads turned at the sound of the noise whilst the napkin drifted off onto the floor. "Now who moved the napkin?"

"You did again... I think." He screwed up his face. "Is this a trick question?"

I grinned. "Sort of. When I blew the napkin I was willing it to move. It was my choice. When I slammed my hat down, that was what I was choosing to do. A violent, angry gesture. But it had repercussions and the napkin floated away because of it. A poltergeist isn't actually a thing, John. It's a by-product, as it were, of someone's emotions. They get angry and things happen that are inexplicable and may not be possible to directly trace to said individual. Me blowing is more like another example of a different phenomenon altogether – telekinesis. That's where an individual moves things with their mind. They are in control of their actions. Do you follow?"

He looked down at the napkin on the floor. "You're saying that the things that have been happening, we need to decide whether they were caused voluntarily or involuntarily by someone. Whether they wanted them to happen or whether it happened because they couldn't control it."

I smiled at the use of the word *we*. "Something like that. Now, when you've put that napkin in the bin, why don't we go take a look at that window?"

Our shoes crunched on cruel-looking shards of glass as we stooped underneath the red and white hazard tape. "Wow. Quite a mess," I mused, taking in the empty frames where the window had once been glazed. "And you saw this happen?"

"Yeah." John hovered uneasily at the barrier.

"It's okay for you to be here, you know. You're with me. Official business," I winked.

He smiled and came further in, albeit somewhat hesitantly. "I know that. It's just it was a really weird thing."

I bent down and pulled a shard of glass from the floor. "I can imagine. I bet you were shit-scared." I tossed the fragment and picked up another one.

"It was so sudden. One minute we were talking. The next..." he fanned his arms out, "crash!"

"Crash indeed," I mumbled to myself as I studied the edges of the glass. Small conchoidal fractures perforated the surface, testament to its sudden impact. "Tell me. Who was here?"

"Me and a couple of guys from form."

I inclined my head and waited.

"Oh. You want their names?"

I nodded. "It's okay, John. They're not in trouble."

He shrugged. "You know. It's a bit weird."

I shrugged back.

"Well," he began, "there was Jack, Sam and Sally."

"Sally? A rose among the thorns?"

"Pardon?"

"A girl?"

"Oh! No!" he laughed, rocking back on his heels making the debris crunch. "No. Sally is Peter Salsworth. An old teacher named him Sally back in year seven and it stuck."

I nodded again. "What were you talking about?"

"Stuff."

I groaned and shoved my head in my hands. "John!" I cried in despair. "You've got to give me more than this, okay? How many times do I have to tell you? You're not in trouble, okay?" I levelled my eyes on the teenager and gave him my best Paddington stare. He smiled back at me. We both chuckled.

"Okay. I can't remember much, what with glass showering down on us and all that. It's a bit blurry. I think we were just talking about others in our form."

I tapped my teeth. "This... talking... would it have been favourable?"

John frowned. "What do you mean?"

"You know, was it 'Bert's a decent sort of chap,' or was it more along the lines of 'I hear Bert's got a one-inch dick?'"

John chuckled. "Ah! Gotcha. Yeah definitely the second one. We don't mean any of it, you know. It's just..." he shrugged his arms wide.

"Stuff," I provided.

"Stuff," he agreed.

"And there was no one else here apart from you, Jack, Sam and Sally?" I stood up and looked once more at the window, then down at the confusion of broken glass.

"That's right. No one."

"This glass isn't very thick, is it?" I mused, kicking at the rubbish with my shoe. "What's more it burst outwards from that window, not inwards."

John looked up at the window. "That's the staircase up to the study rooms. We all go up and down there."

"Can you hear what's going on outside whilst you're ascending and descending the stairs?"

"Yeah. Sure. Like you said, the glass isn't very... oh..."

The fact that I had realised just before him hit John as hard as if it had been the glass from the day previous. The glass had burst outwards because it had been projected away from the source and that source had heard what the boys had been talking about.

What's more they hadn't liked it one little bit.

Afternoon lessons began at quarter to two and I dutifully followed John to his next session: music. If I'd been impressed by the IT room, then I was completely bowled over by the music suite. There was a dedicated block of four rooms set apart from the main school. Two were the standard classroom set out: desks, chairs and white boards. The others were like something from a record producer's wet dream. One was a recording studio with a fully sound-proofed booth and complete mixing desk. The fourth room was a small practice area that seemed to have a whole philharmonic orchestra crammed inside. There were violins and other stringed instruments hung up on the walls. Trumpets rested next to flutes and clarinets. A double bass was propped beside four electric guitars. Then there was a big set of drums next to which stood a beautiful pair of tympani.

John noticed the look on my face as we entered the practice room. "Sam? You okay?" he asked, his brow creased somewhat in concern.

"All we had was a rusty tambourine, one and a half pairs of maracas and a glockenspiel that was missing an F sharp." I grinned at the boy. "We had to play just about everything in C."

He smiled back at me. "You musical then?"

"My dad taught me a bit when I was a kid, you know?" I walked over to the trumpet and picked it up. It had been a while, but the brass beauty sat comfortably between my hands. I placed my right fingers on the valves and wiggled their tips. The valves slid up and down like pistons on a well-maintained engine. I gave a little sigh and shot John a knowing look. I was desperate to give this horn a good old blowing.

"Knock yourself out," he said. "I'd like to hear you."

I could barely contain my glee. I inhaled and firmed up my diaphragm, placed the mouthpiece to my lips and burst into what I considered to be a fairly ragged rendition of Mack the Knife. I was in my own little world once more. I didn't think. I just let my fingers bob up and down and my lips buzz as all the noises in my ears were pushed out by the sonorous warmth of the trumpet's brassy song. I would pay for it later, I knew that for sure – that was why I had quit many years ago, the noise from the instrument always caused my ears to go crazy – but for now, I was just there, in the moment, absorbed by the encompassing arms of my brassy lover.

I pressed out the last few notes and lowered the instrument. I was aware of the fact that John and I were no longer alone. There were a few more students hovering behind him, but also in the doorway stood a slim, bespectacled teacher holding a selection of files. Her eyes were peering over the tops of her glasses and were twinkling with mischief. "Do I have a new pupil?" she asked of me.

I blushed, blew out the spittle from the trumpet and carefully replaced the instrument back where it belonged. "Sorry," I apologised. "I think I got carried away."

The mischief continued to dance in her deep blue eyes. "Okay, you lot," she shouted to the kids behind her, "concert's over. You've got work to be getting on with." They chatted to each other as some went into the classrooms, some the recording studio and some, including John, picked up instruments in the practice room where they started to warm up. "They're working on practical stuff at the moment," the teacher explained. "It'll keep them busy. I'm Abalone Morris, by the way." She stuck out her hand, which I shook. "You must be Mr Spallucci. What have you done to your nose? Did Philip hit you or something this morning?"

"Philip?"

"Sorry. Mr Crash. I know he's quite abrasive, but all the same..."

"No! No, he didn't. I had a bit of an accident before I got here."

"Ah. Looks painful." She stood, looking at me.

I think I was still blushing. "Erm... how many pupils are in this lesson?" I asked, desperately trying to get back on task.

"The usual," she said, walking through to the main classroom and dumping her files unceremoniously on the desk. "Just under thirty. These are a good bunch. Not normally any bother."

I looked around at the signs of studious industriousness. The room was a hive of learning. "What about any other trouble?"

Ms Morris' lips twisted up in a curious smile. "You mean of the inexplicable kind? No. Not with this lot. Not a flicker. Not a murmur. Not a flying keyboard," she winked.

My eyes wandered around the pupils as they chatted, scribbled and composed. They rested on a girl with dark hair that was shot through with bright magenta streaks who was writing rapidly on a piece of music manuscript. "She wasn't in the IT lesson this morning. I would have noticed her."

"It's a different group," Ms Morris explained. "This is a top set music lesson. Philip's group were a middle set IT."

"And all departments are like that? Different sets for different subjects?"

She nodded. "It means that the pupils get quite a mix of different peers and it helps to stop little cliques forming. Also we can teach them at a more appropriate level."

"Have you had any supernatural bother?"

"Nope. None whatsoever. I obviously don't teach a ghost," she grinned.

I sighed. "It's not a ghost. It's a poltergeist."

"There's a difference?"

"Would you call a flute a clarinet?"

She cocked her head to one side in acceptance. "For now I'll take your word but perhaps you could explain the intricacies to me over a coffee some time?"

I was sure that I had now turned completely scarlet as her eyes continued to twinkle at me over her glasses. When it became apparent that I had been hit dumbstruck from being hit upon by a teacher, Ms Morris grinned as she quickly wrote something down on a scrap of paper and said, "Well, you know where I am if you feel like educating me. For now, though, I have to see to my students." Then, with a smile, she tucked the piece of paper into my chest pocket before miming a telephone at me then weaving her way expertly around the class like a queen bee in a hive, carefully coaxing the most out of workers who would quite obviously do anything that she asked of them.

At the end of the school day, John and I walked down the curved driveway that led to the main gate of Saint Edmund's. The sun shone brightly and seemed to bounce off the young lad's mop of blonde hair. For a moment he looked so very, very young, weighed down with an incredibly over-stuffed blue rucksack and his steel-rimmed spectacles perched on the end of his nose. He glanced up at me. "It's been an odd kind of day hasn't it?" he said. "Mind you, I guess you're used to all that sort of stuff."

"I've seen worse," I admitted, shivering internally as I recalled a drained body from behind the Sugar House two nights previous, "but this was rather intriguing."

"Yeah," he whispered, "it was. What will you do now?"

We had reached the large iron gates that sat open under an imposing stone arch and I paused as I saw a multitude of school kids fighting their way onto two large school buses. "Guess I'll go clean up a bit then grab a bite to eat and a drink."

"You gonna chase up any leads?" Palpable excitement was radiating from behind John's glasses.

I chuckled. "Later. I can't think on an empty stomach."

"Cool." Then suddenly he looked glum.

"What's up?" I asked.

He peered down at his feet and let his scuffed, black shoes doodle in the dust. "It's nothing. It's just, well, I never knew my dad and Mum never says much about him. Well nothing polite, that is. I just kinda wish he'd been a bit like you."

I was silent for a bit as I rubbed the bandage on the side of my swollen nose. "Really?" I said, finally. "Well I suppose something would be better than nothing."

We turned our heads in unison at the sound of a car horn blatting across the gabbling of teenagers. "Oh. It's Mum," John observed, "I've gotta go. See ya tomorrow, Sam."

"Yeah, see you tomorrow." I watched as he lolloped off across the road to a small sporty number parked down the way a bit. He waved cheerily as he climbed in the passenger seat and I saw him lean across to say something to his mother. There was a flash of light brown hair as she glanced in her mirror to peer at me, but she was parked facing away so I didn't really get to see what she looked like before they sped off down the road, narrowly missing a few school kids ambling out of their way.

I sighed. He wanted a dad like me? Either I had made a good impression or the poor kid was desperate. I turned round and headed back into town, fishing out a Lucky Strike. I would grab a bite and a drink at the Borough whilst I mulled over the events of the day.

My stomach was rumbling and my head was pounding to the sound of a thousand soldiers re-enacting a hundred different battles in my skull. The school dinner hadn't exactly been filling and my throat was parched. I needed a few hours' peace and quiet to calm myself and mull over the events of the day as well as replenish my energy reserves.

The IT lesson had been rather creepy to say the least. It certainly appeared to have been the subject of poltergeist activity. I smiled at the memory of the bully of a man being felled by a flying bit of plastics and circuitry. He'd had it coming. How long had this being going on for at the school? About a couple of weeks Wetherington had said. I was still somewhat surprised that the press hadn't gotten hold of it even with her confidence in the matter. This sort of thing would have made wonderful tabloid fodder. "Church School Home to Devil!" they should be proclaiming. Yet there was not a sniff anywhere. I'm an avid newspaper reader. I devour them daily, local and national, whenever I get the chance. I would have seen it. It would be bloody hard to miss.

Something, somewhere was wrong. Something was stopping the proverbial from hitting the fan. It just didn't add up.

I entered the Borough and the warm smells of evening service wafted up my one functioning nostril. Familiar aromas. Safety in olfactory indulgence. I saw Grace grin from under her woolly hat and pull my bottle up from under the counter before proceeding to pour me a very large measure. "Do I look that bad?" I asked as I downed the drink in one then refilled it.

"Who won? You or the door?" she giggled.

I started on my second shot and must have looked as confused as I felt until her small hand reached out and gently tapped the dressing on my nose. "Oh! That!" I said. "Neither, actually. It was the floor."

Grace winced. "Ouch. Sounds painful. You hungry?"

"Ravenous. What you got for me tonight?" I asked as I squinted up at the specials board groaning inwardly. It was all dead, dead or dairy – nothing I could eat.

Grace cocked her head to one side. "What do you fancy, Sam?"

I sighed. My head was pounding and my stomach felt like my throat had been cut. "You still got any of those bean-burgers? And some chips?"

"Oh. Okay. I think we've got some."

I paused and looked her in the eye. She seemed suddenly less cheery. "You okay?"

"Yeah," the little redhead said, "just a long day. Spliff!" she suddenly called grinning over my shoulder. "How are you?"

I felt a warm hand clamp onto my shoulder and give it a friendly squeeze. "Fine, my little dust-devil," came the well-spoken Scottish accent. "Nothing that a good drink and a weekend with a Thai lady-boy wouldn't put right." He stopped and stared at my face. "Sam, how many times must I tell you? If you go sniffing around ladies' lavatories you will end up with a tampon up your nose."

"Don't start," I warned him. I turned to talk to Grace but she had gone. There were just our bottles on the bar. I took mine and headed over to the table. "I think there's something up with Grace," I told Spliff as we seated ourselves in the window.

He raised an eyebrow. "You don't say?"

"She seems..." I searched for the right word. "Distracted?"

Spliff sipped demurely at his neat gin. "My guess is it's man problems."

I frowned. "I didn't think she was seeing anyone?"

"She isn't."

"So how can it be..."

Spliff held up his hand to silence me. "Sam, Sam, Sam. You've always trusted me, haven't you?"

"Unfortunately, yes."

"Well, just trust me on this one. Our little friend is obviously pining over someone who has no interest in her whatsoever."

I wracked my brains. A man? Grace had never mentioned anyone to me before. Surely she would have said something? I came in at least once a day. It would have cropped up in conversation wouldn't it? "Who?" I asked.

The priest nearly choked as his drink seemed to go down the wrong way. He pulled a napkin off the table and patted at his mouth. "You wouldn't believe me, Sam. I'm sure she will tell you all in her own time."

A while later we had just about finished our food. My bean-burger had initially tasted of stale cardboard. Spliff suggested that I remove my nasal dressing. Tentatively I peeled back the micro-pore and swore as he laughed at my discomfort. After a bit of inquisitive prodding I yanked the dressing down from my nostril. The pain was excruciating. My friend was quite beside himself with mirth as I bit down heavily on a napkin to prevent myself from screaming the Borough down.

Fortunately, the repair work to the inside of my nose appeared to have done its job and, as the pain began to subside, I was able to eat my food without bleeding over myself. I rolled the bloody dressing in the napkin and stashed it in my coat pocket for disposal later.

As I wiped the red stains from around my nose, Spliff asked, "So what happened to our fanged friend then? You never got back to me."

While tucking into a plate of food that could now be fully identified by taste, I apologised for not ringing him, explaining the events with Nightingale and Marcus in Dave's shop and how I had then made the most of being paid which had indirectly led to one elephant's tampon up my nose this morning.

As Spliff skewered the last remaining sliver of his steak I asked him, "So what's been wrong with your day then? Something has to be pissing you off to bring out the lady-boy desires."

The portly cleric harumphed. "The bloody Arch-Deacon's been on my back again."

I smiled. "Now there's an image."

"Quite," he muttered around the steak. "He's always on my case, that one."

"Which baptism did you forget this time, then?"

"Ha bloody ha. You know that wasn't my fault. They booked the wrong day."

"At least it wasn't a funeral."

"Who the hell do you think I am? Father Ted Bloody Crilley?" He wiped his mouth and grinned. "I love that episode. The hearse sticking out of the grave, bloody hysterical."

I nodded. Spliff and I used to watch *Father Ted* when we were students. If you haven't seen it, it's about three dysfunctional Roman Catholic priests on a god-forsaken island off the coast of Ireland. Absolute bloody genius. You have to see it. My favourite is the one where Ted and Dougal (the younger of the three priests) enter the *Eurovision Song Contest* with a little ditty named *My Lovely Horse*. Look up the video on YouTube – you will be laughing for the rest of the week.

"So what's his holiness been whinging about this time then?" I shoved the last two chips in my mouth. Plenty of ketchup. My stomach was loving me once again.

"The usual," Spliff moaned as he poured himself another gin.

"Parishioners or Parish?"

"Parish."

"Oh."

We sat in silence for a small while. This was a serious matter. As you've probably noticed The Reverend James Francis MacIntyre is not your normal, run of the mill priest. He is the archetypal square peg that the Church tries from time to time to hammer into an unforgiving round hole. His first parish was an absolute disaster. There was the aforementioned baptism, but there was also his inability to keep a control of his paperwork or his libido. As a result, he was moved to somewhere that had been perceived as a safe option. Luneside University was looking for a new chaplain about ten years ago and the Vice-Principal at the time was a good friend of the then Arch-Deacon. As a result, a deal was done and Spliff was placed out of sight and out of mind until such a time that is was felt safe to release him back into the diocese.

Anyway, as with all things, time marches on and, as Spliff settled more and more into a campus life where his little eccentricities were either accepted or overlooked, administrations changed. Both the benevolent Vice-Principal and the Arch-Deacon moved on to pastures new, leaving the lonesome priest to the not so tender loving care of their successors. Admittedly, he did blot his own copy book with the new V-C when they first met. After shaking hands with his new boss' wife he innocently asked when the baby was due.

The V-C rather acerbically pointed out that his wife was not, in fact, pregnant. Ouch.

As for the new Arch-Deacon, he was a younger, more vibrant man who liked to keep in touch with the parishes and his clergy. As a result, Spliff was continually having new parishes shoved under his nose for his approval. The hint was as obvious as a villain in a Disney cartoon – It's time you were moving on.

The problem was, Spliff did not want to move.

"Apparently there's this nice little place out by Blackburn." The sorrow brimmed over his words. "It has a rose garden."

Spliff loves his gardening. He has single-handedly crafted a mini Eden out of one of the more neglected corners of campus. In the spring it is awash with flowering bulbs and cherry blossom. In the summer the scent of roses drifts by you on the warm breeze. In autumn the bright reds of leaves lazily drifting to the ground are a joy to see. I sometimes feel that if people really wanted to get to know the real Spliff then they should look past his brash, camp exterior and spend just an hour or two in his little corner of paradise.

"Have you been to see it?"

He shook his head. "No. Just photos. He e-mailed them to me this morning. It does look rather sweet."

There was a touch more silence. Spliff was my best friend but there were times like these that I really struggled to say the right thing so I just kept quiet. There was the big part of him that would always be the bombastic Bohemian, but there was always that little voice that kept whispering about that nice, quiet country parish that he ought to try out and settle down in. Somewhere he could put down roots. Somewhere he could grow up in.

"I'm investigating a poltergeist," I finally volunteered.

"A poltergeist? I assumed it was a plastic surgeon offering back street nose jobs."

"You know what 'assume' spells."

"Oh stop that. You'll get me thinking about Richard Gere."

I smiled. This was the Spliff that I liked best. The one full of banter and insults. The distracted, depressed one disturbs me. I find it hard to handle. "It's at a local high school."

"Which one?"

"Saint Edmund's."

He nearly choked on his gin.

"What is it?" I asked.

"Not Ballcrusher's school?"

"Pardon?"

"Lindsay Wetherington," he explained, "terrifies the local clergy. She arrived three years ago and turned the place upside down. She chucked out all the governors and installed businessmen and cronies who all see the world the way that she does: driven by results. It's true that the school excels academically, but, my God, she runs the place with a rod of iron. You step out of line and your knackers are on the chopping block." He smiled at me over his drink. “You okay Sam? You're suddenly looking a bit pale.”

“I'd rather hold on to my testicles, that's all.”

“I could always hold them for you, if you'd let me,” Spliff winked.

I shook my head. “You're bloody incorrigible. Now, back to the poltergeist?”

“Okay,” he sighed dramatically, “if you insist. You reckon it's genuine? Not just laddish pranks? I got called to a pub once where they claimed there was this ghost knocking at the bar every night at eleven p.m.. The owner was shitting himself. So I turned up to investigate. They told me the story. Every night, bang on eleven, there would be three hard raps that sounded like they were coming from upstairs. So, that night, we sat waiting and whilst the owner sat concentrating on listening for the knocking I sat and concentrated on the young bar-man and the regulars all of whom kept looking at their watches, the wooden ceiling and the long broom behind the bar. Needless to say the poltergeist never showed up again.”

I chuckled. “Bet you got some free drinks too after that.”

“Damn right I did.”

I described the incident in the IT lesson and Spliff let out a low whistle. “Wow! That sounds quite nasty.”

I nodded in agreement. “I know. It could have been a lot worse, I guess. The question is ‘Where to start?’”

“Find the source, I suppose,” the priest suggested. “Most poltergeist manifestations are normally centred around an individual...”

“Usually an adolescent,” I finished. “I know the drill. However, that school is full of hormonal teenagers, all of them with their own bucket-loads of angst. It's a needle in a haystack.”

Spliff leaned back in his winged chair and frowned at me. “Oh Samuel! Really! Surely it's obvious?”

“What?”

“For the incident to occur the way it did, the child was nearby.”

I tapped my fingernail against my teeth as I thought this over. “You think they were in that lesson?”

He nodded. “Then there is the fact that some pieces of work were left on the wall.”

Daylight dawned. “If I had worked hard on something, I would not want to destroy it. I think I need to see that classroom again tomorrow.”

Come the next morning I was feeling decidedly chipper. The new case was starting to entice me. I did not seem to be in any sort of personal danger for a change: no crazed Satanists, no lurking vampires. It was really quite refreshing. What was more, the morning had that crisp, fresh autumnal feeling that makes one feel glad to be alive. The sky was bright blue with only a hint of cloud and light breeze blew any traces of last night's beverages out of my head.

I even managed some breakfast - the most important meal of the day you know – and even those constant bells were somewhat diminished.

I just knew it was going to be a good day.

You can see where this is going, can't you?

"What do you mean you're not going to help me today?"

John dropped his eyes to his scuffed shoes and carefully ground a piece of dirt into the tarmac path. "I... I'm sorry Sam. I want to. It's just..." he trailed off.

I gave an exasperated sigh as dark clouds gathered on my perfect day.

"Oh, come off it, lad. You owe me more than this," I snapped. "Grow a pair and tell me what's going on? Is it Wetherington? Has she got it in for me?"

"No!" His big brown eyes lifted up to mine and I could see the pain in them. I cursed myself for being too hard. He was only fourteen, after all. "It's not her," he said. "It's... it's Mum."

I frowned. That I had not been expecting. "Your mother? What's she got to do with all this?"

John turned to walk down the path to school. I kept pace with him. "She doesn't want me spending time with you."

I opened my mouth to say something, but no words came for a second. I was totally bemused. What was going on here? I was definitely missing something. Nothing new there. It seemed to be my general state for the week. Then I managed, "How does she know about me?"

"I was telling her all about you last night. About what you do and how great you are. I said that I wished I had a dad like you." He paused. Stopped walking. He looked back up at me. He was actually crying. "Sam, she went mental. Absolutely mental. She started screaming and shouting. She actually threw things around the room. She smashed an old ornament that she's had for years. She loved that little thing. It was cut glass, you know. Then she knelt down on the floor and started to pick all the pieces of glass out of the carpet. I tried to help but she told me to stay away. She said that I would get hurt. Really hurt. I said that it was only glass and I would be fine. Then she looked at me and she looked so sad, Sam, and she said that she didn't mean the glass. She said that she meant you. I asked her why but she just ignored me and carried on trying to clean up the broken glass. I tried to talk to her some more but she just ignored me so I went to my room and stayed there until the morning. I couldn't sleep and I finally heard her come to bed about three. She never stays up that late. Her job's too important to her to be tired in the morning."

The bells were ringing loud in my ears once more. I absent-mindedly rubbed the heel of my hand against the side of my head. My spidey-senses were tingling. There was something... something I was missing here. "What's her job?"

"She's a journalist."

The autumnal breeze whipped through my trench coat and my blood ran cold. In my head I saw another pair of brown eyes, female ones, twinkling with delight as they opened a carefully wrapped parcel. My voice cracked as

I asked, "John, what was the glass ornament?" then I jumped out of my skin as a heavy hand clamped down on my right shoulder. "Jesus!" I swore as I turned to the intruder. A large brick wall of a man was stood there beaming at me.

"Mr Spallucci," he stated, rather than enquired. "I believe I have the pleasure of your presence in my gym class."

My mouth gasped like a goldfish drowning in the air and I turned to say something to John, but he had sailed off amidst a sea of blue blazers and school bags.

It was an impressive sports hall. I was rapidly realising now just how much things had changed since my day. First, there had been all the high tech computers, then the assortment of quality instruments and now this. Again, the room was bright and airy, hardly a whiff of stale jock strap. There was enough room for a small football pitch on the sprung wooden floor which was marked out in different colours for various activities. Basketball hoops lined the walls and cricket nets were tied up on opposing sides.

"So are you going to stand there gawping or are you going to help out?"

I turned and faced the brick wall on legs. He was tall, affecting rippling muscles and a highly polished bald head that sat atop a hooked beak of a nose. "Excuse my manners - forgot to introduce myself," The PE teacher thrust out his right hand. "James Dean. Pleased to meet you."

I shook his hand as he crushed my fingers tightly then raised an eyebrow. "James Dean?"

He shrugged. "We can't pick the names our parents choose."

"Tell me about it," I grinned. I was fast warming to him.

"So you going to ditch the hat and coat and want to grab a ball?" He motioned over my shoulder to a pile of orange basketballs.

I grimaced and started to back-pedal. "I don't know. I've never really been the sporty type. Besides I'm no teacher."

"Who said anything about teaching?" he beamed with big, white teeth. "This is fun!" He winked then grabbed a ball which he flung at my chest. Hard!

The boys were piling in and I had been thrust a fait accompli. I regarded the blank face of my orange nemesis which was staring blindly up at me and I grinned. I heaped my coat, my hat and my suit jacket at the side of the hall then went and stood next to James. "So what's the plan?"

"Simple. I blow this whistle and they start to run." He turned and flashed the big grin again. "Then we hit them with the balls." He blew the whistle and a big cheer rose up from the class as they started to zig-zag around the hall. He was good. Very good. Within the first few seconds he had bagged three lads who then made their way to the edge of the hall out of harm's way. I managed one quite quickly too but he was a short, fat lad who wasn't looking where he was going so I could hardly be proud about it - but hey, a hit's a hit, isn't it? After that it got a bit trickier. My god, they were fast.

Talk about greased lightning. They were obviously used to this warm up and ducked and dived from whatever angle I threw my ball at. It was becoming embarrassing as James notched up more and more victims and I was stuck with just the one.

There was a moment when I should have scored a second but the most curious thing happened. I threw my ball straight and hard. It was targeting in on the legs of a thin-looking boy with greasy brown hair. I was about to whoop with joy when suddenly the ball curved away from his legs. I darted after the ball and whipped it up and threw it once more at the same boy. He glared at me through his greasy fringe and the ball fell dead at his feet.

*Very interesting*: I thought. I walked over, picked the ball up and made to say something but James' whistle blew. "Okay people," he shouted, "enough warm up. Now line up."

The greasy-haired boy walked away and took his place in the line. I examined the ball briefly before depositing it in the basket with its cousins. I decided that I needed to have a chat with the lad later, after the lesson.

After the warm up, James had the class divide into five groups of five and positioned them around various wall spaces with plastic footballs. "Right gentlemen, penalty taking is the order of the day. You know the drill. Off you go."

So it was that the members took it in turns in goal while the other four queued up to kick the ball at them. Repetitive but simple. James watched them for a while then nodded in satisfaction and motioned for me to come and join him on a bench. "That'll keep 'em busy for half an hour or so. Time for us to have a sit down," he smiled. He fished into his kit bag and pulled out a bottle of Lucozade which he offered to me. I politely refused (the caffeine content plays havoc with my ears) and he drank half the bottle in a few quick glugs. "Rumour has it you're a ghostbuster," he said after a little while during which he had obviously been mentally choosing the correct words. "Is that right?"

"In a manner of speaking. It's not just ghosts I investigate."

He nodded. "So you're here because of our little problem then?" As he spoke he never took his eyes of the kids. He looked like a shepherd watching for a wolf amongst his sheep.

"I was called in yesterday morning. You seen anything out of the ordinary in your lessons?"

"These are teenage boys," he laughed. "There's nothing ordinary about them. They're a breed unto themselves. Once those hormones kick in, they're all over the place. One minute they're all macho and hard-man, the next they're running down the hall pretending to be a rubber duck!" He smiled as he continued to survey his charges. "I love 'em to bits. They keep me on my toes and keep me young, you know?"

"I think they'd drive me mad. I prefer a bit more order in my life." I winced as one poor unfortunate took a shot exactly where a boy would least want one. His mates laughed and he was about to show them the V when he caught his teacher's eye and relented. "So apart from adolescent vagaries, how about anything supernatural?"

"Yeah, I've seen stuff," the bluff, down-to-earth sports teacher growled. "Stuff I can't explain. I've seen good rugby players suddenly brought down when there was no one near them. I've seen a lad sent to casualty when the vault he was using collapsed. We stick to balls and mats now. They're less likely to break a finger, you know?"

I winced again. "Does there seem to be a pattern to when these things happen?" I asked.

He nodded. "Why do you think I'm not letting these lads out of my sight? It's always with this class. Every lesson over the last two weeks something has happened with this group of lads. That's why I came and grabbed you this morning before her ladyship sent you off on some cock-and-bull PR fiasco."

"You're not a fan of your exalted leader then?"

He pulled a sour face. "She gets the job done I guess, but she's far too image conscious for my liking. You've only got to take one look at the governors to see that."

My eyes followed his and I tried to take in the faces of the boys as they continued to shoot footballs at each other. I'm no good at telling most teenagers apart, but there were certain faces, builds and hairstyles which I recognised from the IT lesson the day before, one of which was the greasy-haired lad who had avoided my ball. It was now his turn in goal and he seemed to be having a hard time of it. One by one, the other lads kicked the ball at him and, with each ball, the boy flinched and cowered. His partners looked somewhat exasperated. I saw them gesticulate for him to put more effort in, but he steadfastly shook his head before crouching down in a sitting position against the wall.

James grunted and headed over to the boy. I followed behind. "Billy!" he called out. "What's going on here?"

"Make them stop, sir. Make them stop," the boy whined, pulling at his lank hair with his long, spindly fingers.

"Make them stop what, lad?"

"They're picking on me again, sir. Make them stop."

James looked at the other lads and raised an eyebrow. "Boys?"

The four lads looked genuinely gobsmacked. "We done nothing, sir!" one of them protested. "He just won't get the ball."

"They keep kicking it at me!" the greasy-haired boy shouted. "Make them stop!"

James rubbed his large hand over his bald scalp. "Mr Swarbrick," his voiced sounded weary, exasperated, "they're supposed to be kicking the ball at you. You're in goal, lad."

The boy just continued to rock on his heels as the other pupils stopped their target practice and gawped at the peep show that was unfolding. I could hear the occasional throw-away comment and snigger.

"Make them stop, sir! Make them all stop," Billy pleaded again. "I don't like it. I don't like it."

James let out a deep sigh and bent down towards the boy. "Come on, Billy, let's get you out of here." He took hold of the boy's arm to pull him up.

Billy dropped his hands from his face and his eyes shot up at James Dean full of murderous intent. "Take your filthy hands off me," the boy snarled.

As the PE teacher's mouth opened to scold the boy I suddenly felt electricity charge the atmosphere and I was sure that we were not alone in the sports hall. I looked up at the rafters of the immense room and laid a hand on James' shoulder. "I think you'd better do as he says," I whispered.

"Why?"

"Just take a look up above you."

The teacher's eyes followed mine up above us where a mass of black, leathery wings flapped and fidgeted in the rafters and ten small, black faces peered down at us with sharp, beady eyes.

People often ask me what it's like to suffer from tinnitus. Well, there's two reactions or descriptions that I tend to hand out. There's the obvious one: it's bloody annoying. Those sodding bells never shut up. Not once. Not ever. They are always there, ring-a-ding-a-ding-a-ding. Constantly. Permanently. Incessantly. There is no softening them. There is no subduing them. They are there when I wake. They are there as I go about my daily life. They are there when I go to sleep. They are there in my dreams.

Most people look shocked and ask "How do you put up with it, you poor thing." I just shrug and say, "I get on with it. It's no big deal."

Then there's the other reaction I give. Admittedly this is normally if I'm having a good day. I tell them, "They're my constant companions. They are always there for me. They will never betray me. They will never walk out on me. They sing with me when I'm happy. They cry with me when I'm sad. In the deepest, darkest fear in the middle of the night they are there to remind me that I am not alone and they will sit and comfort me. When I'm being pissy or narky then they will be there to scold me for my stubbornness. They are my closest friend and my strictest teacher. They warn me when I am starting to feel ill. They relax me when I feel bored. But most of all they remind me and constantly tell me of one thing more than anything else. One thing that each and every one of us on the face of this planet should remember and hold precious to the day that breath finally escapes their lungs for that final, fatal time.

I am different.

Then people normally look at me quite shocked and there is that awkward little silence as their regimented mind tries to assimilate this profound credo that they had least expected. Then, when they think they understand everything about me, they have the damned audacity to say the most stupid thing in the world. "I wish I could hear them, then I would know what you're going through."

I look them straight in the face and sigh as for the umpteenth time I explain that no, they would not want them, because for all the wonders I have just spouted I would happily be rid of the little bastards in an instant.

As I looked up at the ceiling of the sports hall, I realised with dread that I had been the foolish people who so badly wanted to empathise with me. I had wanted to get into the mind of the individual with the poltergeist and see what made him or her tick.

Be careful what you wish for Sammy, I thought as I rolled out of the way of the vanguard of small, black imps that now swooped down out of the rafters and bombarded us. The next succession of events was somewhat of a blur, so please bear with me if this sounds rather garbled. It is, after all, not every day that one gets attacked by ten black imps dragged up from the paranoia of a dysfunctional teenage boy.

First, the obvious happened, they dive-bombed James Dean. The teacher was the focus of the boy's wrath so the imps swarmed all over him. The man's muscular arms batted frantically at the little dervishes, trying desperately to detach them, but it was in vain. They nimbly avoided any attempt to remove them. They just dug their claws in and flapped their wings in a cacophony of bat-like thrumming.

Next, there was a shout from one of the other boys as he hurtled out of the gym. Whether he was just running in fear or in an attempt to raise the alarm, I neither knew nor cared. I had to remain focussed on the matter at hand: how to safely remove the imps from the teacher. It was as I wracked my brains over this that I remembered the basketballs. "Throw me one!" I shouted to the group of on-looking boys as I pointed hurriedly at the basket containing the orange balls. "Quickly!"

One of the lads darted to the basket and grabbed one, then lobbed it straight to me. I snatched it to my chest, turned and hurled it towards the black melee that encompassed Dean. There was a cross between a bleat and a shriek as one of the imps momentarily detached itself before diving back into the fray. I nodded to myself. They were corporeal, which meant...

"They can be hurt!" I screamed. "Grab more balls!"

The students dived for the basketballs and suddenly their teacher was the centre of the most absurd game of dodge ball that I have ever witnessed. Ball after orange ball pounded towards him knocking imp after imp off. Each time they peeled off they dived back in, but the balls were relentless. The boys obviously cared for and respected their teacher. They were not going to give up. After a few seconds, it became obvious that the imps were reattaching themselves at a slower rate. They were tiring.

I grabbed my trench coat and wrapped it around my arm then dived into the fray. A violent hissing noise filled the inside of my head as leathery wings rained abuse down upon me. I stumbled and staggered under the weight of the blows from the imps and the occasional stray blow of a wayward basketball. But I stayed focussed. I had to reach James Dean. I reached out and latched my bare arm around his waist, then, with my coat for protection I swatted at the black furies, pounding at them until they began to retreat.

The clouds of black that had enveloped me and the teacher began to part but the hissing inside my head grew louder and louder. It sounded akin to my tinnitus, but far more extreme. It sounded alien, invasive.

"Stop this!" I bellowed at the flying creatures. "Stop this now!"

And surprisingly, they did.

I wished at that moment that I had brought a pin with me just to see if you really could hear one drop at such a time, but fancy was soon overtaken by the new noises in my head. It had turned from a violent hissing to a bewildered chattering sound mixed with the sweetest singing I had ever heard. The imps flapped their wings casually and hovered about three metres off the ground. They cocked their heads to one side and stared at me in what could only be described as wonder. As they hovered there, I noticed that their skin seemed to shimmer iridescently in the bright lights of the gym. It seemed almost insubstantial. *Curious for a creature that could be hurt by a basketball*, I thought.

I gave Dean a quick glance. He was scratched and somewhat battered, but otherwise he appeared okay. Then I turned my full attention back to the imps. "Thank you," I said, relief flooding through my voice. "You had no need to attack him. He meant the boy no harm."

The boy.

I turned to see where Billy was, but he had gone. He had left the gym. I cursed, quietly at first then loudly, as I looked back up to the imps and realised that they too had fled the scene.

"Mr Spallucci! Really!" came the strident tones of the tempest that was Mrs Wetherington, her court shoes clacking on the hard gymnasium floor. "I shall have no such language in front of my pupils." She eyed the scattered basketballs and the scuffed gym teacher then turned on her heels. "My office. Now!"

"I believe that you have had an eventful couple of days, Mr Spallucci."

I nodded. "You could say that. It's certainly not been like my old school days, that's for sure."

Mrs Wetherington's face looked sour enough to be the essence of the harshest lemon. "Quite," she managed through pursed lips. She steepled her fingers together and regarded me with a superior air. "Would you mind telling me just what was going on in my gymnasium?"

I described the ten black imps, how they had attacked James Dean and how the boys had pelted them with basketballs allowing me to get in and rescue the man. For the moment I left out the connection with Billy Swarbrick.

"This all sounds somewhat unruly," Wetherington sneered. "Not becoming of this establishment. Basketballs indeed!"

"It was the safest way to distract the creatures without hurting Mr Dean," I explained.

The middle-aged woman harrumphed and asked, "So have you come to any conclusions yet, or is this all proving to be a waste of your time and my budget?"

I ignored the insult. "What can you tell me about Billy Swarbrick?"

The head sighed deeply and sank back into her leather office chair. "Year nine. Constant under-achiever despite excellent grades in his first two years here. He will play havoc with our value-added come the end of key stage three."

"Value-added?" I frowned, unsure that I had heard right. "You have to tax the pupils?"

I was given one of those 'oh, you stupid mortal' looks that you normally only receive from librarians as she went on to explain the terminology. "Value-added is the phrase used to describe how a child has progressed. If they come in poor and they respond well to the education that we give them allowing them to perform well at the end of key-stage, then the school is seen as having given good value for that child. If, however, they are perceived to go backwards or stay stationery at the end of key-stage then that is bad value. In short we have wasted our time and our money on them. Our systems here are faultless as long as the child wishes to put the effort in, Mr Spallucci. Billy Swarbrick has recently started to under-achieve. If anything, he has actually started to go backwards. He should be a high flyer, considering his background. Instead, he has continually shut himself off from the rest of his peers and alienated himself from the teaching staff. He is bad value."

I grimaced. It was so cold, so clinical. How could she write a boy off whose life was really just starting to blossom? Then I twigged on something that she had said. "You mentioned 'his background.' What do you mean by that?"

"Billy is the son of Hector Swarbrick, the chair of governors here," she beamed radiantly.

Realisation slapped me across the face like a cold, wet tuna fish. "By Hector Swarbrick you mean the owner of the *Lancaster Chronicle*?" I groaned. No wonder the local journalists had not dived on the story. The centre of the piece would have been the son of their own boss. Which surely meant...

"Has Mr Swarbrick ever mentioned to you about anything happening around Billy at home?"

Wetherington locked me in a stare cold enough to freeze every Bunsen burner in the school. "Hector is a fine, upstanding man and a rock upon which this establishment is firmly seated. He and his wife are constantly involved in school life as well as being fervent fund-raisers. Not only this, but they are personal friends of mine." This last statement sounded more like a threat than a fact. "Now would you mind telling me why you are so interested in their son?"

I suddenly realised that I was walking across very thin ice and the wrong word or interpretation could give me an extremely chilly dunking. "I have reason to believe that the so-called poltergeist activity is centred around Billy."

"You have evidence for this?"

The ice under my feet started to creak.

"Both of the lessons that I attended which suffered activity were attended by him."

"I'm sure there were other pupils who also attended both of those classes, Mr Spallucci."

A large crack was shooting towards me.

"I'm sure there were, Mrs Wetherington, but in PE, the activity with the imps was focussed on the person who could have been seen as a threat directly to Billy – namely, Mr Dean."

Wetherington's icy gaze held me fast. "I do not like where you are proceeding with this, Mr Spallucci. Are you saying that the son of the chair of governors is possessed?"

Very cold water splashed at my ankles and my legs trembled.

I shook my head. "No, not possessed. I feel that he is troubled. You said yourself that his grades have slipped and that he has become withdrawn. I feel that something has pushed him over the edge. Perhaps something at home..."

She did not let me finish. As the ice separated and the frigid depths dragged me down, Wetherington stormed at me that I was obviously a fraud and a slanderer whilst she stamped over to her office door and bade me leave with haste.

As the solid oak slammed behind me I felt chilled to the bone, and not just from the mental metaphor that had enveloped me. The boy was in trouble and was obviously in need of help. The other boys in the gym had not been taunting him. They just seemed to have been exasperated by his weirdness. Had John and his mates been discussing this trait of Billy's personality in front of the glass window? Had Billy been making his way up the stairs to the study room and overheard them? Right then I could have done with my young friend to give me more information, but that was out of the question down to both his head teacher and his mother.

His mother.

With the glass figurine.

I found my hand sliding around my Zippo in my pocket, my thumb affectionately stroking its relief pattern.

I told myself to stop getting distracted by vague coincidences and to concentrate on the matter at hand. Right now I had to help out Billy. So, if there were problems in his life it seemed most likely that they were coming from home. I was about to walk out of the school when something struck me. I still hadn't revisited the IT suite. In all the swift-moving events of the morning I had completely forgotten about it. I checked that Wetherington could not see me and I headed for the stairs.

I slowly opened the door to the IT suite. The corridor was surprisingly quiet and had that eerie sense that buildings get when there is no one around and you are somewhere that you shouldn't be. What with my previous experience of this room, I had a certain amount of the heebie-jeebies.

It was empty of pupils and relatively tidy now. There was not much mess at all, just the usual detritus one would expect from a classroom: discarded pens, paper and the eponymous shoe. Whenever I entered an empty classroom as a child there was always a discarded, muddy shoe in the corner. It conjured up this image of children the world over hopping home after losing a shoe and devising some lame excuse as to where it had vanished: a dog ate it, my friend ate it, aliens ate it.

What was most definitely still in disarray, though, was the display board at the back of the room. Many pieces of work were still missing and a lot of what was left behind hung in tatters. There were, however, four pieces which were stapled neatly to the wall at perfect right angles. I walked over and peered at them. They were very precise pieces on databasing, spreadsheets, web-links and e-mail. All of them bore the same student's name.

Billy Swarbrick.

If I needed any more proof, this was it, but how was I going to find his address, and quickly? Having witnessed the furious apparitions in the gym, I had the feeling that things were spiralling out of control for the young Mr Swarbrick.

I was checking my watch as I made for the main door of the school (it was just coming up to lunch) when a female voice called out, "Mr Spallucci?"

My shoulders sank. What was it now? Who else had I offended? "Yes?" I turned and saw the receptionist waving a brown envelope in my direction.

"I was given this to post on to you, but you don't seem to have left yet..." She let the sentence drift off implying my guilt.

I stepped over towards her desk and took the envelope. My curiosity was piqued as I thanked her. I decided that discretion was in order and I kept it firmly shut until I was out of the school grounds. Inside was a note written in a firm, masculine hand. It read:

> "You will get nowhere with the ice-maiden. She's far too interested in appearances and, as you have probably found out by now, the Swarbricks are friends of hers.
>
> So, as long as you tell no one where you got this from, Billy lives at 12, Sefton Close out in Slyne. Don't expect a warm welcome, though. His father's a pompous arse!
>
> Thanks for your help this morning.
>
> James Dean"

I grinned as I pocketed the letter in my trench coat. I climbed up into the life-boat that had just cruised up to rescue me from my icy plunge and set sail for Slyne.

Slyne-with-Hest is a small village to the north of Lancaster. It is surrounded by fields and populated by those with enough capital to do so: jewellers, bankers, accountants, retired builders. It's not the sort of place that I ever seem to frequent, so my knowledge of the local geography was sketchy at best. I had my local map gripped in one hand as I turned my VW Polo Classic off the A6 down Throstle Grove and I had to swerve to avoid an on-coming four-by-four being driven by a dapper gentleman and his twin-set-and-pearls wife. I crunched into the hedgerow and swore as I stalled. The four-by-four just ploughed onwards and left me in the gutter. My ageing Polo restarted on the third turn-over and I dragged it out onto the road again. I made a mental note that it was due for one of two things: a major service or scrapping. I had been driving it since my twenties. It was the first thing I had bought after my dad had died but it was a 1983 vintage and was starting to show signs of its age. At some point someone had shunted it up the rear in a car park and now an intermittent leak meant that passengers on the back seat inevitably got a wet back-side when they sat down. As a result, I always carried a supply of black bin bags in the boot for the rare occasion that I ever had anyone else in the car with me.

Sefton Close was just down the road on the left. It was a relatively new-built area: a reclaimed derelict farm that had been replaced with twenty red-brick detached houses. They all had pristine lawns out the front and ivy up the walls. Their owners obviously intended their residences to look rural, hiding the fact that they themselves had grown up and made their money in more urban areas.

The road was quite narrow so I bumped my car up onto the kerb outside number 12 and turned off the ignition.

"Here goes nothing," I muttered as I opened the driver's door and swung my legs out. As my scuffed shoes crunched their way up the gravel path I could hear a very large dog bark maniacally from somewhere close by. I had stopped off at my office and partaken of a bit of Dutch courage before driving out to Slyne and now it was close to four o'clock and the evening was just starting to stake its claim on the sky as it is wont to do at this time in autumn. I reached the door and found no doorbell, just a large, ornate knocker which I grabbed and rapped three times. The dog barked even louder. Great, I thought, death by mauling, dribbling or crotch sniffing. Don't get me wrong, I love dogs, it's their owners that frustrate me. So many seem to see them as little babies that need pampering and spoiling. I know where that leads to. I've seen *It's Me Or The Dog* on daytime television. Even the fluffiest little fur-balls can go psycho when not given any boundaries.

There was a scuffling from behind the door and the sound of yelping as the pooch was dragged away by an unseen owner. I heard a door slam and light footsteps approached. The door opened and I was greeted by a slightly built woman in her mid-forties. Her hair was brown, turning grey, her eyes were green and her dress was plain. I could tell immediately from the way her eyes twitched nervously as they looked me up and down that she was a woman on the edge. "Can... can I help you?"

"Mrs Swarbrick?"

"Yes? Who are you?" The dog continued to bark in the background.

There was the sound of large paws trying desperately to shred a kitchen door.

"Sorry to bother you, but my name is Sam Spallucci. I am investigating certain incidents at your son's school. May I come in?"

"School?" Her eyes glazed over and I could see tears welling up. "Oh god! What has he done? Please tell me he's not hurt anyone!" she wailed.

"I don't think the doorstep is the place for this sort of conversation, is it?"

She considered this for a split-second then opened the door wider and let me in. The inside of the house was as I had imagined: spacious. The wide hallway was floored in a light-coloured wood laminate giving it an open feel as it led onto an open-plan kitchen-diner (I had been mistaken as to where the dog had been shut in, then), three more doors and a sweeping staircase. It was from behind one of the doors that the dog was going frantic. Mrs Swarbrick noticed my gaze wander towards the noise. "Don't mind Dooby," she said. "He just gets excited. We'll go through to the living room."

I followed her through the nearest doorway into a room that stretched the length of the house and commanded a large glass patio door that overlooked the local countryside. Outside, the sky was getting darker. She flicked a light switch on the wall and subtle lighting illuminated the room. A rich carpet cushioned the soles of my shoes as I walked into the middle of the room past an enormous plasma screen television. "Is Mr Swarbrick home?" I asked.

She shook her head. "He will be soon. He's fetching Molly from ballet class."

"Molly? Is that Billy's sister?"

"Yes." The woman stood, obviously unaware of where to take the conversation, so I explained why I was there.

"Mrs Swarbrick, are you aware that there have been a number of incidents concerning Billy's lessons recently?"

Silently, she nodded her head.

I drummed my fingers against my teeth. This was like trying to get a pearl out of a delicate oyster without breaking the shell. "You asked before if he had hurt anyone." Her green eyes shot up to me, tears running down her face. "Let me reassure you that's not the case." Her shoulders sagged as a touch of relief washed over her. "However, you seem fairly certain that he is the centre of these matters even without me saying so. Why is that?"

She was about to answer when the door slammed behind me and a male voice roared, "Who the hell are you and what are you doing in my house?" Mr Swarbrick was well-dressed, tall, bespectacled and very, very grey. He stormed into his living room, his finger out in front of him, pointing accusatorially.

I opened my mouth to speak but Mrs Swarbrick beat me to it. "He's from the school, Hector. There's been more trouble."

Swarbrick's face turned murderous. "Spallucci," he growled. "Lindsay rang me at work and warned me he might show up here. Get out! Now!" He stamped over to me and grabbed the collar of my trench coat. I acted instinctively and thrust my forearm against his, causing him to topple backwards, pulling me with him. We landed on the floor in an unceremonious heap and, as I pulled myself away, I saw a small, brown-haired girl standing wide-eyed at the doorway. "Daddy!" she shrieked and ran to her father. The dog's barking grew louder and was joined by the sound of footsteps running down the wooden staircase.

This was rapidly turning out to be very messy. "Mr Swarbrick," I began, trying to placate him, but he was having none of it. He drew himself up, rounded on me, drawing back his fist and I braced myself for another bleeding nose.

It never happened.

"Stop it."

The voice was quiet but penetrating and had come from Billy. Hector Swarbrick's clenched fist remained frozen next to his face as the lights in the living room dimmed. There was the sound of a pitiful wail from Mrs Swarbrick and then the familiar feeling of air crackling around us like in a thunderstorm. I felt a breeze start to waft across my face and my eyes glanced around the room. A watercolour that hung on the far wall was starting to bang on its hook. A rug by the patio door was flapping up and down. A china vase was rattling on a small table.

"Billy!" I called out. "No!" but it was no good, the boy's eyes had glazed over and he was no longer with us. I felt a pulse of air shove into me and I was sailing across the room towards the patio door. I landed hard, but unhurt. The same could not be said for Mr Swarbrick. The water colour picture dropped with a crash from the wall before he was lifted off his feet and slammed up in its place. The air around his wrists and his ankles shimmered and four of the imps appeared, fixing him rigid in position. The newspaper magnate's eyes bulged with terror behind his glasses and a dark stain spread down his immaculate grey trousers. I winced in embarrassment and tried to reach him but found my feet pinned down by two more of the little fiends.

Then things started to fly.

It was another game of dodge ball but this time Swarbrick was the target and the projectiles were a lot harder: TV remotes, books, the water colour painting and the china vase. They were all whipped up into the air and smashed into the terrified man as Billy's rage grew in intensity.

Then, as the small table on which the vase had once rested rose from the floor, Molly broke through her fear and ran to her captive father. The table sliced through the air and caught her square on her back, pounding the small girl to the floor.

"Molly!" Billy's scream echoed through the room. All levitating objects, including his father, crashed to the ground and the imps vanished. For a moment the boy stood aghast, staring at the limp form of his sister, then he turned and pelted upstairs. His mother threw herself on her daughter and wept as she cradled the little mite in her arms. Swarbrick sat stunned and slouched against the wall.

I crawled over to Mrs Swarbrick. “Here, let me see,” I said.

She protectively pulled the girl closer to herself and turned her back on me.

“Please, I can help,” I tried.

The woman was slowly rocking back and forth. I placed a hand on her shoulder and waited. She stopped rocking and turned back to me. I reached over and placed two fingers on Molly’s neck.

Her eyes flicked open. “What you doing?” the little girl asked.

I smiled. “Checking that you’re still with us. Apparently you are. How do you feel?”

“Okay. Just sore.” She looked up at her mother. “I love you, Mummy.”

Mrs Swarbrick said nothing and just hugged her tighter. I stood up, ignored the man of the house and chased upstairs after Billy.

As I pulled myself up the polished wooden stairs of the suburban house I wondered to myself as to what was going through the mind of the teenage boy who had shut himself in his bedroom. He had so much power and so little control. In his anger he had inadvertently hurt his kid sister and the thoughts going through his head right now must be coming from a dark, terrible place.

I had been to many such places as a teenager especially when my dad had been sick. I had lain awake night after night praying that he would get better, praying to God on High to make the arthritis miraculously disappear. Then I would wake in the morning and he was still the same, hunched, in pain and spiteful.

When my father’s body finally gave in, my hope in miracles were buried in the ground along with him. All hope was lost. I was on my own – me against the universe – a small ant in a sea of sand, desperately trying to grab purchase on an ever shifting ground that threatened to suffocate me at any moment.

But I never gave up hope in a loving God. Even on his death bed my father had been an avid believer. He had kept his rosary and his bible by his bedside even when his fingers were too gnarled to count the beads or turn the pages. They were there to comfort him in his own dark places.

So I carried on my own journey and, as I prepared myself for the selection process for the Anglican priesthood, I continued to study. I studied hard. At first, just those subjects that were expected of me. Then, after my encounter with Gerald and after my graduation, those subjects which my heart craved. Those which would bring me true knowledge of the unseen universe. That which is all around and under our very noses but which we do not see because our minds will not allow us to comprehend it. So slowly, painfully, I peeled away the constraints of the logical mind and I explored the finest details of the world of the paranormal; from ghosts to zombies, from phantoms to mystics, from possessions to... poltergeists.

I took a steadying breath and knocked lightly on Billy’s door. What this boy needed right now was not necessarily answers but reassurance.

There was no reply. I knocked again. "Billy. It's Sam."

There was still no reply. Also there were no little black imps to throw me down the stairs. I considered that a bonus. "Can I come in?"

I waited.

"Molly's fine, Billy. She's just a bit sore. She's with your mum right now."

The door handle turned and the side of Billy's face peered out at me under his lank, dark hair. His face was red with crying. It seemed to be my day for upsetting adolescent boys. I stood and waited, cap in hand. After a little while he nodded and opened the door up then went and sat down on his bed.

As I sat down next to Billy, the old mattress sagged under my adult weight. I noticed that it hardly gave an inch under the teenager. He was as light as a feather – skin and bones. "Thanks for letting me in, Billy," I began. "You know we need to talk, don't you?"

The lank-haired lad nodded mutely and clasped the sleeves of his long-sleeved top tight in his screwed up fists. His eyes stared intently at the floor space between his feet.

I looked around the room. When I had been his age there had been posters on the walls of various pop bands and musicians: mainly Madness and The Specials with a smattering of Mike Oldfield or Tom Waits as my tastes had developed. There was just one decoration on Billy's wall: a poster of the solar system. Other than that, the walls were bare. There was a book case in one corner and a tatty looking wardrobe that seemed to be held up with duct tape and a prayer in the other. Besides the bed, there was no other furniture, not even a desk or a chair.

It was pitiful. I stored my boiling anger for a more appropriate time.

"You like astronomy, Billy?" I asked.

Again, a silent nod.

"I think it's fascinating, all that stuff out there. We must be so very, very small mustn't we? Just little specks of dust on one of nine planets in the..."

"Eight." The quiet voice cut my ramblings dead.

"Pardon?"

"Not nine. Just eight." Billy lifted his head and his dark eyes looked me in the face for the first time. They were ripe with sorrow and hurting. "Pluto is not a planet. It is a dwarf planet, along with Eris and Ceres. It is situated in the Kuiper Belt past Neptune."

"I didn't know that, Billy," I said. "Your knowledge is better than mine, I guess."

"The Kuiper Belt is full of objects," he continued, animation edging into his voice, "over a thousand at last count. Some of them may have moved, you know? Into the solar system? Triton may have been there once and Phoebe too." Excitement was starting to edge into the sad eyes. I decided to pursue the matter.

"I recognise the names," I lied, "but I'm not sure what they are. Why don't you enlighten me?"

"Triton is the largest moon of Neptune and Phoebe is an irregular shaped moon of Saturn," he explained, his hands lifting from his lap and drawing invisible lines in the air as if painting images of the celestial bodies that only he could see. "They may have originated in the Kuiper Belt, but the greater gravitational pull of the planets could have attracted them, so they were drawn into orbit around them. That happens a lot you know," his eyes flickered back down to his lap, "and not just to planets."

I heard a slight thud and noticed a book slip over on the bookshelf. I ran the nail of my index finger over my teeth. "Is that what happened to you Billy? Did some things gravitate in on you?"

A silent nod gave me the answer I was expecting.

"Why don't you tell me about it?" I pressed, my voice calm and soothing. The last thing I wanted was a reprisal of the events in the sports hall or with Molly. "Perhaps I can help?"

"No one can help me," he whispered as another book fell over on top of the previous volume, a puff of dust whispering up into the air. "I don't deserve any help."

I frowned. "Why would you believe that, Billy?"

"Because I'm a bad, bad, boy." The poster of the solar system smacked against the wall and I wondered if I could actually hear the faint flapping of wings, or was that just my fearful imagination?

"I don't think you're a bad boy, Billy," I reassured him. The poster settled slightly. "I also have a very open mind. I've seen a few weird things this week already, and not just at your school."

Billy looked back up at me, curiosity on his face. "Really? Such as?"

I rubbed the back of my neck. What should I say? Satanists and vampires? The kid was screwed up enough already, but I didn't want to break his fragile trust just as the foundations were starting to set. "Let's just say that, in my job, I've experienced enough to know that the things that are happening around you may be considered to be abnormal by most, but they are intrinsically part of you now."

Billy nodded, slowly, tentatively.

"I also know that you need to control them before you really hurt someone. But then I think you realise that already, don't you?"

Billy nodded again, this time a lot more firmly. "How can I do that?"

"Let's start from the beginning, shall we?" I suggested. "Tell me when it first happened. Was there a trigger?"

Billy paused for a moment. He stood and walked over to his bedroom door and, after checking that it was shut tight turned his back to me and lifted his baggy top. The sight of the faded belt mark on his back made me feel sick. I had guessed that his father was a git, but this... This was intolerable. "Your dad?" I asked, just to make sure.

Billy lowered his shirt and nodded. "He gets stressed at work and he and Mum argue lots. And I mean lots." He sat down on the bed again and started to intently study his finger nails. "He first hit me a few weeks back. He was laying into Mum. Verbally laying into her – calling her lazy and stupid. She was in the kitchen, just taking it, crying. I flipped. I told him to lay off of her and let her alone. He turned on me and slammed me up against the kitchen door, screaming at me that it was none of my business and that I ought to be grateful for everything he did for me, everything he bought for me. He was the one who brought the money into the house, not that lazy little tramp. I didn't know what to do, so I ran out of the room crying and came up here. I lay down on my bed and cried so hard that my tears felt like drops of fire. I was scared. I was confused.

"I was so angry.

"Then as I got more and more worked up things started to twitch on the bookshelves and the lampshade started to sway. That brought me up sharp and I jolted in fright. Then a book flew across the room and whacked the wall. I hurried over and picked it up. I was scared that Dad would have heard it and come up to hit me, but he didn't. He was still busy shouting at Mum.

"It was late by that point, so I got myself to bed and tried to sleep, but all I could think about was the book flying across the room. I must have dozed off eventually, I guess, 'cos the next thing I knew was Molly shaking me and calling me to wake up. She was whispering loudly in my ear and she sounded scared. I opened my eyes and saw why. My room was a tip. Stuff was everywhere. Books all over the floor.

"'What happened Billy?' she asked me. I said I didn't know and she helped me tidy up and promised not to tell Dad. After breakfast I went to school and, well, you sort of know the rest. Little things happen all the time - things moving and stuff - but whenever I get stressed or feel like I'm being picked on," he made an explosion shape with his hands, "Ka-blooie!"

"Like the window on the staircase?"

He nodded. "I was heading up to the study room when I heard voices. I couldn't make out specifics but I heard my name and I heard laughter." He shrugged.

"Ka-blooie," I surmised.

"Ka-blooie," he agreed.

I drummed my fingernails against my teeth. The poor kid. What a life? A bully for a dad and adolescent paranoia at school. There was something else though, something that didn't quite fit. Something that he hadn't told me yet.

"What are they?" I asked.

The look of fear on Billy's face confirmed my suspicion. "What are who?" His eyes darted back at me from under his lank hair.

I sighed. "Billy, everyone seems to think this is a *poltergeist*," I accented the word with finger-quotes, "but you and I know it's no such thing, is it?"

The boy fiddled with his fingers and studied the floor. "I... I don't know what you mean."

"Poltergeists are an external phenomenon expressing internal anger and angst. They are unexplained noises and telekinetic activity surrounding a certain individual."

"Yes," he interrupted, "that's right. That's what's been happening to me. A poltergeist."

I shook my head. "That's what it looked like originally, but that incident in the gym..." I waited, hoping he would finish the sentence. He didn't. Instead his eyes lifted and fixed on the wall behind me. I swallowed. Hard. "How many are there, Billy? I'm guessing ten. Am I right?"

He nodded.

I turned, very, very slowly so as not to appear threatening, and there they were, just as they had appeared in the gym, ten black imps, each about thirty centimetres in height, clinging to his wallpaper, their beady eyes scanning me with curiosity. Just as in the gym, their skin seemed to flicker in the light.

"Hello," I said, keeping my voice level and calm. "Now, you should really know by now that I mean Billy no harm. You have been watching us after all, haven't you? What I'd really like to know is what you actually are. Obviously you aren't a poltergeist. That is an invisible phenomenon. And this imp stuff..." I shook my head. "Sorry, not buying that. I thought this shimmering business was the lights in the gym before, but here you are flickering like a torch with a dying battery. You're generating this image just for the benefit of strangers. Why don't you just show your real selves? You know I won't hurt you."

There was a quiet chattering as the imps seemed to discuss the matter then one of them let go of the wall and hopped down onto the bed. It chicken-hopped across the duvet and pulled itself up in front of me before reaching out a black, spindly hand towards me. Instinctively I reached out with my considerably larger paw and touched one of its tiny fingers with the index on my right hand. The imp's mouth widened into a large smile and bright lights pulsed vibrantly across its skin. Its stature reduced somewhat in bulk and the black, leathery surface washed away into a bright iridescent sheen. Dainty clothes fashioned from a glowing fabric adorned its delicate, humanoid form and light butterfly wings thrummed behind it.

I couldn't help myself from grinning back at the little creature and its evolving companions as they floated down to join it.

"My God, Billy," I whispered in absolute awe. "They're fairies. They're bloody fairies!"

A number of the diminutive creatures covered their mouths with tiny hands and their wings shuddered delicately.

I frowned. "Are you laughing at me?" I asked, then smiled as their little faces peered up at me, radiant in a bathing light. "I'll let you off as you're so cute," I said, causing some of them to chuckle again. Others jumped up from the bed and circled around my head before flying over to Billy and alighting on his shoulders. They reached out and stroked his hair affectionately before bending over and whispering in his ears.

"They think you're funny," the boy explained, a smile starting to form on his face for the first time since I'd met him. "I guess they kinda like you."

"The feeling's mutual." For a short while, all I could do was sit and watch the little figures gambolling around the teenager's bedroom. It was truly amazing. I couldn't make out if they were male or female, they all seemed somewhat asexual – pixie-like, I suppose. There were the gossamer wings and the light coloured robes they wore, but they seemed to look like they had rainbows streaking through their light coloured hair. "Do they have names?" I finally asked.

Billy shook his head as one sat in his hand, its head inclined curiously to one side. "If they do, they've never told me. They're not the greatest of communicators."

"But they do talk, don't they? I mean, one just whispered into your ear."

Billy pulled a confused face. "It's a bit more complicated than that, I think," he explained. "It's more like telepathy. I'm more aware of the sounds they make in my head than an actual voice."

I recalled the burst of sonorous tinnitus I had suffered earlier and understood what he meant. "I heard something when they were flying round in the gym. I guess it was them." I sighed deeply. They looked so happy here in Billy's bedroom.

I heard a sniffing noise and looked up at Billy. He was crying.

"They hurt Molly," he murmured through the tears.

I nodded. "It was an accident, Billy. You know that, don't you?" I reassured him.

"All the same, she's my kid sister. It could have been worse, too!" he wailed. The fairies stopped flittering around and hovered nervously, all their eyes on him. One of them floated over and held one of his fingers in its tiny hand. It tugged gently and smiled up at him. "I know you're sorry, but it's not safe for you to be here anymore. I think you need to go."

The light from the fairies dimmed slightly as they considered this, then, as one, they turned their faces towards me, their heads inclined in question. I started, aware at where this was heading.

"Oh no!" I exclaimed. "No way. As cute as you are, I don't need little pixies in my life right now. I can look after myself, thank you."

One of the little folk hovered up in front of me and shook its head then clicked its fingers. A bright, white disk hung in the space between us. Craters pitted its surface where rocks from space had impacted. Ice trickled down the river of my spine as I regarded the full moon. Another fairy drifted up to the bedroom's curtains and pulled them back revealing the night sky. There hanging in the gloom was the same moon with a sliver still covered in darkness. Not much time. I had lost track. Damn it!

"You really think I'm in danger?" I asked the little creatures. As one, they nodded their heads. I considered the matter. I really did. They were obviously powerful, they had shown that over and over again, but did I want that power? Did I really?

Part of me really did. I could feel something deep down and animal hungering for the talents that they possessed and that was a problem. A big problem. Once I started down that path where would I end up?

I shook my head again. "No," I stated resolutely. "I will manage on my own. It is time for you to say your goodbyes then leave."

So they did. They floated over to Billy, covered him in hugs and kisses, then, one by one, their little lights blinked out until there was just one left. This one, after it had said its goodbye to the boy drifted over to me and took one last look at the apparition of the full moon, then regarded me once more.

"I said 'no' and I meant 'no'." My voice was firm but there were cracks at the edge.

The fairy gave a little frown and twiddled its fingers in the air. As it vanished, the picture of the moon dissolved and, for an instant, I was sure that the shadowy outline of a winged dragon hung in the air before melting into nothingness.

The quiet hung heavy in the room. I walked over to Billy and placed my hand on his shoulder. "You did the right thing," I said. "You did the right thing." Whether I was saying this to him or to me, I was not too sure.

That evening, I went home, drew the curtains blocking out any trace of moonlight, opened a fresh bottle of Jack D and turned on some Tom Waits very loud. The hard, raucous lyrics filled my ears, releasing the tension from my muscles and the alcohol from the whiskey soothed my battered nose.

Power is a terrible thing. It can turn good men into monsters. My dad told me that before he died. We were sat watching some politician or other on the television and he turned to me and said, "Sammy, innocent people voted for that bastard. Worst mistake they ever made. He walked in with smiles and manifestos, promising to right the wrongs and do good for the nation. Then a few years later he was oppressing workers and squashing the minorities. He wasn't always bad, Sammy. It was the power that corrupted him. It's a cancer, a growth, a malign tumour that feeds off your insecurities and totally consumes you. Never be like him. Promise me."

So I promised him. There and then I promised that I would never be like that politician. I would never grab power when it was presented to me. I would walk a straight path and keep my nose clean.

The next day the centre of my universe was dead and my life was shredded by the claws of bad luck, but I've always clung to what he said: power corrupts.

So, as the whiskey heated my heart and the music nourished my soul, I drifted off into a deep sleep which was inhabited by dreams of fairies and dragons, mythical creatures that ran and did my will, protecting me from the beast that stalked the night in the light of the full moon, its heavy footsteps accompanied by a ragged breath and the stench of decay.

The next morning was another bright, sunny autumnal affair. I ate cereal in the living room as I watched people scurry around Dalton Square on their way to work and I drank a coffee as I listened to a bit of morning news on Radio 4: more doom and gloom about the Middle East.

Nine o'clock came and I was entering the office of Lindsay Wetherington, invoice in hand. There were no rebuttals. There were no put downs. There wasn't even an awkward silence. She politely took the bill and promised that I would receive a cheque within seven working days and actually thanked me for my help in the whole unfortunate matter.

I was actually starting to smile when I left her office. She had obviously talked to Swarbrick after my visit out to Slyne the previous evening. The conversation would have gone something along the lines of: Spallucci came, hell broke loose, it's all sorted now, pay him off.

Yes, power, that was the thing. Those with power crave it so much that they will do whatever they need to cling to it and if that means paying off a minor inconvenience which could turn into a major aggravation, then so be it.

I was leaving the school when my smile faltered. There, walking down the drive, was Billy, his bag slung low over his back as is the fashion and a nasty, red bruise circling his left eye which is not quite the norm. He saw me and actually smiled before bounding over. "Hello, Sam," he grinned from behind the bruise. "How are you?"

"Seemingly better than you," I observed. "What happened?"

He shrugged. "The official story is that I walked into my bedroom door last night."

"And the unofficial?"

He shrugged again.

"Bloody hell, Billy... I'm so sorry."

"It's okay," he said. "I've had worse. But better than that, I didn't retaliate. I just took it. He can't win if I just take it. And others can't get hurt." A bell rang from somewhere in school. "Look, I gotta go or I'll be late. Catch you around, okay?"

"Sure," my voice cracked. What had I done? I had removed this boy's only line of defence and he was grateful for it. I looked at my watch. It was only nine thirty and I needed a drink. I fished out a Lucky and headed back into town, towards my office. As I left the school premises my phone buzzed in my pocket. I fished it out and read the message, "Get here now. Important. Spliff."

Ah well, another crisis. At least he had a decent drinks cabinet.

# The Case of the Werewolf of Williamson Park

I was guessing that Spliff was at his place. This meant that I had two options: either go back to my office and grab my car or walk over to Luneside University. It was quite a walk out to the Quay but I decided that I could use some fresh air and I loathe it when people drive needlessly through town, so I decided to put my best foot forward and head off on Shanks' Pony.

It was about nine-thirtyish and the main throng of traffic in town had subsided - the school run was over and those subjected to the daily grind were safely ensconced inside their workplaces for the morning – so the walk through the west side of town would be quite pleasant. I like to walk as much as possible, which is not as much as it should be these days. When I was younger, I was always up in the Lakes climbing over hills and ambling along winding rivers. These days... well it's work, isn't it? It just gets in the way. You have the best intentions to do something. You get all the gear ready. You even go as far as making a packed lunch to take with you: hummus sarnies, crisps and a few flapjacks in my case. Then you get the phone call and you drop everything to sort out whatever it is that needs sorting and bang goes the day. The boots get put away and the sandwiches end up as a light supper later that evening to save wasting them.

So now I relish any chance I get to walk whenever it may be, even if it is just across town to see a friend whose idea of a crisis is that one of the students may have looked at him a bit funny.

Thirty minutes later and I had walked through the Infirmary grounds, over the canal, along Dallas Road, down onto the Marsh and through the rear gates of Luneside University. As I climbed the stairway decked with Saint Andrew's flags, I could hear such shouting and swearing that one might hear from Richard Dawkins if he was confronted by a small child who just wanted to believe in a higher purpose. I knocked once on Spliff's door and let myself in.

"Where, the bloody hell..?" One of the funniest things I find about Spliff is the way his accent regresses whenever he gets fraught or stressed. Normally, he is quite clipped and precise – a refined gentleman's accent with the lilt of heather plucked fresh from a verdant Scottish glen. However, as he was busy emptying the contents of a sideboard onto the piles of detritus that lay strewn across his floor, his deep Scottish brogue sounded more like it was forged from a viciously barbed highland thistle that had sprouted from the drainpipe of a Glaswegian tenement. "Och! Where the frig is the wee thing? Ah only had eet yasterdee!"

"If you're looking for your sweet innocence, I think it skipped out with your virtue and eloped off to Gretna many years ago," I smiled as I leant in the doorway. I had not thought it possible for Spliff's living room to be even more untidy, but apparently I had been wrong. It looked like it had been played in by a baby tornado who had then thrown a strop when it had been told it was time to go home. Every drawer was emptied and discarded in a pile, their contents heaped up on the rug in the centre of the room. There were jackets and trousers piled on his red leather sofa like it was Harrods on the first day of the sales. One pile of shirts moved ominously and, as I walked over to my friend, I veered away from it, knowing that a black, furry ball of bile and hatred lurked underneath waiting to pounce on a passing pair of shins.

"Ha, bloody ha," Spliff grumbled without even looking up from his search. "If ye canna help then just piss off, will ya?"

"What you lost?"

The dark-haired priest stood up from his task, peeled his glasses of his bearded face, anxiously rubbed his brow and said, "A small, white card about so big." He gestured a small rectangular shape with his spectacles.

I cast my eye around the catastrophe that was his living room. "And this card is important because..?"

"It just is!" he snapped, kicking at a pile of trash. "Now are ye gonna help me look for the frigging thing or not?"

"It might help if you tell me what the card is?"

His eyes studiously peered into the depths of the amassed detritus. "It's an appointment card," he mumbled.

"For what?"

"For tea with the frigging Queen! What th' hell does it matta, Sam? Just help me will ya?"

I sighed. He was really rattled. "When was the last time you had it?" I asked.

"Last night. It was in ma jacket pocket."

"Have you..."

"Of course I've bloody well looked there, ya eejit! You think I'm simple or something?"

"Okay, okay." I raised my hands in a pacifying manner. "I'll just check it again to make sure for you. Err... Where is it?"

Spliff motioned over towards the moving pile of shirts. The sleeve of the jacket protruded from underneath them and twitched expectantly. Great. "On second thoughts, I'm sure you checked it thoroughly. Where were you when you put it in the pocket?"

"Drinking a coffee and eating ma supper last night."

I nodded slowly. "What were you eating?"

"Sam! What the frig does it matter?" Spliff threw an old diary across the room which hit the far wall with a thud. "I don't need to know what I was eating, do I?"

"Humour me," I said.

"Jam," he replied.

"On toast?"

"No, just jam."

I safely stifled a smirk. I did not want anything being thrown at me. Instead I warily made my way over to his kitchen. As I did, I noticed the occasional red marks dotted on the carpet between the piles of stuff. "Was it strawberry jam, by any chance?"

"Raspberry. Look, what's this frigging obsession with ma dietary habits?" He stood up, placed his hands on his hips and frowned at me as I tapped a small waste bin with the toe of my shoe. I could see a red mess lying at the bottom.

"And you used a spoon to eat this sweet delight last night, then? Like any other member of the civilised culture that we live in?" I crouched down on my haunches, grimaced and reached into the bin. It was like putting my hand into the mouth of a sleeping hippo with really bad tooth decay. I won't describe it any more. I'll just leave you with the image, okay?

Spliff opened his mouth to say something more abusive, then stopped mid-stride. "Oh," was all he could manage.

I stood up brandishing the once white appointment card. It was now red, sticky and somewhat smeary in nature. I smiled as I held it out towards him by my fingertips. "Yours, I presume?"

"Bloody hell, I remember now." Spliff replaced his spectacles and peered across the room at the card. "I had the munchies but couldn't find a clean spoon, so I..."

"Yeah. I think I get the picture." I frowned as a logo leapt out from the card. "Spliff, this is a hospital card." I tried to make out the department, but it was obscured by some pulverised raspberry. "You okay?"

He smiled and took the card from my relieved fingers. "Course I am. Bloody Archdeacon wants me to have a physical before I go and look at this new post, that's all. You up for a drink now? I'll just ring for a taxi."

At eleven we were walking through the doors of the Borough just as Grace was opening up. "Hi, guys!" she smiled. "Be right with you." The young red-head fastened the doors into place then whipped quickly around the pub, giving the tables a quick wipe-over, setting out beer mats, and picking up any rubbish that had been missed the night before.

"Come on, little dust-devil," Spliff called out as he settled himself in his chair. "It's like the Kalahari over here!" His eyes were twinkling, the coarse brogue had been smothered once more by the Armani scented pillow of refinement and he seemed his normal, good-natured self. At least on the surface.

I removed my hat and coat. As I took my seat, I contemplated the jammy appointment card. While we had been waiting for the taxi, Spliff had meticulously wiped the conserve from its surface, read and re-read the details on it and stowed it safely into his wallet. Nothing more had been said. No banter. No derogatory comments. No idle chit chat.

It was done, finished, forgotten.

Something was wrong, I knew it, but I also knew that my best friend was not the sort for relinquishing such details in a heartbeat. There would be a time and a place for gentle probing and now was not it. He would be automatically on the defensive. Judging by his mania this morning, the appointment was at some point today. I would let him go through with it, then in his own time I would let him get round to telling me what was the matter. If I pushed him I would just be met with, at best, bluster, more likely, abuse, or worse still, ice-cold silence.

Grace finally finished her opening up routine and brought our drinks over. "At last," Spliff said, "I thought they had instated prohibition."

The bar-maid chuckled and smacked him lightly on the shoulder. "Behave, you. So, you both, like, hungry?"

"Ravenous, my dear. Bring me a bull, horns and all," the priest beamed.

I smiled quietly.

"Sam?" Grace asked. "The usual?"

"Yes please, and a Valium for my friend."

She giggled. "Don't know about the drugs, but I think I could slip you some extra salad, if you wanted."

"Thank you."

"Pah!" Spliff snorted as she left us. "Sheer favouritism, you know. You're the only one who gets extras."

"Don't be daft. It'll just be stuff left from yesterday."

Spliff sat back in his chair and pensively stroked his small beard, his blue eyes twinkling in the light from the outside morning.

I sipped my whiskey. "What?"

He said nothing.

"What!"

My friend's mouth spread into a wide grin. "Never you mind, Samuel. Just you enjoy your lunch."

Chance would be a fine thing as someone walked into the Borough who was going to ruin my appetite.

She was mid to late forties. Her hair was light brown with definite streaks of grey. Her skin had the appearance of someone who smoked far more than was good for them and her manner was one of someone who was highly strung. The woman walked straight up to the bar and called over to Grace who was on her way back to the kitchen having just delivered our food to our table. "Excuse me," the woman asked. "I'm looking for Sam Spallucci."

"Bang goes the peace and quiet," Spliff moaned.

I shot him a warning glance which the priest dutifully ignored. "I'm over here," I said, rising from my seat to greet the woman. She turned without even thanking Grace and walked straight over towards me. "How did you know I was over here?"

"Your landlord," she explained. "He was fixing something in your stairwell and he said that I would probably find you over here at this time of day." Her eyes quickly scanned the half-empty glasses then focussed back on me.

Good old reliable Harry, I thought to myself. Always looking out for me.

"I tried your mobile the other day," she continued, "but hung up when I was bounced onto your voicemail."

I recalled my phone going off during the IT lesson at Saint Edmund's. "Sorry about that," I apologised. "I was sort of in a sticky situation at the time. Listen, we were just about to eat. Would you care to join us?" I gestured to an empty chair and she sat down seemingly placated.

"Thank you for the offer," the woman said, "but I can't say that I'm hungry."

"Why's that, might I ask?"

She took a deep breath, summoned all her reserve, then came out with something that almost made Spliff choke on his gin: "It's my brother. He's a werewolf."

Her name was Simone Hawkins. She and her brother, Nathan, worked in the mini-zoo at Williamson Park. She had thought that they lived a normal, quiet life. Neither of them had felt any compunction to settle down with a significant other so they had globe-hopped around quite a bit together touring first Europe, then more remote parts of the world. Last year they had decided to set down some roots and had taken jobs looking after animals up at the park. They shared one of the small, terraced old mill-houses in Moorlands. Their life was typically uneventful.

Until her brother had dropped a bombshell last night.

Apparently, while they had been travelling in Egypt, he had been bitten by a wild animal of some description. At the time they had not given it much thought; it had not been serious, just a nip and he had been up to date with all the relevant shots and vaccinations. There had been no infection, no complications. At least he had thought so until one lunar month later... He had hidden his secret from her, going away at the time of the full moon and keeping himself somewhere solitary and away from people. Aside from a few sheep, he had killed no living creature.

Now, however, things had started to change.

Over the last month, Simone had seen her quiet younger brother become more and more outspoken. He had become prone to terrible rages and outbursts of violent temper. On more than one occasion he had been cautioned for these outbursts at work and he was in danger of losing his job. Then, last night, he had confessed to his hidden nature. He was a wolf dressed in human skin and at the apex of this cycle he would finally give the beast full rein. He would not hide. He would not skulk away on a deserted farm like an outcast or a pariah. In two nights he would transform in the park itself and then he would rampage around under the all-seeing full moon ridding the place of drunks, vandals and druggies. He was going to wage a one-wolf vendetta on those he saw as being pollutants to the place that he loved the most.

Simone had been horrified. She had not known what to do until, later that evening, she had seen a news report about a local investigator in the paranormal.

"I was on telly?"

"Yes, the evening news. Didn't you see it?"

I shook my head. "Spliff?" I asked.

He shrugged. "Sorry, busy having a life," then he turned to Simone. "Do you have proof that your brother is a werewolf, or is it all just his word?"

Simone's eyes shot venom at Spliff. "He's my brother. Of course I believe him. We've grown up together and been through so much."

I held my hand up to pacify the situation. "Just one thing. Why was I on the telly?"

"Police are investigating something about you being abducted earlier in the week," she explained. "Surely you should remember something like that?"

"It's been a long week," I shrugged.

She sighed, gathered herself together and made to get up. "Perhaps I'm wasting my time here," she said. "I think I'll leave."

"No, please, sit down," I urged. "Seriously, I have really been having one of those weeks. Of course I'll investigate your brother."

"Seriously?"

"Seriously."

There was a somewhat tense silence until Simone gave a deep sigh then finally conceded, "Okay, but can we go and talk somewhere a bit more private?"

I gave my lunch a quick glance of longing and my stomach growled. "Of course we can. My office is just across the square."

I could just about feel the nerves rolling off Simone as she hovered nervously in my office. "Do you want to sit?" I asked, trying to set her at ease. She nodded, quickly, and settled herself on my sofa. "You look like you could use a drink," I observed, reaching into my filing cabinet. "Whiskey?"

"Yes. Thank you." Her voice sounded fragile, as if the slightest noise would cause it to splinter into tiny shards. I poured two reasonable measures of Jack and handed her one. She sipped tentatively at the glass. "I understand that you are not a charity, Mr Spallucci, and I am willing to pay whatever it takes to stop my brother." She gave a little snort and sipped some more whiskey. "Brother," it was the saddest sounding word that I have ever heard. "My brother is a kind, caring, introvert man. What I have now is no longer my brother. He's dead. Long dead."

I sat, drinking my bourbon, and let her continue. The woman obviously needed to talk.

"When we were kids, I used to care for him. If he fell over and grazed his knee, I was the one he came to. If the kids were picking on him at school, I was the one who told him that they were just jealous. Our parents had very little time for us. We were left to our own devices – latch-key kids, as it were."

"I know the feeling. My parents fought a lot and I had to entertain myself."

Her dark eyes peered up at me. "Did you have any siblings?"

I shook my head. "Only pebble on the beach. I was kind of late coming."

The dark eyes continued to look up to me. "May I ask you something a bit personal?"

I smiled. "That depends on how much it will make me blush."

"I don't think you'll blush at all," Simone smiled back, her teeth perfect and even. "It's not *that* personal."

"Fire away, then."

"You don't look typically Italian. Your hair and your skin are lighter than one would expect."

I laughed. "Ah! That old chestnut."

Simone waited patiently for me to explain.

I downed the whiskey. "It's a bit of a convoluted story which needs back history filling in first." I looked down at those dark eyes and perfect teeth and pondered something inside. Ah what the hell, it had been a long week. "Perhaps, when I've sorted all this out, I could explain it all over dinner? If you don't think that too improper, that is?"

Simone gave a delicate laugh that sounded like a crystal waterfall. "No, it's not too improper, and yes, I'd love that."

I grinned like an idiot. "Great! Brilliant!" My heart was pounding and my synapses were tap-dancing in my brain. "So, now we've organised our social life, I guess you'd better tell me a bit more about your brother."

The laughter vanished from her eyes and melancholy settled itself down once more in its comfy chair. "I'm not sure what else there is to say."

"Do you have a photo of him? That could help me quite a bit."

Simone rummaged in her hand bag and pulled out a neat, red purse. "I have one in here. It was taken while we were in Egypt. Here you go." She handed it over and I took the photo gratefully. There standing in front of the immortal sphinx was a tall, bearded man with long, flowing, sand-brown hair. I had to admit that he looked half wolf already.

"Thank you. Do you mind if I hang on to this?"

"Of course not. To be honest, it's rather painful to look at right now. The happy times just..." she petered out as the tears finally took hold. I grabbed a tissue from a box on my desk and passed it over. "Oh, silly me. I'm so sorry. I'm sure you don't need this," she fussed as she dabbed at her large, dark eyes. "Look. I'd best be going. I'm sure you will be able to take care of everything."

I assured the poor woman that I would and saw her out of my office then closed the door and leaned heavily against it. I took a few deep breaths as I tried to assimilate the situation. My mind raced back a few days to my meeting with Dave and the other vampires. "The Bloodline have eyes everywhere. They will know and they will come after you. Soon," Nightingale had warned. I needed to be prepared. I needed to defend myself.

Also, I had a date! Wow, I certainly hadn't seen *that* coming.

But right now I had to focus on stopping an insane lycanthrope and for that I knew I would need certain equipment.

I headed out to see the only man I knew that could help me right now:

Uncle.

Let me tell you about Uncle. Since the Credit Crunch hit and we were all royally screwed by bankers, lawyers and over-priced plumbers, the pawn-broking business has risen in ascendancy and undergone a beatific transformation. The sharp-suited salesmen and the glamorously attired women that we see enticing us with catchy slogans on television may not go by their age-old title and they may not all have a set of three shiny, golden balls hanging from outside a dusty shop-front, but they are pawn-brokers none-the-less whether they just advertise "Cash For Gold!", "Cheques Cashed Here!" or other such niceties of modern life. They are the like that have not really been a daily necessity since our fathers' or (depending on your age) grandfathers' day. They are the vermin that rise up out of the sewer to feast upon the shit that we have blindly let ourselves be dragged into whilst spending the money that we do not really have from employment that is as stable as the foundations of the well-photographed Tower at Pisa. They are the opportunists of old, the drivers of fast cars that would no sooner blink than drown a five-year-old in the spray from their Merc as they speed down the country lane to their lodge meeting where they will quaff fine brandy, smoke fat cigars and proclaim how wonderful things really are and how it's a shame that those damned liberals got rid of the glorious workhouses because they really did fulfil a valuable task in their day, keeping the riff-raff of the street...

Hmmm...

I seem to be ranting once more. I do apologise. I sort of hate the little shits.

So, yeah, these are the modern pawn-brokers, the fly-by-nights who rise and fall with empires built on sand, feasting on the detritus and decay that they themselves have encouraged us to wallow in. They have made the profession less about pawning something against a debt that you will be able to redeem on payday in order to get by and pay off the 'leccy bill and more about sacrificing your house, your life and your first born child in order to position the latest 3D goggle box in the corner of the room for five months until it is obsolete and needs replacing once again.

Then there are the Uncles of this world.

If prostitution is the oldest profession, then Uncle's is the second oldest. After ancient man had enjoyed a jolly good time with an ancient lady of the morning, noon or night, he would have normally realised that he had not a bean to his name and no manner of transport to get him back home. Now, the wheel having only just being invented, it was still an expensive form of transport, but being tuckered out from a number of hours of intense activity, our ancient man was far too shagged out to walk home, so he would have fancied a ride in one of these new-fangled carts. So it was that, as he stood scratching his Cro-Magnon head, he would have heard a polite cough from behind and would have turned to see a short, stooped elderly man smiling at him and paying particularly good attention to our man's hunting knife that was stashed in his belt.

"My boy," says the old man, "that is a very fine knife."

"Indeed it is," replies our man, "fat lot of good it will do me today as I have no means of getting home in time to go hunting."

"Ah, but that is such a pity," sympathises the old man. "For sure you will go hungry tonight and your status in the tribe will diminish."

The old man waits whilst our not so bright caveman takes a while to ponder this fact. "Perhaps I could sell my knife?" the caveman wonders, eyeing the blade's fine flint edge. "It would fetch at least a goat."

The old man scratches his chin as if mulling this possibility over, then sadly shakes his head. "But, my boy," he observes, "you are a hunter, not a knife-maker. How would you feed yourself without your knife and no knowledge of how to make a new one? A desperate conundrum I think, don't you?"

Our ancient man sighs, "What am I to do, old man? I am lost! If only there was some way that someone would lend me a goat against my knife until tomorrow when I could return with payment from my own stock at home!"

The old man smiles and kindly puts an arm around our, not-too-bright hero and says, "Come into my cave, my boy, and let me see what I can arrange for you. By the way," he adds, "are you familiar with the word *interest*?"

And so it has been for time immemorial. Again and again, people have found themselves between a rock and hard place, be it an unexpected baby, the sudden desire to elope with the neighbour's daughter or even a very big, scary man called Vinny. In these moments of crisis they turn to the one place where they will never be scorned, where help is always at hand (albeit coming at a price and with variable rates), and where their precious goods will be kept safe for a fixed period after which they will be sold to reclaim any defaulted debt.

My dad knew all about these type of pawn-brokers. The one where I grew up was Dad's third home. His second home was the bookies, which is why the pawn-broker could only manage bronze. Every Saturday afternoon I would accompany my dad to the local pawn-broker where each week he pawned his pride and joy; his trumpet. His father had scrimped and saved to buy him that instrument when he had been just a kid and he was never going to let it find its way into a stranger's hand because of a bad debt on the gee-gees. No, first he would pawn the trumpet, then he would take the cash and wander up the street to the bookmakers where he would trust his cash into the hands of a six-year old.

"What shall it be today then, Sammy?" he'd asked me. His pale, grey eyes twinkling in the smoky fug of the bookies. I'd look the betting forms up and down and, as usual, I would choose the horse with the silliest sounding name: *My Cousin's Strumpet* or *Four-legged Glue Pot*, that sort of thing. Then my dad would laugh his deep, baritone laugh, run his fingers through his prematurely white hair, and call out to the girl behind the counter, "Wendy! He's picked a winner again," before placing the bet.

Every week he did this and every week we won. Not just once or twice, but three or four times. I'm not convinced that he always went with my selections, but he always told me that he did and there we would sit, cheering as my horses came in before grabbing his winnings and sauntering back down the road, a couple of swells hitting the big time. We would pay his debts, collect his prized trumpet then go home via the tobacconists where he would buy himself a Cuban cigar, me a bag of pick and mix and my mum a box of Black Magic.

Good days. Very good days.

Before he got ill.

So it was that these warm, sepia memories filled me with a satisfying familiarity as the brass bell above Uncle's shop door tinkled and I stepped through into a rose-tinted part of my childhood. The painful memories of my dad's last days tried to claw at me and drag me down, but I fought them off with a stick sharp enough to fatally wound a mammoth and found myself smiling with genuine pleasure as the old man bustled up behind the counter.

"Samuel!" he smiled. "It's been a while, my boy. How are you?"

I looked through the toughened safety glass that ran the length of the counter and smiled to myself. Yes, Uncle was one of nature's constants. Dickens would have adored him – a complete stereotypical pawn-broker. He wore his Jewishness with pride; small round spectacles perched on the tip of his long nose and a black skull cap fastened securely on his fine, greying hair. He was adorned in a Scrooge-like housecoat over a bulky green woollen jumper that provided much needed warmth to his fragile frame which had shrunken with the onset of old age. His gnarled, arthritic fingertips were stained yellow from the burning tar of countless cheap, self-rolled cigarettes.

"I'm not too bad, Uncle. How are you?"

"Oh, Samuel," he waved a nicotine-stained hand in mock affliction, "it would take me from now to the hereafter to tell you of my woes and ailments. This body gets no younger, you know? My heart flutters, my prostate burns and my kidneys ache. I tell you, my boy, it will be soon that one of these mornings I shall wake up dead! Then what shall I do? Who will run my business? A worry, it is. Such a worry." He slipped me a conspiratorial wink and rubbed a finger against his cheek. "But enough of such pleasantries. I think that you have need of my services, yes? What is it this time, Samuel, hmmm? You have drunk your savings away again, is it? Or perhaps..." he paused dramatically, "Yes, perhaps you have need of capital to bail out that heathen priest friend of yours. Yes, I bet it is that, isn't it?"

I chuckled lightly. "No Uncle. I am neither broke nor at the beck and call of Spliff."

The elderly man's brown eyes twinkled in the dusty half-light. "It is not money you seek, you say? Well, well, well. Perhaps you have need of other services, I feel. Services that might be best discussed in private?"

I heard a dull click and the counter door swung outwards.

"Well come on, Samuel. Make with it. I am old, you know. I do not have all day. I might be dead this afternoon."

I smiled and entered behind the counter before following Uncle into his back room.

Five minutes later and the air hung heavy around us. I sipped nervously at a small cup of the strongest brewed coffee known to humanity and waited. It was all that I could do. Uncle was never one to be rushed. He always weighed up the situation thoughtfully and meticulously. He sat there in front of me, his eyes staring straight out in front of him, the flames from the log fire dancing on the lenses of his small spectacles and his arms involuntarily pulling the housecoat tight about him as if an unwelcome chill had just seeped into the room.

As I waited, I let my eyes flit around the old man's parlour. I had been back here a number of times, but every time I ventured into the inner sanctum I always found something new to fascinate me.

Today my eyes rested on a thing of pure beauty. It was a length of lacquered brass twisted round on itself, narrow at one end and bell shaped at the other, inserted with three mother of pearl inlaid valves in the middle. I longed to hear the resonant sound of the trumpet sing out in the stillness of the room. Instead all I could hear was the crackling of the fire and the ringing of faulty inner ears.

"It is a nice piece, yes?"

I jumped slightly. I had been unaware that Uncle had been watching me. "Yes." My voice croaked in surprise and I sipped some pure, unadulterated caffeine to soothe it. "My father had one almost identical."

The old man nodded. "You have not got your father's instrument?"

"No." I shook my head and looked back up at the trumpet hanging from the wall.

"Where is it?"

"I... I don't know. He has been dead some time now."

Uncle picked up his coffee cup, tipped some of the drink into the saucer and slurped it up. "Your father is dead and you do not know where the thing is that he treasured? Most peculiar... like so many other things."

"Uncle," I took a breath, "I didn't come here for a trumpet."

He shrugged before setting his cup and saucer back down on the rosewood coffee table. "You know I came over from Poland during World War Two, don't you, Samuel?"

I nodded. A large Polish community had established itself here during that period. They had settled and were an integral part of Lancaster's diversity.

"I was very young back then. Ten or twelve, I think. So many years have passed, you know? It is hard to keep track." He leaned back into his winged chair and let his eyes dwell on the crackling flames that snapped and spat in the hearth. "It was my father's brother who got me out. My *uncle*." He smiled at the word. "It was a hell of a journey, across war-torn countryside and taking our chances across borders, but that is another story, my boy. Let me tell you about something that occurred on the day that we left.

"Our village had a youngish rabbi. I can't remember his age, but my father always joked that his beard must have been false as he was not old enough to spit let alone shave. Anyway, as the war dragged on and anti-Semitism grew, our rabbi became more and more introverted. He would be seen less and less at public functions, those that there were and they were few and far between, I am sure you can imagine. Rumours spread that he was sick, and not sick of the body, you know? When people went to visit him, he would barely open the door to his guests, but what they saw was a shadow of a man. He was gaunt and thin, his hair unkempt and he rarely wore more than his pyjamas.

"Then one day, the order came through. *The* order. You know what I mean?"

I nodded soberly. The final solution.

"As the trains rolled into the village and the stormtroopers herded us like cattle into the market square, the young rabbi burst out of his house dressed in dirty, foul-smelling rags and brandishing some sort of spray of herbs. I did not know what they were or how he had managed to obtain them, but the flowers were yellow and the leaves bright green. They smelt almost as pungent as he did. He rolled into the square and positioned himself between the soldiers and the terrified villagers. His eyes rolled with that movement that is only used by those whose sanity has deserted this realm and he shouted out, 'I have you! I have you now! You will fail in this atrocity!'

Needless to say, the Germans shouted at the young man to be quiet and their guns clanked and clattered as they levelled them, nervously training them on him. Looking back, the soldiers were probably even younger than the rabbi and very much aware that, although they had the weapons, we vastly outnumbered them. They would not want to provoke a riot by gunning down the village's holy man.

"But he refused to be quiet. 'This is your day of doom! This is the day of wrath! You think you can destroy our nation? Do you? Pah!' He waved the bitter-smelling herbs at the soldiers and spat at the men in uniform, 'Great powers protect us. Greater powers than most would admit to. One of them came to me and told me this would happen. He said that you would herd us like your heathen swine to the slaughter. Well it will not happen. We are not pigs! He has told me of great things. He has told me how he built the Great Temple of Solomon, of how he commanded creatures of far superior strength than you. He told me how to control you!'

"His eyes seemed to lose the listlessness of insanity and burned with the ire of rage. Standing tall and pointing at the soldiers he declared, 'Do my bidding in the name of the Hidden One! Do my bidding in the name of Asmodeus!'"

Uncle paused and sipped some more coffee from his saucer. I realised that I was literally sat on the edge of my seat and remembered at that point that I needed to breathe. "Well?" I asked, "What happened?"

Uncle gave another one of his little shrugs. "They shot the crazy son of a bitch." He pointed to his forehead. "Pop! Right there, between the eyes. Then all levels of hell broke loose. The riot, that the soldiers had so wanted to prevent, erupted like pus from an inflamed boil. There was shot after shot as villagers started to fall down dead. Those who did not die in the first volley charged the soldiers and tried to overpower them. Some succeeded, most died. I felt a pair of hands grip my shoulders and drag me away down an alley. It was my uncle. As we ran, I glanced back over my shoulder and saw a most curious sight. There, in the shadowed doorway of the dead rabbi's house stood a figure clad in black. At first I thought he was a German officer, but then I realised that he wore no insignia - just black, sharply cut clothes, and he was watching the massacre. Watching it and obviously enjoying it. A wide smile was spread across his pale-skinned face. Then he casually ran his fingers through his dark hair, turned and walked away, unhindered by anyone at all. No one charged him. No shot struck him.

"It was as if he could not be seen by anyone except for me.

"It was as if he were *hidden*.

"Then my feet were running so fast that my brain was struggling to keep up. Thoughts of crazy rabbis and dark strangers had to be cast aside in favour of desires to live and escape." He finished his coffee and settled back into his armchair.

We sat in silence as I tapped my finger tips on my teeth in thought, then finally, I asked, "This is all very well and good, Uncle, but what does it have to do with my request?"

He threw his hands in the air. "Oy vey! What are you? A schmuck? You come in here asking for silver bullets for this little toy," he waved at the pistol that lay between us on the coffee table - the one that I had removed from the John O'Gaunt studios on Monday, "and I tell you a story about a rabbi who consorted with demons only to wind up dead and you do not see the meaning of the cautionary tale? Samuel, Samuel, some things are not meant to be tampered with. They are there. We all know that. We feel them in the shadows, we hear them in our nightmares, but they are best left hidden, out of sight. If they were to be brought out into the light of day, what evil would they wreak on us? What destruction would they bring? My boy, I do not want to see you ending up like my young rabbi." Tears were close to brimming over from his eyes. The old boy really meant it.

I chose my next words very carefully. "Uncle, I appreciate, your concern, but I have reason to believe that this werewolf wants me dead. I don't know why, but I have it on good authority that I am a marked man. I just want to defend myself."

"Defend yourself?" he harrumphed. "This sounds more like a preemptive strike, my boy. And who told you that wolfie was gunning for your blood, eh? A reliable source? Someone you can trust?"

"A vampire." I cringed. The words were out before I could stop them.

"A vampire? A vampire? First a werewolf, now a vampire." Uncle leant across and grabbed my hand. "Samuel, Samuel, do you not see what trouble you are getting yourself into here? Please, I beg you. Let it be, my boy."

I shook my head. "I can't, Uncle. There's something set in motion and I have no desire to be crushed under its momentum. Please, help me."

The old man's shoulder's slouched in resignation. "Silver bullets, you say? The stuff of fancy, I feel. I will see what I can do, but I make no promises, you hear?"

I nodded my appreciation.

He picked up the small gun and tossed it over to me as if it was hot enough to burn his fingers. "Now take this little balloon-popper and get out of here," the pawn-broker growled. "I will bring something of more use round to your office later. Go! Before I change my mind."

Spliff has always been one for research - even more so than me. When we were at university he was the one who would go missing for days on end, chasing up the slightest lead on some obscure cult that existed for a few months on some far-flung Polynesian island, just to confirm that the human psyche was capable of looking at a blade of grass in a certain manner. It was during this period that he started to put the weight on. Now, I'm not saying that my best mate is fat, far from it, but he is, you know, portly. He looks like he lives too much of the high life when in fact he spends most of his time just eating out and microwaving convenience food in order to let him get on with his reading. When I first knew him, back in our fresher's year, he was pencil thin, but as the book addiction grew, so did the waistline.

Now me, on the other hand, I have always felt a tad uncomfortable trawling through the fusty archives. Not that I have anything against the books themselves. Like I've previously commented, I was always one for hiding off with piles of them. However, when I was at university, the ones that I wanted always seemed to be guarded by those ageing librarians with medusa stares. You know the sort. You will be innocently browsing through the stacks for whatever takes your fancy at the moment when the nape of your neck twitches and you feel them there, somewhere. You glance over your shoulder and observe that you are alone, but that twitching little rodent inside you can sense them as clear as if they were coiled up on the top shelf waiting to pounce down on you. You grab the book and hurry to the desk with your heart in your throat only to be greeted by a knowing look that says, "Oh yes, I know all about you. I know I am far, far superior to you in every way and one day, when your back is turned, you will be mine..."

Or perhaps it's just me.

Anyway, these days the information that you seek is more or less at your fingertips. Give me Google any day. The whole cyberspace explosion is a wonder to me. These days we can chat to someone in Australia whilst watching re-runs of *Father Ted* when we should be looking up train times to Preston. It is amazing! This stuff had only just been spawned when I was a student. The whole computer thing was mainly still the realm of pale-skinned, greasy-haired individuals who lurked in a darkened technology lab referred to as "The Pit". Normal people either did not want to or were not able to understand what it was these tech-heads were talking about when they babbled such incoherent phrases such as PC, internet and network. And as for apples? Well they were just fruit, weren't they? But today....

Well, it really is amazing, isn't it?

So, when I got back from Uncle's and after wrapping the pistol up in a tea towel then stashing it in the bottom drawer of my filing cabinet, I booted up my laptop and settled down at my desk for some research. As Google found me the site for Williamson Park, I poured a large whiskey and lit up a Lucky. With two clicks I had read all the facts about its location; "...situated in a commanding position overlooking Lancaster City Centre ...approximately 5 minutes from junction 34 of the M6 motorway," its main attractions; "sundial... Ashton Memorial... Butterfly House... Mini-Zoo," and its visitor's centre opening hours; "10am – 5pm April to September, 10am – 4pm October to March."

Now, why would I need a big, dusty book and a hard stare for that?

After jotting down my newly acquired information I clicked on the link about the mini-zoo. I was greeted with bright, cheery pictures of various exotic reptiles, small, fluffy mammals and brightly coloured birds. Then, at the bottom of the page shone a flashing link that really caught my eye: "New this season: Driver Ants!"

"What the hell are they?" I mumbled as I clicked the link; "Ants in cars?"

Not quite. Driver ants were in fact the famous ants found in Africa that were known for eating anything that got in their way. They could strip a carcass in seconds, carrying every tasty morsel back to the colony and their queen. "Nice one for the kiddies," I grimaced. Well, I supposed it was a handy way of disposing of any dead rabbits or guinea pigs from the fluffier side of the zoo.

As I scanned the page of the mini-zoo, a couple of pictures leapt out at me. There, showing crowds of enthusiastic primary school kids around the birds and the reptiles were the Hawkins siblings. I clicked on a photo of Nathan Hawkins smiling up at a white parakeet that was perched on his shoulder and studied it in Photo Viewer. Was this the face of a werewolf or just a crazed individual? My eyes looked him over for any tell-tale signs. Sure, he was a bit bushier than the average guy and he looked like he shunned the normal niceties of brushed hair, but the guy worked with animals, and in my experience, this was a standard uniform for those whose best friends had more than two legs. I'd been to the cattery with Spliff to pick Dante up a number of times. When you're dealing with animals, then social niceties such as the absence of aroma de cat piss or an immaculate makeup regimen are not a requirement.

Hawkins looked like just a normal guy.

I needed more first-hand details. I had to head up to the park.

A downright miserable mood settled itself on my shoulders as I stomped around Williamson Park in a futile fug looking for clues that either weren't there or had been dragged off by the resident rabbits to the deepest depths of their labyrinthine warrens. What on earth was I supposed to find to suggest that a werewolf worked here? Paw prints? A ragged scrap of fur? Wolf droppings? It was ridiculous and I knew it. Even if Hawkins was a werewolf, how was I supposed to confirm the fact?

I looked at my watch. It was just after seven and the light was starting to fade. I let out a deep sigh and fished into my pockets to pull out my cigarettes. I tapped out a Lucky and, as I lit it, a voice from behind commented, "They really are very bad for your health, you know."

I spun round and stared at a teenage boy with scruffy, dark hair wearing a grey hoodie, a small back-pack slung over his shoulder. "You!" I shouted, almost dropping my ciggie.

Alec grinned and darted off across the park. I took up pursuit, my trench coat flapping behind me like the wings of a rather out of breath bat. He raced past the small lake and over the gravel area in front of the Ashton Memorial. He made it look so effortless. My lungs were already starting to burn as I pounded my legs across the unforgiving surface in an attempt to keep up with him. His young feet swept him nimbly up the brow of the hill by the children's play area to the cafe and mini-zoo. My feet, however, tried to fold together and trip me up on the grass. I refused to let my treacherous limbs confound me and carried on running in a staggering lope as best as I could.

When he reached the zoo, Alec turned and grinned at me. The little git was enjoying this! I ground to a halt, my chest burning hard, as the steep incline took its toll and I staggered slowly up to the top. I tried to gesticulate in an annoyed manner with the ciggie I still held between my fingers. Instead, my poor lungs gave up and I doubled up gasping for air. After a few ragged deep breaths, I was about to swear profoundly at him when I noticed that his hand was pointing to something on the wall of the zoo. Then, just as he had behind the Sugar House a few nights previous, he vanished into thin air.

"Sod! I hate it when you do that!" I dragged myself over to the zoo and crouched down to where he had been pointing. I was rather glad that the park was empty. If anyone had seen me they might have thought that I was a dog piss inspector or something. I mean, why else would someone be inspecting the side of a brick wall about thirty centimetres up from the ground.

At first I saw nothing, but then I realised that the encroaching twilight and raised blood pressure was dimming my vision. I peered harder and saw something etched into the wall. I ran my fingers over it. Yes, there was definitely something there.

I looked even closer. There was a circle scraped into the brickwork and on each side radiated out three straight lines. It looked like a child's picture of the sun. There was one difference though. This "sun" had been painted in with green paint which was chipped and was beginning to fade.

I drummed my fingers against my teeth and grimaced. What the hell was this? Why did he want to show it to me? I stood up. "So what the hell is that supposed to mean?" There was no reply. "Look, I know you're still here," this was somewhat of a guess, albeit a logical deduction that he would want to make sure that I understood his message, "so why don't you just come out and explain it?"

There was a soft breeze behind my right ear and a hand fell on my shoulder. "You really should read more books, Sam," said a young male voice, then everything changed.

I was warm, really warm. Instinctively I went to undo my shirt collar and take off my trench coat.

My hand passed straight through my neck. "Okay, that's weird," I muttered. I lifted my fingers in front of my face and gave them a quick wiggle. They were quite transparent, as was the rest of me. I was aware of my outline and my physical form, but I was quite insubstantial, like something composed from a clear gas. "Well I guess that's kind of cool. Now where am I? Ah." I looked up the street where I was standing and saw a row of sphinxes lining a rather grand looking, sandy boulevard. "I guess we're not in Kansas anymore, Toto."

So, I was in Egypt, psychically if not physically. The question was, *when* in Egypt? Modern day or a touch earlier? I went for a casual stroll down the boulevard feeling rather amused when I realised that I left no footprints in the sand. When I reached the first of the sphinxes I ran my hand through its giant paw. The stone looked smooth to the touch and the edges were sharply chiselled. It was fresh, new. I guessed that I had travelled back in time. The next question was "Why?"

"What do you want, Alec?" I mumbled. "Why have you sent me here?" I continued to walk down the boulevard. It then struck me that it was dark. A full moon hung in the night sky. My stomach automatically felt rather sick. "I've got a very bad feeling about this."

There was a huge building down the end of the street and in front of it stood an imposing statue. From my distance I assumed that it was of Anubis. I could make out the jackal-head that identified the statue as the god of mummification and the afterlife – a big player in the Egyptian Pantheon. However, as I drew closer, I realised that I was wrong.

Terribly wrong.

Whereas Anubis had the sleek face of a jackal, this idol was adorned with a canine head that sported a somewhat more ragged look. Wild fur was sprouting from its scalp and a short, snarling muzzle was bejewelled with an array of vicious-looking teeth. The werewolf stood bare-chested, its arms held out in an aggressive display of raw power and round its stone neck it wore a medallion, a round, green stone that seemed to shine in the bright moonlight.

I suddenly wanted to be somewhere else very quickly, even more so when I became aware of movement. All around me, things were stirring in the shadows: big, sleek, stealthy things which imbued the warm night air with a taste of menace. I started to back my way down the boulevard as one by one the werewolves emerged into the light of the full moon. They ignored me completely and made their way to the base of the statue. There must have been dozens of them. I lost count after about thirty or so, panic had devastated my ability to use numbers of more than one digit. Then, as one, they raised their heads to the sky and howled.

I tried in vain to cover my non-corporeal ears with my insubstantial hands. The sound was sickening to the core, an ululation that would fill anyone lower in the food chain with dread. I had seen enough. I wanted to leave this place. I needed to leave.

Then it was cooler again. Much, much cooler and I was standing, shivering in front of the mini-zoo at Williamson Park, Lancaster. It was a cold, October evening and the wolves were far, far away – a distant memory.

I turned and faced the young psychic, words failing to form in my lips.

"That must never happen again," he stated, then vanished once more.

I left Williamson Park somewhat shaken and despondent. What was it that I had experienced? Had I actually travelled back in time or was it a waking dream, some sort of vision? I didn't know. All I could be sure of was one certainty, that the boy named Alec was exceptionally gifted and incredibly powerful. He didn't seem malevolent, quite the opposite. He had helped me out how many times now? Three? But he did not hang around much. He just popped in, did his thing, then vanished like Will O' The Wisp. There was something about him that disconcerted me.

*Something?* Who was I kidding? There was a bundle of stuff too vast to count. The boy was a complete mystery, but as long as he was a help, not a hindrance, I could hardly criticise him. I would just have to accept him for what he was; a Mona Lisa smile, an enigma.

Then there was the content of what he showed me. Ancient Egypt at the mercy of werewolves? Well that never made the history books, did it? I enjoy my history programmes, especially the archaeology ones and I have not yet seen Zahi Hawass or Robert Richmond standing over the mummified remains of a lycanthrope. So, surely, if it happened, then it must have been a short period, a flash in the pan. The Egyptians were good at erasing people from history, look at what they did to both Hapshetsut and Akenahten. They were both seen as an affront to the natural order of the kingdom so their monuments were desecrated and defaced. As far as their successors were concerned, they never existed and they would not exist in the afterlife, either. Perhaps that was the same with the werewolves? Perhaps their reign of fear was short and not so sweet, then they were overcome and the page of papyrus that they occupied was cast into the four corners of the Sahara?

And what was that medallion, the green stone that shone so bright in the darkness of the night? I thought about the symbol drawn on the side of the mini-zoo. Were they one and the same? Was it a relic that meant something to the werewolves? It had to be, surely? Their leader was wearing it after all.

I needed more information. That meant research. More bloody research. As I walked across Dalton Square I cast my eyes up to the clock tower on the Town Hall. Its baleful eye shone yellow in the darkening sky and told me that it was getting on for ten o'clock. Was it that time already? How long had I been out of it in the park? It had only seemed like minutes. Suddenly I felt oh so weary and I longed for a warm bed to keep out the cruel autumn chill, but research is a cruel mistress and she must be served.

You really should read more books, Sam.

I snorted as I stomped up the stairs to my office and let myself in. Sod that! I clunked the door shut behind me and, as the laptop booted up, poured myself a drink. Then, as Chrome loaded, I selected something loud to keep my concentration alert and, as my eyes grew heavier from trailing legions of hearsay regarding lycanthropes around cyberspace, Tom Waits' gravelly voice intoned that it was time to sail for Singapore. When Uncle Vernon was as independent as a hog on ice, I read that the oldest werewolf story dated to just 1591 in Germany and was a man called Stubbe. By the time the Big Black Mariah came rumbling across my speakers, I had found that the Greeks believed Zeus had turned the King Lycaon into a wolf and this was thought to be at the origin of the word lycanthrope, coming from the Greek words lykos (wolf) and anthropos (man). As some men did it for diamonds, my mind boggled at the various theories that were extrapolated as to how one became a werewolf, the most common being infection from another werewolf's bite.

It must have been when Tom was telling me to hang down my head in sorrow that I realised I had started to snore. I jerked up suddenly and intuitively looked around. My office. I was just in my office. There was no sand, no fur, no god-awful howling. I rubbed my eyes, drained my bourbon and rose stiffly from my chair to stretch. My spine creaked and cracked - it felt so good. I poured another drink to soothe the aches and licked my lips. I reached over to my discarded trench coat and rummaged in a pocket to pull out a packet of cigarettes. As the white packet slid out, something glinted and tumbled out, bouncing on the carpet. I frowned and stooped to pick it up. It was the silver pendant that Melanie Brande, that sweet-talking cherub (note the sarcasm) had been wearing when she and her co-stars had tried to sacrifice me. Was that only a few days ago? It seemed a lifetime away. I dangled the little chimera in front of me, its two heads – one goat, one lion – seemingly glaring at me with a spite synonymous of its erstwhile wearer as it swished its serpent's tail.

My mind was numb with werewolves. I fancied a little change. While horses came down Violin Road, Google instructed me that Chimera was a beast from Ancient Greek mythology which was slain by Bellerophon whilst the hero rode the winged horse Pegasus. The last thing I remembered thinking before sleep took a firm grasp of me and led me into the wonderful world of Nod was, "That wasn't in *Clash of the Titans*."

There was the beating of wings. The wind was whipping across my face as I clung onto the person in front of me for grim death. "We'll soon be there," came the gravelly voice of Tom Waits from over his shoulder. The smell of dark bar rooms, musty perspiration and cheap aftershave crawled up into my nose.

"Where are we going?" I shouted across the deafening beat of Pegasus' snowy white wings.

"To Singapore. We have to stop it."

"The Chimera?"

He turned his head and his sharp eyes bored into mine. "Not exactly," he growled and the wind left my lungs as his callused hand sharply shoved me off the back of the flying horse.

Okay, so I was dreaming. That was okay. I had fallen asleep listening to Tom Waits and reading about the Chimera. It all made sense up until the point where the drunken bastard had pushed me off the bloody horse. Why had he done that? No matter. This was a dream. I would just stretch my arms out, flap them like wings and...

Continue to fall.

The atmosphere screamed past my face as I maniacally flapped my useless limbs like a demented Wile E Coyote. I had been thwarted by a phantasmagorical Roadrunner once more. I was going to plummet to the bottom of the canyon and no amount of Acme product was going to save my neck. The desert floor was racing up to greet me and try as I may, I could not get my arms to work. I could not fly. I should be able to fly.

I shut my eyes and turned my face away from impending disaster as I could start to make out sharp rocks and boulders below, then suddenly I stopped and hung still in mid-air, before starting to move horizontally.

My arms had worked. I was flying.

I made to flap them only to find that movement was impossible. They were being held fast by a number of small hands. The fairies glistened iridescently as their tiny wings beat in a furious manner to keep me aloft. They seemed so vibrant compared to the wasteland that surrounded us. There was a large booming noise and the air around us shuddered. We rounded a corner and I saw the source of the disturbance. There, atop a bleak hillside fought two massive dragons. One was obsidian black with huge, gnarled wings and the other was blood red with seven heads. Primal screams shrieked from their fang-lined mouths as their claws slashed relentlessly into each other. Huge clods of blood and gouges of skin and scales flew across the valley beneath them. Wherever the debris fell, the land burst into immutable flame. The heat from this was intense and scorching. I felt as if I was stood at the brim of an erupting volcano that was spewing out lava.

The fairies set me down in the valley beneath the battle. I turned to protest, but they had vanished. Instead I saw two large armies stood facing each other. Surprise, surprise, I was in the middle. On one side stood an army clad in the purest white. The mid-day sun shone off their beatific faces and their wings fluttered in the breeze. Unmistakably angels. On the other stood creatures the like of which I had never laid eyes on before. They were roughly humanoid in shape, but were totally featureless. What heads they had seemed to be sunken into their shoulders as they were possessed of no kind of neck. Their limbs were long and gaunt and seemed to be the colour of wet clay.

Then darkness fell like a suffocating duvet and the armies changed. Where once stood the faceless creatures, prowled a restless pack of werewolves, their coal-black eyes darting left to right, seeking prey to devour. Where the angels had been, was a group of soberly clad vampires, their pale skin devoid of emotion in the light of the full moon.

I had seen enough and I tried to run but, once again, I could not move. My arms were tied to two stout poles. I tugged and grunted but they would not come free. Instead the cords dug deep into my wrists. I looked the poles up and down. Each of them had an object dangling from its top; green hemispherical stones that pulsed rhythmically in the night like a pair of living hearts. Green vapour teased its way down from the stones and encircled me. It smelt sweet like incense in a church or bread in my mother's oven. As I inhaled the smoke, I felt every sense in my body sharpen. I had been dead before I had known the stones and now I was truly alive. I longed to hold them in my grasping hands, to draw them together and mend their brokenness.

There was a whisper of movement and I knew a vampire stood behind me. "Oh, Sam," came the sad, sad voice of Dave. "How could you?"

Then I was alone, my arms and legs were still bound firm, but now I was lying on the hard floor of a darkened room at John O'Gaunt Media. I craned my neck and saw the ubiquitous pentagram once more. This time there were no crazed actors, but on the wall was a lilac coloured banner. It was emblazoned with a large golden "T" shape that was entwined with two snaking wavy lines.

Footsteps approached and Alec knelt down next to me on one knee. He was holding a small brass bell that was adorned with a jersey cow on its handle. He was ringing the bell back and forth and the tinkling noise was starting to fill my ears. "Why am I not surprised to see you here?" I moaned, laying my head back on the cold, hard floor.

"Oh, there are far more surprises yet to come," smiled a voice I had not heard before.

I lifted my head back up and saw that Alec had been replaced by a stranger. He looked about my age, had dark hair and was dressed in a black denim jacket which bore two small, round badges: one was a CND symbol, the other bore the word "Prefect". As he smiled down (and might I add it was not a very nice smile) from beneath a pair of dark sunglasses a kind of warm penumbra emanated around his person and in the lenses of his glasses I saw two items reflected; a chalice and a sword.

"Who are you?" I asked as the ringing from the small brass bell (which I now recognised as being an ornament on my mother's mantelpiece) started to rise higher and became more and more insistent.

The stranger peered down at me and removed his glasses. Where pupils should have been, fire danced in his eyes. "We," he said, "are one."

For the second time that week my drunken slumber was harshly broken by the discordant hammering of my accursed nemesis, the confounded creation of Alexander Graham Bell. My eyes creaked open and checked my watch: ten-fifteenish, give or take a blur. I lifted my head off my desk and my legs pivoted me round on my chair. My arm shot out towards the phone which my hand fumbled from its cradle.

"Hello?" I croaked.

The voice on the other end was clear, so at least I had it the right way up this time, but my brain was still trying to catch up with my body. "Sorry, could you repeat that please?" I asked.

"Sam? Is that you, you sound awful?"

My forehead creased as I tried to place the voice. It was brisk, well-clipped and had the slight trace of an accent. Indian accent? "Jitendra?" I asked. "Yeah, sorry. I'm fine." I stretched my free arm and yawned into the mouthpiece.

"You don't *sound* fine," the DCI observed. "Listen, if this is a bad time, I can call back later." I smiled slightly. There was genuine concern in his voice.

"No, seriously, I'm fine. Just woke up. Late night. A case thing. I didn't know you guys worked on a Saturday." I paused. "It *is* Saturday, isn't it? I've kind of lost track."

"I'm a policeman, Sam. Always on duty, you know?"

I chuckled raggedly into the mouthpiece, "Yeah, you and me both, apparently." I coughed harshly and my eyes scanned the room for a source of liquid. My mouth felt like the backside of a camel in a sand storm. I spied an open bottle of Jack Daniel's, grabbed it, swigged it, and started to feel somewhat better.

"Okay, if you say so." I heard a rustle of paper at the other end – the rearrangement of notes. "I thought you ought to know that we've just about got what we can out of your abductors."

My mind was blank. There was a stilted silence. Abductors? I was still here - I hadn't been abducted.

Jitendra could obviously read my morning confusion. "The satanic cult? Baines and his little playmates?"

"Oh, yes." My fingers played with the silver necklace that lay next to my sleeping place. "Yeah, sorry. Like I say. Late night. What's going to happen to them?"

"Well, obviously, they will be standing trial, but we need a bit more meat on the bones yet. Needless to say we're starting to probe into their backgrounds and lives, but we will need some more information from your good self. I thought we could meet next week?"

I nodded. My head started to hurt. I rummaged in a drawer for some aspirin. "Sounds fine. Sounds good." I wrestled with a tub and washed two pills down with a swig from the bottle of whiskey. "Oh!" Inspiration hit.

"What?"

"While I've got you, I could use a bit of a favour."

There was a short pause. "Depends on the favour."

"It's to do with this case I'm working on. I could use some info on a suspect. I need to know if he has any previous."

"Okay. Shouldn't be too hard. As long as you're discreet with your sources."

I downed the rest of the whiskey. My stomach started to feel warm and relaxed. "Your secret will remain safe with me. You shall be as nameless as the woman at the house of Simon the Leper."

"Pardon?"

I chuckled down the phone. "Mark 14.9. Just look it up."

"Sure." His voice was hesitant. "When do you need the information?"

I thought about the big white disc that was going to rise that night. "This afternoon?"

"You don't ask for much, do you? Should be alright. What's the individual's name?"

I told him and said that Hawkins had a sister called Simone and that they worked at Williamson Park. We arranged for Jitendra to come round about two and, after hanging up, I shambled off for a shower. Five bracing minutes later, I was almost passable for human. I was clean and smelt of whatever chemicals in the shower gel were trying to pass for flowers and spice, but my head still churned; not so much from alcohol abuse but from the desire to learn more about the case. Hawkins was still a mystery to me and I was loathe to sit on my hands until Jitendra came round in about three and a half hours. That moon was rising tonight and I was far from prepared to meet whatever was going to present itself.

It was at that moment that inspiration hit from one of the other major organs of my body. My stomach noisily reminded me that I had not yet eaten. My eyes watched the long hand of the station clock tick round to the seven. Ten thirty-five – too late for a decent breakfast, too early for a proper lunch. I could grab something on the hoof in town.

Of course! Bob! I would go and grab a burger from Bob with a dressing of information. Burger Bob had his own little business in the centre of town selling grilled produce of questionable definition and heavenly taste. He was privy to all sorts of gossip and I was sure I had seen him touting his wares up at the park from time to time. I grabbed my hat and my coat then headed off to feed my stomach and my head.

I love Lancaster on a Saturday. It really buzzes, you know? The street market is out and people mill around all over the place. It's great just weaving your way through the crowds picking up snippets of conversation, watching the shoppers and savouring the smells of fresh veg and freshly cooked food.

The food aromas have two main sources. The first is around the former fountain in Market Square. The smells here are the firmly traditional blended with the distinctly exotic. Along with the vendor selling freshly baked bread and the huge veg stall with all manner of legumes, brassicas, potatoes, onions and fruit (English and foreign), there's Indian food, Chinese food and a guy who sells falafel and other such delights. The other culinary epicentre is down where Cheapside meets Church Street.

This is the realm of Burger Bob.

Now, I'm no meat-eater and I really don't like the smell of it cooking (the bacon thing does not work with me at all), but I take my hat off to Bob. He always has a string of clientele backed up the way queuing for his "Locally Produced Hand-Cooked Burgers." I dutifully joined the end of the line and waited for my turn to shuffle itself up before ordering my little dose of heaven in a bun served with a garnish of reliable information. You see, the thing with Bob is that he has been here for time immemorial and, as a result, he sees things come and go that others miss. Also, while people wait for their food, they talk to him and, while he grills that little piece of sustenance, he listens. He listens intently, stores it away and is able to recall it with incredible detail.

"Sam!" he called out whilst deftly flipping a trio of his burgers over and reaching for two more. "Good to see you. You hungry?"

"I sure am," I said, "on two counts."

Bob looked me up and down, nodded appreciatively and tossed a kidney bean special on the grill along with some chopped onions and sliced tomatoes. The beanie goodness sauntered enticingly up towards my nose and my stomach growled hungrily in response. I felt like I hadn't eaten for a week.

"It'll just take a couple of minutes," he said as the customers in front of me headed off with their burgers. "You'd better be quick."

"You've catered for things up at the park, haven't you?" I asked. "Quite a few times, am I right?"

"Sure." He pressed down gently on my burger, easing out a seductive hiss. "They always get me in for things during the summer. They may know their flora and fauna, but when it comes to mass catering..." He let the sentence trail off as a mischievous smile filled his face and he chuckled to himself.

"You ever meet a guy called Nathan Hawkins?"

He nodded. The smile vanished as he flipped my burger.

"And?"

"You wanna stay away from him, Sam. He's trouble."

"What kind of trouble? *My* kind of trouble?"

Bob shrugged. "You hear stuff, you know?" He grabbed a white bun and sliced it down the middle. "Weird stuff. He can be sweetness and light on the surface, but underneath..." He squeezed a generous squirt of mustard into the bun, "there's something quite sour."

"Specifics, Bob."

He lifted the edge of my burger to see if it was ready. "Well, summer just gone, there was an incident when a young girl was messing around in the small animals' section. Little kid, yeah?" He flipped my burger into the bun, topped it with the grilled veg and closed the bread lid down. "Just a kid, about six or seven. Well, he went ape shit. Now, I know we all have bad days, but Hawkins..." Bob handed me the burger. "Like I said; sour. Oh, damn it!" A blast of loud pop music blared out from across the other side of the pedestrian precinct. "I thought she wasn't here today!"

I bit into my burger and smiled as I watched the source of the chef's ire. There, next to a large CD player was a young woman in her mid-twenties, made up to perfection and dressed like she was off to attend an executive meeting.

However, executives don't jiggle up and down in the street to Abba's *Dancing Queen*.

"Hey! Betty!" Bob yelled at the top of his voice, waving a spatula in the air. "Knock it off will ya? You'll piss me customers off!"

Betty was oblivious to Bob, just as she normally is to everything else. Betty, or Boombox Betty as locals know her, is widely considered to not just be a sandwich short of a picnic, but a completely empty hamper. Every day she will stand over the road from Bob and every day she will dance to her heart's content to whatever music grabs her fancy.

Like I said, today it was *Dancing Queen*.

I know it really gets to Bob, the poor guy has to put up with it every day, but it does make me chuckle seeing him get so irate over something so innocent. Right now he was reeling off expletives that would make Roy Chubby Brown blush. I decided that I would get no more information, so I wandered back up Cheapside, chuckling to myself and devouring my burger of the gods. I paused at Horseshoe Corner and mentally checked myself. Here I was in the middle of a potentially horrific case and I was finding time to laugh. Was I becoming numb to the situation? Was this week starting to mould itself around me like a snugly fitting glove of everyday reality? Surely not? I shrugged and finished the burger then tucked the napkin into my pocket after wiping my lips clean. As I weaved in and out of the Saturday shoppers and street evangelists of Penny Street, I studied the faces of those who bustled past me, oblivious to my presence. I was just another random Joe in the crowd. I was no one special - another face on a chilly autumn day in Lancaster. These people had no idea what I had been through this week. They were oblivious to what might face me this evening. All they were concerned about was finishing their weekly shop and getting home to the warmth and love of their family homes. Those who had families, of course. Those who didn't... I thought about my empty flat above my office. I had been alone how many years now? Fourteen years? Fifteen, was it? I had lost track. It seemed like only yesterday that Caroline had said we were finished and that she could never, ever love me.

She had said that *no one* could ever love me.

Dull clouds blotted out my bright mood and I thrust my hands into my coat pockets. One of them found my Zippo. My thumb slowly traced the outline of the pyramid that was moulded in the brass finish. I grunted as a burning sensation washed across my chest. I decided it was heartburn from eating the burger too quick and continued back up Penny Street. Enough of these thoughts about the past, I told myself. It was dead and buried. It couldn't touch me anymore.

By the time the afternoon approached two o'clock, the lighter had exhausted an entire packet of Luckies and I had finished off the open bottle of bourbon.

There was a quick, efficient rap at the door. "Come in!" I called out from my desk. The door opened and the brown-skinned figure of Detective Chief Inspector Jitendra Patel strode in attired in a commanding air of no-nonsense authority. He was wearing an immaculately pressed grey suit that complemented his skin tone perfectly. His shoes were pristinely polished with a complete absence of the slightest smudge or stain and he held a leather document wallet under his left arm.

"Good afternoon, Sam." Polite. To the point.

"Thanks for coming," I said and gestured towards the sofa. "Would you like a drink?"

"Coffee please," he replied, his eyes scanning every intimate detail of my office. I tried not to glance at the bottom drawer of my filing cabinet. "You really have got a lot of..."

"Clocks," I finished for him as I made my way over to the kitchenette area next to the main room of my office. "I know. It's a thing of mine." I opened the fridge and frowned. "How do you have your coffee?"

"Black, no sugar, please."

I breathed a sigh of relief and flicked the kettle on. "Thank God for that. I don't have any cow's milk at the moment. I don't drink it myself and tend to forget about it. When I buy it, it doesn't get used and goes off."

He nodded. "Perhaps you ought to invest in some little catering pots of UHT milk? Less wasteful."

I nodded in agreement. "Good idea."

"Besides, when it's in coffee no one can really tell the difference," Jitendra continued. "They *say* they can but..." he shrugged. "People always like to appear knowledgeable."

The kettle clicked off and I poured the boiled water onto the coffee granules. "I can't believe we're discussing the benefits of long life milk." I brought the mugs over to the small coffee table and sat on the sofa next to the policeman. "Is that the normal discussion topic at your place?"

He smiled and sipped the warm drink. "You'd be surprised what we discuss, Sam. *X Factor, Coronation Street.*"

"Not *CSI* or *Hawaii-Five-O*?"

Smiling, he shook his head, then placed the mug back down and proceeded to open the wallet. "Far too depressing watching sun-tanned models prancing about without a care in the world. Have they never heard of budget constraints when they write those things? This fellow, however, would be a cause of much discussion if my colleagues knew you were interested in him."

I let out a low whistle as Jitendra placed a rather large manila folder on the table. "My God, it's half a tree."

"And that's all I've been able to find so far." He slipped a thick ream of A4 sheets from the folder and began thumbing through them. "Mr Hawkins has been exceptionally busy. As far as I'm aware he has gone under at least three pseudonyms, so I am hypothesising that there are more out there that remain to be, as yet, uncovered."

On the top sheet were mugshots of a twenty-something male with roughly brushed, light brown hair and bad acne. "What's his racket?"

"Well there's the usual: GBH, drunk and disorderly, petty theft. The sort you see every day in every town. However, there's some more unusual things." Jitendra pulled out a group of papers that were clipped together. "When he was sixteen, Hawkins was a member of a group that spent most of their time sat in a field waiting for a flying saucer to come and take them away."

"He's a ufologist?"

The detective shrugged. "Oh, it gets better. Obviously, the little green men did not show, so two years later Mr Hawkins was living in a commune dedicated to living their life apart from modern society."

"That's not so bad. I have a certain amount of empathy with that."

"Yes, well I'm hoping that you would not use the commune as a front for taking the members' savings and ploughing them into a lucrative drug-supply ring."

"Hawkins was behind it? He was only eighteen!"

Jitendra shook his head. "No. He was just a disciple, so to speak. The ring leader went down for a good amount of time. Hawkins was cautioned and treated more as a victim than a criminal. However, that changed two years later when he turned up in Surrey heading a new-age church prophesying that the end of the world was nigh and everyone who was not with him would be blown to smithereens when the world exploded."

I groaned. "A doomsday cultist. What happened?"

Jitendra studied the notes. "The usual: allegations of fraud and abuse, lengthy investigations, dawn raid, trial and imprisonment."

"He's done time?"

"Eight years. Looks like he got out on good behaviour and promising never to set foot in Surrey again."

"So that takes us to when?"

"About eight years ago, then he dropped off the radar for a few years."

I nodded. "His sister said that that they travelled around for a bit: Europe, Egypt."

"That would explain the gap. Then, a little while back, he moved up here and got a job as an attendant at Williamson Park. Since then, he's been as clean as a whistle."

I skimmed through the pages of the reports. The early years certainly made interesting reading, just as Jitendra had illustrated – Hawkins had been a serial cultist, meandering from one group to another, stealing to fund his habit and beating up those who tried to stop him. Then, after his conviction and subsequent incarceration, he had emerged as a reformed character. He had seemed to get his act together. After the travelling abroad, he had moved up north with his sister and taken the job at the park where he diligently lived his life as a model citizen. The police records on him dwindled to nothingness about twenty-four months ago. The man seemed totally clean.

The turbulent past did not match the idyllic picture that his sister had so graphically drawn for me, nor did the present day promises of redemption and good behaviour gel with the uneasy feeling owned by Burger Bob. I drummed my fingertips against my teeth and various clocks ticked in the silence of my office as I tried to piece the two characters together.

"You look perplexed."

"This just doesn't fit," I said, looking through the papers once more, almost hoping to find something recently which said, "This guy is nuts!"

"Are you going to enlighten me as to why you are so interested in the man?" Jitendra asked, finishing his coffee. "I presume it's related to a case."

"His sister came to see me yesterday morning. The description she gave of how he is now doesn't exactly fit with the image these recent reports give of him. The earlier stuff... yeah, bang on, but these," I waved the offending articles in front of me, "are a completely different man. A reformed man. The man she described to me... was a psycho."

Jitendra leant forward. "Sometimes appearances can be deceptive."

I looked at him. His eyes were peering off to a place that mine could not follow. "Now, that sounded heartfelt," I commented. "Care to unload?"

The policeman rubbed his fingers over his clean-shaven jaw. "You have something a bit stronger than coffee?" I reached into my filing cabinet drawer, making sure I didn't draw attention to the bundled-up tea towel, and hooked out a fresh bottle of Jack Daniel's which I cracked open then poured into the two mugs. Jitendra sipped gratefully at his. "I've worked bloody hard to get where I am, Sam. Bloody hard. My dad wanted me to follow in the family profession."

"What was that?"

"A sodding shop-keeper," he growled. "Please come again! Have a nice day!"

I laughed at the very passable impression of Apu off *The Simpsons*. "I take it that the family business wasn't for you, then?"

He sipped more whiskey. "It wasn't a job. It was a bloody stereotype! I told him that. I said that I wanted none of it, that I wanted to do my own thing. I had a brain and that I wanted to use it. He told me not to be so stupid. He said that this country was blinkered and that I would never come to anything on my own. He said that perhaps, if the shop wasn't for me, then perhaps I ought to be a doctor. A doctor! That's even worse! What else could he suggest? A role in a seventies' sitcom as the poor Indian sap who doesn't understand innuendo and gets himself in all sorts of saucy scrapes? Pah! So I told him what I was going to do. I laid it on the line and I told him that he wasn't going to stop me."

"What did he think to that?"

"Not much. We haven't spoken since I left home. Parents! Waste of space. They just fill you with neuroses and hold you back."

Inside of me something shivered with cold.

"Anyway," he continued, "I studied. I did well. Very well. Top of my class in Psychology. Took a masters in Criminology then applied for the Force. I rapidly went from strength to strength. I started at the bottom. I insisted on it. I didn't want to be one of those uni boys who waltz in and lord it over the rank and file. God no! You see them looking down their noses at the guys on the beat and it sickens you. The uniforms have no respect for them either and I wanted to make sure that any respect I received had been well and truly earned. In order to do this, I needed to see the job from both sides of the desk. So I slogged my guts out on the beat and patrolled my way up into CID where I really got myself noticed. I had the highest conviction rate of my station. People were whispering hushed things about me in the corridors. Meetings were being held to discuss my glorious future. I was on the up, a rising star. I was to be a model of the new police force for the twenty-first century: a multi-racial body, a tolerant and inclusive office.

"Then I was appointed as DCI here. An external appointment to lead the department down the golden paths of glory."

He paused a moment and sipped his drink, steeling himself.

"On my first day I was shown to my office by a young constable. She must have been no more than twenty if she was a day – straight out of training. She was all smiles and compliments. She had heard all about me. She was excited about working with me. She hoped I liked my office. She was sweetness and light.

"Just after she left and closed the door behind her, I realised that I had left my briefcase in my car. I opened the door and made to go fetch it when I heard the young girl saying to her friend, "Just settled the new DCI in. Seems quite nice for a Paki."

I winced.

"Sometimes, for all the work you put into things, Sam, a leopard just cannot change its spots. You think that it has become a nice fluffy little tabby, but then it turns around and slashes you right across the heart."

We were silent again as we both finished our drinks. I topped them up and we drank some more, surrounded by the ticking of clocks and the occasional hoot from a car out in Dalton Square.

"So what is it that Hawkins' sister has said about him?" Jitendra finally asked.

"She said that he's a werewolf and tonight he's going to go on the rampage around Williamson Park."

For a moment the detective sat, mug in hand, his eyes fixed on me and his face impassive. Then, all of a sudden, he threw back his head, slapped his thigh and my office was filled with deep, braying laughter. "My God, Sam," he roared, wiping tears from his eyes, "that's a corker. Absolutely priceless. You had me going for a second there." His laughing subsided as he brought his mirth under control. After a few composing breaths he asked, "Seriously. What is it you want with this chap?"

I was silent and sipped some more of my drink before fishing out a fresh pack of Luckies. I flipped my Zippo and popped a cigarette in my mouth, saying nothing.

Jitendra looked at me in complete astonishment. "You're serious. You're bloody serious!" He stroked his chin and stared at me. "You have got to be kidding, Sam? Surely you can't be taking this at face value? Sure, Hawkins likes his little groups, shall we say? But a werewolf? She's winding you up, or perhaps she's out to cause trouble for her brother?"

"If she wanted to cause trouble," I replied, drawing heavily on the fag, "then perhaps she would tell your lot that he's up to his old tricks? That would sound more realistic, surely?"

Jitendra shook his head. "Perhaps, but a werewolf? Come on. That stuff doesn't exist, does it?"

I thought back to a vampire sinking their sharp teeth into my wrist. I recalled an exsanguinated body behind the Sugar House. I considered Nightingale's warning. "I've seen a lot of stuff this week that you would not believe, Jitendra." I inhaled deeply and finished the Lucky, stubbing it out in the ashtray on my desk.

He stood up and smoothed out his expensive suit. "Okay, this is insane. You're being taken for a ride, Sam." He pointed to the files on the coffee table. "You can borrow these. Read through them and I think that you'll see sense. The man was a whacko, but now he's clean. His sister is out to spite him and is just reeling you in. I've got to head off, but if you need me, call, okay?" His eyes narrowed on me. "Don't do anything stupid."

I nodded acceptance at the official warning and let him out of the office then stood thinking. As the clocks ticked and my ears rang I thought over the evidence in front of me. Jitendra may have been sceptical but his previous words rang true: "The leopard does not change its spots." Hawkins was up to something, whether he was a werewolf or not. True, he may be a cult junkie, but then again...

I needed to take precautions.

I needed Uncle to get here with my silver bullets. I picked my phone off its cradle and dialled in the number of his shop. After about twenty rings

I hung up and checked the mantle clock on the window-sill. Three in the afternoon. The old bugger must have shut early. I drummed my fingers against my teeth and shut my eyes. The whistling in my ears chased the tumbleweed around my brain. I had nothing, absolutely nothing. I was getting nowhere fast, to walk a well-trodden cliché.

I opened my eyes, lit up yet another smoke and dragged a pad and pen out of the desk, deciding to write down everything that I knew in the hope that it would give my brain some thinking space. At the moment it seemed to be cluttered up with half-truths, vague myth and speculation.

I stared at the paper. Where to begin?

At the beginning of course.

One. I had been told by vampires earlier that week to watch for the full moon. I had helped the Children of Cain and now the Bloodline of Abel would be gunning for my blood.

Two. Yesterday, I had been approached by one Simone Hawkins (potential date, although now part of me was starting to reconsider the sensibilities of that) who said that her brother was a werewolf and intent on going nuclear at the next full moon.

Three. The next full moon was tonight.

Four. Hawkins had history. A colourful past of cults and violence.

Five. Hawkins worked in the zoo at Williamson Park. He was rumoured to still be violent.

Six. I had encountered something mystical regarding Alec at the park. I had seen a vision where werewolves were prowling around in Ancient Egypt whilst being curiously missing from the history books.

Seven...

I paused and drummed my pen on the pad. Was there a seven? I sat and finished off the Lucky, slowly ground it into an ashtray then lit another. The roasted smoke filled my mouth and I blew its tobaccoey flavour out of my nostrils.

Yes, there was a "Seven."

Seven. I was on my own and the sky was starting to darken outside. In about an hour, the moon would rise and I would find out, for sure, what was truth and what was fiction. I would see if Hawkins was just a lunatic with delusions of primeval shape-shifting or whether he would be coming for my jugular.

I got up, walked over to my filing cabinet and opened the bottom drawer. There at the back, wrapped in the red and white tea towel was the revolver that I had snatched from the John O'Gaunt studios earlier that week. Had it only been Monday? It sure had been a full week. I turned the gun over in my hand. I had never used one of these before, but it looked fairly simple. Finger on trigger and don't peer down the business end. It looked like there were still bullets in there. I tentatively pushed a catch on the side and the front end dropped down. Yep, there they were, six little packages of death and destruction.

Not silver, but they would have to do, for now. I snapped the gun shut and shoved it into the pocket of my trench coat.

The sky was starting to dim on a mid-October afternoon and I had somewhere else to be.

Normally, I enjoy a quiet, leisurely stroll through Williamson Park with the sun dappling the paths through the autumnal leaves and the gentle breeze wafting the smell of woodland to my nose, but that October evening my skin was crawling worse than a beach at crab-mating season. As I made my way up the gravel path from just opposite Christ Church on Wyresdale Road, my eyes were scanning the darkening shadows, straining to discern anything that might be animal rather than vegetation.

Specifically, anything that might be rather large, furry and full of teeth.

I tried to walk stealthily but the cruel gravel betrayed my every movement. I felt like I was a herd of elephants trying to tip-toe through a corn-field. My heart was dancing a polka in my chest and stress was pulling the ropes of cathedral bells in my ears. I absentmindedly rubbed the side of my head as I approached the first clearing in the park. I don't know it's real title but I always think of it as the fairy ring. It's a circular grove of trees that stand over a small hillock which is surrounded by rough seats fashioned from preserved tree trunks. I swung my legs over one of the trunks and seated myself down, trying to calm my heart and still my chiming ears. As I let my eyes wander around the ring of trees I thought about Billy Swarbrick's diminutive friends and wondered if they ever came here to dance in the still of the night. They had shown me an image of the full moon. They must have known about the werewolf.

Werewolf.

Damn it! Just last week I would have scoffed at the idea. As you can probably tell, I'm not the sceptical kind of person. I have seen so much stuff over the years – that's why I ended up in this profession – but the idea of a real-life lunar shape-shifter? The idea would have been insane. Such notions were the product of old-time superstitions and fears.

Just like vampires.

Vampires like the ones I had met just earlier that week.

So if there really were vamps then that suggested that there had to be...

My train of thought stopped mid-ramble and that mammalian instinct that stems from once having been a small monkey at the bottom of the food chain kicked in. The hairs on the back of my neck stood proud and to attention like a band of subconscious sentries, all the saliva drained from my mouth as it absorbed back into my body, and my bladder performed a little dance as it tried to decide whether it needed to empty itself thus making me lighter and able to run quicker.

I was being watched.

I was being hunted.

Slowly, trying desperately to blend into the shadows of the umbrella of trees, I lifted my eyes to the foliage that surrounded me. There was no sound. There was no movement. There was only instinct. It was there, I knew it.

Carefully, shakily, I rose to my feet, a hand steadying itself against the gnarled, upright trunk of a tree. The bark felt electric to the touch. Every crack, every ridge stood out against my soft fingertips. My breathing slowed and my eyes travelled from tree to tree, from bush to bush trying to spy my stalker.

There on the opposing side of the fairy ring was a gap between the trees. A muddy slope led up to a higher level. Broken branches and snapped twigs littered the way up. In the gathering gloom I could make out decaying leaves scattered about the woody flooring.

There, in the midst of the dying leaves, stood a furry paw. A very large, furry paw. I was frozen to the spot as my eyes travelled up an incredibly thick front leg that was clad in rough, greying hair, over a shoulder that rippled with pure sinew and muscle, across a thick neck maned in predatory camouflage, past two sharp, pointed ears to a pair of dark, abyssal eyes that were fixed directly on me.

It was the teeth that broke my stasis.

In an instant I had transformed from Greek statue to African gazelle. I bounded across to my left, further into the park, my shoes crashing against the gravel path as I tried to place a distance between me and the wolf that would be akin to the distance between the Earth and Alpha Centauri.

Shit! It was real!

It was here!

It was after me!

As I rounded a curve in the path I allowed myself a glance over my shoulder. The wolf was nowhere to be seen. I should have felt relief, but that scared monkey inside of me recognised the reality that the predator was, in fact, hiding, lurking in the gloomy shadows. I groaned as I realised where I had run into. In the light, summer evenings the park is used as an open-air theatre, with different stages set at different locations. I had just run into one such area. On either side of the gravel path were high rising banks with seats sunk into the earth. Trees obscured my vision at the top of both slopes. The only way out was back the way I came or down the other end of the impromptu stage. It was a rat run and I was the little lab rodent scurrying through the test with the big, furry scientist looking on from above, hidden in the foliage. No doubt a dissection would follow shortly.

I shoved my hand into the right pocket of my trench coat and pulled out the appropriated pistol that I had brought for protection. True, the bullets weren't silver, but surely they were capable of some sort of damage? One foot after another I edged down the path, all the time my eyes scanning the horizon of the high, obscuring tree line.

I glimpsed a movement. The pistol rang out. There was an echoing silence, but no ethereal howl of pain.

Damn! A bullet wasted. I tried to recall how many this thing had. Were there five? Yes, I was sure there were five more.

I walked further.

Movement. Up above. Yes, definitely movement. I raised the gun as I approached the end of the rat run. I could see a tremor in the leaves. Was it the wind or was it my hunter? How could I be sure? I kept moving one foot after another. One foot after another. Just keep moving. Just keep moving. Distance is our friend.

Then, with a roar, the leaves revealed their secret and the wolf leapt down the banking. I ran for the end of the stage area and fired wildly behind me. A high yelp cut through the crash bang of the gunshot. I glanced quickly and saw the wolf rise up backward, one shoulder wrenched behind him. I had winged him.

I made good my advantage and pelted hell for leather across the open grass towards the Ashton Memorial.

Now, when you think of a memorial, you might imagine a little blue plaque on the side of a house - Joe Bloggs, inventor of the toffee-chocolate machine was born here, that sort of thing - or, at the most, a grand statue commemorating some glorious victory over peasants whose greatest crime was to hold a pitchfork in self-defence. The Ashton Memorial is the mother of memorials. It is an entire building. Hewn from white marble and standing God-knows-how high, crowned in a green copper dome, it can be seen from most parts of Lancaster. It was built by Lord Ashton in 1909 and was probably a memorial to his late wife. It is a must-see for all visitors, tourists and investigators being pursued by a slavering beast.

I charged across the gravelled area deciding that the memorial would give me the high ground and a clear view.

I bounded up its fine stone steps two at a time until I reached the first level. I turned and saw my hunter stalking with deliberate menace out of the trees. I had to admit that, in the light of the full moon, he looked quite marvellous. Low to the ground, his eyes still fixed upon me, even at this distance, his limbs working in complete harmony despite a slight limp from his left foreleg. He was the ultimate predator. Part of my mind, the part that wasn't shrieking at me to run for my life up towards the top level, was saying, "Thank God that there's only one!"

I reached the top level of the stairs and approached the building itself. I tugged frantically at the glass door. Locked, obviously. I reversed the pistol in my hand and smashed the hand grip through the glass then reached inside and unsnapped the latch. I flung the door open and threw myself over the threshold. He would be behind me soon. I had to make a plan.

Stairs. More stairs. Stairs were good.

There are viewing areas on the outside of the memorial up towards the roof. To reach these, one has to climb one of two small, tight staircases. I chose the nearest one, ignoring the "No Entry. Exit only." sign and darted up them. I spiralled up with the stairs as they took me to the first landing and I climbed out onto the balcony. I was now facing the other side of the memorial, towards the butterfly house and the mini-zoo. There was a modicum of safety for now. The wolf had to come up to get at me. He could not fly and

I doubted that, with his wounded leg, he would be able to climb up the outside of the memorial, besides I had a good view of the exterior walls and there was no way he could creep up on me, unseen.

I stood in the silence of the cool, October evening. All I could hear was the pounding of my heart, the gasping of my breath and the ringing of my tinnitus. There was no other noise - no heavy animal breathing, no brushing of fur against stone, no clicking of claws against steps. Just silence for what seemed like an age.

I brushed something off my shoulder.

It was replaced by more of the same.

Dust. A light dust was falling on me.

From above.

The little monkey inside me expired as I looked up and saw something large and hairy clinging to the next balcony up. The werewolf had gone up the other stairs and taken the access way to the next level. He had me in his sights.

As I lifted the pistol, I saw his legs bend and his muscles tense in the white moonlight. Then, as my third attempt to use the handgun sent a bullet flying off harmlessly into the night, the wolf was sailing through the air down towards me.

I didn't think. I just reacted in a manner of self-preservation. I shoved my hands out in front of my face and, when I felt the impact of a toothed killing machine, I twisted around and the weight of the wolf was gone. A second or two later there was a blood-curdling thump.

I realised that my eyes were closed tightly shut. I dared to open them and peered down over the precipice. The werewolf was laying immobile on the mosaic pattern of the red Lancashire rose that adorns the courtyard between the memorial and the butterfly house.

I must have stood for about a minute panting heavily, willing my numbed legs to move. Eventually they obliged and I tore down the stairs, almost sending myself for a burton as I did so. As I ventured out of the memorial I could still see the pile of fur and fangs lying immobile on the ground. I raised the pistol and tried to hold it steady with two shaking hands while I made my approach. There was no movement. None whatsoever. Nothing was twitching. I could not discern any rise and fall of breathing.

Nothing.

I leant closer and poked it with the muzzle of the gun.

Still nothing.

In the light of the moon I moved round towards his head and took a better look. "My, grandma..." I began, then its eyes flicked open and all I knew next was nauseating blackness.

Sometime later I came to. Normally, I'm a sluggish waker, the effects of sleep grip me tight and try to pull me back down into the comfy duvet of somnolence. However, on this occasion, the little bunnies of panic were jumping up and down outside their warrens and insisting that we skedaddle.

My eyes shot open and the first thing I noticed was that my head hurt like hell. The second thing was also that my head hurt like hell - which meant that I still had a head. I checked the other extremities. Two arms, two legs, crown jewels; all still intact. The scared bunnies dragged me wobbling to my feet. The world was dark and spinny.

No. Wait. The world was dark. I was spinny. Certainly in no fit state to take on a creature that had survived a fall from the top of the Ashton Memorial then had beaten the crap out of me with one solid blow.

I had to get out of there and recoup.

I had to escape.

I don't remember much about getting the hell out of the park. Adrenalin pumped through my heart and bells rang shrilly in my head. About midnight, I crashed into my flat, ransacked my medicine cabinet for some paracetamol and some betahistine. I poured a large whiskey, downed it, poured another, lit a Lucky and crashed into my armchair.

I was alive. I was alive. I had met the bloody werewolf and survived.

I sipped at the second whiskey and revisited that phrase. It made no sense. Why had he not killed me? Blood drained from my face as I leapt from the armchair, ignoring the wobbling floor, stripped my clothes off and stood naked in front of the mirror in the bathroom, a cigarette hanging from between my lips. Nothing, not a scratch, let alone an infectious bite. There was just a bruised swelling starting to emerge on the side of my head. I decided it would match the ones that were fading around my nose, then dressed again and made my way back into the living room. I was just considering how this made no sense whatsoever when I saw the long parcel propped up against the wall. I had obviously missed it when I had staggered into my flat. I drew heavily on the cigarette and approached the object with caution. It was about forty centimetres long, wrapped in brown paper and tied with string. This was no present from Father Christmas. A scrap of paper was tacked to the wrappings. I snatched it off and read:

> "Samuel, silver bullets at such short notice is a no-no, but this little item should serve you just fine. I do not know if you have used one before, but they are straightforward enough. Flick the switch at the back of the barrels and they open up for you to insert the cartridges which are laced with silver. There is a safety on the side. I suggest you use it so you do not blow your balls off.
>
> Uncle.
>
> P.S. The lock on your door is about as useful as a pork chop at a bar-mitzvah!"

I managed to smile for the first time that evening and carefully unwrapped the parcel. It was a short, stubby firearm with two barrels that ended at carefully filed apertures: a sawn-off shotgun, the favoured weapon of thieves and hoodlums the world over. Reggie Kray would have loved it. There was a *thunk* as a smaller package tumbled out of the parcel and onto the floor. I picked it up and opened the little box. There were a number of cartridges inside and another note in Uncle's scrawled cursive handwriting.

"These contain a high amount of silver as well as
the usual shot. They are expensive. Don't waste them!"

I smiled again and in five minutes I had worked out how to load the gun and turn the safety on and off. I was now a bona fide werewolf hunter. I could track him down and shoot him dead.

My spine crawled. Was that what I wanted? Did I want him dead?

No. Of course not! What was I thinking? Here I was imagining myself as some sort of big game huntsman, when in fact my prey was a normal man. Well, as normal as anyone can be who changes into a wolf once a month and desires to eat up half of Lancaster in a feeding frenzy.

I was no killer. The gun had to be the last resort. But what else could I do? I could not capture him. Even if I did, what would I do with him? Have him neutered and kept as a guard dog? True, it would save having a new lock fitted on my door, but the practicalities...

Then it struck me. I fished Jitendra's card out of my pocket and dialled his mobile number. Surprisingly he picked up after two rings.

"Hi, Sam. I've been waiting."

Jitendra met me at the park. He was leaning against a black four by four, his hands in his pockets in an attempt to defend himself against the insidious cold night air. When he saw me approaching in the yellow glare of the harsh street lights he stood up sharp and stalked over.

"Damn it, Sam. What happened to you?" He reached out with a gloved hand and turned my head to peer at my swollen cheek.

"I told you on the phone. I got hit by a pissed off werewolf."

Jitendra left out short, exasperated breath. "Don't start with that crap again or I'm off home. There's no such thing as... What the hell is that?" he yelled as I drew the sawn off shotgun from out of my trench coat.

"Protection," I explained, coolly checking that the safety was still on. At least I hoped that I seemed cool. My heart was beating faster than that of a teenage boy as he watched his first porn video in a darkened bedroom.

The whites of the policeman's eyes were stark against his brown skin as anger swept over his face. "Sam, you do realise I ought to arrest you on the spot for this? Do you?" His face was close to mine and he spoke in an aggressive whisper. I remained stoic, silent. "Well? What do you expect me to do? Be your Sancho? There's no damned windmills up there! Are you going to shoot a man in cold blood? That's murder."

I breathed slowly. I had expected this and all the way up East Road and Wyresdale Road, I had carefully prepared a little speech. It had sounded convincing to me. I just hoped it sounded convincing to the man who kept handcuffs on his person and could throw me in a cell then leave me there to rot. "This time last week, I would have been the man stood in your shoes," I said slowly, carefully selecting every word before it left my mouth. "I would be saying, 'Shit! What's all this?' But in the last seven days I have been abducted and almost sacrificed by Satanists, played nanny to a newly created vampire, stopped irate fairies from causing havoc at a local high school and now, to top it all, I have been attacked by a creature which stepped straight out the pages of *Little Red Riding Hood*. Now, I'm not sure what I was expecting when I set up shop, but let me tell you it was none of this. Perhaps I was thinking that there might be grannies convinced that their dead husband was moving cutlery around the house and that was why they could never find a teaspoon when they needed one. Perhaps I thought that there would be a neurotic teenager who had convinced herself that everyone was being mean to her because the wart on her little finger meant that she was a witch. Perhaps there was a whole lot of other mundane, trite and easily explainable stuff which I thought would present itself to me. What I did not expect was to be stood at the end of the week outside the local park with a sawn-off shotgun that was loaded with cartridges laced with silver readying myself to blast someone who does more than hump your Aunt Ethel's leg or chase postmen when the moon is full. My life has changed, irrevocably. Now, so has yours. So you have a choice. You can either try to take this gun off me and lock me up - and believe me when I say that I will not go without a fight - or you can come with me and help do anything that needs doing.

"What will it be?"

Jitendra's eyes went from my face to the gun to the park then back up to my face. "Sod it!" he swore and stomped off into the park.

My heart stopped racing. Just a fraction.

We walked in silence for a short while until Jitendra turned to me and asked, "I'm guessing you have a vague idea as to where we're going?"

In all honesty I hadn't even considered the matter yet, but not wanting to look like a total muppet I said, "I think it would be logical to start where I left off."

"In front of the butterfly house?"

I nodded.

So, on we traipsed, through the gloom of the park. It was now the middle of the night and the canopy of trees rose over us blanketing out stars, clouds and even the baleful, all-seeing eye that was the full moon. I gripped the shotgun tight, my finger resting on the guard around the trigger. The last thing I wanted was to fire off involuntarily because my hand was shaking. I was too aware that any sharp noise could alert the wolf to our presence.

That was, if he did not already know that we were there.

I quickly booted that thought from my mind like a drunk cast out of a family-friendly pub. It could not be indulged. It was not worth thinking about. The idea that the creature was there, in the woods, his head low, his eyes sharp and his dagger-like teeth exposed from under his wide, slavering lips as he stalked us silently, purposefully...

Stop it, stop it, stop it. "That's crazy talk. You'll get us both killed!"

"Pardon?" Jitendra stopped, his eyebrow raised.

"Oh. Did I say that? That was supposed to stay inside my head."

My companion gave something that almost passed for a smile as we reached the open area in front of the memorial. "Looks rather exposed, wouldn't you say?" he noted, his eyes scanning the trees that encircled the area. The big, dark trees with all their handy hiding places.

Everywhere I looked there seemed to be wolf-shaped shadows. Between the trees, behind the benches, over by the pond. I really knew how a small rodent felt. "We've got to cross it," I said, reluctantly.

Jitendra nodded and set off purposefully across the tarmac. After a second's hesitation, I scurried over behind him trying to ignore any ominous movement. We climbed the stone stairs and it was only after we rounded the building that he seemed to proceed with added caution. He motioned for me to hang behind him in the shadows and whispered, "So this is where you say you last encountered the werewolf?"

"If by encountered you mean *got knocked senseless by*, then yeah, that was here."

"Wait here," he commanded with no room for discussion and walked slowly out over the rose-tiled esplanade. He circled a couple of times then crouched down and ran his fingers over the ground, nodded and walked back over to me. "Well there are certainly signs of a scuffle there," he said.

"You don't say?" My voice was ladled full of tasty sarcasm which he chose not to digest.

"More importantly," the DCI continued, there is evidence of blood and it trails off in that direction." He pointed towards the entrance to the mini-zoo. "Do you think your wolf is an exhibit? Sharing a run with the rabbits perhaps?"

I looked him hard in the eye under the light of the moon. "You're still not buying this, are you?"

"Let's just say that I'm keeping an open mind, shall we?" He stretched an arm out towards the mini-zoo. "Lead on MacDuff."

I swallowed and looked over towards the attraction. My stomach was lurching behind the shotgun that I had clasped tight to my middle. I so did not want to do this. I thought of my bed, my lovely warm bed and a soothing bottle of Jack Daniel's that could keep me company into the early hours. Then I thought of a splintering crash as a blood-lusting hell hound smashed through my door and pounced on top of me, ripping out my throat as my screams evaporated to a damp, squelchy nothingness.

I really had no choice, had I?

I sucked it up, grew a pair the size of beach balls, and led the way over to the zoo. Jitendra was right, there was a thin train of blood dribbling its way across the floor. It glistened a path in the light of the moon all the way to the main glass door of the entrance. The door hung open, still in the quiet night air. I peered in and saw nothing but a darkened gift shop. I gripped the gun even tighter and nodded for Jitendra to pull the door back. As the door swung silently open, I inched my way in, foot after hesitant foot, slowly swinging the shotgun around the small room. It was soon obvious that the scariest thing here were the prices for the touristy knick-knacks. Jitendra lay a silent hand on my arm and pointed to the other side of the room. The door leading through to the main part of the zoo was also open. I nodded and we made our way over there. Once more, the DCI opened another glass door and we stepped back out into the night.

The door brought us into an open courtyard behind the butterfly house. In the middle stood a large, round aviary, its occupants apparently fast asleep, and down the far side of the courtyard lay the newly renovated bird-house and mini-beast building. Looking down at the floor, the trail led off to this new construction. We continued our hunt.

I froze as my foot crunched on top of light-coloured gravel that paved the courtyard.

"Quietly," Jitendra mouthed.

"Duh!" I mouthed back as I continued to walk, albeit somewhat more cautiously, telling my feet to imagine the old *Kung Fu* trick of walking on rice paper.

After what was in fact a few seconds, but seemed like a number of hours, we made it across the treacherously noisy path in one piece. Once more we found another door (this one solid, not glass) that was ajar. Darkness was recumbent on the far side. Jitendra pushed the door open to the bird-house and the gloom inside was even blacker than that which was outside. I hesitated.

"Go on," he mouthed.

I stared into the blackness of the room and my feet froze. They were not for moving.

"Go on!" Jitendra mouthed more urgently, then, when it was apparent that I would not be budged, he edged past me into the darkened building.

I sighed. I couldn't let him go in on his own, so I followed in behind. The vague light from outside gave me a glimpse of large aviaries similar to the one that I had seen in the courtyard. They reached from floor to ceiling and ran parallel down a path towards the door on the opposite side of the room which I guessed led to the mini-beast house.

Then it all went black.

The door had closed shut.

There was no breeze. It had not closed on its own.

Shit.

There was a small click and a thin beam of light shot out from Jitendra, who had obviously brought a pocket torch. Mine was probably still lying somewhere discarded in the John O'Gaunt studios. I made a mental note to nip into town on Monday and buy a new one. That was supposing, of course, that I did not end up doing a good impression of a tin of Pedigree Chum in the next few minutes.

"This is DCI Patel of the Lancaster Constabulary," he proclaimed with unnerving authority. "Please show yourself."

Nothing stepped into his torchlight, instead there was the unmistakable sound of heavy breathing and was that fur brushing against the metal cages or was it just my panicked imagination? My hands flexed on the shotgun. "Nice shotgun," I thought to myself. "Friendly, safe, protective shotgun."

"Do not play games with me." The detective's voice was calm and steady. I was totally in awe of him for keeping his nerve. Had I tried to speak right now I would have squeaked higher than a castrati on helium. "Show yourself." He swept his torch slowly around the room. All it found was cages of sleeping birds.

The rustling stopped. Was it behind us or was it to the side? The dark was confusing my senses somewhat. That, and the blind panic of a sprinting heart.

Then I definitely heard something. It sounded like gravel being rolled back and forth across a rain-drenched tombstone by the mushy, bleeding end of a severed arm. I wanted to cry as I recognised it for what it was. The sound of laughter; cruel, evil laughter.

"You do not scare me, Mr Plod," came the guttural voice, dripping with contempt. "You are nothing to me. It is the investigator that concerns me."

Then there was the sound of swift movement and a thud followed by a clattering as Jitendra's torch scuttled off across the room. I swore loudly and survival instinct took hold. My legs aimed for the door through to the mini-beast house and launched me in its direction. Three long strides took me there. I held the gun in one hand and scrabbled for the door handle with the other.

Where was the bloody thing? Where was it? I ran my hand over the smooth wood at waist height but found nothing. It had to be here. There had to be one. As I searched frantically for my hope of salvation, I was aware of the cacophony of chirruping and twittering as the birds protested at my rude disturbing of their sleep. "Screw them!" I thought, "I need to get out of here." Then my hand lit onto something hard and round. I twisted it clockwise and it turned. Footsteps, strong, hard footsteps approached from behind me. As I flung the door open, light cascaded into the bird-house. I risked a glance backwards and saw the werewolf approaching. He was pacing forwards on his hind legs dragging the inert form of Jitendra by the collar. I lifted the gun up horizontally and fired. The blast was deafening in the enclosed environment and I almost dropped the bloody thing in fright, but I gripped on tight and legged it into the mini-beast section without looking back to see if I had hit the wolf or not. I slammed the door behind me and leaned heavily, waiting for the inevitable thump of the werewolf pushing against it.

The seconds passed.

I waited.

Nothing happened. Had I shot the beast? Had I killed it?

Or was it playing with me?

I quickly took in my surroundings. The room was not that brightly lit, but in comparison to the black hole that I had just escaped, it seemed like seventh heaven. Vivariums were dotted around the edge of the large circular room and there, in the middle, stood Williamson Park's latest, greatest additions, the driver ants. As my heart started to apply the brakes to my blood-pumping I had to admit that it really was quite a spectacular sight. The colony was enclosed in a circular glass case that stood about three meters tall. Glass tubes ran off from the core at various angles and travelled around the perimeter of the mini-beast house. I could make out tiny figures scurrying along these carriageways with leaves and debris on their tiny, powerful backs. The ultimate workers.

But I did not have time to stand and stare. I had to formulate a plan. A plan, yes, a plan. I needed a plan.

No. I needed a miracle.

"Sam? Is that you?"

I started at the sound of the female voice and my face must have shown such surprise as Hawkins' sister stepped out of the shadows. "Simone? Is that you? What are you doing here?" He must have abducted her, I told myself. Brought her here under duress to witness his horrific cull.

But I knew I was wrong.

There wasn't a mark on her.

Crap!

The door pushed hard against my back and I was sent tumbling into the room. Hawkins stalked into the room, in his malevolent lupine state, still dragging Jitendra behind him. There wasn't a mark on my pursuer. The wild blast from the shotgun had obviously missed. I staggered to my knees and brought the twin barrels round to bear on the huge form of the wolf. I had to take care. There was just the one cartridge loaded now and I knew that I would never stand a chance of reloading it with the spares in my pocket.

The wolf, however, was *also* taking care. He dumped the unconscious but not bleeding policeman by the entrance to the mini-beast house and circled behind the ant colony. "There's no escape, you know, Spallucci," his gravelly voice rumbled. "You will die here."

"I've already heard that once before this week, so you'll have to excuse me if I wait and see just how this pans out." I was impressed with myself: humour in a time of crisis. I must have been getting bold.

"The Bloodline of Abel will squash you like a fly, Sam," Simone declared as she too circled around the ant colony. "They have such power. You are totally insignificant."

"So insignificant that you had to get me here to feed me to Fido?" I asked, pointing towards the werewolf with the gun, whilst trying to circle around the display towards Jitendra who was most definitely breathing and, was that his finger moving? "It all seems rather elaborate to me."

"Even a little thorn can dismount a great leader should it get stuck in the horse's leg." She really seemed to be enjoying the sound of her own voice. And I had actually thought she wanted to go out on a date with me! So much for luck with the opposite sex.

"So Scooby-doo here is a great leader, is he?" I glanced over to Jitendra. Yes, there was definitely movement there, just a little, as if for my eyes only. "Where are his soldiers?"

"The Bloodline are scattered, in hiding." Hawkins growled. "They await their command from one who can lay his claws on that which will unite them."

"And what would that be? A nice bowl of tripe?"

"The Potency." Simone positively glowed as she said the word. A gleam normally reserved for religious zealots filled her eyes as she continued; "It will give such power that has never been seen since the time of..."

"Enough!" roared Hawkins. His eyes fixed on mine. "Time to die," and, as he let a long howl rise from his snout, I felt something hard whack against my wrists. I yelped as my hands dropped the gun onto the floor, then grunted as Simone hit me in the throat with a metal pole before kicking the gun out of reach. As Hawkins started to stalk around the far side of the ant colony to join his sister, Simone brought the pole down on the back of my neck, causing everything to grey and my knees to buckle. I bit my lip and forced myself to hold on. If I blacked out now I was a dead man. I focussed on two distinct things: terror and hope. Terror was personified by the sharp claws that the wolf was flexing from underneath his grey fur. Hope came in the form of Jitendra rising to his feet and focussing his attention on the shotgun that lay discarded out of sight from the werewolf. He dived towards the weapon and swept it up in his hands before taking aim around the ant colony. I took a split second to admire his agility, then I cursed his aim as he let rip a blast which pounded a hole into the ceiling above the werewolf rather than in the chest of the ducking lycanthrope.

A deep, rumbling chuckle rose from the mouth of Hawkins and, darting back, he lurched forwards clipping the DCI with the back of his hairy paw. Jitendra crashed into the wall and slumped to the ground. This time he was truly out for the count rather than just stunned.

I swore as the werewolf's head turned and he focussed all of his venomous attention back onto me. I cast my eyes around as he stalked forwards. I was quickly running out of options. The shotgun was lying discarded by Jitendra's limp hand on the far side of the room and, as well as being far from my grasp, it was empty. Could I drag myself up from my prone position, scramble across the room, snatch the gun from behind the werewolf, load it, aim it and fire a killing shot? I thought not.

Hawkins saw the panic in my eyes and continued to chuckle as he took a mighty leap that sprang him up onto the glass casing at the middle of the ant colony. Beneath him, frantic worker ants clambered up and down the glass with valour to assure themselves that the colony was not under attack. The wolf lowered his head and, through a frothy leer, growled, "And now, Spallucci, it's your turn."

"Not a chance," I whispered, harshly, my bruised larynx screaming in agony. I pulled the revolver out of my trench coat pocket and held it firm in front of me with two hands.

Simone drew back nervously behind her brother for protection, but the werewolf just continued to laugh. "You are such a slow learner, Spallucci. Do you not remember that feeble toy cannot kill me? Look. Look at my arm." He thrust his shoulder forward. New fur replaced that which I had grazed earlier in the night. "I am immortal to human weapons. Only a silver weapon can stop my heart from beating and cease my brain function."

"Really?" I asked, pulling back the hammer on the gun. "Then I guess this is just really gonna sting." I fired off three shots in quick succession. With the first, his left kneecap exploded, causing the werewolf to slump down onto one side on top of the glass enclosure. He would have screamed in agony had the second shot not removed half of his face. Simone shrieked as blood and brains splattered her, then the third shot covered her shouts as the glass casing beneath Hawkins shattered from a bullet impact, causing the disfigured wolf to tumble in amongst the ants.

Very pissed off ants, might I add.

As they scurried over him and started to eat at his broken flesh, Hawkins gurgled through what remained of his mouth only for the noise to gag tight on a swathe of ants marching into his gouged orifice. His arms flailed around trying to grab a purchase on the sides of the enclosure, but all they could do was scrabble in vain and slide down the clear, unforgiving surface.

I should have grimaced at the carnage. I should have been sickened by the sight of an immortal creature being digested by insects. Was he still alive in their guts? Was he aware of his tortuous fate?

But I didn't care. All I could think of was the relief that he was not going to get up from the insectile feast.

I pulled myself up from the floor, avoiding the occasional splinter of glass. My back cracked and I winced as I straightened up. I ignored the gruesome sight of the feasting driver ants and limped over to Jitendra's still form. I placed my fingers on his throat and found a slow, steady pulse. Unconscious but alive. No doubt he would wake with a severe headache.

I picked up the shotgun, fished two fresh cartridges from my coat and reloaded it before firing a shot into the rapidly decreasing remains of Nathan Hawkins. Just to be sure.

I froze as I heard a foot crunch down on a piece of glass behind me.

"You bastard!" Hawkins' sister hissed. "You utter bastard!"

I turned round and stood to face the harpy. Her face was screwed up in anger and tears flowed freely down her twisted face as she waved her pole weapon unsteadily at me. "I presume you're talking to me?" I asked.

"Of course I'm talking to you, you fuck-wit!" she spat venomously. "Look what you've done!" She pointed at the ant display. Hawkins was now nothing but a pile of bones – human bones. There was no trace of the wolf. "He was a wonderful man. He had such vision," she wailed.

"He was an utter lunatic with delusions of grandeur and a severe murderous streak," I countered. "What was I supposed to do? Let him kill me? I think not." As far as I was concerned I was done here. I showed her my back and made to rouse Jitendra.

"You think you're so clever don't you?" Simone continued. "You think you're so smart. Pah! You know nothing. Wait until they find out about you, then you'll know what true wisdom is. Then you'll see real power. The power of the Bloodline!"

I stopped shaking Jitendra's shoulder. He was still out cold. Instead, I contemplated her words.

"What do you mean?"

She raised her head and looked down her nose at me with utter contempt. "The Bloodline of Abel. They are everywhere, Spallucci, and when they find out about you, they will descend upon you and devour you."

"Bloodline of Abel?" I mused. "So they will come and rip me to pieces then?"

She nodded enthusiastically. "Oh yes. They will tear you limb from limb and dine on your vile entrails."

"How appetising. But they don't know about me yet? So who's going to tell them?"

"Well, I will, of course. They must know of this profanity that you have accomplished here. They must know of your vile deeds. They must..."

Her words were cut short by the sound of my shotgun firing its second deadly cartridge. Her eyes opened wide and she looked down at the gaping wound that pumped blood out of her chest, then she collapsed onto the floor. I stepped slowly up to her, looked her straight in her disbelieving eyes and watched impassively as her life drained away.

She would have set a pack of werewolves onto me.

It was self-defence.

It wasn't murder.

It was self-defence.

It was.

I've never really believed crime writers when they say that a dead body weighs so much, but now I can genuinely testify that it is absolutely true. As if trying to dispose of Simone Hawkins' body wasn't bad enough, I had to contend with the driver ants. I had seen what an efficient job they had performed on the werewolf and I had no desire to be their pudding. So it was with much grunting, care and precision that I hauled the deadweight into the massed colony to serve as their second course.

I should have felt sickened as they stripped away her flesh and devoured her insides, nausea should have risen in my gorge at such a repulsive act of feasting, but it didn't, not one bit. I felt nothing.

No revulsion.

No remorse.

No guilt.

It was self-preservation, plain and simple.

As the second body was steadily devoured I turned to the unconscious form of Jitendra. He had certainly experienced his share of misfortune that night. I crouched down and shook him, calling his name. Slowly he started to come to.

"Sam?" he croaked. "That you?"

"Yep," I said, reaching into a pocket and fishing out my pack of Luckies. They were somewhat battered but sufficient. I offered him one and he shook his head then winced. I lit myself a cigarette and helped him sit up.

He gazed morosely at the shattered colony. "What a mess."

I nodded. "We ought to get out of here."

He frowned. "I'll have to call it in. What happened?"

I paused, smoking my Lucky. "An accident," I finally stated.

Jitendra's dark eyes regarded the trail of crimson blood on the floor that smeared itself towards the colony before turning back to me. "An accident? You call that an accident? I see two dead bodies and a swarm of flesh-eating ants."

I shrugged. "They were threatening us, climbed up on the glass and it gave way. Your shot with the shotgun must have clipped it and weakened it."

The detective closed his eyes in despair. "But that's not what really happened is it?"

"How would you know? You were out cold."

We sat silently for a little while longer.

"Sam."

"Yeah?"

"It really was a werewolf, wasn't it?"

"Yeah."

"Let's get out of here," he said.

So we did.

It was about two o'clock on Sunday morning by the time that I got home. After leaving the carnage behind us, we walked out into the cool night air and Jitendra called the incident in. A couple of squad cars were pulled up by the mini-zoo within ten minutes. Within half an hour a forensics team had arrived. I answered a few questions: I had asked DCI Patel to accompany me on a case, the deceased had been armed, they dropped their weapon, DCI Patel fired a warning shot with the deceased's weapon, the glass must have been damaged, chow down time for the ants.

As the officers went about their business Jitendra and I sat quietly by ourselves on the stone steps of the Ashton Memorial. "Two questions," he said.

"Shoot."

"Hawkins mentioned two things in there. The Bloodline and the Potency. What are they?"

"I don't know," I answered honestly. "I'm guessing that the Potency is some sort of object of power." My mind recalled the green stone hung around the Egyptian werewolf's neck and I made a mental note to follow that image up later. "The Bloodline... Well, while you were taking your second nap, Simone referred to the Bloodline of Abel as if it were a group of werewolves."

Jitendra's eyes were horror-struck in the night. "A group? Here in Lancaster?"

"No. Not here. The sister and brother were working entirely on their own." I hesitated for a second. Should I tell him any more about my encounter with the vampires? He was a good man. A trustworthy man. But could he take so much information right now? Could he grasp that there were Children of Cain as well as a Bloodline of Abel hiding out there in the shadows? I looked him directly in the face and studied his square, ordered features.

"What is it?" he asked.

"Nothing. I just need to go home." I stood up and began to walk down the steps, leaving Jitendra behind to clean up the mess.

# Epilogue

It's now early on Monday morning. I have sat at this laptop for God knows how long. I haven't eaten or drunk anything - the thought of food makes my stomach turn. I have smoked countless packs of Luckies and I can barely see my hands in front of my face. I really ought to open a window to let the smoke out.

My back hurts and I need to move around, but I feel somewhat unburdened. That was my first week on the job; warts and all. There have been lunatics, vampires, fairies and homicidal werewolves. Quite a baptism of fire, don't you think? Have I gotten the worst of this job out of the way in the first seven days or is it just a precursor of things to come? I don't know. I guess we will have to wait and see.

Oh. There's someone knocking at the door. Back in a mo'.

It's now three in the afternoon. The air in the office is clear, but the fog in my head is dark and heavy.

Things have gotten much worse than I could have possibly imagined.

The person at the door, it was Caroline.

Sam will return in
Sam Spallucci: Ghosts From The Past.

# Author's Notes: Fact & Fiction

First, thank you for reading my book. I hope you enjoyed it. Second, I felt that I had better say a quick word or two about the Lancaster that belongs to Sam. I say the Lancaster that belongs to Sam, because that is what it is, really. It is sort of a side-step away from the city where I live and write; certain things are the same, certain things are different and others are completely made up.

Dalton Square:

The place where Sam lives and works surrounded by his multitude of clocks and empty bottles of Jack Daniel's is, to a point, an exact reproduction of the real-life location.

The Borough does indeed exist, as do the seats where Sam and Spliff normally imbibe their individual tipples whilst watching the world pass by. It is a rather fine hostelry, recommended by CAMRA and always accommodates an excellent selection of real ales some of which it now brews itself and are in fact vegan (Sam would be very happy, I am sure).

The Paradise Dragon, alas, is a fiction. However, it is based on an equally excellent Chinese restaurant called the Fortune Star. I have eaten there many, many times and suggest that, should you visit Lancaster, you eat there yourself. The owner is lovely and she is always very accommodating and welcoming.

White Cross/John O' Gaunt studios:

A little mixture of fact and fiction here. The White Cross Business Park does indeed reside across the A6 from the Royal Lancaster Infirmary but, whereas TV studios were located there in Casebook, in reality there are workshops and offices, among which is an office for BBC Radio Lancashire. To the best of my knowledge, it's presenters are not, and never have been, abductors or Satanists.

The Sugar House:

Indeed, the Sugar House is a student-run night club behind the old Gillow building. It has been going donkeys of years now and I even went there twice when I was a student. Once I was very drunk and the second time I was on a date. I'm sure it is enjoyed by those who frequent it but, like Sam, it's not really my cup of tea.

Luneside University:

This is probably the biggest fiction in the whole book. It does not exist, apart from in my, and now your, imagination. There are two universities in Lancaster: Lancaster University (situated south of the city at Bailrigg) and the University of Cumbria (situated near the centre of the city in Bowerham). I decided to mash the two up a bit and locate them next to the river Lune in an area of the city which, when this book was first conceived, was occupied by the derelict remains of the old Williamson linoleum works.

Dave's shop:

Now, any fantasy/sci-fi fans who have lived in Lancaster for a long time will know that there did indeed used to be such a shop on North Road. It was a fantastic place that was crammed full with little gems from almost the entire universe of fantasy and sci-fi. Sadly, it closed down a few years back and Vexed Vampire was, in part, a little tribute to this shop passing. I am hoping, however, that its real-life proprietor was not left half-vamped on Caton Road.

Edmund Campion School:

There is a school on Ashton Road, but not the one in Paranoid Poltergeist. Ripley Saint Thomas is such a huge gothic edifice surrounded by rambling grounds that it is practically screaming out for a ghost story and I could not resist adapting it for my purposes. All the staff in the story are completely fictitious but I am sure that we have all come across teachers like them at some point in our times at school, from the bullying class teacher to the hard-nosed PE teacher and the incredibly strict head whose glare could wither a perpetrator at twenty paces.

Cheapside/Lancaster City Centre:

The vague layout I have sketched throughout Casebook is more or less accurate. I feel that I just need to say a quick word on Boombox Betty and Burger Bob, both of whom are vaguely derived from real people.

I did not grow up in Lancaster. Like so many, I was a university import. Where I did grow up, however, had its own version of Boombox Betty and, just like in the book, every Saturday morning she would stand outside the Arndale centre and dance away in front of her ghetto blaster. She was a wonderful sight to behold and I just had to use her. I will be using her again at a later date so Betty fans, stay tuned.

Cheapside in Lancaster does indeed have a chap who sells burgers on the street corner, but then I don't think it is unique here. These sort of street venders are in just about every town and city throughout the world. I thought it would make sense for him to be Sam's man on the street and a convenient source of information as well as good, tasty food.

Williamson Park.

If you have ever driven up the M6 past Lancaster, you will have seen the Ashton Memorial rising above the canopy of the trees from this Victorian masterpiece. Just about wherever you go in Lancaster, you can see its green dome. I kept the layout of the park exactly as it is in real life, but I did take liberties with the mini-zoo in order to incorporate the driver ants which were inserted as a way to kill off a murderous lycanthrope.

Spliff and Grace:

The Reverend James Francis MacIntyre and Miss Grace Darling are both entirely fictitious beings as well as being the two creations that I have enjoyed fashioning the most during my time writing Casebook. As a result, they have both taken upon themselves personality traits and quirks of many old friends and people (some of whom are sadly no longer with us) who have touched my life in really positive ways. On rare occasions real-life situations have and will probably continue to seep in; just don't ask me which they are because my lips are sealed. Just hope that, one day, Spliff will settle down and finally feel at home and that the special someone in Grace's life will finally wake up and realise where the young Miss Darling's affections lie.

# Sam Spallucci:
# Ghosts From The Past

# Prologue

*Anything is possible.*

That's what they say. We've heard it all before: the gurus, the salesmen, the politicians.

*Anything is possible.*

It roughly translates as, "Give us your money, sucker. You're so unhappy with your miserable life that we will sell you a barrel-load of hokum and hogwash which you will drink up with such a beatific smile on your face as you think you're getting a wonderful life-changing deal. Just you wait until we're out of town and you realise that you've been had once again. Just you wait while we're laughing all the way to the bank with your hard-earned cash."

*Anything is possible.*

It never is, not normally. Not for normal schmoes like thee and me. We have to make do and mend with our little lot in life: the ups and downs, the to-ing and fro-ing. No, nothing is possible for us unless someone gives us a break and helps us better ourselves. But even then there is always a catch. Always a bitter pill to swallow when you realise you've sold your soul to the devil.

*Anything is possible.*

Imagine, just imagine if that were the truth. Imagine if you could obtain your wildest dreams. What would that actually do to your life? Would you be happy? Would you be satisfied? Or would you want more? Would you crave that little morsel that was just out of sight? What would that craving make you do? What would you become in order to satisfy your hunger?

*Anything is possible.*

I once met a man who told me about this tribe in India. They were a simple but happy people. Living in a small forest, they hunted pig to feed themselves. They had all that they needed to survive. Then corporations came and told them that they could have so much more. They were shown glossy photographs and hi-res Powerpoint presentations. The world was their proverbial oyster. But there was a catch, as there always is. The forest had to go. It was needed for resources and building space, but the sacrifice that the people made would be worthwhile and their lives would be improved. So the trees were cut down and the factories were thrown up; spewed out of the gut of multi-national corporations. It was only a few months later that the villagers realised that there were no more pigs - the animals' habitat had been ruined. This meant they had lost their staple food and had to depend on the corporation to feed them and sustain them. Within a year the village was no more and the tribe had become just another workforce under the rule of a cruel, capitalist overlord.

*Anything is possible.*

Tell me, what did you do yesterday? Did you wake up, eat breakfast, wander round the house scratching your butt before going to work? Did you idle the day away wondering what your life *might* have been? Did you watch that guy with the green hair shamble past your office at five to two just like he always does? Did you come home, have tea, watch a bit of telly then go to bed?

*Anything is possible.*

Or did you even *exist* yesterday? How can you be sure of that?

"But I remember it!" I hear you say. Says who? Says your memory? How can you trust that old thing? What if yesterday you were someone completely different? What if you had a different job? What if you were, in fact, someone of importance in society? What if you had been wealthy, rich beyond your wildest dreams? What if you were the sort of person that you actually loathed?

How would you know?

*Anything is possible.*

What if someone changed everything?

Because, you know what? Someone did.

# Chapter One

I stood and gawped out of the door to my office.

The previous week had been somewhat stressful, to say the least. Satanists, vampires, fairies...

And one big, bad-ass werewolf.

I had just finished typing it all up. My eyes were sore and every muscle in my sleep-deprived body ached.

Now I had to deal with this.

Caroline. The love of my life from those final days at Luneside University when my face was a mask of glee whilst my stomach was a pit of agony at the knowledge that my father, two hundred miles away, was dying a slow, painful death.

Caroline had been, to put it not too biblically, my succour and my refuge. When the terrors had come, she had been the one to hold me while I shook. When the tears had threatened to drown me in their deluge, she had been the one to dab my eyes with a convenient tissue.

She had given me so much.

But there was that one thing that she had never been able to hand to me on a plate and that was why I had walked away.

She had never given me her love.

So what do you say to someone who you haven't seen for sixteen years and whose heart you crushed? How do you express all the angst and regret that has been bottled up inside your stomach like a dormant volcano ready to erupt at any moment in an outpouring of tears and self-loathing? How do you start to make amends for an unforgivable act so heinous that you cannot begin to imagine the sleepless nights of torment and anger that your former lover has endured? What words can even begin to break down all that anguish?

"Hi," I said.

"Hello," she replied.

It seemed a bit of an anti-climax.

"Can I come in?"

I nodded, stood back and Caroline crossed the threshold. As she passed me, I caught the scent of her perfume - patchouli, jasmine, summer fruit - and I was transported back to that summer of my final year. A warm evening at the bottom of a vicarage garden. The neatly mown grass beneath us. The warmth of her body close to mine. The soft touch of her lips on my mouth. The delicate shades of blonde framing her face.

I blinked.

"Your hair's brown."

She stood in the middle of my office, "Some things change," she said wafting her gloved hand through the fug of cigarette smoke, "unlike others." Her eye caught the numerous dog ends in the overflowing ashtray. "Haven't you quit yet?"

"It's been one of those weeks."

"Nothing new there then." Acid. I flinched inwardly.

Silence descended.

The clocks ticked. She eyed them but said nothing.

Apart from the hair she really hadn't changed that much. Slim, youthful, pretty, immaculately dressed with dark brown eyes. I'd missed those eyes.

Why was she here?

"Why are you here?"

"I need your help."

"I should have guessed it wasn't a social call."

"And why on Earth would you expect one of those?"

"You could have kept in touch."

"Kept in touch? Sam, we split up."

"I know, but..."

"Oh, for Christ's sake!"

"You know Daddy hates it when you blaspheme."

"Don't bring my father into this."

"Why not? He runs your life."

"He just wants what's best for me."

"Like choosing adequate boyfriends?"

"At least my father cared for me."

The clocks ticked.

I clenched my hands.

"And what does that mean?"

Caroline closed her eyes. "Sorry. I didn't mean that. Sam, can we just talk about work?"

"Screw work. Let's talk about Dad. What did you mean?"

"Sam, I said I was sorry..." She opened those dark brown eyes again and she did look truly sorry, but she had waved the red rag to the bull and, after the week I had just endured, there was no stopping me now.

"That was always your problem, you know? So bloody superior. You had the better life. You had the better school. You had the better house. You had the better father. The sweet little vicar's daughter. 'Yes, Daddy. No, Daddy. Butter wouldn't melt, Daddy.' But he never knew the half of it, did he? His little sweetness and light was a minx, a tramp. Out all night and climbing back in her window before dawn. And not once did he suspect. Not once did he have to worry. No, because the next day you were back to Miss Prim And Proper. Miss studious and meticulous at school. You were... you were..."

Caroline was crying.

I stumbled to a stop, breathing heavily.

"Caroline..."

She held up a hand. "No, Sam. It's okay. You're right. You're totally right," she sniffed, drawing a tissue out of her purse and dabbing her eyes, "and one day he found out. So we don't exactly talk anymore."

"Ah..." My words had dried up in the heat of my anger. I tapped my teeth as I wracked my brains for what to do next. Here she was after all these years, just walking back into my life and I was so not coping with it. The emotions inside were complex to say the least. They ranged from the hatred that had made me rant to the desire to just scoop her up and kiss her.

I guessed the middle ground would be best.

"Why don't you sit down while I put the kettle on?" I suggested.

She agreed.

I darted into the kitchen and started to clatter about the place. My hands were trembling as I snapped the lid off the tea caddy. "Get a grip, Sam," I mumbled to myself and the bags of dark brown leaves. "No psychotic Satanists, no vamps, no werewolves - just Caroline." I sighed deeply as I filled the kettle and flicked it on. My face felt hot, my cheeks were flushed. I was exhausted from the frenetic energy of writing with no sleep and I desperately wanted to crash in my bed, on the sofa, on the floor - anywhere - but now this had happened and I was suddenly locking down the harness on the roller-coaster for a second spin and I knew my stomach was going to churn up something unpleasant.

As the kettle started to hiss and crackle, I dumped two teabags into the pot and breathed in deep the soothing, aromatic fragrance.

I closed my eyes and it was just shy of sixteen years ago.

A balmy summer's afternoon. My head was still a touch hazy from the events of the previous night with the phantom Gerald, Malcolm Wallace and Wallace's mysterious high-heeled benefactor. I had consequently chewed so many mints that my stomach could have been dished up as a dessert haggis. Saint Cuthbert's vicarage was very much old school - an ironstone edifice nestled in rambling ivy and climbing roses surrounded by ornate and lengthy gardens which were suitable for tea and cucumber sandwiches in the summer, or stalls selling mulled wine at the Christmas fair in the winter. It was a parish which had obviously been extremely wealthy when it had been founded. The church was an immense size for what I estimated to be a small rural congregation and it dominated the village. The priest's home overlooked the green to the side of the church. A gravel path wound its way through immaculate borders; flowers of all shapes, colour and perfume decorated my way up to the large, oak door.

I looked for a bell, saw none and knocked as loudly as my knuckles would allow on the wood that had been hewn from a tree long before my grandfather had been born. I fidgeted as I waited and ran my hands through my curls in a vain attempt to tame my unruly hair. Sleeping half the night with your head on a kitchen table does wonders for the shabby chic look.

There was a rattling behind the door and it creaked open. A blonde teenage girl stood in the crack between the door and the frame. "Can I help you?"

For a moment I struggled to find any suitable words. My brain had forgotten it possessed the ability to communicate with other beings, it was far too busy taking in what it could see and pumping necessary hormones around my weary body.

She was slight of build, standing just short of my nose. Bobbed hair framed a pretty face with a slightly upturned nose which sat precisely between two deep, dark brown eyes.

And she was smiling. It wasn't one of those, "Wow, I'm really happy!" smiles. No, it was one of those, "Oh, hello. I think you look cute," smiles.

I tried to work my mouth into intelligible consonants and syllables but nothing ventured out past my lips.

She raised a light-coloured eyebrow and half-turned her head to shout back into the house, "Dad! The guy's here about the placement." Then she stood back to open the door and gestured with her hand, "I think you'd better come in."

So I did.

The kettle clicked off, snapping me out of my reverie. I snatched it up and drowned my daydream along with the teabags. The past was the past. It belonged to a time that was gone and finished. What was important was the here and now. I placed the pot, two mismatched mugs, some teaspoons and a bowl of sugar on a tray and ventured back into my office. Caroline was seated nervously on the edge of the sofa. I wasn't sure if she was nervous about being here in general or about the possibility that the accumulated debris of the room would leap up like a garbage golem and grab her by the throat. I chided myself for letting the room slip towards Spliffness and lay the tray on the table.

"Do you want sugar? I'm afraid I don't have any milk."

She shook her head. "Just black will be fine."

I spooned two big heaps into my mug and splashed tea onto the white granules. It was still rather weak, so I prodded the bags with my teaspoon to encourage them in their work. On the second attempt the tea poured somewhat darker. I decided it would do.

Caroline took her mug and blew over the hot liquid causing a small puff of steam to blow up over her face. I sat in my office chair cradling my drink and waited. Even now, after all these years, I was still at a loss as to what I should say around her so, for a while, we just sat and sipped tea, the rumbling of past memories bouncing between us in a noisy silence.

Inevitably it was Caroline who spoke first. "I have a son. He's my life, my all. I never made the big time. Still stuck here in this provincial hole working for a tin pot little rag owned by a self-inflated moron who believes the most effective way to get something decent out his workforce is to berate and bully them until they submit to his will."

She had always wanted to be a reporter and the description of her boss sounded incredibly familiar. "You work on the *Lancaster Chronicle*? For Hector Swarbrick?"

Caroline nodded.

"I met him last week."

That old smile caressed her lips and hormones stroked my palpitating heart along with a slightly baser organ. "I know. I hear you had some fun."

I shrugged. Then I frowned. "Wait. Has he sent you?"

Caroline quickly shook her head. "No! God no. If he knew I was here he would fire me instantly. I'm here because my son's in trouble."

"Your son?"

"Yes." Those big brown eyes kept a firm hold on me. My heart sighed and I desperately tried to ignore it; stay professional, Sam. "He's in trouble, I'm sure of it."

I concentrated on letting my mind pore over the facts. It was hurriedly trying to make a connection here. There was Hector Swarbrick, owner of the *Lancaster Chronicle* and bullying father of Billy Swarbrick. Billy was a pupil at Saint Edmund Campion. I had been at Saint Edmund's last week. My heart waved an image in front of my brain - a glass figurine being smashed in anger - and at once I knew who Caroline's son was.

"John," I said.

"John," his mother confirmed.

It had been there, right in front of me, last week - John's blonde hair, the glass animal, the over-protective mother - but I just hadn't made the full connection. The whole business with Billy had sort of edged it out of the limelight. I thought about the bright-eyed youth and his bubbly demeanour. He had seemed just like any other teenage lad, possibly even more well-adjusted than most. He certainly hadn't come across as the sort to get himself into trouble. Sex and drugs or fast cars had not seemed to be on his agenda. "So what's the problem?"

Caroline fidgeted with her fingernails. They were highly polished and lacquered in a clear varnish - professional, not tarty. "Here's the deal. A few weeks ago John and a few of his mates picked up a leaflet in town about a youth group that meets locally and provides what it calls a "safe environment" for teenagers to go and hang out. There's no drink, no drugs, no hanky-panky - all very clean and above board. I thought to myself, 'Okay, no bad. It'll give him something to do,' and for the first week or so, everything seemed fine, but then he started spending more and more time with the group and I guess the *worried mum* gene kicked in. I challenged him about it and he said that everything was cool. He and his friends were having a great time and learning stuff about how to succeed in life."

"No real harm in that," I shrugged. "A bit driven perhaps, but apart from that...?"

Caroline shook her head emphatically. "No. Something was wrong; I knew it. They all started wearing these wrist band things."

"Lilac-coloured ones?"

She nodded.

"I saw them last week. Lots of kids were wearing them."

"It's not just the kids. I rang school and voiced my concerns. I spoke to some young girl who sounded fresh out of college and she brushed me off saying that the society was perfectly safe and even members of staff there belonged to it."

"She may have a point. It could be nothing," I volunteered. So John had described his little group as life-changing, but then, to a teenage lad, every latest, greatest thing was life-changing: the X-Box Kinect, Facebook, banana-flavoured ice-cream.

Caroline stood up and made to leave. I leapt up after her. "Where are you going?"

"This was a mistake," she snapped back at me. "You obviously think I'm neurotic and don't want to help."

For a split-second I hesitated. This woman was one of the greatest failures of my past. Could I really turn my back on her right now? Whether she was over-reacting or not, surely I had to try and make things right?

"Of course I'll help you."

She turned back to face me. "Really?"

"Really."

A smile tugged at her mouth and my heart melted. "Really, really?"

I nodded, remembering the last time we had exchanged those words. It had been the other way round. We had been cosied up together in her dad's garden and my heart had been pounding louder than an atomic blast. "Really," I said again. "John gave me a leaflet last week. I'll start with that."

"Thanks, Sam," Caroline smiled and all the pain of the previous week melted away. I searched my head frantically for a reason, any reason to delay her departure. It had been so long and my heart had missed her so much.

"I'd better take your number," I finally said, "so I can contact you."

"Sure. You have some paper?"

I grabbed a pad off my desk and passed it over with a pen. As she neatly wrote the number down I darted over to the windows and opened them as wide as I could to remove the stale cigarette smoke. She had always hated my habit. "Cancer sticks," she had called them on numerous occasions. Her father was very high church but also curiously puritanical and certain things had rubbed off on her. I remember her stealing my packet of fags and sitting on them until I promised not to smoke another for the rest of the day. When I had finally extricated them from underneath her, it became all too apparent that those particular Luckies would not be being smoked that day or any other; they had been squashed flatter than a child's innocence when it sees its parents filling stockings over the fireplace on Christmas Eve.

"Here you go." She handed the pad back to me, still smiling that sweet little lop-sided smile.

"Thank you." I took my phone out and entered the number into my contacts. "Listen, you want to stay for a bit? There must be all sorts of things we need to catch up on."

She waggled back and forth uncertainly as if weighing up the pros and cons of my suggestion until finally she said, "Sorry, Sam. I can't. I need to get back to work. Another time, perhaps?"

My heart slouched down and rested its head morosely on its hand. "Sure, okay."

"But how about you ring me tomorrow and we can meet up to discuss your findings?"

My heart bounced out of its doldrums and started cartwheeling around my chest. "Okay. That sounds good." I waved the pad in front of me. "I have your number."

She chuckled then something dawned on me. Something which, as yet, had gone unmentioned. "Erm... what does John's father think about all of this?"

The lop-sided grin fixed me in its grip as her brown eyes twinkled. "I never married him. It's just me and John."

I smiled back at her. "Cool... I mean..." I coughed, "Okay. I'll ring you tomorrow then."

"Tomorrow," she grinned as she turned and left me standing like a young boy excited at the prospect that soon he will be holding hands with the prettiest girl in the class. But that was tomorrow. First I had to knuckle down to some work.

After Caroline left, the first thing I did was just sit and stare blankly into space. Life, I decided, was a funny old thing. It was rather like a trusted old car. It ran and ran for years with no problems whatsoever, then you decided to upgrade something in the engine to make it supposedly better. After the upgrade, things started to happen. You might use more fuel or you might start to hear an annoying rumble every time it went above forty miles per hour. The car that you once loved was just not the same any more. Yes, it was running faster and smoother, but those little things just seemed to bug away at you.

Was this my life now? Had my self-imposed upgrade thrust me into some sort of spotlight that would make me a target for all things weird?

Well at least it would not be boring.

I lit a Lucky and glanced at the mantle clock on the window. It was just past ten. I yawned loudly as my body reminded me that I was still lacking that vital component of rest and rejuvenation: a good night's sleep. I glanced over at the welcoming upholstery of the sofa but shook my head. I had matters to attend to.

John, John, John. What to do about John? I reached over to my jacket which was draped on a chair and rummaged around for the leaflet he had given me. I scrutinised the front cover of the three-fold A4 leaflet.

Emblazoned across the middle was the lilac-coloured emblem that resembled an upper-case T enwrapped with two spiralling lines and there, underneath, was the eponymous call to action: "Anything Is Possible."

Anything? Get that killer promotion? Run the London Marathon? Pass your degree with no student loan? Con your way onto the International Space Station? Or how about something really hard – get to the post office on a Monday morning before the grey-haired attack force of old age pensioners make you stand in the queue out the door for five hours?

Okay, so perhaps I exaggerate just a touch but the organisation, which appeared to call itself Credete, might as well have suggested them as it seemed to promise just about anything. There was healthy living, job satisfaction and international harmony to name but a few. I sighed. I had seen all this sort of stuff before. Before I was a student, I had taken a year out (that's what you youngsters call a gap year these days, just in case you were wondering) and explored the various facets of the rough-hewn diamond called the Church. Many people see it as one coherent body and get all confused when they see it squabbling over such things as gay marriage or women bishops. Well, let me tell you this, the Church of England is somewhat like a swan. It has all the grace and decorum on the surface, but underneath there is a chaos of legs paddling maniacally trying to keep it afloat. The difference between the swan and the good old C of E is that the legs of the swan succeed, whereas the legs of the Church are in constant chance of tripping over each other and splitting it apart. You have the ecumenicals, the catholics, the evangelicals, the conservatives, the liberals and the list goes on and on.

So, during my academic sabbatical, I decided to try my hand at as many of these groups as possible, just to verify where I was most comfortable. Looking back, I'm amazed that I came through it still wanting to wear my shirt back to front, but I did and that led on to Caroline, which in turn led me to this train of thought.

A weird kind of synchronicity, don't you think?

The ones that I guess freaked me out the most were the evangelicals. It all seemed far too happy. I'm the cynical sort, by nature, and I kept waiting for the drop. You know what I mean: they're all aliens, they're all sadomasochists, they're all bank managers. Something bizarre or evil like that.

Anyway, the evangelical meetings I went to always followed the same pattern, there would be lots of singing, clapping, affirmation, praising the

Lord and then utter condemnation of anyone who didn't see the world through their vindictive little spectacles.

I once went to this rally... (Oops! Sorry. That should be *conference*...) which was being held by a society that called itself Jesus Loves Us. It was full of young people bathed in the healthy glow of self-righteousness who continually proclaimed just how much good *The Lord* (yes they did speak in emphasised italics) had imparted on them since they had turned away from darkness to Jesus Christ.

That deep, dark cynical part of me knew it was a farce from the moment that I walked in the door. It was like *Songs of Praise* meets *The Stepford Wives*. There was no individualism whatsoever. They all dressed the same (clean t-shirt with blue jeans). They all sang the same hymns (*Shine Jesus Shine* was normally the one that tended to be the favourite. Whatever you do, don't google it; you'll be humming it *ad nauseam*). They all had that beatific cleanly scrubbed glow to their faces that comes with far too much soap and sanctity.

I was subjected to hour upon hour of pious indoctrination. Time after time I was pounded over the head with the undoubtable fact that Jesus was born from a virgin and that he had to be the Son of God. To think anything else was totally incredible when one looked at the wonderful deeds he performed in the lives of the society's members. Any divergent opinion was the work of The Devil. To believe that there was any vestige of truth in any other religions was the work of The Devil. To over-indulge in any practice that could be vaguely construed as fun was the work of The Devil. To pass wind on a Sunday was the work of The Devil.

You get my drift?

Mind you, being the open-minded sort of bloke that I am (and the fact that I had a specific return train booked to save me a bundle of cash), I was willing to give them the benefit of the doubt.

Perhaps all these fundamentalist tenets were just the face of an overbloated managerial hierarchy?

Perhaps the grass roots members were just good, honest youths who were there to nod and smile sagely during the day but would let their hair down and boogie like there's no tomorrow once the lights were out?

Perhaps penguins fly north for the summer?

"Hi... er... *Sam*." It was a clean-shaven boy in his late teens who was performing a remarkable job of reading the three letters (one of them in upper-case) on my name badge. As he smiled that Stepford smile, the mountain-fresh aroma of middle class Marks and Spencers drifted up to my nose causing my face to grimace. Unfortunately, he took this to be a *welcoming* smile and he continued his introduction. "Peace be with you. My name is Luke."

Fortunately, at that point, my common sense gene kicked in and, realising that the name was biblical, stopped my numpty gene from blurting out something along the lines of, "Great to meet you. Killed any Sith recently?" Instead, I just mumbled a vaguely audible, "Hi."

Unperturbed by my non-committal grunt, Luke carried on in his irritatingly friendly manner, "So what brought you to Jesus Loves Us."

Again, I swerved past the obvious answer, which would have been, "A train." The answer I gave was far more sensible (or so I thought at the time). I explained that I was just kicking my heels for a year before university and was looking for something suitable to stick on my CV.

"Ah!" he sighed as if being lifted up in the Rapture. "God does move in mysterious ways." Whatever that had to do with a CV, I had no idea. "What university are you going to?"

I informed him that it would be Luneside University, where I would read Religious Studies.

This was the point where I had to undertake a little introduction: knife meet atmosphere; atmosphere meet knife.

"Religious studies?" The mask of happiness slipped and a look of perturbed confusion assumed its place. "Does that include *other* religions?"

I explained that yes, it encompassed many other varied faiths.

Luke shook his head. "No, Sam. There is only one *true* faith." His demeanour became that of one futilely trying to explain to a serial killer why he should stop listening to that little voice in his head. "All the others are false religions. The only true faith is the way of The Cross."

I begged to differ with him. I especially thought that there were aspects of Buddhism which were very green...

"The Green movement is New Age, Sam. It is the work of Satan himself."

Words left me as I was stunned into silence.

"Brothers! Brothers!" Luke called out to surrounding members. "We must lay our healing hands on this poor wretch..."

*Wretch?*

"... and pray that the evil demon..."

*Demon?*

"... that is dwelling within him will leave, so that he will return to Christ."

*Christ!*

I rose sharply from my chair and bolted to the door in order to make a hasty exit. As my hand grasped the door-knob, a wicked smile touched my lips and an idea bubbled up in my mind. I turned a raised hand as if in a pseudo-blessing and said, "Don't worry, my friends. I am sure that Crom Cruach will forgive you."

There were screams of horror as I shot out of the building and ran for the nearest main road to hitch a lift home. Apparently, none of them had ever read up on ancient Irish religions. Philistines.

So yes, I have very little time for any group which promises a divine thunderbolt that will bring peace, love and fluffy bunnies into your mundane existence. I'm more of a "stop the whinging and get on with it" kind of guy. If your life is crap then it is up to you to sort it out, not constantly wait for a supernatural intervention.

I am also the kind of guy that needs his sleep, and as I sat there, finishing off my cigarette I felt the abuse of the last few days catching up with me and my eyebrows drooped. Stretching, I curled up on the sofa.

I would just close my eyes for a bit. A little doze would sort me out.

Within seconds I was snoring like an asthmatic camel.

It actually started out like any normal dream. I was wandering through my mum's house: all her toby jugs were smiling down at me, the thick carpet felt warm under my bare feet and sunshine was streaming in through the French windows.

I smiled. For once, a dream I could enjoy.

It didn't last, of course.

I turned the handles on the French windows and the tall glass doors swung outwards into the sweet-smelling summer garden. There, in the middle of the immaculate lawn, a young boy of about seven played with his Action Man dolls. He was dressed like a soldier himself: green jumper and purple beret. As he positioned the dolls in various poses around about him, he made squawking noises that sounded like military radios whilst making the characters in his stories interact with each other.

There were light footsteps to my side and I was aware of someone standing next to me. "You remember this day?" A clipped, educated, female voice.

I nodded as I turned to face the stranger. She was about my height, immaculately dressed in a light-green two-piece skirt and jacket suit. Her dark hair was tied up in a severe bun and dark-rimmed glasses were perched on her aquiline nose.

She looked, for all intent and purpose like a librarian.

I shuddered involuntarily.

"Of course I remember this day. It was the first day that I heard things that weren't there."

She continued to gaze at my younger self. "What was it you heard?"

"Voices."

"Where did you hear them coming from?"

"Well, from..." I paused and looked back at my younger self. He was staring up at me with a frown on his face and the memory of that day clarified in my head. I had been playing in the garden on a hot, summer's day when suddenly I had been aware of voices. They had been coming from my house, but I could not see anyone there. I had not been able to make out any words, but it had felt like there had been two people talking there.

I spun towards the neatly-dressed woman, my mouth open in disbelief.

"Don't forget the child you were, Samuel," she said, her fiery eyes locked on me through her glasses before she faded into nothingness and I was left alone.

Then there was a pelican wearing a purple scarf and Buddy Holly spectacles hovering overhead squawking in an extremely irritating tone.

"That'll be my phone, then," I sighed. "Time to wake up."
So I did.

# Chapter Two

Half an hour later I had splashed some cold water on my face in a vain attempt to awaken my senses, roughly run my fingers through my hair to try and make myself look vaguely presentable and legged it up the road to the police station hoping not to keep a certain punctual DCI waiting.

I think I just about managed the last of this trio, as for the others... ah well.

The first time I had ever been in a police station had been when I was about eight. Our dog, a black and white border collie named Shep (every collie in the seventies was called Shep – such was the popularity of John Noakes and his four-legged friend) had done a runner. Again. My parents had bought him for my seventh birthday. For some bizarre reason, they had presumed that the joy that overflowed from a young lad at snuggling up to his newly acquired furry bundle of fun would form itself into that self-same boy exercising said dog twice a day.

Fat chance.

I was far more involved in curling up in my room with my latest super-hero comic whilst my dad grumbled loudly and slammed the door with extreme volume as he stomped out into the rain with "the sodding dog." A few weeks of this saw Shep exercising himself in the back garden rather than in the fields at the end of our street. This, in turn, led to young Samuel refusing to play out in the fresh air as treading in something warm and brown lying in the grass was not his idea of fun. End result: dog got bored in garden, I withdrew into my science fiction, one very pissed-off father.

I'm sure there are parents everywhere nodding their head in recognition of this scenario.

Anyway, back to the matter at hand. One frequent consequence of Shep being imprisoned in our luscious, green, rear-of-the-house dog toilet was that he tended to get bored and longed for the company of other canines, especially female ones. This inevitably led to an already angry father getting even more annoyed as he wandered the local streets searching in vain for a randy escapee.

On the occasion that I mentioned earlier, Shep had been picked up by a local bobby and driven to the town nick where they kept cells for canines as well as humans. My mum was out when the phone call came in and, as a result, my dad dragged me out of my pit and forced me to accompany him in bailing out the four-legged fugitive.

So, as I sat in the corridor outside of Jitendra's office and my watch ticked its way round to one in the afternoon, my mind was cast back to that little vignette from my childhood and I started to dwell on the various Freudian baggage that went with it. I had the overwhelming feeling that I was in trouble again and that my father was scowling down at me from Heaven whilst muttering profanities quietly enough that I could not pick them up and repeat them but with enough volume to know that I had incurred his wrath.

The look on Jitendra's face when he opened his office door did nothing to allay my anxiety. "Hello, Sam," he said. "You'd better come in."

His office was more or less as I had expected it to be. It was totally pristine: clean and fresh with a delicate hint of an essential oil that I could not quite place. Sandalwood perhaps? I had the feeling that Jitendra was the sort that had to go over a room and titivate it to his exacting wishes after the cleaner has supposedly already done the job. There was a wide open window looking out over Thurnam Street and the side of the town hall. Next to that was a lusciously green Swiss cheese plant with immaculately polished leaves and trimmed roots. Down the wall to my right were bookcases lined with meticulously filed and labelled folders next to three imposing filing cabinets. The third wall of the room was dominated by Jitendra's mammoth desk and this was the sole exception to his rule of precision. It was littered with hastily scribbled notes on sheets of A4 paper which were piled up on top of a number of books that were in the process of being read, annotated and dissected. My eyes were drawn to a reproduction of a woodcut of a werewolf standing in all its slavering glory.

Jitendra noticed the direction of my gaze and quietly closed the book shut, sliding it under the notes which he shuffled together on top of it.

Not a word did he say; not a comment did I make.

For a moment we stood in the ominously awkward silence that occupies the space between two individuals who know that sooner or later they will have to confront the elephant in the room but figure that perhaps now is not the appropriate time to crack out the peanuts.

He gestured to the chair in front of his desk.

I coughed and gladly took it.

"It's regarding your abductors from John O'Gaunt Media." Direct, no-nonsense, to the point.

"Ah. I guess I'd almost forgotten about them." I leaned back in the chair and stretched my arms, stifling the desperate urge to yawn. I really did need a decent night's sleep. "How's it coming along? Have they," I formed quotation marks with my fingers, "confessed?"

Jitendra shook his head. "Not exactly. In fact, three of them were found dead in their cells this morning."

Jitendra did not keep the same sort of liquid refreshment that I did. His filing cabinets may have been purely following the manufacturer's recommendation but someone in the station sure made a decent cup of coffee. I've been told many times that I should avoid caffeine as it affects the ringing in my ears, but right then I didn't give a damn. I was already dropping on my feet from lack of sleep and it now felt like the rug had been viciously yanked out from under the self-same appendages.

Haversham, Baines and Sothwell had been found dead that morning in their holding cells. All three of them had chewed at their wrists until they had ruptured a vein (or is it an artery - I can never remember) before bleeding to death. Apparently it had not been a pretty sight.

I could have murdered for a Lucky, but I didn't dare to mess with the precisely positioned molecules of the air in Jitendra's office.

"What about the other two?" I finally managed.

"Brande tried the same trick but must have hesitated for some reason. As a result, she didn't bleed out as vigorously as the others and we got to her in time. Philips..." the policeman let out a short puff of breath, leaned back in his chair and tossed a pen onto his desk. "Philips is exactly the same as when we arrested him."

I raised a questioning eyebrow.

"Lights on; nobody home," he rumbled as he reached over for a buff-coloured file similar in style to the one he had loaned me regarding a certain lycanthrope. "He flicked through a few sheets of paper, chewing his bottom lip. "There's loads of medical jargon in here, but the long and the short of it is he's switched off. He eats, he sleeps, he performs the usual bodily functions but he will not, cannot communicate with anyone."

I drummed my fingernails against my teeth as little bells rang fiercely in my head. "This is all very well and good, but why did you need to see me. Surely you could have told me this over the phone?"

"True," Jitendra grunted, reaching for another file. "There is, however, something else. Before he died, Baines left us a message in his blood. It's not exactly *The Da Vinci Code* but I need to know if it means anything to you." He slid an A4 colour photo across the desk. There, scrawled in a dying man's blood was the phrase:

"The Divergence is coming."

I looked Jitendra straight in the eye. "I need to see Brande right now."

"Oh, and why would that be?"

"You have to trust me on this one."

The Asian policeman threw back his head and barked one sharp, resonant laugh then glowered at me. “Like I had to trust you to take a walk in the park? Is this to do with the werewolf?”

I fidgeted in my chair. “No.”

He continued to fix me in his scalpel-sharp stare.

I remained silent and fidgety.

“Well?”

“Honest, it's nothing to do with the werewolf... I think.”

“You think?” Jitendra's voice was dripping with the most potent sarcasm that I think I had ever heard. “Well there's a novel idea.”

“It's not to do with werewolves and it's nothing to do with the suicides.”

“Really?” His fingers were steepled and he peered over the top of them. “So Baines just decided to compose a little bit of random abstract poetry whilst his blood oozed out of his lacerated wrist? Is that it? That's what you're telling me? Bullshit, Sam. Tell me what it means!”

I winced as his voice raised. “I've heard the phrase once before, last week.”

He nodded. “Go on.”

“From a client.”

“And...”

“They were a vampire.”

That good old familiar awkward silence walked back into the room and sat itself down neatly between us atop Jitendra's desk. It crossed and uncrossed its legs expectantly before carefully examining its nails and eventually buggering off when Jitendra quietly and calmly said, “I think you need to tell me all about last week, and any other little tales of ghosties and goblins, right now.”

So I did. It was all still fresh in my mind from having cathartically typed it all out. I began with Satanists, moved onto vampires, nipped back some years to phantoms before coming back to poltergeists which were really fairies and then finished with one big, bad-ass werewolf.

You know what, I think he actually believed it. I was impressed.

“So you have no idea what this Divergence is?” he finally asked.

I shook my head. “No. But I got the impression that it's bad enough to share the shit out of Bram Stoker's favourite friends.”

“Then I agree,” he said as he rearranged his desk and stood, straightening his tie, “that you need to speak to Miss Brande.”

The young woman who was led into the grey, oppressive interrogation room was not the same young woman who I had met just the week previous. This creature was a wreck, a shell of a person. Her insides had been scooped out and she had been left hollow: a mere simulacrum. I watched through the ubiquitous one-way mirror as two uniformed constables guided her somewhat unwillingly in. Her hair was unbrushed, her skin missing its multilayered coats of slap and her feet shod in tattered trainers rather than some fancy brand of expensive high heels. Having said that, the vicious little spark was still there. I know that I would have struggled to take the verbal abuse that she doled out without snapping back at her. Some of the things that she suggested they do to one another were quite anatomically impossible but they just carried out their duties and waited patiently until Jitendra led me inside; an inquisition party of two. He silently nodded to the constables and they left us alone with her.

Brande sat scowling at us in silence for a minute or so while Jitendra, apparently unconcerned with her being there, quietly flicked through his file and made notes with his fountain pen.

I thought it best to follow his lead, this not being my field of expertise. Was he trying to rile her; get her to blurt out something without thinking? Was he playing Good Cop, Bad Cop? If he was, what did that make me? Was I supposed to go and lean in the corner chewing on a tooth pick bottling up all my misogynistic anxiety, ready to snap and start berating the woman for the piece of crap that I saw her as? I hoped not. I was sure I'd make a much better Good Cop.

Eventually, my worries were proved pointless (not to mention rather foolish and fanciful). Jitendra fished the same photo out of the file that he had shown me and slid it across the table. Brande's reaction said it all. Her eyes widened and her face visibly paled. "Oh, God," she moaned. "Where was this taken?"

Jitendra answered with his most matter-of-fact voice, "In Baines' cell shortly after he chewed himself to death. Care to enlighten us?"

The actress mumbled something inaudible.

"Sorry, Miss Brande," Jitendra's authoritative voice was cold, hard, "I didn't quite catch that."

She lifted up her head and tears were welling in her eyes. "None of us really believed him when he said it was going to happen."

"The Divergence?"

She nodded.

"What is it?"

"We... I... don't really know," she stammered. "He said it was going to be a wonderful thing. The world would change and all would be peaceful."

Something here did not make sense. I thought back to the cold, hard floor of John O'Gaunt Studios, a pentagram and a very sharp knife. "Forgive me if I don't quite believe you to be the butterflies, bunnies and unicorns type," I snapped. I ignored Jitendra's warning glance and carried on. "I'm still having nightmares about your little peaceful games."

"Oh, my heart just bleeds for you," she sneered, her lip curled up in derision.

"I didn't know ice had a pulse," I shot back.

She was silent for a moment then continued, "Do you know what it's like to be used?"

The question burned into me as her dark-rimmed eyes scoured my face trying to rip an answer from my flesh.

"Yes I do." I thought about another woman. One who had waltzed into my life last week, fluttered her eyelids in my direction, fed me a sob story and tried to feed me to her crazed brother as a human-sized packet of Winalot.

"It cheapens you, doesn't it?" She closed her eyes, tears forcing their way out of the screwed up lids, trickling down her pale cheeks. She raised her arm and wiped them away with the fresh bandage that now swaddled her wrist. Brande opened her eyes and studied the damp dressing as if it was the first time that she had lain eyes upon it. Her eyes darted up and down its folds, examining the pattern of the tightly bound material. The tears started in earnest.

"The bastard!" she cried, "The fucking bastard. He promised us everything!"

I glanced at Jitendra. He gave an almost imperceptible shrug. He had no idea who the actress was talking about.

"Who used you Melanie?" I asked, my voice low and calm. I knew that I needed to win her over, to be a friend in her hour of need. Even if it was a total fabrication, it could win us some answers.

Then, in an instant, the little bitch of the previous week was back and I was looking at a middle finger standing upright. So much for the friendship approach. "You really think I'm gonna help an old perv like you? Get kicks off damsels in distress do you?" She flicked her red hair that was tied back in a rough ponytail and leant back on her chair. "Yeah, that's it isn't it? You swank in and go all 'Hey, babe, you can trust me,' with those big dark eyes of yours and that tousled, wavy hair, but you know what? I see right through you. You're a knob who likes to play with himself when no one's looking. You really get off on..."

"That's enough," Jitendra's deep baritone was calm and unobtrusive, but cut her off mid-rant.

She turned, looked at him as if he was a piece of unidentifiable slime that she had scraped off her shoe and spat out, "Screw you, *paki*."

Jitendra rose smoothly from his chair, walked over next to Brande, looked down into the smug little 'you can't lay a finger on me,' face, sighed and slammed said face down onto the table. His hand gripped the back of her head tight as he hissed into her ear. "Now you listen to me, you cheap little piece of trash. With all the crap you've given me and my people, I couldn't really care less whether you live or die. If you had bled yourself out last night, I actually think the world would have been a better place this morning, but to have three prisoners in my charge simultaneously kill themselves... Well that's just far too much paperwork. Letting another add herself onto that list would make it totally intolerable. So I'm going to let go now and you're going to be a nice helpful, little puppy. Do you understand? Roll over and play nicely."

Brande made a strained nodding motion against the hard surface and Jitendra yanked her upright before resuming his seat.

At that moment I have to say I actually felt sorry for her. She looked terrified, truly terrified.

Jitendra nonchalantly crossed his legs. "I believe Mister Spallucci asked you a question and you were about to answer him in a nice, polite manner that is pertaining to a young lady of your profession. Am I right?"

Brande looked from the chief inspector to me then back again. She opened her mouth to speak, her bottom lip trembled and more tears flooded out from her eyes. "I can't!" she screamed. "Believe me, I can't! He'll know and he'll come for me." She thrust the bandaged wrist forward. "You've seen what he made us do. Well this is nothing compared to what he's capable of. Please don't make me tell you. Please!" She sprang from her chair and darted towards me. Jitendra was up like a shot and lunged over the desk to grab at her shoulder but she dodged his outstretched arm and threw herself at my feet, her hands grabbing onto my trouser legs. "Please," she begged, "please, just go away and leave me alone. I can't take it anymore. He promised us so much. We didn't understand the price. The things he said to us. The things he said. It was too much.

"He came to me in my dreams. It was as if he was there in the cell with me. He kept telling me how worthless I was, how there was no way out of this and that I was a failure."

She drifted off to somewhere unpleasant. When she returned her voice sounded as fragile as a new-born baby's skull. One hard squeeze and she would be totally crushed. "His eyes. His eyes. They refused to release me. He stood there punishing me for my uselessness.

"I just wanted to die. It was all I could do to escape!"

She buried her head against my trouser leg and sobbed and sobbed and sobbed.

I looked up at Jitendra. The interview was over.

The roasted, smoky flavour tasted divine. I leaned my head against the brick wall and blew a rather impressive smoke ring.

"Neat trick. Feeling a bit better?"

I nodded and ran my free hand through my hair. "That was somewhat intense, wasn't it?"

Jitendra nodded, his arms crossed and one immaculately polished shoe resting under him against the wall. "I think it's safe to say that Miss Brande is somewhat messed up."

"Indeed." I drew in heavily and finished off the Lucky. It was only mid-afternoon but I was in desperate need of my bed. However, I wasn't finished here yet. "You don't think she's faking it, then?"

The DCI shook his head. "No. I've seen a lot try to claim the insanity thing, but that..." He let out a sharp breath. "That was pure fear." Jitendra pulled himself away from the wall, straightening his suit as he did. "Whoever played her has terrified her to the core. What do you make of that dream business?"

"She genuinely thinks that this guy made her try to kill herself." I drummed my fingers against my teeth. "Obviously there's part of me that is thinking psychic powers here, but perhaps we could do with looking at the more mundane too?"

He shook his head. "If you're thinking it might have been an inside job,

I've already been there, examined it. Not one officer had contact with all five of them last night." He fished a notepad out of his jacket and ran a finger down a list. "Baines and Sothwell were checked on by one PC, Brande and Haversham by a second, Philips by another. There was no link."

"Hmmm..." I pondered. "All the same, it might be worth just doing a bit of checking up in case the three officers have any connections outside of the force. Perhaps they were being used?"

"I'll look into it." He paused, eyed me up and down then asked, "So, you up for another interview? Want to question Philips?"

"Sure, I shrugged. It can't get any worse can it?"

Little did I realise just how wrong I was.

The meeting with Philips began quite well. Okay, as well as a meeting with a man as responsive as a boiled cauliflower can go. We waited for him in the same oppressive interview room as before. He shuffled in, a PC on either arm, guiding him to his seat where they lowered him down and he sat, just staring off into middle distance.

The man seemed to have aged ten years in a week. The grey in his hair was far more pronounced and his face was weathered, wrinkled. His mole-man spectacles had been removed (I guessed these had been considered a possible tool for harming himself) and his eyes looked so much smaller, giving him a more rodent-like appearance. This was not helped by the manner in which he sat. His hands were drawn up in front of him like a pair of grasping paws and he twitched involuntarily every now and then. He was a small mammal waiting for a bird of prey to swoop down, snatch him up and rip him limb from limb.

My heart could not help but go out to him. He had, quite obviously, lost his mind.

"How long has he been like this?" I asked, my voice barely a whisper.

"Since we brought him in. He eats, sleeps drinks and performs normal bodily functions, but apart from that..." Jitendra waved a brown hand hopelessly towards the television producer. "What you see is what you get."

"Lights on, nobody home," I murmured. Cautiously, I rose from my chair and approached the hapless little man. "Mister Philips," I spoke gently as if trying to wake a slumbering baby, "can you hear me?" He continued to stare off into space, oblivious of my presence. I waved my fedora up and down in front of his blank stare. He didn't even blink.

I drummed my fingers against my teeth and glanced over to Jitendra, who shrugged. "He's not responded to anything?"

"Nothing."

I crouched down, my knees creaking as I did so, until my head was level with my abductor's. Even with me this close, my breath on his skin, he did not move. In his world, wherever that was, I just did not exist. "We're not going to get anything from him," I finally conceded. "We're not going to learn anything about the Divergence."

Philips' head slowly turned and his eyes fixed on mine. His black pupils widened and, as he spoke, the frail, gravelly voice that crept from his lips caused the bells in my ears to shriek.

"The Divergence is coming," he rasped. His stale breath smothered my senses and spittle flecked my skin. "When dragons walk the Earth, then all creation shall tremble.

"Dragons walk among us."

Dragons.

My mind shot back to the dream I had suffered the previous week – two dragons, one red one black, viciously fighting each other, their gouged flesh ravaging the land where it landed. I tried to stand, but my tinnitus rose in volume and the room began to spin. I was vaguely aware of someone calling out my name over and over, a chair falling backwards, but then there was just the grey. Everything blurred and there was an almighty crash followed by men shouting.

I gave in and let it all wash over me.

When I came to, I was lying on the floor in the recovery position with a nicely tailored jacket under my head. My head was still spinning but it was bearable, just. I made to rise and felt a firm hand press down on my shoulder.

"Easy," came Jitendra's deep voice. "You went down heavy."

As I rose, I felt the muscles in my right shoulder groan in protest, a testament to just *how* heavy I had gone down. Then I saw Philips. He was flat on his back on the floor.

Totally still and lifeless.

"What..?" I managed.

"Dead. And so is Brande."

I grabbed a chair and slumped down into it. "How?" I was content to go with sentences of just one word. It was all I could manage for the moment.

The DCI sighed deeply. "As of yet, we have no idea. One minute he was rambling on to you about dragons, the next he collapsed face first onto the table, blood trickling from his nose. We tried CPR but..." He ran a hand over his face. "Then an officer came in and said the same had happened to Brande."

I sat and stared at the body. Philips and Brande both together? She had been terrified of some anonymous threat and he had started to spill the beans about Divergences and Dragons.

This was not a coincidence.

# Chapter Three

I staggered home from the police station. It must have taken me about five minutes but it felt more like five hours. My ears weren't just ringing, they were screeching. Someone had taken a blackboard, wedged it in my cochlea and was dragging a screwdriver down its surface. Bile rose in my throat and nausea swept over me with every staggered step. Passers-by stared in disgust at me, convinced I was some sort of awful drunk as I lurched from one steadying lamp post to the next. It was obvious to them that I had just been kicked out of some dive bar. I'm sure that one woman actually turned her child's head away from me.

Or perhaps that was just paranoia. My condition tends to do that to me. I get convinced that people are watching, staring, plotting. If someone tries to help me, I convince myself that they have some ulterior motive and plough on past them regardless. Later on, when the spin has waned, I run my hand over my face groaning and praying to the god of lost causes that I was not too abusive to some Good Samaritan.

Eventually, I reached the door to my stairwell. I pushed it open and it slammed violently against the wall. I tumbled through, crashing to my knees. I swore, kicked the door back into its frame and gripped the wall with my fingertips to heave myself vaguely upright.

The stairwell was swaying from side to side. I leant my back against the wall and closed my eyes. Almost there. Almost there, I told myself over and over again.

When my breathing had steadied, I tentatively prised my eyes open and approached the bottom of the mountain. So many step-shaped cliff faces rose up in front of me. I decided to use the old tried-and-tested technique; all fours.

I knelt down on the first step and slowly, so slowly, began my ascent. Hand over hand, knee over knee I climbed my personal Everest, eyes once again tightly shut, until I finally reached the door to my office. I fumbled into my pocket, fished out the key and, slouching in a heap on the floor, reached up to unlock the door.

As it swung in, I crawled after it then turned onto my back and closed the door in the same manner as I had the one downstairs. I gave one of my clocks (cannot remember which one) a quick glance. It was about two thirty.

Now came the hard part.

Now came the reason why I surrounded myself with so many time pieces. Lying there on the floor, my trench coat splayed out making me look like a bird that has collided with a window, I breathed deeply and listened.

There they were, my constantly ticking workmates. Slow ticks, fast ticks, low pitches, high pitches. All of them surrounding me in their beautiful, caressing embrace. I let the noise wash over me like I had been forced to do so many times before and their individual songs sang into my beleaguered ears. There was the napoleon hat mantle clock, there was the mechanical carriage, there was the station clock. Those and many more surrounded me and administered to me like angels in the desert. They brought me succour and relief; they fed me life-sustaining manna.

And eventually the ringing and screeching subsided.

It did not disappear completely, it never does, but it became tolerable, ignorable.

I rose to a sitting position and, when I was sure that I was not going to keel over, rose and went to my desk. I flipped my laptop open and there, staring at me, was the end of the work that I had been writing just that morning. Once again tiredness tried to claim my limbs. I looked up at the station clock. It was now three o'clock. I finished off what I had been typing when Caroline had arrived that morning, clicked save and sat back in my chair.

I reached into my desk drawer and rummaged around for a pack of Luckies. After a couple of pat downs and jabbing of sharp objects I found an unopened pack. Smiling, I made to unwrap it.

Then the shaking started. I tried to grasp the plastic tab but my fingers just would not cooperate, they juddered and jinked like a caffeine-addicted spider. "Come on..." I grumbled. "Open, damn it!"

Then I felt it again.

The spinning.

This was not good. I knew instantly what was going on. I had overdone it. Stress, lack of sleep, crazy guys rambling on about dragons: all these things are known causes of Meniere's attacks.

I closed my eyes and tried to listen to my clocks.

They were nowhere to be heard. Not a tick. Not a tock. Instead the ringing was increasing in volume. The old serpent was rising from its shallow slumber and it was right royally pissed off at being disturbed.

I rose from my desk and lurched into the centre of my office as reality spun and swayed around me. I knelt down and curled up in as tight a ball as I could manage, clasping my hands tightly over my ears. It was a futile gesture, rather like King Cnut trying to stop the tide from coming in, but I had to do something. I had to try something.

Still the serpent slithered towards me, its mouth dripping with ravenous intent.

Still the bells rang.

Still the tintinnabulation chimed incessantly in my own personal hell.

I rocked backwards and forwards moaning quietly to myself, desperate to cover up the continual noise.

No good.

I hummed.

I hummed louder.

I hummed louder still.

No good. No good. No good.

The scaly beast was upon me now. It had wrapped its muscular coils around my chest and was squeezing every last breath from my lungs.

Tears were forming behind my eyelids and started to trickle down my cheeks and my nose. Angrily, I brushed them off with the back of my hand before shoving my fingertips in my mouth and biting down hard.

No good. Even the pain could not deaden the infernal noise.

The serpent chuckled its infernal laugh. There was no escape for me now.

I rolled back up into a seated position and immediately regretted it. My head swayed and the room spun, nausea rose from the pit of my stomach to the back of my throat. I lurched forward and grabbed the plastic bin by my desk, strewing its contents on the floor. I crouched there, sweat seeping from every pore of my body, a flush followed by a chill as I fought back the inevitable.

And still the merciless bells continued to peal.

Still the serpent laughed at my hopelessness.

I closed my eyes and pulled my face down into the bin. The vomit was somewhere waiting to erupt, lava from my fiery pit. I rocked back and forth dreading the sensation, knowing it would arrive any second. I tried to take my mind elsewhere, I truly did. I tried to think of open fields and fresh country air. I tried to imagine calm walks along a sandy beach with fresh sea water lapping my bare feet.

The only water I felt was mixed with bile and last night's tea.

I'll spare you the details. Let's just say it was unpleasant.

Afterwards, my body's muscles started to unknot and loosen as the serpent, finally satisfied, slithered back down into its rank, foul-smelling pool of stagnant hatred. I was cold, so cold, from the sheen of sweat under my shirt. I cleared one nostril then the other. Spat out whatever was left in my mouth and dragged myself and my bucket to the bathroom.

My head was still spinning but not quite as much now. I was able swill the bin out and flush the contents of my stomach down the toilet.

Carefully, I pulled myself up to the wash basin. The room began to spin again, but I knew the worst was over now. I ran the cold tap and splashed refreshing liquid onto my warm, clammy face before sluicing my mouth out with handfuls of heaven.

When I felt vaguely abluted, I slumped down against the wall and rested my head not too far away from the toilet pan. Hormones were now racing around my body at an exponential rate. There was relief that I had finally been sick. There was revulsion that I had actually been sick and there was deep depression that I knew it would happen again at some indeterminate point in the future.

Time and time again it would happen over and over with no cessation. This was my life. This was my existence, staggering from one spin attack to the next, the life in between them was only a mild distraction.

The serpent would rise and I would plunge headlong into its crushing embrace.

It had to stop. Dear God, I would give anything for it to stop.

When I felt that my stomach was no longer in danger of belching out any more of its contents, I drew myself up to my feet, lurched sluggishly into the office and grabbed a bottle of Jack before stumbling upstairs to my flat and my merciful bedroom where, after a few long drinks of over the counter anaesthetic, I eventually passed out.

# Chapter Four

The next morning I felt somewhat better. Well, by better I mean I felt as if all the fluid had been wrung out of my muscles and my brain had been walloped with an overstuffed trout, but at least my ears had calmed down.

After half an hour of my body working out which way was up, I levered myself out from under the snuggly safehold that was my duvet and shambled towards the bathroom. I took a slight detour via the kitchen to fill the kettle and flick its switch before stumbling into what they refer to in *Star Wars* as "the refresher". Whilst I sat refreshing myself I took my mind off my current state of bleariness by pondering the matter of toilets in films. I'm all for keeping things clean and artistic but surely there has to be a certain amount of realism or people disconnect from what they are watching? Or perhaps it's just me. Perhaps I'm just far too pedantic and can't help remembering that super-heroes and space captains have bodily functions. Is it just me who, when Picard calls up an away team, wonders why none of them say, "Actually Captain, I just need to nip to the Enterprise's loo." Surely it would be practical to make sure the crew were refreshed before they teleported down to an alien planet? Who would know what might happen if Commander Riker took a leak behind some purple-coloured rock. For all he knew it might contain some extra-terrestrial element that reacted with urine, explode violently thus detaching his genitals and scuppering his romantic notions for Deanna Troi.

Hmmm. Yes, I think it's just me.

I obviously over-think these little matters.

Anyway, suitably *refreshed*, I washed my face, brushed my teeth and shaved my chin to within an inch of its life, the result of which left me awake and cleansed, ready for the day. I brewed a pot of tea, lit a Lucky and was fully equipped for whatever would be thrown at me.

As I sipped my brew I kept thinking over the previous day and the sudden re-insertion of Caroline into my life. Just what were my feelings to her? More to the point, what were her feelings to me? Was there a tiny spark of romance there that needed a slightest breath just to rekindle it? "Don't go there, Sammy," I grumbled to myself, stubbing out my cigarette, "Old wounds can easily re-open especially if they never really healed." That was the problem, of course. I had never really recovered from Caroline.

It had been brief.

It had been passionate.

It had been devastating.

I closed my eyes and thought back to that hot summer, the year of my graduation. I was standing in the cold, verging on frosty, atmosphere that encapsulated the study of my mentor-to-be.

"So, you're the boy they've sent to replace the Wallace lad, then?" Caroline's father was sat behind his desk, his eyes peering at me over the tops of his steel-framed, half-moon spectacles. They were the intense brown of his young daughter's, but whereas hers were overflowing with youthful mischief, the craggy lines that criss-crossed his face gave his windows on the world the aspect of a pair of black holes dragging in all that surrounded them, crushing them to oblivion.

Not a very pastoral look at all.

"I am, sir."

The black holes crinkled up under their eyelids and he snorted out a husking disparagement. "That's Father Adamson, sonny, or did you not notice this wrapped around my neck?" He tapped angrily at his dog collar.

"Sorry, Father Adamson," I quickly apologised, desperate to make a good first impression. "I didn't mean to cause offence."

"Oh, stop grovelling and take a seat."

So much for first impressions.

I was informed about the basics of parish life. The main services were on Sunday: said mass at eight, sung mass at ten and evensong at six in the evening. There were other services during the week; I was to look up what time they were on the notice board outside the church. I was to attend every single service without fail and I was to follow Father Adamson during his duties around the parish. He did not suffer fools and, in his opinion, fools were those who blabbed on about nothing at all whilst not paying attention to the world around them so I was to keep my mouth shut and my ears open.

"And one last thing," he said, his eyes fixing me firmly in their gravitation pull, "I am sure that you will have noticed that I have a beautiful young daughter. Her name is Caroline and she is a sweet little thing as pure as the whitest rose. I am well aware of the licentiousness and crude goings-on that happen within the walls of our educational establishments. If I so much as catch a whiff of it here, you'll be out. Do I make myself clear?"

Back in the present I opened my eyes. "Very clear," I whispered hoarsely, shaking my head. If only the old fool had really known what his precious little daughter had *really* been like...

I chuckled to myself, drained the rest of the tea and glanced out of the window. It was turning into the sort of day that really appealed to me; cold and crisp. I stretched my arms and stood as my joints creaked. I decided that a brisk walk over to Luneside University was in order.

As I made my way through the sprawling campus I watched the students passing me by. Most ignored me; some gave the almost middle-aged guy in the mac and fedora a curious stare. How old did I look to them? I recalled that, when I was their age, anyone over the age of thirty was practically friends with Tutankhamun. They still had their whole lives in front of them: loves, losses, achievements, failures. I had been through many of these already and right now it was seeming that the negative ones were stalking me somewhat. I sighed and resolved to myself that this was going to be a *good* day. The sun was out, the air was fresh and I was arriving at my best friend's flat. I bounded up the stairs and rang the doorbell.

A silhouette loomed up through the frosted glass, the lock rattled and the door swung inwards. What met my eyes almost drew a gasp from my open mouth. Spliff stood wrapped in his silk dressing gown, wearing it like a corpse wears a shroud. His skin was pallid, beads of sweat dappled his forehead and stubble was encroaching on his normally neatly trimmed beard. "Hello, Sam," he managed, his voice barely a whisper and his eyes flinching as if the quiet words were hammering his brain. "Come in, please."

He shambled away from the door and left me to close it shut. I followed him into his living room and my nose wrinkled at the unmistakable smell of vomit masked by disinfectant permeating from the adjoining bathroom. "You look like shit. What's the matter?"

My best friend tossed Dante off the sofa and crumpled up into where the cat had been lounging. The feline considered this rude deposition for a moment but decided to wind his fluid, black body around his owner's legs rather than scratch out his eyeballs. "Nothing, Sam. It's my own fault..." His voice drifted off as he rolled his head onto the back of the sofa. His eyes drifted shut whilst his chest rose and fell in a slow rhythmic manner.

I raised an eyebrow. "You been at the lighter fluid again?"

This managed to procure a slight flicker from the corner of Spliff's mouth – all he could manage of a smile. "It's just so tasty, you know?"

I smiled and sat down on the opposite armchair. Dante lifted his head and peered at my lap. I wasn't sure whether he was contemplating curling up there or pummelling my manhood to death so I took the sensible precaution and crossed my legs. The cat gave a superior sniff and decided to jump up onto the sofa next to safer territory. Spliff let a weary hand drape across his cat and Dante snuggled down, roaring loudly. "Seriously," I asked, "what's up with you?"

His eyes still closed, Spliff gave a non-committal shrug. "I enjoyed myself too much at the Borough last night. From what I recall, I was the life and soul of the party. There's probably humorous pictures of my jolly antics all over the Twittersphere by now."

I tapped my fingernails on my teeth. Something was not right here. I had known Spliff half my life and drink had never reduced him to this state of incapacity. "How much did you have?"

A vague, languid wave. "Too much. Can't remember." He forced an accusatory eye open and levelled it in my direction. "You just come here to make me feel even worse than I look?"

"I just fancied a chat."

"A chat?"

"Yep."

"Really?"

"That's right."

Dante lifted his head and watched our verbal tennis ball lob back and forth wondering which player would default first and give the real reason for their current situation. I gave him the pleasure of being the first to crack.

"Caroline showed up yesterday."

That got the weary priest's attention. He levered himself upright and both eyes were suddenly bright and alert, twinkling with unbridled glee. "Well, well. What grubby little rock did her ladyship crawl out from under?"

"She's not like that," I groaned. "She's..."

"A devious, manipulative, power-hungry little harpy." Spliff interjected, all signs of imminent expiration suddenly evaporating into the ether. "Please tell me you were going say that and not that she adores baking cookies and singing to the animals as she sweeps out the homes of seven diminutive miners."

I groaned and clasped my head in my hands. Spliff had never liked Caroline. He had always felt that she was using me as a means to resolve some sort of father issue. I had constantly needed to remind him that he was studying Religion and Politics, not Psychology. "She came for help."

"Really?" He practically spat the word out. "What does she want this time? Someone to idolise her and tell her how wonderful she is? Oh, wait. She had that *last* time! I guess it must be something new." The frame of the sofa groaned as he heaved himself out of the chair and made to stalk off to the kitchen. "I need a glass of water."

"Her son's in trouble."

Spliff paused as he reached the door.

"She thinks he's involved with a cult," I explained to his back. "I know the lad. I can't turn my back on him."

Spliff's silk shoulders rose and fell causing the dragons adorning his robe to dance slightly on his back. "Where do you know him from?" He still faced away from me, obviously trying to control his emotions on the matter.

"I met him at Saint Edmund's last week. He's a really nice lad."

"What does his father think about his mother going running to her old paramour?"

"There is no father."

"Dear God, don't tell me he's a child of the Force!"

I chuckled slightly. The Anakin Skywalker quip was a sure sign that he was calming down somewhat. "No. Nothing mystical there. His dad's just not on the scene."

"Probably had the good sense to get while the going was good," Spliff harrumphed as he turned to face me. "So what are you going to do?"

"Look into it, I guess," I shrugged. "Apparently he's involved with a group going by the name of Credete." I rummaged around in my pocket and fished out the leaflet. Spliff took it, wobbling slightly on his feet as he did so. I leapt up and grabbed him. "You really are rough. Sit down. I'll get you some water."

He nodded shakily and let me guide him back to the sofa where he lay down gingerly and closed his eyes, the leaflet forgotten. Once I had made sure he was not going to throw up or roll off the couch I went over to the kitchen and located a reasonably clean glass. As I filled it with water I saw a pack of pills next to the drainer. Placing the water on the counter I picked the box up and read the label: Stemetil. I was familiar with the product; it was a brand name for prochlorperazine, a prescription anti-nausea drug. I had used it myself for my tinnitus spins. I frowned as I read more. It was dated last Friday - the day that Spliff had been hunting for his elusive hospital appointment card. I glanced up through the door to my best friend dozing on the sofa. Why had he been prescribed an anti-nausea drug? Had he been expecting to feel rough? What was worse, why was he still being sick four days later? I placed the box back on the counter and carried the glass of water through to my patient. "Here you go."

He opened his eyes and smiled as I handed him the refreshing drink. "Thank you, nurse."

"Small sips," I cautioned, knowing too well from personal experience that too much liquid would make the stomach cramp and regurgitate.

He took the tiniest mouthful.

"Keep the liquid in your mouth for a while. You'll rehydrate quicker."

Spliff did as instructed then, after swallowing, said, "My, aren't you the fount of knowledge today?"

I chuckled, my eyes not leaving him. I wanted to tell him about the deaths of my abductors, but there was no way that he was in any fit state to listen. "Look, I'll be off. Ring me if you need me."

"Okay," he nodded vaguely. "I'm actually a lot better than I was earlier."

*Liar*. I thought to myself.

"I'll feel like eating tonight. Want to meet up? Usual time?"

"You sure you'll be up to it?"

"Of course I will. Now stop fussing will you? Unless you're actually going to wear a nurse's outfit, of course..."

I smiled again, turned and headed to the front door. "I'll see you later, then. Seven o'clock."

He waved me off and I left him to his rest.

Amidst all the hustle-bustle of Luneside's campus there is one small corner that remains forever calm and restful: Spliff's rose garden. Spliff has one true passion in life (aside from gin, verbally abusing those in authority and committing numerous far-from-clergylike deeds that could get him sacked at any given moment), and that is gardening. Where he grew up, his parents had a massive garden. He took me there a few times when we were younger. There were rolling lawns, trellises, flower beds, pergolas and roses. Rose upon rose upon rose. It looked like something out of a Disney princess cartoon. The sweet scent pirouetted in your nostrils as you walked past them, and the velvet of the petals brushed soft against your fingertips. It was paradise.

When he moved away to uni, Spliff lost all that. He found campus life bleak and barren. I sometimes think that was what turned the young Mister MacIntyre into the man that he is now; he was looking for a way to escape the concrete jungle that he saw around him.

Anyway, when he took the role of chaplain at the university, he requisitioned a scrap of wasteland behind the chapel. It had been used as a dumping ground so nobody really minded when one day he was found digging out the discarded rubble and levelling freshly dug topsoil. Then, when the powers that be realised that wooden fencing was going up and stone seats were being set, they started to take notice. They claimed that it was all very well tidying up the rubbish, but construction such as was happening there was not in keeping with the surrounding area of the campus plan.

They even sent him a letter saying this.

Spliff sent the letter back telling them in which dark orifice they could insert it. Sideways.

They backed down very quickly. This was either because they did not want to upset their volatile chaplain or they just couldn't really be bothered with a noisy argument.

So Spliff carried on and, as the days turned into months, his little paradise started to evolve. First there were a few bulbs, then some lavender and shrubbery. Then came the roses. All manner of roses. There were red ones, yellow ones, white ones and black. He even has blue ones which I never knew existed. To this day I'm convinced that it's some sort of alchemy that he brews and applies to the soil. I also think it's this self-same alchemy that encourages the roses to stay in bloom well past their natural flowering season.

So it was that after leaving Spliff's apartment I was sat down on a cold autumnal day drinking in the sweet smelling paradise of rose perfume. It was peaceful. It was quiet. It was Heaven. Just what I needed to clear my mind.

What was wrong with Spliff?

Was John Adamson involved in a cult?

How had those actors died?

I had answers for none of these questions so, for now, I was just going to push them to the back of my mind and take a breather.

There was a light crunch on the gravel path behind me. I turned and saw a young face smiling at me. "Hi there," I smiled back.

"Hey, Sam," Grace replied. "How ya doing?"

I waggled my hand back and forth. "So, so. You?"

"Okay," she shrugged. "I just came here for a bit of quiet thinking time."

"Oh, okay. I'll get out of your way." I made to stand up, but her arm reached out and her small hand touched my sleeve. It hesitated there then snatched back to the rainbow-coloured shoulder strap of her bag.

"No. No, it's okay," she apologised glancing up and down between me and her hand. "Stay for a bit, please? I'd kinda like the company?"

"Okay," I nodded, settling back down. I shifted to one side of the stone bench and she came and sat down next me, shifting her heavy bag down to the floor. "That looks like a lot of reading. You here to ponder an essay?"

I caught the glimpse of a smile as she studied her vibrant red Doc Marten's. "No. Nothing like that. It's a bit more personal."

"Ah!" I recalled a conversation from the previous week and nodded sagely. "Spliff did mention last week that you were having," I used my fingers to quote him, "man problems."

There was a stunned silence and a horrified look on the young barmaid's face.

"What? What's the matter?"

"Well... what exactly did he say?" she blustered, her forehead creasing with worry underneath the brown beanie hat that she always wore.

"Just what I said. I was worried about you last week and he... said..." I trailed off as a look of total relief passed over her face. I fought to find the right words to say. I was definitely missing something here so I decided that the best course of action was to change the subject. "Spliff says he had a great night last night."

"Really? Where at?"

"The Borough, of course."

"Oh." Grace looked perplexed at this. "That's odd. I was on last night and I didn't see him."

Now it was my turn to frown. He had lied. That combined with the Stemetil really worried me. "I'm sure he was just confused," I covered. "He looked pretty hung over."

"Okay." Grace accepted my explanation with no argument which was just as well, I thought, I wasn't sure what was going on myself. So we sat there quietly for a moment, both of us with our own thoughts, mine juggling around deceit, murder and death, Grace's probably something far more pleasant. Eventually her voice drew me out of my reverie. "I think roses are, like, really romantic. Don't you?"

I leaned back a touch and regarded the variety of blooms and colours. "Sure, I guess. They certainly cost a fair bit on Valentine's day."

Grace giggled lightly.

I turned to face her. "What?"

"You always make me laugh, Sam."

"What can I say? It's the big feet and the red nose."

This induced another fit of giggles until, once she had brought herself under control, she carried on with her train of conversation. "Just look at them, so perfect. But what were they originally? A small tight bud, curled up so tight so no one could see its potential." She turned and her green eyes looked up at me. "So no one could see its true emotions until it unfolds and blossoms putting all its heart on display. Do you ever feel like that, Sam? Or perhaps you know someone who needs encouraging to bloom? Could you be capable of unfurling someone's tightly-closed bud?"

I looked down at her bright, young eyes and realised just how much truth there was in her words. There was someone who I needed to help blossom. There was someone who kept themselves guarded from me, but just needed some care and attention and they would open up to me. "You're right," I nodded. "You're so right!"

Grace beamed with delight.

'I'll ring her straight away." I rummaged around in my pocket for my mobile. When I found it I looked up to see Grace frowning. "Oh sorry, you don't know, do you? Caroline turned up yesterday."

"Caroline? Who's Caroline?"

I stood as I flicked through my contacts. "Old girlfriend. We knew each other back when I was a student here." I found Caroline's number and my finger hovered over dial as I had a quick thought. "Grace, could I ask a favour? Could you please make sure that no one grabs my table tonight? I'll bring her in for a meal." With that, I hurried away with the phone dialling the number. The curious thing was, as I turned the corner I was sure I could hear the sound of gravel being tossed at the rose bushes. I think my tinnitus must have been playing up again.

Caroline picked her phone up after only two rings. She was delighted to hear that I was making progress and would love to meet me for dinner at the Borough. Seven? Sure. Not a problem.

All I had to do now was actually *make* some progress before this evening. It couldn't be that hard, could it? I slipped my hand into my jacket pocket to pull out the Credete leaflet only to find fluff, a battered packet of Luckies and thin air. Where was it? I'd had it this morning. Quickly, I rummaged through my other pockets, succeeding only in looking like a crazy guy who has an imaginary friend leaping about his person. I'm sure some of the students pointed and sniggered at me. They do that to people over thirty, you know.

Then realisation struck me.

Spliff! I had left it at Spliff's! I cursed loudly and the staring students quickly averted their eyes as I stormed off the campus with my fingers continuing their knowingly futile search through my pockets. It was when they located something in my chest pocket that I paused. I drew the slip of paper out and read the eleven digits penned in fluid, feminine handwriting and smiled.

# Chapter Five

"Well hello, bugle boy," chirped the sing-song female voice at the other end of the phone. "You're lucky to catch me. It's break time."

"Hi, Abalone. How's it going?"

The music teacher at Saint Edmund Campion chuckled mischievously down the phone. "All the better for hearing from you." Then, dropping her voice to a conspiratorial whisper, "You ready to educate me now?"

I was sure that I was blushing as I walked quickly through town, back towards Dalton Square. "Erm..." Words failed me. She was even more keen now there were no kids around her. "Actually, I'm sort of on a case and I could do with your assistance."

"Splendid! You gonna whisk me off in your TARDIS and take me on adventures through space and time or am I gonna be the stay at home secretary that flutters my heavy eyelashes at you every time you walk past?"

I actually pulled my phone away from my ear and stared at it in total disbelief. Was I really hearing this? "Are you legally safe to teach," I eventually asked, "or do all teachers have over-active imaginations?"

Her chuckling rang not unpleasantly into my ear. "It comes with the job, trust me. After two hours of trying to get twelve-year-olds to stay in tune whilst playing *Ode To Joy* on glockenspiels, fantasy and a good dollop of humour helps to save the sanity."

My lips broadened into a smile. She certainly was infectious. "I can imagine."

"Anyway, Samuel, what is it that I can assist you with?"

I ran my fingers through my hair, unsure what to say right now with people walking past. "Could we meet up at lunchtime?"

"Sure, I can dodge out at one."

"Okay. I'll meet you just after that then. In Starbucks?"

"Sounds good to me, Mister Investigator. It's a date," she laughed as she hung up.

A date? Wow. Two in one day. Not bad.

One o'clock saw me dunking a ginger biscuit in my black Americano. There is, I consider, a subtle art to this practice. Not enough dunk and the action has been somewhat pointless – you still have a hard biscuit minus the coffee flavour. Too much dunk and... Well, I'm sure that coffee shops have gone from supplying teaspoons to these weird splintery stirrers just to provide amusement for harassed baristas. The highlight of their day must be watching unfortunate customers try to fish over-dunked ginger biscuit from the bottom of a mug with the aid of something which looks like it should instead be used by Action Man as a splint.

I am a master dunker.

Not too much, not too little. Careful not to drip coffee on the table, or worse, your shirt, then sit back and smile as the ginger and coffee do a little dance on your tongue.

Bliss.

Mind you, it's not like I can take my pick of any other foods that are on offer in these places. Salted Pop Chips, dark chocolate and the aforementioned ginger biscuit are the only vegan fayre on offer these days. There used to be a fantastic falafel thing which I treated myself to once a week but they ditched it and replaced it with a salad box! I mean, come on, not only did they plonk mayo in there, but the packaging... Really, Starbucks. That totally ruined my day.

Okay, rant over.

Back to the present.

Just as I popped the last of the ginger biscuit in my mouth the door opened and in breezed Abalone, her blonde hair escaping from under a large, furry hat. She looked around, saw me and waved as she made her way over. "Good God, it's freezing out there today."

"I'll get you a coffee," I said. "What do you want?"

Her blue eyes twinkled mischievously behind her glasses and the edge of her mouth turned up.

"I meant, *what type of coffee*?" I sighed, albeit with a touch of amusement.

She shrugged, "Well I suppose we are in public. A latte please."

I chuckled to myself as I went and ordered the drink. When I returned, she had discarded her hat and coat and had made herself at home. "Thanks. So what was it you wanted to ask me about then? Why all the cloak and dagger?"

I sipped my coffee, silently judging my words. Like my ginger biscuit, this would take care and precision. "When I was at your school last week, I noticed that a lot of the pupils wear," I made a circle motion around the base of my hand, "wristbands."

"Sure," she shrugged. "It's not covered by uniform so, as long as they're not offensive, most things are sported as a kind of individuality."

I nodded. In my day it had been socks, bright luminous ones. There had been pink ones, orange ones, green ones. All sorts. Eventually schools had clamped down and black was now the only colour deemed suitable in many places. It was logical that something else would emerge as that little act of rebellion. However, teenager protest fashion was not what I was interested in.

I dunked a little bit more. "Tell me about the lilac ones."

In an instant the atmosphere had changed. The smile was instantly gone, her legs were crossed and the latte was held in front of her like a milky, caffeinated shield. "Bitch," she murmured through pursed lips. "I thought she didn't even like you."

"Who?" I frowned, genuinely confused. My metaphorical biscuit was now seemingly in danger of dropping messily into my drink.

"Wetherington," Abalone snapped. "I know she doesn't approve, but to try and get info this way..." She grimaced and shook her head. "Thanks for the coffee, but I need to get back to school." She picked up her coat and made to rise.

"Whoa! Whoa! What's going on? I'm in the dark here."

The young teacher paused mid-flounce and peered at me the way I imagined she peered at a child who said their dog had been fornicating with their homework. I could see her evaluating my body language, trying to perceive the slightest hint of deception. "Then why are you asking about them?" she finally asked.

"I've been hired by a client who is concerned about their son." The truth, plain and simple. I let it radiate from my face.

"Nothing to do with Ballcrusher?"

I chuckled involuntarily at the nickname. "Not a thing."

She waited a moment, still sizing me up, then lay her hat and coat back down next to her.

I withdrew my metaphorical biscuit intact, saturated to perfection with coffee.

"Thank you."

"So tell me more, then." Her voice was still quite icy, but I could sense the start of a welcome thaw. I tried to apply a verbal heater to push back the ice flow.

"Well, basically, a mother of a child at school has approached me with concerns that her son is involved in, as she termed it, a cult." I watched her face for the slightest reaction. There was none. I continued. "Personally, I think she's overreacting, but I promised her I would look into it." Still nothing. "So here I am."

Abalone sat quietly again for a moment, her lips pursed in thought until she picked up her drink, sipped it and said, "There's nothing wrong with Credete." Her words could not have been any more defensive if she had built a fort around herself first made from those little wooden stirrers.

"I'm sure there isn't." My tone was soft, placating. "I read one of their leaflets, all very harmless from what I can see. Can you tell me more?"

She looked down at her coffee, deep in thought, her fingers drumming pensively against the mug. "Sam, do you know what it's like to lose someone who was so close to you that they were your life?"

"Yes," I nodded. "My father died when I was younger. It almost destroyed me."

Abalone's shoulders rose and fell as she looked up at me, her crystal blues filled with utter sorrow. "You have my sympathy," she said, "but it's not quite the same."

I sat and waited quietly for her to continue.

"Last year, I was madly, deeply, totally in love with the man of my dreams. Russell was another teacher at Saint Edmund's. Geography." Her lips formed a melancholy smile. "Oh, he was so Geography. You know the sort? Corduroy jacket. Unbrushed hair. Totally scatty. Well, he was all of these and more.

"And I loved him with all my heart.

"We were totally one body, one soul. We had the wedding planned for earlier this year.

"Then a black saloon ploughed into him on King Street just after Christmas. My life died instantly, it's body crumpled up in a bloody mess on the side of the road.

"They never caught the driver."

Abalone paused as she sipped her drink.

"My life was ruined. I had no future, no reason to live. I went off long-term sick, never intending to go back. I barricaded myself in my bedroom. My housemate was going spare. She could not entice me out with anything. Not even Hob Nobs." The smile started to lose its melancholia as happier memories began to surface.

"Then, one day, I ventured downstairs and I saw a leaflet sticking through the letter flap. I was hungry by that point and thought it was a pizza menu or something. It wasn't and it changed my life.

"It was a leaflet from Credete. I read it with a scathing cynicism, poo-pooing all their wild claims, dismissing it as fodder for the desperate masses.

"But something inside of *me* was a desperate mass. Something inside of me was calling out to go to one of their meetings. Something was pushing me along a path that I had no idea of where it would lead.

"My life has never been the same since the first time I set foot amongst them."

"Why?" I asked, my throat dry from the inactivity whilst I had been fascinated by this young woman's tale. "What was it like?"

"It was... It is..." She held her hands up, lost for words. "Indescribable. You have to experience it just to see how wonderful it is."

I tapped my teeth with my fingernails and thought over her story. To lose someone so dear then fall into the welcoming arms of such a group... I was somewhat perturbed. Then I realised that she was looking at me expectantly. "What?" I asked, a sinking feeling building inside of me.

"Well? Will you?"

"Will I what?"

"Come to a meeting, tomorrow night at the Ashton Hall? Eight o'clock. See what it's like then tell your fussy mother that she has nothing to worry about."

Oh, this was not good. Nightmarish memories of smiley faces and blue jeans rose up in front of my eyes, but what could I realistically do?

Besides, it would mean that I got to spend some more time with the infectious Ms Morris.

"Okay," I gave in. "I will."

After Abalone left, I struck out from Starbucks and lit up a Lucky. All around me, people were hurrying about doing this or that. As I made my way down Market Street and up Penny Street I gave room to wondering just what people were doing. What was going on in their lives? There was a guy wrapped up in a thick overcoat, a briefcase clutched tightly in a gloved hand. Was he a banker? A businessman? There was a young girl, early twenties, battling with one of those big HGV pushchairs that contained two kids screaming and wailing. Was she happy with her lot? Did she go home at night, put the kids to bed then cry herself to sleep with a bottle of vodka?

I had no idea. All these people around me. All going about their everyday lives. All so normal. Yet, what were they really like? How had their lives formed and shaped them? Now, I'm no psychologist, but I only have to look at my past to know that it has an influence. My hand latched onto my mobile. I drew it out, flicked onto the contacts and typed in M. There she was, in the list. My mother.

A lot of years had passed.

Too many.

I could press her icon right now. The phone would dial and I would hear her voice. That gentle voice that had soothed me when I had fallen and grazed my knee, sung to me when the night terrors had first come bringing the voices that spoke to me in the middle of the night.

The same voice that had scolded me for getting involved with a young trollop of a girl. The voice that had despaired at me following some faddy eating disorder diet.

I pushed the phone back into my pocket.

Yes, we all had back history. We all carried our baggage in a very large back pack that weighed us down when we thought about it.

Why should the outwardly bright, sassy Abalone Morris be any different?

As I entered Dalton Square I cast an eye over to the Borough. What baggage would Caroline be carrying when we met tonight? I dreaded to think. I pushed that thought well out of my crowded mind and made my way to my office. My feet carried me up the stairs in a far more dignified manner than they had the previous day and I let myself in, checking for mail as I did.

There was none.

Good, no distractions.

I discarded my coat, my hat and my jacket then seated myself down at my laptop. I flicked it on and called up a web browser before navigating to Google. I had some time to kill before tonight and I had to spend it productively. That meant research.

I typed in "Divergence". My vision started to blur halfway into the first hit. It was rambling on about a mathematical term in vector calculus. Something to do with vector operators and sinks or something. I exhaled sharply and navigated back to the first set of hits. The next hit gave me the definition, "The act of diverging."

"No shit, Sherlock," I grumbled. This was ridiculous. There was nothing at all. Secret societies were not supposed to keep secrets secret! Someone was always supposed to leak juicy tidbits into the good old Interweb. For example, if you wanted to know the deepest, darkest secrets about a politician's sexual fetishes, all you had to do was Google it and there it would be, displayed on some forum in all its bare-arsed, disturbing entirety.

I tried a different tack.

"The Divergence" found me looking at the webpage for a rock band. Not exactly what I had in mind.

I leaned back in my chair and ran my fingers down my face. This was ludicrous. Surely there should be something out there? Some tiny little fragment? Or perhaps the vampires were just too good at their job? Perhaps they kept an immaculate house and tidied up thoroughly wherever they went.

I shuddered at the thought of someone like Marcus "tidying up".

I needed a drink. I grabbed a bottle of Jack from my filing cabinet and poured myself a good thinking measure. Slumping down into my sofa, I took a large swig and rested the glass tumbler on the coffee table where the pad lay with Caroline's number. I scooped up the pad and clicked out Mr Biro. It was time for a list.

Okay, so what was there rattling round in my head right now?

One. Divergence. Duly jotted down. Top of page.

Two. Suicides. Five names all in a row. I drew an arrow from these to Number One.

There was something else to go with these. I wrote *Dragon* along the arrow and next to that, *What does this mean??? Symbolic???* Let's face it, dragons aren't real. One of Lancaster's greatest showed that. Sir Richard Owen lived just off Dalton Square and was the guy who came up with the term Dinosaur – terrible lizard. He was one of the paleontological forerunners who obliterated the idea of fire-breathing creatures roaming the Earth. Well, for us sane folk, anyway.

However, I digress.

Three. Children of Cain. Vampires. They were involved in this so on the list they went. What were they exactly? I didn't think they were antagonistic. They came across as supernatural safeguarders; there to watch and wait then act when necessary. I tapped my teeth with my fingertips as I re-read their name. Cain? Which Cain? I scribbled down *The Cain*?

This brought me onto number four.

Werewolves. Where there were the Children of Cain, there was also the Bloodline of Abel. I wrote their title next to them on the list and sank into thought again. Cain and Abel. One brother murders the other. In biblical history, Abel was the good, faithful servant. His sacrifice was pleasing and Cain killed him in jealousy before being banished. This was odd. Very odd. How could the goody-two-shoes produce such crazed killers and the murderer spawn supernatural watchmen? I drew a large question mark next to this as I also pondered another thing. Did either of the Hawkins siblings mention the Divergence? I cast my mind back over both their rantings and drew a blank. No, it had only been Nightingale and Marcus. Only the vamps had talked about it. Did the werewolves even know about it? Perhaps they were just a side show, a rather hairy, sharply-toothed distraction? It seemed somewhat likely. Something deep inside me was twirling its fingers telling me to move on, guiding me to more relevant matters.

Five. Credete. I circled this one. Even before the creepy suicides and deaths, this had been my first matter at hand. Next to it I penned *cult?* and *who?* This was the thing. So far I had an entity with a name but no face. Every group had a leader. Who led this little shebang? There had been no name on the leaflet and I had stupidly forgotten to ask Abalone. This disturbed me. I don't like secrets; they never come to anything good. You can be walking along quite happily enjoying the sunshine, whistling away to yourself when suddenly a paving slab becomes an open man-hole and down you plummet into the dark. Not good.

I needed to know who Credete's David Koresh was. Was he some silent psycho, quietly feeding his adoring goldfish into an apocalyptic frenzy or was he just some charismatic wordsmith telling needy folk what they wanted to hear whilst laughing merrily as his current account sucked in their donations.

I seriously hoped it was the latter. Dear God, I did. I did not want another week like the last one.

I scribbled next to Credete, a note to myself that I needed to find out who ran the show.

I read down the list. Five neat jigsaw pieces that I needed to rotate, examine and slot together. There had to be a pattern, a common factor that drew them together. I was just about to lay the pad down and take a sip of the bourbon when there was a discreet cough at the back of my subconscious.

"What?"

"You know what."

"No I don't."

"Yes you do, Sam. You're just conveniently ignoring it."

"The hell I am."

"Really?"

Sulking silence on my part.

"You know you have to put her on the list."

"No I don't."

"Yes you do. She started this. She's a factor."

I sighed, downed the Jack and snatched up pen and pad. Underneath Credete I stabbed out another "C" word.

Caroline.

My inner voice had a point. She was the catalyst. Without her I would not be sat here writing this list. I could, instead be sat back enjoying a peaceful glass of whiskey. Okay, true, Philips and co. would still be dead, but that was not my fault, not my problem.

*Apart from that Divergence business.*

Okay, yes apart from that Divergence business.

*And the dragons.*

Yes, and the dragons. Sheesh, give a guy a break.

So apart from some crazed satanic abductors topping themselves and/or dying horribly after rambling on about unidentifiable events to do with mythical creatures, my week would be relatively normal.

Caroline always had a way of turning my life on its head.

Just as she had in her father's library.

It was the second day of my placement and I was taking a relaxing moment before bed after what had been a manic day of parochial duties. There had been parishioners to visit, services to plan, meetings to minute; all of which had seemed to blur into one, commentated on by the dour authoritarian monologue of Father Adamson.

He would instruct me as to how the parishioners were to be cared for but not molly-coddled. He would divulge intelligence on how services had to be succinct yet spiritual. He would stress that meetings were to be endured for the sake of those who felt that they benefitted from attending them but then casually disregarded as what was determined in them was as much use as a chocolate teapot.

In truth, I actually had a certain amount of respect for the priest, but I needed a small time to myself where I wasn't being lectured on parish matters.

So I found myself wandering the vicarage and ending up in the library, which was situated on the first floor just down from my bedroom. I let a surprised whistle squeak through my teeth as I gazed at the numerous volumes that lined the walls. It was just like being back on campus. I had never seen a private house so well stocked with books. There was high-brow literature, modern and classical poetry, academic texts, collections of bound newspapers. The list was endless.

I lingered by the poetry section and let my finger rest on one particular volume: *Blake's Poetical Works*. I smiled affectionately. I had always been (and still am) a huge fan of William Blake. In my teenage years, when others had been more concerned with fashion and love bites, I had been more inclined to curl up with a copy of *Songs of Experience*. I flicked through the worn pages of Adamson's book and found the verse that I had read to myself over and over again.

There was a creaking noise that made me jump somewhat as the only window in the room swung open. I regained my composure when I saw that it was no burglar breaking their way in, just a blonde-haired teenage girl. "A little help?" Caroline asked as she swung herself over from the huge tree that grew next to the house.

I grabbed my host's daughter under her shoulders and aided her unorthodox entry into her own house. It was a fairly fumbled attempt at gallantry as I still clasped the book in my left hand with my thumb marking where I had been reading. "I thought you went to bed ages ago."

"You and my father, both," she grinned as she settled her feet on the floor and quickly brushed herself down. "There are times I like to get out without him knowing."

"What, so you can go and lurk at some friend's house?" I mocked disparagingly, recalling my not-so-distant teenage years.

"Oh, I don't ever *lurk*," she grinned, her brown eyes gleaming mischievously. "I tend to be quite *energetic*. It depends who I'm with."

I am pretty sure that I went red at that little revelation. "But... but you're fifteen!"

"Sixteen next week," she pouted. "Besides, it's my life. I can do what I want with whoever I want." She noticed the book and there was a waft of patchouli and jasmine as she sidled up close to me. "What are you reading?"

"Words, words, words," I grinned.

"Oooo... educated." Caroline reached over my arm and plucked the book from my grip. "Tut tut. Wrong author. Don't quote the Bard when reading a metaphysical."

I turned and faced the cheeky grin that was twinkling up at me.

I swallowed at the sight of those deep, brown eyes.

"Hey," I protested somewhat lamely, "it sounded cool."

Caroline raised a blonde eyebrow. "You stand here reading *The Tiger* and use a word like *cool*? You deserve to be shot."

"That's a bit drastic, surely? You barely know me." I reached for the book. She hid it behind her back and I suddenly found my face very close to hers.

"No, I don't," her smooth, teenage lips whispered. "But so far I like what I see, so that'll do for me." With that, she placed the book into a pair of hands that I was desperately trying to prevent from trembling, turned and walked out of the room leaving me breathless.

Yes, Caroline definitely had a way of turning things on their head.

# Chapter Six

That evening saw me sat in my chair at the Borough, a faux leather-bound menu in front of me, a very large whiskey in my hand and a thoughtful frown on my face. For all intents and purposes I was just another would-be diner sat waiting for his friends to show up. In reality my mind was running around in circles like a dog with a bone tied to its tail.

I was still turning over the list from this afternoon. I was missing something. There was a link. Or *was* there? Was I just being somewhat paranoid? Why on Earth should there be a connection between Caroline, Credete, the Divergence and the suicides?

Because my gut told me there was, that was why. There was a formless phantom sidling around just outside of my peripheral vision. If I could somehow grab the smoky tendrils of this elusive shadow, then it would complete the jigsaw. There was something that linked the deaths to Credete, I knew it. I had no justifiable reason to think so, but it was there, the suspicion.

Perhaps it was last week being the week from hell.

Perhaps two attempts on my life had left me somewhat jittery.

Perhaps a tree falling down in a forest when no one was around did make a sound.

How was I to know? All I could do was hunt around until something struck me. Something that was hopefully not a large blunt instrument.

"The last time I saw a face like that, the vice-chancellor's dog had farted very loudly at an executive soiree."

"Pleasure to see you too."

Spliff settled down into his seat: gin in hand, grin on his face.

"I didn't hear you come in."

"I think you were too busy planning how to scurry off into Mordor," he observed before taking a large (make that, disturbingly large) swig of neat gin.

"I take it your insides are feeling better?"

"Of course," he purred, settling the tumbler down onto a beer mat. "It takes more than a dodgy drink to floor me."

I thought about Grace's comment that he had in fact not been drinking and said nothing. There would be a time and a place for the truth. This was not it.

"Listen," his mercurial personality quickly flitting onto another subject, "are you doing anything this Saturday?"

I sipped my whiskey, my spidey-senses suddenly tingling. There was that recognisable twinkle in his mischievous grey eyes. My best friend would probably describe what he was going to suggest as a jolly jape. Through a more historically accurate perception of these sorts of events, I was more likely to describe it as an embarrassing disaster. "Can't say that I've got anything planned yet, although I can quickly find something depending on what you say next."

He ploughed on, totally ignoring my sarcasm. "Did you know that *What's It Worth?* is coming here? To the Town Hall?"

I shrugged my indifference. *What's It Worth?* is one of those programmes that just does not appeal to me. The idea of sitting in my armchair watching middle class pensioners pretending that they are not interested in the possible monetary valuable of their Great Aunt Maude's bed warmer is not my idea of an evening's entertainment. Apart from the news, if it doesn't involve lightsabers or laser guns, it tends to pass me by. "So?"

"I thought we could go."

I screwed my eyes up and peered over the top of my glass. "Okay, so I'm going to ask you, 'Why?' and, if you say that it's because you have some antiques that you want valuing, I will roll my eyes to the back of my head and groan in displeasure because I know that's not true and there is some other motive for this as of which I am yet unaware."

"I think you've been spending too much time with PC Plod up the road," Spliff pouted. "It was just a simple question."

"Spliff, with you, *nothing* is ever simple. Now, spill it."

He took a deep breath, steeled himself and whispered conspiratorially, "*She'll* be there."

"She?"

"Harmony."

"Ah," and the penny dropped. Harmony Briers, how could I have not seen it? Spliff is totally smitten by those piercing green eyes and sophisticated Home Counties accent. She was his ultimate gay icon.

Personally, I have never really been able to get this whole gay icon thing. Sure, I can understand the likes of Freddie Mercury, Elton John and George Michael. They were and are gay, so for them to be idolised by people of the same sexuality makes sense to me. But then you get all the prominent women who, as far as I know, are or were straight. Liza Minnelli is one as is Gloria Gaynor. Dusty Springfield had been another and even ended up singing with the Pet Shop Boys. Was Carol Vorderman secretly worshipped in bars named The Blue Lobster? I had no idea. I mean, what is it that makes someone a gay icon? One of these days I must look it up when I have time.

For Spliff it is the purring Ms Briers, former Shakespearian actor par excellence (her Lady Macbeth was the talk of 2012, apparently) and now the presenter of a programme where you hope to take your dead gran's lavender-scented hankie and find out it is miraculously worth an arm and a leg. Of course he would want to go to the filming on Saturday.

I resigned myself to my apathetic doom. "What time is it?"

"They're letting people in from eight in the morning, so I thought we could pootle along about nine?"

Begrudgingly, I nodded. Depriving him of this experience would be like depriving a young boy of ten a smelly little mongrel dog. It would just be far too cruel.

"Fair enough. Meet me at my place and we'll head over."

Spliff beamed and picked up a menu from our table. "Thank you, Sam. You won't regret it."

"Tell me that after the event," I sighed.

"Oh," Spliff continued, gesturing to the three menus on the table, "It seems that you've picked up too many menus. Lost the ability to count to two today?"

I steeled myself for the inevitable tirade of abuse. "We've got company tonight."

"Really? Who?" I could tell from the way that he was mumbling this whilst perusing a menu he already knew like an intimate lover that he was not really bothered as long as he got to eat and drink in peace.

That peace shattered into a hundred fragments when I told him.

"Dear God, Sam," he huffed when I had finally calmed him down. "What the hell do you think you're playing at? Caroline? Here? No, no, no! That's not good."

I sighed in exasperation. I knew he could not stand her but this was somewhat of an over-reaction even for my best friend. "I don't see what the problem is, Spliff. I'm working this case for her and I need to report back. Dinner sounded the most civil way of doing so."

His eyes pierced the air between us. "Civil? Civil? Whenever was that little bitch civil? She makes Joan Collins look like Mother Teresa on prozac!" He drained his drink and glowered at me across the table. "And here, Sam? Why here of all places?"

"Why not?" I shrugged, totally at a loss. "I always eat here."

Spliff started to do that goldfish expression that the fatally baffled get from time to time. "Because... because..." His eyes flicked over to the bar as Grace came over, pad in hand. "Oh, forget it," he grumbled, slouching down into his chair, arms folded over his chest.

"Hi, guys," Grace beamed. "You would be, like, ready to order?"

"Actually, Grace," I smiled up at the young girl, "we're waiting for someone to join us."

She nodded, her beanie hat bobbing happily. "Oh, okay. Who would that be then?"

"That," came the silken female voice from over her shoulder, "would be me."

Three pairs of eyes turned to the immaculately dressed woman in her mid-thirties. I could visibly track the daggers flying from Spliff's. Grace's were their usual bright and jolly selves. "Oh, okay," she smiled, backing off, "I'll give you some more time then."

"You do that." I frowned at the tone of Caroline's voice. It sounded somewhat unnecessarily curt. I had no idea why. I guessed that perhaps it was down to the shield of ice that Spliff was rapidly constructing in front of himself.

"Thanks, Grace," I smiled. "Could you just give us five minutes?"

"No probs, Sam," she grinned and headed back off to the bar. Caroline's eyes followed her all the way then turned round and lanced me to my chair.

"You don't change do you? Still chasing the young ones."

I sipped my whiskey and frowned at her. "I don't get you."

She raised a perfectly shaped eyebrow as she pulled a third seat up to our table and neatly lowered herself down. "Forget it," she said. "Obviously my mistake." There was a slight curl to the corner of her mouth, a sure sign that something had amused her. I had no idea what, so I let it pass for now.

Caroline picked up the spare menu and started to leaf through. I looked at Spliff. He looked at me. It was a *you are in such trouble* look.

"I didn't realise we would have a guest," Caroline finally said from behind the menu.

"Believe me, I only just found out," Spliff snapped back.

I suddenly felt like I was trapped between Donald Trump and North Korea and that there were rather itchy fingers on the big, red buttons. "Spliff, behave," I snapped. "Caroline, I normally eat here with Spliff. He also helps out advising me on my cases. I went to see him this morning to ask his advice about Credete. So, please, just calm down."

The fingers edged back from the buttons and the Borough was saved a nuclear cataclysm as both parties went back to studiously poring over their menus. I did likewise, realised that I would order what I *normally* ate and tossed the booklet onto the table before downing my drink.

Silence pervaded.

This was ridiculous.

I wished I still had some more bourbon left.

It was Caroline who finally broke the impasse. "I'll have the mussels."

Spliff grumbled that he was having the fish.

I waved at Grace and she beetled back over. "Hi guys. You, like, ready?"

"Why yes, *like*, we are," Caroline smiled, her perfect teeth showing neatly between her lips. "I'll have the mussels."

"Surely these mussels won't be stiff enough for your tastes?" Spliff sneered.

I shot him a warning look.

He harrumphed back to his menu.

Caroline held her menu up and waited for Grace to take it which the young girl promptly did.

"Spliff?" I enquired, praying for a more civil answer.

"Fish please, little dust devil," he winked at Grace, passing her his menu.

"And, you'll have the veggie-burger, Sam?"

I nodded.

"Want a top up?" She nodded to the empty glass.

"Please."

"Okay." She went and reached over the bar, stretching on tiptoes to grab my bottle of Jack Daniel's before coming back and topping up my glass with a more than generous measure. "Anything else?" she beamed.

"A sick bucket would be useful," said Caroline, "but failing that, a vodka and tonic, plenty of ice."

For a second Grace was quiet, just standing looking at Caroline, then eventually she replied, "Ice? I'd have thought you could have just snapped off your tongue and dipped it in the drink," before turning round and stamping off.

A muffled chuckle emanated from Spliff's direction as Caroline sat back in her chair and regarded me. "So, here's the deal, do you have any information for me, or shall I leave before your little friend thinks really hard in that little head of hers and gives herself a stroke trying to come up with anymore witty comebacks?"

Oh, dear God. I ran my fingers through my hair. "Don't mind Grace. She's probably just tired and overworked."

Caroline sighed. "She a student?"

I nodded.

"Then trust me, she's not overworked. Now do you have any information for me or not?"

Another barmaid brought Caroline's drink over and, after she had walked out of earshot, I started to explain my meeting with Abalone. Caroline listened intently and I was pretty sure that Spliff did likewise although he was a doing a good impression of someone who was more interested in a solitaire app on his phone.

"So, as of yet, you have nothing?" Caroline did not sound very impressed with my progress, or lack of it.

"Nothing tangible, but I'm going to go along and see what this meeting is all about. See if they sacrifice any goats," I winked.

I'm not the confrontational type. To be perfectly honest I would do more or less anything for a quiet life. Spliff and Caroline, however, have both always been somewhat feisty in their nature. My best friend will rant for hours about the latest thing to wind him up whether it be doctrinal, bureaucratic or boringly mundane. Caroline was always one for chomping at the leash wrapped around her neck by her overbearing father. The two of them had only met once before, but that meeting was one too many times for either party.

It had been the day after I had caught Caroline climbing in through the library window...

"So how's it going?"

Spliff and I were sat on the vicarage lawn enjoying the warm summer evening. My best friend was sneaking a quick cigarette and I was sipping some juice.

"It's okay," I said. "Adamson's a bit of a task master but I think I'm learning a lot of stuff."

Spliff peered up the garden path. "So I see," he murmured.

I turned to follow his gaze and my jaw dropped. Caroline was walking down the path wearing a skimpy polka dot bikini, a large sun hat and round sunglasses. She was all legs and midriff.

Spliff took a long draw on his cigarette. "Sam. Have you ever read *Lolita*?"

I was about to reply when the teenager sauntered over towards us. She looked at Spliff, cocked her head to one side and groaned, "Not another one. Father hates those things."

"What?" Spliff inquired. "Potential ordinands?"

Caroline came and stood close to me. Very close. "No. Cigarettes. If he catches you smoking down here, he'll kill you."

"Murder on the vicarage lawn," Spliff smiled. "Very Agatha Christie."

Caroline harrumphed and draped an arm around me. "I thought you were going to be alone down here."

"Oh, Spliff came over to visit," I told her. "He had the evening off too."

"Spliff? What sort of a name is that? Makes you sound like a junkie."

"Better than being jail bait," he shot back. "Haven't you got a street corner to go and stand on?"

With that, Caroline turned and stomped back off to the house. Spliff shook his head as he watched her march back up the garden path. "Malcolm was right about her. You'd better watch yourself, Sam."

The arrival of our food dragged me back to the present hostilities. As the waitress lay our meal on the table, Spliff was berating Caroline for selling her soul to such a filth-feeding hack as Swarbrick whilst Caroline was protesting that Spliff worked for one of the most corrupt and controlling bodies on the face of the planet.

Somethings in life are a constant.

There was a truce as we started to eat. Caroline eyed my burger. "You still veggie, then?"

"Vegan, actually."

She popped a mussel into her mouth, chewed and swallowed. “Christ, you have got it bad. Whatever possessed you?”

“Just felt right for me,” I shrugged. I put my burger down and looked across the table. “You okay?”

Spliff had eaten about two mouthfuls and was just pushing the rest of his fish around its plate. “I guess, I'm still a bit under the weather.” He dabbed his mouth with his napkin and rose from his chair. “I'll see you on Saturday, Sam,” he said.

“Sure. You want me to walk you back home? You look rough.” He was indeed a disturbing shade of green around the gills.

“No, I'll be fine,” he protested. “Fresh air and all that. Catch you later.” He did not say a word to Caroline as he walked out of the Borough and she in turn said nothing to him.

The rest of the meal was actually quite pleasant. We chatted about this and that. I explained how I had ended up in my line of work and she enquired about previous cases. I told her about Satanic actors and Saint Edmund's. I left out vampires and werewolves. Some things did not need mentioning.

Eventually we had finished our meals. Caroline placed her empty glass down on the table and said, “Well, I guess I'd better be off.”

There was a moment when we just looked at each other. I do not know what she saw, but I saw the young girl in the polka dot bikini trying desperately to play the femme fatale and I smiled. “Why don't I walk you home?”

Caroline lived on Coulston Road, just along from Williamson Park. As we walked side by side past the tall trees, the green dome of the Ashton Memorial glowered down at me, reminding me of the events of the previous weekend. I swallowed down the memories and the aching muscles. Dwelling on it right now would be something of a passion-killer.

Passion-killer? Had I really just used that phrase? Sure, Caroline and I were not at each other's throats right now, but that hardly constituted a romantic reunion, did it? I glanced over at her in the rising moonlight. She too seemed lost in some inner conversation or debate. I could tell by the way she kept sucking her lips back between her teeth as she walked, her head slightly down. Perhaps she was feeling old emotions, old passions, starting to resurface?

Perhaps.

Perhaps not.

“So how long have you lived down here then?” I finally ventured, interrupting the creaking sound of metal wheels within wheels.

“Oh, about five years. We used to rent a small place out in Galgate but, as John got older, we rapidly outgrew it and high school was on the horizon, which would have meant him getting the bus every day after I had gone out to work.”

“And that would have been a problem?”

She laughed gently as she shook her head. "I forget you don't know what it's like to be a parent. Teenage boys are far from organised, Sam. If I was to leave him at home to get the bus in the morning, I would come home that night to find him in his room wearing nothing but socks and pants whilst playing some bizarre Xbox game and with no concept of the day having passed him by." By the streetlights I saw her lips turn up into a warm, motherly smile.

"You love him very much, don't you?"

"Yes, I do."

We walked in silence along her street. It was totally quiet, there was no one else about.

I stopped, took her by the hands and stared down into those deep, brown eyes. "I will find out what's going on with Credete. I promise."

"Really?"

"Really, really."

We both chuckled at the reference and I let her hands drop. She thrust them deep into her warm pockets. We both intently studied the footpath.

"Well," Caroline said eventually, "here we are."

"Here we are," I agreed.

"Outside my house," she pointed out with a nod of her head.

My heart started to hammer and my throat suddenly felt like the Kalahari. "Yes," I squeaked.

"And it's late." Those chestnut eyes had me locked completely in their sights. My bones had turned to putty, willing to be moulded to whatever shape the modeller wished. "I'd better get in. John will be fretting."

Okay, so no modelling tonight. "Sure," I nodded. "You'd better get inside. It's cold."

"Very."

"Very."

Our breath hung on the crisp autumn air under the orange glow of the street lamps. Caroline took a step forward, stood up on tip toe and kissed me softly on the cheek. The scent of patchouli and jasmine was my entire universe for a brief second.

"Thank you, Sam," she whispered in my ear, then she turned and crossed the road.

I think my eyes were shut in wonder when she called out, "If you're not doing anything Thursday, why don't you come over for dinner? Six-ish? You can report back about this meeting you're going to."

I was nodding maniacally. "Sure. About six. I'll bring a bottle."

Caroline grinned and waved silently as she let herself in through her front door.

I turned and began to walk back down memory lane...

A few days after the incident between Spliff and Caroline, she and I were walking down Penny Street. She had just stormed out of a stern lecture from her father about her upcoming birthday. She was not just spitting feathers; she was a peregrine falcon flossing its beak with an entire sparrow. I had decided that a trip into town would calm her down.

"How dare he? He always does this to me!" Passers-by were carefully avoiding the crazy blonde who was shouting at the top of her voice and gesticulating with arms that threatened to take out an eye should it stray within their flailing range. "I mean, it's my *sixteenth*, for God's sake!"

So much for an attempt to calm her down. Instead, all it had seemed to do was to give her space to vent a lava stream of sulphurous anger. She was ranting about her father's designs on her upcoming birthday. Caroline had apparently been planning it for months now. There was going to be a rented hall, a DJ, lots of cake, fun and frivolity.

Her father had disagreed.

"He wants to incorporate it into the Parish Summer Fair!" she wailed. "Can you believe it?"

When all I could manage was a sympathetic shrug, she craned her head back, stretching the neck muscles taut and emitted a guttural groan of frustration to the heavens: "Men!"

This was entirely new territory for me. What was I supposed to do? Was I supposed to tell her to calm down? That course of action looked like it would get my head bitten off in one vicious snap. Was I supposed to placate her? I had a feeling that reaction would end in me being scorned as weak and pathetic.

So I took what I considered to be the middle road. I kept my mouth shut and just let her continue to rant.

"Here's the deal," she grumbled. "I hate him. I truly hate him. He's controlling, possessive and cannot accept that I'm almost an adult. I can't wait to be rid of him. I can't wait. In a few years' time I'll be away from here. I'll be off somewhere like London. I'm going to be a journalist, you know? You'll see me on the telly presenting my own programmes. I'll be really famous and he won't be able to stop me.

"I'll be free of him.

"I want to hurt him so bad!"

This was perturbing to me. I found the idea that she wanted to hurt her father incredibly alien. I thought about *my* father back home, lying in his sick bed awaiting the end and I shook my head. This girl was full of such anger. It was unhealthy.

Caroline was taking a breath between her verbal scourging of her father's soul when we passed Gorrills. Gorrills is one of those places in Lancaster where everyone has shopped at least once. This is because it magically seems to have displays in the window for the ideal gift that you need right at that moment in your life when you need to stop someone from thinking that either they are unloved, need to jump off a building or that Jeremy Kyle deserves a BAFTA. As the summer sun beamed down that day, a sparkling light caught my eye and I gently guided Caroline towards the window. She continued to ramble and rage as I peered through the glass and smiled. I knew what she needed right now.

"Just wait here," I managed between outbursts and I darted into the shop, handed over some cash and came back out with a small gift bag and a big, toothy grin.

She paused mid-rant and half smiled, half frowned at the bag. "What's that?"

I handed it over. "Early birthday present."

Carefully, Caroline peered into the bag then extricated its contents which were wrapped in copious amounts of tissue paper. She looked up at me and her blonde eyebrows knotted together. "Sam?"

"Go on," I gestured. "Unwrap it."

Continuing with puzzlement and care, Caroline peeled the layers back until she revealed the contents and gasped in fascination at the small glass elephant that sat on its haunches with its trunk blowing crystal water into the air. "Oh, Sam, it's beautiful!"

"Did you know that in Africa the elephant is regarded as a symbol of loyalty?"

She shook her head, unable to take her eyes of the small glass model. Then slowly, she lifted up her face and all I was aware of were her dark brown eyes drawing close to mine as she kissed me warmly and deeply before drawing away with an exuberant smile on her face.

"No matter what happens, Caroline." I said with earnest seriousness, "I will always be loyal to you. I will never leave you."

How wrong I was.

A small cough dragged me back to the present. "Good evening, Sam."

I was half-way down Wyresdale Road, heading towards East Road. I had not even been aware that my feet had been moving, let alone that I had acquired a companion.

"You."

The teenage boy nodded. "Me."

I groaned. "Please tell me that this is a coincidence."

"I don't believe in such things," Alec shrugged, "and you should be careful when you paint the past with sepia."

"And why's that?" I quickened my pace, hoping to leave him behind.

He just quickened his step. "Because she's hiding something."

"Oh, really?" I turned the corner onto East Road. "You of all people should know that everyone hides things, Mister Now-You-See-Me-Now-You-Don't."

"True, but her's is a real killer."

I stopped, threw back my head in frustration, grunted and turned on him. "So what might this big secret be then?"

"Sorry. Can't tell."

"Oh, really. And why might that be?"

"You'd get upset."

"I'm upset already."

"Okay. You'd get *more* upset." His eyes flicked down to my fists which were rapidly clenching and unclenching. "Violently upset."

"Right now, I don't need to get upset to feel violent, so why don't you just tell me?"

Alec made to speak then, for a split-second, his eyes glazed over before he was back in the room once more. "Sorry, Sam. I can't. Just be careful."

And he was gone.

One moment he was there in front of me, the next he had vanished.

It was a good job that the street was still deserted as my choice of language right then was not really for polite ears. I stomped off down East Road back into town.

# Chapter Seven

Lancaster Town Hall is quite an impressive building. It was completed in 1909 and dominates Dalton Square with its domed clock tower rising like an all-seeing eye above the city. As well as housing the city council offices it also has a large venue around the back where various concerts and large meetings are held. This is the Ashton Hall, named after James Williamson (Lord Ashton) who had financed the construction work.

The next evening saw me hovering nervously just down the road from the large doors that led into Lancaster's prestigious auditorium. With my hands thrust deep in the pockets of my trench coat and my collar turned up to keep the cool air away from my neck I looked like a decidedly dodgy character. I know that my preferred choice of clothing is not what would be called "everyday" for most people, but I'm just not a fan of denim jeans and brightly coloured t-shirts. Someone once told me I was a typical only child of older parents. I replied that he was the typical product of a whore and a sociologist.

I am just me. I will dress how I want and live how I want. End of story.

However, I cannot help but feel a bit odd when passers-by give me that, "Are you for real?" look every now and then. Hey ho. Their loss.

"Boo!"

I think I screamed, just a little bit, as I was snapped out of my reverie.

"Sorry," Abalone apologised, trying hard not to laugh, "I couldn't resist it. You were miles away."

"Quite," I remarked, raising an eyebrow. "How's a man supposed to contemplate the inner mysteries of life on a street corner when people scare the living daylights out of him?" I peered down the road at the doors that led up into the Ashton Hall and sighed, "Are you sure about this?"

"You want to know all about Credete?"

"Yes."

"You want to be reassured that we're not bug-eyed, green-scaled, child-eating monsters?"

I grinned. "Fair enough. Lead the way."

So she did. We walked down towards the large doors then came to a sudden stop. "Oh, will you look at that?" Abalone was referring to graffiti that had been scrawled across the doors, although *scrawled* was hardly an appropriate description. Neatly penned would have been more accurate. "Spud was here," she read out loud shaking her head. "Vandals."

I frowned. This was not the first time I had seen the slogan. Just the week before, I had come across it whilst queuing outside the Sugar House. The words were identical along with the correct grammar, spelling and punctuation. "Curious indeed," I murmured as Abalone opened the door and led me inside. My mind filed the odd graffiti away for later as my heart started to palpitate at the thought of what I was about to endure.

As those of you who have read *The Case of The Vexed Vampire* already know, I'm not keen on attending large, noisy venues.

First, there's the social side. I will inevitably feel like the proverbial fish flopping around out of water gasping at cruelly asphyxiating air. While others dive in and submerge themselves in the apparent glee of mingling, I will be sat or stood rather awkwardly at the edge of the venue like the poor sap who did not get the message that the party was no longer fancy dress and the latest Klingon fashion would no longer be appropriate for the funeral.

Then there's the matter of my ears. Both the tension of the new experience and the volume of a large crowd play havoc with my tinnitus. My anxiety always rises, increasing my internal tintinnabulation and not only making it hard for me to hear what is going on around me, but actually causes me to feel disorientated and dizzy.

Inevitably, I end up looking like some poor sod that has been dragged in off the street and is desperately trying to make out just what is going on around him whilst smiley, happy people are off partying and generally enjoying themselves. There have even been instances in the past where I have passed out or collapsed and have been driven home in embarrassment. Needless to say this makes me rather nervous about such functions.

So it was that, when I arrived at the staircase leading up to Ashton Hall, the butterflies in my stomach were trying to create a tsunami off the coast of Africa.

"You okay?"

I looked the pretty blonde in her bright blue eyes and the lepidoptera's wings slowed slightly.

"I will be, I guess. I'm just not too much of a social animal."

"You make it sound like a student rave," she giggled. "I can assure you there won't be a drop of hard stuff in sight."

*Shame*, I thought to myself as we headed up the stairs. Right then I could have murdered for a bottle of Jack. My heavy feet climbed the marble stairs, which took us up to the hall, and my mind ran over and over what would be the forthcoming scenario.

Guitars. There would be guitars - lots of them. Some of them would have rainbow-coloured straps. Or was that just found within the province of happy-clappy church groups? I shrugged. There would be a tambourine - probably one of those 1980s George Michael affairs, a semi-circular contraption that says, "'Hi, I'm hip with rhythm," as opposed to a Salvation Army version which is circular and says, "Donate for the poor, tight-wad, because you can't take all that cash with you when you go." Oh! There would be a flute. Just one of these and its player would be young, female, slight and willowy. Probably with wavy red hair - and she'd be Irish. She would be the quiet type who didn't say much, but when she placed those sweet lips on the end of that long instrument she always brought tears of joy and pleasure.

Hey! Cut it out, smutty! That's not what I meant and you know it. Jesus! Some people have filthy minds.

So, enough of your sordid imagination, back to the Ashton Hall. We reached the top of the stairs and paused outside the doors that led inside. Abalone pushed one and motioned, "After you."

"Uh uh," I replied. "Ladies first."

She smiled, leant in so that her mouth was next to my ear and whispered, "Whoever said that I was a lady?" then, grinning as she entered, she passed the door to me, her slender fingers brushing my hand. What greeted us when we went inside made me nearly jump out of my already tense and blushing skin. A man about six foot tall with spiked blonde hair was stood inside the door. Nothing wrong with that you might say - just a bit taller than average. However, it was his face that almost caused the loudest girlie scream you have ever heard shriek from my contorted lips. It was covered in black, stylised tattoos. My eyes instinctively did a check on his legs. They did not appear to be robotic, therefore he was not Darth Maul and was most likely not a Sith Lord.

Still scary though.

"Hi, Matt." Abalone bounced up to the tattooed doorman, her lightweight skirt flowing behind her as she gave him a warm hug. Yep, definitely not a Sith. A force choke would have been more appropriate.

"Hi, Abs. How's it going?" Matt had the kind of voice that matched his face: deep, husky and spoke of long nights drinking and smoking in biker bars. I could see under his long-sleeved t-shirt that muscles rippled and flexed as he hugged her back. A little green-eyed monster in the back of my head snorted in disgust. "Showoff," it spat.

Abalone stepped back and introduced me. "Matt, this is Sam. He's just visiting us tonight."

"Cool, Dude," Matt grinned as he crushed my hand to a pulp in his oversized paw. It was okay. I always kept a spare set of phalanges at the end of my other arm. "Good to see you. New blood is always welcome."

Blood? Blood? I knew what the guy meant, but all the same, he was not allaying my nerves.

"Thanks. I'm just here for the show, so to speak," I replied, carefully massaging the damaged muscles at the base of my swollen fingers. "Perhaps have a chat with a few guys afterwards?"

"No probs. We'll make sure you get to talk to the head honcho, too. He'll blow your mind."

Yeah. Far too many biker bars. Smiling politely, I followed Abalone to the rows of chairs that had been arranged facing the stage area. I held back as she confidently made her way towards the front. When she reached her preferred row and noticed I was still hovering at the back, she cocked her head to one side and made a beckoning gesture with her index finger. I shrugged in response and tentatively inclined my head to the back row. She smiled and walked back up to me. "Nobody here bites, you know."

"I know that, it's just..."

"That's okay, sweetie." She placed a hand on my arm and everything felt sort of okay again. "Let's just slide in here, then."

So, in we slid, taking our seats and I started to observe our surroundings. The first overwhelming thing which struck me was the banner at the rear of the stage. It was a huge representation of the T-shaped motif with descending symmetrical swirls that I had seen on the wristbands and the pamphlet. Atop it danced the legend "Anything Is Possible" in bright, lilac lettering.

I frowned somewhat. Lilac was everywhere. Not only was the logo lilac, but there were lilac coloured drapes, lilac coloured streamers, and lilac coloured t-shirts on group members milling around whilst setting things up.

Someone had quite the penchant for this subtle shade of purple.

My stomach knotted somewhat. This was all rather too familiar. I recalled my dream from the previous week where I had been captive once more at John O'Gaunt Media and there had been a lilac banner with a golden version of this logo.

Coincidence? I surely hoped so. I looked over to Abalone who smiled back at me. "God, you look so nervous, Sam. Chill, okay?" She squeezed my hand and grinned as the music group started up some sort of cheery number.

And so it was that, for the next aeon-like hour, I sat and endured my own personal little bit of hell. Rousing choruses were interspersed with thoughtful readings and heart-rending statements of personal salvation and achievement that were all centred around the phrase for the day, children: "Anything is possible".

Want that promotion? Go out and earn it. Anything is possible!

Need extra cash to pay that credit card? Randomly choose winning numbers on the Lottery. Anything is possible!

Think your living room could do with a new rug? Just wait until Granny dies and get hers. Anything is possible!

I sat and politely cringed inwardly as speaker after speaker rose to the podium and revealed more and more ludicrous examples of chance occurrences that they fervently believed to be manifestations of their own will. I didn't know what was worse - that they believed it themselves or that their audience was lapping up this hokum.

Once again I was starting to wonder what on earth Caroline was worried about. These sorts of shenanigans have been around in many forms over the years, normally at a time when society has lost faith in itself and can see no way out of the hole that it has dug itself into. People desperately want answers and solutions to the mundane that constantly drags them down and, when they find none in the normal day-to-day, they start looking under metaphysical rocks for a gem of insubstantial knowledge.

This was daft, yes, but dangerous? I didn't think so.

I was more concerned that Abalone was totally suckered into it. She was a bright, sparky individual who seemed, on the surface, to have no need for an emotional crutch. Appearances, however, can be so very, very deceptive. What was it that was dragging her down into the mire of society? I recalled her tale of the late, great Russell, Geography teacher supreme. Grief and despair can make people perfect targets for emotional manipulation. Had someone done a Jedi mind trick on her and told her that these were the droids she was looking for?

I was pondering this when Matt the Tat bounded up onto the stage. "Okay, people," he announced from behind a huge, male Dathomiri grin, "here it is! The moment you've all been waiting for." He paused and nodded like a deranged chipmunk as members of the audience gave way to involuntary whooping normally found at Wild West rodeos and semi-finals of the *X Factor*. "The man of the moment," Matt finally continued. "The reason we're all here..."

I stifled a yawn.

"The man who has shown us how anything is possible..."

I peeked surreptitiously at my watch.

"Malcolm Wallace!"

All those around me jumped to their feet and started to scream and shout out whoops of joy. I stumbled up, knocking my chair back as I tried to see the stage. Surely I had misheard? It couldn't be, could it? But as the crowd quietened and started to drift back down into their seats bringing with their attention an awed hush, there he was, standing calmly and quietly at the podium.

My old university friend: Malcolm Wallace.

My list of stupefaction had just grown even longer.

I was stunned, flabbergasted, shell-shocked and all the other corny descriptions one might want to use to illustrate the state of mind one is in when the least likely person is stood in front of you.

I had last seen Malcolm back in the days of my university studies. As I said previously in *The Case of The Fastidious Phantom*, he was responsible for landing a ghost called Gerald in my care before swanning off into the night with his benefactor. This was an action that I had far from forgiven him for.

As I sat pondering how I had not noticed his return to Lancaster, I cast my wary eyes over him. He had certainly aged, but in a way which suggested maturity rather than decrepitness. His hair was now pure white and long enough to be smoothed back over his head, framing his curious orange eyes that held the audience enrapt. He wore a plain canvas-coloured suit and sported a simple tie in the eponymous lilac around the neck of a crisp, white shirt. He had leant against the podium a highly polished walking cane and under the lights of the hall I could see a dress ring glinting on the little finger of his right hand.

For all intents and purposes, Malcolm looked like he was doing alright for himself - more than he would have done had he followed his original plan and entered the clergy.

As the crowd settled, he waited, patiently, not saying a word. His orange eyes drifted over the excited throng in front of him as if seeing all and knowing their each and every hidden thought. Gradually, the hushed chattering and breaths of awe subsided into a silence which hung in the dusty air of the Ashton Hall and framed the still personality of one man. Time passed, it was just seconds, minutes at the most, but it felt like, days, weeks, years as Malcolm just stood passively at the front of the hall, his hands lightly clasped together in front of him. His face betrayed no emotion and he half-closed those curiously coloured eyes as if he was straining to hear the slightest sound. Then, when he was sure that he had the complete and undivided attention of absolutely everyone in the room (myself included), he spoke one word:

"Friends."

He opened his eyes and a smile spread across his face. He held his arms out to his sides, now holding the cane in his right hand. "Welcome," he greeted them in his quiet, well-spoken manner. "Welcome to our time together. Time where we know that anything is possible.

"It is good to see you all here, today." Slowly, he walked up and down the front of the stage, his eyes scanning every face in the congregation whilst his cane tapped a steady, pulse-like rhythm. "It's good to see faces new and old." My heart skipped at that; had he seen me? "We are all here for one purpose and one purpose alone: we want to know where we are going. We have lost our way, our map has been drenched in the downpour of life and all those little B-roads have blurred and smudged into one big sticky mess. Many people are shouting at us, telling us that their way is right, that we should listen to no one but them." He shook his head sadly. "Poor, misguided fools. They are so full of their own petty insecurities that they feel they have to impress us with vain attempts at self-idolization. They harangue us from that goggle-box in the corner of the living room while we eat our meals. They bombard us from the radios when we drive to our places of servitude. They never let us be. Over and over they tell us that their way is best, that they have all the answers. But they are wrong, oh so very wrong. For there is but one truth that shines down on us this and every day, if only we acknowledge it and embrace its purity.

"And what might that be, my friends?"

"Anything is possible!" came the roar in unison.

Malcolm's face beamed with joy. "Indeed it is. Indeed it is, and you, yourselves, are witness to that very fact. You see it in your lives. You do not need the pop stars and media moguls to tell you what to do. You do not need politicians domineering your lives. You do not need your brains pulping by the billboards and flashy images of advertising Nazis. No! You know the truth in your heart. You see it there when you sleep. It visits you in your dreams. It whispers in the dark at the base of your subconscious.

"Anything is possible.

"Anything is possible.

"Anything is possible.

"Whatever you want, you can achieve. Whatever you desire, you can do. It is there inside you, buried under a mountain of detritus that has been heaped upon you by modern society. They have ground us down, friends. They have told us that, without them, we are worthless – lower than the smallest, little earthworm.

"Well, I tell you this, you are so much better than that. You can stand proud like this symbol behind me." He pointed with his cane to the large T on the banner. "You can grab the diverse factors of reality in your hands and bend them to your will, for nothing is stronger than the desire you have within you to create a better life for yourself. Nothing can stand in your way, however impossible it may appear."

Malcolm paused, his chest heaving as he took in much needed air after his monologue that had grown steadily in passion and intensity, then he turned to Matt the Tat who stood waiting at the edge of the stage. "Matt, could you bring the Watts family onstage, please?"

It was at this point that I realised I had stopped breathing. This was not the Malcolm Wallace that I remembered. The twenty-something from my distant past had been shy and painfully quiet, withdrawn from his peers and concerned only with his studies both academic and personal. What had caused this transformation? As a young family were ushered onto the stage, I was aware of footsteps entering the hall and someone settling themselves down into a spare chair behind me. I glanced quickly at Abalone. She had not heard the late-comer. Instead, her eyes were transfixed at what was playing out on the stage in front of us. The young family consisted of a man and a woman in their late twenties with a girl of about ten who was sat slouched in a wheelchair.

"This is Melanie," Malcolm informed us as he crouched down next to the little girl. "She is visiting us here today with her parents, Sue and Keith." He looked up to the couple, his body language a living sculpture of concern and heartfelt sympathy. "Tell us, Sue, what is wrong with Melanie."

"We... we don't know," the young woman stammered. "Neither do the doctors. Mel was fine. She was a happy, smiley little girl, then... then three months ago..." A heartfelt sob stole the rest of the explanation.

Malcolm lowered his eyes and shook his head.

"The doctors don't know," he whispered. "The doctors don't know." Rising to his feet, his orange eyes burned bright with anger. "In this modern, scientific world where great minds are happy to devise bigger and better weapons to bring civilisation to the brink of annihilation, not one of those minds can tell these poor people what is wrong with their little girl. Not one of those supposedly respectable doctors thinks it is possible to heal this child."

There were murmurs of discontent from the audience.

From behind me I could hear a humming so soft and quiet that it almost fell under the radar of human hearing. The hairs on my neck prickled and I felt blood rush to my face.

"Anything is possible!" shouted a man over to my right.

"Anything is possible!" shouted a woman near the front.

"Anything is possible!" shouted Abalone next to me.

"Anything is possible!"

"Anything is possible!"

"Anything is possible!"

Around and around it circled the room, like an eagle hovering ready to strike, growing louder in volume, greater in passion. Faster and faster the shouts came as individuals rose to their feet and shook their fists in sheer, unadulterated anger.

"Anything is possible!"

"Anything is possible!"

"Anything is possible!"

This was the mantra. This was the truth. As the humming behind me took words in a lilting tongue that I did not understand, but in a rhythm that cried out to every cell in my body, I too was calling out, "Anything is possible! Anything is possible! Anything is possible! Anything is possible!"

The wings of the swooping eagle were now a violent storm, a whirlwind and there, at its calm epicentre stood the white-haired Moses of this new age, ready to lead his people through the stormy seas of the violent, modern world.

Raising his cane in one hand, he placed the other firmly on the shoulder of the young girl and, with one word brought a shuddering silence to the clamour:

"Rise."

And she did.

As the little girl who had been a shell of her former self and bound to a wheelchair for three months rose to her feet and ran laughing to her parents, the singing behind me abruptly ceased and the congregation erupted into whoops of applause. I turned in time to catch sight of a slim, dark-clad figure slinking out of the doors through which I had entered. I had to follow her. I *needed* to follow her. My entire body craved to hear that song once more and my libido was busily styling its hair with the finest Brylcreem to achieve that possibility, but to leave now would be to turn my back on someone else that I desperately needed to talk to.

Malcolm Wallace.

As the congregation dispersed a short while later, I rose and made my way with Abalone to the front. My heart was pounding and my palms were sweaty. I rubbed the offending skin on my jacket and prayed to God that I did not look a mess. Wallace was stood in the middle of a small group of followers. He was paying complete attention to their every word and consoling them where needed, encouraging as necessary and generally sending them off in a much better frame of mind than they had been just a few minutes previously.

The Watts family were also stood nearby, chatting to members of Credete. Little Melanie looked over at me and smiled. I wandered over to the child as it was plain that Wallace was going to be tied up for a bit.

"Hello," she said to me.

"Hello," I replied, not quite sure what to say to a child who has just been faith-healed. "How are you feeling now?" I asked as I crouched down to a more child-friendly height.

"Much better, thank you. Look!" She giggled as she wiggled her fingers in front of her. "I couldn't do that this morning. Actually, I couldn't do a lot of things this morning."

"You must have been really scared."

She nodded vigorously. "It was like being stuck inside a lump of clay and it stopping everything from moving."

I frowned. "What happened? What caused your body to," I looked for the right words, "stop working?"

The little blondie shrugged. "Don't know. But it was after the dream."

"The dream?" This piqued my curiosity. "What dream?"

"I was playing in the road outside our house," Melanie explained. "It was dark, but warm. Then suddenly it got very, very cold and someone was stood behind me. I wanted to turn to see who it was, but my body couldn't move. I tried to call out to Mummy and Daddy, but my mouth wouldn't work. All I could do was cry. And that's what they found me doing in bed the next morning: crying. It was all I could do apart from eat sleep and, you know..." She leaned up to me conspiratorially and whispered in my ear, "poo." She giggled again. "But now I'm better thanks to nice Mister Wallace. Cool, isn't it?"

"It certainly is," came a quiet, male voice from my side. I turned and there he was, smiling gently at me. "It's good to see you, Samuel."

I straightened up, my knees creaking ominously. "Good to see you too, Malcolm. How's it going?"

"Surviving," he smiled. "Keeping myself busy."

"So I see. You're looking well."

"Thank you." His orange eyes looked me up and down and he frowned slightly. "I believe you have something that bothers you. Something with your ears."

I kept my surprise in check. There was no need to be a psychic to know I suffered from tinnitus. People with long term conditions have certain mannerisms and tells that give the illness away. Obviously I had one that I was unaware of, plus he had been around me at university. True, he had not exactly been a close friend so I had never spoken to him about my condition, but he had always been the quiet, observant type. "I have Meniere's disease."

Wallace raised a white eyebrow. "And you're here to be healed of it?"

"No, no," I laughed nervously. "I'm just here with a friend."

He nodded slowly, knowingly. "That would be Miss Morris, then." It was most definitely a statement, not a question. "I believe you met her at her school last week. There was a bit of paranormal trouble, it seems."

Okay, now I felt threatened. Someone had been talking. I shot Abalone a quick glance. She was off to the side, chatting and laughing with a group of other very cheerful members of Wallace's congregation. "It was something and nothing," I managed through a forced smile.

"Really?" Wallace's voice oozed concern like a politician oozes sincerity. "I would have thought a poltergeist would be most troublesome. I believe you vanquished your foe in the end."

"Something like that."

"So you come face to face with a poltergeist yet you refuse to believe in the power of one's own mind," he mused, his thumb slowly caressing the two snakes that decorated the head of his ornate cane. "Most intriguing."

"If you say so." I was nowhere near able to string together any long, civil sentences. My hackles were up and I had buckled down into defence mode.

"So, again, I ask myself as to why you are here..."

Wallace's musing was cut off as a man I had not seen before interrupted him. "Mister Wallace..."

My old acquaintance turned quickly to the newcomer. The man was mid-fifties, grey-haired and seemed to favour one leg as he walked. "Ah, Mister Flint," Wallace beamed, all warmth and welcome, "so good of you to join us. Is it that time already?"

The man nodded nervously.

"Samuel, this is Mister Flint, caretaker of this fine hall. Mister Flint, this is Mister Spallucci, a very dear old friend of mine who has decided to make my acquaintance once more out of the blue."

Mister Flint shot me a confused smile. I politely offered him my hand. His touch was wet and clammy. This man exuded a primal fear that was almost palpable. After the shortest of handshakes he stuffed his hand back into his coat pocket and said, "Mister Wallace, I'm afraid I have to be asking you to leave right now. You know you're only booked for the three hours."

I started and pulled my shirt sleeve back in a fast manner. Three hours? Sure enough it was eleven o'clock. How the dickens had that much time passed without me noticing? Okay, there had been the waffle and prattling about how life-changing Credete was but that had not lasted that long, surely? Then Wallace had spoken. That had been what, five minutes? Fifteen at the most? Then there had been the healing followed by a few more choruses and it had been time to finish.

Where had the time gone?

My mind's eye recalled the slender figure leaving the hall and my libido shuddered.

"We will pack up shortly and be out of your hair soon, Mister Flint." Wallace smiled warmly as he said this, but there was a chill to those weird eyes of his.

"I'm sorry, Mister Wallace," the caretaker persisted, "but this isn't the first time that you have overrun. There will be a surcharge."

Wallace sighed as he turned back to me. "I do apologise, Samuel. I have to sort this little matter out. Why don't we catch up later? I have your phone number."

I cringed. Damn it! How much did this guy already know about me? "Sure. Ring me when you have time. I'd like to catch up."

He nodded, placed an avuncular arm around the nervous caretaker and pulled him away, talking closely and quietly into his ear. I let out a deep breath and made for Abalone.

"So, what did you think?"

We were walking up from the Town Hall towards the Moorlands area of Lancaster. Abalone lived there in a small two up two down on Dunkeld Street with her housemate. "It was enlightening."

Her light voice sparkled with laughter in the clear evening. "Oh, I'm so glad you think so. Isn't Malcolm amazing?"

Well that was one word for my former university acquaintance. *Creepy* was another. As we walked up Quarry Road, I cast my mind back to a hall full of people, myself included, stood on their feet crying out the three word mantra.

*Anything is possible.*

Had he really cured that little girl? The cynical side of my mind said, "Surely not," but there was that little niggle scratching away at the back with a marker pen and sheets of A4 paper. It was drawing pictures of werewolves, fairies and vampires. If they were real, then what was a casual bit of faith-healing?

What about little Melanie's dream? It obviously had something to do with her illness, but what? I sighed, deep in thought.

"Penny for them?"

"Sorry, just getting my head around everything." Then something struck me.

"Abalone, do teenagers go to the meetings? I think I'm right in saying that was fairly much an adult affair, so to speak."

She stopped walking, placed her hands on her hips and locked those blue eyes on me. "Is this to do with that client of yours?"

I shrugged. "She's paying the bills. I have to be thorough."

"Fair 'nuff. Sure, there's a teenage group. The kids from school go to that one. I'm not sure what day it meets on." We resumed walking up the hill. "Malcolm could tell you." She paused and shot me a sideways grin. "I think he was really pleased to see you."

"It was very weird seeing him there after all these years," I said truthfully. "The sight of him up on that stage, commanding such respect and love, almost bowled me over. He was a total mouse at uni. Hardly ever spoke to anyone."

"People change."

I nodded. "I guess they do."

We skirted round the corner and headed up Aberdeen Road. Terraced houses flanked our right as we climbed the steep hill. I could see Dunkeld Street just up ahead.

"So then..."

My heart skipped a beat as my ego started to smooth down its hair and check its breath. "So... what?"

Abalone grinned again as we reached the end of her street. "I really enjoyed tonight. I'd like to do it again."

"Me too. Although without all the crowds. Somewhere a bit more private, perhaps?"

"Sounds good to me, Mister Investigator." She reached up and ran a finger along my cheek. My ego started to somersault and juggle flaming clubs at the same time. "Why don't you give me a ring this weekend and we'll arrange something?"

"Will do." I paused then called out after her as she turned to go, "Just confirm one thing for me."

"What?"

"You're not the sister of a deranged werewolf."

The blonde beamed from ear to ear. "Goodnight, Mister Investigator." She blew me a cheeky little kiss then turned and headed off to her house. I stood grinning on the street corner for a few minutes before heading back down into town. It had been a rather nice end to a somewhat peculiar evening.

*This could actually work*, I thought to myself. *This could actually work.*

# Chapter Eight

The next day found me feeling decidedly chipper. I had a beautiful, intelligent woman interested in me who, as a bonus, was not a homicidal maniac. Nice one! Perhaps life was turning a corner and fortune was starting to favour the not-so-brave? I do believe I actually started to whistle to myself as I poured soya milk on some sugary cereal. If my life had been a Disney movie, cartoon bluebirds would have been sat on the windowsill waiting expectantly for me to burst into song.

Munching away through my tasty bowl of potential tooth decay I flicked on the goggle box and settled down into the comfort blanket that is breakfast television. Friendly faces wearing cuddly cardigans smiled up at me telling me what a wonderful world I lived in and how bright and sunny the future was.

For once, I was inclined to agree.

I sat and devoured this morning panacea, lapping up every jolly morsel. They were just getting to an interview with the famed Professor Robert Richmond, who was going to fill them in on his latest archaeological dig in the Indus Valley, when my mobile piped up. I glanced at the display. "Unknown," it informed me. I frowned but clicked the answer icon.

"Hello?"

"Samuel. How are you this morning?"

I flicked the television onto mute and set my bowl on the coffee table. "Hello, Malcolm. I'm well. You?"

"Very good indeed," came the cultured voice. "It was marvellous to see you last night. I thought you might like to meet up today, if you're not busy."

"Sure. What time?"

"About ten?"

I glanced at one of my clocks. That was okay. It gave me just over an hour. Plenty of time. "Okay. Ten it is. Market Square?"

"Very good. I'll see you then."

We said our goodbyes and hung up. I turned the television off just as the renowned Professor Richmond was pointing out details of an image of a horned man sitting cross-legged surrounded by animals.

I picked up my bowl and finished off the cereal before taking the empty dish back through to the kitchen. As I washed and dried it I wondered to myself how had Malcolm achieved all this? How had he gone from being the bookish outsider at university to the magnetic focus of last night's Credete meeting? It seemed as if he had undergone a personality transplant. Perhaps our meeting would shed some light on this incredible transformation.

Malcolm was sat waiting outside the Starbucks in Market Square. He appeared a picture of refined calm in the hustle and bustle of Thursday morning. He wore a light coloured suit over a lilac coloured shirt and dark purple tie. His long white hair was loose but neatly groomed. His cane was clasped between his hands as he surveyed those who hurried past him.

"What do you make of them, Samuel?" he asked without even turning his head. Until that moment I had not realised that he was in fact aware of my presence.

I approached my old acquaintance and sat next to him on the bench. "What do you mean?"

"Look at them all, scurrying from this place to that, their heads down, eager to avoid even the slightest bit of eye contact with anyone be it stranger or friend. Are they even aware that we watch them?"

"I guess not," I shrugged, unsure where this was leading.

"They are selfish, Samuel, every one of them, and that will ultimately be society's downfall. It has turned inward, away from its friends and neighbours." The street philosophy continued as I frowned at the somewhat harsh tone: "Tell me, does the ant see the elephant just before the poor insect is crushed under the pachyderm's mighty foot?"

Okay. This was weird, but I went with it. "I'm sure it does. It must feel the coolness of the shadow." I was rather pleased with that response. Very deep.

"Or does it just think that the path of the wind has changed?" Malcolm turned to face me, watching for my response with his curious orange eyes. "Samuel, people never truly realise when disaster is imminent. They may have a gut feeling that something is intrinsically wrong but they ignore it as they scurry hither and thither with their dull, mundane and," he turned back to watch the fair folk of Lancaster, "ultimately pointless lives."

We sat there in silence for a minute or two, he pondering the deepest philosophies of the universe and me wondering what the hell was going on. Eventually, he broke the silence. "So where would you like to go for refreshment?"

Like I have already mentioned, I have been told a number of times that caffeine is really bad for my tinnitus. Apparently it increases the heart rate which in turn makes the ears pound more, or something such. The thing is, by the time doctors have extolled the virtues of decaf coffee or tea that tastes like it was picked from under a cow pat I have normally lit up a Lucky and swigged down a glass of Jack.

Quite frankly I consider coffee to be the least of my vices. It seems fairly pointless trying to pick away at a mountain with a drawing pin so, until I've given up the fags and the booze, the three shot, black Americano will be my drink of choice.

It was not, however, the desired beverage of one Malcolm Wallace.

"You actually enjoy this?" He was stirring around in his drink as if expecting a kraken to rise from the brown depths and grab him by the throat.

"It keeps me awake." I downed a warm sip feeling the wonder drug start to kick in. "I have a habit of not sleeping well. Bad dreams."

Malcolm raised a white eyebrow. "Really? Anything in particular?" He lay his wooden stirrer down and sat back expectantly, the coffee forgotten.

"Work stuff." That was all he was going to get. This little fishy was not hungry.

His orange eyes bored into me over steepled fingers, his golden ring glinting in the sunlight that streamed through the window. "Some feel that poor sleep is down to an unfulfilled lifestyle, Samuel. Would that be true with you?"

A sarcastic laugh escaped my lips. "No, it's more likely that my tinnitus is just playing overtime while I'm sleeping, giving my brain too much night-time entertainment."

"That doesn't sound like fun."

"You can say that again," I shrugged. "it seems to have gotten worse as I've gotten older and it's been particularly bad this last week."

"That must be awful, Samuel." Concern practically dripped off his tongue. "I imagine you'd do anything to be rid of it."

At that moment a goose jumped up and down on my grave whilst playing a sousaphone. I moved uncomfortably in my chair. "*Almost* anything. I don't think I'd sell my soul just for a good night's sleep."

I laughed nervously.

Malcolm did not.

"Besides," I coughed, rapidly trying to change track, "It's most likely just work. My first week was somewhat eventful."

"Indeed," he nodded. "Apparently you were abducted, so the news report said."

"And apparently everyone has seen it apart from me," I grumbled.

Malcolm smiled serenely. "It was most informative. To be honest, I was wondering when our paths would cross."

"Really?"

"Indeed. Tell me, Samuel, why did you *really* come to Credete with young Miss Morris? I'm guessing it was neither a first date nor genuine curiosity. A case perhaps?"

I shifted even more uneasily in my seat. Oh crap! He was good.

"I see," Malcolm observed, obviously amused at my embarrassment. "May I ask what my devilish cult has been accused of?"

I let out a deep sigh and drank up some more coffee before answering, "I have a client who is concerned about their son. Apparently he has joined your merry band and she is worried."

Malcolm nodded sagely and rubbed his ring between his finger and thumb. "That is understandable. Mothers do have a tendency to fuss somewhat. It would have been nice of her to contact me first, though. I might have been able to allay her fears."

"He wasn't there last night."

"No, we have a teen group that meets every other Monday. The next one is next week. The numbers vary, such are the vagaries of adolescence."

I smiled. "Are they the same format as last night?"

"Good grief, no!" he exclaimed. "I keep the younger group far more light-hearted and lower key, so to speak. It tends to be games and activities. I'm sure you know the sort of thing."

I did. The staple of youth groups all over the world: table tennis, board games and intense discussion on the latest, greatest computer game or television programme. Hardly life-threatening or soul-destroying. "Tell me about the wrist bands."

A warm smile filled Malcolm's face. "Pure marketing," he admitted. "The teenagers love them. They get something that creeps through their uniform regulations and I get a walking advert for Credete. It's a win win situation."

I nodded. That did make sense.

"May I ask who the concerned mother is?"

I pondered this for a moment, drumming my fingernails against my teeth. Should I tell him? I had to say that so far I could see no real harm in Credete. Sure they were a bit driven and charismatic but in the last week I had certainly come across far worse. However, what if I was wrong? What if there was more; dark secrets lurking in the shadows? Also, what about client confidentiality?

I shook my head. "Not just yet. It wouldn't be proper."

Malcolm nodded understandingly. "I see. Don't worry yourself about it. Tell her to contact me and we can have a chat. I imagine it's all a misunderstanding. Besides I'm sure she would listen to you."

My mind drifted back to a time that I had been the one listening to Caroline...

It had been a warm summer's night and we had snuck away from the madding crowd of the summer fair that had doubled up as her sixteenth birthday party. We exited quietly through the kitchen of the vicarage and found a secluded spot under the full moon. Her hand gently clasped mine, leading me through her garden. I still remember the sweet scent of some sort of lavender and rosemary that lined the winding path. As we ran our fingers through the foliage the aromatic scent enveloped us in its embrace.

Eventually, we arrived at the foot of the garden; the hubbub of the party was just a dull, distant hum - a world away. Caroline sat herself down on the curved stone seat that nestled underneath a large tree and she patted the surface next to her. I obliged and sidled up. Her eyes shone beautiful and dark in the moonlight, contrasting against her fine, blonde hair which my fingers were itching to stroke the same way that a small child cannot help but stroke a pet cat or a crazy person their stuffed raccoon. She must have been reading my mind as she took my hand in hers and rested the side of her head into my palm, closing those dark eyes.

"This is nice," she whispered. "I could stay like this forever."

"You might get a crick in your neck," I grinned.

She sat up and giggled, holding my hand in hers. It felt so small. "Oh, I have something for you." She stood up and felt around in the pockets of her tight jeans before fishing out a small, neatly wrapped package. "Here."

I took the proffered gift and looked down at it, bemused. "What's this for?"

"I saw it and thought of you," she shrugged. "Go on, open it."

I smiled and set to unwrapping the small package. A brass Zippo lighter tumbled into my lap. It was adorned with a pyramid, atop which was an all-seeing eye. "Cool."

"I know I hate those wretched things you smoke, but if you will insist on torching your lungs, you might as well do it in style. Turn it over. There's an engraving."

I thumbed the lighter over and saw there in curling script: "*Nil illegitimi carborundum.*" I chuckled. "You know that's not a real Latin phrase, don't you?"

"But it sounds good." She nodded up towards the vicarage. "I'm sure if the Romans were in your position, then they'd say that all the time."

I grinned. Her father had been constantly on my case all week. At times I feared that he knew about us but then logic stated that I had not yet been turned out of the vicarage on my backside. "Thank you," I continued to beam. Standing next to her I took her in my arms. "Thank you so much." Then we were kissing: me stooping down, her tiptoeing up, my hands stroking her flaxen hair, her arms wrapped around my back.

When we pulled away, there were tears trickling down her cheeks. "What's wrong?" I asked.

She shook her head vigorously, the back of her hand wiping the tears away. "Nothing, nothing at all."

"Then, what is it?"

For a moment she just stood, staring up at me, those dark eyes surveying all that I was, all that I had been, all that I might be, then she said the three words I had been longing to hear all week:

"I love you."

My heart was probably skipping a few beats, but my brain didn't notice as it was too busy reeling the audio track back to make sure that it had heard right. When it was sure that it had, I asked:

"Really?"

Caroline smiled. "Really."

"Really, really?"

Her arms linked up behind my neck. "Just kiss me again." So I did.

It was paradise.

The next day was hell.

"Samuel?"

The gentle, enquiring voice snapped me back out of my reverie to the present day. "What? Sorry. I drifted off a bit there."

"So I noticed." Malcolm's cup was empty. I had not even seen him touch it. I must have been well away.

"Like I said, last week was rather tiring."

"I think it's more than that." He leant forward and gripped me with his strangely-coloured eyes. "Tell me, Samuel. Just how much do you trust this woman?"

I remained silent as, in my heart of hearts, I could not find an answer that I truly liked the sound of.

"Look, enough of such things." Malcolm's voice was now much lighter and convivial. "I think we have so much to catch up on, don't you? I'm going to the Grand tonight. I have a box reserved. Why don't you come and join me?"

I thought about my dinner date with Caroline and John. "I'm afraid I can't. I already have plans."

Malcolm regarded me silently.

"Otherwise I would love to come."

"Very well," he said. "If you change your mind or if you feel you need to, I'll be in box number one from seven thirty. I would most enjoy your company." He lifted his arm and checked his watch. "Now, however, I must be off. Things to do and people to see, as it were. It has been most illuminating catching up like this."

We stood and shook hands before he headed off out into Market Square. I resumed my seat and finished off my almost cold coffee. Most illuminating? How could that be? I did not think that I had told him all that much about me. I got up and headed out of the café feeling somewhat disturbed.

# Chapter Nine

I arrived at Caroline's half an hour early, bottle in hand. I stood in front of her yellow front door and took a deep breath. I could do this. Yes, I could. It was just a meal with a client and her son. That was all. There was nothing special about it whatsoever.

Liar, liar. Pants on fire!

Who was I kidding? This was such a big deal for me. Caroline was my greatest mistake of all time. We had been entwined in something beautiful and it had gone suddenly, rapidly sour. One minute she had loved me deeply and completely, the next...

There had been nothing.

What had I done wrong?

Had it been something I'd said? Something I'd done?

To this day I was still in the dark.

And here she was, suddenly back in my life, begging for my help. I could not refuse. I had to make amends for whatever it was that I had done even if that was just telling her that John was not in mortal peril.

Then, of course, there was Abalone. Damn you, bad timing! Something was developing there, I was sure of that and I did not want to prune that particular rose before it had flowered. It was a far too beautiful and delicate thing.

So, what to do?

Well, for now there was only one thing that I could do. I knocked on the door. My knuckles rapped three hard pulses and I took a polite step back as my heart pounded in my chest and bells rang wildly in my ears. There was that age long silence that always follows as you wonder to yourself whether the person in the house has heard you knock or not. You stand in front of the door, rocking back and forth on the balls of your feet trying to decide whether you should knock again or not. You glance at the windows and try to see if you can discern whether there are people inside without appearing to be a peeping Tom. Next you have to decide whether you knock again or not. Has it been long enough? If you knock now, will it have been too soon and will they answer the door whilst making some sarcastic comment about you being impatient? So you raise your hand and quickly lower it again a number of times, unsure what to do. You look like a worried marionette with a cruel puppeteer lifting and dropping your hand over and over. Then, just as you are about to knock one more time, you hear footsteps approaching and you smile with relief as the door opens.

"Hi, Sam," John beamed as he swung the door open. "Great to see you."

"You too," I smiled.

"Wanna come in?"

"Sure. Sorry I'm early."

"That's okay." He led me down the short hallway through to the second door on the right which took us into the dining room. The smell of cooking reached my nose and my stomach rumbled noisily. "You sound hungry," he laughed.

I grinned. "Apparently I am."

There was a doorway on the other side of the room which led through to the kitchen. Caroline appeared, framed by the light of the kitchen which appeared to be a hive of industrious activity. I could see pans boiling, something baking in the oven and copious amounts of flour. In fact, it looked like a snowstorm had happened through there, she even had streaks of white through her chestnut brown hair.

"Everything okay through there?"

"Mum doesn't entertain much, but when she does she gets creative," John informed me, much to the embarrassment of his mother whose cheeks flushed bright red.

"Does she indeed?" I raised a knowing eyebrow towards Caroline as the double-entendre flew straight over her son's head as soon as it had bounced out of his mouth.

Ever the professional, Caroline cleared her throat and greeted me. "Hello, Sam. Why don't I put that," she motioned towards the wine, "in the fridge?"

I nodded and followed her through into the den of creativity. As I walked behind her, the aroma of patchouli and jasmine drifted up to meet me. "Something smells nice."

"Thank you," my host replied, slipping the bottle into the door of the fridge. "It's a tart."

"Pardon?"

"In the oven. Hence all the flour," Caroline explained. "John's right. I don't entertain much and I tend to get in such a flap." She bit her lower lip as she surveyed the white drifts that lay piled up around the room. "Oh God, it looks like I had a fight with Mister Kipling."

We both laughed at that. It was nice.

"Do you need any help?"

"No." She shook her head and a cloud of flour billowed out from her hair. "Believe it or not, everything is under control. Why don't you go chill out in the other room while I finish off in here?"

"You sure?"

Her head bobbed up and down emphatically as she shooed me out of the kitchen. "Go. Talk boy talk or something."

I conceded defeat and gave up the role of Good Samaritan as I ambled back into the dining room where John was busying himself setting the table and not watching what was going on in the kitchen, honest guv. I shed my hat and jacket before picking up some cutlery and finally managing to make myself feel useful as I placed knives and forks around already positioned place mats. "So, how are you keeping?" I asked.

"Same old, same old," the teenager shrugged non-committally. "You?"

I chuckled quietly to myself. "Oh, rather busy."

"Ghosties and goblins?"

"Ghosties and goblins."

"Cool."

My chuckling intensified.

John frowned. "What is it?"

"Nothing," I smiled as I lay the last knife on the table. "I just love how you're so enthusiastic over things. It reminds me of when I was your age."

He appeared to ponder this for a moment then asked, "Don't you get excited about things these days?"

I stood and regarded the young lad as I pondered this. When was the last time I had truly gotten excited over something? I wracked my memory for some glimmer of an image, but nothing was forthcoming. If there was a book, a film or even a curiously shaped potato that had made me jump up and down fanatically then it had been buried beneath images of vampires, fairies, Satanists, dragons and werewolves. "I guess work's just getting in the way a bit at the moment." I looked up and gave an involuntary shudder as I caught sight of the picture that hung on the wall above the fireplace.

"You okay?"

I forced a smile. "Sure. I'm good. That's quite a picture."

John turned and followed my gaze. "Oh, yeah. It's great."

Great was not the word that I would have used. There, dominating the dining room, was a large print of the Ashton Memorial. It was a Chas Jacobs – a local artist. I could tell by the bold, striking colours and lack of shading that were his trademark. A very popular artist, his work could be found framed in every art gallery in town and on greetings cards in every newsagents. His style was described as "simplistic" and "childlike". I had no simple, childlike feelings as I stood staring at the dark green trees that lined the stone staircase up which I had fled not long ago to escape the slavering

Hawkins. There, framed against the night sky, was the very stonework from which the murderous beast had leapt in an attempt to kill me. All it needed was a full moon hanging watchfully behind the green dome and the nightmarish image would have been complete.

"I used to play there as a kid."

"Sorry?" His words snapped me out of my nightmare. "What did you say?"

"I said that I used to play there as a kid. When I was young, mum didn't have much cash so she'd take me up there every weekend. It was a very special place where I ran up and down those steps fighting imaginary battles with monsters and stuff, you know?"

My mind saw Hawkins stalking up the stone steps after a younger version of John. My stomach lurched. If my face was showing any of my horror, he did not seem to notice. The boy was transfixed, staring up at his infancy. This was incredible. How could a place that had been hellish for me be so paradisiacal for someone else?

"We used to pretend it was a palace. We would hold court for imaginary nobility." He smiled softly as he continued; "People would look at us gone out as we sat on the steps addressing our lords and ladies. It was all very daft - a queen and her prince – but truly wonderful.

"Once, I asked Mum a question." His voice took on a softer, more melancholy tone. "I asked her why there was no king. Every royal family had to have a king, I said, so where was ours?

"I remember Mum going very quiet. For a moment I thought she hadn't heard me, but then she turned to me and said that ours had run away and left us.

"It was the saddest moment of my childhood.

"That night I crept out of the house and snuck up to our palace. In my eight-year-old head I must have reasoned that our king was really hiding there – perhaps playing hide and seek. So I toddled up to the park and hunted through," he pointed to the swathes of dark green on the picture, "those trees, but the king wasn't there. I decided that perhaps if I waited for him, he would come and find me.

"So I waited and waited.

"But he never came.

"However, my mum did. Needless to say, she was not very happy. No, not at all. I don't remember too much, but I do remember her crying lots as she brought me home. She made me promise never to do something so stupid ever again and she took me into her bed and curled up with me so we went to sleep together."

He turned and grinned at me. "The things you remember."

I heard a noise from the kitchen doorway and turned to see Caroline watching us. Her eyes said it all.

The things you remember, indeed.

The food was great. Caroline had excelled herself. It was a red pepper and tomato tart. She had found the recipe on, as she put it, some lentil-eating, hippy website. There was a great deal of conversation, albeit not from the adults. A number of times Caroline had to scold her son for talking with his mouth full. As I watched the young lad eating his food and whiffling away about this thing and that thing, I couldn't help but smile. He had a truly infectious enthusiasm for life which radiated from him like light from a candle. If the world is in the hands of a generation like him, I thought to myself, then it is in very *safe* hands.

After the meal, Caroline told John to tidy the plates and wash the dishes. I was amazed at how agreeable he was to get on with the chores. He just scooped them up and headed off into the kitchen, whistling to himself. "He's a good lad," I said.

Caroline's eyes followed him out of the room. "I know. That's what worries me so much about this Credete business. He's a soft touch. He'd do anything for anyone."

"Well, that's something I don't think you need to worry about," I said, leaning back in the dining chair, my stomach contentedly full. "I checked them out. Apart from being a bit free and easy with the happy vibes, they don't strike me as any sort of threat. My guess is it will run its course and dissipate." Caroline said nothing so I carried on. "I went to one of their meetings and it was all about self-confidence and faith healing – not exactly sinister. Then I met with the group leader and he said that if you had any concerns you should get in touch with him." I paused. Her brown eyes were staring off across the table into the middle distance. Something was wrong, something I was missing. "Caroline, you okay?"

She shook her head. "No, that can't be right. It can't be. I was sure there was something." Her manicured nails drummed impatiently on the dining table and she turned to face me. "Here's the deal: you're wrong. You have to be. There must be something."

Okay. So I was *definitely* missing something here. I dialled it back a bit and trod cautiously. "Sorry, Caroline, but I really don't think there is."

"No." She shook her head vehemently, causing her brown hair to swing violently from side to side. "There is. I know there is. It just appeared from nowhere overnight. How did Wallace manage that? How could he afford it?"

I frowned. How did she know Wallace's name? Had John told her? Had she mentioned it before now? I recalled Alec's mysterious warning that she was hiding something. "Caroline, is there something I don't know?"

"You guys alright?"

Both our heads snapped to the kitchen door. John was stood there holding a red and white tea towel, a look of consternation on his face.

"It's fine, sweetie," his mother reassured him. "Nothing to worry about."

It was obvious that he did not believe her as he twisted the damp cloth anxiously between his hands.

"Your mum's just a bit concerned about you, that's all," I explained.

"Why?"

"Sam, we really don't need to..."

I held my hand up, cutting off the protest. "Actually, I think we do. John, your mum's really worried about the group you're hanging around with. Credete."

Confusion crept into his brown eyes. "Really?"

"I know. I've just been explaining to her that they are not so bad and she should not be worried about you having joined a cult or anything."

"I should hope not." The corner of his mouth turned up as he started to laugh. "I mean, after all, she was the one who suggested that I join them."

Next there was a stunned silence.

Then there was shouting.

"So you set this up? You made your own son join a group you were suspicious about just for a scoop?"

She tried to explain, she tried to be reasonable.

I was not for listening.

"It wasn't like that, Sam. It really wasn't." Caroline's voice was starting to take on a thin and reedy petulance which was beginning to get on my nerves.

"So what *was* it like then? Why don't you tell me?" I had abandoned my chair, all post-dining contentment flushed down the drain, and was pacing back and forth like a trapped lion. Right now I felt like biting someone's head off and Caroline's was the obvious choice. "Come on, *Wondermum*, enlighten me."

Caroline tore her eyes away from me to John who was still stood in the doorway silently watching us fight. She opened her mouth to say something to him but shook her head and let her lips snap shut before turning back to me. "Sam, look at me," she begged. "Just look at me. I'm a failure, a bloody failure. I was supposed to go off and become a hotshot journalist, but instead I'm stuck in a backwater city writing garbage for a *What's On* section in a local rag. To make matters worse, I'm shunned by my family and alone with my son."

"My heart bleeds for you," I sneered.

"Hector Swarbrick was on my back," she continued. "He said I wasn't pulling my weight and my section was going to be cut. My neck was on the block if I didn't get him some juicy stories for the paper. So I hunted around, all over the place. I scoured everything: bars, courtrooms, the net. Then I came across Credete and I thought, Bingo. Here was a group that had sprung out of nowhere and was offering its followers the world.

"They had to be dodgy.

"So I told Hector that I was going to get dirt on them and he asked me just how I planned to achieve this. Then it hit me that I had no idea. If I walked in, they would see right through me as a reporter. So I said the first thing that came into my head."

"You said you'd send me." John was slouched against the door frame, all traces of *joie de vivre* expunged from him. Poor kid.

"You willingly sent your own flesh and blood into what you expected to be a nest of vipers?" I shook my head unbelievingly. "And I'm guessing you got nothing."

Caroline hung her head and kept silent.

"You didn't realise that the teens had their own meetings which were effectively just a youth group. You needed another strategy. You needed someone who could get in with the adults."

She nodded, sullenly.

"So," I continued, "what should happen but your employer and your son have chance meetings with an old flame of yours. Not only that, but said person actually went to university with the very founder of the group you wanted infiltrating. It couldn't have been planned better. You turned up on my doorstep full of sob stories and heartache and lured me in to do exactly what you wanted.

"Only, you've *not* got what you wanted, have you? It was a waste of time. Credete is harmless. Creepy, yes, but totally harmless." I shook my head and grabbed my hat and coat. "I'm leaving." I turned to John. "I'm sorry about this. I really am."

His head gave a set of small, nervous nods and he returned to the kitchen leaving us alone. My heart broke for the poor lad. I turned on Caroline. Her wet eyes looked up at me through her dishevelled hair and I felt nothing but anger. "Don't you ever contact me again," I hissed. "I'm through with you. We have no connection. None whatsoever."

As I grabbed the door handle, a small, pathetic voice whispered, "Yes we do. We have our son."

# Chapter Ten

I stormed into my flat and opened the bottle of Jack that I had purchased on the way home. My head was pounding and my ears were screaming. I needed something to silence them both. On my way to the kitchen I took three deep swigs from the bottle and, as the liquid heat spread down my chest, I half-filled a whiskey glass I'd snatched up from a table.

Breaths, deep breaths. I stood clasping the kitchen counter as I tried to control the rhythm of my gasping lungs. It was no good. I drank some more bourbon, this time from the glass.

I should have known it.

I should have seen it.

It had been there in front of me all the time, hidden in plain sight. There had been the crystal elephant, my secret gift to Caroline just before her sixteenth birthday. Then there was the age of John, for crying out loud! How could I not have noticed that one?

Perhaps I had not wanted to.

Perhaps I had subconsciously been in denial.

Perhaps I had not wanted to suffer rejection once more.

I had a son.

I had a son, and I had screwed up once again. I had just turned and walked away. I thought back to the last time I had walked away.

The day after Caroline's birthday party, I woke refreshed and renewed. I was a different person: alive and joyful. The pain of my father's imminent death had been transported somewhere else entirely – a different planet, galaxy or universe. Right now I was invulnerable; nothing could hurt me.

I lay in bed looking dreamily out of the window at the morning sunshine and wistfully touched my fingers to my lips. Caroline had kissed me there. Lots.

That had only been the start of it.

We had made love down at the bottom of the garden. It had been so sweet, so tender. Hidden away from prying eyes in our own paradise we had become one body, one soul. An intimate union had occurred that nothing could ever split asunder.

I clambered out of bed and dressed hurriedly, eager to face the coming day, excited at our lovers' secret. We had something that was truly ours and no one else knew. There would be knowing glances, snatched kisses and more love making.

But right now, breakfast.

I practically skipped downstairs and when I entered the dining room Caroline was already sat there, toying with a grapefruit.

I grabbed some cereal and plonked myself down next to her. "Morning, you!" I beamed.

"Hi." She continued to prod the flesh of the fruit with her spoon.

"How are you?"

"Okay."

I leant across to kiss her.

She drew away. "Sam. Don't!"

"Ah, right. Okay. I understand." I glanced out the door of the room and saw no one but it paid to be careful. I poured some milk on my cereal.

Caroline sighed and pushed the grapefruit away, uneaten.

"You okay?"

She shrugged.

I reached up and ran a finger through her blonde hair.

She reached up and drew my touch away. "Please don't."

It was about this time that I realised something was wrong. "Caroline?"

She sat staring at her discarded breakfast.

I was also starting to feel less than hungry. "Please. Talk to me. Have I done something wrong?"

Slowly, she shook her head.

"Then what is it?" I glanced over at the door again to make sure we were still alone and whispered, "Are you having regrets about last night?"

No response.

"Caroline, it really meant something for me. I love you."

She turned. Her brown eyes rimmed with tears held mine as she said, "But I don't love you." She stood, slid the chair back under table and dumped the discarded grapefruit in the bin. "I could *never* love you." She turned away from me. "Father wants to see you. You'd better not keep him waiting."

And she walked out of the room.

I sat there for a moment, crushed and deflated as a dark void began to rise inside my chest and crept up inside my ears, causing bells to toll. I fought the darkness down and pushed my inedible breakfast away before rising to go see Father Adamson.

Caroline's father was stood looking out the wide window behind the fastidiously tidy desk of his study, his hands clasped tightly behind his stiff back. The sun was bright outside and he cast a long, foreboding shadow across the room.

"You wanted to see me, Father Adamson?"

His shoulders rose then sagged in one fluid motion. "I do not *want* to see you. I *need* to see you. There is a difference."

It did not take an idiot to realise that I was in deep, deep trouble. Surely he did not know. I swallowed nervously then asked, "Is there something the matter?"

He continued to stare out of the window, down the long, grassy lawn as he spoke in a low, threatening growl, "Could you not keep your filthy little hands to yourself?"

Okay, so he *did* know.

I tried to offer an explanation. I tried to volunteer some logical fact that would prove my innocence, but all that came out was an unintelligible stutter. I was screwed.

"I took you into my house. I fed you and gave you somewhere to sleep. I provided you with experience for your chosen career path – a career path I must say you will now never follow." All the time he kept his back to me. He was a dark silhouette in the bright summer sun.

"But, I can explain..." I finally managed. "I..."

"Enough!" Adamson roared, whipping around and slamming both his hands palm down with a thundering crash. I took an involuntary jump back. It was not just the sudden noise; his face was a study of terror. He looked like a creature from the lowest pit of Hell. I had never seen such a scowl, such a grimace of sheer fury. "My daughter has told me everything. I know all that I need to know. I know how you two..." His face contorted as if he was tasting the bitterest poison on his tongue. "I know enough," he repeated, finally bringing his bilious wrath under control.

She had told him? Why on Earth had she done that? A large part of me wanted to curl up and wither right there. I had been rejected and betrayed by the girl that I had given my heart to. The delicate little ember of my unrequited love had been ground under foot into the dirt and pulverised into extinction. However, a tiny voice at the back of my head screamed to be heard. "Don't you dare!" it yelled at me. "Don't you give her the satisfaction. This is not your fault."

So I pulled my shoulders back, took a deep breath and said, "I'm not the only one."

For a terrifying moment Adamson said nothing. He just stood there, hunched over his ornate wooden desk, his dark brown eyes glaring at me. I was convinced that if he had been in possession of a gun he would have mown me down and spat on my rapidly cooling corpse. However, something else happened. Slowly, he lowered himself down into his padded leather chair and, as he did, the mask of malevolence slid from his face revealing a look of haunted despair. His eyes lost all their wrathful fire and turned dim as he said quietly, "I know, Sam. I know.

"Now pack your things and get out. You are no longer welcome here."

"That's okay. I no longer want to stay."

And I left.

The crystal glass smashed against the wall. Shards splintered off around the room and golden liquid cascaded down. The bitch! The absolute bitch! How could she do this to me? She had waltzed back into my life, tugged at my heart strings as if it was a marionette for her cruel amusement, and played me for all it was worth.

She had used me once again, just as she had used me before. Last time I had been blinded by young love; this time my mature eyes had finally seen through the vicious little game that she had been playing. Last time she had wanted to strike out at her over-domineering father; this time she had wanted to improve her career by getting a trashy inside story on my old friend.

What a bitch!

I stood panting heavily in the middle of my office, my shoulders rising and falling in a ragged rhythm. My broken heart banged in my aching chest and scalding tears of rage welled from between my screwed up eyelids. I screamed out loud in an incomprehensible roar, sank to the floor and pounded my balled fists into the carpet. Over and over they struck the synthetic fibres which burned against my skin. I relished the feel of the pain; it was real, unlike Caroline's affections for me.

I had been such a fool - a bloody, stupid fool. She was chip off her boss' old block, selfish through and through. How had she produced such a nice lad in John? Heaven alone only knew.

The thought of John made me bring my carpet thumping to a halt. Instead, I rested my forehead on the floor and rocked back and forth. The poor boy. It was just not fair that he had such a conniving little cow for a mother. What must have been going through his mind right now? Had he overheard her little revelation? If not, would she tell him?

I sighed and rocked back onto my rear, sitting cross-legged on the floor, staring at the shards of glass and rivulets of Jack Daniel's. The initial tension was leaving now, but the anger was still there, simmering away in the pit of my stomach like an over-cooked stew of bile and remorse. I had refused to believe Wallace when he had said, categorically, that all humanity was doomed because of its blind selfishness. Now, however, I saw his point entirely. He had spoken truthfully; possibly the most truth I had heard in a long time.

I glanced up at the station clock. He had told me that he would be at the Grand from seven-thirty. I still had time to clean up this mess and freshen up. I needed some truthful company.

Insistent chilling rods of October rain hammered down from darkened autumnal skies onto my wide-brimmed fedora as I stormed my way across town. My feet sloshed in pools of muddy water that congregated down Great John Street and probing headlights flashed across my eyes as I drew my collar up close to prevent the worst of the weather from penetrating my clothing.

It was a vile night and I was in the foulest of moods. I had been used, betrayed and spat upon. I felt abandoned and alone. I needed someone who would listen without judging me, someone who had been right from the very beginning.

I needed Malcolm Wallace.

He had warned me; oh, how he had warned me. People of this day and age were users. They were selfish to the core and had lost all respect for those they claimed to love. They were blind to those around them and their own fate. I too had been blind but now I could see clearly. You could not rely upon anyone else. You had to draw upon your own convictions and pursue them to the fullest.

Anything is possible.

The trouble was, I was scared to trust my newly reborn vision. I needed guidance.

I darted across Moor Lane, dodging more puddles in the worn, cracked cobbles and made my way over to Saint Leonard's Gate. This had once been the site of a leper colony. The pariahs of society had been rounded up and locked away from sight of the general public. They were afflicted and different, made to fend for themselves as best they could with little resources. I knew how they felt.

The rain was coming down so hard now that it was actually getting difficult to see through the precipitation. People scurried past me, barely visible; spectres in the night. They were not real to me. They had no purpose in my life so I paid them no attention. I had to focus on what I wanted now. I had to take charge of my life and pull back together the fragments that Caroline had smashed apart.

The smell of take-away food assaulted my nostrils and my treacherous stomach rumbled. How could I be hungry already? Caroline had fed me before her deceit had been revealed. Besides, it was irrelevant. I had to ignore the want of my body and concentrate on what my mind and my soul longed for.

Truth.

The Grand Theatre is one of the older buildings of Lancaster. It has stood since the late 1700s and suffered from such fates as fire, flood and local planning. It has the ubiquitous hauntings of dead actresses and the even more numerous groups of local am-drams who step to the stage in whatever play takes their fancy from time to time. I've never really been a theatre-goer; my attention span is far too short and, besides that, sci-fi never really translates well to the stage. I mean, can you imagine *Star Trek On Ice*? I rest my case.

I stepped through the main door, out of the downpour and indeed out of the twenty-first century. Middle-aged men in black tie stood amongst the bustling theatre-goers, showing them to circle or stalls. The décor of the foyer was mainly of a deep red wallpapering and dark wooden furnishings that one would expect from the era of pre world war two. I half expected young flapper women to bustle in, swinging their bead necklaces and babbling on about the Charleston or some other such care-free whimsy.

I removed my hat and a flood of rainwater drenched the carpet at my feet. I grimaced as I saw a dark-suited man approach me. He was about six foot five, had short-clipped grey hair and a pencil thin moustache crowning an incredibly stiff upper lip. A muscular physique rippled under his evening attire and from his posture I could tell at an instant that he took no crap. Ex-military, I surmised; typical Sergeant Major type. He probably excelled at barking underlings into an ear-bleeding submission and then firing shells out of a Freudian cannon onto ramshackle villages of helpless natives.

I didn't think we were going to be good buddies.

"You look lost." The voice was sharp, clipped and to the point. What the words actually meant were, "Piss off out of my theatre, you scruffy little urchin."

I drew myself up and met him in the eye as best I could, and by eyes I actually mean chin. "I'm here to meet a friend," I explained.

The towering Sergeant Major's immaculately groomed eyebrows rose with military precision. "Oh, really?" His piercing blues slowly appraised my drenched and bedraggled attire as if trying to locate a target. "A female friend?"

I sighed. I had endured enough crap for one night and I made to push past the jumped up dictator of the theatre foyer.

His arm shot out and a vice gripped my arm. "And, where do you think you're going, Sonny?"

"Like I said, to meet my friend," I spat, my contempt now very vaguely concealed. Anger was boiling up and I seriously wanted to lash out at this pompous arse, but I had somewhere to be and someone to see.

"You got a ticket then?"

"No."

"The street's that way, then," he pointed with a fat finger on the end of a rigid arm.

"My friend is waiting for me in box number one."

The grip slackened on my arm and I saw hesitation creep into the man's eyes. "Box one?" he repeated, his mouth suddenly sounding dry and his voice less sure that the world was actually round.

I nodded, my eyes narrowing with caution.

It was when I saw the ultimate tell of his Adam's apple bobbing that I knew I had won the battle and he could only fire duds. His hand dropped to his side and he motioned up the stairs with his head. "It's up there on the right hand side of the circle, sir." He paused, awkwardness dancing merrily between the two of us. "Sorry about the fuss, sir. It's just... well..."

I didn't give him the opportunity to finish his half-baked apology and made my way through the crowded foyer, up the stairs and into the theatre. It was as I politely squeezed passed people down the side of the circle that I realised I didn't even know what the play was. I looked for someone selling programmes, but couldn't see anyone and just gave up, walking over to the doorway of box number one.

For a moment I paused outside the box, looking up at the gloss-red door. Should I just walk in? No. I raised my knuckle to knock when the door swung inwards and there he was, sat in one of the two padded chairs that overlooked the stage: Malcolm Wallace, the bringer of truth. He turned to me and smiled warmly. “Samuel, you came. Wonderful! Do come in and could you close that behind you, please?” He motioned towards the door.

As I closed it behind me, the fact dawned on me that I had not touched the door and Malcolm was sat over the other side of the box.

*Anything is possible.*

But surely...

I dismissed the notion. This was an old building; perhaps I had just stood on a loose floor board which had caused the door to swing inwards.

Well, that's what I wanted to believe for now, anyway.

There was a row of hooks on the back wall of the box. Malcolm's overcoat occupied one of the pegs. I hooked my mac and my hat up on the other end of the row so as not to dampen the material of his finely tailored outerwear then I made my way over to the spare chair and seated myself.

So, here I was, the eager student ready to learn from the wise master. Questions, so many questions, but how to pose them without looking like a complete muppet? I drummed my fingers against my teeth and words stumbled and stuttered over each other in my head. They would not behave themselves. They were all there, every one that I wanted to say, but they would not form themselves into coherent phrases.

All the time Malcolm just sat calmly, his meticulously neat white hair framing his pensive orange eyes as they peered out over the theatre and surveyed the members of the audience as they clambered into their seats.

“Do you think they know we watch them,” his low voice suddenly cut into my awkward silence, “those people down there? Do you think they realise that we sit here high above their heads, gazing down and watching their every insignificant footstep? Why should they? We are not part of their mundane lives. We are not their TV dinners or their soap operas. We are not their *Jeremy Kyle Show* or their *X Factor*.” If the names of the shows had been liquid, they would have been potent enough to stun a blue whale. “Look at them, Samuel. Really look at them.”

I turned and followed his gaze out over the stalls beneath us. There, down below, sat a young couple, he with his arm around her shoulders, her with a face like thunder. Further along sat a family: man, woman, three kids. The kids were bouncing and yammering whilst the mother had the weary look of, “Oh, dear God, not here,” on her face whilst the husband idly played on his smart phone. Then there was the young woman bending over to sort out her handbag completely unaware of the old man behind taking great interest as her skirt rose rather too high.

"Do you see them, Samuel?" Malcolm asked. Even without looking at him I knew that those intense eyes were now fixed on me as his hand grasped his ornate, serpentine cane. "Do you see them for what they really are?"

My broken heart shrivelled in my aching chest and wept with no control. "Caroline..." I eventually whispered as I turned to face him.

"Caroline, the girl who broke your young heart after university," Malcolm soothed, his face full of sadness. "Caroline, the woman who walked into your life and played with you as if you were a yo-yo on a string or some sort of cat's toy to bat around the floor until it falls apart from the savaging of her claws." The sage words from my new master continued. "Caroline, the trashy rag reporter who sent you into my midst to find as much dirt as you could for her to plaster over her little provincial newspaper."

My jaw fell.

A hint of a smile formed at the corner of Malcolm's mouth. "Was she worried about that nasty cult, Samuel? Was it going to snatch her beloved baby from her? I am not a fool. I knew the boy was her son from the moment I laid eyes on him." He shook his head and turned to look out over the darkening theatre. "Do I really look like a man who would kill a child?"

"No... no," I said. "You don't." And the thing was, at that point, he really didn't.

The play was fairly dreadful. I can't recall its title as my mind was racing with all the stuff that was bombarding it about Caroline, Malcolm and everything. I just seem to recall it was some depressing little number about these guys who take a tramp into their care and end up shouting at him lots. I think I must have yawned at least half a dozen times during the first act. Malcolm, however, was totally caught up in the piece and hardly shifted position as his eyes remained fixed on the characters on the stage, his left hand clasping the head of his cane and the thumb of his right hand twiddling his ring which bore two snakes. I decided that he really had a thing about snakes.

Eventually my boredom was relieved by the interval. The curtain lowered and the house lights came up. Malcolm gave a small sigh of satisfaction. "Fascinating," he murmured, lifting his right hand and caressing his lower lip with his ring. "Fascinating."

"Yes," I said, surreptitiously flexing my shoulder blades, "it was."

My companion turned to me and raised a white eyebrow as there was a tentative knock at the door. "Enter!" he called out, his orange irises not drifting from me for a second. A young woman entered, carrying a tray with a silver tea pot and two china cups. She set them down on a small table and left without a word. "Tea?" Malcolm enquired of me, lifting the pot and pouring himself a pot of steaming hot liquid. "It's Earl Grey."

"Thank you." I gratefully took the second cup after he had filled it and sipped slowly. The aromatic flavour danced soothingly on my tongue. "I didn't realise the theatre provided such a service."

"They don't. At least not to anybody else." Malcolm sat back in his chair, saucer in one hand and cup in the other. He looked for all to see like a gentleman at home in his study. "I have an... *arrangement* here. I have been very successful financially and as a result I contribute greatly to the Grand. As a result, there are certain," he gestured around the box with the tea cup, "benefits."

There didn't seem to be much to say on that matter so I kept quiet and tried not to appear stupid. I was totally out of my depth here: theatre, luxury box, expensive tea, incomprehensible dramatics. Definitely a time to keep schtum.

Malcolm finished his beverage, placed the cup lightly on the saucer and smiled at me in a way that a genial uncle regards an inept nephew. "You don't attend the theatre much, do you Samuel?"

I sighed deeply. I had been sprung. "God's honest? I think the last play I saw was a rendition of *The Very Hungry Caterpillar* by Miss Harper's class back in primary school. I seem to recall it was very well received by the critics. Well, Danny Clough said that Amy Johnson looked "well fit" as the piece of cherry pie."

Malcolm smiled as his thumb rocked his ring back and forth. "And we all know how harsh a critic a child can be, don't we, Samuel? Let's face it, Caroline wasn't much more than a child when you first met her, was she?"

At once the tea in my gut turned to bile and I felt anger start to boil within me once more.

Malcolm nodded in appreciation. "Yes... yes... she makes you so angry, doesn't she? And quite rightly so, Samuel. That little tramp ruined your life. She lured you in like a sweet smelling flower draws an unsuspecting insect, then just when you were all warm and cosy, her jaws snapped tight around you like the *Dionaea muscipula* she is and she devoured your future, snatching away all confidence that you ever had in yourself. You've blamed yourself for so long now," his soft voice soothed. "Poor, poor Sammy, devastated that he could never love another soul without getting hurt, yet eternally doomed to punish himself for taking advantage of a sweet, sixteen-year-old girl."

There was a loud crack as his cane rapped the floor between us.

"Well enough is enough, Samuel." Malcolm's voice was low but penetrating; commanding and forceful in our enclosed, private space. "Enough is enough. Caroline was no shrinking violet. She used you then and she used you now. You know that to be true or you would not be here tonight."

My head drooped as I nodded in mournful agreement.

"The question is, Samuel," he pondered, absentmindedly stroking his cane, "what are you going to do about it?" The lights dimmed and the audience hushed down below. "Well for now, I think that we should watch the second half of this play." He smoothed down his lilac-coloured lapels and turned towards the stage. I rubbed my hand across my forehead and did likewise. The actors shambled out and meandered messily around the stage. I really had no idea why people paid to come and see this sort of stuff; it did absolutely nothing for me. I felt that it was just pretentious twaddle; a collection of longing stares and pregnant pauses mixed up in a solution of heartfelt monologues and diatribes. The words drifted over me as I sat there occasionally glancing at my watch. As the play dragged on, I began to feel that this had been a mistake. Yes, Malcolm had been somewhat sympathetic, but had he really been the help that I had expected? Had he given me any real answers?

A gleeful chuckle bubbled up from my companion as his thumb played once again with his snake ring.

"What is it?" I whispered, daring not to be heard.

"Oh, this is just marvellous," he crowed, his eyes darting about the stage in frantic animation. "The things, one learns."

"Really?" I asked, somewhat perplexed.

Malcolm turned and looked at me, his orange eyes twinkling mischief in the half light. "Oh, not the play, Samuel. That is utter," he waved a hand dismissively, "balderdash and piffle - especially in the hands of rank amateurs. No, it's what one can learn about the actors. Most fascinating."

I frowned. "What exactly do you mean?"

"You see the tramp?" Malcolm gestured with a tilt of his chin. "He is so desperate to improve himself. The actor that is, in real life, so to speak. So much so that he is looking for a way to leave this little troupe. What's more he's intending to do it by stealing an upcoming part from his best friend, the young chap there."

I looked at the two men arguing on the stage, their arms waving like windmills and their mouths flapping like castanets. "Did you read that in a magazine or something?"

Malcolm shook his head. "No, Samuel. The best of it is though is that the third chap down there, the one who keeps fiddling with the plug, knows about the older chap's designs and has already informed the young fellow, who is seething with such rage. Oh, such delicious rage. In fact, he is fit to explode and any second now... any second..."

*Smack!*

The audience gasped as the younger actor floored the older man with a vicious right hook. The tramp collapsed to the floor. The look of absolute disbelief painted on his face was soon replaced by terror as the younger man fell on him and started to pound him around the head with clenched fists. I saw a commotion at the side of the stage as the third actor dashed into the fray, trying to drag the younger man away from his victim. The attacker was having none of it; he screamed and cursed as his fists connected with the face of the tramp, one after the other. The last thing I saw before the curtain quickly fell down sealing off the carnage was the sight of the older man's nose exploding in a spray of blood.

"I'm guessing that wasn't in the script." I turned and looked at Malcolm who was sat back in his chair smiling as if he was the proverbial cat with the cream or the estate agent with the gullible newly-weds.

"Not the script of the play, perhaps, Samuel. But it was certainly inevitable. It was there for all to see as long as one believes one can."

"You're saying that you had no knowledge of that before you came here tonight?"

He shook his head. "Nothing. Not a jot."

"I find that very hard to believe," I protested. "Okay, perhaps you could read their body language and see where it was heading. All this stuff about the old man snatching the young one's role, well that could just be speculation." I ran my fingers through my curls. "I can't really believe you know what is actually playing out in their lives."

The satisfied look did not leave Malcolm's face as he gave me his full attention.

Suddenly, I felt distinctly nervous. "What? What is it?"

"Tell me, Samuel," his words were low and seductive, "what was it like?"

"What was what like?"

"Killing her. Gunning her down in cold blood."

I felt as if the floor of the box had been removed and I was tumbling arse over tit down to the floor of the stalls below.

"How?" My voice cracked. "How?"

Wallace leaned into me, his unnaturally coloured eyes dancing like fire. "Samuel, Samuel, anything is possible. You are in such a dark place right now. Your life is at its ebb and you know not how to proceed. Life has been such a trauma for you. There is blood on your hands and guilt in your broken heart. But do not worry, I am sure most of us would have done the same. You had no idea who she would tell, did you? And those ravening beasts... that," he spat the words, "*despicable Bloodline*... you could not have them pursuing you, hunting you down.

"But it can all go away now. It can all be made better."

The world was spinning. I could feel nausea rising as the ringing started to scream in my ears. I could not stop my hands from clasping at the sides of my head as they tried to rip out the very noise itself. I shut my eyes to try and steady my other senses. I had no way of knowing which way was up and which way was down. I needed my clocks, my comforting, ticking companions, but they were not here.

It was all going wrong.

It was all going wrong.

Then, amidst all the chaos of the senses, a cool pair of hands covered mine and a soothing spring breeze drifted through my ear drums and into my inner ears. I felt it stroking at my terrified cochleae and an intoxicating aroma of spices and scent filled my nostrils. An overwhelming feeling of peace and serenity washed over me.

Then there was nothing.

There was no noise.

My ears were quiet.

"It's okay," Malcolm said as I opened my eyes to my new life, "I am here to save you."

# Chapter Eleven

The soft warmth of autumnal sunshine bathed my face as I strolled down Market Street with my mentor on Friday morning. It was one of those rare moments of seasonal beauty that the weather graces you with before the bitterness of winter starts to bite. Around us the folk of Lancaster hurried about their business: teenagers huddling in groups, mother's dragging demanding children or perplexed husbands, suited office workers nipping out on a coffee break.

And I could hear every word around me.

I had not stopped grinning since the previous evening. A lifetime of incessant, high-pitched noise gone in an instant. Instead, there was the normal humdrum of the everyday world. It was bliss. I could hear the chatter of children discussing the latest electronic toy. I could hear the cantankerous moaning of an old couple berating the proposed building work down on the quay. I could hear birds.

I stopped outside Morrisons and gawped up at a sparrow perched in a tree on the edge of Market Square. It was sat there, chittering away to its little heart's content. I could hear every single, sweet note. I could not help but grin.

"Wonderful little chap, isn't he?"

"Not a care in the world," I agreed to Malcolm. I turned and faced him. "Right now I know how he feels."

Malcolm nodded and sat on a nearby bench. I followed him and did likewise. He gripped his ornate cane in his hands and let his eyes wander around the square. "Tell me, Samuel, who do you think is the most blessed this Friday morning? This mass of consumers with all their gadgets and wealth, their overflowing shopping bags and their comfortable houses or your little feathered friend up there in the tree who does not know where his next meal will come from or whether he will survive the night safe from a predator's hunger?"

I groaned audibly. "Don't go all Yoda on me, okay? I know you want me to say that I think the people are better off because they won't get eaten tonight, then you'll jump in and say something like, 'Aha. Blessed the sparrow is for unburdened with pressures of consumerist society is he.' Am I right?"

My white-haired friend smiled, "Know me well, you do, my young apprentice."

We both chuckled. Then quiet settled between us before he asked, "But tell me, Samuel, which life would you choose for yourself? Safety and the tedium that it brings with it or total happiness and freedom with the constant risk of death?"

"Well I can't say that my life has been very tedious, recently," I snorted. "If it carries on the way it's going, I'll soon have as many white hairs as you."

Malcolm nodded in agreement. "True, true. But consider this fact; these shoppers do not really know where they will be this time next week. They assume that they will be living their monotonous little lives, day in, day out, the usual routine. But how can they be sure? What if some great predator swooped down and devoured them? It could happen. Look at the Twin Towers."

"I hardly think that Lancaster is the same political target," I scoffed.

"People thought that about the London underground and a shopping centre in Nairobi. Terror can strike anywhere, Samuel. It doesn't even have to be political. What if an asteroid struck us?" He hammered the tip of his cane down on the floor between his legs. "We are totally unprepared! The politicians of this world are far more concerned with lining their own pockets than planning for possible futures. We need to take a hold of our existence and shape a future that suits us. Sacrifices have to be made to ensure this happens."

I frowned at him. "Sacrifices? What do you mean?"

Malcolm gave a deep sigh, composing himself back to his normal, unruffled self. "Enough of this talk for now. Let us go for a cup of tea, or, if you prefer, some of that hideous coffee you drink." With that, he stood up and led the way. I followed, a touch perturbed by his little outburst, but willing to follow all the same.

When I was a kid in the seventies, tea in a café was served in a light green mug topped up with milk. You drank it at a table that had an easy clean surface of laminate or melamine upon which sat the usual condiments of salt, pepper and vinegar along with tomato ketchup and brown sauce in their individually coloured squeezy bottles. In some establishments the ketchup bottle was actually in the shape of a tomato.

However, things change. These little retreats from the stresses and strains of everyday life gave way to fast food restaurants with their shakes and fries which, in time, retreated from the relentless product that was the infinitely versatile coffee bean. So the High Street became dominated by ubiquitous coffee shop chains such as Costa and Starbucks with their Cappuccinos, Lattes and other such socially recognisable beverages.

However, in the back alleys and dusty arcades of our towns and cities, a silent revolution has begun to take shape. Small establishments have started to provide journeys into other times and distant lands. Yes, they still provide a range of coffee-based drinks for the less adventurous, but their star turns are birthed from the leaf not the bean. Here you find Darjeeling, Assam, Ceylon and the lord of them all, Earl Grey. They are served in china cups that come atop a saucer and they have fresh, home-made cakes of all shapes and sizes depending on your budget and your appetite.

These are the tea rooms and there is not a tomato-shaped ketchup bottle in sight.

Such an establishment was Guy's Café. Tucked away down Sun Street, the humdrum of the main trawl passed it by, letting it revel in all its neo-Victorian splendour. The thing that struck me, as the rather overweight proprietor effused over Malcolm and thanked him for his patronage, was the doilies. The place was overrun with them. Every cake stand stood atop one. The condiments on the polished tables rested on them. Was there even one poking out from under the till?

"Pardon?" I snapped out of my doily pondering when I realised that Malcolm had asked me a question.

"I said, 'Shall we sit here?'" he smiled, gesturing to a small table in the corner of the room next to a parlour palm.

"Sure."

The proprietor saw us to our table and beckoned for a young waitress to come over and serve us. She took our orders (mine was a black coffee, Malcolm's was an Earl Grey) as the middle-aged man hovered behind her, watching her every move. My companion, in turn, was intently watching the man and the girl. As they headed off to prepare our drinks he nodded silently to himself. "Well, what did you make of that?"

Make of what? "Sorry?"

Malcolm smiled and shook his head as the young waitress brought our drinks over. "Thank you, my dear," he said.

The girl smiled nervously and headed back off to the kitchen. Malcolm nodded again then turned his attention to me as he sipped from his aromatic tea.

"Tell me, Samuel, why are there so many things in the way?"

"In the way of what?"

"Life, Samuel. Life." His eyes watched the steam rising from the hot drinks as if it was a troupe of dancers on a stage, his orange irises tracking every twirl and pirouette. "You know the sort of things that I mean. There will be things you want to do. Say, that holiday you wish to take, that book you want to read or," he paused to sip his tea once more, "that girl you want to woo."

I swallowed as my thoughts crossed their arms and let out an irritated snort.

"All these things you want," he continued, "yet time after time the mundane, boring, little day to day things get in your way. Your house needs a new roof so no holiday that year. Your neighbour has lost their dog so you spend the day hunting for Fido rather than curled up with Jane Austen. The girl you wish to woo..." He sipped his tea. "Well, we both know how that one ended don't we? Work got in the way. The need to further herself was far more important to her than your emotions.

"Imagine if there was a way to remove those barriers. Consider, if you will, a life without barriers, a world where you can achieve your dreams.

"All people need is to be liberated and then anything will be possible.

"All the world needs is change."

I frowned. "Surely the world *is* changing? Look at all the new technologies we've created in the last century. The world is changing all the time."

Malcolm gave me a small, knowing chuckle. "You actually think that the world is any different now to how it was in the Stone Age? Sure, we have all our nice, shiny toys, but is humanity actually any different? We may have evolved intellectually but do we actually know what we should be doing with all our electronic marvels?

"Tell me Samuel," Malcolm settled his fine china cup onto its saucer with a delicate clink, "if the world was to end tomorrow, what would people do?"

I sipped from my black coffee and instantly countered, "What sort of end are we talking about: supernova sun, nuclear bomb? What? It would affect things, surely?"

He nodded, sagely. "Good point. Indeed it would. To clarify then – something apocalyptic, something out of this world. An event so unlike anything that humanity has seen the like of. An event of singular cataclysmic significance. What then?" He placed the cup and saucer precisely on the table, leaned back in his chair, and awaited my reply with steepled fingers.

As I pondered this, my eyes were drawn to his ornate ring. Two serpents entwined around each other, one with a red jewelled eye, one with black. I shuddered involuntarily and shrugged, "I guess it would not make much of a difference. There would be widespread panic. People would hide as best they could. Some would pray to their god, others would seek out their families. Some..." My words drifted off into obscurity as I saw him chuckling quietly to himself. "What? What is it?"

Malcolm's oddly-coloured eyes twinkled over his steepled digits. "Tell me, Samuel, how would they possibly know? How could someone in Africa seek shelter in his village hut if this event had occurred right here in Lancaster? How could someone scaling the sides of the Grand Canyon know if a cataclysm had occurred?" He slipped his mobile phone out of his jacket pocket and lay it purposefully between us on the table. "This is how, Samuel. This is how. Should an event causing the end of the world occur, two things will indubitably come to pass. First, all those in the vicinity will reach for their mobile phones, their little umbilicals to the rest of the world, and begin to tweet away or start snapping photos for Facebook. Then, shortly after that, they will most certainly start to complain that they have no phone signal." He stared intently at me for a moment until a clap of laughter thundered from his mouth. When he had brought his mirth under control, he dabbed at his eyes with a handkerchief. "You know that I tell the truth, Samuel. These things will come to pass."

And, unfortunately, I knew he was right.

"The earliest evidence we have of *Homo Sapiens* is from about two hundred thousand years ago, give or take, since then we have stopped evolving. We have become dependent on these little gadgets," he stated, waving the phone around before popping it back in his jacket, "and other similar niceties. We started with stone axes, worked our way through bronze and iron receptacles, onto plastics and circuitry always passing the hard work onto another little toy whilst shrugging off our own responsibilities and consuming more and more of the planet's finite resources. We think we are so clever to have made all these wonderful discoveries to make our life *easier*, more *comfortable*." He sneered the words as if they soured his tongue. "But what is life without evolution? Where will we go? We will stagnate, that's what!"

I shook my head. "So what, you think we should follow Pol Pot's nice little idea of going back to a Year Zero and wiping out all the intellectuals? We both grew up with those images of mass burials in Cambodia."

"Not at all, Samuel." Malcolm's voice had taken on the gentler tone once more of a patient uncle explaining a hard subject to his less than bright nephew. "What I am saying is that change is inevitable, no matter how much we, as a race, seem to be slowing down in the evolutionary process. It is all down to sheer logic. As we continue our lifestyle we consume far more than this planet can produce. Our lifestyles are bleeding creation dry. They are totally unsustainable. We have nothing entering our system. We are consuming all around us like ravening beasts hungry for more and more. The time will come when there will be nothing left."

"And you feel that will be the end of the world?"

"Oh no. The end will arrive before humanity has had a chance to wallow in the toxic detritus of its entropy. The end will come when some right-minded individual stands up, says, 'Enough is enough,' and brings the whole thing to a surgically precise end.

I downed the rest of my coffee and sat back in my chair. I wanted to counter him. I wanted to say that I had faith in humanity, that everything would work out okay. I desperately wanted to say that we would turn things around and make it all better.

I just couldn't.

Right there at that moment, after all that Caroline had put me through, my broken heart knew that he was right. We were devouring our world at a cataclysmic rate whilst ignoring the wars and poverty that raged on around us. They were an inconvenience that we did not wish to see; a huge elephant trumpeting its trunk in the corner of a room where everyone wore earplugs of reality television and viral clips of cats doing stupid things.

We had become blind to our fate and steeped in a selfishness that drove us to use our planet and our friends as we saw fit.

The young waitress came back over to our table and asked us if we needed anything else. Morosely, I shook my head, not wishing to meet her happy, little face.

"One thing, my dear," Malcolm said. "A bit of information."

My ears pricked up as the girl replied, "Sure. What do you want?"

"Are you happy in your job?"

She shrugged, "I guess so. I haven't been here long, but it seems nice."

"Seems nice?"

"Well, yes. I guess."

Malcolm nodded quietly, his orange eyes not leaving the girl and his thumb casually rotating his ring around his little finger. "But you're not too sure, are you, my child?" he whispered, his conspiratorial voice not audible to anyone out of our circle of three. "There are little things, aren't there?"

The girl shuffled back and forth on her feet. This was clearly making her uncomfortable.

"It's okay, my child," Malcolm purred seductively. "You're among friends. You can tell us."

She gave a quick, furtive glance around the tea room, at the lacy doilies, the fresh flowers and the decidedly middle-class patrons. All the time, her fingers were playing with the smartly cut blouse.

"Ah..." her inquisitor sighed. "I see. It's like that, isn't it? He makes you feel uncomfortable. The way he *looks* at you." He almost sang the word as his voice rose in knowing emphasis. "And you really don't like it, do you, my child?"

The waitress snapped her head from side to side, her dark fringe bobbing across her eyes which were now tightly shut as she fought to hold back the tears.

"You hate the way his eyes follow you around the room," Malcolm continued, relentlessly pursuing the matter, "always studying your figure when he thinks you're not looking. He insists that you wear the smart clothes and spray yourself with seductive scent. Your make up has to be just so. 'It's for the customers,' he says. 'We have an image to present.' But you know different, don't you? He just likes to watch you. He lusts after you."

"Malcolm..."

He waved a hand to cut me off, his eyes never leaving the poor girl, who was now close to exploding. "You feel trapped, don't you, my child? Your employer is keeping you trapped underfoot. It makes you feel worthless."

She nodded vigorously, a single tear escaping her tightly shut eyes and tracing down her impeccable make up.

"You need the money. Desperately need the money because..." He closed his eyes and seemed to concentrate for a brief second. "Because of your child."

She gasped and her eyes flashed open in shock, causing a stream of tears to waterfall down her cheek. "How?" Her voice was cracked and hoarse. Other customers started to crane their necks in our direction.

"Anything is possible, my dear," Malcolm crooned. "Once you understand that, then you are truly liberated. He looks at you with his lustful eyes, wanting you for himself. You allow that so that you can scrape a meagre crust together to feed yourself and your little one, all the time dreading that he will find out about your secret infant. A single mother would not sit comfortably with his doilies and his chintz. But anything is possible. *Anything is possible*. All you have to do is decide to take the first step." He rose from his chair and placed our payment on the table. "You can stop him from abusing you with his gaze, from holding you and your little one to ransom. You truly can."

And with that he walked out of the tea room, oblivious to the gaping and gasping that followed him.

I grabbed my hat and my coat, stumbled out of my chair, made to say something apologetic to the girl, failed miserably and ran after him. By the time that I had caught up with Wallace, he was already out of Guy's Café and heading back into town. I grabbed him by the arm and spun him around. "What the hell was that about?"

My companion silently fixed his eyes on my tight grip and waited patiently. I withdrew my hand and took a step backwards. "Thank you," he said before continuing to walk down the road.

I huffed in exasperation and followed behind him. "Well?" I demanded. "Are you going to tell me or do I get the silent treatment now?"

Wallace's cane clicked rhythmically on the cobbles. "I would have thought it obvious, Samuel. I just liberated the girl."

"Liberated?" My voice had slipped up a register with disbelief. The arrogance of the man! "Humiliated, more likely. Did you see the way the other customers looked at her? You reduced her to tears!"

"That is of no consequence. The opinions of others do not matter. She now knows that she has the power to control her own destiny. She will do what needs to be done."

We emerged onto Market Street and into the hubbub of the weekday business. "Oh? And what might that be, I ask?"

Wallace turned, his strangely-coloured eyes fixed on mine and stated simply, "That is for her to decide." With that he casually walked off into the crowds leaving me stood seething and bubbling over with contempt.

I stomped off in the opposite direction through Market Square. What the hell was the man playing at? Was this the same guy who had made a small girl walk and had healed my infernal ringing? How could someone I had gone to for solace in my darkest hour suddenly turn round on a sweet kid and reduce her to tears like that? My mind was racing as I barged my way through the mass of shoppers. Had I been played with once more? Had my emotions been batted around like a ball of string in a game of cat and mouse? It just did not make sense. What did I actually know about Wallace? Where had he been all these years and what had he been doing?

I needed answers.

I headed for Cheapside.

"Hey there, Sam. You hungry?"

"Sure am, Bob. What you got for me?"

The street vendor idly flipped some onions over on his griddle. "Depends what you're after, I guess."

I looked around in a somewhat furtive manner. I was the only one in the queue, which was something of an unusual occurrence. "Information."

Bob nodded. "Hawkins? 'Cos I got nothing else on him."

My stomach lurched at the thought of a slavering beast bearing down on me up at Williamson Park. "No. That's dead. Buried."

"'Kay. What you need then?"

"Someone's walked back into my life. Someone I haven't seen for many years. Name of Malcolm Wallace. Heads a society called Credete. You heard of him?"

The smell of grilling onions drifted up to me as Bob chewed his bottom lip for a moment. "Can't say that I have," he finally volunteered as he deftly assembled a veggie burger in a bun. "Name doesn't ring any bells. He local?"

I shook my head. "He studied at uni with me and now he's back in town all successful and something smells wrong."

Bob handed the burger over. "I'll listen out for you. If I hear anything, I'll let you know. That one's on the house."

I smiled. "Cheers, Bob." I gestured to the lack of customers behind me. "Quiet today?"

The vendor scowled across the other side of the street. "Too bloody right. She's off on one today. Driving them all away with some depressing dirges. Bring back bloody Abba, I say."

I chuckled slightly and looked over at Betty. There she was, as immaculate as ever, just selecting a track on her CD player. A low drone emitted from the speakers followed by a laconic male voice; "It begins with a blessing and it ends with a curse. Making life easy, making it worse." She stood with her eyes staring up into the ether and swayed slowly from side to side as heavy guitars and drums pounded out a beat.

"She's been like that all day," Bob grumbled. "Don't know what's caused it. Don't want to know. I just want her to bloody well stop. It's ruining business."

I stood and watched Boombox Betty, away in her own little world. She raised her arms in the air and looked all the bit a charismatic preacher caught up in the ecstasy of the spirit as she remained in her own private little universe, absorbing the music. Passers-by gave her just the quickest of glances before hurrying past.

"Now people are watching, people who stare," continued the singer, "Waiting for something that's already there."

I smiled. It seemed somewhat apt.

The next line, however grabbed my attention to the full.

"Tomorrow I'll find it. The trumpeter screams, then he remembers that he's hungry and he drowns in his dreams."

The trumpeter.

Dreams.

"Sam. You okay?"

I snatched a glance back to Bob. "Yeah, sure. It's just... It's just a bit weird." I finished off my burger and walked across the street to stand before Betty. Smoother music was playing now from the track, the sort you would find in a neon-lit dive bar, it drew me in as the singer sang about his head being a night club with glasses and wine. Then the song exploded: "Get out of my dream...!"

I couldn't move. My feet were set in the paving stones of the street and people I was oblivious to jostled past me. Betty opened her eyes and looked straight through me as she sang along to the music: "Once I awakened, my eyes filled with tears. I had been sleeping for thousands of years, dreaming a life full of problems and sadness, endlessly turning in spirals of madness."

Then, suddenly, as if I had slapped her, her eyes focussed sharply on me. She gasped, her hand flying to her mouth and she stooped down, deftly flicking off the CD player and scurrying away.

It actually took me a few seconds to wake up to the fact that she had gone. She was hurrying down towards Damside. I pursued her. "Wait!" I called out. "Betty!"

She ignored me and continued tottering as fast as her high heels would permit her with the boom box cradled protectively in her arms like a new-born infant. Eventually she reached Damside, just as a double decker bus pulled round. It blocked her way and gave me the chance to catch up. "Betty, please wait. I just want to talk."

She turned towards me and worry was written over her face. I pointed to the CD player. She pulled it as close to her chest as was physically possible and gave a vigorous shake of her head.

I hold out my hands placatingly. "No, it's okay. I don't want your player. I just want to know about the song you were singing. What was it?"

Warily, she cocked her head to one side and had the look of a child that doesn't really believe you when you say that you're not going to break their favourite toy.

"Please, Betty," I begged. "I think it's important."

She leant forwards over the top of the CD player until her nose was almost tip-to-tip with mine and she stared intently into my eyes. I stood there, playing along, ignoring the stares and sniggers of passers-by. Finally, she pulled back, nodded and ejected the CD from the player. She held it out and gestured for me to take it. "Dream," she said, turned around and walked off towards the bus station.

I stood where Cheapside meets Damside and looked with great interest at a CD I had just been given by probably the craziest woman in town. It was bright yellow with green writing. "Kevin Ayers: The Confessions of Dr Dream and other stories" it read. I pocketed it and headed back up to Dalton Square. I had some music appreciation to undertake.

I dropped my newly acquired CD next to the pile of my usual listening material and went through to the kitchen to make myself a coffee. The kettle boiled, I poured the water over the granules and trudged back into my living room where I slouched down onto my old sofa.

My shoulders ached with tension and I could feel the beginning of a headache starting to niggle away in my head. I closed my eyes and breathed deeply to try and relieve the symptoms. I smiled as the aroma of the coffee drifted up to greet me. Its flavourful vapours wafted up into my nose and danced lightly with my senses.

I actually started to relax.

"Hello Sam."

I damn near jumped out of my skin as the two words snapped me out of my stupor. "Jesus!" I cursed. My hot coffee sloshed down my front, scalding me through my shirt. "Bollocks!" I swore. Instinctively, I grabbed my hankie from my pocket and started to dab at the searing, brown beverage.

After a few dabs my brain caught up with the fact that I was not alone.

"I've so got to get a new lock on that door."

"Indeed."

It was a female voice: quiet, clipped and precise. It made me think of long, hot afternoons spent toiling in the local library with a middle-aged harridan patrolling the stacks on the hunt for comics, contraband porn or, even worse, food and drink - horror of horrors!

Slowly, I stopped rubbing my crotch with a damp hankie and looked up at the source of the voice. It was the woman from my dream about the first day my ears had decided to hear things that weren't there. She was the definition of demure. She wore the same light green woollen two-piece skirt and jacket over a light blue blouse along with polished, flat-soled, sensible shoes. Her dark hair was again positioned atop her head in a neat, precise bun (there was not a single stray hair out of place) and she wore dark-rimmed glasses that twenty years ago would have been totally unfashionable but nowadays screamed (albeit very politely in this case) retro. Definitely librarian material, but looking younger than I remembered from my uni years - or was I just getting older? Policemen, doctors, dentists - did librarians start to look younger too when you neared the magic forty?

"Although, I have to say," the librarian continued, "that no lock could have kept us out."

I frowned as something hit me. "Wait a minute. I'm not dreaming." I pointed an accusing finger straight at the woman who had previously taken me back to my childhood. "So you're real, then, and not some weird Jungian archetype of my deepest fears?"

There was a soft, familiar, fluttering of tiny wings and she was gradually surrounded by things that I was sure no other librarian would have been accompanied by.

"Fairies," I whispered, feeling myself slump further back into the warm, safe embrace of my threadbare sofa. This was getting worse.

My guest seemed slightly amused by this. "That term will suffice for now. It serves our purpose."

I let my eyes wander around my room and I counted about ten of the little folk bobbing up and down, looking around inquisitively. One was even typing something into a search engine on my computer. "I'm guessing that this isn't a social visit. Hey! Leave that alone!"

I lunged out of the sofa and bolted across the room to the mantle clock. One fairy had opened the glass and was about to turn the hands... backwards!

"Get off that you little sod!" I bellowed, swatting it away with the back of my hand. "Don't you have any manners, you trumped up luminous gnat?"

The fairy scowled and buzzed around my head, crossly twiddling its tiny fingers at me. I swished my hands around in an inanely futile gesture as if I was trying to swat an annoying insect, but it kept lithely dodging away out of reach before darting back in and poking at me. I could hear a tinny high-pitched whistling which I surmised to be its voice displaying annoyance.

There was a polite cough and my assailant flew away, perching itself on the woman's shoulder. It continued to scowl at me and its diminutive lips were moving in a manner that suggested it was mentioning very un-fairylike words under its breath.

"My companion," the woman explained in her smooth, matter of fact manner, "was just fascinated by your obsession with time."

"Obsession? What obsession?"

She just raised an eyebrow.

"Okay, so I have a few clocks. It's not like they control me. I don't go out and buy them all the time. I don't need to look at them. They're just there for... recreational use." God, that sounded lame. "Damn it! It could have broken it, that's all. Besides, you've made me jumpy, just appearing here like this and that. I thought you had gone off and left us."

Casually, she walked around the room, looking from clock to clock. She closed her eyes and appeared to be reading something that was only apparent to her. "These timepieces are your solace, Sam. They bring you comfort in your darkest moments, when the creature that rages inside your head threatens to break free and consume you."

My throat suddenly parched, I stood and listened. I thought about lying flat out on the floor, eyes closed ears open to the all-pervasive ticking as it calmed me, soothed me.

"You draw on their ability to tell the time to centre you in this reality," she continued, running an immaculately manicured finger over a cheap carriage clock. "From the smallest to the biggest, each of them plays its part in subduing that monster within. You depend on time to chain the beast." Her fiery eyes snapped open and snared me with the precision of a finely tuned animal trap. "What if time was not what you expected it to be, Sam? What if it went wrong? What if it were to split in two? What if it were to... diverge?"

I tapped my fingernails against my teeth. There it was again. That word. "I'd need twice as many clocks," I quipped, ignoring the growing panic in my gut as I imagined something snarling and squirming within me. Something brutal, primal.

She shook her head. "No," she said, her voice brimming over with sadness, "you wouldn't." Then she lay her hand on my shoulder and everything shifted.

It was a ruin. There was rubble everywhere. Buildings were either fallen or in the process of decay. Wild grass grew up through pavements and moss clung to broken brickwork.

"I know a builder who could fix this up. He'd be done by next Friday, if you're interested?"

Lighting up a Lucky, I blew cigarette smoke over towards my existential abductor before sitting down on the creaking remains of a park bench. It wobbled ominously as the rusted joints shifted under my weight. She remained standing whilst the fairies (or whatever they were) flittered around us, their little faces looking like puppies that had lost their favourite chew toys. Bless.

"What is it with you people? I mean, why do you have to drag me away from the same old same old to places of devastation and universal depression? I can be just as depressed at home, you know? Why didn't you leave me there? You could have come on your own and sent a postcard or something. You know the sort of thing: 'Wish you were here - instead of me!' or 'Happy Sunshine Apocalypse in Morecambe.'" I took another puff from my Lucky. "Christ I don't even know where we are. Are you going to tell me?"

There was no immediate reply.

I scanned my eyes around through the detritus and ruins. "At least there's no bloody wolves this time. Tell me, you're not related to a young lad by the name of Alec are you? This is one of his party tricks."

"Friend of the family." The woman neatly lowered herself down on the bench. There was no shifting of metal or scraping of rust. It was as if she were weightless.

I shivered. It wasn't just a bit nippy; I was chilled to the core. The sun was out high over the ruins and there was no breeze, but I felt as if a gale was gusting around my bones. This place felt like a pleasant little New England village in the hands of Stephen King; it was just *wrong.*

"Okay," I sighed, "so here we are, happy as can be and there's nothing I can do about it. Can you at least answer two questions for me?"

She sat quietly, her eyes of fire inspecting the devastation. I took that as a yes.

"First. What is your name?"

"Sophia."

I chuckled. "Nice one. Wisdom. I like it. Is that for real or do you just treat this," I gesticulated to her impossibly neat form as ash dropped off my cigarette, "librarian getup like some sort of virtual avatar?"

"It is my name," she replied succinctly. "Second question."

"Well if you are Wisdom," my voice was heavily laden with sarcasm, "shouldn't you already know what the question's going to be?"

"Wisdom is not the same as all-knowing, and there are certain things that even *we* cannot foresee."

"Such as?"

Her head twisted and her steely eyes locked onto me. "Who is Kanor?"

I recalled a night from the previous week and the reaction of Marcus and Nightingale to hearing that name for the first time, not to mention the abject terror in Dave's description of his nightmare.

"Apart from some badass vampire killer? I haven't got a clue. But we're skipping ahead here. My second question."

She nodded slightly.

"Where the hell are we?"

"We are in a place where things have gone terribly, terribly wrong, Samuel. Where time as you know it was supposed to proceed down one path. Something prevented the physical realm from heading in that direction. Instead, it diverged and ended up here.

"We call it the Divergent Lands."

I shivered in the cold. "So what caused this?" I looked down and saw that all the fairies were now sat at our feet. They were enrapt and listening intently like school-kids around a teacher at story time. Now children, let's all listen to the tale of the Happy Apocalypse.

"Not a *what*, Samuel. A *who*."

"So?"

She dipped her head slightly. "We don't know. Our viewpoint does not extend that far. The Divergence obscures it. All we know is that it is near and," her eyes locked on me once more, "you are involved."

I jumped to my feet and windmilled my arms in disbelief. "You think that *I* caused this? Jesus, I don't even eat meat!"

"But you are a killer, Samuel. You have taken a life in cold blood."

I stopped mid-rant.

She sort of had me there.

"It wasn't cold blood," I mumbled. "It was self-defence."

They were silent and just watched me.

I squirmed. People knowing my darkest secrets was becoming an unsettling occurrence.

"It was."

Sophia sighed and stood up. "That is beside the point. All we know is that the Divergence will come about and that it will occur near you. You may not be the cause but you will, however, be intrinsically involved. You cannot avoid it. Perhaps it may be someone you know. Has someone entered your life recently? Someone with great power?"

Instinctively my hand tugged at the lobe of my silent ear. Sophia saw the tell for what it was.

"There is, isn't there?"

"No," I protested rather feebly.

She crossed her arms and peered at me over her dark-rimmed glasses. It was fifteen years ago and I had forgotten to bring Kinsley's *Hindu Goddesses* back on time. People were muttering behind me as I meekly handed over both the book and the appropriate fine.

"Name."

"But he couldn't do something like that." My voice was high and whiney. It had that *it's not fair* quality to it. "Yes, he's odd and he's creepy, but so are the Addams Family and everyone loves *them*."

"Samuel, I need his name." the voice was like ice, penetrating.

Damn it! I'd had enough. I was going to grow a back bone and stand up to my demons. I gave her my best Paddington Bear glower.

Sophia sighed and nodded to her tiny companions.

I realised that I had made somewhat of a miscalculation in my time to grow a spine. Paranormal creatures had no time or respect for rigid vertebrae. They darted towards me and, as I ducked, throwing my hands over my head, I felt them not only hit me at full tilt, but actually slide into my skin. My body started to jolt and leap all over the show as the fairies rummaged around inside, making their way up to my brain. It was not really painful as such, just somewhat awkward and intrusive. Then, as they reached the top I saw images of the last few days flash before my eyes. There was Caroline, the lying little bitch, pleading for my help in my office. There were Brande and Philips just before they both died. There was Spliff looking god-awful in his flat. Finally, there was Malcolm Wallace. Malcolm Wallace in front of the adoring masses. Malcolm Wallace sat in the shadows of the box at the Grand Theatre. Malcolm Wallace reducing the waitress to tears at Guy's Café.

I heard a schlurping noise as the little dervishes extricated themselves then reported back to Sophia. She listened intently to them before lancing me with her attention once more.

"And you think that this man is not capable of great destruction?" Her voice was quite incredulous.

"He healed me," I protested. "He's given me back my life."

Sophia shook her head and waved a hand in front of us. An image of Wallace appeared. She pointed at and it focussed in on his right hand. "Do you see that?"

I shrugged. "It's his hand." I was feeling rather peeved and uncooperative after having been interfered with by fairies.

"His ring," she glowered. "Look at it."

The image enhanced and the two coiled snakes were crystal clear: one with a red eye, the other with a black. I felt sick. I could see where this was going.

"You studied mythology, Samuel," the crisp librarian tone berated me.

"You know what snakes represent."

"Dragons," I sighed.

"Dragons," she agreed. "What's more, there is something about this man. Or rather someone. He is not alone. I am sure of it. He has someone behind him. Someone old and powerful. I can smell her on him."

I thought back to the lilting voice singing at the back of the Credete meeting but kept my mouth shut on the matter. Instead I asked, "What now?"

"You distance yourself from Mister Wallace as soon as you can, Samuel. He is Death. He is Destruction. He is a danger not only to you but also to all those you love. His mistress is a jealous being and she will stop at nothing to get what she wants."

"And what do you think she wants?"

"To put it simply? Devotion or death."

I surveyed the wasteland around me and felt sick to the pit of my stomach. Everything was gone. Everything was destroyed. I could see no sign of life; not human or animal. Perhaps there was some somewhere, but here, where people had once bustled about their normal, mundane existences, there was nothing. Not a breath of vitality.

It was a barren land.

A *divergent* land.

Then a thought struck me and I turned to Sophia. "Another question. What was it supposed to be like? If the Divergence hadn't happened, what would have been here instead?"

She cocked her head to one side and I could tell that she was formulating a response that would be easily understood by a mere mortal like myself. After a small pause she said, "The Lord your God would have descended from Heaven on a throne of winged beings. The last trumpet would have sounded after which Heaven and Earth would have converged into one. The dead would have woken from their dark slumber and all pain would have ceased. The angels would have walked alongside their human cousins in a realm of perpetual bliss and harmony."

I closed my eyes, tears blurring at the edges. "You mean Paradise."

"Paradise," she said.

I opened my eyes. I was alone in my living room. A discarded coffee cup lay on the floor and rain beat against the dirty window on a cold, autumnal evening.

"Shit."

# Chapter Twelve

Saturday morning crept up on me like a flea-infested, worm-ridden, three-legged dog. I kicked hard at it from under my bedclothes but it refused to leave me alone and eventually I surrendered to its tenacity and crawled out of bed. I showered, shaved and had just finished my breakfast when there was a resonant knocking at the door to my flat. I glanced at the carriage clock on the nearest bookshelf: nine o'clock. An early visit for a Saturday morning. I instantly began to worry but tried to reassure myself that at least they were knocking and not just appearing in the middle of my living room.

However, when I opened the door, my worry upgraded itself to panic. Jitendra stood there with a uniformed officer. He saw my eyes clock the bobby and said, “Good morning, Sam. May I come in?”

I stood back and gestured for him to enter. He did so on his own, leaving his companion stood with his back to my door. “Your friend not joining us?”

“I sincerely hope that he won't have to.”

Oh, this was not good. I eased the door shut and stood facing the DCI. “What is it?”

“Yesterday afternoon, a young waitress at Guy's Café decided that she'd had enough of her employer. Now, whereas most would just hand in their cards and offer up a bit of verbal, she went a bit further.”

My stomach was starting to sink. I could see where this was leading, and not to a happy ring of pixies in a forested glade where children go to drink ginger beer on long, hot summer afternoons.

“She went into the kitchen,” Jitendra continued without even consulting a note book, “propped the door shut with a stool, picked up the nearest knife and stabbed her employer twenty times in quick succession before plunging the knife deep into her own stomach. Customers and other staff tried to intervene, but the jammed door prevented their access to the kitchen. By the time the paramedics arrived, both employer and employee had lost a drastic amount of blood. He died on the scene; she passed away in the ambulance."

I staggered over to the sofa and collapsed like a limp bag of bones and disconnected tissue. In my mind's eye I still saw the young girl dissolving under the acid touch of Wallace's tongue. "Dear God."

"When we questioned the witnesses, they stated that just prior to the act, the girl in question had undertaken a rather curious conversation with a pair of customers who had just left. One was described as a refined looking gentleman with striking white hair and orange eyes, the other was said to look like something out of a Mickey Spillane novel." He raised an eyebrow and awaited the inevitable response.

There was no point denying my being there. "I'd had a coffee there yesterday afternoon."

"Obviously." Jitendra gestured towards the mac and coat draped over my sofa. "You are somewhat distinctive in your attire. Care to tell me who your friend was?"

"An old uni friend."

He waited for more information like a heron waits quietly before spearing a minnow.

"His name's Wallace. Malcolm Wallace."

Jitendra nodded. "You have his address?"

"No."

"Phone number?"

"No."

"Not much of a friendship then," his voice loaded with sarcastic disbelief. "How are you supposed to meet up every now and then in order to encourage young waitresses to go psycho?"

"Now, hold on!" I surged from the sofa and started pounding my finger in his chest. "How dare you suggest that? I had nothing to do with what went on yesterday. Wallace dragged me along and all seemed fine until he just turned. One minute he was sweetness and light, the next he was turning that young girl's life upside down. And you know what? I think he was enjoying it. There was a look of total relish on his face as she realised that she was never going to come to anything. It was horrible to watch." I stopped, realised that jabbing a finger in the chest of a policeman was tantamount to assault and lowered my hand to my sides. "Please find him, lock him up and throw away the key. I'm done with him." I stomped off to the kitchen, yanked a cupboard door open and took out a bottle of Jack. I sloshed a good measure into a tumbler and marched back into the living room.

Jitendra was still stood waiting for me. "Anything else that you want to add? If I take him into custody will he inexplicably die under questioning?"

I snorted my contempt at the cheap shot. "Trust me, right now I'd see that as a blessing." I threw back half of the bourbon; it added extra heat to my ire. "Wallace is toxic! I was employed to investigate a little group that he runs. He tells people that anything is possible and they, in turn, treat him like some sort of Messiah."

"You mean Credete?"

That struck me like a fish across the face. "You know of it?"

"Of course we do, Sam. What do you think we do all day? Watch television? We've known about that little group for some time now and I don't like having a cult on my doorstep, trust me. I've tried to get it infiltrated before now, but to no avail." He paused, thinking. "Did you get in?"

"Yes," I answered carefully, worried about where this conversation was going. "I went to a meeting a few days back with a friend, Abalone Morris. She's a music teacher at Saint Edmund Campion. That's where I met Wallace, at the meeting. I didn't even know he was around here until then."

Jitendra slowly paced around my living room, his polished shoes making next to no noise on the cheap nylon carpet. His eyes wandered from clock to clock in a carefree manner, but I knew that his mind was honed like the sharpest scalpel and he was about to make a critical incision close to the heart of the matter. "I want you to get in touch with Wallace again and gain as much information as you can on him: what he's up to, how he holds sway over people, where he's been before he set up this little shebang of his."

I shook my head violently. This was all I needed. I was not only being manipulated by paranormal entities but now also by the mundane and corporeal. "Not a chance. No way. I'm done with Wallace and I'm certainly not going all James Bond for anyone else. I'm forgetting the whole sorry mess and getting back to my ghouls, ghosties and goblins. I'm sick of people or entities pressing my buttons or tugging on my heart strings. I'm finished with it!"

Jitendra stopped his pacing, stood square in front of me and locked his eyes on mine. "Really?"

"Really." Although part of me was now having serious doubts on the matter.

He nodded to himself. "Right now, we are the only two people who know what really happened in Williamson Park. The constable outside is a new lad, a bit green, one might say. Also, he's very eager. He's not nicked anyone yet. I'm sure he'd bring his granny in if there was so much as a whiff of trouble about her. I think you'll do this little favour, just for old times' sake." He walked up to me, took the remains of my drink and downed it in one. The bastard had me exactly where he wanted me. "I'll be in touch next week for my information."

After the door swung shut and the footsteps of Jitendra and little boy blue retreated down the stairs, I slouched down into the padded comfiness of my sofa to consider my lot in life. Had I done something truly evil in a previous existence? Had I been a ruthless dictator or, even worse, a banker? What had caused me to be the butt of so many people's machinations? All I wanted was a quiet life. A few DVDs, the television remote and a decent bourbon. Was that too much to ask for? Instead, my life was rapidly spiralling into the plot of a Dan Brown novel – intrigue and conspiracies teasing and trailing the hapless hero as he stumbles his way through a repetitive series of dastardly dangerous events.

I had hoped that my first week on the job had been a hiccough, a blip on an otherwise sedate and calmly satisfying career. However, it was becoming apparent that it was to be the norm.

Perhaps I could just run away, leave it all behind? What would I do? I would have to live off cash only, no tech lifestyle so that Jitendra's boys would never find me. Yes, that was doable. I could manage that... for about a week! Then I would realise that I had no perceivable life skills to earn said cash and that I was missing my television with such devastating force that I would come crawling back and have to face the music.

How about if I found somewhere quiet where I could just go and *be*? There was a Buddhist retreat centre up in the Lakes. Perhaps I could spend my life there in peace and solitude. The food would not be a problem. Buddhism was compatible with veganism. But was it compatible with sci-fi? How would the monks feel when I started making lightsaber noises during morning classes of Tai Chi? I didn't think they would be too impressed.

No, I was stuck here, not through any third party keeping me here, but through my own inability to actually make do without the things that made my life fun. What was the point of a life on the run if it was miserable? A life without the comforts of home would be no life whatsoever. I would just have to stay put, grinning and bearing it.

"Hello, Mister Rock," I said to a point of space just to my right. "I'd like to introduce you to my friend here," I gesticulated to a space on my left, "Miss Hard Place. Now, I know she looks like a cold-hearted bitch with a face set in granite, but I assure you that she's quite the party girl. A few vodka martinis and she'll be on the table boogieing away to *Dancing Queen*. What's that, Miss Hard Place?" I turned to my left. "You think that Mister Rock is a rather fetching young man, but he really needs to pull his trousers up because he's showing far too much of his Calvin Klein underpants? Well I must agree, he does need to do something about his attire, but I'm sure you'll be able to whip him into... *What the hell am I doing?*" I yelled to my empty room. There are times when your sanity can be pushed just that little bit too far.

Fortunately, at that moment, my mobile rang. I fished it out, saw who was trying to contact me and smiled. Perhaps today was going to get a bit better after all?

"I'm just coming down Penny Street. I hope you've got some coffee brewing."

Good old Spliff, straight to the point, no messing around.

"To what do I owe this impromptu visit?" I switched my mobile to speakerphone as I started to prep the coffee machine in the kitchen. "It's not even ten. Isn't this early for you?"

There was silence.

"Spliff?" I yelled across the kitchen. "You still there?"

"You've forgotten."

Uh oh. "Forgotten what?"

"Oh, Sam. How could you?"

I started to wrack my brains as I poured the water into the coffee maker. What the hell had I forgotten? It wasn't his birthday; that I was sure of. It sounded important though. I switched the coffee maker on and picked the phone up as I wandered back through to the living room. As I did, I couldn't help but notice the unusual amount of people milling around Dalton Square in front of the Town Hall – people and a great, big outside broadcast van.

"Oh no," I groaned.

Spliff did not even bother to knock on the door to my flat; he never does. Instead, he barged in and did what he always does upon entering my alleged Fortress of Solitude: he complained bitterly. "I can never understand why the hell you have to live up so many stairs? It's worse than going for a stroll up Kilimanjaro."

"Good morning to you too," I smiled. "What's that?"

My old friend beamed from ear to ear as he thumped a parcel which had been hastily wrapped in dog-eared newspaper onto my coffee table. "This," he proclaimed dramatically as he unveiled the layers of some trashy tabloid, "is our ticket to get to see her."

"That?"

"Yes. This."

"It's a dog."

There on my table was the scruffiest piece of chinaware that I had ever had the misfortune to lay my eyes upon. It was a black china dog, a terrier of some kind with wiry hair and squinty-looking eyes. I felt that if anyone from the Ming Dynasty were to lay their eyes on it they would have gone away and taken up metalwork.

"It's bloody awful!"

Spliff gave me a look. "What do you mean?"

"Oh, come on, Spliff," I laughed, fishing out a Lucky. "It's just... It's just..." I lit the cigarette and drew on the nicotine for help in searching for the right form of criticism. "It's just so scruffy. It's all black and wiry and looks like it hasn't seen a good clean for at least twelve months."

"Well, it's just like your scrotum, then," he snapped back. "Anyway," he sulked, picking up his supposed meal ticket, "I only just bought him from Oxfam. I saw him in the window and thought how cute and adorable he looked – perfect for getting me onto the show. All he needs is a little cleaning up."

I shook my head and continued to draw on the Lucky. "He needs something, that's for sure. Perhaps a flea treatment?"

Spliff's icy silence slapped me in the face.

"Okay, okay. If you want to clean him up before we go over the road, help yourself."

Spliff swept past me, muttering something about bloody useless friends and stomped off into the kitchen. I heard the water run as he started to bathe his china dog. I followed behind, chuckling quietly to myself, then the image of Jitendra and his boy in blue drifted into my head. I opened my mouth to tell Spliff about Wallace and the waitress just as he turned round, drying his beloved pooch in a tea towel. "What's up with you now? Catching flies?"

Slowly, I closed my gaping mouth. I would keep things to myself for now. I would tell him later.

"No. Nothing's wrong. Let's go see your beloved Ms Briers."

The Ashton Hall was quite different in atmosphere from my last visit. The happy, smiley faces of enthusiastic group members had been replaced by expressions that were a mixture of concern and excitement as owners of antiques carefully ferried themselves about from queue to queue in the hope that their great-aunt's hand-embroidered silk bloomers (which they had no intention of selling whatsoever) would gain them five precious minutes on prime time television.

The lilac-coloured banner adorned with its stylised logo had been replaced by mobile studio cameras, bright lighting and boom microphones. I couldn't help but smile. The transformation was quite extraordinary.

"So where do you think she is?" Spliff asked, raising himself up on tiptoes to peer over the crowds.

"If you mean the wonderful Ms Briers, I have no idea. I guess she's cozying up with some photogenic little old dear ready for her next greatest photo shoot."

He shot me a withering look. "Harmony's nothing like that at all. She'll be mixing with the masses, bringing them joy in their otherwise dull, dull existences."

I shook my head. He was totally smitten.

So, for now, we were pursuing Spliff's own personal little piece of icon-worship that made him go all kittenish and trembly at the knees: Harmony Briers demurely sexy actor of the Shakespearian stage and champion of old people's even older bits and bobs. He waded through the mass of individuals carrying their great aunt's china urns or whatever it was they had and stood on tiptoe again to try and gain a sighting of his quarry. I contented myself to shamble along behind him.

I glanced at my watch. How long was this going to take? I was supposed to be finding a way to reingratiate myself with Wallace. It crossed my mind that I hadn't told Spliff about my morning visitation. Was there a reason? Was I being deceptive? Was it that I felt like I was being used as a spy by Jitendra? I ignored the questions and just followed my antique-laden friend.

"Damn it!" he cursed, gaining himself a reproachful look from an elderly woman in her seventies, "I can't see her. Oh, Sam, what am I to do?"

I was about to suggest giving up and heading over to the Borough when I heard a silky smooth voice say from behind, "Can I help you, Reverend?"

Spliff turned, about to launch into some diatribe about stuffing one body part up another when he clocked the man's ID badge, marking him as part of the production crew. "Why, young man," he effused, all sweetness, light and buttered crumpets, "I certainly hope you can. We have come here, desperate to have my grandmother's china dog valued." His arm that wasn't clutching the hastily-wrapped dog bear hugged me to his side. "Could you possibly point us in the right direction. It would mean so much to both of us."

"What?" I gasped.

"Oh!" exclaimed the runner. "Of course, I can. Why don't you follow me?"

He turned and headed off towards a corner of the hall. Spliff made to follow him but was jerked back violently by the grasp of my hand. "What the hell are you playing at?" I hissed under my breath. "*Us*?" I demanded, my eyebrows threatening to shoot off the top of my forehead.

Spliff rolled his eyes. "Oh, come on, Sam. Everyone knows that the gay demographic is so vitally important on the Beeb these days. You should know that being all sci-fi and what not. Look at *Doctor Who* and *Torchwood.* I'm surprised they haven't painted the TARDIS pink yet."

There are times when my best friend causes words to fail me and the only sane response I could give would be with a very sharp machete. This was one of those moments. My mouth flapped open and shut as Spliff wrapped his arm around me, bundling me off after the runner. "Come along, darling. We mustn't keep the good man waiting, must we?"

As we made our way through the crowds of antique holders I noticed a face in the crowd. There, at the edge of the room was a grey-haired man whose eyes seemed to follow me. I strained to get a better look at him, but a rather large lady wearing a horrendously flowery dress and carrying a parlour palm in an art deco vase sailed in front of me. By the time she had finished eclipsing the light from the windows, the man was nowhere to be seen. I frowned. He had looked familiar, but for now I needed to keep up with Spliff.

We were led directly to a table that was set up with an expert, a camera man and someone who, judging by the large headphones, appeared to be a sound technician. A number of people who had obviously been waiting in the queue for quite a while chuntered and murmured amongst themselves. If looks could kill, then the antiques mafia would have been taking out a bounty on our heads. Spliff, of course, was either totally oblivious or just didn't give a monkey's bottom. I lowered my head and tried to avoid the glares.

"Trevor! Trevor!" the runner called out to the seated expert. "I have a perfect one for you. This is Reverend..." he turned to Spliff who was beaming jovially from ear to self-satisfied ear, "I'm sorry, I didn't catch your name."

"MacIntyre," he provided. "Reverend James Francis MacIntyre. I'm the chaplain at Luneside University."

"Marvellous," the runner simpered. "Reverend MacIntyre and his partner..."

"Actually, I'm not his... *Ow!*"

"... have brought an item in for you to look at."

"Jolly good!" Trevor was a rather red-faced man in his fifties with the sort of moustache that normally deserves a good twirling. He leaned over the table and shook hands vigorously with both of us. He had something of a perspiration problem and I had to resist the urge to wipe my hand on my coat. Spliff was now in full flow and slid onto the empty seat next to the man without even being asked. "So what is it you chaps have for me then?"

I sighed in resignation and dropped down next to my best friend as he dug his china dog out of his shopping bag. "It's this little fellow, Trevor. I inherited him a few years back when my dear mother died. She in turn had inherited him from *her* mother, so he's been in the family for quite a while now. We're all very attached to him."

I had to admire his balls. As far as I was aware, Spliff's parents were still alive and kicking north of the border. I wondered what they would make of this if it was aired then I decided that after almost forty years of him, they were probably used to his various shenanigans by now.

Trevor took the dog from Spliff and, turning it over in his hands, started to comment on such things as its glaze, its colour and its markings. I, in turn, started to tune out the event and let my eyes wander around the room. There were huddles of onlookers surrounding us, peering over each other's shoulders and pointing at the charity piece that Spliff had brought along. If only they knew: I thought to myself. Then, through the undulating current of the crowds, I caught sight of the grey-haired man once again. He was stood off to one side and, when he saw me, began to walk slowly in my direction. As he did so, I saw that he was limping and realisation struck me: it was Mister Flint, caretaker of the Ashton Hall, the man who had annoyed Malcolm at the end of the Credete meeting on Wednesday. I smiled at him and he nodded a silent acknowledgement.

"Well this is interesting." These words from Trevor The Expert, caught my attention and I swivelled back to see what was going on. He was carefully examining a marking underneath the china dog. "My, my, I don't get to see many of these at all."

"What is it?" Spliff was perched on the edge of his chair, rapt. "Is it good?"

"It most certainly is. This mark here," the expert leant over with the dog and pointed to a series of blue smudges on its base, "tells us where it was made and indeed by whom. It was cast right here in Lancaster, by none other than Robert Gillow."

I frowned. "Correct me if I'm wrong, but wasn't he a furniture maker, not a potter?"

"Indeed he was," Trevor beamed, "but just after his marriage in 1729 and before he set up shop the year after, he experimented with china wares. Some say it was boredom, some that it was a failed business venture. Personally I think they were gifts for his new wife, but then I'm an old romantic at heart."

There was a pause as the unasked question circulated the table. Robert Gillow. Chinaware. How much?

It was Spliff who voiced what we were both thinking. "So, not that I'm ever thinking of parting with it, but, you know... is it at all valuable?"

Trevor stroked his chin and motioned for the runner. "I think we need Harmony on film with this one."

I thought Spliff was going to explode, not only was his bit of tat seemingly valuable, but he was going to meet Ms Briers as well. I chuckled quietly to myself then saw Mister Flint beckon to me with a sideways nod of the head. I leant over to Spliff and whispered in his ear, "Listen, I have to go."

"What? Oh? Okay." He was in shock. I decided to leave him there. Patting him on the shoulder I made my excuses to the television crew and made my way over to the caretaker.

"Hello again," I smiled.

"Not here. Too public. Follow me." He limped off through the crowd. I shrugged and followed him.

He led me away from the masses of tat-laden hopefuls to a small corridor off the main hall. Carefully, he closed the door behind us and looked up and down to make sure that we were alone. "I saw you here on Wednesday," he said.

"That's right. A friend dragged me along."

"A friend?" He shook his head in disbelief. "No friend would bring you to that... that..." He searched for the right word. "Monster."

I arched a somewhat shocked eyebrow. Harsh words indeed. "You mean Malcolm Wallace? I hardly think overrunning a bit for a few weeks makes someone a monster."

"That's not what I mean. He's evil. Perverse."

I drummed my fingernails against my teeth. This was getting rather high on the weirdness factor. "Okay, friend, you'd better explain what you mean."

"You saw them. You saw what they were like. They all went off their rockers. You did too. I saw you. You were all standing up yelling his little slogan over and over again. It's not right."

"He also healed the girl. You saw that? Made her get up and walk."

Flint nodded his head quickly, nervously. "Sure he healed her. He healed her good and proper. But tell me this, how d'you think she got sick in the first place? Hmmm?"

"She told me it was after a dream."

"A dream? A nightmare more like," he shouted then snapped his head left and right scared witless that he had been overheard. "Since when did dreams start to make people sick? Really, you believe that's natural?"

He sort of had me there, so I let him continue.

"Don't you think it strange that a man who can turn a group of normal folk into a bunch of gibbering loons is presented with a little girl who was crippled by a dream? Don't you think it's possible that he had something to do with her illness? Don't you think he was responsible for that dream, that nightmare? If he fixed her, then perhaps he was the one who broke her?"

My stomach churned. I had not even fully considered the girl's story. Wallace had interrupted us before I could ask her anything. "Tell me, what other sorts of healing have there been?"

Flint opened his mouth to speak then, as if a breeze had brushed his face, he shuddered and his eyes glazed over. "I... I have to go," he murmured and he dashed past me back into the hall.

I swore under my breath and chased after him. I caught a fleeting glimpse of the caretaker diving into the crowd of people and made to follow him. Unfortunately, the same woman as before walked in front of me and glared across her ample bosom as I almost knocked her parlour palm out of her hands. I apologised and dodged around her only to feel a hand close on my arm. I spun around, my fist raised instinctively and stared down into the cringing face of the runner. "Oh God, sorry," I apologised. "Somewhat on edge."

He backed off slightly, nervously watching my fist as I lowered it down and thrust it deep into a pocket. "I thought you might like to see this." He motioned over to the table where Spliff was still sat, only now he was accompanied by the demure Ms Briers.

I glanced around the hall. Flint had disappeared. There was no way I could catch him now. I would ring the Town Hall on Monday morning and arrange to meet him. For now, the sight of Spliff sat smiling like Tinkerbell on Prozac would be a much welcome diversion.

"So," Harmony Briers purred, "I believe we have quite a find here."

"Indeed we do." This was Trevor The Expert, hamming up his time in front of the camera for all it was worth. "This charming little dog came in this morning with Reverend MacIntyre here."

"It sure is a curious little piece." I had to admit there certainly was something about her. Was it her eyes, her voice or just her mannerisms; I could not tell. What I *could* tell though was that Spliff had it bad. Oh, so bad.

"It was my mother's."

"Really?"

"Yes. I call it Scrotum."

I slapped my palm over my face and did my best not to laugh, I really did. Peeping through my fingers I saw a perplexed Ms Briers shoot a look at the cameraman. He twirled his fingers: *carry on.*

Ever the professional, she turned to Trevor The Expert and asked, "So what makes this little chap so special?"

Trevor puffed out his chest and entered into his little spiel about Gillow and his wife as Spliff just continued to sit and stare in awe at his own object of wonder.

"So, Trevor," Harmony Briers smiled, "this begs the question, how much is Reverend MacIntyre's Scrotum worth?"

*Did she just say what I think she said*: I wondered, open-mouthed. Trevor The Expert was also exhibiting an expression of jaw-dropping shock, but the words that came were nothing to do with Spliff's valuable china dog.

"Dear God!" he gasped, staring up behind the camera.

I turned and followed his gaze. There on the balcony level, overlooking the hall stood Flint. He had a noose tied around his neck. There was a rush of feet as a number of people dashed out of the hall towards the stairs to the upper level. I manoeuvred myself away from Spliff and his moment of joy. The fat woman in the flowery dress got in my way once more. This time I just shoved her and ignored the complaints and abuse she poured onto my back. What the hell was going on? I heard a loud hammering as people pounded on the doors leading to the balcony. They must have been either locked or jammed shut.

Flint climbed tentatively up onto the wooden wall surrounding the balcony and sat there staring off into space. His eyes were fixed on something that we could not see, something in his own field of view that was driving him to this final act of desperation. Tears were streaming down the man's cheeks. His hands were gripping the edge of the balcony, their knuckles corpse white. His lips were moving over and over in some sort of silent litany. Rapidly flickering over his teeth, they told of the hidden motive for this scene but I could not make out a word of it even with my new, improved hearing. Then, as if waking from, dare I say it, a dream, Flint's eyes were bright and full to the brim with terror.

"You cannot escape him!" he screamed, a tremulous falsetto grasping his tense vocal chords. "He will come for you in your dreams!"

"Oh no," I whispered. This was not good. Not good at all.

Flint tugged at the noose; it pulled taut against the railing. There were gasps from the crowd and the pounding on the doors increased. It sounded as if someone was hitting them with something heavy like a fire extinguisher.

Satisfied that the noose was secure, Flint gripped the side of the balcony once more and opened his mouth shouting out, "The Divergence is coming!" before pushing off. There was a deep twanging noise as the rope stretched to its maximum and a resonant smacking as it hit the wall of the balcony. An almighty crash came from the doors as someone finally broke their way through and clambered between the seating to the railing. Arm over arm they heaved the dead weight of the caretaker up, but I, like everyone else in the Ashton Hall, knew Mister Flint was no more.

We were still there an hour later. The police had turned up alongside the paramedics. The ambulance guys had found little to do apart from shake their heads and respectfully cover Mister Flint's body with a cloth. The boys in blue, however, were definitely at the peak of their game. Everyone was questioned from shocked members of the public through to horrified production crew.

Then they reached me.

At this point they rang for backup.

Backup stormed into the hall wearing a perfectly pressed suit and a face like thunder. It grabbed me by the arm and dragged me away from prying ears and eyes as it growled under its breath, "I leave you alone for less than three hours and I have another body on my hands. Three hours, Sam! Are you trying to prove a point or do you just think I love my paperwork?"

I snatched my arm away from his grip. "Back off, Jitendra! It's not my fault!"

"Really?" His face was nose to nose with mine. I could smell peppermint on his breath and his pupils bored into mine. "Tell that to the bodies that seem to be following you around right now? One yesterday. One today. Not to mention five stiff actors."

I frowned. The actors. Two attempted and three completed suicides. My mind raced back to Philips, his terrified eyes and his gravelly voice. "The Divergence is coming," I whispered.

Jitendra backed off shaking his head. "Don't go all hoodoo on me, Sam. I need answers here."

"No, no. I'm not." Running my fingers through my hair I paced in a small circle. "Just before Philips dropped down dead, he said, 'The Divergence is coming,' didn't he?"

The DCI nodded. "Go on."

"Well, so did Flint."

"You're sure?"

"Positive. Ask your men. I'm sure all the other witnesses will have heard it. It was pretty hard to miss as he had centre stage somewhat."

Jitendra frowned. "So, you're saying that Flint was connected to your abductors?"

"No, not exactly."

"Well, what then?" Exasperation was touching the policeman's voice. "Come on, Sam. Give it to me straight."

"You're not gonna like it."

"I'm a big boy."

"Okay," I shrugged. "I first met Flint here during the week when I came to the Credete meeting. He had a bit of a run in with Wallace about the meeting overrunning. Then he seeks me out today and starts rambling on about how Wallace is a monster and how he somehow sets up people's illnesses by entering their dreams and how he controls the crowds and gets them whipped up into a frenzy.

"Flint was scared for his life. He was a man on the point of running away and hiding in a deep hole up a very tall hill, but then he just suddenly changed. It was as if someone had gotten inside his mind and told him what to do."

"You think Wallace made Flint kill himself?"

I nodded.

"You think Wallace killed those actors?"

I nodded again.

"Shit."

"I said you wouldn't like it."

Jitendra stood staring off into the middle distance, his mind working overtime. The longer he thought, the more I started to worry. I felt like I was in one of those situations where you find you have somehow backed yourself into an awkward corner. I had been unknowingly treading step after step, toe to heel into a very tight spot with zero space for manoeuvrability. There were long jagged spikes protruding from sheer walls and they would snag me whichever way I tried to turn.

"I need more info," he eventually said.

I groaned as the metaphorical spikes snagged me and held on tight.

"I want you to meet up with Wallace again and get as much information out of him as is possible."

I desperately tried to twist and turn away from the barbs of my mind. "I don't have his number. I can't contact him."

"But I think you know someone who can."

"No."

"Is that *no you won't* or *no you don't*?"

"You know damn well which one it is." I pictured those sparkling blue eyes framed by light blonde hair. Anger began to well up inside me. How could this arrogant copper ask this of me? "It's too dangerous."

"Sam, people are dying. You want that to continue?" He turned and left.

I stood on my own, panting heavily. I had an awful feeling about this. My stomach was churning and I felt like a total cad, but he was right; people were dying.

More would die.

I fished out my mobile and flicked through the contacts.

"Hi, Abalone. How's it going?"

# Chapter Thirteen

It was a crisp autumnal afternoon as we drove out of the city. We went east along Ashton Road out towards Glasson. Just past Conder Green, Abalone instructed me to turn down a freshly tarmacked drive. I let out a low whistle when I saw chez Wallace. It was immense; a wide stone construction that looked like it had been crafted by Hebrew slaves. There were wide stained glass windows overlooking the rolling fields that surrounded the house. Stonework had been carved and fashioned into all manner of animals mythical and real along the roof top. Everywhere I looked the building screamed, "Money!" It had seen one hell of a financial investment over the years.

"I know," she whispered reverentially as if approaching the Holy of Holies, "it's an amazing place. A real testament to his message."

I forced a smile whilst feeling sick inside. How could such a bright, intelligent girl be completely suckered in by this guy? Then I remembered the dead fiancé. A car crash had claimed his life and Abalone had gone running into the avuncular arms of the reassuring Wallace.

A dark thought crossed my mind.

Had it really been an accident? What if..?

No, surely not. How could Wallace have orchestrated something like that? Yet, Flint had insisted that he could control peoples' dreams; that he had made the little Watts girl sick in her dream. Was it really beyond the realm of imagination that he could have contrived the death of Abalone's fiancé? Could he be responsible?

Possibly. But why?

"Therein lies the rub," I muttered.

"Pardon?" Abalone raised a blonde eyebrow as I pulled the car to a halt in front of the huge, rambling pile. "You quoting Shakespeare for some reason in particular?"

"Sorry. Just thinking out loud. It's a bad habit."

She leant across the hand brake and breathed into my ear. "I *love* bad habits."

I felt my cheeks glow hotter than a television bought down the local pub and she pulled back giggling lightly. Smiling, I let my eyes look at her there in the passenger seat. She was truly an amazing woman, full of life and vitality.

And I had lied to her.

I had rung her up and told her that Malcolm and I had argued the other day and that I wanted to go see him and apologise. I stressed that it was really playing on my mind (at least that bit was not a lie) and that I wanted to see him that afternoon. Could she arrange it? She had said that of course it was possible. She would ring Malcolm and arrange it while I drove over to meet her.

She had believed me implicitly like a child believes their parent will always be kind, careful and loving.

I had kicked this child in the face.

"What's the matter?"

"Nothing," I said dismissively, whilst building another falsehood. "Just worried about seeing Malcolm."

"I told you, it will be okay," she reassured me. "Now come on, let's go and see him."

Abalone, dear sweet Abalone, opened her door and climbed out of my VW Polo. I did likewise and as I followed her up across the drive we saw the front door swing open and there he stood: Malcolm Wallace, who some claimed to be the most evil man I had ever met. What did he do right then? Did he stare me down with those freakishly orange eyes of his? Did he shout tirades of abuse at me and slam the door in my face? Did he greet his darling disciple whilst giving the estranged acquaintance the cold shoulder?

He did none of these.

He walked across the drive, arms outstretched and enveloped his prodigal son in one all-forgiving hug.

The inside of Wallace's house was just as impressive as the out. The creatures that had lined the rooftop were also to be found carved into oak panelling that lined the hallway and the study to which he led us. I made out lions, panthers, dogs, crocodiles...

And dragons.

Lots of dragons.

Dragons were starting to follow me everywhere now. It was creeping me out somewhat.

*When dragons walk the Earth then all creation shall tremble.*

What was the connection between them and the Divergence? There had been two dragons in my dream the previous week: one red, one black. Was Wallace one of them? Was he really going to be the cause of the Divergence? What was his connection to this mysterious Kanor? Was *he* Kanor?

All these loose ends and unanswered questions made my head hurt but I kept my discomfort well-hidden and said nothing. I just smiled amicably as we sat on a plush upholstered sofa that looked like it cost more than my father used to earn in a year and Wallace poured us all a cup of what smelt like Earl Grey tea; its delicate lemony fragrance danced in my nostrils as I slowly sipped from the fine china cup.

Classical music played quietly from discreet speakers as Wallace told us how pleased he was that we had come out to see him. He had been terribly concerned about how he and I had parted company the other day. He had wanted to ring me but did not want to intrude. He had been so terribly afraid that I would just hang up on him. It would have broken his heart.

Damn, he was just as good a liar as I was.

"Tell me, Malcolm," I smiled, settling the china teacup down on its delicate saucer, "your collection must have increased quite a bit since you showed it to me at university."

"Collection?" Abalone asked, genuinely curious and oblivious to the swathes of deception that swaddled her.

Wallace chuckled to himself. "Samuel is referring to my collection of esoterica. Something of a hobby and yes indeed it has grown immensely. Would you like to see it?"

"If it's no bother." I settled the cup and saucer down on a coaster.

"No bother at all." He rose and made his way over to a door at the back of the room. "This way."

Abalone and I followed him out of the comfortable study with its background orchestral accompaniment and delicately flavoured tea. To begin with, the ambient light in the back room was low; there were no windows, just electric illumination. Wallace fiddled with a switch on the wall and the lighting rose.

Abalone gasped.

I had to admit that I was also rather impressed. His collection had certainly expanded. What had once been confined to a box under his bed was now displayed in glass cases around a room that was roughly the same size as the ground floor of an average-sized house. Abalone was wandering around from cabinet to cabinet with her mouth open, obviously blown away by this side of Wallace that she had never seen before. There were scrolls, brooches, robes, pendants. All sorts of paraphernalia.

Wallace acted the benevolent guide, talking us through the most interesting pieces. "Most of my artefacts, as Sam knows, are pre-biblical. Here we have original texts from ancient Ur. Totally impossible to put a price on. Here is some Hittite cuneiform."

Abalone peered down at the small clay tablets he was pointing to. "What is it?"

"Cuneiform? It's an ancient alphabet, my dear. Very hard to translate.

Fortunately, I have someone in the know," Wallace winked knowingly.

"Would that be your mysterious benefactor?" I asked, my eyes scanning the cases for anything familiar.

"Why indeed it would, Samuel. Indeed it would."

The thought of killer heels clicking on a kitchen floor flashed across my memory. "She must be getting on a bit these days?"

Wallace let out a bray of laughter. Abalone looked at me, perplexed. I shrugged. "Oh, Samuel. You still have no idea, do you?" He tapped his index finger against his lips in thought and his curious ring glinted in the light. "Come, let me show you both something familiar."

Abalone and I dutifully followed him to a wide cabinet at the back of the room. She gasped and I felt my mouth drop open in disbelief. "How on Earth..?"

There, tucked away reverentially in Wallace's private collection was a vast array of small clay figurines. They all depicted a similar form: the bust of a woman presenting her breasts. Not only that, but in the middle of them stood a cast statue of about one metre in height. It was of a woman staring straight in front dressed in a long gown whilst holding two serpents apart, one in each outstretched arm.

"Is this Minoan?" I asked, peering closer at the statuette. "it looks like one I've seen before but..."

"Very good, Samuel," Wallace purred as if lavishing praise on a somewhat dim student. The patronising tone made me feel sick inside. "You're close, but not quite there. It is like the famous Minoan deities, but it is in fact Canaanite. Very old, very precious and totally unique."

"Why's it not in a museum?" Abalone frowned.

"Because it is mine, dear. And whatever I want I shall have because..."

"Anything is possible," I finished.

Wallace nodded silently.

I looked around the base of the statue. There were wooden sticks entwined with black and red ribbons. My mind darted back once more to Luneside University, this time examining Wallace's room. I had picked up something similar. Spliff had identified it. "It's Asherah," I whispered. "This is the goddess Asherah." In my mind's eye I saw Credete's banner of a capital T wrapped in two swirling lines. I glanced at the two snakes that made up Wallace's ring. "You worship her, don't you? That's what all this is; it's your personal shrine to your goddess."

Wallace bowed, his arms out to his side. "Guilty as charged. I became infatuated with Her Ladyship back when I was younger. I live to serve her."

"So you worship an ancient goddess?" Abalone's eyes were bright and wide in wonder. "That's rather cool."

"Thank you, my dear. Now, why don't we go back to my study? I shall fetch us some refreshments."

We turned and headed back to the door through which we entered. As we did, my eyes wandered up above the door frame and I caught sight of another statue. This one was displayed on a large shelf above the door. It was a creature with the heads of a lion and a goat and a tail in the form of a serpent.

The Chimera.

The same image that I had seen as a statue on a set at John O'Gaunt media, as a painting at the house of Howard Baines and as a necklace around the neck of Melanie Brande.

I snatched my eyes away from the beast of Greek mythology and couldn't help but look at our host.

He was smiling knowingly.

In my heart of hearts I now knew for sure that I was looking at a serial killer. Five actors, a waitress and a caretaker. How he had done it, I was not sure. All I could think of was his little mantra: *Anything Is Possible*. I shuddered and walked through the door into the study.

As I seated myself down, Abalone discreetly enquired of Wallace as to where she could powder her nose. Being the gentleman that he liked to appear, he offered to show her where the relevant room was as it was on the way to the kitchen, where he would brew us some more tea.

As soon as they had left the room I was over to his desk in a flash. I needed information. What information, though, I was not sure. I was guessing that he would not have a list lying around on his desk entitled, "Innocent people I feel like killing on a whim". One by one I pulled out his desk drawers and rifled through them whilst classical music continued to be piped through his hidden speakers. The drawers contained the usual things one would find: pens, staplers, scissors and a hole punch. No luck there. I rummaged through the books and papers he had neatly arranged on the desk's work-surface. Again, not much of any use. There were books regarding translations of ancient languages and archaeological finds and what seemed to be printouts of testimonials by members of Credete claiming how Wallace had changed their lives.

I shook my head and turned on the monitor to the computer. The screen flashed into life and I was presented with a login screen. I groaned.

Now, if this had been a film, I would have probably found the password on the third attempt. The first attempt would have been Credete as that was the name of Wallace's organisation and always the first attempt of film hackers. The next would have been Asherah as that which means something to the user is always the second choice. Then, if it had been a film, my trusted sidekick would come up with a comment that started something like, "Wait a minute. Don't you remember..." and we would input something blindingly obvious from three scenes previous. As it was, this was *not* a film and I had no perky little sidekick so I just turned the monitor off and gave up on that idea.

As I tapped my fingers against my teeth, my eyes were drawn back once more to the testimonials. I riffled through them again and paid them a bit more care and attention.

Here was a woman who had received a massive raise at work. She had been on the verge of suicide after her brother had gone missing the previous year.

Here was a man who had suddenly rediscovered the will to live after having been diagnosed with a mysterious illness a few months before joining Credete.

My heart started to pound as I read on. They all followed the same pattern: some sort of tragedy, join Credete, tragedy cured or relieved. They all also contained the names of the individuals. I whipped out my notebook and started to scribble down a list as I mentally made a note of their stories. I kept one ear cocked for the sound of footsteps approaching the study down the hallway. How long had Abalone and Wallace been gone? I had no idea. I had lost track of time. Was the same piece of music still playing? If so, how long for? I ignored the sound of violins and wind instruments and carried on with the matter at hand.

As I started to write down the tenth name, I heard a noise from outside the room. I quickly shoved the printouts back where I thought they should lay and sidestepped over to a bookcase where I pulled a random book off the shelf and pretended to peruse the volume of literature.

"You reading?" I turned to be greeted by a pair of sparkling blue eyes.

"It appears I am," I replied in as casual manner as I could manage.

Abalone looked over her spectacles at the book and frowned, "*Fly Fishing* by J.R.Hartley. I never knew that was really a book."

"Neither did I," I managed, closing the book and sliding it up on the shelf. What followed was one of those awkward little silences that seem to stalk me. It was broken when I realised that Abalone had placed a hand on my arm.

"Sam..."

The moment was broken by a polite cough from the doorway. "If I'm interrupting..?"

Abalone quickly snatched her hand back and a slight red hue blushed on her cheeks. I turned to Wallace who was brandishing a silver tray containing a fresh pot of tea and some scones. "Actually, Malcolm, I've just had a text. I'm afraid I need to be heading off."

He actually looked disappointed at the matter. "What a shame. Ah well, can't be helped. I'd better let you two lovebirds fly out into the night."

"Lovebirds..." I floundered. "Oh no, we're not... I mean, we're just..."

He raised a hand to quell my babbling. "Say no more, Samuel. Well, thank you for dropping by. It was good to put things straight, so to speak. I hope you found what you were looking for."

Ice shot down my spine. "Pardon?"

"I hope you found resolution to our unfortunate incident."

I nodded. "I got just what I needed."

As I parked up opposite Abalone's house on Dunkeld Street, she unclipped her seat belt and smiled at me. "I really enjoyed that."

"Good." I managed. I had been scared somewhat shitless, personally, but then I had been there under rather false pretences.

"Listen," she cocked her head to one side and her blonde hair fell down onto her shoulder. "How do you fancy meeting up tomorrow?"

The little man who lives inside my head with a trumpet for when nice things happen to me rushed to open his instrument's rather dusty case. "Sure. You want to go for coffee again?"

Abalone giggled softly and shook her head. "Been there, done that, Mister Investigator. How about a meal? You choose where. Pick me up about seven."

As I drove back down to Dalton Square, the gleeful music of trumpet fanfares was playing inside my head.

# Chapter Fourteen

I woke Sunday morning after sleeping like the dead, and that was the powerfully rested kind, not the zombified or vampiric kind. There had been no dreams, no dragons and, best of all, no librarians. Instead I had been lullabied to sleep on Saturday evening with the knowledge that Sunday was going to be a better day. The statue of the Chimera had linked Wallace to the John O'Gaunt actors which suggested that he was probably linked to Flint and the waitress. I had a list of members of Credete. I had a date planned with Abalone.

Yes. Things were definitely looking up.

*Anything is possible.*

I shuddered and kicked that corny little phrase into touch. This was all my own doing, my hard work. I had put the time in and now I was reaping the rewards, that was all.

I swung myself out of bed and headed for the bathroom.

After a shower and a shave, I decided to hit the list. Ten names. No addresses. No telephone numbers. What to do? First the obvious. I flicked my computer on and brewed some coffee while it booted up. Then, warm drink in hand, I lit up a Lucky before navigating to an online phone directory. Out of the ten names, two struck out. At a guess they were ex-directory. Of the rest, seven had multiple entries but one, Matthew Slesinski, gave me a single hit. I checked the nearest clock. It was just past noon. I hazarded that Mister Slesinski could be at home unless he was church-goer, so I dialled the number and listened to the dial tone. On the fourth ring, someone picked up.

"Hello?"

"Oh, good afternoon," I said in my brightest, breeziest voice. "Is that

Mister Matthew Slesinski?"

"It is. Who's that?" I detected that note of suspicion most people get when an unfamiliar voice rings them up and they start to think, Call centre? Double glazing? Crazy guy?

"Sorry to bother you, sir," I continued as if all were sweetness and light and this was the most natural conversation in the world, "but I'm from the *Lancaster Chronicle* and we're running a feature about the group known as..." I pretended to read my notes, "Credete and I was wondering if you could give us an interview?"

There was a slight pause before he replied. "Oh, well, I don't know..."

Bingo! I had snared the right guy. Now I just had to lure him in. "I can assure you, sir, that it's all above board. We have heard all about the great things that Mister Wallace has been doing there and we would like to tell our readers all about his marvellous work."

There was another pause. "And it's all above board? Malcolm really is a great guy. He saved my life. I wouldn't want to be part of anything seedy."

Slowly reeling. Slowly reeling. "Quite right, Mister Slesinski. I could meet up with you this afternoon if you were okay with that? It would only take a few minutes and a first-hand perspective could really paint Mister Wallace in a most favourable way."

There was a deep intake of breath on the other end of the line. "Ah, what the hell. I'm sure Malcolm would love the coverage. He'd love some new blood in the society and your article could do that. Okay. Let's meet up."

"Splendid, sir," I beamed. "How about two at the Borough? I believe that's just over the road from where your group meets?"

"Okay. Two it is."

"Could I just ask how I'll recognise you?"

There was a blast of laughter from the other end and when he told me what to look for I grinned from ear to ear. This would be a piece of cake.

Some people like to drink at a number of different watering holes. They like the variety of beverages and constantly changing sea of faces. Not me. I have to sit in the same chair, looking out of the usual window, drinking the constantly appealing bourbon surrounded by familiar faces. It brings me comfort in an otherwise manic world. All creation can be going to hell in a handbag, but you sit me down in the Borough with a glass (or two) of Jack and I'm like a five-year-old on a bouncy castle. No matter what may come up and smack me in the face I will bounce back up, laughing.

Besides, where else in Lancaster would I have Grace as a barmaid? I don't even have to go to the bar; I just settle myself down in my chair and she brings over a good-sized measure of straight bourbon.

"Hey there, Sam," the young girl smiled down at me as she placed my glass tumbler on the table, "not seen you since, you know, Tuesday. How's it going?"

I sipped at the whiskey and smiled as it warmed my insides. "Interesting, Grace. Very interesting. How about you?"

"Oh, you know," she shrugged, "the same old, same old. Lectures, essays, coursework. Spliff joining you?" she gestured to the empty chair opposite me.

I explained that he was not but I was expecting somebody else.

"Oh." A slight crease formed on her forehead. "Caroline?"

I almost choked on my bourbon. "Good God, no!" I spluttered. "I don't think I'll be seeing her for a very long time. Turns out she was using me all along."

"Oh, what a shame. Well if you need anything, you know where I am," she beamed and I am sure she was whistling as she made her way back to the bar.

It was just past two when the door to the Borough swung inwards and the pub descended into silence for that briefest of moments as drinkers turned to surreptitiously gawp at Matthew Slesinski or, as I had previously christened him, Matt the Tat. His spiked-blonde head swivelled from left to right, looking for the reporter that he had arranged to meet. I lifted my glass and he frowned. So it appeared that he recognised me. The facially-tattooed six-footer loped over to my table and peered down at me. "Abalone didn't say you were a reporter," he rumbled. I had to tread carefully here. He might not be a Sith Lord, but I still had the feeling that he could rip me in two if I pushed the wrong buttons.

"I'm not, Matt," I confessed, "but we need to talk. Please, take a seat. You want a drink?"

"I don't do that shit no more." His voice was quiet and threatening as he lowered himself down into the chair. "Just tell me what you want."

"A question first." I downed my drink and placed the heavy tumbler on a beer mat. "Tell me, Matt, why do you follow Malcolm? What's the attraction?"

His eyelids formed narrow slits as he tried to get the measure of me. "He saved me," he eventually revealed.

"From what?"

"From myself."

I nodded sagely. In fact, my earlier suspicions about Matt had been correct. He went on to tell me that he had indeed been a biker and not one of those kind, hippy types that sell New Age jewellery at fantasy fairs. No, he had been a rather vicious leader of a gang that had hung out round Devil's Bridge over in Kirkby Lonsdale. For five years his gang had terrorised the local community, beating up those they saw as weak and extorting money out of local businesses. Then something had happened.

"How did you meet him?"

Matt leaned back in his chair and there he was, the biker of old. Cynicism adorned his face and anger glimmered in his eyes. "What's this about, man?"

"You had an accident, didn't you?"

"So?" he shrugged his colossal shoulders. "Abs tell you that?"

"No. But that wasn't the end of it, was it?"

Silence. Cold, glowering silence. I had hit a nerve.

"You were paralysed in a hospital bed after a fall from your bike, and I'm betting that you were dreaming some crazy dreams while you lay there."

The eyes flickered. Something was edging the anger out of its way: uncertainty. Matt shifted uncomfortably in his chair.

"What did you dream, Matt? What visited you while you slept?"

He ran his fingers through his spiked hair and let out a sharp breath. "How the hell do you know about that? No one knows about that."

"Just a hunch. You're apparently not the only one at Credete who has been dreaming."

"Seriously?"

I nodded. I started to pull back on my fishing rod. Come to Sammy. "And I'm betting that the docs could find no physical reason why you were paralysed either."

Matt swore quietly under his breath. "Look, man, it was real freaky stuff. I can't remember half of it. At the time I thought it was just the morphine and stuff, you know? But remembering it..." His train of thought wandered off into somewhere unpleasant. "There were snakes."

"Snakes?'

"Yeah. Snakes. Big wriggly, slithery snakes." His hands undulated, illustrating the phantasmagoria that he was revisiting. "They came at me out of the grass and wrapped themselves around my legs and my arms. They felt so heavy. So heavy that I couldn't move. And all the time they were squirming against my skin. Damn it, I was naked under those things! It was awful. I felt violated. It was as if they just wanted to pin me down, keep me immobile. Every night it was like that. I'd dream of those wretched snakes, slithering and sliding all over me. I could feel the muscles of their long bodies undulating on me. I used to wake up soaked in sweat every morning. The nurses were constantly changing my sheets.

"Then one day it was different.

"I had the same dream. The snakes came up out of the grass and wrapped themselves around me, pinning me down. They even coiled themselves around my face. I was gagging for breath as they forced their way into my mouth! But suddenly I knew I wasn't alone. There was somebody else there. I could hear his breathing. I could feel a coolness as if a shadow had fallen across me.

"Then there was a word. One single word. 'Leave.'

"I woke up screaming and lurched upright in bed only to be caught in a pair of arms.

"He was there by my side."

"Wallace?"

Matt nodded. "He'd healed me."

Now it was my turn to sit back in contemplation. Slowly, I drummed my fingernails against my teeth. "Matt, what was he doing there? In the hospital, I mean."

Matt frowned. "It never came up. I was just so grateful for him saving me. I guess he must have been visiting someone."

"Hmmm. Or perhaps, you were the one he had come to see."

"What d'you mean?"

Okay. Now was the time to tread really, really carefully. "Matt, Malcolm has incredible powers. You'd agree with me on that, yes?"

He nodded. "Sure. I've seen him do wonderful things. You saw him heal little Melanie on Wednesday. That was fantastic."

I placated him. "It sure was, Matt. It sure was. But here's the thing." I leant in close and beckoned for him to lean forwards too. This was going to be our own little secret. "Don't you think it's just possible that he may have been the *cause* of those illnesses?" I leant back and waited for the reaction.

Well, he didn't hit me, so that was a positive.

"That's not possible."

"Yes it is, Matt. Think about it. How many members do you know have all experienced a similar tale to you? Quite a few, I bet. All these mysterious illnesses which Wallace miraculously cures. It's far more than coincidence that he finds you. Perhaps he's in the right place at the right time, or perhaps someone gets handed a leaflet just when they're at their lowest. Hell, they might even have a dream about going along to one of your meetings. Let's face it, with Wallace, anything is possible!"

Matt's eyes turned to steel once more and lanced me to my chair.

Uh oh. A step too far, perhaps?

"I don't like what you're suggesting." His muscles rippled as he rose from his chair in one fluid movement. "I'm going now and I don't ever want to hear from you again, you hear?" With that he stomped out of the pub.

I sat back into my chair and pondered the conversation. No physical violence, another mysterious illness and a miraculous healing. All in all, I considered it a success.

As I rang the doorbell on Dunkeld Street I checked the time on my Tissot. It was bang on seven. I prayed that Abalone was not one of those types who took forever to get their gear together and leave the house. I had planned this almost to the minute. The door swung inwards and I was greeted by a tall, willowy woman with dark hair and brown eyes. "You must be Sam," she smiled, amused by my obvious confusion. "I'm Heather, Abalone's housemate. Come on in, she's almost ready."

I glanced again at my watch as I stepped over the threshold. Almost was good. I could do almost.

It was a neat little house which was currently occupied by a blonde tornado that was hastily whipping things up into its cyclonic grip: shoes, handbag, phone, keys. Then the storm subdued and there she was stood in front of me, grinning lopsidedly, the picture of demureness, all her hairs in the correct place and those bright blue eyes shining out from behind those cute glasses of hers.

"Well?" she asked.

"The lady doth impress."

She giggled then said to her housemate. “Right, not sure what time I'll be back.”

“No probs,” Heather winked mischievously. “I'm off to Tyler's for the night so you'll have plenty of privacy.”

I'm not sure who blushed most as I ushered my date out of the front door.

“So, Mister Investigator, where are you taking me then?”

A cab pulled up outside right on cue and I opened the door for her. “Alessandro's.”

That one word brought a visage of stunned shock followed by a look of total glee.

Nice one, Sam, I congratulated myself. Nice one.

There is one word and one word alone that describes Alessandro’s: “Swanky.”

I’ve eaten out a lot of times in my life and a number of the dining establishments have tried to achieve that certain finesse but have just missed out somehow: the lighting’s too low, the music’s too loud, the staff are too patronising. This place, however, had it just right. The maître’d was pleasant, not fawning. The tables were smart and well-presented. The open log fire in the waiting area. I could just go on and on. I loved the place.

“I just hope there’s something I can eat. I forgot to check when I booked it,” I mumbled to myself, expecting it to be too good to be true. Abalone smiled up at me, her blue eyes twinkling in the glow of the fire.

“Don’t you fuss,” she soothed, stroking my arm in a manner that I had to admit was rather pleasing. “We had a work's do here a while back. The menu is extensive and they cater for all sorts.” She grinned, “Even nut munchers like you.”

“Nut muncher?” I smiled. “Well I’ve been called a lot of things recently, but that is a first.”

She tinkled a small giggle and handed me a posh-looking, leather-bound menu as we sat ourselves down on the very comfy couch. “Here, look at the pasta. They have a chilli version. I bet you like a bit of spice, don’t you?”

My throat dried up. I was so out of practice at this game. “That would be nice,” I managed eventually to yet another one of her mischievous giggles. “I think I need a drink first. Bourbon, if that’s okay?”

“You don’t need to ask, silly,” she chided. “You’re not one of my pupils, you know?” She called the drinks waiter over and placed our order. When they arrived, I noticed that she had ordered me a double. I drank it swiftly, all the more to her amusement. “You don’t get out that much, do you, Sam?” she mused over her glass of white wine.

“That obvious is it?”

“It’s sweet.” She laid a hand on mine and lightly kissed my cheek. “Not to mention quite appealing.”

As we mulled over the menu, the little men inside my brain who normally make sure that everything runs to order were having somewhat of a panic attack. Apparently someone had been tidying up and had decided that, as I had not been on a proper dinner date for a very long time, that the manual on *How to talk to a good-looking woman who wants to get into your pants* was just sitting around cluttering up the place so had stashed it somewhere. Consequently, at that moment in time, my head was full of the sound of running and shouting as the little men inside were trying to Google what I should do. They weren't having much success, but Abalone didn't seem to mind. She even held my hand as we were led over to our table.

The waiter took our coats and our order, then it happened.

The silence.

You know the one. The one where you know that you should be saying something, but nothing comes, so the silence gets broader and broader, an all-enveloping monster that is going to gobble you up whole. All the time you are aware of the silence and its all-pervading presence and the fact that the very sweet, pretty person you are sat with is patiently waiting for you to *fill* that silence.

Scenarios start to run through your head. Should you mention the weather? Too mundane. Should you comment on her dress? Too obvious. Should you say that you were traumatised as a child and are incapable of small-talk? Too freaky.

In the end, the silence gets bigger and bigger as sentences rise up to your tongue only to be swallowed up by the silence's voracious appetite. You may even go so far as to make a slight gesture before realising that there are no words to accompany it and this makes you look like a mild sufferer of social Tourette's.

No. The silence is always victorious. You cannot win. You just have to sit back, bite your lip and hope that your death by verbal insufficiency will be quick and painless.

"Not much of a talker are you?" Abalone finally ventured.

"More, out of practice," I corrected her, relief washing over me as the silence was beaten back into its box with a very large stick.

"That's okay. I can't stand men who are always banging on about themselves. I prefer the quiet types."

I shrugged nervously. "My lucky day then, I guess."

Abalone's mischievous blue eyes twinkled as she lifted her glass of wine and took a sip. "So," she began, settling the drink back down on the restaurant table, "do you actually believe in all this stuff you deal in? You know, ghosties and goblins and the like? Isn't it all mumbo-jumbo?"

I thought first about a dark-haired vampire offering me as nutritious snack to her new-born and then about and insane, power-crazed lycanthrope being devoured by flesh-eating ants.

"There's *some* truth in it," I said.

She cocked her head to one side and her loose blonde hair hung over her shoulder. "Really? Tell me about it?"

I recalled firing a bullet into the chest of an unarmed woman.

"Not much to tell really. Early days. Besides, you saw what was going on at Saint Edmund's."

She gave an indignant snort and downed the rest of her glass.

"What?"

"You really think the Ballcrusher let that live as some sort of ghostly phenomenon?" she reached for the bottle of pinot grigio, then paused and started to wave her finger up and down. "We all saw what was going on. We know it was something spooky and, whatever it was, you stopped it." Her finger continued to gesticulate. "But that sanctimonious cow has absolutely squashed it flat. 'Schoolchild high jinks,' she says." I watched her hand sway closer and closer to the wine bottle. "School-child high jinks my arse! We all know it was a ghost of some sort, but that bitch..." She let out a frustrated growl and swung her arms out.

My hand shot out to catch the toppling bottle, so did Abalone's. Mine got there first, hers a second later closing around my fingers. We stood the bottle upright. Neither of us removed our hands.

She smiled, not just with her mouth. Her eyes were studying my face, intently. I felt her thumb casually stroke the top of my fingers.

I shifted a bit in my chair.

It had been a while.

A long while.

Having said that, I had no desire to move my hand right away. That would have seemed rude, wouldn't it?

Eventually I nodded to her empty glass: "More wine?"

"Are you trying to get me drunk, Sam?"

"No. No! God no!"

"Pity," she grinned, then removed her hand and offered me her glass for a refill.

I obliged and quickly brought the conversation back round to safer topics. "So what's it like working at Saint Edmund's - Wetherington aside?"

So we chatted, laughed and relaxed into the arms of each other's company. As the courses came and went, we tucked into what was really splendid food and she told me all about how she loved her job but hated having management on her back all the time, pushing harder and harder for impossible results.

"I'd love to work for myself," she said as she finished off an incredibly indulgent chocolate fudge cake. "In fact, why don't I come and work for you?"

I chuckled. "I don't think I need a music teacher on my books."

"No, no," she shook her head as she scraped every last dribble of cream and chocolate sauce out of her dish. "I could be your secretary. You know the sort, the stay at home girl who secretly hopes that she'll be able to tame her boss so that they could drive off into the sunset. I'd spend half my time daydreaming about my fit boss and the other half answering the phone." She put her hand to her cheek and mimed a phone call. "Hello. Spallucci Investigations. I'm afraid the incredibly buff Mister Spallucci isn't here at the moment, but when he comes back I'll give him a message once I've extricated my tongue from his mouth." She looked at me intently with those blue eyes for a few seconds then dissolved into uncontrollable giggles.

I smiled. This was a welcome release from current events.

"Oh!" Abalone started, "that reminds me, Mister Spallucci, I've been meaning to ask, what part of Italy are your folks from?"

I laughed. "Oh God, that one."

She sipped her wine. "What one? A dark secret?" She showed mock conspiracy as she leaned forward into the candle light. "Are they *mafiosi*?"

"Anything but," I smiled. "You want the full story about my name?"

Abalone nodded as she refilled our glasses.

"Okay, my dad was born Eric Smith. As well as being a damn hot trumpeter..."

"Just like his son."

I shrugged off the compliment, "he also used to be a compulsive gambler. If there was anything you could place a bet on, my dad was there. From the gee-gees to the dogs to the toss of a coin. It was always double or nothing. Anything for a bet.

"Anyways, he met my mum, Marion Short and they started dating. Everything was going swimmingly until the stag night."

"I'm guessing we're not just talking a stripper here?"

"Did they have them back in the forties? I'm not sure they did. Anyways, I digress. It was a few weeks before the wedding and Dad was enjoying his drinks with some of his mates, all of whom were gamblers like himself. When one of them says, 'Hey Eric. Don't you think Smith is a boring name for your new lady?' My dad said that it had been good enough for his mum then it would be good enough for his wife. His mate then goes on to say, 'Yeah, well you always play it safe.' My dad denied this vehemently. An argument ensued, the outcome of which being that my dad's mates bet him he would not change his name to something bizarre before the wedding and furthermore, they dared him not to tell my mum-to-be until the moment of the vows."

Abalone was gobsmacked. She sat with her hand over her open mouth. "God, that's terrible! Wait a minute, what about the banns? Surely they would have been in his new name?"

I nodded. "They were indeed, but my dad was the canny one and persuaded my mum that she wasn't feeling well the first day that they were read out in church. As for the second and third reading, she must have missed them. They were never much in the way of church goers."

"So the first time she heard his surname..."

"Was when the clergyman said, 'Do you, Eric John Spallucci....'"

Abalone fell into fits of giggles. "Well I guess she still said, 'I do.' It must give them something to look back on and laugh at in their old age, I guess. Oh. What is it?"

I downed my glass of wine. It tasted bitter compared to my normal tipple. "My dad died about fifteen years ago."

"Sam," she reached out and took my hand, "I'm sorry."

"S'okay. You weren't to know."

"I guess you and your mum must be quite close then."

I let out a dry chuckle. "Not exactly. We haven't spoken in about five years."

"You're kidding? How come?"

"We argued."

"What over?"

"Me refusing to eat her Christmas dinner."

"Sam!"

"Hey don't get all school ma'am with me. I'd been vegan for ages and every Christmas it was the same: 'Haven't you got over this silly phase yet?' I'd had enough."

"But she's your mother!"

I shrugged.

Abalone looked down at the table and whisked up my phone.

"What are you doing?"

"What do you think?"

"Don't you dare!"

"Try to stop me and I'll scream."

I sat and seethed.

"It's ringing," she smiled. "Oh, hello. Mrs Spallucci? Yes, sorry to disturb you, but I'm a friend of your son's. He'd like a word with you." She thrust the mobile out to me and cocked a blonde eyebrow behind her spectacles.

I took the phone and started to speak. "Mum?"

"Sammy? Is that you?" After all the years, she still sounded the same and I could not help but smile. This was the woman who had raised and nurtured me.

She had been there when the noises in my head had brought night terrors.

She had been there as I had stumbled my way through an awkward adolescence.

She had been there when my life had imploded after Caroline had trampled on my heart and Dad had died.

"Yes, Mum. It's me."

There was no, "Well, it's been a long time," or, "Are you still eating stupid food?" Instead, the first thing that my mother asked was, "Who's your friend? Are you dating?"

"Mum!" I sounded like an embarrassed teenager whose parents have told their teacher at parents' evening that they fancy them.

"Oh, I know. None of my business," she apologised. "I can't help but fuss. I am your mother after all."

I grinned. So did Abalone. "Yes, you are. It's good to hear you."

"Well, all you have to do is pick up the phone. You know that, don't you?"

I nodded. "Yes, Mum. I do." I swallowed and fought back the tear that was rising behind my right eye. "Listen, Mum, I have to go. I'm sort of..." I drifted off. What was I sort of doing?

"That's okay, Sammy. You go have fun with your girlfriend. What's her name?"

"Abalone."

"Pretty name. It's a fish, isn't it?"

"A shell, Mum."

She paused before saying, "Don't be a stranger, okay. Ring me again soon."

I promised that I would. We said our goodbyes and hung up.

"Well?" Abalone was sat back wearing a mischievous grin, her arms crossed.

"Well what?" I was also smiling. In fact, I was probably grinning like a loon. Five years of avoidance, animosity and fear had been swept away in one fell stroke by this remarkable young woman.

"A thank you would be nice."

"I think I can manage more than that." I rose from my chair a new man, confidence swimming in my blood stream. I took her face in my hands and pulled her mouth to mine. She resisted not a jot. As her lips worked slowly against me, her floral scent filled my nostrils.

When we parted she groaned contentedly, "Well that's definitely worth top marks."

I chuckled.

"You see," she beamed as she affectionately stroked my hand, "anything is possible."

"Perhaps it is," I agreed. With my new-found mettle I was about to suggest we could go back to my place when her phone chirruped an interruption.

"Sorry. I'd better check this," she apologised, blushing and smiling. She tapped the phone and read the text message.

Her smile faded.

She stood up.

"I'm sorry, Sam. I have to go."

"What? Are you okay?"

She drew some money out of her purse and lay it on the table before turning and making for the cloakroom.

"Abalone? What's the matter?"

"Please. Sam," she said, her voice dull, lifeless; her blue eyes downcast, avoiding me "I have to go now." With that she walked away, retrieved her coat and left.

I sat back in my chair, my gast truly flabbered. What the hell had happened? One minute there had been smiles, orchestras and cherubs; the next... I made to rise then thought again. No. I wouldn't pursue her. That would be the wrong thing to do. Something had obviously upset her. Something in the text. Something that she couldn't share with me. Something personal.

Yes, that was it. Something personal had cropped up and she had to attend to it quickly. It would be wrong for me to intrude.

That didn't make it any less of a bummer, though.

I sighed, tossed my half of the bill on the table and rang for a taxi. Ten minutes later, I was half dozing in the back of a cab on the A6 back to Lancaster. The sweet scent of flowers kept enveloping my memory, causing my drooping eyes to turn up at the corners. The touch of her skin had been divine; her soft, beautiful skin. I longed to touch it once more. As I dozed off in the back of the cab, images started to prod my memory. There was something odd. Something was nagging me. How could a personality change so quickly? My mind wandered as the headlights from other cars splashed over me. I saw Flint from the town hall, anxious and afraid as he told me about his concerns. Then just a short while later he was dead. Next I saw the young waitress who had been a bright, chatty thing until Wallace had apparently turned her into a self-sacrificing, murder machine.

Wallace.

Anything is possible.

Anything...

My eyes snapped open. Dear God!

I leant forward to the cab driver as we drove down Scotforth Road. "Quick, I need to get to Dunkeld Street right now!"

I rocketed out of the cab and charged across the pavement to Abalone's front door. As the car drove away, I hammered heavily on the dark blue wood. To hell with anyone watching.

The door swung inwards and my stomach lurched. I stepped over the threshold into darkness. "Abalone!" I called out into the unlit house. Unlit, that was, except for one light worming its way into the gloom from an upstairs room. I bounded up to the next floor two steps at a time until I reached the closed door with the light seeping out from underneath. "Abalone?" I knocked tentatively at the door.

There was no reply.

Cautiously, I grabbed the handle and turned. The door swung inwards and steam wafted over me, causing me to blink as I entered the small bathroom.

The thing that struck me more than anything else was how red the bathwater looked. There were no words, no expletives. I had no time for that, none whatsoever. I flew across the tiled floor and grabbed Abalone's slashed wrist. Blood was still seeping out into the warm water. I pushed my thumb down on the cut and raised it above her head to try and stem the flow. With my other hand I felt at her neck

No pulse.

"Abalone!" I yelled, my voice echoing round the small room. "Abalone!"

There was no movement. Not a flutter. I dropped the wrist and decided more action was needed. I drove one arm under her shoulders and the other under her knees – this was not a time for modesty – and hoicked her clumsily out of the tub onto the floor. I lowered my mouth to hers, pinched her nose shut, and gave two deep breaths then placed my hand together below her breasts and applied thirty quick compressions.

I swore violently as, with each compression, dark blood spurted out of her savaged wrist. I grabbed a towel and tied a tight tourniquet to her arm then went back to the CPR.

Two breaths. Thirty compressions.

Two breaths. Thirty compressions.

Two breaths. Thirty compressions.

Two breaths. Thirty compressions.

Two breaths. Thirty compressions.

Two breaths. Thirty compressions.

Two breaths. Thirty compressions.

Again.

Again.

Again.

Again.

Over and over. Each time I checked for breath. Each time I came back up and continued the same pattern.

Eventually, I realised that my hands were wet and it wasn't from her body which had begun to dry out. It was from my tears. They were flooding from my eyes as they realised the hopelessness of the task.

The compressions grew slower and slower as I gradually ground to a halt.

I had lost her.

This bright, young spark that had only just entered my life had been so awfully removed. I sank back on my haunches and there, for the first time, I saw it; drawn on the tiled wall above the bath in her own blood:

An upper case T surrounded by two swirls. An Asherah.

My phone rang.

I tore it out of my pocket, slid the accept icon across and spat with venom into the mouthpiece, “You bastard! You utter bastard! Why are you doing this?”

“Now now, Samuel,” Wallace's patronising voice sauntered across the airwaves into my ear. “I did nothing apart from inform Miss Morris that the man she was sat opposite was in fact just using her to acquire knowledge about me and my machinations.” He paused. Then with a wicked twinkle in his voice said, “I take it that she did not receive the news lightly.”

“I'll kill you! I'll kill you!” I screamed down the phone. “I'll come looking for you then I'll rip that black heart out of your smug, puffed up chest.”

“Yes, Samuel,” he crooned, “such passion. Like when you dispatched that wolf and his wretched sister. Feel that anger. Use it. Come find me. It will be quite the family reunion.” With that he hung up.

I slumped back against the wall and shut my eyes. I wanted none of this. I wanted a simple, quiet life.

And I would kill to get it. I would hunt him down, corner him, wrap my hands around his neck and...

My eyes shot open.
Family reunion.
Oh no!

# Chapter Fifteen

I thought my lungs were going to explode as my legs pounded left right, left right up onto Wyresdale Road and past Christ Church parish church. I've never been much of a runner, never had the need, but now I was calling on every last unit of energy I had to charge my way up to Caroline's.

He knew! The bastard knew, but how? I had not told him that John was my son. The old maxim came back to slap me round the face: *Anything is possible*. Sure, anything is possible, but how was he doing it? What was his secret? He had talked time and time about his benefactor about how she had changed his life. How could it possibly be the same one from university? If so, was she somehow pulling his strings? Was she this mysterious woman that Sophia had mentioned? "Devotion or death," that was what the curious librarian had said that Wallace's mistress demanded. Well she seemed to be getting plenty of both, but who was she?

After our little episode with Gerald the phantom caretaker, Spliff and I had discussed who Wallace's mysterious companion had been. Spliff had been insistent that it was some old, lavender-drenched spinster who was releasing some frustrated sexual tension with a young plaything. I disagreed. I had heard the killer heels and the seductive voice of Wallace's female companion that night and I was convinced that she was more of a leather and scent girl rather than wool and humbugs. Then, not to mention there was that voice at the Credete meeting in the Ashton Hall. The weird thing was, if it was the same person then it did not sound like it had changed at all. Wallace had said that she was old, but both times the voice had sounded young and, dare I say, sultry. A vampire perhaps? As I rounded the corner onto Coulston Road, past Williamson Park, I quickly discounted the idea. It didn't feel right.

Not only was I known to the Children of Cain but it didn't seem their style. They were creatures of the shadows, watching waiting for whatever this Divergence thing was. They did not seem the type to be manipulators.

No, Wallace's benefactor was someone or something else. Of that I was fairly sure.

I pulled to a halt just down the road from Caroline's house. All this speculation was, right now, just that: speculation. I had to concentrate on the present, on the moment. Wallace had threatened Caroline and John, my family. He was either planning something or, more likely, had set something nefarious and spiteful into motion. The image of Abalone lying drained of blood in her red-stained bath flooded back into my memory. I pounded it back into the darkest recess with a big stick and cautiously crossed the road, looking up at Caroline's windows for any signs of life. There was none. No lights escaped from behind the curtains. No noise came from the house.

I walked up the small path to the house and pressed gently on the front door. For the second time that night I found a door swinging into pitch black. This was most definitely not good. There was no shouting this time around. I walked as carefully and as stealthily as I could. Gently, I swung the door back into its frame, making sure not to close it in case the latch gave away my presence. I stood for a moment, allowing my eyes to adjust to the insidious gloom. The hallway led off in front of me, terminating at the foot of the staircase to the upper floor. To my right were two doors, first the living room and then the dining room which led onwards to the kitchen. I edged my way along the wall and found the door to the first room. The handle turned silently and I nudged the door open, my heart pounding. Inside was a sofa and an armchair facing a large flat screen television. I closed the door and made for the next room.

Next was the dining room. The rear window's curtain had not been drawn and the moonlight aided me in noting that there was nothing amiss here. The dining table was clean and tidy; there was no trace of their evening meal. The Chas Jacobs still hung on the opposite wall. I progressed onwards to the kitchen. Pots and pans lay washed on the drainer, waiting to be put away. I ran a finger over a saucepan. It was dry. At a guess, they had eaten tea as usual, washed up and left them to dry on their own. From the lack of water on the pan, this must have been at least a few hours ago. If something had happened here, it had happened very recently. I scanned the rest of the kitchen. Everything was neat and tidy. There was none of the detritus on the counter that I would find in my kitchen: a packet of cereal, breadcrumbs and the ubiquitous stray teaspoon. What's more, there was no sign of any struggle.

I turned to my left and my eyes fell on the door down to the cellar. Rather than having a handle, there was an old-style latch which I lifted silently and tugged on to open the door. As I peered down the old wooden stairs I could make out a dim light permeating from somewhere down below. I leaned my back against the wall and crept foot after foot down the stairs. Passing down below the dining room I could make out a room that seemed to run the length of the house. There was a slight musty smell that is found in most cellars due to the lack of air flow, however there was also the unmistakable scent of expensive aftershave.

"Do come down, Samuel," Wallace called out. "I think we need to chat."

With all attempts at stealth foiled, I walked with fake calm down the rest of the stairs. Most of the cellar was in darkness apart from one corner where Wallace was sat casually behind an old desk upon which were set a CD player of some sorts and a candle, which was the only source of illumination.

"Making yourself at home?" I was fighting back the overwhelming urge to lunge forward and choke the man to death but I knew it would be futile. I had yet to establish the whereabouts of Caroline and John. He was my only link to their safety.

And he knew it.

"So, Samuel," he purred, the glow of the lone candle giving his face a skeletal appearance, "how's life treating you?"

"It's been somewhat better." I descended from the bottom step and stood across the room from him. A quick lunge; that's all it would take. I could throw myself at him.

"Oh, I imagine that's probably the case, isn't it? I believe your little date didn't go so well this evening?" Those perverted eyes were dancing in the fire of the flame.

I clenched and unclenched my hands. My face stayed turned to him but my eyes flickered quickly around my surroundings. They saw nothing, just darkness.

"Nothing to say? What a pity." He wore a mask of mock sorrow. "Mind you, Miss Morris had very little to say either, when I told her about how you were just using her to get to me. I imagine it upset her... somewhat."

I could feel the muscles in my legs and my shoulders tensing. They were wanting to charge at him, right here, right now. I could end this. My hands around his throat, grasping, clawing, tearing; watching the life drain from those orange orbs.

But I had to wait. I had to wait.

The sorrow faded and was replaced with glee. "My, my, you really are playing the strong, silent type tonight. No little quips? None of your dull, little sci-fi anecdotes? Not in the mood are we?" Wallace shook his head. "Perhaps this will loosen your tongue?" He raised his right hand in an upward motion and, around the edge of the cellar, candles burst into flame illuminating the far end of the wall. Caroline and John were there. She was bound to an old wooden armchair the stuffing of which had seen better days and John was curled up in a tight ball in the far corner of the cellar with a circular chalk marking around his foetal form.

I had what I needed to know. Nothing held me back now. I surged forward, hands outstretched like talons. I made it halfway across the room until I felt my feet leave the floor and my momentum stopped to a shuddering halt.

Frantically, I tried to move my arms but they were locked by an invisible force, as was the rest of my body. I tried to twist and turn but to no effect. All I could do was scream in frustration at my captor who now walked up to me and inspected me as an artist inspects his canvas.

"So volatile, Samuel. So predictable." Wallace's voice was soft and low. He sounded like a cat preaching to a canary that is about to be served up as an *hors d'oeuvres*. "What did you really hope to achieve? I can see right through you. You wear but one face, whereas I, like the Chimera, wear many."

Chimera. I thought frantically back to my thespian abductors and the statue in Wallace's collection.

Wallace nodded. "Yes, you see it now. Well, part of it, anyway. Those bumbling fools were to serve my purpose. I drew them together, trained them and led them down a path that they thought would bring them riches and reward. Unfortunately, they decided that they had to take care of you. Fools! You were a nobody, a hack. What harm could you have done? All they had to do was keep themselves hidden until I needed them and they couldn't manage that." He shook his head. "The five of them couldn't even kill themselves properly. Two botched attempts meant that I had to intervene.

"And then there was you." He stood before me, his arms crossed, pondering something. "I could have killed you straight away, be done with the matter. Your little girlfriend there would have taken the hint and scurried back to her news desk where she could have penned sweet little anecdotes about brave puppies saving drowning toddlers or whatever tripe it is she writes. However, my benefactor was quite insistent. You were to be kept alive. You were to be brought into our fold.

"She had plans for you. She alone knows why. Personally, I think you're a failure. Look at you: you chain smoke, you reek of bourbon, you have no life. I offered you a way out of your pitiful existence but you threw it back in my face." Wallace shook his head. "Very disappointing, Samuel. Very disappointing.

"What was it that my benefactor saw in you? I wondered. Then I realised that, for some reason hidden from me, she must have been afraid of you. Perhaps she feared that the two of us together could have risen up and wrested her power from her hands. I decided that like primordial dragons we could turn on our mother, breaking free of her constraining grip.

"But no, it wasn't to be. Your reaction to that young waitress proved that all too clearly. You are just like everybody else, Samuel, weak and pitiful. You do not have the strength to make the necessary sacrifices for the benefit of creation.

"I however suffer from no such compunction whatsoever."

As Wallace walked across the room towards Caroline and John I felt myself moving, gliding with him. He stopped and my body tilted backward to a horizontal position before being folded into a chair next to Caroline. I flashed my eyes to my left. I could just make out the rise and fall of her body breathing. At least she was alive.

"Now," my captor clapped his hands together as if about to explain the boundaries of the play area for children on a picnic, "I'm going to loosen your bonds. Not entirely. No, I have no doubt that if I did that then you would try something stupidly pointless again, but just enough for you to talk. All of you. What a gay conversation you could have." He blinked and I felt the muscles around my mouth loosen. I gasped a ragged breath and immediately tried to wrench myself from the chair. It was no use. Whatever power he was using, I was still held fast. There was a groaning from my left and I found that I could now turn my head towards her. "Caroline," my voice was dry and croaky, "can you hear me?"

"Sam?" Her voice was muffled and tired as if waking from a deep sleep. "Is that... What? Where?" She wrestled with the straps that held her bound. "Sam!" She screamed. Her dark eyes shot at me then across the room. "John! John!" she wailed as she tried desperately to free herself.

John started to come round. He rolled over onto all fours and climbed heavily to his feet. "Mum? Sam?" He took a step forwards and was met with a blinding flash of light as his foot touched the chalked circle and he was pushed back into the centre of the ring. Panic rose in his eyes as it did in Caroline's. "What... what's happening?"

Caroline was now wriggling frantically against her bonds, her bobbed hair swaying back and forth against her cheeks. "Let me out! Let me out!" Her head snapped up in the direction of Wallace as he made a deprecating tutting noise. "You!" She was a trapped lioness whose cub was in danger. The problem was that her claws had been tied and she was in no position to attack.

"Just calm down," I said quietly. "You'll achieve nothing."

"Piss off!" she spat. "This is all *your* fault. It's *always* your fault." She turned back to John. "It's okay, sweetie. Mummy will get you out."

"Oh, really? And how do you propose to do that then?" I was tired. I was cranky. I couldn't help the sarcasm. I had left a lovely young woman dead in her bathroom to come here and what was I getting? The same old, same old. "In case you hadn't noticed, we are both somewhat incapacitated."

We both looked up at Wallace as he chuckled quietly to himself. "Ah, the wonders of the modern family unit. And we wonder why humanity never progresses. Samuel is quite right Ms Adamson; you cannot possibly escape. All you can do is sit.

"And watch."

My blood ran cold. "Watch what?"

"Samuel, Ms Adamson, I have somewhat of a predicament facing me. For some time now, I have been planning the future, not just of humanity but of creation. As Samuel knows, I rather feel that our situation at the moment is corrupt, devoid of hope and totally irretrievable. As a result, I have found it necessary to implement a plan that will ultimately rectify this.

"I am going to bring about the Divergence.

"My benefactor tells me that it is quite simple. All it requires is five willing sacrifices. Five individuals who are known to me that feel they have nothing left to live for. Five individuals who see this life for what it really is: totally devoid of prospect and hope.

"Now, I had those individuals prepared and ready to give themselves for the greater good in the form of the John O'Gaunt production team. However, something went terribly wrong. One went insane and did not receive my final call and then another seems to have hesitated and performed a less than satisfactory job."

"Philips and Brande," I growled, frustrated and annoyed at having to listen to my captor revel in his own story once more.

Wallace nodded at me. "Very good, Samuel. You've been paying attention. Anyway," he continued, obviously relishing every moment in the spotlight, "I had to dispatch the two failures and start again. I needed a clean canvas on which to create my masterpiece, so to speak."

Caroline: "Five new sacrifices."

"Indeed, Ms Adamson. Five new lives to extinguish of hope and remove from this mortal coil. So far, I have clocked up three: a waitress in a dead end job, a scared caretaker and a betrayed lover. Of course, their predicaments alone were nowhere near enough to merit them taking their own lives, but I can be *very* persuasive.

"My benefactor has taught me well."

"You need two more." My blood had gone from chilled to frozen.

"Indeed I do. Indeed I do. I wonder what could make such loving parents lose all hope?" His orange eyes drifted over to our son, trapped in the magic circle.

All anger drained from Caroline's face. Her mouth hung open and her eyes widened. "No. Please, no. You can't he's all I have."

Wallace crouched before her, his eyes level with hers. "Oh dear. Does that make you sad? Does that make your little heart hurt? How does it feel to have something snatched away from you? Can't you play with it anymore?"

"Please... please..." Tears came with the words.

"Why should you really care, Ms Adamson, ace reporter? You were the one who gave your son the wrist bands. You were the one who wanted him and his little friends to join my group."

Wallace turned his head towards me. "Such a caring mother, isn't she? Using her only son just as much as she used you. She willingly jeopardised both your lives for a news story. Such a doting lover and mother, don't you think?" He walked back to the table and started to fiddle with the controls on the CD player.

I looked at Caroline, tears flowing freely as she sat slumped in the chair. She was a broken woman. John stood over in the circle, helpless, wanting to run to his mother. There was a click from the CD and stringed instruments started to play a slow, doleful tune. Wallace closed his eyes and breathed deep. "Ah, Beethoven's *Seventh*. Magical. I had considered the *Moonlight* for this, but it had been used before in some film if I recall correctly, so I thought it would be a touch cliché."

"The captor wasn't murdered in cold blood in *Misery*. Just incapacitated."

Wallace raised an eyebrow at me. "Murdered? Oh! Ha ha! You think..." He clapped his hands together with glee. "Oh no, you have me quite wrong, Samuel." Woodwind joined the strings as he continued. "As well as changing reality for the better, I have a little side project that I want to try out. Have you ever heard of Beyond? It's a charming little place that was a sort of accident at the beginning of time. So I am told, three realms were created: Heaven with all its angels and love etcetera, etcetera; Earth and the physical realm with all its... well you know what *that's* like; then there was Beyond. Beyond was the place where the eye of God never looked. It was the place that even the angels feared to go. It was a place with no time or sustenance. If one was to go there, one would be separated from all creation.

"One would not exist.

"Well it appears that a travelling companion of my benefactor accidentally found a way to open Beyond. I've been dying to try it out for years and now I have a suitable subject."

My head played tennis between Wallace, smug and puffed up at his imminent victory, and John, forlorn and captive – not really sure what was happening. "Why? Why would you do that?"

Wallace frowned in confusion. "Why? Because I can." He turned side on from me and faced John as the music started to swell in volume. He closed his eyes and his mouth opened to speak.

"...

"...

"..."

There were words, there really were, but I could not possibly describe them. They were as if someone had taken the sounds and removed them. I could hear him speaking above the crescendo of music but my brain could not translate the uttering into anything that made sense. It left the space in my auditory processors blank.

What was not blank was the space in the circle behind John. It split open and a black maw widened behind the terrified teenager. Caroline rocked back and forth in her chair, moaning and crying. I tried to free myself but could not even stretch my fingers.

Wallace raised a hand and tendrils of blackness reached out from the split in reality, wrapping themselves around my only son. They snaked around his jeans and along his arms dragging him into a doomed embrace.

"Dad!" He cried out. "Dad!"

"John!" I screamed, my neck taught with grief, frustration and anger as he slid backwards into the darkness. "John, I'll find you! I'll find you!"

And with that he was gone, sucked into God knows where. Wallace lowered his hand and the portal shut. The chalk markings rose from the floor and dissolved into the air. The music reached the end of the track and there was silence. Wallace walked to the table, unplugged the CD player, glanced casually over his shoulder and the next thing I knew, everything was black.

# Chapter Sixteen

When I came to, the first thing I realised was that I had the mother of all headaches. The second thing I realised was that I was completely alone. It wasn't just being in the cellar with nobody else, there was just that feeling. You know the one, don't you? It's the one when you wake up in the night after having that terrible nightmare: your pulse is racing and your skin is soaked with sweat. You wake up with a start into the grim reality of the night and realise that you are all alone to face your fears. There is no one there to roll over towards and cuddle up against. There is no one there to tell you that it was just a dream. There is no one there to gently take your hand and stroke your fingers until you drift back off to a restful sleep.

You are totally alone and have to deal with the horror of the previous night completely on your own.

I lit a Lucky and poked around a bit. There wasn't really much to discover. Wallace had meticulously cleaned up after himself: the CD player was gone as were the candles. I decided that the cellar was a bust and ventured back upstairs.

As I entered the kitchen I saw the light of morning creeping its way into the house. It was one of those grey, tiresome mornings where you would normally crawl back under the sheets and ignore the rain that drizzled down the window panes. I did not have that luxury. Even here, in the normally bustling heart of the home, there was that feeling of emptiness, that something had been untimely ripped from the womb of domesticity.

"Dad! Dad!"

John's last words rang out and I forced myself not to blink or shut my eyes as I would be forced to look upon the nightmare of him being dragged down into that creeping portal once more. Instead I proceeded to give the rest of the house a quick once over. It was, as I had suspected, totally empty apart from a useless investigator and a nearly burnt out cigarette.

My tour brought me back to the dining room. Where was Caroline? Where had she fled to? I wanted to track her down and make things right with her, check that she wasn't doing anything foolish. As I drummed my fingernails on my teeth, my eyes lit upon the picture that dominated the wall and I nodded to myself.

I headed for the front door.

She was stood by the viewing stations that overlook the city. I thought she was crying, but it was hard to tell as she was drenched from the continuous drizzle that had crept into town that morning. I walked over the mosaic pavement under the Ashton Memorial and approached her with extreme caution. "Caroline?" I ventured. There was no response. "Caroline?"

"I heard you the first time."

I winced at the simmering anger in the voice.

"Sorry."

"Sorry? Sorry? Is that all you have to say?" Her arms were wrapped tight around her middle and she turned her back to me. Her shoulders were shaking. There was no mistaking the tears now.

"I couldn't do anything."

Silence.

"I was held tight."

She turned on me, her hands clenching and unclenching by her sides, the increasing precipitation running down her brown hair and onto her face.

"You think that makes this any better? Do you?" Her face contorted in grief and anguish, her eyes half open as tears forced their way out to mingle with the rain. "He was all I had. My son. My boy. All I had."

I walked over towards her and made to put my arms around her.

"No!" she screamed, batting my arms away furiously. "No! Don't you dare. Don't you dare! Don't you touch me."

"Caroline, please. I want to make it right."

She shook her head frantically from side to side, the rain flicking off her fringe. "No. You can't. You know that. He's gone, Sam. Gone.

"And it's all my fault!" She crumpled down onto the floor, her head in her hands and cried in a manner I had never witnessed before. The sounds from her mouth were barely human and she tugged frantically at her hair as if trying to pull it out by its roots. "I set this up. I set this up. I condemned him!"

I bent to comfort her but she exploded up from the floor, her arms pushing me backwards causing me to stumble slightly. "I don't deserve your pity, Sam. I'm poisonous. I'm toxic."

I backed off, hands outstretched. "Okay, I get it, but tell me one thing."

"What?"

"Did you ever really love me?"

She stared at me through the rain, her brown eyes wide in disbelief.

"You're asking me that? Now?"

"I need to know."

And we stood there, two people drenched by the rain and I looked deep into those brown eyes. What did I see? Did I see love? Did I see regret? Did I see any little glimmer to make me think that she had any care or compassion for me?

I saw nothing.

"Goodbye, Sam." With that she turned and ran out of my life, her tears for her lost son blending with the rain that washed down her face.

I stood and watched her go. My heart ached to chase after her, to calm her down and bring her comfort but, for once in my life, my brain won through. It would be useless. She would just push me away, consumed with guilt for having sacrificed her child. My face would be a constant reminder of what she had lost. Every time she looked at me she would never see my love for her, but the pain of her ultimate loss. Besides, she would never love me. She had lost the one person that she had ever truly loved. Her greed for personal advancement had sent him into danger and the universe had punished her.

I shoved my hands into my pockets and sighed. What was I to do now? I was no challenge to Wallace. The man had powers that outstripped my mere mortal imaginings.

I needed something close to a miracle. I turned and made to walk away when I noticed something odd. Just off to the side was a dry patch of ground. All around it was drenched from the rain pouring down on top of it, but this little area looked as if there was something there – something stood there. I paused, lit up my second Lucky of the day, slowly inhaled whilst walking over to the curious patch of dry and puffed out a stream of smoke about head height. I was rewarded with a short, strangled cough.

"Peek-a-boo," I smiled. "I see you."

The air in front of me shimmered and there stood the mysterious Alec.

"Don't you think that's getting a bit tired now?"

"People never tire of a classic," he shrugged.

I tilted my head to one side. I'd let him have that one. Then, drawing slowly on the cigarette, I raised an inquisitorial eyebrow.

"There's been another suicide," he said.

# Chapter Seventeen

I watched the world through a fug of malaise whilst seated on an unforgiving metal bench at Lancaster train station. "1900," proclaimed an ornamented guttering on the opposite platform, a testament to the typically Victorian construction. Formal light brown blocks of neatly chiselled sandstone sat cemented one upon another, forming regular symmetrical patterns in the stout walls; just like so many of the older buildings in Lancaster – those which had not been turned into trendy wine bars. These old relics were memories of the Blakeian mills and the dark times of the slave trade (so conveniently forgotten: "How did we finance that fine building? Through linen and blood, my son. Linen and blood.") Also, like so much of Lancaster, this natural stone-work had been mutilated and scarred by more than a century of the vagaries of architectural fashion. Corrugated metal sheets and rust-reddened rivets made shabby canopies – a testament to the height of 1970s good taste.

The olden times were hidden behind the new; disregarded, reviled, forgotten. Just like the thousands of black slaves whose lives and travail had brought their taskmasters the vast profits that paid for the construction of these once grand buildings. Not many know. Even less seem to care. Some things never change. The wonderment that is humanity. Beauty and cruelty walking hand in hand: married, entwined, inseparable.

I sighed.

It was indeed a depressing line of thought, but then it was hardly surprising that my mind was wandering down that particularly grey and dismal avenue. Caroline hating and loathing me more than ever, had walked out of my life for good. John, my sweet, new-found son of only a few days, had been snatched away from me and taken God-alone knows where.

Beyond.

What sort of a place was that? How can something be truly *beyond*? Surely there is always something? There cannot be a complete absence of something if someone is there? Surely?

Then there was Wallace. Malcolm Bloody Wallace.

Still out there.

Still superior.

Still killing.

I looked down the train track to where police seemed to be wandering around aimlessly, occasionally bending down and picking things up from between the dark sleepers. I did not want to know what they were putting in their little plastic bags. Christ. My stomach turned somersaults and I prayed for Alec to get a move on and get back here.

I needed a smoke but even that was *Beyond.* All around me posters proclaimed that it was against the law to light up in this place. So is getting some poor bastard to jump in front of the nine o'clock express service from Glasgow. Perhaps Wallace hadn't read that particular poster.

I felt the pack of Luckies in my pocket and was about to say “Sod it!” and pull one out, but then I remembered that not only does a kick in the ass from some officious little prick hurt, but it would not pay to get people's backs up when we needed to get down and see the site of the suicide.

There went my stomach again.

Had I eaten yet today? I didn't think so. I had just gone home to change out of my blood-stained clothes before meeting up here with Alec. The mysterious Alec. He had snapped his fingers and I had come running, just like I seemed to be doing for everyone else that walked into my life at the moment. “Grow a spine, Spallucci,” I grumbled to myself and kept my little lucky companions stowed away in discreet secrecy whilst sitting on my hands waiting for Mystery Boy.

I didn't have to wait that long, thank God.

“It's just down the track,” he motioned to the milling of police I had been watching as he came out of the Supervisor's Office, “Let's go.”

I lifted myself off the bench, its ridges still fresh on my behind, and followed after the youth. Down the track was good. Down the track was away from the station, away from a public place of work.

There I could have a smoke.

I knew that when I saw what was waiting for us there I would need one.

They had hardly made any impact on the mess when we arrived.

It's very hard to describe what the scattered, drawn out remains of someone who threw themselves under a speeding locomotive look like. The feel of the macabre is immense. There is an overwhelming air of disgust at the pools of blood between the lines and the splayed edges of torn limbs lying casually by the wayside.

"Pesto sauce," said Alec. "When you get the mix wrong and it goes runny with lumps in it."

I ignored the flippant comment and, pulling my collar up close round my neck, made my way to the scene of the carnage. I felt ever so slightly unnerved as a uniformed officer marched over towards us. "I'd ask what your plan was," Alec whispered, "but you seem to make things up as you go along."

"What do you think you're doing here, Spallucci?" demanded the officer. I wasn't surprised that he had recognised me. The police seemed to have been my constant companions recently.

"I'm on a case."

"Well you can piss off back to your tarot cards. This is a suicide and nothing else, understand?"

I was about to plead my case when Alec stepped forward.

"It's very important that we see the remains." There was a certain lilt to his young voice. "You will let us through."

For a moment the copper just stood and stared at us. Then he nodded and stepped back to let us pass. "Thank you," said Alec.

As we made our way down to the train track I questioned the youth, "Where did you learn that trick, Obi Wan?"

He smiled. "At the Academy."

I let the matter drop. There would be a better time and a place for explanations later on, I hoped.

We encountered no more resistance. It was organised chaos down under the bridge. Police were scurrying about left and right. As of yet there was no sign of a forensics team and certainly no sign of an ambulance - the remains of the jumper were very visibly dead. You don't tend to survive losing both your legs and having your head ripped off while your internal organs are being pulverised along a train track.

"Quickly," urged Alec, "We don't have much time. We need to look closer at the body."

I decided to let him do the looking. I just kept watch. Sensitive stomach, you know.

"He jumped alright."

I dared a quick look over my shoulder to see what Alec was doing. He had removed his right glove and had actually placed his bare hand on a piece of fragmented tissue. "*Jesus*," I moaned as my stomach started to lurch. I fought down the urge to foul a crime scene with hot, steaming vomit and wrenched my gaze away from Alec's examination.

"There's something else though," he continued. "This man had lost all total hope." I grimaced as I heard a squelching noise from behind. What the devil was he doing? Treating it like Play-Doh? "He was afraid that his past was going to catch up with him. Terrified in fact."

I caught a sight of something amongst the strewn carnage and picked my way over carefully.

"This man," Alec continued, "must have had a real chequered history. He had gotten himself a real respectable life recently, but before..." He took a sharp intake of breath. "Well he was no saint for sure. There were girls, drugs, alcohol and lots of-"

"Bikes." I finished, peering down at the remains of a familiar tattooed cheek. "Lots of motorbikes." I heard raised voices and noticed that people were starting to look over in our direction. Apparently the little Jedi mind-trick had started to wear off. "Company's coming, Alec. Time to leave."

So we did. Quickly.

"You've gone quiet."

We were walking back down Market Street towards the city centre. Lancaster is quite small as cities go and most places can be reached on foot if people are willing to put the effort in. The train station is just a couple of minutes' walk from the main shopping area, an area where the shoppers and workers would be busying themselves that autumn morning, unaware that an innocent man who had turned his life around from vice and violence to clean living had been ritually murdered by the man that he regarded as his saviour.

I took sweet relief from the tobaccoey heaven that was a Lucky Strike.

"Those things are really bad for you, you know?"

We stood outside Waterstone's book shop, waiting for the lights to change so that we could cross the one-way system. I blew out a long puff of smoke, looked at my new companion and gave a short chuckle. Companion. It made me sound like Doctor Who. Shaking my head, I decided I couldn't be bothered waiting for the lights and walked out into the flow of traffic. There was much screeching of brakes and presenting of fingers but I ignored them. A pair of trainers ran after me.

"Why do you do that?"

"Why are you here?" I had stopped next to the estate agents on the corner to stub the remains of my cigarette out on the nearby bin. "Tell me. Why this sudden interest in me? You were quite happy to lurk in the shadows before, all..." I flapped my arms, "guardian angel style. Now, here you are, talking ten to the dozen, a mouth full of questions without so much as an explanation. I've had a really shit couple of weeks Alec and, quite frankly, right now I feel like finding the nearest pub and drinking myself to oblivion. So, just for once, give me a straight answer, will you? Why are you here?"

His dark eyebrows knotted together. "You need help."

I crossed my arms and let my eyes survey him from his feet upwards. His trainers had seen much better days; they were worn and muddy. His blue jeans were scuffed at the edges and covered in grass stains. His jacket was crumpled and had been roughly stitched back together in numerous places. His chin was slightly stubbled in the sort of growth that teenage boys would normally call in prideful delusion a beard. On his back was a grubby, well-loved back pack, that had the corner of a sleeping bag poking out of the top.

He shrugged. "That, and I need a place to stay for a while."

For some weird reason, I couldn't help but grin and I don't think it was one of his mind tricks.

He talked almost incessantly on the way over to Dalton Square. About what, I'm not too sure. I think I zoned out once we turned onto Penny Street. I was still in a morose stupor from the events of that morning and the weekend. Suicides, deaths, one mystical disappearance and a shed-load of hatred from your ex can do that to you. Alec didn't seem to mind. He just seemed pleased to have someone to talk to. From what I recall, there were comments about the smell of coffee when we passed Starbucks, opinions on the decline in the economy when we passed the empty Next shop on Horseshoe Corner and other little snippets that washed over me as we headed south on Penny Street. To be honest, it was rather soothing to have someone who seemed more concerned with the day-to-day stuff for once rather than being bombarded with the paranormal horrors that had been dogging me recently.

It wasn't until we had entered my flat and he had dumped his pack on the floor that he said, "You did the best that you could, you know? Wallace is incredibly powerful."

I shrugged. It was little consolation. "I'll put the kettle on," was all that I could manage. I meandered off into the kitchen, leaving Alec to investigate his new surroundings like a puppy in a new house. At least he would not pee on the carpet.

"I love the clocks!" he called out cheerily as I spooned some instant coffee into two mismatched mugs. One was slightly chipped and I ran my thumb over the damaged glaze. So functional yet so fragile. The slightest thing could turn this simple utensil into a pile of shattered fragments. All you had to do was pick it up then drop it from a great height.

Just as Wallace had done with Matthew Slesinski.

Then, once more I was stood over his tattered remains, chunks of flesh strewn along the train track and pools of blood thick in the gravel. My stomach churned and I ran for the bathroom. I made it just in time as my guts puked up into the toilet. This was just too much. How could I cope with all this? I felt like I had become an angel of death and everyone I touched was dropping down dead from an unseen plague. My stomach churned and more vomit spewed into the pan.

As I groaned to God on the great, white telephone I became aware of footsteps behind me. My cheeks flushed with embarrassment but I did not dare let go of the toilet as more bile began to rise.

Then suddenly it was gone.

The churning had quelled to a soft eddy and the burning bile tasted like clear fresh water which trickled softly back down my gullet. I knelt up, wiped my mouth with some toilet paper and looked up at the boy standing behind me.

"Better?" he asked.

I nodded. "Much. If you wouldn't mind?" I motioned to the wash basin.

"Sure." He filled the glass tumbler there with water and offered it to me. I drank it down slowly. Then peered in surprise at the clear liquid. It tasted of...

"Ginger is good for nausea," Alec explained.

I raised an eyebrow. "I didn't know I had it on tap."

"You don't," he shrugged, "but for now your brain thinks you do."

"Neat trick."

Another little shrug. "I found Israel far too hot so had to learn how to cope. That helped."

"Israel?"

"The kettle's boiled. I'll go finish those coffees for you." He turned and hurried out of the bathroom.

Curiouser and curiouser: I thought as I sipped at the clear liquid which, this time, was just water. I heaved myself up to my feet and followed him. As I walked through, Alec was bringing two steaming hot mugs of coffee through to the living room. He set them down on the table and settled himself on my sofa. I took the armchair. "So, here we are," I said.

"Here we are, indeed," he replied.

We sipped our coffee and the rest of the conversation went unsaid. It was just not the right time. I had far too many questions and I had the feeling this young fellow was not going to surrender any answers too quickly.

So we sat and drank our coffees in silence.

Eventually I decided that it would be best to remain focussed on practicalities. "There's an attic upstairs. You could sleep up there if you wanted. It would give you some privacy and I'm guessing that you're not heavy-laden with possessions."

Alec smiled. "That would be great. Thank you."

"I'll get hold of a mattress or something you can use for a bed."

"Okay. The floor will be fine for now. At least I'll have a roof over my head."

I pointed towards the back pack. "You've been on the road for a while?"

"Yes," he nodded. "Talking of which, could I use your shower? It's been, as you say," he grinned, "a while."

I chuckled to myself. "Sure. Help yourself."

So he wandered off into the bathroom and I drained my coffee before turning back to matters at hand. First things first: what day was it? I flicked on my phone. The screen announced that it was Monday and that the battery was incredibly low. As I sat the device in its charging cradle I shook my head. Where had last week gone? Also, was I any further to reining in Wallace?

The answer to both these questions was that I had no idea.

What was Wallace actually doing? Yes, he was running riot in his own little serial killer fantasy, and for what aim? He was convinced that it would bring about the Divergence. But how?

"Not too sure on that one."

"Jesus Christ!" I snapped jumping out of my skin in shock. "Alec, don't do that."

"Sorry, Sam. Old habit." He stood in the doorway bare to the waist and hair wet. I frowned as I noticed seven dark marks across his chest. They looked like the remnants of old wounds. Another question to file away for later. He wandered over to his pack and fished out a slightly less crumpled t-shirt. "I'm not used to being around people."

"Sure, I get that, but house rule number one: no head poking."

"No probs," he grinned. "But like I said, I really don't know how the suicides should bring the Divergence about. It doesn't really make sense."

I leaned back in my armchair. "So you've had a bit of experience in this already then?"

Water droplets dripped off his wet hair as Alec nodded. "I've seen similar."

"Really? When?"

Alec shook his head sending more water flying. "That's not important right now. What we need to be focussing on is numbers. Wallace needs five sacrifices, yes?"

"How do you..?"

He tapped the side of his head.

"Fair enough," I conceded. "Yes, he needs five."

"And he has how many so far?"

I counted them off on my fingers. "The waitress and Flint were two. Abalone made three and Matt Slesinski was the fourth."

"Which means?"

I sat gobsmacked. "He only needs one more to bring about the Divergence."

At that moment there was a loud hammering at the door.

This time Jitendra had brought more than just one playmate. Three burly boys in blue muscled their way into my flat after him.

Oh, I was in deep trouble.

"Two more!" the DCI yelled into my face. "Two more victims, one of which I can place with you less than an hour before her death." He stood invading my personal space, breathing heavily as he ran his fingers through his jet black hair. "What the hell, Sam? I asked you to get close to Wallace, help me bring him down, not get him to up his kill rate."

"Jitendra..."

"No! Enough!" His nostrils flared as his normally well-guarded anger flooded over the brim. "Not this time. No, not this time."

I glanced over to the corner of the room where Alec was stood propped up against the door frame. The police officers were totally oblivious to his presence. Hope started to puff frantically at the small ember that it was desperate to nurse back to life.

"No," Jitendra continued, "this time... this time..." He wagged a finger vigorously in the space before my nose. "This... time..." He stopped and stared at the tip of the finger as if it was the first time he had ever seen such a strange looking object. "This..."

The uniformed muscle gave each other confused looks. "Sir?" one of them asked. "What are..."

I saw a smile touch Alec's lips. He combed his fingers through his wet hair. "Go back to the station. Forget you were ever here. Go and save some puppies."

Jitendra's eyes snapped back into focus, alert, resolute. "Come on, men. We've got work to do. There are innocent canines out there that require our help!"

"Yes sir!" The bobbies snapped to attention before charging out of my flat in pursuit of their dog-saving boss.

I started to breathe again and closed the door behind them. Then, looking back to my young companion, I said, "Yes indeed, you are very useful to have around the place."

He grinned.

"But now, young Alec," I frowned as I slumped down into my armchair fishing out a cigarette, "I have questions and you will answer them." Flicking my Zippo, I lit my Lucky. Breathing in deep, the tobaccoey goodness warmed a pair of lungs that were still chilled from the blind panic caused by Jitendra's sudden intrusion. I gazed out of the window across Dalton Square and observed that winter was starting to breathe down my city's neck. It always comes early in these parts: the leaves fall, the geese fly and little black and white pied wagtail birds can be seen bobbing their long plumage up and down around town.

What never seems to change, though, is the lack of clothing that people seem to wear when they go clubbing. Even on a night when the sky is clear and frost is starting to turn tarmac into ice-rinks, young girls wear the shortest dresses and young lads sport silk shirts open halfway down their chests with no jacket. I shook my head as I thought about how they would stagger through Dalton Square later on, oblivious to any apocalyptic threat, then turned and faced my new lodger.

"So," I said, "here's the thing. I set myself up in what most would consider to be a less than conventional career and suddenly I find myself with a young shadow. This shadow appears from nowhere. Now, it is not a malign presence - far from it. Indeed, on certain occasions it has indeed appeared to be quite useful. In fact, one could call it a life-saver." There was a glimmer of a smile from the young boy's worried mask. "For that, I thank my newly-found guardian angel."

"You're welcome," he replied, graciously, his eyes trying to look everywhere but at my face.

I paused. "Indeed." A draw of nicotine suffused my bloodstream before I continued. "However, there seems to be a catch. Said shadow seems to have been dealt a better hand of cards in the game of poker that is my life at the moment. It knows things that I do not and seems to possess attributes that would not really be welcome by other players at a game of cards."

Alec's head raised and his eyebrows knotted. "Actually, I think it would be more correct to use the word *powers* rather than the word *attributes*. An attribute is a quality or feature regarded as a characteristic or inherent part of someone or something. The ability to manipulate minds or make someone perceive you to be invisible could not be defined as qualities or features. They are something that I do, they're not part of my character."

I raised an eyebrow as I drummed my fingernails on my teeth.

"Fair point." I stubbed the cigarette out and leaned back in the armchair, its soft embrace cushioning my tired joints. "Does being a walking dictionary also count as being a power too?"

The youth flicked his head to one side. "I have had a rather more extensive education for my years than most of those my age."

"And what would your age be then?"

"Seventeen or eighteen," he shrugged with an air that did not really care. "I've lost track a bit."

"Why would that be?"

"I've been travelling."

"Far?"

"Yes."

"I'm guessing not a standard gap year then."

A little head flick. "No."

I let out a sharp, exasperated breath. This was like trying to knock down a stone wall with a tooth pick. Alec was not for giving. It was not as if he was hiding anything, as such. He was just not telling me anything unless I asked him in a completely direct manner.

I stood up, poured myself a Jack, downed it in one, poured another and began to pace the room. "Why are you here, Alec?" I finally asked.

He paused, gathering his thoughts, before answering. "To help you and to stay safe."

That caught my attention alright. "To stay safe? What from?"

He shook his head.

I turned that over in my mind as the whiskey slid down again.

"Okay, not *what* from. *Who* from?"

"That is very difficult to answer, Sam."

"Why? Do you not want to tell me?"

For the first time in the conversation he looked straight up at me and those bright blue eyes were full of the deepest sadness I had ever seen. "Because there are just far too many people to list that would want me dead if they knew of my existence."

Wow! I hadn't seen that coming, but then... "Is that how you got those marks on your chest?"

He nodded silently.

"How did it happen?"

"I was shot seven times." He unconsciously ran his fingers over his cotton t-shirt.

I sat down again, my knees suddenly weak. "Shot? When?"

"A month ago."

I had no voice. A month? Seven times? But the marks looked so old, not to mention the rather alarming fact that he should almost certainly be dead! My mind was racing now. There was so much that I wanted to know, that I *needed* to know, but I had to be so very, very careful here. I was going to have to tease the pearl-like information out of this tightly-closed oyster without managing to damage the shell.

"Who shot you Alec?"

He crossed the room and sat down on the sofa. "That is complicated and it might upset you."

My stomach lurched, but I had to know. "Try me Alec. Please tell me. It's important."

His blue eyes shot to the front door. "The police."

"Oh shit," I groaned. I had a wanted felon sat here in my living room. A wanted felon with supernatural powers who had just mind-warped the very authorities that had tried to kill him. The day was just getting better and better.

"I did say it might upset you."

"That's okay."

"Besides, it's not like most of them were *real*, anyway."

I frowned. "Not real police?"

"No," he corrected. "Not real humans."

Okay. Curiouser and curiouser. I filed that little snippet in the *come back to it later* box. "So how did you survive?"

"I heal quickly."

I snorted a quick laugh. No joking he healed quickly. "So, I'm guessing that you're not human."

His eyes drifted off again as his thoughts once more processed my question. "Again, that is complicated."

"Is it likely to upset me?"

He shook his head. "Oh no. Not at all. Sam, do you believe in angels?"

Okay. So I had to admit, this was a new one. In the last few weeks I had encountered vampires, fairies and a werewolf. Wallace had briefly mentioned angels in passing when lecturing me about his beloved Beyond. So did this mean that I had some sort of cherub sat in front of me? Alec did not strike me as the type to spend all day sat around on a cloud strumming a harp so I asked, "Are you saying...?"

"What?" He sat bolt upright, a mixture of surprise and amusement on his face. "Oh, God no! I'm not an angel."

I felt a sigh of relief escape my lungs and I tipped the glass of Jack back. Hooray for almost normal.

"It's my *dad* who's the angel."

I nearly choked as bourbon sprayed from my mouth.

"And *possibly* my mum, but we're not sure on that at the moment," he continued as I gasped for air, rasping staccato coughs through alcoholic vapour.

*Dear Lord, why me?* I thought to myself. I had never known that life could get this complicated. First a week from hell, then Caroline turning up, then Wallace, then John and now *this*. I sat and stared for a while. Alec contemplated his bare feet.

"When you say *possibly* your mum," I finally ventured once I'd calmed down. "Does that mean you're not sure who your mother is?"

He shook his head. "No. I know who my mum is. It's just we're not sure whether she was an angel at the time or not."

Okay. More weirdness.

"You say *we*. Would that be you and your father."

Alec nodded.

"So he's still on the scene, so to speak."

He gave a quiet chuckle that managed to unnerve the pants off me. "Oh yeah, Sam. He's very much around. It was him who said I had to come and find you. He said that you could keep me safe."

My fingers did their little tooth tap dance. "He knows me?"

"Yes. In a manner of speaking."

My shoulders rose and fell as I gave an exasperated breath. This really was getting me nowhere apart from five steps closer to the cuckoo nest. "Look, Alec," I held my hand out to him, pleading, "you've got to give me more than this. These little riddles are doing my head in."

For a moment he looked up at me and, when those blue eyes locked on mine, I swear to God above that the pupils were burning with fire. Not only that, but they suddenly seemed far older than they should.

They were eyes that had lived.

They were eyes that had wandered.

They were eyes that had suffered.

Those eyes stayed fixed on mine for about thirty seconds before he checked his head to the side and looked away once more. "I'm sorry, Sam. I can't tell you anything else about me right now. Dad doesn't want me to. It's very, very complicated and there is a definite chance that you will not like what you hear."

He looked up once more and there were those attractive blue eyes of a young lad who was alone in the world and needed someone to watch over him, someone to protect him.

Someone like me.

I nodded. "Okay," I capitulated, fishing out another Lucky. "But do me this, if you can. Why don't you tell me about angels?"

Then suddenly, it was like a massive amount of pressure had been unburdened from his shoulders. He leaned forward, his eyes bright and his face animated. "Sure, I can tell you about angels, Sam. I can tell you everything that I know about them."

And he was off.

As he started to talk he rose from the sofa and paced the room, his arms gesturing in the air as he described things for me. His eyes wandered around the room although it was clear that they did not see a thing that was in front of him. Instead they were off with the very beings that he was describing.

I have read numerous books over the years which describe how theologians and mystics throughout the ages have stated that there is a hierarchy to angels. Alec told me that this was a reality, though not as any old chap in a cave had described it.

At the bottom were the Angeloi. These were what most people thought of when it came to angels. They were white-robed, golden-skinned and possessed a single pair of feathery wings. They spent their time wandering the realm of Heaven contemplating God and His works.

Next were the Archangels. Of these there were only four: Michael, Gabriel, Raphael and Uriel. They spent their time in the Sanctuary actually in the presence of God. They were similar in appearance to the Angeloi, but they seemed to hold themselves somewhat different. You just knew that they were superior. I figured them to be sort of middle management types, but then I had an image of *The Office*'s David Brent as cupid and quickly shoved the picture out of my head.

One point of interest that all Archangels and Angeloi shared was a specific power. There were those who could create matter from nothing. Some could shift time. Others had more elemental powers such as control over fire and water.

I asked him if, perhaps these powers could be hereditary?

He grinned, catching onto my point. "My mum has the ability of psyche; she can get inside people's minds. She can see what they are thinking and distort what they perceive to be real."

"Neat trick," I observed.

He nodded.

I rolled my fingers à la Roland Deschain, encouraging him to continue.

Next came the three mystical groups of angels: Thrones, Dominions and Powers. Thrones sort of spoke for themselves. They were the angels that made up the throne of God - small cherub-like creatures that made cute noises from time to time. *Angelic Furbies*, Alec called them. Dominions were somewhat elusive. All the other angels knew they existed, but none had ever seen them. It was believed that they dwelt here on Earth in the physical realm. Powers were the mad hermits of Heaven. They had no true form apart from what they felt like assuming for their own purposes and they spent all their time in a specific part of Heaven that was separate from the rest. Sometimes other angels went there to contemplate or seek their wisdom, but most of the time the rest of the Heavenly Host stayed well away. There was only one who ever went there on a regular basis, but he would not be going back anytime soon.

"Why's that?" I asked.

Alec stopped pacing. Suddenly the air was a touch too tense for my liking.

"He's the only member of the highest order of angels - the Seraphim."

Clocks ticked into my once ringing ears as I guessed the name that Alec was about to say

"Lucifer," I whispered.

He nodded. "Lucifer, the six-winged Seraph who spent most of his days, years, aeons dwelling in the heart of the Presence of God until one day he saw something that filled his heart with fear, causing him to leave Heaven."

"Filled his heart with fear?" Now that was different. "What do you mean by that? Most texts say he fell from grace through pride and such stuff."

Alec shook his head. "Lucifer was a tragedy. He existed from before the beginning of time. He was the first of all angels, dwelling deep in the heart of God. As he slept, he sang and God was so pleased with his song that He created Heaven and the angels. Then, aeons later, when Lucifer saw that God was to create a physical realm, he looked along Creation's timeline and saw something so horrific that it filled him with dread. He saw the timeline split in two.

"The Divergence."

There it was again. That phrase that seemed to be stalking me closer than a sad, greasy loner in Hollywood.

"Down one way there was Paradise. Heaven and Earth would unite. Love and Peace would rule for eternity. We would all be at one with God.

"Down the other... Down the other was Kanor. Kanor and his Divergent Lands, the time of the constructs. Heaven and Earth would not converge. There would be no peace. there would be a living hell on Earth until finally everything was put out of its misery.

"Total Oblivion."

"Crap," I whispered.

"That's not all."

"You've got to be kidding? There's more?"

"Sam, the Divergence is imminent. It will be caused by a man who is alive now. We will see it happening in our lifetime."

My blood chilled to sub-zero. "Wallace," I hissed.

# Chapter Eighteen

Four down, one to go.

Four down, one to go.

Four down, one to go.

I was smoking yet another Lucky as I paced back and forth in my flat. Dark vapours hung heavy around the room. Alec had made his excuses and gone to explore his attic room.

Alec.

I shook my head. So here I was, babysitting again. Last week a vampire, this week a... a... a goodness knows what child of one angel and one angel or human.

Oh, for the simple life!

Plus all the time Wallace was out there planning to take another innocent life in order to reform creation into some sort of post-apocalyptic paradise. Who would it be? Someone I knew or a complete stranger? Who was that monster going to reduce to such a wreck that they would end their own life?

Then there was the small matter of the Divergence.

What would happen when that final victim popped one too many pills or walked out into oncoming traffic? Would life as we know it cease? Would we enter into a new realm of horror and despair or was Wallace just a deluded sociopath?

The vampires had talked about the Divergence. Hell, they were even waiting for it, it had to be something tangible, but could it be brought about by just five suicides?

*Anything is possible*. Those three words, the little mantra of Wallace and his beloved disciples. Was it possible that five little acts of random cruelty could bring about the end of the world as we knew it?

My head was screaming. I was going round in circles. Literally. I paced round and round the room trying to grasp some slight straw of certainty in a field of confusion.

I needed to stop and rest.

I needed some music.

I flicked my stereo on and rummaged through the usual suspects of CDs that sat patiently next to it. I grumbled noisily as nothing grabbed my fancy. Too loud, too quiet. Too frantic, too chilled.

Then something struck my eye. A single CD lying there on its own with no cover. I picked it up and turned it over in my hand. It was the one that Boombox Betty had given me on Friday: *The Confessions Of Doctor Dream And Other Stories* by Kevin Ayers. I shrugged.

I might as well, I thought.

I popped it into the CD slot, lay out on the sofa and closed my eyes as the doleful voice of Kevin Ayers wafted over me.

The next thing I knew...

Rain hammered down like stair-rods but I remained remarkably dry.

"Another dream, then," I sighed to myself. "Ah well, let's go with the flow."

I surveyed my location. It was a dark, wet alley. Lancaster's full of them, a hangover one might say from the wonders of Georgian development that decided every last square inch ought to be put to good use as long as it didn't impact socially on those who actually funded the building of the store-houses and mills. To my left was the side of a building that I recognised as a furniture warehouse on Saint Leonard's Gate, which meant that on my right was the Grand Theatre. Okay. Not so bad. Hardly an apocalypse. I let my feet lead me around the corner to the front of the large Georgian building. The rain kept me company in its hammering manner, miraculously parting before me as I walked. Saint Leonard's Gate was bustling with theatre-goers hurrying out of the rain that seemed to prefer soaking them rather than me. They didn't seem bothered, however. There was not a scowl or a curse amongst them. They all seemed remarkably cheerful, which seemed unsettlingly unusual as, at the first drop of rain, Lancastrian folk will normally inform you, "It has never rained this hard as long as I can remember." Their other meteorological comments also include, "It doesn't snow anywhere near as bad as it used to," and, "The summers were definitely hotter thirty years ago, so don't you go telling me about this global warming rubbish." There were people of all ages piling into the theatre: parents dragging along chattering children, elderly couples reminiscing about the last play that they had been to see and young couples entwined arm in arm.

My heart ached at the sight of them.

"Losing someone makes you sad, makes you think that life is bad."

I turned at the sound of the voice next to me. There, crowned with his mop of unruly hair stood the late, great Kevin Ayers himself. I raised an eyebrow. "The last time I dreamt about a musician, they threw me off a flying horse. You're not planning something similar, are you?" I asked.

He just smiled and gestured for me to lead the way.

As I passed the billboards, I caught an unmistakable flash of lilac and saw emblazoned in large letters: "Tonight only, Doctor Dream!" I groaned inwardly. It had started out so promising, too.

Presently, Ayers and I were sat in the same box that Wallace and I had occupied the other night. I had no memory as to how we had arrived there, but there we were. The audience, as they had previously, were settling down and the lights were starting to dim. As a stuttering hush crept through the stalls, the curtain rose and the unmistakable sound of *The Confessions Of Doctor Dream* struck up from the speakers. "Take your partners for the dance, quick before you miss the chance," Ayers spoke into my ear in an exaggerated stage whisper.

I had no partner right now. I was totally on my own. Caroline had used me. Wallace had... I wasn't sure what. I shook my head slightly, oozing melancholy, and watched as the show began.

A lone man stepped into the middle of the stage. He was clad head to toe in lilac: a lilac suit, a lilac shirt and lilac shoes. All this was topped off by a lilac top hat and an elaborate lilac cane that was entwined with two snakes: one red, one black.

"I take life!" he proclaimed to the audience at large who responded with whoops and shouts of joy.

"My knife cuts deep!"

I leaned forward to try and get a better view of the man but, from my angle, the brim of his gaudy top hat obscured any chance of glimpsing his face.

"Brings sleep..." He raised his arms out to his sides, his cane clasped in his right hand.

"Looks like a crazed Willy Wonka and an inebriated Robbie Williams mated and produced some weird love-child," I murmured.

Kevin Ayers touched my arm and whispered, "Watch out for Doctor Dream."

I could hear something else now. Behind the psychedelic tunes of Ayers' music, there was another voice; one that was sweet but insidious. It was a female voice humming low and quietly, just within audible range. Ice slipped down my spine as the members of the audience started to rise from their seats and gradually ascended into apoplexy. They were waving their hands in the air as they vied for the attention of Doctor Dream. Lovers pushed each other aside, parents fought to free themselves of their offspring, the elderly were trampled over as a body of grabbing hands and beatific smiles rushed towards the foot of the stage.

I caught a glimpse of Dream's mouth. It was smiling cruelly. "I'll fill your skies with promise that you'll fly," he hissed and the humming grew louder and louder in time with the incessant beat of the music. The audience were now totally hysterical, screaming and wailing for him to reach out to them. They wanted him to look at them, to touch them, to save them.

Dream raised his cane high in the air and it started to squirm. With languid fluidity, the two snakes detached themselves from the stick and started to elongate out into the air above him. Their eyes glittered with orange malevolence as they grew rapidly in size. In a few seconds they went from being extravagant ornaments on a walking stick to filling half the stage with their rippling bodies.

They slithered their way hungrily towards the edge of the stage, their huge muscles undulating along their bodies, causing a harsh rasping sound as their bellies crawled along the wooden floor.

"I will return to feed on you!" he screamed out.

"Oh no," I whispered hoarsely. As the snakes opened their cavernous mouths, I made to rise from my chair but the hand of Kevin Ayers resolutely fastened me tight. "Watch out for Doctor Dream," he repeated once more.

Down below, there were no screams of terror as the audience were systematically devoured by the oversized serpents. Instead there were welcoming cries of, "Take me! Take me!" before the sickening sound of those voices being muffled out one by one. The snakes spared no one; adult or child, male or female, they devoured everyone and not one person protested. Each meal gave itself willingly and joyfully to the vile creatures. All the time, Doctor Dream stood on the stage, his arms outstretched, a look of satisfaction on his cruel lips, as if he were bathing in the glow of a beautiful summer's day.

I tore my eyes away from the horrific spectacle and looked in the one direction that I could to avoid the massacre, the opposite box.

A familiar pair of sunglasses were staring back at me.

The stranger from my dream about John O'Gaunt Media lowered the glasses and his eyes of fire fixed on me.

If ever there was a face that described anger, it was his. His hands gripped the sides of his box and smoke began to rise up in wisps from the painted woodwork. I was suddenly very aware that the temperature in the theatre had risen quite dramatically.

There was an enormous flash of flame and I awoke, drenched in sweat.

"I have got to stop listening to music before I go to sleep," I groaned.

# Chapter Nineteen

Monday lurched its way towards Tuesday. I spent most of the day brooding over my incapacity to achieve even the slightest action. Whenever I closed my eyes I saw the two monstrous serpents gobbling up willing sacrifices as Doctor Dream looked on with glee.

Then there was the other guy; the one from the opposite box, the same one from my dream of the John O'Gaunt studios. Who the hell was he? Like I needed any more to worry over.

I could not cope with this. It was all too much. In the end I got myself totally rat-arsed and collapsed in a heap on my bed.

The next day, I sluggishly made my way through to the bathroom then the kitchen and back in circuit to my bed where I sat, drank coffee, ate toast, downed paracetamol and grumbled inwardly at how the world had been put in place just for the sole purpose of torturing me.

What had I ever done?

What was my crime in a previous life? I was too old to have been Pol Pot. Surely I was too young to have been Hitler? Was there some other crazy serial-killing lunatic politician who had died the year I had been born? That must have been the case. It could not be surely down to just plain bad luck, could it?

A depressive cloud enveloped me as I finished off my toast. Eight-thirty, proclaimed my vintage Mickey Mouse alarm clock. No rest for the wicked. I had to get my backside into gear.

But to do what?

Good question. I considered hollering upstairs to my new lodger but something inside me resolutely shook its head. Right now I needed clarity of thought not brain-aching cryptology. I felt like I had been handed a pile of enigma codes and been told to decipher them without the slightest help from a code book.

In short, I was in an impossible situation. All I seemed able to do was constantly mull over and over images and actions that I had no hope in understanding or preventing. Wallace was always that bit too far ahead of me. He was a dark Pied Piper casually playing a haunting jig whilst everyone, myself included, merrily danced along to their doom.

Well, not today.

Today I was going to walk in a different direction. I had spent far too long chasing my tail and it had only brought me heartache and misery. Today, I was going to turn my back on the whole affair and clear my head before I came back to the task at hand refreshed and reinvigorated.

I glanced out of the window. It was a bright, crisp autumnal day. Perfect for a walk. I needed a long, refreshing tramp either down the canal or up Clougha, the hill to the east of Lancaster on the edge of the Trough of Bowland. Either would do the trick. Just one foot in front of another; tread after tread, pace after pace. With each footfall, dust would be dislodged from the nooks and crannies of my congested mind and the cogs would be allowed to turn once more, letting me see all around in a fresh light. Illumination would fall into the darkest recesses and that which was staring me straight in the face would be unmasked.

So what was it to be? The canal or Clougha? Only one way to decide, really. I fished a pound coin out of my pocket and tossed it high. Heads for the hill, tails for the flat.

The coin landed on the carpet with a dull thud. Heads it was. I scooped the coin up and pocketed it once more then rummaged under my bed for my walking boots.

I had to admit, I was kind of glad that the coin had landed heads up. Clougha is probably my favourite walk in the area. You drive out to Quernmore, look up and just go. I normally choose the route via an old, abandoned farm just to the east of the village. It provides a nice sloping ascent over rough grassland, then a slightly steeper incline over peat and heather before a final push over the short rocky outcrop.

I drove out of town and headed east along Wyresdale Road out past Williamson Park (not somewhere I wanted to visit right now) and off into the countryside. The Leisure Park and the Brewery skipped past my right, the motorway roared over my head and suddenly I was surrounded by a vast expanse of fields, fields and more fields. There, straight ahead of me stood my destination: Clougha Pike.

In a short while I had parked up in the village of Quernmore, pulled on my old, battered boots and was trekking away from civilisation. I had trod this path many times over the years, especially when I had been studying at Luneside University. Once I was out of my car, everything was left behind. There was the still air and the slightly acrid smell of rural industry.

I felt like I was home.

I walked out of the village and, turning off the road, headed up to the base of the hill. The footpath, as ever, took me past the old, run down farm house that had stood vacant for at least ten years now. At least it had used to be empty. Right now it was a hive of activity with builders buzzing around its walls and up in its exposed rafters. Obviously someone had bought it and had decided that it needed renovating. I shrugged and passed by on to the access point to the land of Clougha.

I carefully closed the gate behind me and smiled as I looked up over the few miles of farmland that stretched upwards in front of me. First, there were the fields; mainly grassy with the occasional tractor ruts. Next, there was the heath land, riddled with becks and deep, boggy peat areas; the claimer of many a carelessly-fastened boot. Then finally there was the pike itself, a rocky outcrop rising up above the softer surrounding areas, fashioned by scraping and sliding glaciers of the last ice age. This was my *Ultima Thule*; my far destination. Once there, I would be free of all cares and separated from all that was dragging me down into the mire of everyday life.

For what felt like the first time since Caroline had walked into my office, tension truly slipped from my encumbered shoulders. The give of the ground under my well-worn boots felt friendly and reassuring. "Come on, old friend," it was saying to me, "let me take all your strains and burdens." Time was irrelevant as I continued to place one foot in front of another and ascended the slope. Cool, fresh air penetrated my lungs and the distant bleating of sheep danced delicately in my ears.

Before I realised it, I had reached the base of the pike and the rocky path climbed sharply in front of me. I loosened my walking jacket to allow my skin some room to breathe on the final push and progressed at a calm pace up the last stretch.

Then I was there. I have climbed higher peaks - Skiddaw, Snowdon, even the great Ben Nevis – but whenever I crest that last rise onto the summit of Clougha, I always feel that I am on top of the world. Sometimes, when I know there is no one looking, I even do a god-awful impersonation of Jimmy Cagney.

But not today.

Today was a day for peace and quiet not daft black-and-white gangster movie antics.

I picked my way across the jutting rocks, made my way to the trig point and just stared out across the vast expanse of space. It was a glorious blue-sky day and I could see out across Morecambe Bay in one direction and over to Yorkshire in the other. I fished a fruit bar out of my jacket and nibbled at its juicy yumminess in a very satisfied manner.

This was how life was supposed to be: no creatures looming out of the dark, no ex-girlfriends, no big bad always around the corner. This was paradise. I could stay like this for ever.

I stretched and felt all the clawing pressure from my spine unkink. I wriggled my neck and the tension crackled out from between my loosening vertebrae. I yawned as I sat down on the ground with my back to the trig point, looking out over the beautiful, verdant valley below. Yes, this was truly an unspoilt paradise.

I just had to rest my eyes for five seconds, didn't I?

There was a sound that would turn a man's heart inside out with terror. It was a cross between a shriek of an eagle and a roar of a lion but seemed to stretch across all possible boundaries of the human auditory range.

Then there was the smell. Charred ground and trees permeated with the unmistakable, sickening tang of blood.

I kept my eyes tight shut.

"This isn't real. It's just a dream. I am on Clougha. This is my special place. It will go away."

"I'm afraid it won't, Samuel."

"Sod off," I groaned. "Why don't you please just leave me alone?"

"I'm afraid that's not possible," stated the clipped, educated female voice from right next to my ear. Even over the vicious sounds of carnage and devastation her quiet voice commanded total authority that demanded silence from boisterous readers of books.

I turned my head towards her then opened my eyes. Two pools of pure fire held me locked from behind a pair of dark-rimmed spectacles. "I hate you," I whined. "Don't you have returned books to file or happy children to terrorise?"

The librarian look-a-like cocked her head to one side. "You don't hate me at all and no, I don't." She stood up in one graceful movement that left her trim and immaculate whilst the world around her went to hell in a handbag. Casually, she walked with supreme confidence to the edge of the pike and looked out at what could only be described as an apocalypse.

What was worse was the fact that I had already seen this montage before.

There they were, the two dragons – one red, one black – lashing out at each other with talons and claws, gouging chunks of flesh from each other that hurtled to the ground and spawned fires which consumed whole tracts of land. As their blood sprayed from their wounds it rained down on the devastated ground. From the rivulets, creatures arose. From the blood of the red dragon with seven heads angels were spawned; from the blood of the black, those faceless creatures of clay. Both sets of new-borns turned on each other and fought as ferociously as their parents; bloodied wings were torn apart and clods of clay were cast up into the sky.

"Is this for real? Will it actually happen?"

"When dragons walk the Earth, then all creation shall tremble."

There it was again. The same little psychotic soundbite I had heard from Philips shortly before he had shuffled off this mortal coil. I turned on my companion, my fists balled in anger. "Don't give me this prophetic crap!" I yelled across the noise of the war. "Will this happen?"

"One dragon already prepares for battle, Samuel." She squeezed my shoulder with her perfectly manicured fingers. It felt like I was gripped in a vice. "Do not let your inactivity cause the other dragon to join the fray!"

Then, as usual, I was left standing on my own.

"I'm really starting to hate my life," I groaned and my eyes flicked open to the once more calm scene of the Trough of Bowland. I let my heavy head sink into my hands and I rocked back and forth against the trig point. Dragons, dragons. What was it with dragons? First the late, not-so-great, Philips, then Wallace and now my ethereal, book-loving stalker.

And what the hell did she mean by, *Do not let your inactivity cause the other dragon to join the fray*? More cryptic codes even here at my fortress of solitude!

I delved into my pocket and fished out a packet of Luckies. Sod the healthy living fix; I needed the good old-fashioned crutch of roasted tar and nicotine. I flicked my Zippo and lit the cigarette. My hand paused as I was about to return the lighter to my pocket. I lifted it up and studied its pattern. Over sixteen years old and it still looked like new. It had certainly been made to last.

It had lasted a damn sight longer than our relationship – mine and Caroline's.

It had lasted longer on this planet than our son. Tears welled in my eyes.

I turned the Zippo over as I rubbed away the stinging tears and read the fake Latin saying that my son's mother had had engraved for me. *Nil illegitimi carborundum.* "Don't let the bastards grind you down," I whispered to myself. Right now I was between a sod of a rock and an infeasibly hard place. I was being bashed about and smashed to a pulp.

I was not going to let them grind me down.

I didn't care about all their supernatural, mystical hoodoo.

I had no time for their dragons or their blessed Divergence.

Wallace had stolen my son. He had played his flute and my only child had been dragged screaming to the land beyond the mountains.

From the top of Clougha I could see that clouds had started to gather over Lancaster. They were dark and ominous, harbingers of an oncoming storm. As I made my way back down towards my car I let the storm swirl inside my guts, churning and gusting at the thought of Malcolm Wallace, self-proclaimed Messiah and destroyer of lives.

The bastard would pay.

# Chapter Twenty

Arriving back at my flat, I unscrewed a fresh bottle of Jack and poured myself a generous measure. I had boarded the train to righteous anger with a first class reservation and I was hurtling along the track at full speed. I knocked the bourbon back in one swift glug and poured another.

Doctor Dream. Wallace was Doctor Dream, promising people that anything was possible, drawing them in like a fisherman with a tasty morsel hooked onto a cruel barb. Then, when they were close enough, all adoring and all worshipping, he devoured them. He drew on their devotion like a hungry ancient god obsessed with immortality.

Caught up in this supernatural feast had been my son, John. He was an innocent bystander removed from our reality on a casual whim, a sideshow.

Thunder cracked outside rather dramatically. I rasped a rude noise and poured myself more whiskey. Right now I was impotent, unable to stop him. He was far too powerful. How could I bring down a guy who could send people to other dimensions with just three words.

I grimaced as I felt those three syllables slide around my brain. They writhed and wrestled with my synapses, eager to be free. I felt my mouth twitch involuntarily. I slapped a hand across my mouth. They were not going to escape.

I needed a momentary distraction.

Slouching down into my armchair I flicked on the goggle box. It was the lunch time news. This was just as depressing as my life. In the Middle East people continued to blow each other up in the name of God. I sipped the whiskey as images of homeless children flashed across the screen followed by footage of young men with guns burning American flags.

Some things never changed.

Ironic really when Wallace was determined to change everything into a model that he would carefully shape with his own hands.

I drank my way down the glass as the national news gave way to the local. Murders, deaths, abductions. Even the local news was depressing. I didn't remember it being like this when I was a kid. Surely there were lighter topics that had been covered in my youth? Or perhaps that was just the rosy tint of approaching forty colouring my view of the long lost past? The long lost past of playing with an Action Man on my parents' lawn.

"*Don't forget the child you were, Samuel.*"

Then I nearly choked on my Jack.

The local news was showing live footage of an all-too-familiar location. There was Market Square in all its drizzly glory. I could make out the library, TK Maxx, Vodafone.

And a crowd of people.

My heart started to race as I downed the rest of the whiskey. I had a very bad feeling about this.

The reporter was prattling on about how in this time of despair people needed hope and how, here in Lancaster, one man was determined to bring people that hope. Indeed, that man was determined to show everyone that anything is possible.

There he was, the new Messiah, standing tall in the drizzling rain, his white hair immaculately groomed and his orange eyes looking straight to the camera.

His hands placed firmly on the shoulders of the same little girl that he had healed the previous week.

*"Do I look like a man who could kill a child?"*

*"You wear one face whereas I, like the Chimera, wear many."*

I dashed out of my flat and down the stairs to my office. As I pulled open the bottom drawer to my filing cabinet and pulled out the heavy weight wrapped in an old tea towel, one thing alone was racing through my mind:

I had to stop Wallace by any means possible.

I would not let him take another innocent life.

Thunder rumbled in the distance as I hurled myself down Penny Street, knocking innocent bystanders out of my path. I had no time for social niceties as the fine mist of rain soaked my face and the storm brewed ominously above. I had one hand firmly planted on the revolver in my coat pocket. The last thing I wanted was for that little beauty to tumble out and cause me some interesting explaining.

My lungs started to burn as I reached Horseshoe Corner and darted up Market Street. I chided myself once more with the fact that I really needed to get into better physical shape as I saw the mass of people milling outside the City Museum. I slowed down somewhat, approaching the rear of the crowd and took slow, steadying breaths. Two weeks ago, chasing across

Williamson Park, I had endured the added inconvenience of raging tinnitus and poor balance. At least I did not have that to contend with this time as I hunted my new quarry. No, my prey had made sure that my affliction was a thing of the past. All he had wanted in return was my soul.

That was never going to happen. Just as he was not going to harm a hair on the head of the young girl he had healed the previous week.

I slowly elbowed my way through the thick mass of onlookers. None of them noticed the rumbling of the approaching storm or the wet drizzle that plastered their skin. They were all focussed on one voice, on one moment. There he stood, calm and majestic on the steps to the City Museum, his words cutting clearly across the growing crowd. I glanced around, suddenly aware of just how many people were here. There were far more than there had been at the Credete meeting the previous week. Were they all new disciples to his rallying call? I didn't think so. Some were dressed for work, others carried shopping bags. These were the good old general public; the Average Joes who felt that they had to take a good look at what was going on. What was this new and interesting development in the heart of their city?

Each and every one of them hung on Wallace's every word.

I tightened my grip on the revolver in my pocket as I fell in behind the front row of the adoring populace. If only they knew.

He stood there, his kind, avuncular voice instructing all who would listen that they were destined for a better life. He explained that the world would change this very day, that in a few moments all the heartbreak and woe of their mundane lives would be washed away with one simple act.

My blood ran cold as I looked at the child who stood in front of him, his hands placed firmly on her shoulders. His reassuring words drifted in front of me like a translucent veil that was attempting to hide a ravening beast. I had heard them all before and they just did not wash. The man was a murderer. Just look at how many had died at his hands in an attempt to change reality and bring about this Divergence. There had been the five actors to begin with then, when that had failed, he had started again. The caretaker from the museum, tattoo guy from Credete, the young waitress and of course Abalone. Poor Abalone. The thought of her smiling blue eyes almost caused me to squeeze the trigger and shoot myself in the groin by mistake.

Then there was John; not dead but sent somewhere else. Beyond, wherever that was.

This man was a destroyer not a healer, and now he wanted to destroy one more time to bring about his idea of paradise on Earth. He wanted to terminate the life of a young innocent girl who, just the other day, he had healed.

Not while I still had breath in my lungs.

I stepped out of the crowd and pulled the revolver from my pocket. There were shouts and screams as people around me suddenly backed off in fear. I was the madman to them, not the calm, controlled harbinger of a new dawn who stood on the steps in front before them, his gentle smile framed by a halo of pure white hair.

"Well, good afternoon, Samuel." Wallace smiled. "So nice of you to join us for this momentous occasion."

"Screw you," I spat. "Step away from the girl." I motioned with the gun. Wallace just smiled at me with a curious look. It was as if I had asked him to walk around on his hands whilst playing a recorder from his butt hole.

"Really, Samuel? Now why would I do that?"

"Because if you don't, I'll blow your sodding head off!" My eyes flicked from side to side. I was aware of a surprising lack of movement from the crowd. In the back of my subconscious I seemed to be expecting someone, perhaps one of Wallace's devoted acolytes or an off-duty cop, prowling stealthily through the people, positioning themselves somewhere where they could pounce on me and save the day. In reality, there was nothing. All that had happened was that those around me had backed off, giving me a wide space and centre stage. Good old British bystanders.

Above, the thunder rolled deeper and the rain started to increase in volume.

Wallace shook his head, a faint smile touching his lips. "Ah, I think I see what this is now. You think that I want to kill little Melanie here. How amusing. I've never killed a soul in my life." He bent forwards, lowering his mouth to her ear, his orange eyes never leaving me - mocking me.

"Don't you dare!" I pulled the hammer back on the revolver. "One word! I swear to God, one word..."

"Run along, dear," Wallace said, ignoring the gun, and the girl trotted off to her parents without a care in the world. There was no crazy guy waving a revolver around in front of her. There was no psychopath wanting to destroy humanity from the steps of the City Museum in a small, north west city in England. "So here I am, Samuel." Wallace spread his arms to his sides, his cane held in his right hand. "What now?"

"Now you die."

"Ah yes, of course. I was forgetting. You are a killer, aren't you?"

"No." I swallowed. "You're the killer. All those people."

"Really?" He stroked his chin in dramatic thought. "I don't seem to recall laying a hand on anyone. Now you... Now there's a different story." A cruel smile formed on his lips. "Does it feel *good*, Samuel? Does the weight of the gun feel like the weight of someone else's life in your hands?"

My hands dipped slightly as the gun suddenly felt heavier. I raised them up level again, aiming the barrel straight at Wallace's chest.

"Tell me, Samuel," he continued as he walked down a step towards me, what did her eyes say when you pulled the trigger, that poor woman in the park? Were they shocked? Were they pleading? Or were they just dead - lifeless as her heart was ripped open and her soul expired?"

I took an involuntary step back and the gun wobbled once more.

There was a flash of lightning and Wallace's orange irises glowed like burning embers in the flashing unnatural afterglow. "Why do you want to kill me, Samuel? Tell me. Tell all these good, trusting people."

"Because... Because you have to be stopped." My throat was suddenly as dry as an abstainer's pint glass and the words were hard to form – tangled behind my rasping tongue.

"I have to be stopped? What from?"

"The Divergence." Rain streamed down my face and I blinked it out of my eyes. "I've seen it. It can never happen."

"And it's your task to decide what must happen? Your task to decide the future for these good people?"

The weight of the gun was unbearable. Sagging once more, it took all my concentration to lift the barrel up. My head was light and my knees gave way as I sank down onto the paved square. Once more the gun sagged. I hefted it up with my right hand as my left propped me up on the pavement. This time, however, I felt like I had no control over my own hand. The gun seemed to rise up out of its own volition.

"Tell me, Samuel," Wallace was now just a couple of metres away from me, triumph radiating from his smile, "what makes you so different from me? Surely we are just the same?"

"Never." It wasn't my voice. It wasn't my lips that moved. My body was displaced from my control of my basic motor functions. I felt like an observer, just another face in the swarming crowd. All I was fully aware of was my right hand lifting the gun up level with my head, the cold, wet muzzle pressed hard against my temple.

"Poor Samuel," Wallace crooned. "Poor, deluded Samuel. He came chasing demons only to realise that he was one himself – a monster in human flesh. An unbearable thought. Certainly not one that he could bear living with."

And he was right. I had killed a woman in cold blood – pulled a trigger and watched as she had bled to death.

What right did I have to judge this man? I was a far worse killer than he was. Wherever I walked, bodies followed.

Lightning forked across the sky and I heard an almighty crash.

It was not thunder.

# Chapter Twenty-one

*Anything is possible.*

*Anything is possible.*

*Anything is possible.*

My head hurt.

My head hurt.

My head *hurt*!

I sat bolt upright. Could I do that when I was dead?

Damn, my head hurt! I placed my palm against my temple and rubbed, gingerly.

No gooey mess, that was a plus point.

Wiggled my toes back and forth. My shoes waggled at the end of my feet.

Okay, nerves and muscles seemed to be in order.

I looked around. It was dark. It was Williamson Square, the heart of Luneside University. It was also raining.

"This is Heaven? You've got to be kidding me!"

"It would appear that you misunderstand your situation."

I recognised that prim, crisp female voice. It was the voice that immediately made me want to check the dates in the front of my library books.

There was the light fluttering of wings and half a dozen or so of my little winged friends settled down on my legs and my shoulders. Sophia walked round into my field of view, her plain, sensible shoes making no noise whatsoever on the flagstones.

I noticed that, even with the night-time precipitation, she was bone dry.

But, then again, so was I.

"Well I'm guessing I'm not in Kansas anymore, Tonto."

She stood still and raised an eyebrow. "Curious, you have a wide-ranging knowledge of fantasy fiction yet you fail to remember that the dog from the *Wizard of Oz* was, in fact, named Toto. Tonto, on the other hand was the Native American companion of the Lone Ranger."

"Well, *kee-mo sah-bee*," I sighed, "perhaps that little slip was something to do with me blowing my brains out just now."

Sophia cocked her head to one side in thought. "No," she replied, "I feel it is more in keeping with your trying to outsmart me in a witty manner. You failed. You cannot outsmart me."

I shrugged. "Yeah, yeah. Wisdom and all that." I gently removed the fairy-folk from my clothes and pulled myself to my feet. "So then, oh, fount of knowledge, perhaps you will tell me what it is that I'm doing here and, in fact, where here is exactly?"

"You are at Luneside University the night after you found out that your father was dying and you have brought yourself to this place and time for the same reason that we want you here."

"What might that be?"

"We both want Malcolm Wallace erased from history."

I tapped my teeth with my fingers as I pondered this little matter. Erase Wallace from history. Right now, that did seem like a dream come true. Here I was, the very night that he went off with his mysterious benefactor and started down the path that ultimately led him to make me point a gun at myself and blow my brains out.

"What the hell," I said, smiling darkly, "I'm in."

Sophia cocked her head to one side and frowned. "Curious."

"What is?"

"You did not ask why we want him removed."

I shrugged. "I'm sure you have your reasons, but right now I'm sort of dwelling on the fact that I'm as dead as a third season of *Enterprise* which is something I would gladly correct." I paused. "The fact that I'm dead, not *Enterprise*, that is."

Sophia nodded, "Agreed then. You will dispose of Wallace and your life will return back to your timeline. Any act he committed after this night will never have happened."

"Sounds sweeter than my mother's apple pie." Not only had this man made me kill myself, but he had pushed my son into some sort of hell dimension. Oh yes, I wanted him gone from my life. "Where will I find him?"

"He will be here shortly. Approximately half an hour or so. He is due to rendezvous with *her*." The word was fuelled with pure venom.

"Wow, am I detecting a history there?"

"No. We just feel that she has interfered in this realm's affairs too many times. She must be stopped on this occasion." The small fairies fluttered up from their resting places and hovered around Sophia. The air started to shimmer and as they started to disappear, Sophia said, "I believe there is a small matter you have to attend to before Wallace?" and with that, she and the fairies were gone.

My brow knotted. A matter?

Then it struck me and I smiled my first genuinely happy smile that night.

Luneside University had not changed since I had graduated, but then of course it wouldn't have as I had not yet graduated yet. I shook my head as I climbed the stairs to Borrowdale Hall. I had to admit that I was rather enjoying this little trip down memory lane and as I walked through (yes, through – rather cool isn't it?) the door to my old kitchen I couldn't help but chuckle at the sight of Gerald the ghostly cleaner sitting forlornly at the head of a table upon which slumbered the forms of rather younger versions of myself and Spliff.

"Hello, Gerald," I smiled.

The moustache twitched as he took a rather comical double-take at me and my doppelgänger.

"Sam?" he enquired. "Is that you?"

"In the flesh." I spread my arms to my sides. "Well, sort of."

"You look older."

"I feel it too, mate. How you holding up?"

"Well, your buddy lasted about ten minutes before he 'just had to close his eyes a minute'. Then, well.... here we are."

I grinned. "He's good at that, trust me. He'll apologise in the morning." I rounded the table and crouched down beside myself (never, ever thought I'd get the chance to type that phrase) and gave myself a good looking over. "Less grey in the curls," I murmured to myself, "and less wrinkles, too." I was still smiling as I stood up. "So, Gerald, I believe you are in need of a psychopomp."

He nodded.

I waved my arms dramatically. "*Ta da!* Tonight's your lucky night."

My younger self snored and rolled in his sleep. I remembered what I saw back then and knew what I had to do. I stood in front of the cleaner and said, "So we need to get you home then?"

Gerald nodded. "Do you think you could do it?"

My hands suddenly felt pleasantly warm. I lifted them up between us and Gerald gave out a low whistle. I was aware of a slight moan from my left as the yellow glow from my hands started to spread out around me. "It would seem that I am adequately equipped. Must be some sort of after-life gift." Instinctively, I reached out and the glow spread towards Gerald. It snaked itself around him, shrouding him from head to toe. As he disappeared, his mouth didn't utter a word but his eyes quite clearly smiled a, "Thank you."

There was a small noise and I kept smiling as I turned to the source. There I was, about sixteen years younger, looking up at me. My younger self made as if to speak and I shook my head. There was no need for words. Instead, he closed his bleary eyes and passed out again.

I chuckled to myself and looked out of the window.

I had to go.
I had a job to do.
I had things to put right.

When I saw him, whatever passed for blood in my dead form ran cold. There he was, the cold-hearted, murdering bastard. There in plain sight, waiting under the overhang of Williamson Square as if he hadn't a care in the world, as if he didn't have it in him to destroy the life of an innocent boy, my son, John.

Quietly, I walked up behind him and stood for a moment, collecting my thoughts. He was here, within my reach, ready for me to end it before it had begun. I reached out to grab him and he spun in an instant, the side of his arm batting mine out of the way. The recognition in his eyes was instantaneous. His mouth formed an "O" shape and he backed away, rapidly. I advanced and his legs twisted together causing him to fall flat on the floor.

I lunged forwards and grabbed him by the front of his jacket, not taking my eyes off his for a moment.

I had no weapon, but I knew exactly how I wanted to kill this slime. Oh yes, I knew exactly what I intended for him. I bent my knees and leapt up into the summer night. The warm air streaked passed my cheeks as we sailed up towards my destination, the top of the boiler chimney.

My ears were deaf to the screams of my victim as he flailed vainly in my granite grip. I had a purpose, a mission and I was going to follow it through to the vicious end.

My feet alighted on the red brick and I turned to survey the panoramic view. Off in the distance, I could see the lights of Barrow-in-Furness across the bay, beyond that the hills then the mountains of the Lake District.

And in my hand I held a worm. It squirmed, twisted and writhed between my fingers. It was a deformed worm as it had arms and hands – hands that gripped at my wrists in desperation. Deformed as it had a mouth that could speak and eyes that could weep.

"Sam! Jesus, Sam! What's going on?" the worm shrieked as I dangled it precariously over the edge of the chimney, its shoes scraping on the old, crumbling brick trying to seek out any form of life-saving purchase. "Sam! Sam!"

"Don't you *DARE* use my name, you filth!" I spat in the worm's face, at his creepy orange-tinted eyes. "You lost the right to address me like that a long, long time ago."

"What? Why?" Those freakish eyes were desperately scanning his situation, flitting from me to his feet to the long, fatal drop that awaited him. "What have I done? What in God's name have I done?"

"You killed my son!" I bellowed into the night sky. "You took a sweet, young lad and sent him to a hell dimension where there's no time, no joy, no life."

"When? When?" His feet scrabbled loose and one leg swung back causing him to sway in my grip.

"In the future. Your future, my past." My knuckles were white, tight with gripping his jacket.

"No! No! I wouldn't. Couldn't!"

The first niggle of doubt started to squirm its way into my thought process. Would he? Would he really now? What if I had changed things? What if I had altered the future? How would I know?

Involuntarily I pulled him slightly closer towards me.

"Yes, Sam! Yes! Pull me in! Please pull me in. I won't do anything. Tell me about it and I'll make sure it won't happen. Honest to God, I won't let it happen."

His eyes were wide open. Those orange irises glistened with tears, warm wet tears of a terrified man. I recalled a woman's look of shock as she died from a gunshot to the chest.

What the hell was I doing?

I pulled him in and wrapped an arm around his shoulders to steady him.

"Hold on," I said. "Hold on tight."

"Thank you, Sam. Thank you." His hands gripped me firmly as he looked down at his feet on the narrow rim of the chimney. "Thank you." He frowned. "Tell me. What did I do exactly?"

I was about to tell him when I saw his lips move around an empty word.

"..."

I pushed.

He fell.

There is an episode in *Doctor Who* called *Day of the Moon* where River Song (or Mrs Doctor as Spliff sardonically calls her) takes a backward swan dive from a ledge of a skyscraper in New York. Her arms fly out to the side and it all goes slow-mo as she gracefully plummets backwards until the TARDIS materialises behind her and scoops her away to a swift rescue.

The same was for Wallace.

There was shock in those orange eyes as his arms spread wide.

There was a rush of air that whipped at his hair.

There was, however, no TARDIS.

There was, instead, a sickening thump.

I think I may have smiled. Just a bit.

I stepped off the tall chimney and felt the warm summer night air brush against my flushed cheeks as I glided down to the floor below. As I descended, my eyes stayed fixed on the motionless bundle of flesh and bones that had been Malcolm Wallace – one-time student, one-time potential priest, one-time wannabe bringer of Armageddon. The body was so still, so straight, so...

Not bleeding?

Surely there should have been blood. I mean, he had fallen from a terrible height. He should be oozing from jagged rips in his torn skin where fractured bones should be jutting out at grotesque angles. I knew this. I had read Stephen King novels as a teenager.

My feet lightly touched down and I walked cautiously over to the body, prone on its back, arms out cruciform and eyes closed.

Drumming my fingers against my teeth as I held my breath, I crouched down and lay a tentative hand on Wallace's chest. There was no rise or fall. There was no heartbeat.

Nodding to myself, I was assured that he was dead.

It was then that his hand grabbed my wrist.

I let out a shout as his eyes flashed open, the cruel orange irises glaring in the glow of the illuminating lights around Williamson Square. He snarled like a wild animal as he flung himself upwards and lunged towards me. Instinctively I moved with him and he stumbled forwards, letting go of my hand. I had no time to think, only act. I rugby-tackled him roughly to the paved floor. We hit with a smack and I felt the side of my face tear harshly against an unforgiving man-made surface. We both scrabbled with our hands and our feet like beetles trying to avoid the burning rays of a magnifying glass in the hand of an immoral child. I was first to my feet and let loose a wide kick which he grabbed with his hands and twisted round causing me to fly over onto my side. I swore as I landed and yelled as Wallace's foot achieved what mine hadn't. My lower back hated me.

"You fool!" he hissed. "You damn fool. Do you think you can better me? Really?"

I twisted over and lurched up to my knees as my face and my back wailed louder than a cat on heat. I wanted to come back with a witty one-liner, something to put him in his place, but the words were just not there. The pain had sent them packing to a land of no return. Instead, I just knelt there slumped, dejected.

Wallace was towering over me now, his hair wild and his eyes ablaze. "You have no concept of what I'm capable of, Sam, of what I'm destined to do."

I chuckled wearily. "Oh God, it's that speech again. Blah blah blah.... mankind is corrupt... blah blah blah... only I can right all that is wrong. Please change the record, already!"

For a second he was dumbstruck, amazed that I had mocked him, then he said, "I don't need words to silence you."

The little panic monkey in my head realised just what he intended and screamed for me to act. As Wallace opened his mouth to speak the first silent syllable, every desperate ounce of energy slammed into my legs causing me to pounce up onto him and slam him to the floor kneeling on both his chest and, more importantly, his mouth.

Angrily, he lashed at me with his arms which I pinned with my hands and my feet while his head tried to twist free from the pressure of my knee.

"Ah, ah," I chided him mockingly, not for once letting up on my body weight. "Two can play at that game."

I opened my mouth and this time the horrible non-sounds tripped from *my* tongue.

"...

"...

"..."

There was a flash and a hiss as the reality of space time opened up in front of us. Wallace was now writhing even harder underneath me and was screaming muffled pleas into my trouser leg. Evidently he was no longer so sure of himself.

Then I heard slow, high-heeled footsteps echo across the square accompanied by a slow, appreciative clapping.

"Oh, well done. Well done indeed." I had to admit it was the goddamned sexiest voice I had ever heard and, apart from a few lilting hummed notes, I had only heard it twice before – once in the Ashton Hall and once on this same night many years ago.

I looked up and caught a proper sight of Wallace's benefactor for the first time, and what a sight she was. The ultimate femme fatale: there were the killer heels that I had heard before (scarlet of course); black, tight trousers that left no part of her legs to the imagination; a fashionably cut black leather jacket over a silky red top; reasonably long black hair cut perfectly to frame her beautifully cruel face.

Part of me actually thought, "You lucky, lucky bastard," until my more rational side reminded me that this was probably the last thing that went through the head of a male praying mantis, if you didn't count the teeth of the *female* praying mantis.

But *what* a female praying mantis!

She came to a stop and eyed some stone steps that rose up near to us. A small plume of dust rose away from their worn surface, leaving them spotless. Gracefully, she eased herself down into a casually seated position, stretching her long legs out in front of her. "Well go on then," she smiled.

"Pardon?" My voice cracked. I must have sounded like a hormonal teen. I certainly felt like one right then.

She pointed to the portal with a finely manicured finger. "Finish him off. I don't have all night and I've been so looking forward to this." She smiled callously, her upturned lips making her appear even more beautiful.

There was a grunt of protest from beneath me and I was rolled sideways as Wallace clambered to his feet. "What do you mean?" he whined. "You can't be serious!"

His benefactor gave a tired sigh and admired her fingernails. They actually changed colour three times before she smiled with satisfaction and deigned to looked back up. "Oh, are you still here? Not taken over the world yet? You know that gets so dull in the end. 'Look, look, here's the universe I destroyed for you!' *Bor*-ring." She turned her attention to me. "I've had an eternity of that you know. It's okay the first few times, but it gets dull ever so quickly."

"You can't do this," Wallace groaned, running his fingers through his hair. "We had plans."

"*You* had plans," she snapped. "I was just having fun and now I'm not. You're boring, Malcolm. So damned boring." She stood in one fluid move. "I'm through with you. Finished."

Her one-time student fell on his knees in front of her and actually began to weep. "Please, please don't leave me. What will I do without you?"

She shook her head. "Actually, after what you are *going* to do to his son, I really don't think that's an issue. Goodbye, Malcolm." She turned and left, leaving the two of us alone in the square with a portal to some weird hell dimension, Wallace with growing confusion, me with growing rage.

He stood and asked over his shoulder, "Will I really do what you said? To your son?"

No words could form a decent reply. I just grabbed him by the shoulders and shoved him through the portal. Wallace screeched in frustration as the whirling material of the portal enveloped him and sucked him in.

I slumped down onto my knees, panting hard. I had done it. I had eliminated the source of my troubles. I had caused Wallace to cease to exist, cut him off from time.

The portal still hummed in front of me.

I stared at its spinning lights.

There was a dark spot at its centre. My stomach turned.

A hand slowly clawed its way through the undulating surface. It was followed by a shoulder then a head. Wallace glowered at me like a demented thing. He opened his mouth to say something when there was a loud bang and a black dot appeared briefly on his head before he was sucked back in once more and the portal hissed shut.

I spun around on all fours and saw a dark-clad figure in the shadows of Williamson Square. He stepped forward and the artificial lights showed the cruelty that inhabited his sallow face. A pistol was gripped in one hand and electricity appeared to spark from the other.

I made to speak but he just shook his head and my mouth closed shut.

He looked from me to where the portal had hung then turned and walked away before disappearing into the shadows.

Then everything changed.

# Chapter Twenty-two

I was sat at my desk, my fingers resting on the keyboard of my laptop.

"There's somebody knocking at the door. Back in a mo'," were the last words that I had typed. I rose quickly, darted across the room and flung the door open.

There was nobody there.

Of course not. In this reality Caroline had not needed to come and see me about Wallace. She would not have been chasing that killer story. Yet I had still typed it out.

I opened the bottom drawer of my filing cabinet. The revolver was still there, wrapped in an old tea towel. I took it out, looked it over and set in down on top of the cabinet as I fished a bottle of bourbon from the top drawer and slugged down a good number of mouthfuls.

"And you don't even offer me one," sing-songed a feminine voice from the gloom. "Mind you, I would prefer a glass."

The bottle clunked to the floor as I whipped the pistol off the top of the cabinet.

There was a deprecating tutting followed by the sound of killer heels grinding into my carpet. "Now look what you've done. You've spilt it."

The intruder emerged out of the gloom and I recognised her at once. "You were there. In the past, egging me on."

She smiled. It wasn't a pleasant smile either. "Mmmm, yes I was, and I have to say I'm very impressed."

I kept the gun trained on her, although I had the growing feeling that this was a fairly pointless gesture. "Why would that be?"

"Power." She made the one word sound like a lingering orgasm. "It's rolling off you. Malcolm was powerful, true, but so, so gullible." She chuckled to herself, her laughter sounding like a stream eddying over the polished pebbles of a summer's brook. "Divergence indeed. As if he could bring that about."

"But the deaths. The storm brewing around him at the end..."

She slowly shook her head, her dark hair swaying hypnotically from side to side. "No. His little *Danse Macabre* was far from bringing about the end of your world. But it amused me to watch it." She held her hand out in front of her and casually examined her nails. "The Divergence will come and Kanor will rise."

Her eyes levelled with mine, fire burning in her pupils with glee.

"And then we will have a ball!

"Poor Malcolm," she sighed dramatically. "He was so sincere in his quest. He so believed that he was going to be the focus, that he would be the ruler of the Divergent Lands. That made him so biddable.

"But you, I sense you are different." With that she started to hum under her breath. It was a tune I had heard many years ago when I had been lying semi-comatose on the table in Borrowdale Hall and again, more recently, during the Credete meeting in the Ashton Hall. Once more the tune drifted into my head and danced seductively around my brain. However, unlike on the previous occasion, that was where it's effect on me stopped. There was no paradisiacal euphoria, no longing to follow this woman to the ends of the earth. I just stood there, the gun straight out in front of me.

The song stopped.

She smiled.

"Yes," she said, her voice brimming with curiosity, "different. Something has happened to you. Perhaps it was your little time walk. Perhaps it was blowing your brains out then coming back. I shall have to ponder the matter." She turned her back on me and made to leave.

"So that's it?" The anger and frustration of the last few days was overwhelming me now. "You're just going to walk out of here and leave me dangling like a marionette, ready to jig up and down at your pleasure? Well, let me tell you, that's not going to happen. I'm sick of being played by women, using me for their latest whim and then discarding me. I've put things back to how they should be! I have! I'm going to drive over to Caroline's house and see my son. Then I'm gonna spend the rest of my life being his dad and no one's gonna stop me. Not Caroline, not you!"

She turned and grinned wickedly. "Oh? It's going to be happy families is it? You and your little boy. Going to go and play football are you? Buy a puppy? Yes, you've changed things, alright, Sam, but consider this: how *much* have you changed?" and with that she walked out of the door.

She was playing with me.

She was toying with me.

I had killed her devotee and she was giving me payback.

I lay the gun down and fished out my mobile. I tapped the contacts icon and scrolled down to the "A" entries. There was no Adamson, Caroline.

My stomach turned.

I flicked on my internet browser and Googled the *Lancaster Chronicle*. I flicked to the *What's On* section. There grinning at me was some young chap with a neat goatee. Not Caroline.

No, no, no.

I drew up a telephone directory and entered her details. Nothing.

Then it started to sink in.

My last conversation with Wallace at university had been regarding my parish placement. He was going to give me the details the next day. As it had transpired he had run off with my visitor and left me a note.

Oh, God!

He had given me a note after I had killed him.

"But I still remember going," the words choked me.

"That's because you did. Just not in *this* timeline."

I turned and Alec was sat on the sofa. "How long have you been here?"

He shrugged in a manner that only teenagers can. "I got here before Asherah."

Asherah. I remembered the statue in Wallace's collection and a little wooden stick in his room as a student. He had laughed when I had asked if she was older.

"Asherah." My voice was dry. My head was spinning. "*The* Asherah."

Alec nodded. "Strange to see her on her own, though. Asmodeus must be nearby, I guess. Either that or he's off looking for his..."

I cut across him. "Asmodeus? As in the book of *Tobit*? You're serious?"

He nodded again. "Last time I saw them was back in ancient Israel. He had this racket going with Solomon and the building of the temple. Then she waltzed in and things got kind of messy."

Two images melded together in my head. One was from the story Uncle had told me about a dark stranger in a Jewish ghetto, the other was of similar figure shooting Wallace through the portal to Beyond.

I grabbed the discarded whiskey bottle off the floor. Fortunately, there was still some left in the bottom. I downed the lot. A goddess and a demon? Here? In Lancaster?

"Bloody hell," I groaned. Then the whiskey took hold and the tears started to force their way out of my ducts. "John! What about John?"

"You never met Caroline. He was never born."

The bottle almost made a satisfying sound as it smashed against the wall. I threw myself after it, screaming, pounding my fists time and time again against the hard surface. They must have started to bleed eventually as red smears streaked on the wallpaper. "Nothing," I sobbed. "All for nothing." I slouched down on the floor, put my head in my bleeding hands and wept openly. "What's the sodding point?"

I felt Alec crouch down next to me. He put his arm around my shoulders and guided me to the sofa. "It's a bit more complicated than that.

There is still hope."

He looked blurred through my tears. "What do you mean?"

The youth took a handkerchief from his pocket, moistened it with his saliva and dabbed at my abraded hands. "Remember what I said Wallace had done with your son? Where he had sent him?"

"Beyond."

Alec nodded. "Well, Beyond is outside of our physical universe. The laws of time and space do not apply there. He'll still be there."

"Even though he never existed here?"

Again, a quiet nod. "There's a sort of paradox. If you look through your laptop all the things from your first week will still be there: Satanists, vampires, fairies and one big, ugly werewolf. This is because they did happen in *your* past."

"So I really met John at Saint Edmund's"

"In *your* timeline, yes. Just as the John O'Gaunt team were under Wallace's control. However, in *this* timeline things will be different. Perhaps those actors had different motives for kidnapping you and perhaps you had a different guide around Saint Edmund's. I don't know for sure, but we will just have to see what other people say or mention."

I looked at this young lad who seemed far wiser than I could ever be. "But *you* remember what happened in my timeline?"

"Yes, because I'm special."

"Angels?"

He smiled. "Angels."

I thought about my son trapped in some timeless hell and tears welled up inside me. "How do we get him back?"

"I don't know, Sam, but I know someone who might be able to help."

The next day must have been a week day. I didn't have a clue which one but people were bustling around outside earlier than I would have liked so it must have been somewhere between Monday and Friday. I glanced at my watch. It was just after noon. How long had I been asleep? At least there had been no dreams.

I crawled out of my pit, rummaged in the drawer for some paracetamol and downed them before lying back and listening to the silence.

No. Not silence.

Listening to the bells.

The fucking bells.

I think I screamed.

I hadn't realised that they were back the day before with all the comings and goings of supernatural folk, but I guessed it was inevitable.

No Wallace, no miracle cure.

Ah, sod it. I'd coped for almost forty years, I'd carry on coping.

I got out of bed, showered, shaved and dressed. As I entered the living room I saw my laptop on the table. Drumming my fingers against my teeth, I opened it up and pulled up Google Chrome. I typed in Caroline's name and waited.

"Well, well," I muttered as her face grinned up at me from the top hit. "Daddy's girl did good after all then." She was still a reporter, but not for some provincial little rag. She was working for a national TV network heading an investigative show that interviewed people with quirky lifestyles and obscure professions. Apparently it was quite popular.

I couldn't help but smile. Good for her, I thought. Perhaps the bitchy little cow that I had known and loved was just a result of a life that had never achieved its full potential.

I typed in another name. Again there was a result. I checked my watch. It was now just gone one. I had a couple of hours at least. I'd grab a bite to eat before I caught up with this one.

I arrived outside Saint Edmund Campion School just before three. God alone knew what I had in mind. First, would Abalone have actually met me? I remembered going to the school to investigate the so-called poltergeist, but did it really happen and, if so, did I meet her there or not?

Also, how could I be sure that I would see her come out of school and at what time? I didn't want one of Jitendra's boys picking me up as a potential paedo.

Jitendra. There was another one. I had met him because of the little group of Satanists who had been devotees of Wallace. Damn. I was going to have to check over everything with Alec and see what had actually been going on in my life for the last week or so.

I was just about to Google the good policeman on my mobile when a flash of blonde hair caught my eye. There she was, over the other side of the road! Not only was Abalone still alive, but she was as cute as ever. There was a definite spring in her step and her locks shone in the dying light of the late autumn day.

But I soon realised that she was not alone. There, jogging up to meet her was a man of a similar age who stood about six foot and sported a corduroy jacket with elbow patches. She rushed to hug and him and, as they kissed, I recalled the dead boyfriend. Had his accident been instigated by Wallace to draw her into Credete?

I turned and walked away.

She would be better off without me anyway.

I thrust my hands deep into my pockets and felt my fingers slide around my phone. I remembered with fond sadness the meal at Alessandro's which had now never happened. I remembered how Abalone had made me feel and I remembered the wonderful deed that she had done.

I pulled my phone out and hit speed dial. It was answered after three rings.

"Hello Mum."

I took my time walking home. It meant I was able to natter to my mum. She told me she was well, that the neighbours were well, that their pets were well and that someone who I had never met before but was a very nice man was also well.

I think this meant that she was happy to hear from me.

As I entered my stairwell she asked, "So when am I going to see you, Sammy? It's been a very long time."

I smiled. Indeed it had. "Tell you what, why don't I pop down later this week?"

She thought that was a fantastic idea and I said I'd check my diary then get back to her. We said our goodbyes and I unlocked my office door.

I groaned at the sight that met me.

"What the hell is a gargoyle doing in here?"

Sam will return in
Sam Spallucci: Shadows of Lancaster.

# Afterword

So there you have it, my second foray into the beleaguered life of Samuel C. Spallucci, investigator of the paranormal. I hope you liked it. Please look out for the next two instalments: *Sam Spallucci: Shadows of Lancaster* and *Sam Spallucci: Dark Justice*.

I ummed and aahed over the format of *Ghosts*. I had really enjoyed playing with the format of *Casebook*, using five individual stories that contained a background arc weaving through them and, at one point, it was my original intention to do the same with *Ghosts*. I had thought about using five or six cases with Malcolm Wallace lurking ominously in the background but it soon became clear as I developed his storyline that the topics of Credete and the Divergence were far too big to share the space in a book with other independent stories. So it was that *Ghosts* became a novel-length story and I'm rather pleased with the end product. This let me play about with older characters and bring in new ones hovering on the fringe, hopefully teasing you as to their purpose and identities.

One character I really enjoyed using more was Sam's mysterious guardian angel, Alec. We shall be seeing a lot more of him as the stories develop. Indeed, he has his own novel formulating in my head at the moment, explaining his back history and all the little tidbits that he feeds Sam from time to time including the identity of his parents.

Another character that I have been very excited about unleashing is Asherah. She is one of my favourite creations, first seeing the light of day in the as yet unpublished fantasy novel *Fallen Angel*. The ultimate bitch, she is self-serving, self-worshipping and lacks any sort of compassion for any other lifeform including her various lovers and her long time on and off companion

Asmodeus. She will return to torment Sam, albeit not imminently as it is possible to have too much of a good thing. Also, look out for a story I'm working on set at the fall of Troy where she will play a pivotal role.

So in the meantime, feel free to look me up on Instagram, Twitter and Facebook. Don't be afraid to say, "Hi!" I don't bite. Well not all the time, anyway.

ASC. February 2018.

# Sam Spallucci: Shadows of Lancaster

# Prologue

How do things end?

Is it with a bang? A cataclysmic explosion of passion, anger or relief? Giving in to those creeping hormones as they revel in the desired attention from a fellow workmate, leading to an office *thing* going just that bit too far for matrimonial harmony? Harsh words in a moment of irritation that can sever a relationship of many years? Is it the strength to walk away from a lifetime of degradation and humiliation, to pack your bag, walk out the door and just leave no matter how much they claim that they love you?

Or is it that they just fade away...

Into the shadows.

Do those dark recesses of your life reach out with Cthulhuesque tentacles and drag back into their gloomy embrace that which used to be theirs but which you unknowingly borrowed for just a short period of time?

All things come to an end; that is unavoidable. Grass is devoured by hungry sheep or cattle. Geriatric hearts finally beat their last and our terminal breath rattles from our tar-stained lungs. A star collapses in on itself forming a gravity well so ravenous that no planet in its orbit can escape its final meal.

But what is the true cause of this finality? Is it really written in stone? Yes, things come and things go but why must their passing to oblivion occur at a set moment in time? Can it be predetermined, sought after or stalled?

Can that which has happened many years ago bring about the final moments and actions of those who walk this planet today? Can repercussions echo through time?

I say that yes, they most certainly can.

# The Case of the Grotesque Graffiti

There are certain things that you expect when you walk through a door. If it is your house, then there might be a cosy armchair where you can crash out and flick through the latest book you recently acquired: Stephen King, Anne Rice, Bernard Cornwell or even Jeffrey Archer. Alternatively, there might be an enthusiastic household pet, say a cat or a dog, which comes bounding up to you with unselfish glee at your arrival home. If it is your workplace then you might expect there to be a utilitarian desk or a bland, beige counter, somewhere that you perform whatever cerebrally putrefying day-to-day task it is you tolerate to pay for the gold-plated food for which your fawning animal companions *really* love you.

These are the *normal* things.

I am now fully aware that my life as a paranormal investigator has far transcended that which is considered normal just in the course of my first week on the job. I had already come up against numerous supernatural creatures only then to be pitched against an old university acquaintance who was hell bent on bringing about the end of reality as we knew it. After apparently blowing my brains out at his behest, I slipped back in time to prevent his tutelage under a fallen angel before I returned to an alternative present where he no longer existed. Not only this but my recently acquainted son was now stranded in some obscure purgatory and the previous week had been wiped from time, causing me to have to relive it again and work out what in my head were real memories and what were echoes of things that had never been.

Therefore, it should have been of no surprise that, when I opened the door to my office, I found a gargoyle sitting in the middle of the room.

It was a big feller: taller than me, broad, with wings folded neatly behind its back and huge stone claws digging into my unfortunate carpet. I issued a deep sigh as I closed the treacherous door that seemed to want to admit any manner of creature, be they vampires, angels, pawnbrokers and now gothic roof ornaments, into my office. I was exhausted both physically and mentally from my recent escapades concerning Malcolm Wallace. He had dragged me right to the edge and mercilessly pushed me over with a firm shove. Yes, I had bounced back, but right now I just felt like crawling upstairs to bed and sleeping for a week after downing a bottle of Jack. Instead, I settled for slumping against the door and sliding down until I was sat on the floor.

I fished a Lucky out of my mac and regarded my latest intruder whilst inhaling the smoky goodness from the only true constants in my ever-evolving life. "So," I said, puffing out a smoke ring, "as you managed to bring yourself here to see me, I'm guessing that you can communicate."

As the gargoyle's head tilted to one side, I expected there to be the noise akin to a boulder scraping along the side of an expensive car. Instead, its movement produced no sound whatsoever until its mouth opened and words plodded out like a mammoth going for an afternoon stroll. "Indeed, this one can. When it is necessary. As it is at this moment in time."

I took another drag on the cigarette. "I take it that talking is something gargoyles are not used to."

There was a low rumble that I guessed was a clearing of a stone oesophagus before the stone creature loomed in my face. For such a large being with such a ponderous voice, I was again amazed at the lack of noise with which the massive form moved. Perhaps it spent many hours rubbing oil into its joints? An image of a gargoyle massage parlour flitted into my mind and I discarded that idea as just plain silly. "This one is not a *gargoyle*," it growled, the overwhelming stench of damp moss assaulting my nostrils. "Does this one look like a moronic water spout?" It straightened up, crossed its arms and huffed, "This one is a *grotesque*."

"My apologies." I dragged myself up to my feet and stubbed my Lucky out on a nearby saucer. "I meant no offence." The grotesque inclined its head slowly to one side as I made my way to my filing cabinet.

"That is acceptable," it rumbled.

I took a bottle of Jack out from the bottom drawer and poured myself a large measure. "Do you..?" I asked, waggling the bottle towards him.

It shook its head. "No, thank you. This one has no need." In a drawn out, lumbering movement, it turned to face me. I grimaced as its stone feet mangled my increasingly pathetic excuse for a carpet even more.

"So, what can I do to help you?" I enquired.

The grotesque's shoulders rose and fell in a deep articulation of a sigh that caused its stone wings to tremble. Something was clearly bothering my visitor. "This one has been sent for your assistance. These ones are quiet creatures," stated the deep, gravelly voice. "These ones sit. These ones stay. These ones watch."

I sipped some bourbon and looked the stone creature up and down. "You look familiar. Which building are you from?"

"These ones reside atop the Priory."

I nodded as recognition provided a certain amount of illumination. Saint Mary's is the central parochial Anglican church of Lancaster. Being one of the oldest surviving buildings in the city, it is situated next to the Castle. The two edifices can be seen with ease from any vantage point. It contains beautiful stained glass windows and a number of intricate stone carvings.

Apparently some of which were alive.

"You say, 'These ones.' Does that mean that all the grotesques on the Priory are living things?"

Its head moved down then up in a single nod. "These ones sit. These ones stay. These ones watch."

"You must see quite a lot."

Again, a single nod.

"So, as I asked before, what brings you here?"

"There is one that does not do this. There is one that abandons its position. There is one that wanders. There is one that *writes.*"

The sound of utter disgust in the final word made me shudder and I downed the bourbon. "I take it that's a bad thing, then?"

"These ones do not write. These ones sit. These ones..."

"Yeah," I interrupted. "I get the picture. Wonderful sandstone tranquillity and meditation. What does he, or is it *she*, write?"

"These ones have no gender. These ones are just grotesque," explained the creature. "That one is not satisfied. That one has taken a name. That one writes that name around the city."

"And again I'm guessing that's bad?"

"These ones do not possess names. Names are not necessary for just watching."

I nodded. It made sense. If all you did all day was just sit and watch the world go by with no communication, then surely a name was fairly pointless? "So what does this grotesque call itself?"

"That one calls itself *Spud.*"

"I know that name." Indeed I did. I had seen it neatly written on both a wall and a door. The former in Sugar House Alley when I had been accompanied by an abandoned vampire, the second behind the Town Hall when I had attended Wallace's little Credete shindig. "It graffitis 'Spud was here' doesn't it?"

The grotesque nodded once more. "That one must stop what that one does. These ones do not write."

"Have you tried to stop him?"

"That is a problem." If the grotesque's lips had not been chiselled from stone then I was sure that it would have been worrying at them with its teeth right then.

"How come?"

The grotesque lifted a taloned hand to its face and pointed at its blank, grey orbs. "With these, these ones see. With these, these ones *all* see. These ones see everything. This one looks, other ones see. Other ones look, this one sees. Even if this one is not there, still this one will see." It craned its head to one side to see if I understood.

I thought that I did.

"You have a collective consciousness? What one of you witnesses, so do all the rest of you?"

It nodded.

I frowned as I briefly drummed my fingers against my teeth in thought. "So, how is that a problem?"

"These ones see all the writing. These ones see that one's hand reach out. These ones see the hand at work yet these ones do not know which one the hand belongs to."

This started to make sense. "So, let me get this straight. You know one of you is off writing their name around town because you all see it through their eyes, but you don't know which one of you it is because you are static and just facing your own direction."

"Yes."

"But you are here. You moved to come to me."

"These ones are desperate. These ones just wish to watch. These ones do not wish to be disturbed. That is why this one was sent."

"And if you tried to work out who the vandal was then people might notice."

"Yes, that is correct."

Without wanting to make a pun of it, the grotesques were between a rock and a hard place. They knew what was happening. Indeed, they could see it with their own eyes. However, to cause a fuss would bring unwanted attention so one had been dispatched to find help.

"Okay, I'm in. Do you have any suggestions how I can track this chap down?"

"That one wrote again last night. You should go there."

Normally, when I'm on Cheapside, part of the main pedestrian area of Lancaster, I am frequenting the small burger stand on the corner owned and run by one of my sources of local information: Bob. With afternoon getting ready for some treasured time at home with its feet up on the sofa and flicking through the television channels and evening readying itself for a night out on the town, Lancaster's purveyor of all things in a bun (white, wholemeal or seeded) had already packed up and headed home.

Cheapside's other resident, however, was still in full flow.

As I headed towards the site of what I had been told was the latest outbreak of graffiti, the sounds of *The Show Must Go On* were belting up the street. I smiled then realised that the late, great Freddie Mercury was not singing the lyrics, but instead the words were coming from the mouth of Lancaster's very own Boombox Betty. I frowned as I paused and watched her pouring her heart out to an instrumental backing track of the classic Queen hit. Now, I know that this sounds not run of the mill in any sense - Betty is a local legend and well known for her eccentric behaviour and choice of snappy numbers – but the peculiar thing was that she never normally sang to the songs, certainly not without being accompanied by a recording of the original singer. She normally played her music and just danced along with exuberant enthusiasm. I was not the only one to be drawn in by her voice. A number of passers-by had stopped and stood watching in what appeared to be true admiration.

Lancastrians mostly love Betty, seeing her as a free local attraction, and as the song drew to its close, there was a quiet pause before applause rippled around the surrounding crowd. Awkwardly, Betty performed a small curtsey and started to busy herself with her CD player.

The crowd dispersed and went their separate ways.

I turned and looked at the building behind Betty: Nowell's restaurant.

I am not much of a fan of fine dining. Never have been, never will be. It's not just the fact that I'm a vegan and most high-class restaurants serve up food that previously had a pulse, it's more the fact that the whole thing is a con-job and everyone seems to buy into it. If I go out to eat, say at the Borough or at the Paradise Dragon, I get a good plateful of food that will fill me up and sustain me. Whether it be a large burger with a mountain of chips or a sweet and sour with enough rice to brew fifty bottles of sake, I will walk away from the table satisfied with a warm feeling of contentment in my belly.

When most people walk away from a fine dining joint they normally stop off at the nearest takeaway and wolf down as much carbohydrate as they can to quiet their rumbling stomach that is complaining of a promise that has not yet been delivered on.

Now, the more *educated* would say that the delicacies delivered at these establishments of haute cuisine are, in fact, mini *objets d'art.* They might then go on to say that the arrangement of the food is there to entice the diner and the aromatic fragrances are layered to tantalise the senses.

I say back to them that they need to get a life rather than making *Masterchef* sound like upper class porn.

So, needless to say, I had never entered let alone dined at the phenomenon that was Nowell's. As I stood outside its glass-fronted dining area that overlooked Cheapside, I puffed away thoughtfully on a Lucky. As my stony-faced client had informed me, the errant roof ornament had done quite a job on the frontage of the building. “Spud was here.” was neatly painted across the wide window. Once more the spelling was correct and the grammar perfect, so unlike most graffiti one would find in toilet cubicles which offered unmentionable services or cast into question the purity of random individuals' lifestyles.

There was something else. Even though the paint had been applied direct to glass, there were no runs or smears. The letters were formed correctly and without the slightest error. I ran a finger around the base of the final “e” in “here” and could find neither the slightest wiggle nor bump. I knew for a fact that if I had attempted to spray paint onto such a smooth surface then the result would have looked like something Jackson Pollock had attempted using a melted felt tip pen whilst wearing a horny koala on his face. This was so clean and clinical. I was impressed.

Someone else, however, was not.

“Bloody vandals! Nothing's sacred these days.”

I turned to see a squat man who was almost as broad as he was tall. His thinning dark hair was neatly combed into place and his angular chin was shaved to within a nanometre of perfection. His was the sort of chin upon which stubble dared to emerge at its peril. Muscles rippled out from under immaculate, starched chef's whites and fury burned behind his piercing blue eyes.

“I imagine it's quite annoying,” I volunteered.

The chef snorted in disgust. “*Criminal* would be more accurate. The yobs have no respect for anyone else's property. Probably high on crack when they did it.”

I raised an amused eyebrow. If only he had caught a glimpse of his artistic vandal. Perhaps then his righteous indignation would have been dampened somewhat. “Sam Spallucci. Investigator.” I extinguished my cigarette and stuck out a hand. “Pleased to meet you.”

“Colin Nowell.” He squeezed my hand in a vice, reminding me that I really had to work on a firmer handshake. “Owner, head chef and target of moronic hoodlums.” He looked up at me and frowned. “You said, 'investigator.' Are you here because of this?” he snapped, waving a hand at the graffiti.

There was a clatter from nearby. We both turned our heads in the direction of the noise. Boombox Betty was fiddling with her CD player and seemed to be trying to ease it into a small holdall.

“What are you staring at?” Nowell growled at her with no lack of animosity.

Betty flinched and looked desperately like she *also* wanted to fit in the small bag.

I frowned. “Perhaps we could speak inside?”

Nowell continued to glare at Lancaster's harmless eccentric for a moment more then gave a small shrug and opened the door to his restaurant. “After you.”

I had to admit that it was rather nice. The ambient temperature felt just right without being blown away by an over-enthusiastic air conditioner. Well-tended palms broke up dull corners and the smell of strong coffee caressed my olfactory nerve.

Nowell was obviously perceptive and had noticed my reaction to the enticing aroma. “Sit down. I'll get you an espresso.”

I slid into a booth next to the far wall. A copy of the *Chronicle*, the local rag owned by incredibly rich bullyboy and family beater, Hector Scarisbrick, lay on the table. The front page was divided between two stories. The side column was telling of a local pimp who had been found dead and the police were somewhat quiet over the details of his demise. The editorial shed no tears over the death but wanted to know what exactly the local fuzz were withholding. The main headline proclaimed that Frontierland, the derelict ex-theme park on the front in Morecambe had been burnt down in suspicious circumstances. The journo who had penned the article saw it as yet another sign of moral decline, anti-establishment aggression and probably a threat to all things British. I shook my head, pushed the paper away and eased myself back into a chair the comfort of which matched the sleek décor or the restaurant. Normally when I sit on a long bench or other such affair I find myself wriggling and desperate for personal space. Here, however, every muscle of my back and behind was catered for. There was the right balance of give and support that informed me I would never feel discomfort whilst in its secure embrace. As I relaxed into my sedentary bliss I cast an eye up to the wall and let out a low whistle. There, for all to see, was a detailed tree of Colin Nowell's family and ancestors. I craned my neck to follow the neat script and connecting lines as it took his lineage back through generation after generation. I have always had a penchant for this sort of thing. I think it's fascinating to know where we come from and whether it bears any resemblance to where we are today. "Nice," I whispered.

"Bloody should be," Nowell grumbled as he slid in opposite me with two coffees. "Cost a sodding fortune."

I dropped three sugars into my drink. "You paid to have it researched?"

"Nope. All the blood, sweat, tears and sore eyes from staring at online databases were mine and mine alone. Some of these sites are running a right little racket. Costs an arm and a leg to get hold of a certificate that you can't even be sure is correct until it drops through your letterbox. Mind you, it was worth it. Found out some fascinating things." I noticed his eyes drift out the window to where Betty had finally packed up and was scuttling off down Cheapside. "Yes, very fascinating things," he murmured.

I stroked the handle of my coffee cup with my thumb. There was obviously history of some sort between Betty and the restaurateur, but that was none of my business so I pulled him back on track to the family tree. "How far back does it go?"

My host sipped his coffee and looked up appreciatively at the timeline. "To a time when people knew it was wrong to break the law. This one here," he pointed to *Alexander Nowell*, "produced the first bottled beer."

"Seriously?" I was genuinely impressed.

"Yep," the modern day Nowell nodded with pride. "Did it by accident when he went fishing one day."

I peered at the dates under the name. "That's back in the fifteen hundreds. Amazing. I always thought it was modern."

"Oh, they knew a thing or two back then. Like how to keep order. Take Roger Nowell for instance." His finger pointed to a name in the seventeenth century. "I hold him in very high esteem."

"Why's that?"

"He was a Justice of the Peace and kept order over in East Lancashire during some dark times. A fine man." Nowell's brick-built chest practically burst out of his chef's whites with pride. "Yes, he could get to the bottom of that monstrosity, I'm sure." He inclined his balding head to the graffiti on the window. "So, tell me, why are you here, then?"

Now, that was a good one. I could hardly tell him who my client was. I sipped the espresso as I carefully chose my words. "I'm working for a family who believe that their son might be responsible. However, they need proof. Did you see anything at all?"

"Nothing. It was here when I came in this morning. Been glaring at me all day. Didn't remove it in case the police wanted a look-see, but they've not been near. I was about to scrub it off before you got here." He leaned back in the booth, his thick arms crossed across his wide chest. "So, tell me. Who are they?"

I grimaced. "Sorry. Can't do that. Client confidentiality."

Nowell leaned menacingly across the table. "Bullshit," he hissed into my face. "I want to know who's been scrawling on my window so I can wring their sodding neck and you're going to tell me."

I was about to mouth back at him when something curious happened. I felt an insistent tug at my sleeve. I glanced around but there was nobody there. Looking back at the angry bulldog that sat opposite me, I shrugged, stood up and made to leave.

"Hey! Where do you think you're going?"

I had encountered men like Colin Nowell many times before. They fuel themselves on self-righteous indignation. The universe spins around them whether it wants to or not and everything must run to their own personal drumbeat. If you oppose them then they will march right over you, both metaphorically and with every physical sense of the phrase.

There was nothing else that I could glean from him so I ignored his challenge, carried on walking and left the restaurant, turning back up Cheapside towards Penny Street.

"How long have you been there?" I asked.

"Long enough." The voice was disembodied but distinct. It belonged to my new lodger and companion, a teenage boy by the name of Alec who had already saved my life and proved most helpful with my investigations into Malcolm Wallace.

He had very special talents.

"I did not like the man."

"You and me both," I agreed as I turned down Ffrancis Passage. It was empty. There was a slight shimmering of substance and Alec was stood next to me. "What did you get from inside his head?"

The youth shrugged. "Much the same as came out of his mouth. The man's an intolerant bigot who believes that hanging's not good enough for the likes of them. That and he's obsessed with his family history."

I chuckled. "Yeah, that's about right, but it doesn't really give me anything else to go on, does it?"

"Perhaps."

I groaned. "Oh, come on. Don't go all Yoda on me. What do you mean?"

"I was just thinking that this is the second time that you've lived this week, yes?"

I nodded.

"Where were you tomorrow, last week?"

The days bounced through my head. It was Tuesday evening, which meant that tomorrow, when I had previously lived this week before I had reset it, I had gone to the Credete meeting with the poor Abalone at...

"The Town Hall!"

Alec nodded. "All you have to do is be there when Spud shows up to graffiti the doors around the back."

I looked up in the sky. There was definitely more darkness up there than light and I made to head off to the Town Hall. I was halted by an almost embarrassed cough. "What is it?"

Alec kept pace with me as we walked up Dalton Square towards the Paradise Dragon. "There is one small thing. What with last week not happening and all that went on, are you still okay for me to crash in your attic?"

There are three storeys above Harry Kim's outstanding Chinese restaurant. The first is occupied by my office, the second by my flat and the third by a small, spare attic room. As we entered this unused space, our shoes left deep imprints in the accumulated layers of dust that looked like it hadn't been disturbed for many years. I was sure that I heard something scuttle off in a dark corner – something with far too many legs than can be considered natural.

"I'm afraid it's not much..." I began.

"Trust me," Alec butted in, "compared to where I've been kipping the last few weeks, it's paradise." He began to explore what little there was up in the roof space of 15, Dalton Square and discovered a small Velux window that he proceeded to polish with the sleeve of his hoodie. "I can see out across the city centre from here," he grinned. "Cool."

I eased myself down onto an old mattress that had been left discarded up here for some unknown reason. A musty smell of decaying bedbugs assaulted my nose. "I thought you'd rather be up here than on my sofa. Privacy and all that."

Alec squatted down next to me and patted the mattress appreciatively. A mushroom cloud of festering matter billowed up into the stale atmosphere. "It's perfect, what with me being on the run from the police, and all."

I shuddered. "Yes, we will need to have a chat about that in a bit more detail..."

"Just not right now," the teenager finished. His eyes locked on mine in the gloom and there it was again, the older soul that I had seen before. The one that had lived a very long time and seen far too much. It was not to be argued with.

"Some other time," I surrendered. "Look," a wonky plug socket hung precariously from the wall. "You've got power up here."

The old soul vanished as quickly as it had arrived and the young lad was back in the room, excited to have a place of his own, albeit shared with numerous spiders, insects and whatever else had their beady little eyes on us. "Cool. I'll have to get myself a stereo or something."

We sat there for a short while, the late thirties paranormal investigator who only last week (or was it this week?) had shot himself, died and come back to life whilst resetting reality around him and the mysterious teenage boy who was apparently part angel and could perform tricks the like of which most people would just scoff at.

It really is a funny old life.

Eventually, I stood up, brushing dust off my backside. "I guess I'd better go find myself a grotesque."

The sun had well and truly set by the time I had ensconced myself behind some trees opposite the rear of the Town Hall. Even surrounded by a town planner's vague attempt to make urban renewal look *green*, I still felt somewhat conspicuous. A lone man obviously hiding behind a tree in a city centre? Not easy to explain, especially when the magistrates' court was behind me and the police station was just over the road.

I nervously drummed my fingers against my teeth hoping that I would not have to wait too long for my graffitier. *Graffitier:* was that even a real word? Like correct grammar was the worst of my worries.

There was the sound of approaching footsteps and I pulled myself behind my tree as best as I could. A young couple walked down George Street; arm in arm and deep in conversation. The girl giggled as the lad cracked some sort of joke. She batted him playfully on the arm and he feigned mock pain. Young love. Very sweet but, right now, somewhat of a hindrance. I willed them to keep on walking. Instead, they paused in front of my tree and started to do what most young couples do.

As their mouths slurped and their vocal chords moaned, I tried desperately to be an errant leaf or twig. I sucked my stomach in and pulled myself as close to the tree as physically possible.

They would move on soon. They had to.

My mouth fell open as the girl smiled when the boy slipped his hand up inside her top. Oh, come on! In the street? For pity's sake! Did they have no decency?

My eyes skittered from side to side desperate to not see anyone spot me lurking like some dirty mac man behind a tree watching a young couple making out. That would not look good in the local rag, no sir.

Suddenly the girl extricated her mouth from the boy's and looked around quickly. I held my breath. Had I made a noise? Was I discovered?

"What is it?" he asked.

"Did you hear that?" she said.

*Oh, crap*: I thought.

With a quick inclination of her head, the young couple quickly rearranged clothing and trotted off into the night. I was about to let out a sigh of relief when I heard what had caught her attention. There was the sound of scrabbling, something moving on stone. I looked up and saw a huge figure leap down from the roof of the Town Hall. With one solid flap of its stone wings, the grotesque landed lightly on the pavement before approaching the large doors, spray can in hand.

From my hiding place behind the tree, I could not help but smile. The artistic felon was identical to the grotesque in my office in every way bar one.

It was wearing a balaclava.

I mean, come on, it was a huge, stone, winged creature walking around in a Lancastrian back street! It really needed a balaclava?

Quietly, I emerged out from behind the tree and proceeded to cross the road.

I should have remembered my Green Cross Code. There was a flash of headlights and the blatting of a horn as a car screeched to a halt less than a metre from my side. My eyes were drawn through reflexive panic to the car; it was left to my ears to hear the scraping of stone on asphalt as the startled statue made its escape.

"Wait!" I called out, ignoring the startled look of the driver. "Just wait!"

The grotesque glanced over its winged shoulder and I saw it start to flex its muscles. I chased after it and jumped wildly onto its back just as its wings beat hard and its feet parted company with the ground.

This was not good. Not by a long shot.

I frantically scrabbled with my arms and my legs, trying to shimmy myself into a relatively secure position on the fleeing creature's back. I am not a good flyer at the best of times. I hate that feeling when a plane lifts away from the ground and there is an increasing distance separating me from good old *terra firma*. Clinging onto the back of a stone creature whose wings were pounding so hard that they threatened to dislodge me at every beat was indescribably worse. My stomach lurched and rolled as my ride swung around to the left and headed out over the city centre. Familiar landmarks shrank away as did my feeling of surviving this new experience. A gust of wind snagged at us and my hand instinctively flew to my fedora. I felt the grip of my other arm weaken and I slipped down the grotesque's back. Hat still in hand, I desperately rammed my wrist over the joint where its wing met its back. The creature grunted and we skewed to one side causing my legs to slide to the right. I was now hanging precariously with both legs flailing wildly in thin air. My hat crumpled in my palm as I gripped both it and the creature's wing, desperately trying to pull myself back up.

The grotesque's head turned and its eyes peered through the slit of its balaclava. I saw its mouth crumple into what looked like a frown and I felt us start to descend once more.

"Hang on," came its deep voice across the rushing wind.

I had no intention of doing anything else as the evening skyline of Lancaster loomed up to meet us. We had flown over to the western side of the city along the River Lune and close to Luneside University. As the grotesque's strong wings beat through the air, we circled out over the River Lune before beginning our final descent towards landfall. It was at that moment that I gave up and closed my eyes, my lifelong tinnitus now not just ringing but shrieking in pure panic. My stomach cartwheeled up into my gullet as we swooped down to earth and a jarring halt caused my grip to slacken. I rolled onto the greatest thing that the Lord had ever made for me: hard, solid ground.

For a while, I lay curled up in a crumpled heap breathing heavily as I tried desperately not to vomit. I thought about relaxing fields in the summer sun, lapping ripples of a babbling brook and the pleasant warmth of a soothing ginger tea.

It was no good. The ringing was too loud and the nausea too great. I could feel a full-blown vertigo attack starting to build behind my eyes. I screwed my eyelids tight and did the only thing that I had left in my self-help arsenal. I screamed loudly into the night, oblivious of whom or what might be around me, watching and listening. I gave in to the rage and anger that had built up inside me over the last two weeks. I had been abducted, beaten, bitten, scorned, mocked and worst of all, had the entire history of my life rewritten so that it now no longer included a son whom I had only just had the fortune to meet. Then, to top all of this, I had been nearly dropped to my death by a fleeing grotesque that seemed to consider itself a sandstone Banksy.

I must have screamed for quite a while, as the only thing that made me stop was the fact that my voice croaked to a halt once my mouth had run dry. Slowly, I calmed myself back down and stood, eyes closed, feeling for any errant swaying that might cause me to double up and revisit the contents of my stomach.

There was none.

I nodded in satisfaction. Go, Team Sam.

Carefully, I opened my eyes and began to investigate my surroundings. I could not help but let out a low whistle. I was in a ruin of a building but it was far from unloved. Every space of the shattered walls was covered in spray art, from an abstract Ashton Memorial, through to a wonderfully intricate red rose of Lancaster that had details from around the city crafted with exquisite finesse in its petals. I wandered from wall to wall taking in each and every piece of graffiti, my jaw slack with wonder. I fished into my mac pocket and pulled out a pack of Luckies. Before lighting one, I looked over my shoulder at the balaclaved grotesque who was watching me like a child watches a teacher that holds a big, red pen. "Is it okay if I..?"

"Be my guest." The voice was still deep but, unlike the visitor to my office, it had a softer lilt to it. I nodded and lit a cigarette before crossing my arms and just stood there breathing in both the tobacco smoke and the artistic beauty.

"So you must be the eponymous *Spud*." I said whilst my eyes flitted from one painting to another.

The grotesque gave a courteous bow. "Indeed, I am."

"How long have you been doing this?"

"Some weeks now." I felt the floor tremble somewhat as he lumbered up next to me. Nervously, I glanced up at the ceiling where a large hole marked our entrance. The rest of the roof seemed secure. For now, at least. "The others, however, do not approve."

"I know. But then, of course, you know that I know, don't you? What with that whole shared consciousness thing."

The grotesque nodded once more. "I saw you through its eyes."

I looked around and spied a piece of seat-sized rubble. I settled myself down. "Okay, so now I'm here, and as they obviously know I've found you, let's talk."

The grotesque settled itself down onto its haunches and cocked its head expectantly.

"First," I drew deep on the Lucky and looked up at his covered face, "what's with the midnight mercenary look?"

Spud raised a stone claw to its face and pointed tentatively at the balaclava. "You mean this?"

I nodded.

"Isn't it obvious? I don't want people to recognise me."

I stared in silence at the two-metre-tall stone depiction of a winged hell beast as smoke from my fag drifted up between us. "For real?"

It nodded solemnly. "I keep my identity a secret so that people will marvel at my work and not thrust me into the cult of celebrity. I have to remain anonymous."

Once more, I looked at the stone musculature and bat-like wings that had borne me across the night sky of Lancaster. I sighed. "If you say so. Secondly, then: why do you do it?"

The grotesque rose from his crouched posture and began to pace around the perimeter of the broken room. "The others," he rumbled as he let his eyes wander over a brightly coloured representation of Market Square, "are not content with their lives. They sit above the Priory and look down upon the world around them with their hearts of stone. They see humans and other life forms scurrying about their daily business. They witness love and death, charity and murder. Yet they feel that they must never, ever intervene. They feel that they must stay where their creator placed them, rooted in stone on the rooftop. They tolerate their lives." It turned to me, the creature that had taken a name and had rebelled against its kind. Although its eyes were blank circles of stone, they bored into me as it stated with passion, "Life is not there to be tolerated. It is there to be enjoyed. What is the point of having a self-aware state if all that one does is ignore what is within? I know that I can paint. I see the beauty around me and I have to worship it in my own, individual manner. I take spray cans of paint that the builders leave behind and I make my own things of beauty.

"But soon it will have to stop. Soon the builders will come here and develop what they see as wasteland. The machines will bulldoze my art and my legacy will crumble.

"I have nowhere to go, so I protest. I make my mark around town so that people will wonder as to who or what I am. I write it with precision and clarity so that they will see I am not just a random vandal. In every grotesque heart is the precision of the artist that created us, so it must be in my artwork and my message. The people of Lancaster will talk amongst themselves about this mysterious character that dwells amongst them. My name will be on their lips and questions about me in their minds. Then, when their curiosity has reached saturation and they can tolerate the question no longer, I will draw them to this place so that they can witness the beauty of their city as I perceive it through these plain stone eyes. Enlightenment will touch their hearts as they come to realise that, if these bare carvings of stone can see such beauty then they, with their living, organic orbs, must see even more of this incredible creation."

As I sat their listening to the impassioned sermon, I cast my mind back to Colin Nowell. "Not everyone appreciates your signature mark."

Spud shrugged. "There will always be those who disagree with what I do, with the beauty that I create."

"Such as your kindred at the Priory?"

He nodded. "They did not tell you about this place and yet they must have seen it through my eyes. They have seen the wonders that I have painted and the beauty that I have witnessed yet they saw fit to withhold it from you. Why do you think that is?"

Why did anyone ignore the elephant in the room? "They're scared by it, aren't they? They see you as an aberration that needs correcting rather than a seedling that needs nurturing into maturity and full bloom."

"Exactly."

"My guess is that they know this place will be gone soon and your work destroyed. They just want you stopping in the meantime before you draw attention to yourself and them." My eyes wandered again around the artwork. "That would be a shame." With this, it began to dawn on me where we were. "We're on the derelict site near Luneside University, aren't we? On the quay."

Spud nodded. "I came here so that I would be undisturbed in my creation but then I saw the men in hard hats and watched as they measured with their small devices and sprayed markings around the rubble as they surveyed. At first I saw it as an opportunity to acquire free paint but then I realised what they are planning to do."

"They're going to flatten the site and start again," I finished for him. "It's all over the local press. Some big shot from down south has bought up all the land and wants to regenerate it."

A snort of disdain erupted from the grotesque's mouth. "I saw him once. I did not like him. He arrived in a big, fancy car wearing a sharp suit and looked at the ruins with pound signs in his eyes."

I shrugged. "He's a businessman. They're all the same."

"No, no." Spud paced the room once more, clearly agitated. "There is more to him than that. He is wrong. *Very* wrong."

*Uh oh*: I thought to myself. Where was this leading? "What do you mean?"

Spud's clawed hand rubbed frantically at his balaclava as he tried desperately to find the right description. "I cannot truly say. There was something about him; the way that he presented himself, the way that others cowered in his presence and the way that he... he..."

"What?"

"The way that he *walked*."

"The way he walked?"

Spud's head inclined from one side to the other as he thought long and hard about the correct words to explain what he meant. "Us grotesques," he eventually said, "spend all our life watching those down below. We are masters of observation. We can deduce a great deal of information about individuals from the way that they present their bodies and the way that their bodies move."

"You mean body language?"

He pondered this, a stone talon stroking the side of his balaclava as whatever passed for brain cells in his stone head ticked over the matter. "Yes. That feels appropriate. For example, you are tired. Weary. You have been through a lot. I can tell from the way that your shoulders slump downwards and your eyes look dark around the edges."

"Well, I have just had an impromptu flight across the city with no seat belt, nor even the security of four walls."

"No." His voice was steady, firm, concerned. "There is more to it than that."

Okay, now was not the time to discuss my random vicissitudes. I wanted to know about this mystery developer. "Tell me more about this man you saw."

Before he could answer, the grotesque raised his head to the hole in the roof.

From above came the sound of boulders being catapulted at a castle wall. "That is not its concern."

We had company.

There are moments in your life when you cannot avoid the unmistakable fact that things have gone irredeemably wrong and have seriously started to resemble the shape of an over-ripe pear. You know the sort of things I mean. There is the car journey out into the countryside to where you are meeting a cousin in order to scatter a loved uncle's ashes only for your sat nav to guide you in a cheery voice to a wooden shack in the middle of nowhere, outside which is sat a guy with big ears playing a banjo who looks like he has a thing for pigs. Then, perhaps even worse, is the time when that cute girl takes you home to meet her parents and behold, there on the mantel piece, they have a framed picture of Nigel Farage that is smeared with lipstick. Yes, it is in instances like this that you feel fate has taken a very big rock and barricaded the end of the tunnel so securely that not even the smallest iota of light can penetrate the overwhelming darkness and causes your mind to scream, "Get me out of here! Now!"

Well that was the self-same situation in which I found myself that night at Spud's ramshackle art gallery down on the quay.

My newly acquainted friend and I both raised our faces to the hole in the ceiling through which he had carried me. There, framed against the night sky, were half a dozen identical faces peering down. With their features being carved from stone it was hard to read any type of emotion from them, but I was guessing it was not a social call.

"Hello there!" I called up in as cheerful voice as I could manage. "I found your artist."

The ground shuddered and flakes of plaster detached from the broken walls as one of the grotesques thumped down into the room. "These ones know," it stated, its voice devoid of any emotion. "These ones saw."

I nodded. Of course they had. They would have seen everything through Spud's eyes.

The grotesque leaned forward menacingly. "These ones are not pleased with your progress."

"Now, wait a minute," I blustered, aware that things were about to turn rather nasty, "I've not exactly had a long time with him. It took me a while to find him and then there was the business of sheer terror as I clung onto him over the city. So, in reality, we've only just started talking about what's going on."

"Talking, yes," growled the gravelly accusation. "Stopping, no. These ones require that it be stopped. Now. That is why these ones have taken the grave decision to intervene."

Then all hell broke loose.

The five other grotesques crashed through the hole in the roof at the same time causing plaster, slate and timber to come cascading down. They and Spud were seemingly unaffected. I, on the other hand, was somewhat aware of the fact that I was not crafted from stone so I dove for cover against what looked to be the strongest of the walls. Even so, I was still showered in dust and muck from the grotesques' entrance. I coughed and spluttered amongst the flying detritus and managed to roll somewhat awkwardly out of the way before my location was suddenly impacted upon by a speeding piece of ecclesiastical statuary.

Spud, however, was not going down without a fight. As the others charged him, he took them on, one by one, and hurled them effortlessly around the room. Evidently his time alone grooming his own independence was giving him somewhat of an edge in the scuffle and he was able to bat off the individual attacks from his kindred masonry.

I decided that it was probably safest if I left him to it and concentrated on not becoming a piece of collateral damage or, to be more precise, a sticky red smear between a grotesque and a wall. The strangest thing about the fight was the lack of noise. Yes, there was the crashing and banging of the participants smacking into each other or the occasional wall, but none of the combatants uttered a single word. They just advanced, took aim and flung themselves at their target. After a while, I actually found myself watching the scene with a certain amount of appreciation just as one might regard the vivacity in a lifelike painting. It was a work of art in itself, albeit somewhat threatening to my existence because of my close proximity to it.

However, all good things come to an end and this was no exception as the reality of the matter started to drive away all thoughts of sublime beauty. The enemy grotesques gradually came to realise that their individual attacks were ultimately futile and slowly they started to learn from their mistakes. They changed tactics and started to attack Spud in pairs. He was immediately thrown by this alteration in their manoeuvres but, being resourceful, he adapted, ducking and diving, using his opponents' body mass against themselves.

Then they attacked him in threes.

This was too much for the lone artist. He tried desperately to dodge the attacks but inevitably they hammered their way through his defences. One grabbed a wing as another latched onto a leg. The third drew itself back then barrelled into Spud's midriff. The result was that Spud was catapulted violently across the remains of the rapidly disintegrating room. In a split second I realised that I was directly in his path. I cowered on the floor and, as the felled grotesque collided with the wall above me, I caught sight of something that chilled me to the bone. There on a fragment of broken plaster was half a face glaring up at me. It was male, with dark hair and sported sunglasses.

I had just the fraction of a moment to realise that I knew this face before something cracked me on the head and darkness descended.

I became aware of Light.

Yes, Light with an upper case letter.

It permeated the darkness, twisting and spiralling out of the gloom like a serpent, insidious of intent and threatening of purpose.

How could this be? Light was good, surely? It protected us from the monsters of the night and was left glowing on the bedside cabinet of many a toddler who knew that creatures stalked the shadows.

Light was our saviour.

Light was our redeemer.

The Light snaked around me and crushed me in its overwhelming grip. I tried to breathe but its coils encased my ribcage, preventing my lungs from performing their most basic task. I tried to scream but the Light twisted up around my throat, squeezing hard against my larynx so that only a strangled squawk could escape my tortured vocal chords.

And yet, I could not die.

I hung there, suspended in the Light as I saw movement in the distance.

There came the sound of measured footsteps and the source of the Light emerged from the dissipating gloom. It was the man, dressed in black and sporting the dark sunglasses. The Light emanated from him as a corona from around an eclipse and in each hand he held an object. In his left was a cup, a chalice like one might find in a church and in his right was a sword, the blade of which gleamed in the brilliance of the Light.

I quaked and wished to fall to my knees, covering my eyes in terror, but the Light would not let me. It gripped me fast and peeled my eyelids back so that I had to watch the steady approach of the dark figure.

Then, when he was no more than a few centimetres from me, he leaned into my face and hissed:

"We are one."

I think I actually screamed as I started to come to. Weak and exhausted from the nightmare, I kept my eyes closed as my head screamed out for paracetamol, ibuprofen, a daytime soap opera - anything to numb the nauseating pain. Slowly, I began to surmise that I was sat slumped against what felt like a wall. My hands went to the floor and I frowned. My fingers were not feeling the rubble or detritus of the grotesques' attack on Spud and his works of urban art. Instead, they were running over a surface that was very smooth apart from overlapping ridges at regular intervals. I dug a nail at the surface and it made a slight impression suggesting that the material upon which I sat was durable but malleable.

My heart started to sink as I realised what substance owned such properties.

Lead.

I seriously did not want to open my eyes, but I really had no choice. Squeezing my eyelids apart a millimetre at a time, I let my brain try to accept the horrifying fact that I was now sat on the roof of Saint Mary's Priory with my back against the top of a buttress. A number of stone heads turned to regard me as I groaned my displeasure.

"You are awake," said one of the grotesques that stood guard over me. "You will come with this one."

"Can't I just have a minute?" I pleaded in a voice, which even to my own ringing ears sounded like a futile whine.

"No," came the reply and a hard grip clamped on my shoulder causing me to wince as I was pulled to my unsteady feet.

Curiously enough, this was not my first time on the roof of a church. When I was a kid I used to be a chorister at my parish church and every Ascension Day we would clamber up a dark spiral staircase and sing to the assembled parish down below. Well, most of us sang. One of us stood there miming, frantically praying for the whole terrifying event to be over as soon as possible.

I will let you guess which choirboy that was.

Correct!

I kept my eyes straight forward. Every instinct was screaming that I should look around, take in my immediate area and plan for a sudden escape. The trouble is, when you are God knows how many metres up above the skyline of Lancaster, the only route of escape involves leaping to an ignominious end. This was not a route that I wished to explore.

It was now very dark. I had obviously been out for a while and the moon hung bright in the sky. I shuddered at the thought that it looked unnervingly closer than I was used to then I let my resolute guard frogmarch me across the roof to where more of his kind were assembled. In their midst, shoulders slumped and wings drooped, stood Spud. I could tell it was him as he still wore the ridiculous balaclava albeit the fabric was now scuffed and ripped. My heart ached for the poor grotesque. He looked as if all life had been sucked out of him. The vivacity with which he had shone so radiantly whilst telling me about his art had been terminally dulled. He looked, for all intents and purposes just like any other statue, just one that had been yarn-bombed with a discarded piece of winter headwear.

"This one," one of the other grotesques rumbled, "has been found."

"This one," said another, "must be stopped."

"This one," came yet another voice, "must never act in that manner again."

There was a clicking of feet and wings, which I took to be signs of agreement from the amassed group.

"This one must be *punished*." This voice rolled like a ferocious avalanche descending on an unsuspecting alpine village. All heads on the roof turned to its source. A grotesque stepped forward that I had not seen before. It was identical in its makeup but distinctly different due to a blanket of moss covering one side of its face and one of its wings. It also had a number of claws missing from its feet. This lack of digits caused it to walk with a pronounced limp. "This one," it continued with ultimate authority, "must never threaten our way of life again."

Uh oh. This was turning into a lynch mob, but as the thought of hanging a statue seemed somewhat ludicrous, I could only guess that Spud's punishment would be somewhat nastier. "What are you going to do?" I asked.

Moss Face gave me the briefest look of contempt then nodded to the grotesques nearest to Spud. "Hold that one," it commanded. Then, turning back to me, it leaned down towards my face and whispered. "That one is an abomination. It is an affront to all that these ones are. These ones sit. These ones watch. This one," it roared with the absolute conviction of a being that would happily dunk an old granny in a lake for talking to her black cat, "sent another one to you for assistance. You failed. As a result, that one," it pointed at the deflated Spud, "will be disassembled, piece by piece. That one shall have its pieces rent apart bit by bit. Then," Its eyes levelled with mine, "these ones shall do the same to you."

So, this was definitely not good. I had to think of something smart and put it into action fast. The thought of those stone creatures exacting punishment on poor Spud and my good self filled me with dread. I had already seen them at work: the way they had relentlessly flung themselves at their quarry, coming at him time and time again, their fluid moves silent in the night air.

Deadly beauty.

Something fired off in my brain. I was not sure what it was but I hoped to God it was the start of a plan. As the grotesques lumbered their way over to the prostrate artist, I twisted out of my captor's grip and hoped that my plan would form quickly enough in my head for me to use it to save our lives.

"Wait!" I called out. "Wait!"

There was a pause in the movement of the grotesques and Moss Face turned towards me. "What is it?" he withered.

Synapses began to fire in my brain and started to dribble words into my frantically blabbering lips. "Are you enjoying this?"

Moss Face twisted his head to one side, shrugged and turned his winged back on me once more.

"Really?" I continued, my hands running through my hair desperately trying to drag my emerging idea out from my follicles. "Are any of you enjoying this?"

There was the sound of hesitant clicking of talons and wings as some of the grotesques turned away from Spud and towards me. I had their attention, now all I needed were the right words.

"How... How does it feel to be moving," I asked, my eyes wide open, my mouth moving rapidly, "after all this time stood still, facing in just one direction?"

More clicking, louder this time. Spud's head raised just a touch. That was good.

"How did it feel to fight," I pointed at the doomed artist, "that one?"

The clicking evolved into a roar as wings clapped together and feet hammered on the roof of the old church. It was a good job it was the middle of the night. Had there been any worshippers inside, they would have thought it was the Rapture.

"It... felt...*good*," came a small voice trying to form the right words for an emotion it had never felt before. "It... felt... *new*."

"Enough!" Thunder ripped from Moss Face as his word split the night sky. "Enough, this one says. New is different. Different is bad. Different is wrong." He paced back and forth along the roof, his posture challenging any who dared to stop him. "These ones sit. These ones stay. These ones watch."

"But what could you watch if you moved? What could you accomplish if your limbs were given freedom?" Here it was! Here was the idea and blowed if I was going to let some bedraggled, lichen-covered roof ornament stop me. "Imagine if you were to move like you did tonight every night! No one need know. No one could see you up here. You were so silent, so stealthy. No one would hear. By day you could watch; by night you could..."

"Be free!" All eyes turned to Spud who now stood erect in the middle of the roof, his tattered balaclava clasped in his taloned hand. His stone eyes shone like diamonds in the moonlight and his wings spread out to their fullest. His spark had rekindled and now he was on fire. "These ones shall be free!"

I grinned as wings flapped and feet stomped in perfect unison. I had done it. I had won them over and saved the day. The grotesques had been emancipated and had chosen to explore a new life of creativity and...

My thoughts were cut painfully short as Moss Face charged at me and sent the pair of us free falling over the edge of the roof.

I had faced death before. Who am I kidding; I had *died* before, slipped behind the smoky veil, trotted up the stairs eternal, knocked upon the pearly gates...

I had not enjoyed the experience then; I was not enjoying it any more now.

After catapulting me out into the less than supportive air over the Castle area of Lancaster, Moss Face's instincts seemed to fail him. Perhaps it was because he had just been driven by overwhelming rage or that he was not used to using his six limbs (two arms, two legs, two wings). Whatever the reason, he plummeted, if you will pardon the pun, like a stone, leaving me to watch his catastrophic impact in the car park below as I followed at a slightly slower velocity.

Now, when I say *slower velocity* that does not imply that I was floating casually down to Earth like a discarded feather that sways back and forth, gently riding the currents. No, I was pinwheeling, turning head over heels and screaming random obscenities when the howling wind that insisted on buffeting my lungs would let me. I was aware neither of time nor distance, just the overwhelming fact that I was about to be spread over a very wide area next to one of Lancaster's buildings of outstanding beauty.

Nice one for the tourists. Here's the Sam Spallucci memorial. It's a modern installation and quite abstract. Take care where you walk, as it can be quite slippery.

The ground drew nearer and nearer. Faster and faster, my fate rose up to greet me with outspread tarmacadam until, at the last moment, I felt myself lurch back up into the air. I wriggled around and looked up to see the angelic sight of a pair of chiselled wings beating strongly into the night. My saviour looked down at me and smiled, its eyes glinting in the moonlight.

It was Spud. Whereas darling Moss Face had been unused to moving his heavy form around, my rogue graffitier was adept at the process and had plucked me from an untimely demise. In a few strong flaps, we were stood once more on the roof of the Priory. I sank down on my shaking legs as another grotesque plodded over and handed me my fedora. "You dropped this," it said matter-of-factly.

All I could do was grasp my battered hat to my chest and smile weakly before keeling over onto my back and passing out with stone cold relief.

When I awoke, I was lying flat out on the sofa in my office. My hat was still gripped firmly in my hand. Spud was crouched in the middle of the room. I sat up, every muscle in my body screaming with tension, and turned to face him. "Thank you."

The grotesque graciously inclined his head. “It is we who should thank you. For too long our lives have been mundane and sedentary. Now...” He let out what in a human would have been a long breath. From him it sounded like a car skidding on gravel. “Now we can explore what it means to be alive. It is scary, yes, and I think that is why that one acted the way it did, but we shall embrace it. We shall be *different*.” He rose and made to leave. “We are in your debt. Should you ever need our help, you will know where to find us.”

With that, Spud eased himself out of my door and made his way silently out into the night.

I went over to my filing cabinet, pulled out a bottle of Jack Daniel's and poured myself a very generous measure.

# The Case of the Bondage-Loving Banshee

Most of the next day was spent in a haze of aching limbs, terrifying flashbacks and one chronic hangover. I eventually tumbled off my bed about five in the afternoon. It was already getting dark outside. I had missed what precious daylight this latter day of autumn had deigned to surrender. Was this to be my life now, staggering from night to night? Dwelling in a shadowy world that no one else knew existed? No one with a normal life, that was. There were certainly those out there who knew of this alternative lifestyle and they revelled in it. They were the stuff of nightmares, the creatures in the closet, the boogeymen under the bed. Hell, they were even the sock monster that always manages to burrow holes into your finest, new hosiery. They were there and they had welcomed me into their hidden universe. Grotesques, vampires, fairies, werewolves — the list seemed to keep getting longer and longer.

I stubbed a toe against an empty bourbon bottle. My big toe peeked up mockingly through a hole in the black cotton. Perhaps there really *were* such things as sock monsters. I sighed and headed to the bathroom. I needed to freshen up.

Fifteen minutes later I was scrubbed, shaved and smelling somewhat more of aftershave than alcohol. I padded barefoot through to the living room and flicked on the goggle box. Thumbing the remote, I scanned through a plethora of channels with minutiae of content. Plastic faces grinned up at me as they tried to win their way out of their humdrum lives. Others tried to sell me the latest fitness video. I watched mindlessly as bombs exploded somewhere in the Middle East and a serious-looking man in a grey suit tried to dazzle the watching world with his perspective on why we were now officially in the middle of World War Three. I shook my head, clicked again then frowned.

I had seen *this* programme before.

I dragged back a series of images from the previous week that had now not happened and there it was. The famous archaeologist, Professor Robert Richmond, was sat on a sofa with a rather cheery interviewer.

"Indus Valley," I mumbled.

Sure enough, the esteemed shoveller of sand and bones proceeded to inform the smiling cardigan person that he had just returned from the Indus Valley and had made some fascinating finds.

I drummed my fingers against my teeth. Something here was not quite right. The program was the same but... I happened to glance out the window and saw the streetlights flickering in Dalton Square. Nodding to myself, I remembered the difference: the programme had been on during the daytime. Now, apparently, archaeology was prime time. *Better than cooking, dancing or wannabe nobodies locked up together in a house*: I mused.

I settled back to enjoy the show as Professor Richmond started to point out details on an image of a horned man who was sat cross-legged and surrounded by animals.

The phone rang.

I groaned and flicked off the television. Apparently, I was doomed never to find out the identity of this ancient animal lover.

"I'm bored," drawled the well-spoken Scottish voice as I picked up the phone.

"Nothing new there, then," I replied, smiling. Dear, old Spliff. Apparently, something else had not changed. "What are you going to do about it, or do I not want to know?"

"Well, I guessed that you were sat there being miserable in the dark and I thought you could come round here so we could be bored together."

I cast my eyes around the flat. He was right. I had not realised that I was now sitting in complete darkness.

"I'll be there in half an hour or so."

It took me a little longer than I had anticipated to complete my walk over to Luneside University. I took the back route through Marsh Estate, unable to walk leisurely down Saint George's Quay as that would take me past a certain grotesque's devastated art gallery. My stomach lurched at the thought of hanging on for grim death as Lancaster sped past below me, wind tugging at my hair and my hat. No, a more indirect route was much more favourable tonight.

As a result, it was getting on for half past six when I knocked on the door to the chaplain's flat. The sight that met my eyes when the door opened almost caused me to faint: Spliff in a pinny, brandishing a feather duster. He was also talking on his phone.

"Yes... yes... that's right. Oh, yes it is." He beckoned me in with the duster. "*Coffee*," he mouthed, inclining his head to the kitchen. I got the hint and made my way across the living room. As I did, I could not help but cast my eyes around in complete amazement. The room was spotless. Gone were the mouldering coffee cups, the overflowing ashtrays and random piles of Kleenex that had been utilised for purposes unmentionable in polite company. The flat, instead, was adorned with freshly cleaned cushions, smelt of Pledge and was that a bowl of potpourri?

One element that had not changed was the ever-threatening presence of Dante, Spliff's black bundle of venom and spite. The cat lay draped over the back of the red sofa scowling in disapproval as Spliff continued to ramble away on the phone whilst cleaning behind the radiator with the duster. "Yes, it is. Very dirty. Sliding in and out. Up and down."

I frowned and shot Dante a confused look as I left the perplexing scene. If he had been human, or even given a damn, he would have shrugged his shoulders and said, "Don't ask me. I just live here."

The cleanliness continued into the kitchen. The sink was not piled high with unwashed crockery and the draining board was clear. There were no random half-open tins of green-topped contents discarded on sticky surfaces. There was just a recently used bottle of Cif and a scrubber.

There was also a freshly brewed pot of coffee. I grabbed two sparkly clean mugs from the ordered and regimented cupboard where a row of china handles saluted me, ladled in a few sugars with a spoon that did not adhere to my fingers and poured the drinks. As I did so, I recalled my visit here the week previous – the week that had not been. Spliff had been ill. He had claimed it had been due to too much drink but Grace had denied having seen him at the Borough. Then I had found a pack of anti-nausea drugs in his kitchen.

I calculated a little mental maths. It was the day after I had visited him during my phantom week. If he had been on the pills for a bad stomach or an evil dose of alcohol then they should have sorted him out and got him back to his chipper old self. My best friend was a creature of habit, though, and they should still be here somewhere. I let my eyes wander over the counter. As well as the cleaning liquid and the coffee pot, there was a teapot with a flowery tea cosy next to it. I lifted the woolly item up and there they were, a pack of Stemetil that was again dated from last Friday, the day of Spliff's mysterious hospital appointment.

It seemed that certain things had not changed.

I replaced the tea cosy and carefully carried the beverages through to the living room leaving my ponderings stored away for another time. Spliff was still chatting away on the phone and, more miraculously than Lazarus rising from the dead in order to host a daytime chat show, he was still cleaning. He motioned for me to put his drink on the coffee table. As I did so he proceeded to pick up a can of polish from the immaculately hoovered floor. "That's right. I've got it in my hand now." He eyed the polish up and down quizzically. "Well... it's long, hard and quite the handful." Something that was said on the phone made him smile. "You would, would you? Well, why don't I shake it for you?" He proceeded to agitate the aerosol, slowly at first, but gradually with more momentum. I sat back, sipping my coffee, watching the curious performance. "Oh, it's getting faster now," Spliff purred into the handset, winking at me. "Much, much faster. Yeah, that's right. The pressure's building up." The can was practically a blur in his hand. "Oh, I know. I do. Here it goes. Yes, here it goes..." He bent over and sprayed the polish over the coffee table, carefully avoiding his mug. "Oh, yes!" he moaned, "It's gone everywhere." There was a pause as he listened to the voice on the other end before raising an amused eyebrow. "You would, would you? Really?" I could hear the suppressed mirth in his voice. "Well why don't I wipe it all up?" With a dramatic flourish that was obviously wasted on the person down the other end of the phone, he pulled a cloth out of his pinny and proceeded to rub the polish into the woodwork. "There, I'm working it into the wood right now. My hand is circling round and round, firmly caressing. It's starting to glisten. It's..." He held the phone away from his ear and the sound of the loud cry from the other end almost made me choke on my coffee. Spliff gave a shrug, switched the phone off and tossed it onto a nearby armchair.

"Now, whenever I tidy up," he said, picking up his coffee, "I'll feel like having a cigarette afterwards." He lit himself a Silk Cut, breathed in deep and purred, "Damn, I'm good."

I shook my head. "Please tell me that wasn't what I think it was."

"I was bored," he explained. "You were taking forever to get over here so I had to distract myself. Besides," his eyes twinkled, "it *was* rather fun."

I looked around the spotless flat. "You're not telling me you tidied this place up in forty minutes."

"No, it's taken most of the day. I think I might have a very big phone bill this month."

I chuckled as I drained my coffee. "Just when I think you can't stoop any lower..."

"Hey! At least my sex life is existent, albeit carried across the telephone network. Plus it helped get the place nice and clean. Besides," he continued, "yours isn't exactly anything to write home about. What?"

There must have been a look on my face. I was thinking about a sweet young woman lying dead in a bath after receiving a phone call from Malcolm Wallace. I slid a concealing mask over my grief. "It's nothing," I smiled. "I'm just jealous."

"Of course you are," my best friend grinned. "Who wouldn't be. Mind you, I might be able to sort you out."

I was just about to ask him how when the phone rang. "Back for round two?" I inquired.

"I might have to get the hoover out," Spliff murmured as he answered the phone. "Hello. Reverend MacIntyre here... Okay... Right... Not again." he groaned. "Okay. Well there's bugger all I can do about it right now, is there? I'll be over with a maintenance team tomorrow morning... Well don't do anything stupid... I don't know. Like sticking your finger in it." He hung up and tossed the phone away again. "Although it would be doing the world a favour."

"Problems?"

"Bloody students complaining again."

I let a chuckle escape and he glowered at me. As well as being the university chaplain, some bright spark in the admin department decided a year or so ago that it would be a brilliant idea for Spliff to be assistant dean of Patterdale College as his flat was just around the corner from that particular hall of residence. Having been trying to work his way back into the vice chancellor's good books since an incident with the V-C's Jaguar, half a bottle of gin and no convenient public toilet, my errant friend had begrudgingly agreed to what he referred to as his term in purgatory. This meant that as well as catering for the spiritual needs of students he was also at the end of the phone should the slightest mishap occur be it blocked drains, attempted suicides or inappropriate relationships with academics. If it was the last of these, Spliff did not really mind as he enjoyed all the juicy details, but as for all the other stuff...

"What is it this time, then?"

"They think I'm a sodding electrician!" he stormed, marching over to the drinks cabinet and pouring himself a large gin and me a fairly substantial bourbon which I accepted gratefully as I sat back to enjoy the rant. "Me! I don't know one end of a screwdriver from another. As far as voltage is concerned all I know is that the more you use, the greater the thrill!" He knocked back half of the drink and slumped into his armchair. "Apparently they're having problems with mini black outs. It's being going on all week. For no apparent reason the lights keep flickering on and off. My guess is that some randy little sod is humping a light socket for cheap thrills."

"Wouldn't they need a step ladder?" I grinned.

All I received in return was a sneer.

I politely quelled my amusement as I sipped my whiskey before steering the boat back onto calmer waters. "So you were interested in improving my sex life then?"

Once more, the chaplain's eyes twinkled and he stroked his neatly trimmed beard. "Sam, have you ever been speed dating?"

It was ostensibly a charity fundraiser. I had no idea what the charity was, but I was fairly convinced that the attendees were more interested in hormonal gratification rather than providing water for an African village or the rights of political prisoners. There were about two dozen of us filing into the back room of the campus bar and, as we entered, we handed over five pounds which was quickly stashed away before we could change our minds. We were then handed a badge onto which we were instructed to write our names as legibly as possible. I was inscribing mine when Spliff sidled up to me.

"Tell me again how you convince me to take part in these sorts of things," I growled under my breath.

"My natural charm and infectious enthusiasm," he grinned.

I raised an eyebrow. "Really? Are you sure it's not those photos you have of me locked away in a safe deposit box somewhere?"

Chuckling, we headed over to the bar. "Seriously, Sam. You need to get out more. Relax and enjoy yourself."

I ordered a Jack Daniel's and looked around the room. It was full of students of varying shapes and sizes but not one of them looked over thirty. "Perhaps fraternizing with those of my own age might be more appropriate?"

Spliff sipped his gin. "Beggars can't be choosers, dear. Oh, look. Here's a friendly face for you."

I smiled warmly at the sight of Grace, the barmaid from the Borough, bounding over to us. "Hey guys! I, like, didn't know you were going to be here."

"Well, Cupid here," I pointed at Spliff, "is one of the organisers."

Spliff held a hand over his chest. "Just spreading true love wherever it's required."

I shook my head in despair.

Grace giggled. "What about you?" she asked me. "Are you, you know, helping out?"

"No," I sighed, "apparently I am taking part."

"Really?" the young girl beamed, her smile filling most of the space beneath her woolly hat. "That's totally awesome!"

"You think so? I'm not so sure. I mean I'm practically a fossil compared to most of the others here."

Grace's head was shaking rapidly from side to side. "Not at all," she said, ordering a soft drink from the bar. "You just need to find the right person and they might, you know, actually be in this very room."

"Thanks for the support," I winked. She wandered off sipping her drink. "Sweet kid," I said.

"That she is, Sam. That she is."

I turned and saw my best friend looking at me in a very peculiar way. "What?"

He said nothing, just shook his head and walked off to start the proceedings. I sipped my drink and surveyed the rest of the attendees. Had I been that young once? I was convinced that most of the males had not even started shaving yet. They were grouped in small gaggles dotted around the edge of the room: some male, some female. Most seemed to be with their friends, the fellow students that they had tagged along with. There was the obligatory group of blonde girls that go everywhere together, all immaculate and groomed. There was a lone girl sat on a table in the corner reading a book, another one playing with what looked like a tail attached to her short, black skirt and a pair of young women who seemed to be having a very heated silent discussion. You know the sort of interaction: one person goes to say something but the other one cuts them off by turning away quickly or throwing up their hands. The first one then gesticulates a *what the hell* as the other storms off to the bar shoving people out of her way. I was busy watching this little scene when I felt someone tap me on the shoulder.

He was tall, clean cut, sporting a rugby shirt and stank of too much cheap, oversweet aftershave. "Hey, there, granddad," the youth winked. "You here to make sure we don't get too rowdy?"

Eyes tracked across the room from the various little cliques and fastened onto me. I internalised a groan of despair. "Actually, I'm here for the speed dating."

Rugby Shirt radiated what could only be described as one hundred per cent insolence and looked knowingly over his shoulder at the others before turning back to me. "Seriously? You want someone to take care of your Zimmer frame?" He laughed at his erudite wit and looked once more at the crowd, giving them a *can you believe this guy* shrug. A blonde girl who looked more bust and bum than brains tittered into her hand. Rugby Shirt winked lecherously at her. I sighed. Some things never changed. I remembered boys like this holding court back when I was an undergrad and dinosaurs still roamed freely. I did the only sensible thing possible, downed my drink, patted him on the cheek and walked away.

His two brain cells had just collided again and were about to utter another little humorous gem when Spliff rang a bell and began to inform us of the rules for the evening. The females were to remain seated at the small tables whilst the males travelled from one date to another. We would have four minutes to tell each other about ourselves before the bell rang and the males were to move on to the next table. On no account were we to exchange details during a date. Instead, we were to tick a *yes* or *no* box on a sheet that we would be given to show our preference for wanting to date each individual. At the end of the evening the organisers would tot up who wanted to date who and, where both people matched, they would be contacted.

The female students took their places and the evening's entertainment commenced.

My first date was Harmony. She was the vacuous blonde who had laughed at Rugby Shirt just before. We shook hands and I was somewhat amazed that she did not immediately wipe hers on her skirt in disgust at being tainted by a lower, non-Instagram life form. Perhaps the material was too expensive to be sullied with my degenerate skin cells. From the outset, it felt incredibly awkward and I am sure that she looked at her watch about five times in the first minute. The problem was, what on earth was I supposed to say to her? I was a thirty-eight-year-old paranormal investigator and she was, surprise surprise, a cheerleader.

I tried my best.

I really did.

"So, have you been on many of these speed dating things, then?" I asked.

"Some," she shrugged. "You normally get to meet fit guys." I saw her glance over at Rugby Shirt and my ego rolled its eyes heavenward in disdain. Whilst she was distracted, I looked over at the clock on the wall. Had it only been two minutes? Heaven help me! I could feel my palms starting to sweat and I was actually having flashbacks to Melanie Brande, sitcom actor and wannabe Satanist. There was something in the *I'm hot, you're not* attitude that made my stomach churn. The back of my mind pondered something: the little harpy and her fellow actors had been in league with Wallace. What had happened to them in this new timeline? I would need to check up on that.

Dragging myself back to my *current* sacrificial predicament, I decided to change tack and impress Harmony with my knowledge of popular culture. "You must get a lot of comments."

"Pardon me?"

"About your name."

"What do you mean?"

"Well, being blonde and called Harmony, people must keep asking you where Spike is."

The silence that followed suggested that they did not. However, like an unfortunate climber plummeting down a gaping crevasse, I was on a roll and could not stop. "It's a *Buffy The Vampire Slayer* reference. Spike is a vampire and Harmony, his girlfriend is also... a...

"So what do you do for fun?"

The bell rang. I was out of my seat quicker than a politician that had been asked about his recent expenses claim and whether he liked his pork well done.

The next date, Juliette, provided me with a quick, precise handshake. No sooner had I seated myself than she demanded, "Are you Italian?"

"Pardon?"

"Your name. It looks Italian." Her voice was, clipped and precise as if she was aware that any excess time spent on a lingering syllable was a nanosecond wasted.

I smiled. At least talking about my name was safer territory. "No. Actually, it's a funny story..."

"How much do you weigh?"

"Pardon?"

The slim woman sighed and pursed her lips. "Really, I don't want to have to keep repeating myself we only have," she checked her watch, "three minutes and twenty-five seconds left."

Okay. This was different. "Well, why don't we start again? I'm Sam and I..." My words drifted off as I realised that she was leaning forwards and furrowing her brow somewhat. "What are you doing?"

"Maintaining eye contact."

"I think that's more like staring."

"No, it's definitely maintaining eye contact. It's what you do to increase levels of phenethylamine."

"Sorry."

"Phenethylamine," she repeated, her unblinking, hazel eyes still boring into me from under the contorted eyebrows. "It's the love hormone. Although if you produce too much it can turn into a flight response."

The bell rang and I swiftly made use of my increased phenethylamine levels.

To Cynthia, I was a huge juggernaut with bright headlamps that was steaming down a country lane about to squash her flat whilst she choked on the remains of a tasty carrot. This metaphor was somewhat accentuated by the huge, dark-rimmed glasses that she wore under a severe basin haircut. All she needed was a thick, orange sweater and I would have expected her to be out solving cases with Scooby and the gang. Instead, she sat rigid opposite me and made curious little noises whenever I spoke.

"Hello, Cynthia. My name is Sam."

"*Squeak!*"

"What are you studying here?"

"*Eep!*"

"Do you get into town much?"

"*Meep!*"

"Do you have any hobbies?"

"*Awk!*"

I sat back and blew out a long breath. I was not so much extracting teeth here as trying to remove an entire mandible. A glance at the clock showed that there were still two and a half minutes to go – an entire geological epoch.

"Why are you here?" I asked in desperation.

"Because my so-called *best friend* made me come."

Okay. A response. A somewhat envenomed one, but a response nonetheless. "You make that sound like a bad thing."

She turned her head to a young woman who was sat three tables down. She was dressed completely in black, had kicked off her heels and was comfortably schooshed up onto the chair as Rugby Shirt was giving her the moves. I looked from Cynthia to her friend then back again and realised that they were the two who had been arguing in thunderous silence earlier.

"The bitch always does this," Cynthia continued. "She drags me along as a Plain Jane so that she shines out better to all the guys." Then, for a moment, a smile touched her lips. "She hasn't learnt yet, but she will. Give it time and the lesson will sink in."

I was about to enquire what the lesson was but whatever the student's machinations happened to be were saved by the bell.

This could not get any worse, could it?

What do you think?

Adele seemed like a nice girl. She had a soft, feminine handshake and informed me that she was a sociology undergrad. We chatted about bits and pieces: how we were finding the evening, the places we liked to go in town and what she hoped to do when she left university.

Things started to go wrong when we got onto the subject of hobbies.

"I collect badges," Adele said as she pulled up a large, canvas bag, the shoulder strap of which was adorned with a plethora of small button badges. "I normally buy them when I go somewhere special or if they have a special meaning."

I dutifully inspected the badges. There was nothing wrong with collecting badges. Certainly a healthy past time. Adele singled out a few which she regarded as special. "This one was my first ever badge," she said, tapping an image of Felix The Cat. She then went on to introduce me to Garfield, Tom, Simba, Salem, Puss-in-Boots and numerous other fictional felines.

"I'm sensing a theme here," I smiled encouragingly. So she had a thing about cats. That was no problem as long as she was not in the habit of wandering around town in her slippers with various mangy felines mewling from inside her shopping trolley. I decided she looked far too well presented for that.

Yes, yes, I know now that appearances can be deceptive.

Adele beamed from ear to ear as she clapped her hands together in unadulterated glee. "Oh, you noticed!" the girl squealed then she leant across the table and her face took on a more serious frame. "Are *you* one too?"

Uh oh.

"One what?"

"A cat."

My subconscious sat with its jaw hanging slack in disbelief.

"I've always known I was one," Adele continued, her misty brown eyes drifting off into some place far away where happy little elves fed friendly unicorns crayons and watched them poop rainbows. "I drank nothing but milk all last year and lived on a diet of sardines and tuna." She reached under the table and yanked up the toy store cat's tail that she was wearing. "Look! I grew this!"

The bell sounded and I moved on in dumbfounded silence. There really was nothing that I could say.

The next date saw me mooring my ship in an undoubtedly safer haven.

"So," Grace smiled, "how are you, you know, doing?"

I sank back in my chair and let out a long breath of air.

"That good then?" She giggled and took a sip from her drink.

"If that's got alcohol in it, I could really do with a swig."

"Sorry. Absolutely part of my five a day."

I stroked my chin in thought. "You know, I don't think I've ever seen you with an alcoholic drink."

"That's because I don't drink, remember? Alcohol, that is."

I nodded wearily. Yes, of course. She had told me back when I had been babysitting a certain new-born vampire.

"Worried it'll impair your postgraduate perceptions?"

There was slight pause. "Not exactly. So what are we going to chat about then? You know, date-wise."

Her green eyes looked up at me from under a tangle of red hair that had escaped from her omnipresent hat and I shifted in my seat. Something somewhere was tapping me gently on the shoulder. It bore in its hands an important message for me that I really ought to read to but for some reason I was not taking visitors at the moment. I cleared my head and said, "How's the course going?"

Grace smiled slightly and her eyes broke contact. "It's good, thanks. All research and note-taking at the moment. I'll start writing up in the next few months. Really enjoying it.

"What's the subject?"

"It's sort of to do with transmission of symbolism through ancient cultures. You know, looking at, say, how trade and war led to religions being proliferated through the pre-New Testament period."

I let out a low whistle. "Impressive. Then what? You'll drive off into the sunset as Doctor Grace leaving dusty old Lancaster in your educated rear view mirror? Perhaps follow in the esteemed footsteps of the likes of Professor Robert Richmond?"

She ran a finger around the rim of her glass and gave a small sigh. "Nah. I don't think I could ever leave, you know? There's things I sort of wouldn't want to leave behind."

The bell sounded and her cryptic words remained unexplained as I moved on.

"So, tell me, what does a fat polar bear weigh?"

My next date's eyes twinkled with mischief from behind a striking swathe of mascara and eye shadow as I sat opposite her, obviously confused at her first words.

"I have no idea," I finally managed.

"Neither do I," she shrugged, "but hey, it's an icebreaker."

I could not help but chuckle as Lydia grinned at her awful joke. "I'm guessing that you don't believe in being a wallflower then?"

The young woman spread her arms and said, "What can I say? Life is for living. Unfortunately, some people just don't see it that way." Her eyes darted quickly to her left and I saw her not so best friend, Cynthia, scowling at us. "So, you read much?"

"When I have time. Work keeps me rather busy."

"Everyone should read." Lydia leant forward and her dark eyes, framed by the black, dyed hair, held me tight. "A book is a portal to a fantastic realm where our imagination reigns supreme."

I thought about my recent adventures and said, "Sometimes reality can be just as fantastic as fiction."

My date smiled. "A man of mystery. I *like* that."

Three things happened at once. First, my libido had no doubt in figuring out just *how much* the woman in black *liked* this man of mystery. Second, I swallowed nervously. Third, the lights in the bar flickered for a moment.

Heads bobbed up as they always do when things like that happen before settling back down when realising that the building was neither caving in nor that there was any imminent threat of danger from fire, flood or a rampaging Godzilla.

"Cheap university maintenance," I quipped as I turned back to Lydia. She was leaning back in her chair and giving me the sort of once over that I would give a new suit hung on a shop mannequin.

"Still," she said, "there are some books which can be quite useful as a guide, don't you think? Show us the paths less travelled, so to speak."

"Never been much of a travelling man," I muttered. "There was an incident with some Marathon bars when I was younger..." She was peering at her watch. My heart sank. "Am I boring you?"

"Nope. It's just that we have sixty seconds before half time and," she peered around the guys that were following me, "I don't really like what's coming up on the menu. So what do you say to us skipping out and getting to know each other in a somewhat more relaxed timescale?"

Okay, this was serious! I opened my mouth to explain that I was really only there to make up the numbers and help out my friend who was the organiser but instead my libido slapped its hand tightly over the mouth of my common sense and produced the word, "Sure."

So it was that, when the bell rang, we both got up from our seats and made for the door. I could not help but glance over my shoulder at Mister Rugby Shirt who was sitting open-mouthed watching us leave. I walked over to him, patted him once more on the cheek and with a satisfied wink said, "Still got it, sunshine."

Now, I am not usually the kind of guy who throws care into the wind. I am normally the chap who, when something new and unexpected rears its head, sits there feeling decidedly nauseous and worried that the morning's breakfast will make a distasteful reappearance. I think it all stems, like so many things do, from when I was a kid. One long, hot summer, my dad decided that we were going to drive over to France. I had never been abroad before and got highly overexcited as only a seven-year-old that has eaten far too many Smarties can. It was a long drive; a hell of a long drive. Not only that but we happened to get caught in traffic jam after traffic jam. This led to the inevitable infant boredom and marital disharmony. In order to block out the sound of my rowing parents and to assuage my feeling that I was trapped in a four-wheeled prison, I decided to gorge myself on a stash of chocolates that I had smuggled into the car. They were Marathons - sweet, melted, peanutty yumminess.

I ate about seven of them.

Then we went on the ferry.

You can probably see where this is going.

I am eternally amazed that the vomit fiesta which ensued only put me off travelling and not peanuts as half-digested nuts up your nose whilst you are retching over the side of a ferry with your father swearing loudly behind you is a fairly traumatic experience.

Anyway, after that I was always somewhat timid around new experiences and events, so to find myself in a self-assured young woman's room after knowing her for just half an hour was rather surprising to say the least. The campus room reflected what I had already gleaned of her personality. It was not overly neat but far from messy. Posters of bands whose lead singers wore a considerable amount of eye shadow adorned its walls and there was the lingering smell of joss sticks.

"Want a drink?" Lydia opened her wardrobe and I think I actually let out a low whistle at the cornucopia of beverages. "I like to be well stocked," she explained whilst dragging out a fresh bottle of tequila, "as I never know who I might be entertaining." A knowing look flickered out from behind the mascara.

"That would be a regular event?"

"Sometimes," she shrugged, pouring the drinks into a pair of matching shot glasses. "It depends on who I find to be entertaining."

I took the offered drink and knocked it back in one. "And do I fit the bill?"

"What do you think?" The young woman pushed herself up against me and kissed me firmly on the lips, moaning deeply as she did so.

I was about to make some sort of smart remark when the lights flickered. "There they go again," I said. "That's becoming a habit."

Lydia downed her drink. "I know. Just ignore it and make yourself comfortable. I'll put some music on." She picked up an mp3 player and started thumbing through her tracks as I looked for somewhere to sit. The options were rather limited as they usually are in student rooms: the obligatory desk chair (which, although functional, is far from comfortable) or the bed. I removed my hat and coat and decided that they could have the chair. The bedsprings squeaked under my weight and Lydia turned at the sound of the noise. "Good choice," she winked. "Ah, here we go." She found what she wanted and slid the player into its docking station. Soft, synthesised music drifted out from the speakers along with a deeply sensual female voice. I recognised it immediately.

"Enigma."

"Can't beat the classics," she said. "Really gets me in the mood." She closed her eyes and started to sway to the rhythm of the music. I had to admit, it was a rather pleasing sight. After the stresses and strains of the past two weeks, this was a fine distraction. With her eyes still shut, Lydia danced her way over to me and stopped when her legs bumped gently into mine. Her dark eyes opened and she lowered herself down, straddling my lap and slipping her arms behind my neck. Resting her forehead against mine, she continued to sway slowly to the hypnotic music before bending to kiss me again. I responded as the taste of tequila danced delightfully on my tongue. My hand slid up her back and she moaned once more in obvious pleasure.

The lights dimmed again.

I pulled back, frowning.

"No, no," Lydia complained. "Just... just ignore it and kiss me."

"But, don't you think it's weird?"

"Just bad wiring. Always doing it." She gripped my face in her hands and ground her mouth passionately against mine.

The mp3 player went silent.

Lydia swore. I glanced over at the docking station. Its power had gone off and the player sat dead in the cradle. "More bad wiring?"

"We... we don't need music," she stammered, dragging her black painted nails through her hair in frustration. "We can improvise."

Now, if there is one word that fills my heart with dread, it's *improvise.* To me, its basic definition is *let's make things up as we go along until we have a total disaster on our hands.* Governments improvise with billions of pounds and ruin economies. Musicians improvise with old hits and end up sounding as if they are playing a discarded washbasin with a perforated plunger. Comedians improvise with throwaway lines and end up clearing an auditorium.

Lydia's idea of improvisation came in a pair with a short chain dangling between them.

I did not even see it coming. I was too busy with the gothic frenzy that was smothering my face in kisses as she pushed me back down onto the bed. I felt her manoeuvre my hands to the top of the bed then there was the brush of cold metal and a rasping noise as the cuffs locked around my wrists.

"What the hell?" I tugged at the handcuffs, but they had been securely fastened through the head of the bed.

Lydia bent down and made a shushing noise as she placed a finger on my lips. My protests were quieted albeit more through shock than compliance. She knelt back up, still straddling me, and lifted her top up over her head. I will not describe much of what my eyes were presented with as I am far too much of a gentleman. All I will say is that there was lacy black underwear and numerous tattoos then leave the rest to your imagination.

She leant forwards and kissed me again. I felt her fingers unfasten my shirt buttons one at a time. As her fingers moved down, so did her mouth: over my chin, down my neck and to my chest. "Like I said," she breathed, "there are books which can guide us down paths that we wouldn't normally travel."

I groaned. "You mean *Fifty Shades Of Grey*?" I quickly looked around the room. No whips, no paddles and (thank God) no ball gag were anywhere to be seen.

My seductress laid her warm cheek on my stomach and gave a small, throaty chuckle. "Oh, that's just the new shiny version. There are books going back years telling us how to spice things up."

"Sure. My dad kept them in the garden shed along with his 1970s photography magazines."

Now, at this precise moment in time, my subconscious was rapidly trying to find its own appropriate guidebook that was stashed deep down in the depths of my brain which would give the correct advice on what to do in a situation like this. It had discarded *How To Beat Off A Shark, How To Strip Down And Repaint An Antique Set Of Drawers* and *101 Ways To Survive When Stranded In The Desert.* As useful as these learned volumes might have been in other possible times of my life, right now they may as well just have been used as kindling at a good old American Baptist book-burning shindig.

Should I protest?

Did I *want* to protest?

Lydia was obviously enjoying herself (I could tell from the soft moans that were gradually building in volume) and I had to admit that it was a far from unpleasant experience. It was just that there was something that was niggling me at the back of my head. I felt that there was another very useful book that I had forgotten about and really should be reading right now.

Lydia was now busy kissing my stomach and starting to moan louder.

The lights flickered again. What was it with them? It was as if...

"Lydia..."

She ignored me and carried on kissing my skin.

"Lydia!" I shouted.

Her moaning changed in pitch. Where there had been a warm undercurrent of pleasure now there was the background of what sounded like an old kettle starting to whistle.

I tugged frantically at the handcuffs and the cold steel dug into my wrists. Something was very wrong with this picture.

Lydia's shoulders started to tremble and the keening noise increased in volume. I shouted her name again and the lights flashed on and off far more violently this time. She threw her head back and I jolted into the bedstead. Her eyes were rolled up in her sockets and her mouth was wide open, emitting the ever-increasing shrill noise. I frantically tried to cover my ears with my arms, but it was no good. The inhuman sound just continued in its relentless crescendo. Lydia grasped the bedclothes tight in her hands and the shriek filled the entirety of the room.

At that moment the lights went out permanently as the bulbs sparked and shattered.

Lydia exploded in a shower of expletives and fell off the bed onto the floor. I strained over in the dark to see her pounding the utilitarian carpet with a fist. I hitched myself up the bed slightly to get in a rather more comfortable position and called over to her. She ignored my voice and continued to punish the synthetic mixture of rayon and nylon. Eventually, her anger gave way to sobs and she curled up in a ball crying loudly as her long dark hair covered her face.

Well, this was new.

I surmised that calling out to my distraught captor was going to be ineffectual so I did the only thing that I could right then; I waited quietly and I listened. There was the distinct sound of annoyance coming from the corridor. Doors were opening and slamming shut as occupants tried to work out what had happened. I had a good idea, but right now I was in no place to enlighten them. Then there was a new noise, an intermittent knocking at doors followed by low-level grumbling.

This had to be the college authorities coming round to assess the situation. Somebody must have rung them. Lydia's whimpering ceased. She had heard the knocking too.

"Hey," I called out, "can you undo these?" I rattled the cuffs.

There was a knock at the door.

Lydia wiped her wet face with the back of a hand, smearing a streak of wet mascara across her cheek, got up and headed to the door.

"Hey!" I yelled. "What do you think you're doing?" This was crazy! She was half-dressed and I looked like a candidate for the aforementioned *Fifty Shades Of Grey*. "Lydia!" I hissed, but it was no good. She ignored me and opened the door.

The maintenance guy's face was a picture. He stood, his mouth flapping open and shut like a demented goldfish as Lydia placed a hand on her hip and pouted. "What is it? I'm *trying* to be busy here."

"Indeed it looks that way, my dear," chuckled a smooth Scots accent.

I groaned as a certain college chaplain and college dean popped his head around the door.

"Quite busy indeed."

I slammed my head back against the metal headboard and closed my eyes in despair. "Hello, Spliff."

He strode into Lydia's room and surveyed me under the piercing scrutiny of a very bright torch. I could not make out his face as the bright beam burned into my retinas, but I could distinctly feel an eyebrow rise.

"Don't you dare," I growled. "Just... don't."

There was movement rather than mockery and I opened my eyes to see Spliff retrieve Lydia's top from the floor. "My dear, I think that perhaps you ought to put this on before," he motioned to the maintenance worker, "Harry's eyes pop out."

Silently, Lydia complied.

"Good girl. Now, perhaps some keys are in order?"

My amorous captor surrendered a shrug of resignation and fished a small silver-coloured key from her black jeans. Spliff took it with a gracious nod of thanks and sat down on the bed next to me. "Well, Samuel," he smiled as he fiddled far too slowly with the restraints, "I know I told you that you needed to sort out your sex life, but really..."

"Just undo the bloody cuffs," I growled.

There was a click and my wrists fell free. "As you wish."

I levered myself up and started to button up my shirt. "Thank you."

"Don't mention it," my best friend twinkled. "Now, unfortunately Harry and I have to press on and leave you to your night's... *entertainment.* We have a mysterious electrical conundrum to solve."

"Actually," I looked over to Lydia who was leaning against the wall, arms crossed and face scowling murderous intent, "I think I might be able to help you there."

There are two constants in my life: whiskey and nicotine. As I sat outside the college bar slowly sipping a soothing Jack Daniel's and inhaling the roasted tobacco flavour of a Lucky Strike, I knew that at least these two things would never, ever turn around and bite me on the rear. They were exactly what they said on the packet: bad for you.

However, did I care? Not a jot.

We spend so much time worrying in our short, fragile lives about what is good for us and what is bad. We spend hour upon hour pounding a treadmill in a stiflingly hot gym when in fact we could be out walking in a luscious green park with a loved one, inhaling the sweet aroma of summer flowers. We reduce the sugar in our coffee from two spoons to one and a bit, convinced that this token sacrifice will stave off diabetes yet we greedily gorge on the biggest, tastiest cream cake we can lay our hands on the moment we realise that whatever we do, whatever we try, we cannot escape the inevitable.

There is only one way off this careering, careening runaway train that we call life. At some point we will crash into the buffers at the end of the track and our carriages will tumble off the rails, never to travel again.

So, we might as well enjoy the time that we have and stop wasting it by spending every precious second of every day worrying.

That was more or less how I was feeling at that moment.

It was also the creed by which young Lydia rocked and rolled. However, she had a problem.

"She hates that I get all the attention." Lydia was pacing around our table, waving her hands in the air whilst swigging from a bottle of beer. "She just can't stand it!"

Spliff raised an eyebrow over the rim of his glass of gin. I shrugged. I was just as baffled as he was. How was I, a late thirties male, supposed to understand the ravings of a female undergrad who could apparently wipe out all things electrical when she got turned on? "Who can't stand it?" I asked.

The girl slumped down next to Spliff and chugged at her beer. "Cynthia. That's who."

I cast my mind back to the speed dating earlier that evening. "That's the girl you were arguing with earlier, isn't it?"

She nodded sullenly. "She's so jealous."

"Okay. Why do you think that?"

"Because she can't get laid. She's all Miss Prim And Proper, Miss Daddy Wouldn't Approve."

My conversation with Cynthia bimbled back into my memory. "She didn't sound like that, when I spoke to her earlier. Shy perhaps, but not prudish."

Lydia just snorted derisively.

I let out a long breath and looked to Spliff for help. "Lydia, my dear, do you think that your friend is somehow involved with your *condition*?"

"Involved?" she started, disbelief on her face. "Damn right she is. She bloody well hexed me!"

I shot Spliff a look, which he returned with a slight incline of his head.

Lydia rolled her eyes. "Typical. You don't believe me. What a surprise." She made to leave but Spliff placed a gentle hand on her arm and guided her back down.

"Far from it," he said quietly, reassuringly. "Samuel here and I have indeed seen many things which mean we need very little convincing."

The girl's mascara laden eyes shot back and forth between us, trying to weigh up the situation. "Really? You don't think I'm some sort of whack job?"

I rubbed my wrists involuntarily as I remembered the handcuffs. Sure, that was a bit of a quirky peccadillo but certainly not proof of insanity. "Not at all, Lydia. Besides, how else can we explain the power outages? I'm guessing that has happened before?"

She seemed to relax and her shoulders slumped as her head nodded in resignation. "Every time I get a guy up to my room and get... you know... weird shit starts to happen. I feel this energy start to well up inside me and I just have to let it out. First, it's a giggle or a laugh, then a moan, then finally it's a shriek and all the electricity goes *whammo*. Normally I kick the guy out and lock the door until the maintenance guys have gone by. It's not the sort of thing you want to talk about, you know?"

"I can imagine. Yet, tonight you let them in. Why?"

She chewed her bottom lip for a second then whispered, "I don't know. I'm tired. I think I've had enough. It's grinding me down and I want help." A tear trickled down her cheek taking a blob of eye shadow along with it.

"We'll do what we can," I reassured her. "Now, tell me about Cynthia."

Lydia rolled her beer bottle between her hands. "At first I thought she was my friend, you know? My *BFF*. She was the first person I met when I came here. She's local, her dad has a business in town, and she knew all the cool places to hang out. This place is so different from where I come from. I'm used to the big city lights, you know? Lancaster is so... so..."

"Small?" I volunteered.

She nodded. "Don't get me wrong. I like it, it's just so not what I'm used to. Anyway, I hooked up with Cynthia and she'd show me all the cool places to hang out in town. We had a blast.

"That was, until the boys started to show an interest in me.

"Obviously, she knew all the local crowd, so she introduced me to them to make me feel welcome and, well, I have hormones, you know? She sort of got royally pissed off that the guys wanted to hang with me and not her. I tried to apologise, I mean it wasn't my fault, was it? But she was having none of it. She was all, "You're a skank!" and got so huffy with me. I tried to smooth things over, I really did, but still the boys came a-calling and I'm a friendly girl.

"Then, one day last week, she hammers on my door and starts yelling in my face saying that she's fixed me and the guys won't want me anymore. I ask her what she's done and she says that she found out about this woman in town who her dad had been researching and she got the woman to show her how to hex me. Well, I just laughed and shut the door in her face thinking she was off her rocker.

"Then, the screaming began, and the power outages."

She sipped the remains of her beer. "I tried to fix things between us tonight by bringing her to the speed dating thing. I thought if she found someone nice then she'd see that I wasn't stealing the guys on purpose. She just got all antsy and said I'd just brought her along to make myself look better and asked if I liked being a banshee then started to goad me. She's lucky I didn't slap her."

Spliff sat up straight and his eyes wandered over to the door of the bar. "If that's the case," he murmured, "then you might want to sit on your hands."

My eyes followed his and I saw Cynthia coming out of the bar. Her head turned and a smug grin crept across her face when she caught sight of her so-called best friend. However, the smile slipped off quicker than a fried egg on Teflon when Lydia leapt from the bench and flew at her with nails outstretched. Both girls started to shriek as Lydia sank her clawed fingers into Cynthia's hair and dragged her hexer to the ground. A crowd started to form around us and I made to get up and intervene but Spliff laid a hand on my shoulder. "Give them a minute first. You go in there, you'll lose an eye... or possibly a testicle."

I winced at the thought but nonetheless I got up and edged cautiously to the flailing mass of arms, hair and legs. From my safe vantage point, it seemed to be somewhat evenly matched. Neither girl was gaining the upper hand and both were giving as good as they got. So much for being bosom buddies.

After a minute or so, the initial aggression seemed to subside a fraction and I spotted a gap between the two sparring girls. I inserted myself sideways, careful not to be accidentally castrated by a rogue fingernail, and pried them apart. Lydia lunged forward and grabbed at Cynthia. She caught the bespectacled girl's handbag which was still miraculously slung over her shoulder. As I pushed them apart, the bag was pulled free and skittered to the floor.

A silence fell over the two as something spilled out and rolled to my feet. Cynthia lurched forward and tried to snatch the object up but I was too quick. I bent down and lifted it from the floor. The item was a small plastic doll, the cheap sort you pick up in your local poundstore. It was naked except for one thing. Around its face were a few strands of dark hair tied across its mouth like a gag.

The hair was the same shade as Lydia's. She was a sharp girl and noticed immediately. "Where the hell did you get my hair from?"

"When you were passed out from tequila," Cynthia grumbled sullenly.

Lydia frowned. "I don't remember." She glanced at her friend's raised eyebrow then said, "I suppose I wouldn't."

I pulled the hair off the doll. "Feel any different?" I asked.

The goth looked around the crowd of onlookers and walked over to a tall, male student. “Hello, Handsome.” She reached up and latched her lips onto his.

Seconds passed.

So did some more.

And even more.

Eventually we heard moans of female enjoyment coming from the clinch. No lights flickered. Lydia came up for air, linked her arm through the boy's. “So what books do you like to read?”

Her new plaything just shrugged, unable to believe his apparent luck. Lydia, now free from the hex, slipped us a wink as she led him away to her hall of residence.

Cynthia gave a deep sigh and slumped down onto the bench as the crowd dispersed. Nothing to see now. Entertainment over.

“Well?” I asked.

“Well, what?” There was no anger in her voice, just sad despair.

I placed the doll and the hair on the bench. “How did you learn to do this?”

She picked the doll up and regarded it, her body language screaming that she was not sure whether to tell me or not, but finally she gave a shrug of submission. “My dad was researching stuff and came across this woman in town who is a bona fide witch. Okay, she doesn't do the whole pointy hat or candy cottage thing, but apparently she's descended from a *family* of witches. So I looked her up.” A chuckle escaped her mouth. “It's not like she's hard to find. She didn't want to help to start with, but I spun her this sob story of how I was being wronged and needed to set things right, so she told me I could do this as a temporary thing until Lydia learnt her lesson and stopped using me as a Plain Jane.”

“Only Lydia wasn't for quitting, was she?”

Cynthia shook her head.

“She didn't think she was doing anything wrong,” I explained. “She was never using you. She's just a natural...” I searched for the correct word. The correct *polite* word. “Man magnet.”

“I guess so.” Cynthia got up. “I'm going now. I promise I won't do it again.”

I felt as if I was the head teacher reprimanding the naughty schoolgirl and not in some sort of pervy fantasy way, either, before you jump to any sordid conclusions. I'd had enough of other people's fantasies for one night.

“Okay,” I nodded. “Just one more thing. Who's the witch?”

The student smiled. “Oh, she's the crazy woman on Cheapside. You know, the one with the music.”

As she walked off, Spliff and I gawped at each other in disbelief. *Boombox Betty?*

# The Case of the Marauding Mummies of Morecambe

By the time I had made it back to Dalton Square, I was in a somewhat pensive mood. So far this week I had been abducted and almost executed by sentient stonework as well as being manacled to a bed by a hexed bag of hormones. It would appear that I was never again to have a peaceful life.

At least this week was not turning out as bad as it had the first time around. No bodies had started to pile up.

Yet.

I flicked my Zippo open and lit myself a Lucky. As I snapped the petrol lighter shut, I inspected the worn brass case. There, on one side was the All Seeing Eye and on the other was the inscription, "*Nil illegitimi carborundum.*" I frowned. The item that I held in my hand was a paradox. Caroline had bought me this lighter and had paid to have it engraved yet I had never met her due to the early demise of Malcolm Wallace. How could it still exist?

What else had not changed?

A police car rocketed through Dalton Square, siren blaring and lights flashing. "Someone's put the kettle on at the station," my dad would have said. It made me think of something else entirely and I turned to my computer. I typed in "Jitendra Patel Lancaster Police" and pressed enter. There he was, Lancaster's Detective Chief Inspector, dressed to the nines, his calm demeanour radiating his *don't mess with me* confidence. So, he was still here. Had I already met him? Had he accompanied me to Williamson Park to take out Hawkins the werewolf? My fingers drummed my teeth as the cogs in my head clicked over in thought. I had first met him when he had arrived on the scene at John O'Gaunt Media during my little satanic soirée.

I typed in "John O'Gaunt Media" and was presented with links to John

O'Gaunt School and John O'Gaunt Golf Club.

It made sense. Wallace had been the dark manipulator of the production company. He had brought them together and then ensured that they had catapulted to success. The once unknown actors had literally sold him their souls. The question was, had they still abducted me somehow for some other reason? One by one, I typed their names into the search engine and each time I drew a blank. It appeared that they were lost in the mists of obscurity.

Then there was the werewolf.

Had that happened? Was Hawkins still out there? I navigated back to the image of DCI Patel. Did he know me in this reality and was he involved with any possible lycanthropic slaying?

Questions, questions, questions.

Just no apparent answers. I needed to clear my head.

The wheels of the desk chair mewled a high-pitched squeak as I wheeled myself over to the filing cabinet. I reached into the bottom drawer, fished out a bottle of Jack Daniel's and poured myself a good measure. I downed it in one and poured another.

One to soothe; one to savour.

So much mental dandruff was drifting around my brain that it was near on impossible to gain a clear picture of what I should be doing. It needed purging. A mental enema.

I needed to relax.

I smiled as I recognised what would do the trick.

I have mentioned before that I have a somewhat diverse collection of music. There is the heavy thrash stuff that helps me deal with angst and frustration. The poppier stuff helps my brain switch off when the housework needs doing in mindless repetition. The likes of Tom Waits are just perfect to get drunk to.

Then there is Kriss Foster.

"Kriss Who?" I here ninety-nine point nine per cent of you ask.

Okay, how to describe Lancaster's very own whimsical wonder...

That would be like asking a blind philosopher to describe a cluster of cumulus.

Let me just say that he has an incredibly unique surreal music style that perfectly suits the home made leopard print onesie that he wears whilst performing. As well as having a liking for a nice cup of tea and having a thing for football magazines, he has also written songs about falling between the station platform and the train, a homicidal Dale Winton and Vimto.

The one I wanted right now though was Morecambe.

This is my go to default when I just need to lie back and think of those long hot summers that we never have now when ice cream tasted so sweet and the only clouds in blue skies were fluffy cumulus, unseen and therefore unable to be described by aforementioned blind philosophers.

I selected the track on my laptop's media player and as soon as I clicked play, the acoustic guitar tugged at the corners of my mouth. I sipped more bourbon and lay down on the sofa.

"Morecambe," sang the soothing Lancastrian voice, "it's a place that's by the sea."

"It's just like Venice," I joined in, "but it's not in Italy."

I let the Jack warm my insides as Kriss continued to sing. "Oh, I do like to be beside the seaside, but I do really miss my favourite sea ride; the big one, the Polo Tower, had so much power."

"But it can't have made a mint," I mumbled as drowsiness started to overwhelm me, "because it closed." Then so did my eyes.

I looked down at my hand. It was no longer holding a glass of whiskey. Instead, it was gripping a selection of Panini football stickers. I flicked through them: Kenny Dalglish, Phil Neal, Trevor Francis, Peter Shilton to name but a few. All classics from the 1980s.

"That's a rare one. Want to swap?"

"What have you got?" I asked as I walked over to a large white table where Kriss Foster, the minstrel of Morecambe, had his own collection neatly laid out in what appeared to be teams. "I can't remember who goes where."

"Let's have a look then."

I passed them over to the leopard-spotted aficionado and sat down on a spare plastic chair as he mused over my stack. He shook his head, his fluffy ears twitching. "You've got them all mixed up. Look, this one goes here." He laid Peter Shilton next to a card that was emblazoned with a set of shiny fangs. The former England goalie transformed into Dave Nichols, former comic storeowner and now apprentice vampire. "This is team Cain," Kriss explained as he pointed to the other cards in the group.

I recognised the petite Nightingale, Dave's blood mother, and Marcus, her aloof partner. "Who are these?" I asked, pointing out two females: one with long blonde hair, one sporting a closer crop of red.

"You've not met them yet, but you will do. Soon."

"Can't wait," I frowned. I pointed to a gap above Nightingale. "Who goes there?"

Kriss stroked his chin in consideration.

"Well?"

"Later. Now this one," he produced Kenny Dalglish, "he's a born leader." He laid my former Liverpool striker then serial manager next to a card that bore two doors. The word Divergence emerged into view as Dalglish morphed into an all too familiar face with white hair and orange pupils.

"Malcolm Wallace. But he failed. He was misled."

"True, but the Divergence was his motivation and its effects are like a ripple in a pond." He placed five cards in front of Wallace. The five so-called Satanists of John O'Gaunt media. Then he drew my Trevor Francis and placed it directly above the card with the doors. It turned totally black with an undulating border. An image seemed to shimmer in the gloom as if it was trying to break free of the shadows but was being held captive by something.

"Who's that?"

"You know who that is. The chairman of the whole event."

"Kanor."

Kriss nodded.

I stared into the black mire. The shape within it turned and twisted. I caught a glimpse of sickly white skin and the edge of a cruel lip but that was all. "Who?" I asked.

"That is not for now." He began to deal out more football stickers, five of them, adjacent to the vampires. His finger touched the top one and a pair of feathery wings fluttered into view. "Team angel," he said.

The first face that came into view made me sigh deeply.

"I believe you two are acquainted."

Cruel eyes and a seductive smile looked back up at me from beneath fashionably sexy dark hair.

"Asherah," I growled, then, "and I guess that is Asmodeus," as the card next to her coalesced into the image of a male. He was the one who I had seen shoot Wallace.

"Where there is one there is always the other."

"Rather like bankers and austerity measures?"

Kriss ignored my quip and ran his hand over the next two cards. Two teenagers looked up at me: Alec and a blonde girl with red streaks in her hair. I drummed my phantasmagorical fingers against my teeth. "Okay, so I know my little friend there. Who's she?"

"She will cross your path soon enough, but not just yet. She is not yet aware of whom she really is."

I studied the cards: vampires, bad guys and angels all laid out in front of me and I frowned. "You've laid the angels and the vamps out in a very certain way." I tapped the space for the chairman of team Cain. It was equidistant between the vamps and the angels. "Does he run two teams?"

Kriss held out my final card: Phil Neal. Its transformation was quite spectacular. It would be quite the understatement to say that this one was different to the others. For starters, it was made from fire. The material flickered and danced as he lay it down on the table.

Then there was the noise.

It was the shrieking of wind screaming past at speeds that the human brain could not possibly comprehend. As I stared at the face that started to materialise I felt that I was going to be sucked down into an abyssal vortex. I actually clasped my hands tight on the table.

"Who is it?" I shouted across the infernal noise.

Kriss was gone, vanished from this hellish place, but his calm voice drifted into my ears, "You already know."

Before I looked down at the card, I knew what I would see. There they were, a pair of black glasses staring up at me masking a face of pure hatred. A face that burnt with incandescent fire.

I woke with a start, my heart pounding and my face slick with perspiration. My eyes darted back and forth, desperate to recognise my surroundings.

It was my office.

It was morning.

I was safe.

"Who the hell are you?" I whimpered.

"Bad dream?"

"Jesus!" I felt my heart make use of my rib cage as an impromptu climbing frame. "How long have you been there?"

Alec, my newly acquired flat mate and teenager of mystery, pulled a chair over and sat himself down. "Not too long." His clear blue eyes did not blink once as he looked me over. "Do you always sleep here?"

Running my fingers through my hair, I gave myself a shake and thought about standing up. Bells chiming maniacally in my ears persuaded me that remaining seated for a moment would be a better idea. "I guess I nodded off. What time is it?"

Without even glancing at one of my many timepieces, he said, "Eight thirty."

"I'm hoping that's morning, not evening."

"The daylight would suggest so."

"Smart arse." I rummaged in my pockets and found a rogue Lucky. As the tobaccoey goodness danced in my lungs, I heard the bells start to subside. Experimentally, I rocked my feet back and forth on the carpet. No wobbles. I stood up and stretched as joints popped noisily and muscles silently screeched.

"You didn't answer my question."

"About what?"

"Bad dream?"

I performed a quick impression of Smaug and let smoke drift ponderously out of my nose as I debated what to tell this newcomer in my life; there was still so much that I did not know about him. Trust had yet to be fully earned. Eventually, I nodded. "You could say that. I'm guessing my subconscious has been working the night shift."

The blue eyes followed me as I paced restlessly around my office. "You've been wondering about the events of the last two weeks."

I raised an eyebrow. "I told you not to read my mind."

"I don't need to. It's just obvious."

"Guess so." I explained about my internet searches returning diddlysquat. "I just want to make sure of what has actually happened."

The youth's mouth broke into a smile. "Well, that's easy enough. Why don't we go and find out?"

"This is a *very* bad idea."

Alec ignored my whiney protest in much the same way that scantily clad archetypal horror genre females ignore the fact that the lights do not work in the deserted gothic mansion that they have just inherited from Great Uncle Silas after he died in *mysterious circumstances*. He just continued to walk down the corridor as if he owned the place.

The corridor that, might I add, was crawling with Lancaster's constabulary going about their day-to-day business.

I felt like I was a zebra who had walked into his local bar only to find it had been turned into one of those trendy lion bars that seemed to be popping up everywhere all over the savannah. What was worse, my friend who had dragged me along, was completely oblivious to the fact that we were probably going to be grabbed, sliced, deep fried and served in a little wicker basket along with some limp lollo rosso and an over-acidic hollandaise sauce.

"Alec!" I hissed.

He paused, turned to me and said, "There's no need to whisper. They can't see or hear us."

I let out a highly agitated sigh of deep discomfort and nervously edged up to my young companion. "As long as you are fiddling with their minds. What if you lose concentration? You might sneeze or... or... go running after a cute puppy."

"I'm not into puppies."

"Okay, a sloth. The internet's full of cute sloths these days. What if you inadvertently see one on a copper's laptop?"

Alec cocked his head silently to one side – his version of a teenage *seriously* eye roll. As if anything could distract this unique boy. He seemed to be the paradigm of focus. When I was his age, my mind had flitted from one thing to another: computer games, comic books, inadvertently touching Justine Munroe's left breast with my elbow through my shirt, my sweater, my coat, her coat, her cardigan, her blouse and her bra and could I justify that as copping a feel? Alec however, seemed the complete opposite to my permanent flush of adolescent hormones. He had his sights set on something far off on the horizon; he was playing the waiting game and was truly focussed on the journey ahead.

I raised my hands in surrender, duly admonished, and gave in to his guidance. "Lead on, MacDuff. But seriously, not even sloths?"

"No... Not even sloths."

Even with his reassurance, I still felt incredibly uncomfortable just waltzing into the heart of the police station as the boys and girls in blue walked blithely past. The weirdest thing was that none of them collided with either of us. They would be walking down the corridor and, as they approached, they subconsciously sidestepped around without missing a beat.

In a short while, we were standing outside Jitendra Patel's office. The frosted glass door announced his presence in a neat black font that perfectly mimicked his staid and precise personality. The lights were on inside and I could make out movement. The good inspector was home.

"Now what?" I asked, motioning with my head to the firmly shut door. "We can't just open that."

Alec gave the trademark shrug of teenage nonchalance. "Yes we can," he said and turned the steel handle. I scurried in behind and was amazed to see that Jitendra was paying us not the blindest bit of attention. "He can't see that the door's open," Alec explained. "To him, it's still shut."

He closed the door and walked into the room which was almost exactly as I remembered: lined with filing cabinets, gently scented with furniture polish and anally neat. A perfect representation of its occupant's inner self. I was sure that even his intestines were regularly washed, tumble-dried and, after a thorough cleansing, were inserted back into his abdomen in numbered order. Okay, perhaps a slight exaggeration, but you catch my drift?

There was, however, one exception to this rule of ordered tidiness. On a square table in the corner of the office there was piled a stack of books and printouts that lay in haphazard heaps of varying size and usage. I felt my spidey senses tingling and approached the cluttered anomaly. The books were of random sizes and bindings, quite unlike the more formulaic reading material that lined the DCI's bookshelves. They looked like the type of books I had been used to perusing in the depths of Luneside University's stacks many years ago. They were big green tomes with ridged binding that creaked and crackled when you opened them and inhaled the years of knowledge that lingered within their musty depths.

The knowledge that the volumes in Jitendra's office contained were on one specific topic: werewolves.

"Well, I think it's safe to say that our little encounter at Williamson Park has not been erased." The books contained old woodcut prints that would have a bible-bashing evangelist frothing at their mouth: scantily clad women dancing in the moonlight with wolves, wolves devouring what appeared to be first-born young, men wrapped in ragged furs and drenched from head to toe in blood. The printouts were more clinical: professional reports on lycanthropy, dualistic personalities and other conditions that you needed a joint postgrad degree in Greek, Latin and Psychology Of The Crazy Person to understand.

"He certainly takes all this seriously." Alec was leafing through the papers, his light coloured eyes flicking from item to item. "It would appear that you made quite an impact."

"Indeed." I drummed my fingers against my teeth. Quite the impact, but what exactly were the events? I glanced over to Jitendra, sat at his desk, typing up what looked like a report. I frowned. Was that an image of the Eric Morecambe statue?

For those of you who don't know (and how could you not?) Morecambe is Lancaster's next-door neighbour. It is situated on the coast and, in its Victorian heyday, was a hub of fun, frivolity and long-legged stripy bathing costumes. Then foreign package holidays took hold and gradually choked the life out of this little coastal jewel of the north. The holidaymakers stopped coming and the hotels stood empty. The grand Midland Hotel fell into disrepair, the Winter Gardens was boarded up and the promenade became a watery ghost town.

There was, however, one bright spot in the resort's bleak retirement. Eric Morecambe was a locally born lad who teamed up with one Ernie Wise and went on to become one of the greatest comedy double acts of the late twentieth century. They stormed first the stage and then the screen, becoming the staple diet of Saturday nights before reality television started bludgeoning viewers over their heads with its crass lowest common denominator form of "entertainment". Then, one evening in 1984, Eric walked off stage and dropped down dead. The world of comedy was stunned and Morecambe had lost its shining light. It was as if the death of this cheery chap with the thick-rimmed spectacles and cheeky grin was the last nail in the coffin for the already ailing town. The resort descended into a downward spiral from which no one thought it would ever emerge.

They were wrong. It has been a hard, painful task but Morecambe is finally on its way back up. The hotels are reopening, cultural hotspots are starting to glow like expectant embers and, as if to represent all this, there is a crowning glory on the promenade. The statue of Morecambe's finest is cast in bronze and stands skipping with gay abandon just as he used to at the end of every show. People flock to it from all around the country to have their photo taken with the long dead idol. Toddlers smile in wonder at the funny man who died before their parents were even conceived.

From beyond the grave, Eric Morecambe has breathed fresh life into the place that gave birth to him and had long mourned his passing.

As to why it was on Jitendra's monitor, I did not have a clue.

"I need to know what happened on Saturday night. From *his* perspective."

Alec nodded and walked up behind the detective, bent over and whispered in his ear, "Doughnuts."

Jitendra sat up and frowned as his stomach produced an urgent rumble. As he stood, he made to log out of his computer.

"No need to do that," my young Jedi whispered.

Jitendra's hand hovered over the mouse before he cleared his throat, grabbed his coat and left us alone in his office.

"I have to say, that *is* cool," I muttered, sitting down in the desk chair, "freaky, but nonetheless cool."

I minimised the open windows and started to look through his immaculate filing system. Praise the Lord for anal retentiveness! It was all in date order. I flipped through to Saturday's date and opened the appropriate folder. There it was, a document entitled *Williamson Park Incident*.

Alec leaned over my shoulder. "I'm guessing he's not referring to an errant flasher."

I shot my young companion a glance. "Was that humour, young padawan?"

"Your ways are rubbing off on me, my learned master," he smiled.

Smiling myself, I opened the document and we began to read.

Jitendra had not met me before the werewolf case. I had contacted him that morning looking for information on Hawkins. From his report, it appeared that there had been something troubling him but he had gone round to see me nonetheless. He had then met up with me at the park where we had confronted Hawkins and his sister. From there it read just as the official story had previously: gun, ants, terrible tragedy.

I looked over my shoulder at the pile of research. Apparently the case had had quite a profound effect on DCI Patel. There was no mention of a werewolf in the text but he had obviously believed what he had seen and was now doing his homework.

I found this somewhat disconcerting.

I closed the document and its parent folder before maximising the picture of Morecambe's finest and its accompanying document. As I did this, something in the text caught my eye and my jaw dropped.

"You've got to be kidding me!"

Feet are funny things. They were crucially important in our evolution. They led to us descending from the trees to hunting prey on the forest floor. They gave us the ability to cross from one continent to another in order to follow migrant food sources and to flee from encroaching ice ages. They enabled armies to march into battle and conquer vast lands. They are also one of the first things we rub when we get tired after a long day at work.

The world seems to fall into varying camps when it comes to feet. There are those who loathe them. People who hate their feet to such an extent that they have to keep them shrouded in occultation away from public view. They see them purely as knobbly extensions of their legs, abhorrent to the touch and a blight on their body.

Then there are those who see their feet as objects of adoration. They have them pummelled and pumiced, every scrap of dead skin removed. Their nails are trimmed, polished and coloured in every hue under the sun before being displayed for everyone to view and admire in an array of strappy footwear that could have catered for the entire legions of Rome should they have admired Dolce And Gabanna and been able to march across the field of Europe in stiletto heels.

Then there are the group that are really into baby oil. I think I shall just leave those guys to your imagination.

As for me, I can take feet or leave them. I give them a good pair of shoes and, when they ache, a warm soak. I look after them; they look after me. I have a symbiotic relationship with my pair of path pounders.

The foot that I was currently looking at was definitely not feeling the love.

One of Eric Morecambe's feet stood all on its own on Morecambe promenade, separated from and abandoned by the rest of its cast metal body. It was a most sorry sight to behold.

There was blue and white police tape strapped around the podium but as there were no boys in blue nearby I just ducked under to take a closer look at the solitary bronze shoe. Lighting a Lucky, I crouched down to study the unusual scrawlings that encircled the lonely piece of footwear. Back at the police station I had clicked on a hyperlink in Jitendra's document. It had pulled up a video of them being scratched into the stonework. There were all manner of shapes and squiggles: the ubiquitous pentagram (upside down of course), moons, winged beasts and what appeared to be either magic wands or anatomically inaccurate phalli. Each pattern was inlaid with a sticky red liquid, the blood of a white hen that I had watched have its neck slit before it's still twitching feathered corpse was smeared around like a gory paint brush.

I blew smoke out of my nose and my head cleared slightly.

There was on first appraisal, nothing at the crime scene that told me anything about the apparent perps – the vandals that I had watched over and over again with bemused disbelief in order to check the accuracy of the report. According to DCI Jitendra Patel, the most sober and serious person that I had ever known to walk this sceptred isle, and backed up by the incontrovertible evidence of CCTV footage, last night the bronze statue of Eric Morecambe had been stolen not by drunk youths, not by dodgy scrap metal dealers but my a group of mummies.

Yes, that is right – bandage-wearing, long dead but lovingly preserved mummies.

They had driven up to the statue in a pickup truck, proceeded to amputate Eric from his foot with the use of an oxyacetylene torch and then, after daubing chicken blood into all manner of occult symbols that they had etched into the dais, had driven off down the prom.

You just couldn't make it up, could you?

"Morecambe, it's a place that's by the sea," I whispered to myself. "It's just like Venice, but with embalmed iconoclasts." Being careful, so as not to smear myself with coagulated poultry blood, I ran my hands around the foot. The bronze had been carefully sheared away by the torch. Because of the thickness of the material, this meant that it had taken quite a while, yet they had not been disturbed. True, it had been about four in the morning, but surely someone must have seen something? I looked up and down the promenade. There was the usual mix of pubs, shops and boarded up premises. It was autumn, not the busiest season, therefore a passing tourist would have been unlikely.

I turned my attention back to the foot and something caught my eye. A small scrap of fabric was fluttering in a slight breeze. It was caught in a chip in the stonework where a piece of pink bubble-gum had secreted itself and acted as involuntary adhesive. I pried the scrap away from the masticated gum and held it up to my face. A grubby white flexible material.

Bandage wrapping.

There was something else. I carefully sniffed the fabric and caught the acrid odour of burning. This was not the burning of metal, that sharp iron taste. This was the bitter aroma of melted plastic and it was combined with... was that wood smoke?

Wherever this cloth had been singed, it had not been here. It had not been caused by the slip of an acetylene torch.

Curious.

I pocketed my fabric clue and straightened up before looking over at the shops once more. The nearest was The Magic Toybox. I smiled. It was either a quaint little children's toyshop or a lurid little adult emporium. As the puppets in the window were not clad in accessible clothing of the PVC variety, I guessed it was the former and headed over.

A bell chimed as I entered and for an instant I felt as if I had entered a Wild West saloon. True, there were no gunslingers lounging around sipping red eye, neither was there an old timer, sporting a waxed moustache and those curious little arm bands, tinkling out something merry on a discordant piano. There was most certainly no overly dressed harlot peering over a balcony eyeing up her next client whilst dreaming of a better life back east.

I think I must have watched too many black and white westerns as a kid...

But there was the silence, the one where the conversation stops and all eyes turn towards you.

There was the sum total of three people in the shop: a teenage boy fiddling aimlessly with a display of rubber ducks, an elderly woman with blue-rinsed hair who was wearing a drab coloured anorak and the proprietor, a middle-aged man whose three strands of thinning hair were perfectly plastered over a bald scalp in such a manner that a nineteen-seventies' footballer would have wept with joy. He turned from his conversation with the elderly customer, eyed me up and down then asked, “Can I help you?”

I turned on my most charming of smiles and walked over to the counter. I noticed the young boy's hands continue to pick up ducks whilst his eyes actually kept track of me. “Hi! I notice you've had some bother outside.” I inclined my head towards the shop window.

“It's a disgrace,” the retailer bristled, his ferret-like features screwing up in disgust. “Nothing is sacred these days.”

His customer chipped in, “I know. And have you seen all those writings they've left behind? Bloody foreigners.”

I frowned at the old woman. Had I missed something at the crime scene? “Pardon?”

She crossed her arms defensively across her ample bosom, handbag clasped tightly like a shield. She disturbingly resembled a member of Monty Python wearing drag. “I was looking at it this morning. Poor Eric hacked away like that. Then they go and write all their darkie lingo all over the thing.”

Okay. This was somewhat baffling. “Darkie lingo?”

“I remember them coming over here in the sixties. All on the banana boats stinking of rum, none of 'em speaking a word of English. That's who's done this! The darkies! They've chopped him up for scrap metal and bragged about it in their heathen picture language.”

Was I really hearing this? I had thought that this sort of racism had died out when Bernard Manning had joined Hitler underneath Satan's sulphurous sphincter. “Actually, I don't think that the vandals were immigrants.”

The shop owner voiced his support for my more racially tolerant opinion. “See, Mrs Crombie, I told you. It wasn't anything like that.

“It was a witch!”

Okay, perhaps not so tolerant.

“She raised the dead and got them to do her evil work. That's what those symbols are. They're a *cult.*"

I raised an amused eyebrow. "I think you mean *occult.*"

This correction knocked around inside the man's head for a few seconds before it took hold. "Yeah, that's what I meant to say. Occult. That's what the witch does."

"So you saw this witch, then?"

"No... But I've seen her writing. And it's covered in blood. She got her mummies to come and nick the statue and write a curse there. That's what the writing is. *A curse.*"

I drummed my teeth with my fingers and proceeded to do my own bit of cogitating. Darkies? A witch? Mummies? Well, the first two were obviously absurd, but as for the third... I had seen them with my own eyes on CCTV that had been filmed during the night.

When the shops had been closed.

"How do you know it was mummies that took the statue?"

The balding man looked like I had just squeezed his shrivelled balls in a vice. His face flushed red while his mouth flapped open and shut like a skylight in a tornado.

"The statue was stolen during the night. Are you telling me that you were here, watching?"

"I... I... I think you'd better leave."

I smiled. Well, this was very interesting. However, I had outstayed my welcome and turned to make my exit. The teenage boy had finished perusing the rubber ducks and gave his head a quick nod in the direction of the door. I returned his use of the universal symbol for, "I have something to tell you, but not here," with an "Okay. I'll meet you in a minute outside where we can talk freely," in other words, another slight nod of the head, and left. The youth followed a few seconds later. I lit up a Lucky and waited. "So?"

"Didn't look like you were getting far there."

"You'd be surprised."

"You a cop?"

I could not stop myself from smiling. "You an extra for *Miami Vice*?"

He looked confused.

"Don't worry. Before you were born. So what have you got for me?"

"Not much," the boy said, "but I probably know someone who does. There's a guy who sees everything around here."

After blowing a smoke ring above his head, I asked, "Who might that be?"

"Stinky Pete."

"Stinky Pete?"

He nodded. "That's right. He sees everything while being ignored by everyone."

"Where might I find this all-seeing eye?"

The boy checked his watch. "It's almost lunch time, so he'll be round the back of the market hoping someone feeds him some scraps."

"Scraps, eh?" I spied a pasty shop just down the road. "I think I can do a bit better than that."

Stinky Pete was certainly not hard to locate. For one thing, he was exactly where my young informant had said that he would be, behind the Jubilee Market. For the other, he was very noticeable by the large space that encompassed his dishevelled form as passers-by gave the old tramp an extremely wide berth. It would appear that he certainly lived up to his name. Either that or they just didn't give a damn.

I took my recently purchased pasty in hand, girded up my olfactory senses and crouched down next to my potential source of information. As I handed the warm meal over there was one thing that struck me even more violently than the smell of filth and urine, the total lack of hope in the beggar's eyes. I could not begin to comprehend what had led to his life being reduced to this – cowering under a filthy blanket on Morecambe promenade hoping that the generosity of passing strangers would allow him a few discarded scraps with which to sustain his pitiful existence. Had he once been a happy, smiling boy with loving parents who had doted on him, given him endless cuddles and cleaned his grazed knees whenever he had stumbled? Had he once known the love of a wife or partner and the doting affection of his own children? Had there once been a successful job where he had felt like he was the king of his own little world?

What had reduced him to this?

I doubted that I would ever know.

I sighed then immediately regretted the action as his acrid aroma made me gag. So much for sympathy.

"Hello there," I said, fighting back the urge to vomit. "Are you Stinky Pete?"

The tramp eyed me suspiciously through half-open, wary eyes. He looked at my face then at the pasty that he turned over in his grimy paws. Again, his eyes looked up at mine and there was a rustle. I glanced down and the pasty had vanished under the folds of the blanket, squirrelled away for consumption at a later time.

Not a word left his mouth.

I carried on, regardless. "I believe you saw what happened down on the prom last night." I motioned along the road with my head. "Would you be able to tell me what you saw?"

"Weren't me. Was 'Arold." His voice was thin and laboured as if the words were foreign and little used, their pronunciation almost forgotten. "Was 'Arold."

"Harold?"

"'Arold. Told the police. Earlier."

"I was told that you would have seen whoever took the statue. No one mentioned that you had a companion."

"'Arold saw them. Not me." He leaned forward to me and whispered. "Heard them too, 'ee says."

I drummed my teeth in thought. Clearly the poor guy was a white-sliced sandwich short of a picnic. Not surprising considering his wretched lifestyle. Was Harold an imaginary friend? Was he something that the tramp had conjured up to help him get through each monotonous day of hunger and destitution? "So where's Harold now?"

"Right 'ere 'ee is."

I nodded sagely and decided it would be best to play along. Turning to the empty space next to the tramp, I addressed it in a friendly manner, "Hello Harold. Nice to meet you."

The tramp gave me a look that suggested I had told him the Queen had just invited him to Buckingham Palace for afternoon tea. "What you doin'?"

"Talking to Harold."

There was a wet chuckle as the old man showed his amusement. "'Ee's not *there*," he explained. "'Ee's *'ere*." There was rippling movement from under his filthy blanket and I instinctively leant back expecting a baby Xenomorph to burst forth. Instead, I was greeted by a sight that would melt the coldest heart: a white albino baby rabbit. "'Ere's 'Arold," the tramp grinned, cuddling the little *lago*morph to his bristly chin. "'Ee likes it down there. Nice and warm for 'im."

I could not help but smile. Here, in the shape of a small furry animal, was this poor man's hope. Something to comfort him when he was down and to look out for when there was trouble about. I reached out and stroked Harold between his ears. He twitched his pink nose and craned his neck to sniff my fingers.

"'Ee likes you."

"So it would seem. Do you think he will tell me what he saw and heard last night?"

"Might do."

"*Might* do?"

The tramp shifted uncomfortably. "The thing is you see, 'ee has this filthy 'abit. I keep tellin' 'im that they're no good for 'im, but 'ee does like 'em." His eyes looked up hopefully.

I smiled and fished two Luckies out of their pack. "For Harold," I said, passing them over.

"For 'Arold," the tramp agreed as the cigarettes vanished, sucked into the same bottomless pit that stored the pasty. Absentmindedly stroking his furry companion, Pete looked up at me and asked. "So, what was it you wanted, then?"

I pointed back down the prom again. "Last night, when the statue was stolen. Did Harold see anything?"

Pete glanced back down at the rabbit, which was casually nibbling the already frayed cuff of the tramp's stained overcoat. "'Ee don't sleep very well, does 'Arold. What wiv it bein' cold an' damp, you know?"

"I can imagine."

"An' last night, there was all manner o' noise."

"By the statue?"

"Tha's right. By the statue. It really kep' 'im wide awake, it did, poor little thing."

"So what did he see?"

"Well tha's the most curious thing. With all the kerfuffle, 'ee thought it was the kids who come and make fun of us. They're cruel, they are, calling us names and kicking us. We, don't like 'em, do we 'Arold?"

I was sure that Harold didn't.

"Anyway, 'Arold had a little peep, 'ee did. To see who it was making the noise. An' what a surprise 'ee got! Monsters, 'ee saw! Four of 'em. They used some sort of contraption on the statue and cut it down, leaving a foot behind. 'Arold knows this because 'ee went and watched them. 'Ee can move very quietly and stay 'idden, being a bunny. So 'ee went an' 'id in the shadows an' watched them monsters cut poor Eric down an' throw 'im in a van before they painted all sorts of stuff over what was left."

"Did he notice anything unusual about them? Apart from being monsters, of course."

"Well, you see, tha's the thing, innit." Pete's eyes glinted with excitement. "They were them Egyptian monsters, the ones that wear all them bandages and wander round the big tombs in foreign lands. 'Arold knows this cos 'ee's seen 'em on the tellies in shop windows. An' there's one thing 'ee knows for sure about them monsters. They don't wear fancy watches!"

Well, well. I raised an eyebrow. "Fancy watches? What do you mean?"

"Them monsters on the tellies have been dead a long, long time. They didn't 'ave watches back them, let alone none of your Rolexes or Omegas and tha' sort 'a thing. But those ones last night did. 'Arold saw them shining in the moonlight. So 'ee crep' a bit closer, like and 'ad a listen. An' you know what?"

"What?"

"Well 'Arold and me reckon that those old monsters being foreign and such wouldn't be speaking like folk from roun' 'ere."

"You overheard them?"

Pete nodded his head adamantly.

"What did they say?"

"Well one of 'em was in charge, by the looks of it. 'Ee kep' telling the others that they 'ad to be quick and make it look like someone else 'ad done it."

I frowned. "Who?"

The tramp leant back and almost disappeared into his bundle of rags. "I daren't say."

"Why?"

"Dangerous, tha's why."

"Pete, what could be more dangerous than four mummies running around Morecambe?"

He seemed to weigh this up in his mind then finally said, "They said it was a *witch*!"

"A witch?"

"Tha's right," his head nodded up and down so fast that it looked like he was being controlled by a caffeine-addicted puppeteer from inside his rags. "Tha's why they painted all them symbols and stuff. They wanted a witch to get the blame."

"Did you hear anything else?"

Pete shook his head. "Not me, nor 'Arold. 'Ee was too scared."

I could imagine.

"Did you see where they went after they loaded the statue into the van?"

He pointed a grubby finger down the prom. "They took their van off in tha' direction. Down towards the West End."

I stood up and felt my muscles creak. None of this made any sense. Well-to-do men dressed up as mummies, stealing a beloved statue to blame it all on a witch? Madness. "Pete, you said that the police came and spoke to you. What did they have to say?"

"Not much," he shrugged. "They just asked question after question, but I didn't give 'em any answers. Tha's cos I don't know nuffin. It was 'Arold that saw everything an' they didn't ask 'im."

I smiled. "Well you tell Harold that I'm very grateful for all his help," and I headed off down the road towards the West End of Morecambe.

Back in its heyday, Morecambe was a tourist boomtown – the Venice of North England. If you look in the local history books or peruse the life-size displays in Lancaster's city museum, you will come across sepia-toned images and jolly reproductions of happy Victorians in knee-length swimming costumes daringly dipping their toes in the healthily bracing waters of Morecambe Bay. Moustaches and boater hats were the uniform of the day (normally for the male folk), upper lips were buffed up with extra stiffener and a marvellous time was had by all.

So it continued for many years. Fashions changed along with demographics but still Morecambe thrived as a bustling seaside town - the pearl at the centre of the Morecambe Bay oyster. The powers that be even built a theme park that evolved into Frontierland, promising a Hollywood-style Wild West experience for all its visitors.

However, the foundations on what Morecambe had been built started to crumble in the 1980s. Tourists were wooed away to sunnier climes by glossy brochures and silver-tongued salespeople. The hotels started to haemorrhage guests and desperate hoteliers, in order to make ends meet, started to take in individuals and families who were claiming government benefits. A downward spiral set in: more social security residents meant fewer vacationers which, in turn, led to more social security residents, and so on. Even the construction of the Polo Tower on the decaying remains of Frontierland failed to draw much of a crowd and the amusement park finally closed its doors in 2000.

Not a very prestigious way in which to mark the passing of the millennium.

As a result, Morecambe is now very much a town of three parts. To the east there is Bare, the more affluent neighbourhood populated with retired jewellers, bankers and upwardly mobile builders. In the middle, centred around the Eric Morecambe statue (or rather, right now, its foot), is the promenade where new seeds of growth can be witnessed with shops and hotels starting to blossom once again as people begin to yearn for simpler holidays rather than the stress of chasing illusive baggage around such exotic places as Stansted Airport. To the west, however, the land is still somewhat soured by years of neglect and abandonment. This is the West End of Morecambe where former glory slouches despondently in the decaying detritus of self-loathing and hopelessness. It gazes listlessly across the sea to the beautiful mountains of the Lake District and wonders where it all went wrong before scratching its expansive butt, belching loudly and tossing an empty can of Special Brew into the sea.

As I headed down past the train station, the bowling alley, Morrison's supermarket and other such local landmarks, the ruin that was Frontierland loomed on my left hand side. Corrugated iron provided a rusty rampart to a bygone age that was now derelict and in ruin. Ungrammatical graffiti was scrawled across the discoloured, jagged partition between Morecambe and its past failure. Numbers offering sexual acts, comments on alleged parental ambiguity and anatomically incorrect genitalia were the order of the day.

No one ever came here apart from junkies looking for somewhere to grab a secluded fix and piss-heads on the way home who required an impromptu latrine.

It was the perfect place to hide a heavy bronze statue in a hurry.

As I looked over the metal wall for a possible way in, the light breeze that had been carrying the scent of the sea to my nose changed direction and my nostrils wrinkled at the unpleasant stench of charred wood and plastic. This was the same odour that I had recently smelt on the piece of bandage that I had discovered at the remains of the Eric Morecambe statue. My memory suddenly became very excited and thrust it hand up in the air: "Me, sir! Me, sir!"

"What is it, Memory?"

"We read about this, sir. The other day, sir."

"Did we?"

"Yes, sir. It was in the paper, sir."

"Well done, Memory. Give yourself a house point."

"Thank you, sir!"

"Oh, and Memory..."

"Yes, sir?"

"Stop being such a fornicating little arse-licker."

Of course. According to the copy of the *Chronicle* at Nowell's there had been the suspicious fire here. All it would take would be for a careless mummy to lean against a piece of burnt material and voila, smelly bandages and a clue to point Yours Truly in the correct direction.

My mind thought things over as I casually gave the boundary a once over for entry points. What if the so-called mummies had been planning ahead and had started the fire.

All the more reason for people to stay away.

All the more reason for me to get inside.

I shot a quick glance up and down the road to make sure I couldn't be observed then jumped and grabbed the top of the fence, heaving myself up. It was as I scrambled my feet up the worn metal and to the top of the barrier that I realised I was now in somewhat of a predicament.

How to get down?

The floor on the other side was lower than the pavement. I wobbled frantically as I stretched myself out along the precariously thin metal. Ragged edges gouged into my hands and I swore under my breath before realising that I was moving.

Downward.

My legs rattled against the rusty panelling as they hurriedly tried to grab a purchase, but it was no use. I was falling. All I could do was roll myself up into a ball and hope for the best as the floor rushed up to greet me in a less that welcoming hug.

I came down with quite a loud crash as tattered bunting, discarded fabric and the ubiquitous abandoned pallet enveloped me. I lay for a moment as I mentally checked off that all my limbs were both still attached and fully functional. When I had ascertained that this was the case and I was not doomed to calling out for help, I rolled gently onto my side and surveyed my surroundings.

It was certainly not Disneyland.

When you think of a theme park what normally comes to mind are swooping roller coasters, brightly coloured attractions, neatly kept lawns and the tantalising smell of sugary treats. Here there were overflowing skips, decayed and crumbling benches, rampaging bracken and the acrid stench of burnt polymers.

"Must bring the kids," I muttered to myself whilst limping through filthy puddles of water left over from the fire brigade's valiant attempt at preventing such an iconic piece of seaside history from being further devastated.

You can choose where to insert the implied sarcasm wherever you want in that last paragraph.

I shuddered as I looked around the carnage. It was all too reminiscent of the vision that I had been shown of the world post-Divergence. I kept expecting little fairies to flutter over and start annoying me. They didn't, however, so I decided to be grateful for small mercies. What I did see was one vaguely upright structure in the middle of this pseudo-apocalyptic wasteland. I slowly clambered over the detritus and rubble until I stood in front of the last remaining edifice: The Hall Of Mirrors.

"Cliché," I grumbled as I snuck up to the door. A gentle push proved it to be unlocked so I ventured inside. The door swung shut behind me and I was enclosed in ominous darkness. I fished out my small penlight and, cupping the device in my hand, switched it on. Using the device's tight beam, I carefully investigated the floor around me; the last thing I wanted was to trip over something say, like a dead body. That would be most unfortunate. As my eyes started to adjust to the gloom, I risked sweeping the torch around in larger arcs. All I saw was a cracked version of me squinting back. It *was* a hall of mirrors, after all. I registered which way the corridor veered and headed of in that direction.

There are certain things in life that one can rate as truly unpleasant: having to bathe in a tub of warm vomit, dental surgery with no anaesthetic, listening to a slimy politician explain why he stuck his flaccid genitals in the mouth of a dead pig when he was a student. For me, trying to navigate around a pitch-black building that kept casting gruesomely distorted reflections of my lost and confused self back in my face rated up there with such experiences. Even when I was a kid, I had never really been a fan of mirrors. I was convinced that when I was brushing my teeth or squeezing a prominent zit that my reflection would wink at me or perform some sort of independent act. Even worse, I was always concerned that someone would appear behind me in the mirror; someone who was not in the room. I would see myself standing there watching this stranger, my shaking hands gripping the washbasin as I mustered up the courage to turn around and confront the apparition.

Fortunately, this never happened when I was kid.

Right now, though, my mind was telling me that there was a first time for everything.

The corridors seemed to drag on for eternity. How big *was* this building? It had not seemed too vast from the outside. Around every corner that I turned there lurked a distorted parody of my face mocking me. A thin face grimacing at my stupidity. A fat face laughing at my predicament. Again and again, they mocked me. After what seemed like fifteen minutes or so I came to the only logical conclusion: I was going around in circles. I swore under my breath and closed my eyes. I was being distracted by the varying reflections and I had to try utilising another sense. I held my breath and tried to reach out beyond the non-stop ringing of my tinnitus. I could hear small sounds around me. There was the hush of a breeze drifting through a hole in the roof, the flapping of a torn tarpaulin that had come loose from somewhere, the creak of a fragile piece of wood.

Another creak.

Then another.

I listened harder. There it was again, repetitive but irregular. Short bursts then pauses. There was something else too: murmuring.

I was clearly not alone.

As silently as I could and barely breathing, I made my way towards what I hoped was the source of the noise. Ignoring the glares from the cracked mirrors, I felt my way along the winding corridors, my spare hand running along the charred wall until my fingers came across a ridge in the woodwork. I stopped and listened again. There was the creaking and the murmuring once more, nearer this time.

I flashed my torch over my hand and ran it up and down what was a gap in the wall just a centimetre or so wide. It ran from floor to ceiling. Prising my fingers into the small space, I pulled gently and there was movement as, in the dimness of my surroundings, the wall seemed to come towards me.

It was a door.

I clicked off the penlight and eased myself into the erstwhile hidden room. As I edged forwards, I could hear voices. They were not sounding too happy. Neither did they sound very Egyptian.

"For Christ's sake, look what you're doing with that!"

"Sorry. These bandages keep getting in the way."

"Well, roll them up then!"

"But then I'll get paint on myself..."

As I closed in on the voices, light started to permeate the surrounding gloom and I could make out a balcony looking out over a lower room. Crouching down, I manoeuvred to a vantage point. What I saw made me raise my eyebrows somewhat. Down below were what passed for three Egyptian mummies. They were not doing what you would *expect* mummies to do: wandering around aimlessly with arms outstretched, throttling unsuspecting archaeologists or abducting beautiful archaeological assistants, nothing like that at all. They were spray-painting the Eric Morecambe statue.

Now, when I say *spray-painting*, I use the term very loosely. They seemed to be getting more paint on each other than actually on the simulacrum of Morecambe's finest comedian. However, what did make its way onto the cast bronze was reminiscent of the symbols I had seen around its base. There were pentagrams, moons, snakes and various other pseudo-occult images.

Right now, though, the smallest of the mummies was continuing his argument with one of the taller ones. "Besides," he whined, "I've only just got them on and by the time I get these bandages off, he'll be back. And he'll be pissed off that we're not finished."

"He'll be more pissed off that you seem to be painting me more than the statue!"

The widest and tallest of the mummies grumbled to the others. "I thought we were supposed to be doing this tomorrow."

The small one started yapping again (I had subconsciously christened him Scrappy because he was small and annoying), "Is there anything apart from cotton wool in that thick skull of yours? I told you, someone was sniffing around the statue today and asking questions." He hastily sprayed a pentagram on Eric's head. "I rang the boss and he damn near bust a blood vessel. Said we had to get this finished and move it out."

Middle-sized mummy gave a quick, sharp laugh.

"What?" demanded Scrappy with his hands on his hips. "Something funny?"

"He's afraid that someone would come looking in here? We really did a number on this place. No one's gonna be coming around."

"That's what you think," I whispered to myself.

"Like I always say," came a threatening voice from behind me, "you just can't be too careful."

I started to turn but all I saw was the shadow of something heavy descending very quickly, then there was blackness.

My head hurt.

This was becoming a habit. When I first set myself up as a paranormal investigator, I sort of had the idea that I would be sipping cups of tea with old dears who thought that their cat was a psychic channel for Doris Day or that the strange knocking in their pipes was Great Aunt Ethel rather than an airlock.

I did not expect to have permanent concussion.

"Jesus!" I yelped as someone grabbed my hair and yanked my already traumatised cranium backwards.

"He's awake."

"I can see that."

"So, what are we gonna do with him?"

Then there was silence. I did not enjoy the silence; it implied that my future and well-being hung somewhat precariously in the balance. I eased my eyes open. There were now four mummies in the room with the freshly daubed statue: the original three lackeys, Scrappy, Medium-sized and Plus-sized, and the one that was quite obviously their boss. He was standing in the centre of the dusty room, his bandaged arms crossed and his dark eyes glowering furiously in my direction.

"I said, 'What are we gonna do with him?'" came the question, once again. It was Scrappy yapping away.

"I heard you the first time."

"This is him. The guy that came in the shop."

So that identified the smallest of the four. It was the toyshop owner. That figured, considering his little slip at mentioning mummies earlier.

I adjusted my position and winced as my head throbbed and my wrists ached. They were bound to some sort of pipe. "Don't mind me," I groaned almost cheerfully. "Just passing through."

The leader continued to survey me as if I was a problem in the plumbing to which I had been tied captive. "Somehow, Mister Spallucci, I don't believe that."

"You know me? I'm flattered." He knew me. That was worrying. Also, his voice. Did I recognise it? It sounded familiar. The dexterous fingers of my internal filing system blurred into overdrive. If I could remember who he was then I might just be able to save my life.

The mummy turned his back on me, his drab, ragged bandages flapping somewhat. "We can turn this to our advantage. Is the paint dry?"

There were nods from the others. I had obviously been out for a while.

"Gather some wood and some diesel. We're going to rid ourselves of a witch-lover."

"What?"

The leader grabbed his underling, Scrappy the shop owner, by his bandaged throat and smashed him against the nearest wall. "You agreed to follow me."

"We didn't agree to murder," voiced Medium-sized.

Dissent in the ranks. This was good.

The leader dropped the first rebel and turned on the second. "And what do you suppose we should do now? We want to be rid of the witch. That was the idea."

"I know... but..."

"No buts. He knows what we're doing. He's seen us."

"But he's not seen our *faces*, Colin!"

All around the room realisation hit in a number of ways. The leader realised that I now knew he was Colin Nowell of the eponymous restaurant in Lancaster. The three stooges now knew they were in for the scolding of their lives. And me, I knew I was dead.

I raced my memory back to the day that I had been flown across Lancaster whilst gripping for grim death onto an animated grotesque. I had visited Nowell's as it had been a target for Spud's graffiti. Nowell had taken me inside and we had chatted, or rather he had proceeded to turn aggressive and I had left. There had been something else, though. His family tree. *Justice of the Peace. East Lancashire.*

Mummies rambling on about witches.

Something was nagging away. There was a connection. I just could not put my finger on it. It was like a greased chickpea skittering away from a blunt fork and rolling out of the salad onto the table. Perhaps it was down to the permanent pounding my skull kept receiving?

"What is it with witches, then?" I had to stall for time. Get him talking. "Everyone knows they're all just celery-eating, sandal-wearing hippies these days. Long gone are the pointy hats."

Nowell's shoulders rose and fell. "You think you're so funny, don't you? Such a comedian." I watched as his ragged fists clenched and unclenched. "Well you couldn't be so wrong."

"Okay. And why would that be then?"

The bandaged restaurateur loomed over me. "Every day I have to put up with her. Every day she stands there, her very presence mocking me. She's an abomination."

So, this was getting weird, as if being held captive by men dressed as dead Egyptian pharaohs was not weird enough. "Who? Who are you on about?"

"That crazy bitch outside my restaurant," he roared. "That's who! Standing there all day, singing and dancing to her infernal music."

The penny dropped. "You mean Betty?"

"Call her what you want. She is a bride of Satan."

That precise moment called for the ultimate in tact and diplomacy. My life hung in the balance at the whim of a madman.

I laughed.

In hindsight, it was probably the wrong thing to do.

"Stop it!" Nowell screamed in my face. "Stop it, now!"

"Oh, come on," I managed between chortles. "Betty? Boombox Betty is a *witch*? Where on Earth did you get that?"

The big ox lurched forward, grabbed me by the throat, and then started to shake, hard. As the surroundings started to tremble and blur I was aware of his underlings grabbing in vain at his shoulders to try and pull him off. There was shouting and swearing but to me it was all starting to fade away. Everything was starting to look somewhat watery as the ringing in my ears began to crescendo.

Then there was nothing. Again.

When I came to, I was alone, untied and exceptionally sore. The mummies were gone along with the Eric Morecambe statue. I closed my eyes and waited for the world to stop swaying before eventually dragging myself to my feet and limping away.

What had happened during my period of unconsciousness? Why wasn't I toast?

I closed my eyes and gently struck my head against the pipe.

I had endured enough for one day.

No, I had endured enough for a lifetime.

# The Case of the Gambling Ghost

I like bourbon. I know it's not fashionable at the moment what with the middle classes clamouring for limited edition single malts or hoppy-tasting beers from microbreweries, but for me a good swig of Jack always hits the mark. Besides, who are these people trying to kid when they sit around after their fancy dinners in their nice suburban houses? Just because a bottle has a picture of a happy looking bee or a genteel Scottish lassie plastered on its label does not mean that it will not pickle your liver any less than a white-labelled bottle of vodka from a budget supermarket. It is all about perception and, more importantly, marketing. Buying into the fancy alcohol branding is like buying into the better schools or the latest 3D television. It's all about social appearances being used to cover up the cracks in the plasterwork that attempt to hide the god-awful truth that haunts us all.

One day we will die.

I have witnessed this too much in my life. I saw my first dead body when I was about eleven. My parents received a phone call in the early evening and I was whisked around to the home of my two elderly great aunts, Mary and Tots. What my parents neglected to tell me was that Tots had just passed away whilst watching *Bullseye*. Mary was in such a panic that she had not known what to do and had rung us first. As a result, we got there before the undertaker and there Tots was - still propped up in her comfy chair with Jim Bowen rambling on about "magic darts" and "Bully's special prize." She looked mostly like she was asleep. Her eyes were closed and she was slumped cosily into her armchair. The one thing giving it away that she had terminally lost interest in a couple from a council flat in Staines possibly winning a speedboat by hitting double top was the pallor of her skin. It looked like someone had fabricated a life size simulacrum of my great aunt from wax. There was a weird sheen to it that reminded me of the Autons from Doctor Who and it was a yellowy-beige colour like custard mixed with a drop of Bisto gravy.

So, I sat politely and quietly as my mum comforted my aunt and my dad sorted out the necessary arrangements. All the time I expected Tots to open an eye and send me a sneaky little wink to show that she was not really dead, but it was all just a trick.

She never winked.

The bedtime after that incident, the terrors that I had suffered on and off throughout the nights of my childhood came to stay and never left.

From that moment on, the notion that at some point in our lives we would never open our eyes again and that there would be nothing, not even a sense of blackness or solitude, terrified me. It was a peculiar oxymoron as, on the other hand, I was a devout Christian. I believed firmly in the ministry of Jesus and his death and resurrection, his message of love and forgiveness, but there was always that voice of Thomas Didymus whispering away in the back of my head, “But he is divine. Of course he cannot die. The same can't be said for you.” So on Sunday mornings I would sing, pray and serve at the altar of my parish church whilst on Sunday evenings I would ram the sheets of my teenage bed into my mouth to ensure that my parents did not hear the mournful screams that told of one who dreaded that final, inevitable breath and the oblivion that ultimately followed.

All of that changed when I encountered Gerald, the ghostly janitor of Luneside University. Suddenly there was light at the end of the tunnel. The dark veil that clouded the afterlife was torn down and I could doubt no more. I had seen first-hand that there was life after death. Someone had come back from the grave and had told me so.

He had told me not to worry for my dying father.

As I sat in the Borough ploughing my way through my third or fourth glass of whiskey I dwelt on this. Surely it should be okay now? Surely all that doubt and terror should have been swept away by an extremely tidy phantom? Yet, as the bourbon warmed my tense gullet and gentle heat soothed my unsettled stomach I could not help but hear that insidious whisper at the back of my head once more.

“Eternal rest and the life hereafter are not for you.”

Damn it! I had died hadn't I? I had blown my own brains out and survived the experience. Or had I? The previous week had been a paradox, which I was now living under different circumstances. Circumstances, which it seemed, had distressed me.

I could not get over the vile hatred of Nowell. What was he doing? He had dressed up as a fictional wanderer of Egyptian tombs and, with his cronies, had defaced a local landmark. And for why? To make it look like Boombox Betty was a witch!

I shook my head and drank more alcohol. It was too hard to comprehend. My brain cells needed numbing. Once again in my life I felt that I was missing the most important piece of an infuriatingly complex jigsaw. Okay, Betty was, well... individual. But a witch? Not to mention that Nowell saw her as all black pointy hat and dancing round a cauldron summoning Satan style rather than dancing through a meadow singing to daisies. The mousey girl, Cynthia, from the speed dating night had procured some sort of voodooesque doll from "the crazy woman on Cheapside." She surely had to have meant Betty. However, there was something else that she had said. Her father had been researching stuff and found out that Betty was a witch.

I closed my eyes and an intricate fractal of carefully scripted names danced behind my eyelids. I groaned. Was Cynthia actually Colin Nowell's daughter? Was this why he was so anti witch? Did he fear that Betty's harmless eccentricities might lead his daughter down some sort of dark path?

Families really did mess with your head.

I drank more bourbon.

"Hey there!"

I glanced up from my glass and felt a genuine smile touch my lips. "Hi, Grace." How are you?" My smile faltered as she hesitated before answering.

"Oh, you know, so so."

I frowned as this was most unlike the little happiness dragon. Normally she served my alcohol with an infectious grin. "What's up?"

Her shoulders rose and fell as she perched herself down on a stool. "You know that I'm, like studying for my doctorate?"

I nodded. As well as pouring a mean drink, Grace was also a bright bunny.

"Well, my flatmate, who was on the same course as me has pulled out and moved back home to her parents'."

"So what's the problem?"

"I now have twice as much rent to pay and I can't afford that on," she waved her hand around the bar, "this job."

"It shouldn't be too hard to get another roomie, surely?"

Grace winced. "There's a problem. She's not been paying her rent and the landlord is being, you know, a complete douche. He sorta wants the new tenant to pay what she owes him."

My jaw dropped. "That's awful! He can't expect anyone to move in with that hanging over them."

Grace nodded. "I know. So he goes and says that because, you know, no one else will pay so I will have to."

Her deep green eyes looked up at me and it was truly heart breaking. This poor kid was trying to better herself and not only had her friend run out on her, now her sleaze of a landlord was trying to strong-arm her into paying double. "Have you been onto legal at the students' union?"

"I rang them this morning. They said they'd look into it for me."

I reached over and held her tiny hand in my somewhat larger paw. She immediately smiled. "Let me know how it goes," I assured her.

"Will do," she smiled, squeezing my hand before blushing slightly for some reason and getting up quickly. "I... I'd better get back to work. Catch you later."

"Sure."

I smiled. Oh, to be young again when the biggest traumas revolved around awkward landlords and flighty friends who went running home to mummy when things got hard.

My train of thought paused as it mulled over that last part.

I pulled out my mobile and hit the same speed dial that I had called a few days previous.

The phone rang twice before a female voice answered.

"Hi, Mum. It's Sam..."

I grew up in a small market town called Wellington, which was situated in the East Midlands. Apparently, in the long dusty annals of time, there had been a spring in the centre of town that had been famed for its healing properties. People from far and wide would come by horse, cart or even stagger along the muddy roads in ill-fitting shoes for just a taste of these refreshing waters. Chroniclers catalogued all manner of miracles from the healing of plague to the raising of the near dead. All manner of miraculous feats had been attributed to this one single wellspring.

Then sometime in the Middle Ages, something happened. The Church moved in. The ground around the well was deemed to be holy and therefore belonging to the Church. So it was that the edifice of All Saints was constructed.

And what a construction it was.

Its locally hewn limestone was forged into a spire that towered above the burgeoning town. Bells were placed in said tower that, when pealed, could be heard across the surrounding villages calling the faithful to prayer. They prayed in their droves, filling the intricately carved pews week after week. A life-sized painted wooden sculpture of their saviour was placed up on the rood screen to watch over them and to demonstrate His love just as he had to his disciples.

Then, in under a generation, the well that had been the fount of so many miracles, was forgotten. Today, people only know of its existence because of those early records, but not once was its specific location ever mentioned.

I have my theory though.

At the opposite end of the nave to the rood screen stands a stone font. It is plain grey except for a single inscription around its rim: "Knaves are not our responsibility." That reference alone is puzzling enough and is alleged to have been a quote from some bishop regarding work on the church in Victorian times. Whether it is or whether it isn't, whether the knaves in question were parochial lowlifes or the engraver just could not spell the names of certain parts of the church, I always feel that it would make sense for the font to have been located over the site of the original spring, the natural wonder upon which the man-made wonder was placed.

As I stood looking at the font that autumnal day, the pall of incense from a previous service still hanging in the crisp, cold air, I was sure that I could hear the susurration of distant water coursing through the bedrock.

But, then again, it could very well have just been my tinnitus.

"Can I help you?"

I turned and saw a middle-aged man in clerical blacks approaching me. *There but for the grace of God...* I thought to myself. "Hello. Sam Spallucci." I introduced myself and stuck out my hand. "I'm just visiting family and thought I'd pop in for a look see."

The priest took my hand and shook it firmly. "Alan Walters. I'm the vicar here."

I smiled. "So I see. The old place hasn't changed much. Less dustier than I remember, though."

The priest positively beamed at my compliment. "Well we do our best, being short-staffed and all."

I raised an eyebrow.

"I'm currently without a curate. Expecting a new chap any day now. Apparently he's some sort of high flyer. Lincoln's his name. Peter Lincoln. Have you heard of him?"

"Can't say that I have."

"Well as long as he's capable with a spanner and furniture polish then he'll go down okay here," Walters chuckled. I joined him.

"People forget that there's more to a church than Sunday worship, don't they?"

His head nodded, light glancing off his bald scalp. "Indeed they do. Most of them just turn up, say their prayers and go. Not a thought for the day to day running of the place."

"It's the small cogs that drive the engine," I said.

"Indeed. Indeed." Walters frowned. "I say, do I know you? You look somewhat familiar."

I grinned. "You might have seen me quite a bit without realising it."

A minute later, we were standing in the choir vestry gazing up at what we used to call the Rogue's Gallery back when I had a much higher voice and regularly wore a red cassock. "Well, bless my soul!" my new friend exclaimed. "You haven't changed much, have you?"

Looking at a teenage version of myself, I supposed I hadn't. "Not lost the curls yet." There I was, beaming down in my surplice, cassock and ruff along with all my predecessors and successors. All head choristers of All Saints for their brief moment of power and glory. Well, that's what it felt like back then. I had to admit, looking back on it, it was hardly a post of international supremacy but at least I got to use a nice, new copy of the church's hymnal and that had to count for something.

"Is the choir still thriving?"

"Oh, yes. Most definitely. They sing twice every Sunday and for high feast days. Do you still sing?"

I expelled a short bray of laughter. "No. Not anymore. I sort of, drifted away. Life has a habit of sometimes dealing you cards that you don't expect."

"True. True," Walters nodded sagely. "So, may I enquire as to what it is you do these days?"

I fished out a crumpled business card from the depths of my trench coat. "I'm a paranormal investigator. Sort of still working for the same side."

After smoothing out the small piece of card, the vicar nodded and slipped it into his shirt pocket. "Well, you never know. We might have need of you sometime."

I guessed that he was just being polite. What would a parish church ever need from me? I gave a small sigh. "Well, I'd better be off."

"Very good. Visiting family, did you say?" I recognised the change in the tone of voice. It had shifted gear from welcoming to pastoral.

"My mother. We've not seen each other for quite a while."

Walters followed me out of the vestry, through the organ chapel and into the nave. "Well you're here now, aren't you?"

"Indeed I am." Indeed I was.

Inclining his head to one side he observed, "You don't seem too thrilled at the prospect of this family reunion."

"We... didn't exactly part on good terms last time."

"Ah... one of *those* situations. Worried that harsh words are going to be on the menu?"

"Something like that."

"Sam, there's only one thing that you need to remember. She is your mother. You will always be that ruffed little choir boy that she listened to in adoration all those years ago."

Twirling my fedora around in my hands, I nodded. He was right. Of what did I have to be scared?

I said, "Goodbye," and headed out of the church. As I did, I heard the sound of rushing water again, the water that healed those in need. I turned and out of the corner of my eye, I was sure that I saw a shadow fall across the font.

Most likely the sun being obscured by clouds as it shone through the stained glass, I told myself.

Well, I can guess that you already know I was wrong about that.

Thirty minutes later saw me sitting in my car in the middle of a sub-urban street that ran for about half a mile through a neat little housing estate. As I switched off the engine of my Polo Classic, I looked out at my mother's semi-detached sanctuary. There were the pruned rose bushes, the neatly trimmed grass, the finely polished double-glazing and gleaming woodwork. "Immacurate," as she would say. No, I didn't spell that wrong; that is how she actually says it.

The windows were shut tight against the chill autumnal air and a slight fog blew on my breath as I exited the car before taking the long walk up the tarmacked drive. With each step, the long years of separation seemed to shrink to just a few hours.

I had never left.

I had never been away.

This was where I belonged.

As Father Walters had said, *she was my mother.*

I pressed the doorbell and Beethoven's *Ode To Joy* jingled away inside. I looked up and saw the bedroom nets twitch slightly. Thinking it was my mother, I smiled, but then the door opened and there she was, smiling at me with that infectious beam of joy. It must have been a draught in the curtains.

"Oh, Sammy..." Then I was completely engulfed in a monumental hug, which was quite a feat considering that my mother is about half my size. "It's so good to see you. Come on in." She pulled away and let me carry my bag inside. "We've been expecting you."

I frowned at the word, "We." *Please tell me she hasn't invited the neighbours round*: I pleaded with the universe at large. My mum has always been one for social events and what could be larger than the return of her only son?

Fortunately, as I removed my hat and my coat, the lack of noise from the house made it quite clear that we were alone. I breathed the proverbial sigh.

"Are you tired, Sammy? I know it's a long drive."

"No. I'm fine, Mum. Just glad to be here."

"Are you *sure* you're not tired? You do *look* tired."

"No, Mum. I'm fine. Really."

She gave me that mother frown; the little pout and wrinkle that show that she knows I am keeping something back, as she said, "Okay. Well why don't you go and sit down? I'll put the kettle on."

I nodded and went into my mother's living room.

Now, let me tell you about my mother's inner sanctum. The first thing you realise is that you have a great number of eyes watching you. From inside and on top of her long, g-plan china cabinet, the faces of about fifty toby jugs stare lifelessly at you as you enter. As well as the traditional ones sporting a tricorn hat and pipe, there are various others from innkeepers to sailors, from tennis players to knights. There is even one in the shape of Goofy!

Then, above the gas fire, there is a selection of little Wade figurines called Whimsies. Technically, they are mine, but I have never really contested ownership of them as they were bought for me in a distant youth where such things were not yet overshadowed by computer games and 2000AD comics. So the selection of cute woodland animals remained forever with my parents when I left home.

Finally, one turns around as one collapses into the soft caress of the floral sofa and one is confronted with the *Hall Of Sam*. There, on the wall above the television, is the complete life story of Yours Truly framed in photographic posterity. There's the cute one of baby Sam coming home from hospital after the traumatic forty-eight-hour delivery. There's the amusing shot of one-year-old Sam sat butt naked in the kitchen sink having an impromptu bath. There's the various ages of Sam as he travelled through his school career from sweet little newbie to embarrassed, spotty teen. Also, how can one miss the proud centre piece of ruffed and cassocked chorister Sam as he poses for his Head Boy's photo, the green ribbon of the parish church's first ever Dean's Chorister hanging around his neck – a copy of the one at All Saints.

As I looked up at the framed history of me, I could not help but think that all it needed was a few candles and it would make quite the shrine.

"Now then," my mum bustled back into the room carrying a tray of food and drinks, "I've made you your favourite sandwiches, cheese and onion. And, before you complain..."

My mouth snapped shut.

"I went into town and got some of that soya cheese, what with you being... *you know*."

My mother was one of the few people I knew that made being vegan sound on a par with being a registered sex offender. "Thanks, Mum." I took a sandwich and tucked in. It was like being seven again: coming in from running around the garden to a supper of sarnies and a swig of juice. I couldn't help but smile.

However, I was smiling nowhere near as much as Mum was. "Oh, it is so good to see you. Have you grown?"

"I don't think so. I was fairly much an adult when you last saw me."

"You'll always be my little boy, though."

"I know, Mum."

So we chatted and caught up with what each other had been up to. Well, I gave her the edited version: own business, doing well, no mention of vampires, werewolves or shooting myself and going back in time to change the past. Parents are always touchy about such matters, I find. From her end, it seemed that things were very much the same: not too many of the neighbours had died, Marjorie down the road had a new conservatory that my mother was envying.

Then my mum dropped the bombshell.

"Of course, I knew that you were going to ring me."

I raised an eyebrow. "How come?"

"Your dad told me you would."

My eyebrow went into spasm and refused to come back down.

I suppose there comes a point in everyone's life when you start to wonder whether or not your parents are slipping down into the gaping pit of dementia. To use a Star Wars image, it's like the Sarlacc at the Great Pit Of Carkoon into which Boba Fett, the once mighty Mandalorian bounty hunter was so ignominiously shoved to be slowly digested over millennia. However, as all Expanded Universe fans know, Fett managed to escape. Unfortunately, our elders are not clothed in the most durable of *beskar'gam* let alone being equipped with all manner of weapons and rocket launchers. No, once we meet our Sarlacc of senility, it is a slippery slope down into gradual digestion and despair.

So, the notion that my mother believed my long departed father to still be alive and kicking... well, that was rather worrying.

I tried to talk to her about it that evening, but where does one begin? Do you start with, "So, Mum, is that nice Mister Churchill still Prime Minister?" or how about, "Have you started keeping your slippers in the microwave?" You see? It's not easy. Instead, I just let her chatter on about what she was watching on television, what the neighbours were up to. All the safe stuff really.

And so the next week followed suit. I remained focussed on non-threatening chores. I painted woodwork, gave the lawn an incredibly late final cut on a rare sunny day before the chill winds of winter set in and generally pottered around my mother's semi-detached suburban paradise. I was not pursued by mummies, bitten by vampires or molested in any way possible by any manner of supernatural creature.

I actually started to relax. I felt knots that had held my shoulders wound tighter than a clock spring start to loosen. Headaches that I had not really noticed were a perennial problem cleared, blowing fog from the ocean of my mind, enabling me to see further than I had in a long time. This in turn led to the constant companions in my ears, the screaming tinnitus and other such annoying noises, abating through lack of stress.

I was in a safe place. The life that was currently trying to bludgeon me to death with random events was now far, far away.

It was just me, my mum and my mum's occasional references to my father who she was definitely convinced of being around the house somewhere. True, I found this troubling, but I decided that she was far from wandering down to the shops in her nightie and rollers so I was best just letting it be for now.

The strangest moment of this ilk was one afternoon when it was raining hard outside. The fire was on inferno setting as members of the older generation tend to use at the first sign of wintry weather and my mum was clattering about in the cupboard under the stairs.

"It's in here somewhere," she chunnered as stray shoes, woolly hats and errant bags were discarded until, eventually, she pulled out a box the size and appearance of a small suitcase. "Here it is!" she proclaimed. "Your dad said it was under there."

I looked up from my cup of coffee and watched as she opened the box and brought in something that I hadn't seen since I was a child: my dad's trumpet.

"Wow! I didn't know you still had it."

Mum laid it on the sofa next to me and I picked it up, my fingers instinctively fiddling with the valves. "They're seized up."

"Just a minute." She opened a drawer and extracted a small vial of yellow liquid. "Here you go. This should help."

I unscrewed each valve in turn, careful to not get their order mixed up, and applied a small quantity of the oil that I rubbed in with my fingers. Next, I pulled the slides out and oiled them too, enabling me to adjust the tuning.

Then, when the instrument was prepared and looked a little bit more cared for, I placed the mouthpiece to my lips and blew.

I didn't stop for a very long time.

It was very literally a blast from the past.

I had never taken proper lessons in the trumpet; my parents had never been able to afford them. Instead, my dad had shown me the ropes. He had explained that the music came from proper control of the diaphragm and not through using your cheeks like bellows. You had to open your arms wide to allow the best use of oxygen in your lungs and keep upright, not slouched, so that the air glided easily into the instrument.

I played all manner of pieces from classical to jazz and other bits and bobs that my dad had passed on to me before arthritis had claimed the flexibility of his fingers. All the while, my mum looked on in adoration.

We finally realised that it was nine o'clock: Mum's bedtime. "Oh, look at the time!" she cried. "I'm so pleased that your dad told me to dig that out for you. He said that you'd love to play it again. He wants you to have it, you know."

I locked the trumpet back into its box and paused as I snapped the clasps shut. This had to stop. "Mum..."

"You know, I was so sad when he died. I thought that my life was over. He had always been with me, ever since we met that night outside the working men's club in Irchester."

I smiled. I had heard this story so many times before. My mum's date had stood her up and dad had been playing in a band at the club. He had come outside and found her fuming. Ever the smooth talker, he had persuaded her to forget her missing date and come listen to him blow sweet music from his trumpet. The rest, as they say, had been history.

"Mum," I tried again.

"Then," she interrupted, "when he came back... well I was a bit shocked to say the least. But he's here now and that's a good thing. I'm not stupid, though. I know it's only a temporary thing and he'll have to go again soon.

"But it'll break my heart and at *my* age..."

We sat in silence after she trailed off. What the hell could I say now? She was totally convinced that dad was back in her life. If I tried to persuade her otherwise, it would destroy her.

I kept my mouth shut and my rational view on the world to myself. Let her believe what she wanted. It was harmless, after all.

"Right, time for a nightcap," she proclaimed, her words pouring light into the gathering gloom of my thoughts before she proceeded to pour herself a pint of sherry. "I'm having trouble sleeping," she said defensively as my face must have been a picture. "Feel free to help yourself to anything." She kissed me on top of the head and wandered off upstairs.

So that was that. In my mum's head dad was still very much with us. He was talking to her and telling her what to do. There was nothing that I could do about it and she would not let me raise the issue.

I grabbed a malt whiskey from the drinks cabinet and poured myself a good measure. Life, I decided, was becoming far too complicated. At least, here in my mother's house, I was just confronted with things psychological. I was free from all things supernatural.

As my eyelids drooped and I started to snore gently on the sofa, a black shadow flickered in the corner of the room.

It was the middle of summer, not the tail end of autumn. I could feel the heat of the sun on my bare legs.

I wandered aimlessly round the front garden of my granddad's small house on a dreary council estate in Glossop. My mum and dad were inside. So was Granddad, Dad's father. I could hear Granddad's broad Mancunian drawl as he made his opinions known a bit too loudly. I guessed that he was probably criticizing my dad about something.

That was normal.

I picked up a stick that lay on the grass.

However, it wasn't a stick.

It was a sword.

The most beautiful sword in the world. I looked up and down the sword in wonder, clenched in my eight-year-old hand. It shone in the bright light of the day. Its metal was iridescent and the rainbow rays of the sun danced tangos on its reflective surface.

I squinted as the fiery light bounced up into my eyes.

People were walking past outside the garden. I never talked to them. I knew that you did not talk to strangers. They were dangerous. They promised young boys that they had puppies but instead they took you away and did horrible things to you.

I just waved my new sword at them. I was so excited by it that I had to show someone.

No one noticed, though. They just walked on by to wherever it was that they were headed.

I scowled.

Then I listened. I could hear something. This was not unusual as I heard lots of things these days; things that other people couldn't. It was normally bells but sometimes there were voices too. I would be on my own and then there would be a soft susurration in my head that gradually coalesced into voices of people I knew. It was normally Mum or Dad. Sometimes it was a teacher or someone else from school.

More often than not, though, it was a high-pitched ringing or whining that sounded like a small fly dancing next to my eardrum.

However, this was different.

There was music playing somewhere. Beautiful music. I closed my eyes, listened and smiled. The music sounded like the songs my mum would sing to me when she came to me in the night.

When I woke screaming.

Because of the dark.

The dark.

The dark was a horrid place. It slithered into my bedroom and hovered over the edge of where I lay before descending down and smothering me. I would wriggle and struggle against its shadowy form, trying as best as I could to fight it off. But the dark was relentless.

There were other noises in the dark. Shouts and screams. People in terror and agony.

Then there was the one voice that I heard as I lay there, blanketed in my nocturnal oppressor. It was a man. A nasty man. A vicious man who whispered cruelly in my ears, "I will rise."

My eyelids shot up. I hated the dark and I hated the unseen man. He scared me so much.

Only my mother's songs made things better, soothed me to sleep.

Right now, I was thirsty. I looked around.

There on the step of my granddad's porch was a plastic beaker, filled with juice.

My young forehead creased. Had Mum put it there for me? I did not remember. Holding my beautiful sword, I ventured over to the porch and picked up the beaker. Then I began to drink.

The music seemed to get louder. As I gulped down the cold liquid that tasted of honey, strawberries and a million other sweet things I tried to see where the music was coming from. Surely, it had to be a radio somewhere?

Was it coming from inside Granddad's house? No.

Was someone playing a radio in the street? No.

I shrugged and carefully placed the beaker down on the step next to me as I perched myself on the hot stone.

Only, it wasn't a plastic beaker any more.

It was a goblet, like the big chalice that the priest used in church, cast in a lustrous, silvery metal.

Just like my sword.

I picked the goblet up and inspected it closely with my curious young eyes. There was not a mark on it. It was perfectly smooth and highly polished, just like the sword in my other hand.

Then I realised where the music was coming from.

It was coming from the goblet and the sword.

I smiled as I listened to the music. This was not like the noises that I heard in my ears or those which emanated from the dark. This was soothing, enchanting and somehow wise. It spoke of times past and a future yet to come. It sang of the beauty of creation and how it had been there to witness the birth of life itself.

Moreover, it did this without uttering a single word.

I smiled even more when I saw the big black dog that came padding into the garden. I liked dogs. I liked them a lot and so did my dad who had promised to buy me one when we got home, before I went back to school.

I cradled the goblet in the crook of the arm that held the sword and waved at the dog. It turned and looked at me before trotting over. "Hello," I said.

The dog sat down in front of me, its huge, black head level with my small face. It raised its muzzle to the sky and started to howl. It howled so loudly that I could no longer hear the music from the radio.

Then there was another noise - a splitting, cracking noise and little me gasped as the dog's fur started to melt away in front of him. The skin sloughed off and a black shadow oozed out.

It was the dark!

It had found me!

I clutched my newfound treasures close to my chest as the darkness swirled in front of me. I could hear the bad man whispering again: "I will rise... I will rise... I will rise..."

Tears started to form in my eyes and I wanted to scream, but I dare not. This was not a dream, a night terror. This was real and the man in the dark would kill me if I shouted out.

Then the darkness began to take shape and there in front of me stood a creature with a scaly, serpentine tail and two fierce heads: one a goat, the other a lion. Four eyes bore down on me and in their white pupils I saw reflected, not me, but a huge black dragon with fire pouring from its cruel mouth.

"I will rise!" screamed the dark creature.

I tried to back away in terror but banged up against the wall of my granddad's house. I whimpered and my tears dripped freely from my eyes whilst the monstrous thing growled at me from its two mouths.

However, I did not let go of the sword or the goblet. I could not. Then, as I gripped them tight in my hand, holding them close to my chest, the most amazing thing happened. I could hear the music that sounded like it came from a radio once more as the sword and the cup started to glow. They felt warm to the touch and all my fear dissipated. I stood up, all four foot of me, and held the two objects out in front like a protective shield. As I did so, the music turned into the roar of a waterfall and the glow from the objects became like the fire of a sun. The fire enveloped the two-headed creature, causing it to scream in agony as it burnt to ash.

Then there was silence once more, apart from the gentle tinkling of the music.

I sat once more on the doorstep and listened as I heard footsteps approaching. I looked up and saw what looked like a man made of pure sunshine standing beside me. The light around the man dimmed and there was a man that I had seen many times before - the man in black with the sunglasses. He held out his hand and commanded:

"Give those to me. They are mine."

I jolted out of the dream and awoke on my mother's sofa gasping for air.

What the hell was *that* about? Goblets? Swords? A disembodied voice in my head? I shook my head. Nevertheless, there were two images that I definitely recognised: the guy in the glasses and the two-headed beast. A chimera.

I had seen that mythological crossbreed too many times before – in the possession of certain satanic actors and one erstwhile doom-bringer.

Wallace.

What was the connection? What was I missing? "What's the significance of a beast with two heads?" I muttered to myself.

"Perhaps it gives two points of view," came a quiet reply from behind the sofa.

I catapulted across the room, narrowly missing the coffee table, but tripping nonetheless over the floral hearthrug. I recognised that voice. One I hadn't heard for many years now and my heart was pumping faster than the crew who had tried to save the Titanic.

I looked up from my unceremonious heap on the floor, my mouth wagging like a floundering goldfish, unable to find suitable words for the man who stood before me, just as I remembered him: about five foot ten, bright grey-blue eyes, white hair.

"Hello, Son," he said.

"Hi, Dad," I eventually managed.

Five minutes later, I was sat nursing a mum-sized glass of sherry. Dad was sitting in his armchair, his hands laced together as he watched me with obvious concern - his eyebrows knitted and his forehead furrowed.

It was as if he had never been away.

Been away? That was an understatement. He had been dead for over fifteen years!

"You okay, Sammy? You looked like you were having a bad dream."

I nodded. "I seem to be having a lot of them recently." Then I chuckled, shook my head and downed half the sherry.

"What?" he asked in his soft, northern accent. "What's up?"

I smiled and looked at him. "Do I really need to spell it out?"

He smiled back, his grey-blue stars twinkling. There he was, the old gambler, ready for the next bet. "I guess you don't. Sorry if I startled you."

"Don't apologise," I said, a slight grin now forming on my face. "I should be used to all this by now."

"So I see. An investigator of the paranormal. Your mum's very proud. She hasn't got a clue what you do, but she's very, very proud of you."

And that was it. I leant back in the sofa and chuckled away in silent mirth being careful so as not to wake up the woman who had given birth to me. It was just like old times. My dad was here making wisecracks about my mum and everything was going to be okay.

Everything was going to be okay. It really was.

A tear trickled down my cheek.

Then I felt something that I had not experienced in over fifteen years. The touch of my father's fingers on my face as he wiped away the salty liquid. "It's okay, Son," he whispered. "It's okay." I recognised the touch, the hard calluses on his fingers that had come from working in a shoe factory for far too many years, the slight tremble as he struggled to show his emotions without appearing soft. I put my half-empty glass down and my hand reached up, cradling his against my cheek. It felt cool but not deathly, pleasant to the touch. I squeezed it hard, then remembered his crippling arthritis, the cruel disease that had stripped him of his trumpet playing, his job and eventually his life.

"I'm sorry. I didn't mean to hurt you."

Dad smiled. "Don't worry. There's no more pain. Look." He withdrew his hand and wiggled his fingers easily in front of my amazed eyes. "All better now." He grinned and picked up his drink before seating himself on the sofa. His eyes looked up at me expectantly. "I hear you've been having troubles. Why don't you tell your old man?"

So I did. Once more, I was a sad, little ten-year-old pouring out my heart about how the bigger boys were picking on me and how I could not take it anymore. How it was stopping me from sleeping and making me not want to go to school. Only this time there were vampires, werewolves, cults, grotesques and mummies.

My dad's answer was the same now as it was back then.

"Well isn't that crap? What are you going to do about it?"

I gave a tired, little sigh. "I haven't a clue. I feel like I've been hit by a steamroller. All my energy is drained and I just want to curl up tight in a ball. That or..." I paused, feeling the mixed emotions churn around in the pit of my stomach.

"Or what?"

"Or lash out."

My dad sat back in his armchair and silently regarded me for a few seconds before leaping up. "Right, grab your coat. I know just what'll sort you out."

When your old man suggests that you go out and "Have fun," you expect it to be something from your childhood like kicking a semi-deflated football around the back garden or watching a supposedly famous steam train pumping carcinogenic pollutants into the air as you stand and shiver on a platform populated with about twenty *Where's Wally* clones.

What you don't expect is to be bundled into a taxi and carted off to a newly opened greyhound racetrack.

As I sat uncomfortably on the back seat of the cab, I listened while my father rambled on excitedly about the Alhambra Dog Palace. Apparently, it had only opened the previous month and had caused all sorts of controversy. The locals had not wanted this den of iniquity in their backyard but the owner was alleged to be sleeping with someone high up on the council so planning permission had been a breeze. Not only that but it had been built on a long-derelict brownfield site so was being plugged as an example of *prime urban regeneration*. My dad didn't care about any of that. He just wanted to get down to his favourite past time and hear the clatter of the gates opening, the mechanical whirr of the hurtling hare and the pounding of the chasing hounds mixed with cheers of encouragement and exasperation from excited onlookers.

Whilst he waxed lyrical about the feel of tattered betting slips between his fingers, I shot a nervous look at the taxi driver who, in turn, peered cautiously at me in his rear view mirror. "Sounds excited," he said.

"I know," I replied. "It's been a while."

"God, tell me about it!" my dad let out, slapping his palms onto his knees. "Over fifteen years. Can't wait to get back into it."

"That's... quite a while. You sure you really want to do this?" I could hear concern in the driver's voice. "It's just my brother... he had... you know... a problem..."

The cab fell silent for a second then my dad erupted into laughter. "Oh, I see what you mean. No, it's nothing like that. It's just that for the last fifteen years I've been..."

"Far too busy," I interjected. "My father's been busy at work and now he's..." I flicked through my mind's rolodex for something appropriate, "*retired* and wants to enjoy himself a bit." I smiled nervously at the cabbie.

The poor driver continued to frown but gave an *if you say so* shrug.

We drove the rest of the way in silence as I sunk down into the chair wondering what the hell I had gotten myself into.

Eventually, we arrived at the Alhambra and I had to say that from the outside it was indeed very impressive. It looked more like a modern football stadium rather than a run-down dog track of the sort that had populated various pockets of the country in the seventies. The walls were sleek and white. Shops, bars and restaurants were dotted around the perfectly polished plaza that extended down the side of the arena. Massive floodlights towered from the track and rent the night asunder with their powerful beams, causing shadows to dance between excited punters waiting to enter the turnstiles.

My dear, departed father was practically dancing as he bounded his way up to the queue. This was not the disabled man of my youth, riddled with crippling arthritis. He had been born anew, baptised into a fresh body with not the slightest twinge of pain or discomfort.

There was one problem, however.

"No money?"

Dad shrugged his shoulders like a naughty schoolboy and leant in close so as not to be overheard. "It's not as if I have a national insurance number now being, you know, *dead*. I can't exactly go out and get a job."

"What about your pension?"

"Yeah, about that." He rubbed his chin. "Well, your mum sort of has that, again with me being, *you know*, and well, she sort of..."

I closed my eyes in despair. "She doesn't know where we are does she?"

My dad smiled pathetically. Some things never changed.

"Okay," I relented, "how much?"

He told me.

I made to walk away and his hand grasped at my sleeve. "Sammy..."

"For crying out loud, Dad. This isn't Premier League football; it's a handful of psychotic inbred canines trying to rip to shreds a moth-eaten Bugs Bunny reject!" I snatched my arm back and shoved my hands deep in my pockets. "Not only do you have no cash but you expect me to sell a kidney to get in."

"In fairness, Sam, it does cover a free five pound bet," he pleaded. "I can easily win your cash back by the end of the night. Honest."

I was furious, both at my dad for his dragging me into this and also at me for *being* furious. This was my dad, for Christ's sake! He had been dead for over fifteen years and here I was squabbling about spending a few quid to enjoy an evening with him.

I looked at his sad face then at the queue of people filing into the stadium. "Okay," I gave in, "but if Mum's cross then you take the blame."

His face lit up and those grey blue eyes danced under his white hair. "There's a good lad," he said. "It'll be just like old times." Then he frowned and held me by the arm again. "Come on... we'd better get inside. Get good seats, you know." As he guided me quickly towards the turnstile, his eyes flickered past the crowd of people. I looked where he was staring and saw nothing but moving shadows.

I had been to the races a number of times with my dad when I was a kid. Both horses and dogs. Going to see the horses race had always been a major day out for us. We would set off in his banana-coloured Vauxhall Viva at the crack of dawn and normally arrive at a certain racecourse for the second or third race. There would be lots of standing around getting cold, undercooked hot dogs and lots of whoops of joy when Dad's horses inevitably made him a few quid. Going to the dogs was different. This was where we would normally go in an evening. Dad would knock off early from the shoe factory on a Friday afternoon and we would catch the bus to a local venue. We would sit under flickering lamps and cheer on the mutts as they hurtled around the track at break neck speed.

I loved this time with my dad. It was special. Moments for the two of us etched in time.

These days I have a far different opinion of animal races. I see them as exploitation of both those who are enticed into placing the bets and the beasts who are forced to run and know nothing more than the eternal circuits of a racetrack. People end up losing all that they have far too easily and when an animal is injured or past its best, then it's either dog food time or abandonment on the hard shoulder of the M6.

As I followed my excited father to our seats, I made sure that my younger thoughts were foremost rather than those of the adult that I had grown into. I was determined to enjoy this evening come hell or high water. This was a special moment that I had never expected to revisit ever again.

Dad was having no such battle of conscience. He was in his element. He had already placed his complementary bet and was sat on the edge of his plastic seat, ticket grasped tightly in his hand, wound between his thumb and third finger, straddling his middle and index as he always did out of habit and gambler's luck. As his dog was led obediently to its trap, my dad slowly tapped the slip against his teeth just as I had seen him do so many times before in the days of yore. The tension was palpable as his eyes remained fixed on the one dog wearing green and yellow in the number three trap. Then the hare was off and the dogs were in pursuit. It was a one lap race and Dad's dog never lost its footing. It streaked into the lead and stayed there, finishing about three lengths in front of its nearest rival. The whole thing took just under a minute.

Dad gave a little nod of satisfaction then turned to me and grinned.

I could not help but grin back. I was seven again.

So the evening continued. Dad won one race then piled the winnings onto the next. He won every single time. Each time he just sat there, tapping his ticket against his teeth, eyes fixed on his hound until the inevitable win when he would nod and grin. Not all races were straightforward; some had my heart breaking up concrete in my chest cavity with a pneumatic drill when Dad's dog would suddenly falter or not leap to the head of the pack at the outset. But even those little slips recovered. Not one of his dogs failed to come first.

By the tenth race, he had made considerable profit on my initial ticket money. When he got up to place his next bet I tugged at his sleeve. "Don't you think that should be it for the night?"

His eyes sparkled in the light of the giant floods. There was almost a mania to them. "Don't be silly, Sammy," he chided. "We're only just starting."

"Just starting? That's been ten races. Your luck can't continue forever."

He chuckled to himself and walked off to the betting office.

Okay, now I was annoyed.

"Hey!" I clambered out of my seat and stalked after him. "Hey!" Heads turned and watched the ensuing argument. "Dad. Seriously, this is enough. Let's quit now."

My father waved a dismissive hand at my concern. He might as well have waved a red rag as I lowered my horns and charged.

"That's my money, there, don't forget. At least give me back what you owe."

"If I bet more I win more."

"Or lose more."

He stopped in front of the betting office, took a deep sigh and rolled his eyes heavenward. "Sammy, Sammy, I'm not gonna lose."

"I've heard that before. I listened to the rows."

With his hands on his hips, "Not a chance. I will win every time to-night."

My mouth dropped open. "You can't seriously believe that!"

"Oh, yes I can! I've been waiting for this for so long."

*Plonk!* That was the sound of the penny dropping. "You know what the winners are, don't you?"

There was a guilty silence.

"Dad? Answer me. Do you or do you not know which are the winning dogs?"

Hands flapped in front of me. "Shush, Sammy! Do you want to get us arrested?"

"Well that would be interesting wouldn't it? I'd like to see how they write up your distinguishing features: 'Five foot ten, white hair and slightly chilled from having been dead for over fifteen years.'"

"Sammy! Please!"

"How? Just tell me. How do you know?"

My father turned and looked longingly at the betting office just as an alcoholic looks at a prize bottle of scotch, then sighed and lowered his eyes. "Okay. But not here."

We sat in silence nursing coffee and contempt. Around us, folk were chatting about their evening: their wins, their losses. Between us, however, a storm cloud was brewing stronger than my Americano. As my dad sat idly twirling his wooden stirrer around his drink, I saw the mixed emotions flittering across his face as he tried desperately to work out an excuse for what he had done, a way to dig himself out of another hole. When I was young, it had always been my mother sat in my chair, but now it was up to me to listen to the feeble excuses.

"Barry from work said that the horse was a dead cert. Sorry about the Christmas bonus.

"It was only a small round of cards with the mates. It was only a bit of fun.

"Now, I know we were saving up for that new cooker..."

I had heard all these and many other gems over and over as my mum and dad had argued time and time again.

"Well?" I finally asked him. "What's the excuse this time?"

Eyes fixed on his coffee. "There's no excuse. I screwed up."

I was stunned. Well that was a first. I sat quietly and waited for him to continue.

"It's rather odd being dead."

"You don't say?"

"Please, Sammy. I'm trying to explain."

I shut up the wisecracks.

"It's not what I expected. I guess I thought it would be like this, you know? Just another life but with wings and harps. But it isn't. It's all sort of blancmangey."

"Blancmangey? You're saying that Heaven is a stomach-turning dessert from the seventies that is moulded in the shape of a fat rabbit?"

There was a small chuckle and his eyes looked up at me. "I never was good with my words, was I? No, it's like one big mass. You're aware of yourself, but you know of everyone else there too, not personally, just... well...

you know..." He drifted off as words failed him.

"Go on."

"Anyways, there is a certain sort of quirk to this existence. I'm guessing it must act as some sort of amplifier or microphone. You hear echoes. Voices through time. Past and present."

*Plonk!* There went another penny. "You learnt what dogs were going to win tonight when you were dead?"

He nodded.

"But how did you get out, so to speak?"

"If you want something hard enough, then you can get it."

I sat back and glowered. "Well, aren't you the piece of work."

"Sammy?"

Anger was starting to throb in every one of my veins and arteries. "Here I was, thinking that you had come back to see Mum and me, but in fact all you wanted to do was have a night out at the racetrack. You bastard!" I made to leave.

"No! No! Wait!" Dad lurched forward to grab me. His coffee cup was knocked by his arm and spilt across the table. "You've got it wrong. So wrong.

"Sammy, you're in danger."

Okay. That had my attention. I sat down again.

"What do you mean?"

Dad took a deep breath. "The dogs were just a nice little side trip. I wanted to spend time with you like we did when you were a kid. Before you grew up. Before... all sorts of shit happened to you.

"You know your grandpa fought in the First World War?"

"Sure. You told me he lied about his age. He was only fifteen when he signed up."

"He told me it changed him. He went in a devout Catholic and came out angry and bitter. He got heavily into Nietzsche. Really heavily. The guy had only died in 1900, the year my dad was born, and dad lapped up all his works, all the really nihilistic stuff.

"Anyway, his favourite quote was, 'Whoever fights monsters should see to it that in the process he does not become a monster.' He actually wanted that on his headstone but, after he died, we went for something a little less confrontational.

"Well, while I was drifting in that seventies' dessert that is the afterlife, these words kept coming to me over and over, along with betting tips, and I had no idea as to what it meant.

"Then I met someone."

*Plonk!* "Gerald."

Dad nodded. "Your friend might have been OCD when it came to cleaning your university, but he was also really worried about you. His presence found me, I don't know if it was by chance or by design, and he showed me how you had set him free and I knew, because of that, that you must be dead."

I remembered the night of setting Gerald free from the physical realm. It had required a psychopomp: a dead spirit guide. As I had just blown my brains out, I had fit the bill quite nicely.

"But you were not with me," Dad continued. "You were supposedly dead but nowhere to be found in the afterlife. I was terribly worried.

"So I had to break out and find you. I guess I should have come straight to you, but for some reason I ended up with your mum and just couldn't leave. Then you arrived and I wanted to talk to you, but I couldn't. For some reason I couldn't make myself known to you. Something wasn't quite right. I could talk to your mum and she could quite obviously see me, but to you I was just the delusion of an ageing female parent."

"I couldn't really believe that you were there."

"Perhaps, but then tonight, something felt different. It was as if you had unlocked something within yourself and I could walk into your life again. And, when you told me all you had been through, those words my dad wanted on his gravestone made sense.

"Sammy, you must stop what you're doing. It will destroy you."

Well this wasn't where I had expected the night to go. I sat back down in my chair. "What do you mean? Some *big bad* is out there waiting to gobble me up?"

My father shook his head. "I don't know about that. From what you've said, I wouldn't be surprised but I'm more concerned about *you* being the danger. Look at what you've done." He leaned forwards and whispered, "In the park. At your university."

There was blood on my hands.

"They were self-defence."

"Really? You really believe that? Tell me that there is not even a squidgen of you that got satisfaction from those acts. Tell me."

I couldn't.

I really couldn't.

"You will turn into a monster. A darkness will grow inside of you and consume you if you carry on down this path. Let's face it, it's not bringing you any happiness, is it?"

Damned parents. They're always right.

"So you're saying that I should quit?"

He said nothing, just nodded.

I thought about it, a life without constant mortal peril, no strangers breaking into my flat, no benders, no nightmares. A life like the one I had been enjoying over the past week.

"Okay. I'll quit."

Dad couldn't have looked more relieved had he found a winning Lotto ticket intact in a freshly laundered pair of jeans. All tension flowed out of his face and he closed his eyes, sinking back into his chair. "I'm so glad to hear that," he murmured, "but now I have to go."

I felt a familiar chill tugging at the edge of my senses and a shadow seemed to split away from the corner of the room.

"Dad? What's happening?"

"It's okay, Sammy," he explained, crooking a beckoning finger at the shadow which slithered across the floor to his feet. "I knew this was to come. I just had to do what I wanted to do first. I had to save you and now I can go back to where I should be. My get out of jail free card has expired." The shadow started to curl up around his feet and his legs.

"No, no, no," I stuttered, "this can't be happening. Please, you can't go."

"Sorry, Sammy. That was the deal. I had until I got you running down a straighter track. I've done that and now I have to go back. I don't belong here."

The shadow twisted its way up around his waist to his middle. From his chest down, my dad was just a black, empty space. I looked around the coffee shop. No one was looking. No one noticed that my father was being dragged away from me. They were all far too busy with their own lives.

His words rattled something in my head.

"Deal?"

"Pardon?"

"You said, 'That was the deal.' Who did you make a deal with?"

His arms and neck were now in shadow. All that was left was my father's head. "Sammy, please just drop it. You promised. I have to go back."

"Dad..." My eyes were starting to burn and my voice cracked.

"Goodbye, Son." The shadow crept up over his features. For a moment there was a dark silhouette of a man-shape then gently, delicately the shadow faded, allowing light to pass through once more and all that remained was an empty plastic chair.

I stood up and walked away.

It was extremely late, or should that be very early when I got back to my mum's house. It was still dark, so I took that as a good thing. I always feel there's something very wrong about coming home when the sun is creeping up above the horizon.

I felt like a disreputable teenage stop-out as I quietly closed the door behind me. At least I had not been drinking. That would be guaranteed to make me enter so overtly quietly that I would make enough noise to wake the dead.

And I was done with the dead waking right now.

Dad.

Why was life so unfair? He had been snatched from me not once now but twice. I crept through to the kitchen and opened the top drawer next to the cooker. There, next to a pack of Benson And Hedges, was a battered old ashtray. *Greetings From Portugal!* It declared. My mum's little habit, stashed away where everyone pretended not to know.

Some things never change.

I lit myself one of my Luckies and sat at the breakfast bar tapping ash into the face of some random Portuguese orange seller. Mum and Dad used to go to Portugal every winter right up until I was born and the price of another mouth to feed dug away at their disposable income. Mind you, from what they told me, their trips were hardly enjoyable affairs. They had normally started arguing by the time that they had embarked on the plane. I sometimes think that they only used to go so that my mum could bring back masses of duty free cigarettes and a couple of fancy watches shoved down her knickers. I looked down at my Tissot that had once been my dad's and shuddered.

Oh God! How would she take the fact that Dad had gone? Well I wasn't going to wake her now. I would let her sleep her sherry-enhanced slumber and break the news in the morning.

I stubbed out my Lucky, disposed of the evidence and made my way up to bed.

The morning saw me wake about eleven o'clock. There had been no bad dreams and I actually felt relatively refreshed. I swung my feet out of bed and ran my hand over my couple of days' worth of stubble. Once dressed, I opened my bedroom door and noticed that Mum's door was shut. Guessing her to be up and about, I headed downstairs. She wasn't in the living room and there were no sounds of curious concoctions in the kitchen.

This worried me.

I ran back upstairs and knocked on her door.

There was no reply.

Carefully, cautiously, I pushed the door open. The usual aroma of lavender-scented Febreeze assaulted my nostrils.

Mum was still in bed.

"Mum?"

Nothing.

"Mum?"

Still nothing.

I already knew what to expect before I touched her cold skin.

I knelt down next to her bed, gripped her stiff fingers tight in my hands and wept.

# The Case of the Warbling Witch

I have always thought that winter is the ideal time for funerals. In spring, everything is putting all its stored energy into growing like crazy and plants are bursting out of the ground with vigour and vitality. Daffodils and tulips, so bright and uplifting, do not seem appropriate to me for funeral wreath material. Being the get down and boogie members of the flower world, they lack the melancholy and serenity that one finds in lilies. Summer is a joyful time when we think of long hot holidays on the beach with a teasing blue sea tickling at our toes. It is not the time to be planning Aunt Gertrude's wake, carefully having to work out who should sit next to whom so as to prevent a family massacre not seen since the Borgias thought it would be a nice idea to invite a few cousins round for wine and canapés. As for autumn, well there are the practicalities to consider. It's normally wet and leaves are drifting on the ground as they fall from the sleepy trees. If a pallbearer were to slip on one of those little sods then Uncle Bertie would be skidding off to the afterlife in a wooden, jet-propelled Porsche.

No, winter is the time of slumber when animals and insects lay themselves to rest in the hollows of trees, warm caves and the deep, dark earth. Therefore, it is only fitting that we should lay our deceased relatives alongside them at this time of year as we stand mourning by the dead, frosted earth and our tears of lamentation chill upon our mournful faces.

It was an excellent turn out for Mum's send off. She was well known around town, having held a number of small jobs before she reached the age of retirement and even one or two afterwards. So it was that many and varied friends from different walks of life came to pay their polite respects. All Saints was truly full to the rafters. I'm guessing that Father Walters gave a good service. On the whole, I was oblivious to the goings on. I was aware of just three things: Grace was holding my hand (she had come down with Spliff for the service), I had two more hymns that I would never be able to sing without breaking down into tears (*Morning Has Broken* and *Praise My Soul The King Of Heaven*) and the undeniable truth that the sweet, slightly bonkers little old woman that was my mother was now lying dead in a wooden box in front of me which meant that ye olde sherry sellers of fair Wellington town would probably go bankrupt overnight.

After the church service, we drove over to the cemetery on the far side of town. Spliff and Grace rode with me in the main car behind the hearse, others followed Tusken style – single file to hide their numbers – and we planted her deep in the cold, dark earth where my father had been interred over fifteen years ago. I think I placed a rose on her coffin; I'm not sure. I just remember it being bitterly cold. No, make that *damnably* cold. After we had finished and with the gravediggers standing politely but expectantly to one side, face after face filed past me. Names that I vaguely recognised from my mother's past were mentioned and condolences were offered. I smiled vaguely at each one and immediately forgot them as soon as they had passed.

All except one.

"I'm terribly sorry for your loss."

He was a touch taller than me, dark-skinned with neatly cropped afro hair. He wore a smart overcoat and a dog collar peeked out from the neckline. I frowned in slight puzzlement. I was sure that my mum had never socialised with members of the clergy.

Noticing my confusion, the priest took my hand and shook it in a firm but not crushing manner. "I'm Peter Lincoln, the new curate."

"Oh, at All Saints?"

"That's right. Father Walters suggested that I come along and see how he ran things, so to speak."

I shifted on my feet, retrieved my hand and slipped it deep into my coat pocket. There was something about this guy that gave me the willies and I felt the hairs on the back of my neck rise to the occasion. "It was a lovely service," I said. The words seemed appropriate even though I remembered next to nothing about it.

Lincoln's dark, penetrating eyes never once left mine as he spoke. "Yes, it was. I think I shall learn a lot here."

Why did I feel as if I was in possession of an overdue library book? The man was being perfectly civil yet I felt that he was dissecting me and was about to scold me for being too noisy. "Well, I hope you have a good time here." That was lame. What was I thinking?

Salvation came with a pair of twinkling eyes and a refined Scottish accent.

"Well, hello. I don't believe I've had the pleasure. And believe me, I would definitely remember if I'd had *your* pleasure."

Lincoln's eyes shifted from intense interrogation to worried bewilderment as Spliff casually draped an affectionate arm around him. All the curate could do was mutter and stutter as my saviour carried on, "*My my*, that's a rather fetching overcoat." Fingers stroked the material and lingered on the collar. "I must admit I tend to wear a cloak at funerals. The expected image, you know. But this really is quite striking. Which supplier did you get it from?" Lincoln was left bereft of words as Spliff guided him away down the path.

I felt a small, familiar hand slip into mine.

"You okay?"

"Yes."

Grace looked up at me. "Really?"

"No."

"Let's go now."

"Yes. Let's."

A short while later Grace and I were sitting in my mum's living room. My petite companion had made herself a cup of coffee. I had refused one when offered and instead I raided the drinks cabinet. I didn't think Mum would mind, being dead and all.

We just sat and drank. Grace, numerous warm, soothing beverages; me sherry, port, whiskey and, dear lord, even crème de menthe. I had nothing to say; she was marvellously patient. If I had been her, I would have slapped myself around the face and told me to snap out of it. Instead, she sat next to me on the sofa, her beanie-attired head on my shoulder. Then, when night drew in, she pulled the curtains shut, flicked the lights on and rustled up some sandwiches for us. It had been almost three weeks since Mum had died. There had been an autopsy – heart attack, her pints of fortified wine and secret cigs had apparently caught up with her, although I knew different. She had given up on life. She had somehow known that Dad had gone so she had followed. Then there had been a delay with the undertakers. As a result, I had been stuck here, not wanting to leave until everything had been sorted.

At the sight of the hummus sandwiches, my stomach started to rumble. It was the first normal sensation that I had felt all day.

"Thank you."

"That's okay."

I drained my glass of green devil's semen, grimaced and devoured the food.

"What are you going to do?" At last a question, now that I had broken the silence.

I looked up at the toby jugs, decapitated heads atop a G Plan traitors' gate. My eyes skimmed over the photographic history of Little Sammy. That was a life that had passed me by. I wasn't that person any more.

I had promised my dad that I would give my job up. Return to a normal life to save my soul.

How could I? What was there for me? A semi-detached family home full of painful memories? No. That would be unbearable. Lancaster was my home now. I had a purpose there and I was not going to desert it.

"I'm going to head home. Tomorrow."

Grace's smile was all that I needed at that moment to know that it was the right decision.

Still, something deep inside of me was not so sure, no matter what I thought.

Grace stayed over that night, sleeping in Mum's bed. I had no idea where Spliff was, but I was sure he would turn up before we headed back up north the next day. I had already spoken to lawyer types before the funeral. It was all straightforward. Mum had actually left a will rather than jotting a few things down on a post it note stuck to the fridge. The house would go on the market once it had been cleared out and they were hopeful that it would sell quickly.

Quite frankly, I didn't give an owl's hoot about the whole thing. I told them to sell off all the big stuff and I would pop down to collect the small personal items that I wanted to keep before the sale went through.

There was nothing here for me now.

That was what I told myself over and over as I lay in my childhood bed trying to drift myself off to reluctant sleep. I tossed and turned as images kept scurrying into my head and biting my subconscious on the ankles.

My mum, dead.

My dad, engulfed in shadow.

The sight of a solitary rose on a plain coffin.

A stone font at the west wing of a church.

My footsteps echoed as I walked down the nave. My breath fogged in the cold night air. Moonlight glimmered through the stained glass, casting coloured patterns across the perplexing words: "Knaves are not our responsibility."

I reached out and traced the first letters of the words.

K.A.N.O.R.

"You should not be here."

The voice was a poisonous hiss, as if a snake could speak and damn the one that had cursed it to walk upon its belly.

He was waiting there on the opposite side of the font, the man in black. He wore no glasses now and his eyes burned with the intensity of dying galaxies.

"You must not return to this place."

As he spoke, I saw tendrils of smoke drift from his nostrils. His skin shifted in colour. It reddened and seemed to harden. Scales formed on his face as his head started to lose consistency. I was frozen, petrified to the spot, my hand still resting on the font as the creature, for that was what he truly was, metamorphosed into something that I had seen before, a vision from another nightmare. His neck stretched up to the ceiling and his head split apart into seven strands, each coalescing into a serpentine neck with a fierce head at the end. His body stretched and contorted as his hands morphed into vast claws that scraped and scratched at the stonework of the font. They smashed the baptismal basin apart and boiling water geysered up out of the ground. I felt my skin pucker and scald. The dragon's hands flexed and in one appeared a sword, in another a chalice.

"The Cup and the Blade are mine," hissed the seven mouths in seven tongues. "They will *never* obey you."

It opened its mouths.

The heat was intolerable as I burnt in the ensuing inferno. My skin peeled away and my organs dissolved.

I was sure that I was screaming but my tongue had gone, burnt to ash by the dragonfire.

I gasped for air.

I tried to run but I was paralysed, fixed as if arms held me tight.

*Sam...*

I wanted to escape. I had to escape.

*Sam...*

But I couldn't. The dragon raised its powerful hind leg over me...

*Sam wake up...*

and brought it crashing down.

Frigid air barrelled into my lungs causing me to gasp and choke as I tried to free myself from the terrifying apparition. I shouted out incoherent words and attempted to break free of the imprisoning arms.

"Sam. Sam. It's okay. You were having a nightmare."

As I calmed down and started to breathe in a more regular pace, I recognised the sweet, citrus scent and the small arms that were wrapped around me.

"Grace? Is that you?"

"Well it's not Minnie Mouse."

I couldn't help but smile. She was curled up behind me on the bed - red, tousled hair falling around her face that was close to my neck, her breath warm on my skin.

"I heard you yelling in your sleep and tried to settle you."

"Thank you."

A warm finger stroked my curls. "You okay?"

"No."

"You want me to stay?"

I paused.

"Sam? You want me to stay?"

"Yes. Please stay."

So she did.

The next day saw me heading back up the M6 motorway to Lancaster. Spliff accompanied Grace in her little VW Beetle, which meant I had a quiet, uneventful drive home. Before we left, he dropped by Mum's house for his ride. Whilst Grace was busying herself upstairs packing or some-such, Spliff took advantage of our alone time to give me a quick once over.

"So?"

"So what?"

"How are you?"

"As good as can be expected, I guess."

"You look like shit."

"Screw you."

My best friend chuckled as he sipped the remains of a rather strong coffee. "Well at least you still possess the Spallucci wit and charm," he winked.

I sat back in the overstuffed sofa. "Dad was here."

His cup paused just a touch before it reached his mouth. "Really?"

"The night that Mum died." I told him about how Dad had shown up and taken me to the dogs before warning me off my career path. "That's why she died. She knew he'd gone."

"Sam..."

"It's okay. I got it out of my system last night. I was pretty cut up but Grace came and checked on me and sort of cuddled me back to sleep."

The twinkle in his eyes said it all. "*Cuddled*?"

The roll I gave my eyes would have impressed even the most infuriated teenager. "Yes. Cuddled. Nothing else. Jesus, Spliff, she's a kid! She just came and sort of rocked me back to sleep. That's all."

His raised eyebrow begged to differ.

"And again... screw you." I frowned. "Have you lost weight?"

Spliff threw a hand up in the air. "At last he notices! It's marvellous. Just dropping off. Soon I'll have all the university rugby team wolf whistling me when I walk past wiggling my pert little booty."

I smiled but a notion at the back of my head was coughing politely to grab my attention. There was something missing here - something that he wasn't telling me.

"What are you going to do when you get back home?" and the moment was gone.

"I'm not sure."

"You going to do as your dad said? Quit?"

I really didn't know. "I'm not sure it's that easy." I thought about Alec, my semi-angelic lodger. How could I really stop what I was doing when he was still in my life? I had spoken to him by phone a couple of times since I had come here. The place hadn't burnt down and no apocalypse had swept across Morecambe Bay. "It's not really the sort of profession that I can just walk away from."

Spliff nodded thoughtfully. "I see what you mean. Well, look, why don't you drop by for coffee tomorrow? In fact, why not come to the Saturday mass first? That way you'll have doubled your church attendance for the last week."

I chuckled, began to protest but then changed my mind and agreed.

I staggered into my flat late that evening. At once, something struck me. It was spotless. Now, I'm nowhere in the league of Spliff when it comes to untidiness, but with my absence over the last few weeks and the time before that being somewhat chaotic, a certain amount of housekeeping had gone undone. You know the sort of things I mean: surfaces remain dusty, windows build up grime, that bank statement which fell behind the sofa last month that you keep meaning to fish out and put in the bin just sits there and mocks you every time that you walk past in a hurry to go somewhere else.

In addition, with me having been at my mum's for a few weeks, I had expected there to be that aroma that is the half-breed of stale socks and curry farts that miraculously conjures itself up from an alternate universe and decides that ours is the best place to linger when no one else is using the space.

Instead, there was the aroma of something far more pleasant.

"I used a jasmine-scented polish." Alec walked in from the kitchen whilst snacking on a bowl of dry cereal. "I also kept your clocks wound up. I hope that was okay."

I smiled. "Thanks. That's appreciated." I dumped my luggage and walked over to the long case timepiece that sits in the corner of my living room. I affectionately ran a hand up and down its oak case. It had belonged to a great aunt who had left it to me when they passed away. It had been a constant companion for many years now. The deep tick-tock noise of the weight and pendulum mechanism was always soothing. "It's good to be home. So what did I miss?"

"Oh, the same old, same old. Fire, flood and famine according to the local paper."

I raised an eyebrow as I wandered through to the kitchen. "What is it this time? Students want to liberate frozen turkeys from the supermarkets in the run up to Christmas?"

"Actually, it's a bit more in your league."

I paused from spooning coffee granules into my mug. "Go on."

"They're saying that Lancaster's infested with witches."

The memory of a group of ramshackle mummies painting esoteric symbols onto a stolen bronze statue stomped into my head. I turned to face my lodger. "Specifics?"

"Your not-so-friendly restaurateur has been mouthing off."

"Nowell," I groaned. "What the hell has he done?"

"Morecambe's finest comedian turned up while you were away."

"Go on."

"It appeared one morning outside his restaurant."

"Of course it did. CCTV?"

"Let's just say that it was placed there by individuals more accustomed to sleeping in the peaceful depths of a pyramid. The *Chronicle* was full of it. Someone leaked images of the CCTV and it made the front page along with Nowell ranting on about how Lancaster was being dragged into the dark ages."

I gave up on the coffee and instead grabbed a bottle of whiskey off the counter. After a long slug I asked, "What about Betty?" I had images of pitchforks and bonfires creeping into my imagination.

"He's blaming it all on her, saying that she 'resurrected minions from the land of the dead' I think was his phrase. He's gone on record saying that she tried to corrupt his daughter and that she needs 'dealing with'."

I had a good idea of what Nowell's *dealing with* entailed. "Public reaction?"

"Mixed. Most think that he's off his rocker and it's a publicity stunt. Others, however..." Alec faded off.

"What? What's happened?"

"Nothing too substantial yet. Harsh words. A little bit of noisy argy bargy. I think an egg was thrown once, but she keeps on singing. It's as if she's oblivious."

I drank more whiskey.

It was late – too late to do anything productive. I was meeting Spliff in the morning. After that, I would go and see for myself just how much of a hotbed of witchery Lancaster had become in my absence. "Okay. Listen, do you mind if I have a bit of space?"

"Sure. I was just heading out, anyway."

I gave my lodger an interrogative look as I flicked on the television and the news came on. "Out?"

"Out," he shrugged.

I surrendered to his lack of forthcoming information and slumped into an accepting armchair, kicking off my shoes and loosening my shirt. I had no right to ask questions as to what Alec did with his life and I guessed that he would just evade an answer if I pushed him. "Have fun then."

"Will do," and he left me in the company of a pretty blonde woman reading over the events of the day. I stared at the television. Was it me or were newscasters getting younger. I started to shake my head but the movement was interrupted by a yawn. I drained my bourbon and gave a tired grunt of interest when images of Lancaster appeared on the screen. Apparently, witches weren't the only local news story and this one had made the nationals.

"The murders started three weeks ago with the suspicious death of local pimp and drug dealer, Darrel Barnes." Barnes' less than flattering mug shot zoomed into the foreground before shrinking to a smaller size and being joined by four others. I let out a low whistle. Someone had been busy. "In the following weeks..."

I let out another yawn and felt my eyelids start to droop. I'd just let them rest – watch with my ears.

"...more murders of known criminals have followed. Lancaster police have..."

I was aware of a deep snortling sound and fidgeted in the armchair, making myself more comfortable.

"...refused to comment on what the local press are now calling the V..."

The rest of the news was drowned out by my snoring.

Now, humour me and just take a moment here to contemplate something. What do you think the Reverend James Francis MacIntyre's place of worship looks like? Go on. Have a go. By now, you've been acquainted with his drinking habits (neat gin in copious quantities), his home décor (a life size statue of Michelangelo's *David* in the vestibule), his nocturnal habits (not going to go there right now as children might be reading this) and his housekeeping (whatever he needs is normally on the floor somewhere next to a mutating virus that makes rabies look like a mild dose of teenage acne). So I can sort of guess what you're imagining right about now.

Well, you are so wrong.

The chapel on the Luneside University campus is a perfect little haven of calm in an otherwise hectic hubbub of late teen, early twenty-something whirlwind of hormones and hassle. When the doors swing shut behind you, the delicate aroma of cut flowers leads you to a cushioned seat where you sit and gaze upon the stained glass images of classic Lancashire countryside – perfect reproductions of the Crook O' Lune, the Trough Of Bowland and Clougha Pike. Not a glaring postmodern assimilation of primary colours to be seen anywhere. No depictions of savage crucifixions or wailing, disembowelled saints adorn the walls. There is one hand-painted statue of Saint Francis of Assisi in a side alcove and a lattice work cross fashioned from local wood that hangs on the wall behind the plain altar which itself is dressed in pure white linen and two simple candles.

Bet you didn't see that coming, did you?

This is why Spliff always has been and will always remain my best friend. What people see on the surface is just the mask that he wears to divert the turbulent world around him away from the sensitive soul that he is inside. Yes, he may have a habit of forgetting funerals. Yes, you may contract a debilitating neurological disease unknown to modern science from his sofa. Yes, you cannot trust him with your son's virtue and innocence. However, you can always rely on him to be a shoulder to cry on, to be a calm, quiet pair of ears that will listen to and a priest that has a solid, unshakable faith in his God whom he believes to be the fount of all love and compassion. I consider myself to be extremely fortunate.

His Saturday lunchtime services reflect this. Rather than being all pomp and circumstance with choir and organ, they are instead quiet and contemplative, normally no longer than twenty minutes or half an hour in duration. They follow the Anglican liturgy and are sometimes interspersed with some meditative chant or music and an acceptable, non-suffocating amount of incense. You come away feeling like you've just had a spiritual massage; your soul has been gently pummelled and stretched until you feel that the world is a much better place. There are normally only a handful of communicants: a couple of students, some staff and a few passers-by.

This Saturday, though, there was a face there that I was not used to seeing in that particular location.

Boombox Betty.

She had seated herself at the back of the chapel, her CD player tucked tidily behind her chair. As immaculately dressed as ever, she seemed oblivious to the other worshippers as they drifted in and, in turn, slipped her a quizzical look. As the service started, it became apparent that she was not exactly reading from the same prayer book as everybody else or indeed the rest of the Anglican Communion. I occupied a seat a few rows down on the other side of the nave and every now and then a movement from her would catch my attention. When we crossed ourselves, she would follow suit then proceed to run her thumb in a cross pattern over each of her eyes. When Spliff read the gospel, she stood with her arms crossed over her chest, rocking back and forth mumbling quietly under her breath. Most unusual of all, as he read the Eucharistic Prayer, Betty quietly rambled on to herself as if she was reciting her own version. The words were not clear but certain phrases crept out: "When the sea shall be split asunder, then shall he ride the sky," and "In the light they are encompassed, those that have been forever from before the beginning of time." Finally, after receiving communion, she walked back to her seat, picked up her CD player and walked right out of the chapel, not waiting for the blessing or the dismissal.

At the end of the service, after the other members of the congregation had drifted out, I asked Spliff, "How long has Betty been coming here?"

He rummaged around under his robes, produced a cigarette and lit it using one of the candles on the altar. "Just a couple of weeks. She only comes to the weekday and Saturday services, not the Sunday mass. Why you asking?"

I momentarily thought about shoving the cigarette up his nose but decided that a random act of violence in a chapel was probably not the done thing. "You really have to ask? What about all this witchcraft nonsense?"

He looked blank.

He had no idea.

"You don't know, do you?"

"Know what?"

"You remember sweet little Cynthia from the speed dating? Claimed that Boombox Betty had hexed her mate?"

I received a cautious nod.

"Well her father owns Nowell's and has been blowing off steam in the local press about how Betty is a bona fide witch."

I watched the information start to sink into Spliff's face. "Oh. When was this?"

"While I was away. Not only that but he and his buddies nicked the Eric Morecambe statue and blamed it on her. They claimed she raised mummies from the dead to do it. Also, they roughed me up in the process. You won't have seen *that* in the papers but trust me, I was there."

My friend stood there, saying nothing. Well, not verbally, anyway. His face was screaming out something that I could not translate. Not yet, anyway. "Sorry, Sam. I didn't know," was all that he managed.

"You didn't know? How the hell could you miss it?"

He fidgeted awkwardly. "I've been... a bit preoccupied."

My eyes looked him up and down as they had in Wellington. His robes were hanging off him and his face definitely looked thinner than it normally did.

"Well, right now, I'm heading into town to see if I can avert a cosy little witch burning. However, when I'm done, we're going to have a seriously long chat."

My feet echoed in the chapel as I left my best friend standing admonished at the altar.

I steamed into town, smoking one Lucky after another. I was the *Flying Scotsman* in a trench coat and fedora as the tar and nicotine-imbued vapours trailed behind me. What the hell was going on with Spliff? He was hiding something from me, I was sure of it. First, there was the mysterious hospital appointment, then the anti-nausea medication followed by an alleged hangover from hell. Now there was weight-loss and an apparent disinterest in local news and gossip.

How could he have missed the goings on between Nowell and Betty? What was the matter with him?

I flouted a number of littering laws as I discarded an expired butt and struck up another smoke.

Nowell and Betty. Now *that* was another matter entirely.

What the blazes was I to do about that?

Now, in any sane world I would head straight over to the police station and report the goings on in Morecambe a few weeks ago; spill the beans over my tête-à-tête with Nowell's little cadre of mummies. However, in a sane a world, the local DCI would not have helped me hunt down and exterminate a werewolf in a local petting zoo. I had no full understanding as to what Patel was aware of in this reality. Previously, he had been unconscious, oblivious to me feeding Hawkins to the ants and blasting his sister to kingdom come. In this reality, one without Wallace, what was my relationship with the darling DCI? Alec and I had seen his perfunctory report but we had also witnessed his pet side project on werewolves. Had I inspired that or was it his way of working through a paranormal trauma and an execution he had been witness to and powerless to prevent? Would he arrest me for insectile homicide as soon as I set foot inside his police station?

I had no way of knowing.

For all I knew, if I walked into the nick with stories of a fine upstanding member of society dressing up as a deceased pharaoh and trying to pin the theft of a statue on one of the town's slightly less balanced members of society then I could end up spending an amount of time getting to know the inside of a holding cell.

No. It was up to me and me alone.

I stomped over Damside and stormed up Cheapside. There she was. As usual, she had her CD player going full blast and she was swaying side to side. As she had the other week, she was now singing along to the music. Along with the late, legendary David Bowie, Betty was telling all the passers-by that they ought to put on their red shoes and dance. The singing seemed to be drawing more of a crowd than back in the days when she just used to boogie on down to ABBA, Queen or whatever took her fancy. There was a rough horseshoe formed around her that saw people drift in, gawp a while, then wander out from the other side.

I hovered near the edge, wondering what to do. Then the smell of grilled food reached my nose and I took that as a hint from the wider universe.

"Hey, Bob!"

"Sam! How's it going?" Burger Bob was busying himself at his usual pitch, flipping over a couple of burgers for some hungry diners. "You after some food?"

My stomach tried to growl through my skin that yes, it was indeed after one of his famous veggie concoctions, but I overruled its demands and said, "Looks like Betty's getting more of a crowd these days."

Bob huffed in obvious annoyance and slapped a piece of grilled meat into a bun. "Don't get me started. It's a bloody nuisance."

"I would have thought it'd be good for trade, all these extra bodies."

The burger man wrinkled his nose. It's not the crowds I'm concerned about. It's, you know, the other stuff."

He flicked me a look that begged me not to press him for any more.

I was ignoring my stomach so I was damned well going to ignore somebody else's organs too. "What other stuff might that be, then?"

Bob handed out another burger to a waiting client. "You know what I mean. That statue turning up the way it did."

I waited patiently for him to continue.

"I know the police say that they can't prove anything but... well it ain't natural, is it?"

I shook my head and turned away. If the likes of the normally rational Bob believed in Nowell's claptrap then the poisonous little turd was well and truly sowing his seeds of hatred deep, allowing them to germinate and grow. I went and hovered behind the crowd, not quite sure what to do; it wasn't as if they were crying out for her to be dunked in the River Lune. Lighting up another Lucky Strike, I let my eyes wander around Betty's audience. They were apparently from all walks of life. Some were old, some young. There were office employees in their smart suits and workmen in their paint and plaster-splattered high-vis clothing. All of them stood intently watching her as if it was the first time that they had ever encountered such a sight even though she had been a regular fixture here for as long as I could remember. Perhaps they were just genuinely curious? Perhaps Betty's alleged notoriety had awakened a curiosity from deep within that bade them to search out that which was different from their normal, mundane lives.

It was just as I had started to ponder the more positive side of the human psyche that an egg was thrown. I didn't see where it came from but it hit

Betty hard on the shoulder and its sticky innards ran down her pristine jacket. She shrieked in fear and a roar erupted from the crowd as their true, baser intentions became apparent. Other items were lobbed: more eggs, fruit and less savoury materials. Betty cowered under her arms as she tried in a vain attempt to deflect the incoming projectiles.

Then the horde moved in for the kill.

I attempted to push through as they pressed in on the defenceless woman. I elbowed and kicked my way into the throng. On one occasion, I felt my feet part company with the paving stones of Cheapside and I was dumped on the floor sending a sharp judder up my spine. I swore in anger and grabbed onto someone else in order to pull myself up. They tumbled to the floor and I kicked them hard to ensure that they stayed down.

The gloves were off.

I was now all fists and feet as I punched, kneed and stamped my way to the front where Betty was lying on the floor next to her pulverised CD player. The thugs at the vanguard of the assault were actually grinning as they laid into her with punches and kicks. I grabbed the largest, a guy in a grey, pinstripe suit, and delivered a hard blow to his right kidney. He fell to the floor screaming where I delivered a kick to his midriff. Then I turned on the next attacker, a young woman in a parka coat, and grabbed a handful of her long, blonde hair. I pulled it down and, as she raised a heel to stamp on Betty, she tumbled backwards, landing in a flailing mess of limbs and curses.

I dove towards the stricken singer and firmly inserted myself between her and her assailants. "Back off! Now!" I yelled and a stunned silence fell over the mob. A bulldog of a guy stepped towards me. "Really?" I threatened. He stepped back, intimidated by the fury in my voice.

I reached down and hoisted Betty to her feet. She wobbled unsteadily but managed to stand. Her jacket had been ripped and blood trickled down her face.

"We're leaving now," I growled at the crowd. "You're not going to stop us."

A wary gap parted in front of the two of us as I guided the unsteady woman away. I made to head to my office but she pulled me in the opposite direction. "My house, please," her shaky voice whispered.

I nodded and we headed down Cheapside. My mind was raging. How could people turn like this? How could they be suckered into believing such nonsense?

*But was it nonsense?*

I stiffened at that other voice in my head.

*You've seen what she can do. Think about Cynthia and her friend.*

That was just suggestion. It had to be, surely?

*Okay. What about the CD she gave you in your Wallace week?*

Coincidence.

*Quite.*

Even so, she does not deserve to be beaten to a pulp.

*Well at least we can agree on that.*

Yes, we can. Thank you.

*Thank you, too.*

"Do you normally talk to yourself?"

"Oh," I almost tripped as we crossed North Road. "Sorry, I didn't realise..."

A smile blossomed in amongst the cuts and scrapes. "Not with your mouth. With your eyes. I could see the conversation darting between them."

I breathed a sigh of relief. At least that was something, I guessed.

"Up here," she motioned and we headed up behind the Sugar House. I cocked a glimpse and noticed that Spud's artwork was long since painted over.

"He still keeps watch, you know?"

"Pardon?"

"Your stone friend. I see him sometimes circling overhead, normally at night." We crossed over Saint Leonard's Gate. "Others must see him too but not believe what their eyes show them so they ignore him. People cannot handle that which is not normal to them. If it is thrust in their face, then they will act irrationally.

"You must not feel anger towards them."

"What happened just now was malicious, not irrational."

Betty shook her head as we half walked, half staggered across the car park. "No, Sam. Of course it was irrational. If a bee thinks it is in danger, then it will sting its attacker even if that means the loss of its own life. They are no different to a bee. They are afraid and fear breeds irrational behaviour."

"If you say so."

"Oh, I do." We reached a green door on Alfred Street. Betty reached into a pocket and fished out a key. "My family has been well acquainted with irrational behaviour in the past. Are you okay with dogs?" Betty asked as she entered the house.

"I grew up with a border collie."

She radiated a warm smile at this. "Of course you did. That figures."

I shot her an inquisitive look.

"The collie is always darting from here to there, protecting and rounding up those in its care." Betty waved a manicured fingernail at me. "Just like you." Before I could pull her back on subject or even comment on my apparent canine similarities, she opened the living room door and a small Chihuahua bounced out. It yipped enthusiastically at its mistress then sniffed my feet, its tail wagging at hypersonic speed. "This is Mister Tibbles," my host explained. "He is very friendly and mostly well-behaved. He is good protection for me. Chihuahuas were originally hunting dogs, you know?"

I tried to imagine the diminutive Mister Tibbles bringing down a bison and dragging the oversized corpse to its master. I really did try, but all I could envisage was the chicken hawk trying to take on Foghorn Leghorn. I bent down and tickled the dog behind his ear. He returned the affection by licking my wrist.

"He likes you. That's good." Betty settled herself down in a floral armchair not too dissimilar to my mother's and began wiping her cuts and grazes with tissues from a small patterned box. I sat myself on her sofa. "He's always a good judge of character." The little mutt bounced up onto my lap, spun around a couple of times then settled down to sleep. I could not stop myself from smiling.

"I miss having a dog. Perhaps I ought to get another pet? Something low maintenance."

Betty nodded. "A very good idea. They help to keep us grounded in the here and now." She sighed, disposed of the bloodied tissues and placed her hands on her knees. "But we are not here to talk about our furry companions, are we?"

I hadn't known quite what to expect upon entering Betty's house. I mean, what does the city's resident eccentric use as décor? Would there be rows of clown toys, creepy ventriloquist dummies or a plethora of ABBA posters? Knowing her taste in music, my money had been on the latter. So it came as a bit of a shock as my eyes travelled around the immaculate living room. All the woodwork was polished and the windows gleamed. Doilies nestled under every possible item and the pillows on the spotless sofa were fresh, clean and plumped to within an inch of their upholstered lives.

There was, however, one thing that immediately caught my attention as being somewhat prevalent.

There were angels everywhere. There were small, white china ones, ornately painted resin ones and pictures of all shapes and sizes. Each one was artistically positioned with a little electric tea light flickering in front of it.

Well, I suppose I had my clocks...

Above the mantelpiece was hung a watercolour of a long green mound set above a rolling valley. My spidey senses tingled and I carefully set Mister Tibbles down on the sofa as I rose to take a better look. The canine sat expectantly, waiting for me to come back and provide a lap once more. I could see immediately that the painting was old. Very old.

"It's a family heirloom." Betty's voice was wistful, sad. "Passed down for over four hundred years. Painted by an ancestral aunt."

Something that Nowell had said chimed in my subconscious, that and the intricate family tree in his restaurant.

"Betty, you said that your family was well acquainted with irrational behaviour. Is this Pendle Hill?"

She looked down at her lap. Mister Tibbles gave a concerned whine and snuffled up next to her. "I help people, that's all." It was the voice of a small child, confused and upset at being scolded for doing something that it did not see as wrong. "People who know me come to me for help with things that other people can't fix. Help with a promotion, cures for things that pills can't sort. Matters of love. My family have been doing it for generation after generation.

"I've helped you now. Twice."

I frowned. "Twice?"

"Yes. Twice. The first time was the CD. I take it that you listened to it?"

Well this was something. "But that week never happened. How can you remember it?"

"I have grown quite adept in my arts, Sam. It's not all *word magic* and just getting people to believe in themselves. I remember that week as well as you do, as if it had happened to me.

"I know how much it scarred you, which is why I helped you a second time.

"Which is why I sent you your father."

Okay, now I was speechless. I felt as if I had been sucker punched and all the air had been expelled from my lungs. "You?" was all I could eventually manage, followed by, "How?"

Betty gently tickled her pet dog behind his ear. "When I became aware that I was living a week for the second time, I concentrated on the events that I was experiencing. I meditated and prayed for answers. All the time, the answers came back as *you*. I saw you standing at a threshold to a door or on the pivot of a balance. Your experience with your university friend was drawing you to a dark place and you needed guiding back."

My knuckles were white as I gripped my hat. "He was no friend of mine."

"As that may be," she continued. "Anyway, your dreadful experience left its mark on you. Sometimes these marks are indelible. They cannot be erased just by rubbing at them over and over again. That just causes anguish and irritation. You must not make the same mistake that my ancestors did. They revelled in their so-called powers and it destroyed them. I used certain practices which lifted me up from this place and allowed me to travel where very few mortals have been before."

"You're saying that you went to the afterlife?"

"If you want to call it that."

Now my head was spinning. This could not be happening, surely? This was Betty, the crazy woman who stood on street corners whilst singing and dancing. Was she some uber-powerful mage who could transcend our physical plane? Surely not. She had a Chihuahua for Christ's sake! Surely if she was a witch, she should at least have a black cat or some sort of brooding hellhound? "I find this very hard to believe."

"Really? After all you've witnessed during your first few weeks in your chosen profession?"

Okay. She had me there. I shrugged in defeat.

"Your father was already anxious to leave so I just helped him along his chosen path with a temporary pass. When I came back I found myself somewhat transformed. I had already been hearing voices from beyond this realm, but now... Now I realised that I had unleashed something else within me. I started to go to church for guidance."

"But you recite your own words in the liturgy."

She nodded. "That is because of what I saw when I was in this other place."

"What did you see?" My throat was dry and the words croaked out of my mouth.

"All in good time. I believe you asked me about my lineage."

My heart was a runaway stallion. I tried desperately to rein it in, offering niceties such as straw, carrots and that pretty, young filly in the neighbouring paddock. Eventually it slowed from a manic gallop to a brisk canter and I nodded. "Did they possess the abilities that you do?"

Betty gazed up to the painting of Pendle Hill and I could see her walking over the green grass with those who had trod the same path before her. "They certainly thought they did. In truth, it was probably just psychology and such stuff. Not that it mattered when their notoriety tore them apart. Accusations started to fly and families accused each other of terrible, terrible deeds.

"They should have taken a step back and kept themselves out of the public eye, then they wouldn't have come to the attention of the local Justice Of The Peace."

And suddenly the jigsaw was complete. All the pieces had been there. I just hadn't seen what order it was in which they locked together. "Roger Nowell. Colin Nowell's ancestor."

Betty's eyes returned to mine and they were overflowing with sadness. "Mister Nowell had been researching that dratted family tree and found out about my heritage. He must have left notes lying around somewhere because, one day, his daughter, Cynthia, came to me saying that her supposed best friend kept stealing all her boyfriends. I said that I could do something to make her stop but it had to be removed once she had learned her lesson."

"I witnessed the result of that first hand. Quite impressive."

Betty nodded. "It's very powerful magic, that one."

There was the word: *magic*. I glanced up at Pendle Hill once more.

"I don't call myself a witch, not like they used to. It's such an umbrella term and people get the wrong idea. I just try to fix things. What happened then..." She shook her head. "It all got out of hand."

So there it was. "Are you descended from the Pendle Witches?" I asked.

Betty Nodded. "From one of the eldest children of Elizabeth Southerns, Old Demdike. Apparently, they left the area for some reason or another before all the troubles in 1612. Before they were hunted down by Roger Nowell."

I stood back and admired my metaphorical jigsaw: Nowell, *his* ancestor, Betty, *her* ancestors and Cynthia the unsuspecting catalyst.

"When he found out that I had helped his daughter, he went crazy. Accused me of being in league with the devil, he did! As if!" I was taken aback by the anger in Betty's voice. "Ignorant little man. What does he know? Has he seen what is to come and what will be? Has he been visited in his dreams by those from above?"

Okay. This had suddenly taken a turn down an obscure little alley. "Betty, what do you mean?"

Lightly closing her eyes, the neatly dressed woman said very quietly, "You dream a lot don't you, Samuel? You've rarely had a peaceful night's sleep recently. Your thoughts and your worries haunt you. As mine do me. And not just since I released your father. They have been there long before. I hear voices whispering to me from over great distances. They tell me things, things that will happen and they conflict with what I hear when I go to church to find peace and forgiveness. They echo what I saw in that realm of the dead. Echoes of the future paint pictures in my head and I, in turn..." She drifted off.

I leaned forward.

"What, Betty? What do you do?"

She paused a moment before rising out of her armchair. Mister Tibbles' head snapped up alert and he bounded down to her feet. "Come with me."

I did as I was asked and followed her upstairs. As we ascended to the next storey, Betty said, "These days it seems to be quite fashionable for people to want to follow their dreams. The young girls want to be singers, the young boys footballers. That is all very well, but following your dreams will never truly put them in your grasp. They will always be one or two steps ahead of you. Follow them and they will just dance around in front of you, continually skipping out of your grasp like an elusive Will O' The Wisp or," she glanced knowingly at me, "a feisty little fairy." We reached the landing and Betty stood with her hand on the handle of the first door that we came to, the back bedroom. "What I say is this, that chasing your dream is pointless, Samuel. Instead, you should confront your nightmares. Only then will you be truly free."

The door swung open and I looked inside. What I saw was... well, everything.

There were pictures. Not like in my mother's living room that iconified the passing years of little Sammy through spotty teen to young adult, but graphite and pastel sketched images of my nightmares.

Plastered in every conceivable wall space were feathered beings with faces that showed sometimes adoration, sometimes concern, sometimes anger. Four characters in particular made a plethora of appearances: one walked with shoots of grass springing from where his feet touched the ground, one opened his mouth and rainbow-coloured notes illustrated his voice, one's hands were shown to bring health and restoration to those whom he touched, one stood looking worried whilst clad in golden armour.

I trawled the depths of my studies in mythology. "Michael?" I asked, pointing at the last one.

Betty nodded. "The soldier of God."

I frowned. He looked vaguely familiar. "So these other three must be..."

"Gabriel the life-giver, Uriel the worshipper and Raphael the healer."

The images were fascinating. I could not take my eyes away from them. Alec's little chat about the angelic hierarchy drifted back into my head. "They are the archangels that dwell in the presence of God. Or so I'm told."

"Correct."

I continued to stare up at the eyes of Michael. Small flames burnt brightly in his pupils. "He doesn't look very happy for someone who lives with God."

"That's because he has a mission to prepare for here on Earth. It concerns him somewhat."

*I bet it does*: I thought to myself. Out loud, I said, "Is he going to cross my path?"

"Perhaps he already has. However, there is one far more powerful who has his eyes set on you."

I glanced at Betty and saw her eyes gazing at the opposite wall. I knew what I was going to see even before I looked. There he was, the man dressed in black. The man from my nightmares. In some images he wore the dark glasses, in others his eyes burned bright like stars. In one he stood tall and proud with six wings spread out behind him and his hands, formed from incandescent material, grasped a large sword and a beautiful goblet.

Six wings.

Oh no. Once again, I was reminded of Alec's little Angel 101 lecture.

"You've got to be kidding me."

I felt Betty's reassuring hand grasp my shoulder. "What you see here are the Eternals. The Light holds the Cup and the Blade. These things existed way before creation's first breath and will still stand after it has finally expired."

"But he is..."

"Yes, Samuel. He is Lucifer, the Light of Lights."

I was so screwed. But, hey, it could only get better, couldn't it?

Sure, you know my luck. There were more pictures.

Betty turned me and what I saw made me want to weep. There on a massive drawing that had been pinned to the wall behind me fought two dragons: one as black as coal and one blood red with seven heads.

"*When dragons walk the Earth then all creation shall tremble.* One dragon already prowls this realm, Samuel, whilst the other slumbers dreaming dark dreams."

It was then, at that moment, that I knew one thing for sure, above all others. "I want none of this." My voice was harsh, dry and panicked. "I never wanted this. Never, you hear?" I heard my voice start to rise, anger edging its way in. "All I wanted was the quiet life: go to school, university, work, wear slippers and a cardigan in my old age then pass away quietly in my bed. Yet here I am, confronted with *this*!" I was shaking as my finger pointed from picture to picture. "I can't cope with this. I have too much to deal with in my normal life, let alone my *para*normal one."

There was a soft whimper and Mister Tibbles rubbed hesitantly against my leg.

Betty's sad eyes wrapped their arms around me and hugged me tight. "We cannot choose our path, Samuel. What will be will be no matter how much we rant, rave and protest. I already know what my fate is and I accept that I cannot escape it as it comes running to greet me."

I was about to ask her what it was, but at that moment all hell broke loose.

There was a smashing sound and the bedroom door burst inwards followed by three Nowellesque mummies. In the confusion I couldn't tell which one was which but I launched myself at the nearest. I was aware of a small growling noise followed by a strangled yip as a bandaged foot kicked Mister Tibbles across the room, then two pairs of hands were dragging me backwards. I saw one of the pseudo-mummies grab Betty and pull her out of the room. I struggled against my attackers but all I received for my efforts was a crack on the skull as the back of my head collided with the wall.

I greyed out yet again.

It was hot. Damnably hot. Even before I opened my eyes I could hear the screams of tortured souls.

Was I in hell?

Well, that would be just about the perfect end to the perfect day, wouldn't it?

A shoe kicked me sharply in the ribs.

"Get up."

I recognised that voice. Precise, refined, cruel.

I did as I was told. Opening my eyes, I crawled to my hands and knees and took in my surroundings. I was back in All Saints but something was far from right. The building seemed to be in a serious state of disrepair: the pews were broken, starlight streamed in a shattered roof and the smell of burning wood and flesh made me screw up my nose in disgust.

One thing that still stood unaffected by whatever had ravaged the rest of the building was the font.

He sat astride it.

The man in black.

Lucifer.

He looked at me through his dark glasses and smiled none too kindly. Pointing at the inscription in the stone he asked, "So have you worked it out yet?"

I re-read the words: *Knaves Are Not Our Responsibility.* K.A.N.O.R.

A waft of smoke caused my eyes to water. "Is it you?"

His cruel smile widened and erupted into a harsh bray of laughter.

"Son."

I turned and my parents stood there.

"This must end now," Dad said, his blue-grey eyes full of sadness.

"Oh, Sammy," Mum fussed, "you've got dirt on your cheek." She whipped out a tissue, moistened it with her spittle then proceeded to wipe my face.

"Mum!" I whinged. "You're embarrassing me in front of Lucifer."

She ignored me and continued to wipe my dirty cheek. The tissue pressed harder and my face felt wetter. I wriggled, trying to back away.

Mum barked.

I opened my eyes. A huge, black beast of a dog was insistently washing my face with his tongue. I tried to rise and took in a deep breath of air. This was immediately regretted as I started to cough my guts up.

The bedroom was on fire. All the pictures had burnt to a crisp as had the wallpaper. The flames were currently busy consuming anything that was wooden. I had a feeling that other organic matter would be next on the menu, which included Yours Truly.

Crouching down I tried to make my way to the door only to have the dog (where had this thing come from?) wrap its mouth around my wrist and tug me away. I saw the reason why. The former door was now a curtain of flame and resembled a portal to a hell dimension; there was no escape that way. The dog yanked at me again, this time with even more insistence. I felt myself topple forwards as it manoeuvred itself under my weight. Instinctively, my hands grabbed around its neck and I felt its powerful muscles tighten as it charged to the other side of the room.

I saw what it had in mind and quickly closed my eyes.

There was an almighty crashing of glass as we flew through the first floor window. This was followed by the rush of cold winter air, Yours Truly screaming like a baby, then the thud of four furry feet settling heavily but securely on the concrete floor of the backyard.

I rolled off my canine saviour and turned over in time to see it shimmer in the half-light. Its form collapsed in on itself until it was a fraction of the size and Mister Tibbles was standing there, yapping at me with all his diminutive might.

I crawled somewhat shakily to my feet. "Thank you," I managed. "I'm guessing you know where they've taken her?"

The Chihuahua gave an affirmative yap then hurtled off out of the yard. I followed in close pursuit, thinking to myself: *Bet Lassie couldn't do that.*

Shortly, I was following Betty's canine companion back up Cheapside. It did not take a genius to work out where Nowell had taken Betty. His restaurant, obviously. I shot ahead of Mister Tibbles and tried the door. It was locked shut and the "closed" notice hung against the glass.

The small dog yapped at me.

"What?"

He barked again and chased off to the end of the road.

"Hey, Pussy!" yelled a spotty teenager loitering with intent alongside his fellow future inmates, "Your little rat's run away."

On another occasion I might have dealt up a dish of sarcastic wit accompanied by a side salad of eye roll, but right now other matters were far more pressing than the putdown of an irritating little oik wearing a baseball cap. So instead, I did the next best thing and flipped him my finger before chasing after Mister Tibbles who had dashed around the corner onto Church Street. He sat in front of a steel gate that hung ajar. I pushed it open, letting the pair of us into a small alleyway that led behind the Cheapside buildings.

My furry friend bounced over discarded rubbish and black bin bags before scuttling up to a battered glass door where he hunkered down on his rear legs and began to whimper.

"What?" I said in disbelief. "You can jump out of a first floor window but can't open a door?" I was sure that he shrugged at me.

I tried the door. Unlike the gate, it was locked. I picked up a stray brick and smashed the top pane as near to the handle as possible. Then, reaching in, I flicked the latch and swung the door inwards. I was immediately confronted by a confused mummy. Judging by the lack of height, it was Scrappy, the toyshop owner.

He started to raise the alarm but stopped immediately. The reason? An angry Chihuahua hanging from his privates. I grabbed him by the side of the head and slammed him face first into the wall. He dropped satisfyingly to the floor like a bundle of dirty laundry.

"Teamwork," I whispered to the little bollock-muncher.

I received a satisfied "woof" in return.

We carried on down the short corridor. Mister Tibbles alternated between growling and whimpering. I felt like doing the same. I settled instead on nervous perspiration. When we heard voices coming from behind a door we stopped and listened.

"Colin! What have you done?"

"What needed to be done."

"But... but... she's..."

"Shut up! Let me think!"

Mister Tibbles' growl rose.

"What's that?"

I kicked the door with the heel of my shoe and it flew into what was obviously the kitchen. I charged the first thing that came into sight, another mummy. I grabbed him by the shoulders and thrust my knee up a la Mister Tibbles. He collapsed, sobbing. That left two more.

"I didn't want any part of this!" shrieked another one, pointing wildly at the other who, judging by his burly build, was Nowell. "It was all his idea! I tried to talk him out of it."

Out of what?

And then I saw Betty.

I saw her stripped naked and tied to a metal work-surface. I saw a funnel that had been rammed into her mouth. I saw the hose running from a water tap to the funnel. I saw her distended belly.

I also saw that she was quite dead.

Mister Tibbles started to howl.

I went very quiet, clenching and unclenching my fists. She had been an innocent, an eccentric individual who had only wanted to help. What was more, she had seen the future and possessed answers to questions that I desperately wanted resolving.

And this little shit of a man had killed her.

"Leave. Now." My voice was barely audible, but it needed no repetition. The flunky darted out of the kitchen grabbing his semi-castrated buddy as he went.

Betty had said that I was at a tipping point. She was right. I could feel it in my blood. My hairs were all on end and my ears were screaming so loud that I could barely hear Nowell begging for mercy. He was rambling on about how he had been mistaken, how the family tree had convinced him that he should carry on his ancestor's work. His voice pitched into falsetto as he claimed not to know that his actions would kill her and that he hadn't thought it through. I closed my eyes and all I could see was the man in black, Lucifer, sat on the font, laughing at me.

My fingers flexed open and shut.

Open and shut.

Open and shut.

In one reality, they were clenched around the wretched neck of this worthless piece of night soil who had snuffed out a unique, beautiful life. They grasped his throat, first restricting the blood flow to his brain, then crushing his windpipe and asphyxiating his worthless carcass. The joy of disposing of this vile little piece of excrement flooded my body with pleasure-giving hormones and I laughed loudly as he collapsed dead at my feet. Then, as he lay there, still and defeated, I took my foot and kicked his pathetic face to a pulp, smashing in his nose, splintering his teeth and gouging out the eyes that had watched with glee as he had drowned someone who had done him no harm whatsoever.

But not in *this* reality.

"You have nothing to fear from me," I said as I turned to walk away.

There was a stunned silence then Nowell fell to his knees and started to thank me profusely.

I sighed as I reached the door. "You misunderstand. I said that you have nothing to fear from *me*. The same cannot be said for," I pointed to the growling little dog whose fur had started to shimmer in the neon lights, "*him.*" I walked out of the room, closed the door and sat down against it, barring it shut.

I heard the rippling sound of metamorphosing flesh, then the growls followed by screams.

Screams.

Screams.

Screams.

Silence.

I got up, brushed myself down and walked away.

I was done.

# Epilogue

I didn't even bother heading across town to the Borough. I crawled into the nearest pub and just started to drink. I think it was the one across from the rear entrance to the restaurant. I didn't care. The barman lined them up and I knocked them back. What sort of a life was this? Week after week people died and my own life was in constant jeopardy.

I'd had enough.

A cheer went up as a group of lads including the spotty youth from earlier watched some overpaid knuckle-dragger kick a spherical object past someone lying face first in the mud. It looked dull as dishwater but they seemed to be enjoying themselves. *Let them have their fun*: I thought.

The spotty youth caught me watching. "Where's your dog?"

"Wasn't mine," I shrugged and downed another drink.

He seemed to ponder what to say next. "Sorry about earlier."

"S'okay. We all do things that we don't want to."

He gave a toothy smile at his apparent absolution and went back to cheering at the game.

I summoned over another drink. As it was being poured, a glossy flyer on the bar drifted into my booze-infused sphere of attention. I picked it up and read:

"*Ghosties and Ghoulies in your attic?*

*"Let me scare them off for you!*

*"Wayne Diamond: Paranormal Investigator."*

It took a few seconds for the realisation that I had competition to push its way through the alcohol molecules that were partying in my brain. When it finally dragged itself up to the bar of my grey matter and managed to wave a brown beer voucher for attention I gave out a rather large snort.

"Let him have 'em," I muttered. "I quit."

Sam will return in
Sam Spallucci: Dark Justice

# Author's Notes

So, there we go, the end of another Sam Spallucci adventure. I can now put my feet up for a few days and raise a glass to the troubled adopted son of Lancaster. I hope you enjoyed reading it and I hope that you didn't find the ending a bit too worrying. Don't fret too much; do you really think Sam will be able to keep away from his chosen profession? He will return in *Sam Spallucci: Dark Justice* and, if you've been reading the vampire short stories in *Oh Taste And See, All Things Dark And Dangerous* and *Let All Mortal Flesh*, then you should have a good idea as to who he will be up against in his next outing.

Besides, there are so many other things that could draw him back in. What is wrong with Spliff? Are things starting to blossom between Sam and Grace? Who is the notorious vigilante stalking the streets of Lancaster? Then, probably the biggest one of all, what does the fallen angel Lucifer want with our investigator of the paranormal and what is the relevance of the Cup and the Blade?

Moreover, there is the small matter of a stone font with a certain inscription...

Oh yes, there is plenty yet to come. So far, we have only just scratched the surface. In the meantime, though, here are a few little factoids that you might find interesting.

I have actually moved the grotesques on Lancaster Priory from Lancaster's Roman Catholic Cathedral, where the story was originally going to be set. I had it all written, right down to the last word. Then I realised that the Cathedral had an incredibly steep pitched roof, which meant that the last scene would have been total nonsense. So, I picked the sandstone ornaments up and transferred them across to the other side of the city where, in this version of Lancaster, they now reside. If you visit Lancaster (which you really should do one day) then you must go and see both of the churches. The architecture of both is truly stunning and most inspirational.

*The Marauding Mummies Of Morecambe* has had a long, tempestuous history. It was originally intended to be the final story of *The Casebook Of Sam Spallucci* and Sam ended up being saved by Alec. However, storylines changed and *The Werewolf Of Williamson Park* became the tale that took its place. Also, the story was not originally set in Morecambe. I first thought up the idea of a troupe of rampaging mummies when I was on a hiking holiday as a teenager and I had just passed Monmouth. I decided that this would be a great place to set such a story and it sort of just sat as an idea for many years. Then, when I was writing *Casebook*, I came back to it and thought about locating it in Milnthorpe, a small village on the Lancashire/Cumbria border. Spliff was going to drag Sam up there on some wild goose chase and they were going to get pulled into the case. However, this idea dwindled as I wrote *The Werewolf Of Williamson Park* and was shelved until, just before I started *Shadows*, the weirdest thing happened. Someone actually tried to steal the statue of Eric Morecambe. Well, needless to say, this sparked off the old ideas and the rest was, as they say, history.

*Shadows* has taken an incredibly longer time to write than I had planned, and this is down to one story: *The Case Of The Gambling Ghost.* Dealing with the deaths of one's parents is exceptionally hard. Both of mine died years ago now, but the memory of their passing is still raw. I got to the point in the story when Sam's dad reappeared and I just stopped. I found it nigh on impossible to continue, so the laptop remained shut for a few months. However, I eventually plucked up the nerve to return to it and thoroughly enjoyed the send-off that I gave him. I was watching a lot of *Once Upon A Time* when I was working on the story and I can't help but see Robert Carlyle portraying Sam's dad in a similar manner to his magic-addicted Rumplestiltskin. The death of Sam's mum was totally spontaneous. I had not planned it whatsoever; it just happened when I was writing it and I feel it worked very well. So very often writers glamorise death in books and films, but in reality most people die on their own or in their sleep. I felt that a peaceful passing was most suitable for Mrs Spallucci.

Unfortunately, Boombox Betty did not meet a similar fate.

The case of the Pendle Witches is a dark hour in Lancashire's history. Suspicion, rumour and fear destroyed the families that were hunted down by Roger Nowell in his witch-hunt. The subsequent trial in 1612 led to the unjust hangings and deaths of those involved. There is a plaque on the wall of the Golden Lion public house on Moor Lane commemorating the victims of Nowell's righteous fervour. Again, if you come to Lancaster, I suggest that you go and spend a minute reading it in thoughtful silence. The books I used for the background surrounding this horrific act were *Wicked Enchantments: A History Of The Pendle Witches And Their Magic* by Joyce Froome and *Tales Of Witches And Sorcery* by Ken Radford (which illustrated the method of drowning by which poor Betty met her fate).

So, I'll stop rambling on now and let you get back to your everyday life. Once again, I hope you enjoyed this latest instalment. If you did, please leave some kind words for me on Amazon and Goodreads. I, like many writers, have a very fragile ego and it needs encouraging every now and then with little tidbits of praise and thanks.

All the best,
ASC, January 2019.

# About The Author

A.S.Chambers resides in Lancaster, England. He lives a fairly simple life of walking in the countryside, gazing at mountains and rescuing his cat from the net curtains.

He is quite happy for, and in fact would encourage, you to follow him on Facebook, Instagram and Twitter.

There is also a nice, shiny website:
www.aschambers.co.uk

www.ingramcontent.com/pod-product-compliance
Lightning Source LLC
Chambersburg PA
CBHW020534310726
48979CB00014B/2331/J
* 9 7 8 1 8 3 8 4 5 7 3 9 6 *